Love Unscripted

Love Unscripted

THE LOVE SERIES, BOOK 1

Tina Reber

ATRIA PAPERBACK
New York • London • Toronto • Sydney • New Delhi

ATRIA PAPERBACK
A Division of Simon & Schuster, Inc.
1230 Avenue of the Americas
New York, NY 10020

This book is a work of fiction. Any references to historical events, real people, or real places are used fictitiously. Other names, characters, places, and events are products of the author's imagination, and any resemblance to actual events or places or persons, living or dead, is entirely coincidental.

First Atria Paperback edition January 2013

Manufactured in the United States of America

10 9 8 7 6 5 4 3 2 1

Library of Congress Cataloging-in-Publication Data

Reber, Tina.
Love unscripted : the love series, book 1 / Tina Reber. — 1st Atria Books trade paperback ed.
p. cm.
1. Women—Rhode Island—Fiction. 2. Motion picture actors and actresses—Fiction. 3. Love stories. I. Title.
PS3618.E35L68 2013
813'.6—dc23

2012037056

ISBN: 978-1-4767-1868-2
ISBN: 978-1-4767-1869-9 (ebook)

Dedication

To my husband, Cory, and son, Ryan
For all of your patience, understanding, and support
in making my dream a reality.

To my dear friend, Janelle
Thank you for talking me down off the ledge
so many times when I wanted to give up.
Without you, this novel would be nothing more
than a 2 meg Word file.

And to all the celebrities
who deal with the paparazzi
and the invasion of your privacy
with grace and dignity.

Love
Unscripted

Preface

"You never know which way the wind blows" was one of my father's favorite expressions. I used to think it was silly; just one of those sayings we tell ourselves when we don't think we have control over our own destiny.

But I've since come to realize that sometimes when those winds of change blow, they're strong enough to toss you into a whole new world, and you really have no control over where you fly or how you land.

I'd always been quite content with my life; it was fairly easy and predictable, with only a hint of drama here and there caused by an occasional light breeze. There were a few times when Mother Nature hit me with her best shot, but I always managed to land on my feet.

Somewhere along the line I actually thought I had gained control over the weather, keeping the possibility of a terrible storm always at bay.

That was until the day the wind blew through my door and carried me away.

CHAPTER 1

Eye of the Storm

"OOH, OOH, TARYN, turn it up!" Marie pointed frantically in the air while making a gin and tonic with her other hand.

Her sudden excitement caught me off-guard and made me jump. I quickly grabbed the television remote, fumbling to adjust the volume of the evening news. I should have known better; there was only one thing Marie or any of the other women in town felt was newsworthy these days, and it wasn't that the mall was having a shoe sale. I don't even think "free shoes" could have been more exciting to them.

Soon after my thumb hit the button on the remote I became slightly perturbed, but it was too late to correct my mistake. The damage was already done.

"Looks like the obsessive fans caused *another* traffic jam today," I said, laughing lightly, trying to pretend as if I actually cared.

For a moment, I thought I was watching a repeat of yesterday's news report. The camera panned a large crowd of frantic girls who lined up alongside the road—*again*. They were trying to spy on the movie crew as they filmed on one of our local beaches—*again*, hoping for the random chance to get a glimpse of "him."

Between all of the cars that were parked haphazardly and the girls running back and forth across the street, traffic on Ocean View Drive was almost at a standstill. The police were trying their best to move the chaos away from the area, inadvertently creating more chaos in the process.

"I'm sure all of their 'I Love Ryan' posters will capture his attention," I stated jokingly, rolling my eyes at the absurdity of it all.

From what I had seen and heard about him, I presumed he didn't care the slightest bit about the teenyboppers and their childish signs of love and adoration. Still, their actions perplexed me to no end. What possessed these girls—many of them grown women—to take the time out of their day to decorate poster board and stand alongside a busy roadway? Do they actually think he may just stop one day?

"Darling, your sign with my name written in fluorescent pink with silver hearts is such a brilliant artistic representation of my life. It validates my existence and makes me *so hot*. Please . . . come . . . run away with me . . ." I tugged on Marie's arm, pretending to be "him."

A few of the patrons sitting at the bar laughed at my theatrics, while the girls who were being interviewed by the news reporter on TV screamed just a bit louder. I pointed the remote back at the television and quickly lowered the volume of their ear-piercing shrieks; I really wanted to change the channel.

"Hang on a sec, I want to see this," Marie defended quickly, dismissing my actions with her hand. Her eyes stared intently at the screen.

"Ah, see, he's on again," Marie squealed with excitement. Several ladies sitting at the bar lurched off of their stools to get a better view of the television.

"Hey—watch what you're doing." I pointed.

Marie was so preoccupied watching the news, she speed-poured vodka on the outside of the glass.

"Damn, look at him. He's so freakin' gorgeous," Traci, one of my regular customers, shouted.

A group of businessmen sitting at one of the tables nearest to the television booed loudly and then requested that I turn ESPN on instead.

Unconsciously, my eyes flashed back to the television to see what the big deal was, but I only saw part of his head as he climbed into the backseat of a car.

It had only been about two weeks since "he" and "the cast" descended on our town, but I was already tired of hearing about them. The local news and radio stations talked about the actors incessantly, to the point of overkill. I tried desperately to remember what life was like *before* they landed, but it was difficult.

I quickly diverted my attention to more important things, such as the two well-dressed young men who'd just sat down at the bar near the first cluster of beer taps—customers. One of the men caught my eye as he loosened the knot of his brown paisley necktie, taking a moment to unwind after a long day at the office no doubt. I had seen him once before in the pub, and now he was smiling brightly at me.

I let out a tiny sigh while waiting for the stream of amber beer to fill the glass mug in my hand. My fingers gripped the large wooden handle, and with a quick flick of my wrist, I cut the flow from the beer tap.

I slipped the ten-dollar bill out from under his fingers and went on with my day.

"He's cute," Marie muttered privately.

I punched the keys on the register to ring in the sale. "He's married."

Marie looked back at him. Her eyes examined my assessment.

"No ring," she whispered, appearing slightly puzzled.

She obviously didn't look hard enough. "You can see the indentation."

I carried his change back to him. Marie looked astonished that I'd noticed that. What she didn't know was that the last time this particular man was in my pub, he was wearing a gold band around his left-hand ring finger. Poor man . . . somehow his wedding ring must have accidentally slipped off before he sat down.

While I mindlessly washed some dirty glasses in the sink, the setting sun beamed its final rays, casting beautiful hues of pink and purple through the large windows that dominated the front of my pub.

My pub—I could say that now with absolute authority, although the heartache that I was put through to be in this spot would never, in a million years, be worth it. It was not worth the personal loss. But then again, when has life ever been fair?

I had prepared myself properly . . . college education with honors, plans for a master's degree to follow. Still, despite my best efforts, fate apparently had some other future in mind for me, and it wasn't to worry about other people's financial situations.

I gazed at the windows, imagining that the view of the evening sky over the Atlantic Ocean was even more breathtaking. I thought about running upstairs to the rooftop to watch the sunset over the water but I couldn't; customers were already filtering in for happy hour.

Even though there was an enormous influx of new people in our little town of Seaport, Rhode Island, recently, my customer count oddly remained the same—probably because all of the mayhem was located at the other end of town.

It had been almost two months since the tractor-trailers loaded with expensive cameras and filming equipment first rumbled through our streets. An extensive production crew immediately followed. They came in droves.

In the blink of an eye, police barricades blocked off selected roads, and huge, white tents were erected in the empty parking lot next to the vacant warehouse by Pier Seven. Towering lights were brought in to illuminate the entire lot and several large mechanical cranes were parked on standby near the new fence.

Long, white camper trailers were arranged in rows, and it reminded me of the times when the carnival would come to town. The only thing missing was the Ferris wheel.

Everything, for the most part, was calm; that was, until the big-name Hollywood actors arrived. With them came the news crews, photographers, and mobs of obsessed fans. It was like having rabid dogs unleashed in the streets. Everyone was in a tizzy.

The biggest commotion, however, was caused by a twenty-six-year-old actor turned mega-star overnight…

Ryan Christensen

Six foot two, dirty-blond hair, blue eyes, incredible body from what I've seen in the magazines that Marie keeps stuffing in my face, and reportedly single again.

Oh, how they all swooned—everyone, except for me.

Marie and several of my female customers were completely flustered just from getting a quick glimpse of him on TV. I was relieved that they didn't behave like the mob of screaming fans who were shown on the news.

I could never understand what drove women to the point of hysterics when they saw a famous singer or movie star. I remembered seeing video clips of women going out of their minds from seeing Elvis or the Beatles—screaming, crying, and passing out from getting their glimpse. I knew it was thrilling, but there has to be a limit before you lose control of your emotions and behavior. I just couldn't relate.

Growing up, it wasn't in my personality to hang pictures of teen heart-throbs on my walls. By the time I was in my teens, I had discovered fine art instead. My bedroom was covered in the classics, with my own artwork dotted in between. That was more my style, more . . . realistic, tangible.

I slid a fresh pitcher of beer over to my current customer. "That's five-fifty please." I smiled in return, dancing slightly to the song playing off my iPod over the pub's sound system.

One of the firefighters from the Seaport Fire Department, who was sitting with a group of co-workers at the large, round table in front of me, raised his empty beer pitcher in the air to get my attention.

"Phil really likes you," Marie whispered.

"Who's Phil?" I asked, pulling my long blond hair back to remove the few strands that annoyingly stuck to the corner of my mouth.

Marie rolled her eyes at me. "Taryn!" she scolded.

"Sorry, but I don't know who you're talking about." I honestly had no clue who Phil was.

"Fire department?" She motioned the direction with her eyes. "The cute guy smiling at you? The one who is recently divorced and now on the open market?"

"Him?" I pointed with a tilt of my head. "I thought his name was Todd."

"No, it's Phil," Marie corrected, laughing at my confused expression. "He's been asking about you."

I opened a new bottle of vodka, wondering where I ever got the name Todd.

"Well?" Marie asked impatiently, waiting for my response.

"Not interested," I muttered while I prepared a dirty martini. Sandy had asked for three olives in this one.

Marie put her fist on her hip, just like she always does when she feels the need to lecture me. I started laughing at her stance; it reminded me of when we were teenagers, leaning on our school lockers and talking about boys.

I was thankful that she at least kept her voice down this time to reprimand me, so all the people sitting at the bar wouldn't hear her every word.

"Taryn, what's wrong with him? He is freaking good-looking," Marie whispered.

I sighed. "Nothing is wrong with him." I quickly hurried down the long bar to deliver the martini. It didn't matter how handsome he was; I did not want to be any man's second choice for a wife.

"What about Dan over there?" Marie suggested. "That poor guy asks you out at least once a week. He's adorable too. Or Jeff, or Kevin, or Andy?" She pointed inconspicuously around the pub.

I glanced around at the faces of the men that she was referring to. Several of them had asked me on a date at one time or another and I had lied to each and every one of them, telling them I already had a boyfriend.

"You need to give a few of these assholes a chance . . . you just might find one that fits," Marie teased me. "Besides, if I had a body like yours, I'd be putting it to good use every day."

She didn't need to shake her butt for me to grasp her innuendo.

I rolled my eyes. "No you wouldn't. And you've known me long enough to know I'm not like that either."

"Tar, it's been like eight months. This existence you're in is not healthy."

"Healthy in comparison to what?" I asked. My chest still had a lingering, dull pain from the last man who shattered my heart into a million pieces. I didn't need to explain further; Marie knew exactly what I meant. "Besides, I like my existence," I informed her with an exaggerated grin. It was safe—predictable—painless.

"I just want to see you happy again," Marie uttered in defeat.

"Don't worry about me. I'm fine." Actually, I had grown quite accustomed to lying to her, too. Little did she know, I had another stupid dream, or should I say nightmare, about Thomas again this morning.

"I don't need some divorced guy on the rebound to make me happy," I said to her in passing.

"Ahem, Taryn?" I heard a man's voice call my name. Phil the fireman was standing at the bar.

Instinctively my shoulders hunched from the fear of having been overheard. I hoped like hell that he didn't just hear my comment; I would feel awful if he did.

I looked at Marie for confirmation. Her eyes opened wider and she shrugged the slightest bit, which was absolutely no help. I started to panic a little inside; the last thing I wanted to do was to hurt his feelings.

Phil waved a twenty at me and gestured for the new pitcher of beer I still held in my hand. "I wanted to ask you if you've tried that new steakhouse over by the mall yet?" he mumbled nervously, almost to the point that I didn't understand him. As I processed his question, my eyes closed briefly and I took a deep breath through my nose. This was his opener to ask me on a date.

"No, I haven't, but Marie has." I hurried away to the cash register with his money in hand and punched the keys slowly, trying to figure out how to let him down easy. I could sense what was coming.

"Do you, I mean, maybe sometime, can I take you there for dinner?" It was hard for him to ask. I felt really bad for him and for what I was about to say next.

"Phil, that's very sweet of you to offer, but I'm already seeing someone. I'm sorry." My candy-coated lie sounded so convincing I almost believed it myself.

"So who are you dating these days? Your right hand or your left?" Marie jeered after Phil walked away.

I couldn't help it—some juvenile instinct made me react. I stuck my tongue out at her.

"You know what your problem is? You need to get laid," she mumbled under her breath. "And I'm not talking about the do-it-yourself kind of laid, either. Just pick one of these guys and go have meaningless, mind-altering, sweaty sex already."

I retaliated for her snide remark by snapping her in the butt with my damp bar rag.

"So is that what *you* would do if you weren't already married?" I laughed. "I just want to be clear about this wonderful advice you're giving me, because I don't recall you selecting Gary from the masses here."

"Ah . . ." She waved a disgruntled hand at me. "You're hopeless."

I let out a loud, agreeing sigh.

"Why don't you go over there and be nice to him? I heard the fire department was called out to the movie set this morning. Maybe *he* could get us in?" Marie shrugged; a glimmer of hope infused her voice.

I wrinkled my nose and countered her suggestion with one of my own. "Why don't *you* go be nice to him then? I have no desire to go flock around some movie set like a pathetic groupie."

"Speaking of groupies, did you hear that the police had to escort his limo to his hotel last night?" she asked, tapping one of her long fingernails on Ryan Christensen's picture in today's newspaper. "Article says there was a mob of women there; they had his hotel surrounded again."

I rolled my eyes and continued wiping the bar with a towel. I really could not be bothered with the trivial, but it was hard to ignore. Everyone wanted to know the most minuscule details about him and his fellow actors and their glamorous lives. The photographers and reporters hunted them down daily.

It was all too absurd for my taste, but Ryan Christensen was a drug that everyone seemed hopelessly addicted to.

"Girls have been trying to sleep out on the sidewalk and everything . . . cops had to tell them to leave," Marie babbled to a few female customers sitting at the bar as she shuffled the newspaper into a neat pile.

I shook my head while trying to imagine what the payoff would be to even consider sleeping on cold concrete in 50-degree weather. It was still nice out during the day, but it was the last day of September and the evenings were chilly.

"That's ridiculous," I muttered.

"They'll have to sleep down on the beach now," Sandy, our local beautician, chimed in. She took another sip of her martini while everyone waited in anticipation for her to explain.

"One of the girls who work at the Lexington Hotel was in the salon this afternoon," Sandy babbled, like the information she had was no big deal.

"She said it was all hush-hush, but the hotel staff was informed that all of the actors were being relocated there today. Apparently the Lexington has better security and private garage entrances. I don't know—whatever. Anyway, it sounds like they're going to be right down the street from us now."

"No shit!" Marie screeched excitedly. "You mean to tell me that Ryan and the entire cast are going to be only three teeny blocks away?" She pointed out the window in the direction of Mulberry Street.

"I still can't believe they're filming the second *Seaside* movie right here in our town. This one is going to be even better than the first," Marie gushed.

"Okay, that's like the hundredth time you've said that," I teased.

"Well, maybe if you bothered to watch the first movie you'd know what all of us are so excited about," she snapped back.

"I read in one of the magazines at the salon that he's sleeping with the girl who starred in his last movie . . . what's her name, Suzette, Suzanne something?" Sandy said.

"No Sandy, that's not true," Marie shot back, shaking her head in disagreement. "He was dating Lauren Delaney from that TV show *Modern Times*, but they broke up."

Marie's tone was almost sympathetic. She tossed her long chocolate-brown hair off her shoulders, looking as if she felt sorry for this man she didn't know personally.

"I heard that someone stole some of his clothes from the hotel last week and tried to sell them on eBay," Traci added.

"Oh, that's just wrong," I blurted out, trying to imagine what type of sicko would buy some guy's used shorts. The thought made me shudder. "Why on earth would someone do that? Well, whoever did it, I hope they got arrested." My mind could not rationalize the actions. "It sure is a twisted world we live in."

"If I had the chance, I'd twist on him several times," Marie growled. I laughed when she wiggled her hips.

"Why don't you twist your way over to the big table with this pitcher for me? Please? Our fire department looks like they still have fires to put out."

I felt bad for turning Phil down, so I was trying to make it up to him with a free pitcher of beer. Secretly, though, I didn't want to go anywhere near him.

"Why don't *you* take it over and at least talk to him? He's a really nice guy, Taryn."

"Marie, I'm not interested, okay?"

"Well, since you seem to have sworn off men . . ." she muttered, "here, I've got something for you. It's not porn, but it's close enough." She laughed while rummaging in her huge purse.

She held out another gossip magazine with a big, glossy picture of Ryan Christensen on the cover. The caption under his picture read:

THE TRUTH ABOUT RYAN:
His ex-girlfriend tells ALL!

I pursed my lips and turned away, slightly disgusted that anyone's ex-girlfriend would have the audacity to "tell all." He was probably better off without her.

"Hey, let me see that," Traci yelled, reaching for the magazine.

"What's your problem, Taryn?" Marie grumbled and stamped her foot. "Don't you think he's hot? I mean, look at him."

"It doesn't matter. He's just another guy who is all full of himself. Besides, I have better things to think about—like why George and Ted look mad because I'm not bringing their drinks fast enough."

"Yeah, like those two old farts are in a hurry. The only place they're going to is their next alcohol-induced coma," she declared.

I gave her my most dramatic, horrified look. "Who are you all going to gossip about once the celebrities leave town? You'll need to find someone else to talk about." I couldn't help but laugh.

"We'll just talk about you, Tar. We'll sit around and reminisce about how much fun you used to be while using the cobwebs growing between your legs to knit hats for the poor." Marie nudged me.

"You're such a bitch." I snickered at her.

"Yep!" She grinned, pretending that she was going to spray me with the soda wand. "But you'll never fire me because I'm your best friend and you love me."

Damn her for being right.

THE NEXT day I woke to the sun beaming brightly through my window. I yawned while my fingers carelessly fumbled to shut off the alarm clock. I contemplated going back to sleep, but it was already nine o'clock and there were things I wanted to get done today.

With a groan, I tossed the covers off and landed my bare feet on the cold wooden floor of my bedroom. "Brr," I muttered as frigid oak planks sent a shiver through my body.

Outside my window, truck brakes screeched loudly, causing me to flinch. Curiosity made me tiptoe across the floor to find the source of the noise.

Ah, Maggie is getting a delivery, I noticed, peering out the window at the back alleyway behind my building.

I lingered in the hot shower next, my mind focused on creating my agenda. The longer I thought about it, the longer my to-do list got.

I picked my favorite jeans out of the basket of clean laundry and slipped a white T-shirt over my head, tousling my long blond hair with my fingers to separate the waves.

After adding the final touches of makeup and mascara, I skipped down my stairs and through the door that led directly into the pub.

"Good afternoon, my lovely bar," I said out loud to no one. "Time to wake up and greet a new day."

I opened each of the window blinds, watching the microscopic dust motes float in the sunlight. I thought about cleaning the windows again—they were looking a bit dirty. I'd have to remember to ask my friend Pete if I could borrow his extension ladder.

That would have to wait. It was Wednesday already and I still hadn't updated my entertainment sign for the weekend. First things first.

This weekend Live at Mitchell's Pub:
Fri 10/3 Mark Tercha
Sat 10/4 Stay Nogo

I dropped the piece of chalk back into the box and carried the updated slate-board sign out to the sidewalk.

I had to squint; the sun was bright—even more so since I'd just emerged from a darkened pub. *Wow! It's beautiful out here.*

I leaned back against my open door, taking a deep breath and closing my eyes for a moment to feel the warm sunlight on my cheeks. Even the air smelled better today.

Perhaps if I open late today I could enjoy this nice weather up on the rooftop with a good book in hand? Oh, that thought was very tempting. Reasons to goof off were starting to outnumber my to-do list, but the responsible part of my conscience quickly snuffed that. *No, I have a lot to do inside. Better get at it . . . in a minute . . . the sun feels so nice . . .*

My reluctant eyes popped open when I heard the frantic sounds of women screaming. My vision was blurred by the sun and it took my eyes a moment to adjust to the pandemonium headed straight for me.

That's when I caught sight of him—what appeared to be Ryan Christensen—running full speed down the sidewalk. His body was on a direct collision course with mine.

"Back door?" he asked in a panic as he almost knocked me to the ground. I stumbled backward awkwardly into the open doorway, grabbing the frame to keep myself from falling down.

"Door," I quickly answered, my shaky hand pointed in that direction, but he was already running through the pub.

Instead of escaping through the kitchen door around the corner, he flew through the first door he saw.

"No, not that door," I breathed out, tripping over my own feet as I followed him inside. It was too late; he'd disappeared through the door that led up to my apartment.

"Damn it!" I cussed.

A split second after he vanished from view, the front door flew open and smacked loudly into the wall. A small group of women barged in; behind them were men with cameras, but oddly they stayed outside.

"Whoa, hold on there. Wait! Oh no, no!" The words were just spilling out of my mouth as I ran toward the door. Instinct told me I had to stop them before they got too far into the bar. It was obvious that *they* were what he was running from.

"We saw him come in here," one of the crazed-looking women barked as she tried to press past me.

"No, he's not in here—he ran out the back door," I shrilled, blocking her advance with my arms. "If you run down the street you might catch him." I hoped my lie sounded convincing.

"You all have to get out of here. NOW! Don't make me call the police," I yelled as I herded them back to the door.

The instant they were out, I locked the door behind them and hit the light switch. *Shit, what do I do?* I started to panic. There was a large crowd of photographers and people starting to pile up on the sidewalk. Many of them were already mashing their faces to the glass, trying to look in my windows.

I moved as quickly as I could, sliding on my knees across the wooden bench seat at the first booth by the door. I felt like the hapless human, the last survivor, who has to fend off the attacking zombies all by herself. My heart was pounding in my chest when I dropped the blinds down on their intruding faces.

My thoughts spun in circles as I ran from window to window. I was so preoccupied with obscuring their view that I hadn't even noticed where he was.

I tried to replay the last sixty seconds in my mind. Was he still inside, or did he manage to make it out of the building after all?

Did he slip out the back door when I was distracted?

CHAPTER 2

Open Doors

I SLOWLY CRACKED THE door leading upstairs to my apartment, my eyes straining to see if I could spot him. There he was, sitting huddled on the top landing with his face buried in his arms. His hands were shaking ever so slightly.

I could see that his shirt had been ripped; part of his stomach was visible through the large, frayed tear. *Oh my God! What happened to this poor guy?*

I felt a little more courageous since he was obviously in distress, so I opened the door wider and cleared my throat so he would know I was standing there. I had no idea what to say.

"Sorry," he pleaded, cautioning me with open hands. "I'm not some crazy maniac. Please, please don't scream."

"It's fine . . . it's fine. I know who you are," I said in my softest voice, trying to calm him down. "Um, are you okay?"

"Not really," he whispered. He was gasping for air, his hand covering his heart. "Can you give me a minute?"

"Sure," I whispered. "Take as long as you need."

"Not the back door, I take it?" he barely uttered, pointing his thumb over his shoulder to the door behind him.

"Ah, no. That's the door to my apartment."

I wanted to give him some privacy, so I started to back up out of the doorway.

"Are *they* down there?" His trembling fingers covered his eyes, his palms pressed into his cheeks.

I looked back up at him. "No. There's no one here." I had to take another deep breath; my heart was still pounding from the surge of adrenaline.

"I threw everyone out and I locked the door. All the blinds are down, too—no one can see in. It's okay, you're safe here. I'm, um, going to leave you alone now."

I quickly shut the door and returned to the bar to continue stocking the coolers with bottled beer. I needed to calm myself down. I needed a distraction.

A few minutes later, the stairwell door creaked and I saw him glance around the wall to see if the bar was truly empty. The poor man looked absolutely terrified.

Slowly he walked to the edge of the bar.

"Do you mind if I just sit here for a while?" Ryan was speaking so softly I almost couldn't hear him.

"Yeah, sure. Please, have a seat," I whispered, matching his tone. "Can I get you something to drink? Soda, or a beer . . . maybe even a shot or two?"

He was holding his head in his hands, his elbows rested on the bar.

"Can I, um, have a beer?" he breathed out.

He looked in no condition to decide what kind of beer to drink, so I quickly grabbed a mug and tapped him a draft. He started to fumble through his pockets; his hands were still trembling.

"That's okay. Please, don't worry about it, it's on the house."

"Are you sure?" he asked timidly. "You don't have to do that. I don't want you to get in trouble."

"No, it's all right. It's my pub. I'm the owner," I said, shrugging slightly.

Ryan's eyes narrowed on me. "Thanks. You don't know how much I appreciate this." He pushed out a big, relieved sigh. A little smile appeared on his lips.

"It's no problem. Please, just sit and relax, and don't worry, I promise I won't bother you," I said softly. I held up my hands briefly to let him know that I'd be keeping my distance.

I grabbed another six-pack of beer out of the cardboard case and opened the cooler again. My nervousness caused me to almost drop the pack, knocking over more bottles inside the cooler in the process. I had to lean far in to reach the bottles that had tipped over and out of the holder, and for a moment I almost fell into the cooler myself.

I felt so uneasy about my careless fumbling, knowing that he must have just seen my feet come up off the floor, that I started to become flush. Fortunately the cold temperature in the cooler counterbalanced the heat rising to my cheeks. *Perhaps if I stay in here I won't have to look at him?*

Just then I heard a phone ring. I popped my head out of the cooler and felt my pocket for my cell phone, but it wasn't mine that was ringing.

"Hey, Mike. Yeah, I'm safe. I'm at some bar," Ryan muttered, trying to sound like he was fine. The hand that rubbed his forehead was still shaking.

He looked at me as he held his phone away from his face. He was blinking rapidly and he looked confused for a moment. "Ahh, what's the name of this place?"

"Mitchell's Pub." I slid a new napkin with our family name on it to him.

"A place called Mitchell's Pub. Listen, I'll call you when I'm ready. I'm just having a beer."

"My driver," he stated, as if he could read the question in my mind. "I suppose he thinks he might get fired by the studio for losing track of me."

I had no idea what to say, so I gave him a brief smile and darted into the kitchen. I figured he wanted to be left alone anyway; distracting myself by stocking the coolers sounded like a good idea. I took my time loading up two cases of beer onto the metal cart and wheeled them back into the bar.

He was still sitting there as I unloaded the cases by the bar refrigerators. I tried not to look at him. *He's probably so sick of people bugging him. As soon as he finishes that beer, he'll call his driver. What would be the point of talking to him? Just leave him alone.*

He stared at me while I emptied the cases of beer into the coolers. I could see out of the corner of my eye that his head turned and his eyes followed me when I took the empty boxes back to the kitchen. I still couldn't make myself look at him.

Ryan cleared his throat when I returned. "Well, you obviously know who I am. Can I ask what your name is?" His tone was very polite and friendly.

"Taryn," I replied, glancing at him for a split second through the curtain of hair that spilled over my shoulder. I pulled it back out of my way and tried to refocus my eyes on putting away the clean glasses that remained on the sink counter.

"It's nice to meet you, Taryn."

"It's nice to meet you too." My nervousness made my responses sound unintentionally indifferent.

"So, Taryn, do you have a last name?"

"Mitchell?" I squeaked. *So much for appearing casual and unruffled!*

"Ah, I see," he murmured as he held up the bar napkin with the Mitchell's Pub insignia. "Are you *sure* you don't mind if I stay for a few minutes? Then I promise I'll be out of your hair."

"It's no problem, really," I whispered, giving him a brief, friendly smile.

My nerves were tangled in knots so I had to keep busy. I grabbed a new liquor order form and took it to the other end of the bar to fill it out.

I could feel him watching me, even though I refused to look up and confirm it. *Maybe I shouldn't have worn this top today? Could he see down the front when I bent over?* I fixed my shirt at the shoulders, trying to inconspicuously see if *I* could see any cleavage. *I'll have to change my shirt after he leaves. His beer is almost finished.*

I tried not to make eye contact, but I could still tell that he was following every move I made. I felt a little strange as he gawked at me, so I picked up the television remote and turned the large flat screen on; maybe he needed something else to look at. But he didn't seem to notice the television.

I allowed myself another quick look and observed that his brow was knitted. He looked confused; either that or he was deep in thought.

"Are you doing okay?" I asked, concerned.

"Yeah, I think so." He nodded and combed his fingers back through his hair. "I was just wondering, are you always this talkative?"

I was trying to appear preoccupied by filling the garnish holder with swizzle straws. I smiled bashfully at his comment.

"I thought you'd prefer to be left alone. I'm sure the silence and peace must be refreshing," I said, assuming he'd agree.

He laughed lightly.

"It is, but it's also nice to be able to talk to a woman who isn't screaming at me," he said, looking a bit more relaxed. "You're not going to scream at me, are you?"

"No," I said in my softest, most nonthreatening tone. That's when I noticed the laceration on his face.

"Are you sure you're okay? I don't know if you realize it, but you have a pretty big scratch on your face." Now that I was able to look at him more closely, I saw the dried streak of blood that ran down his neck.

Ryan rubbed his eyes and sighed heavily. "Unbelievable," he murmured.

I opened up the first aid kit I kept behind the bar and picked out an alcohol swab.

"Is it that bad?" he asked.

I nodded gently. "There's some blood. It's not *that* bad, but you should clean it just in case."

"I can feel it," Ryan muttered as he ran his fingers over the raised marks. "My jaw hurts."

"Don't touch it," I cautioned. I attempted to hand him the swab, but he seemed perfectly fine with letting me tend to him.

"Um, can you tilt a little bit more?" I asked nervously. My hand trembled slightly as I wiped the swab across his wound, trying to be as gentle as possible. There were actually two distinct fingernail marks across his jaw, though the stubble on his face covered up most of it. I saw his eyes scrunch together; the alcohol must have stung a little.

"I'm sorry," I whispered. "Almost done."

Ryan was gazing at my face while I put some antibiotic cream over the raised scratches. I noticed his eye color was a lovely mix of blue and green, making them very striking. It was hard to look at anything else.

"Thanks," he said, softly and sincerely.

I wiped the remaining cream off my finger. "I don't mean to be intrusive, but may I ask what happened to you today?" Secretly I was dying to know how he got in this condition.

"Um," he began, "I had some errands to run but I guess I didn't get too far." A broken smile appeared on his lips as he scratched his eyebrow with his thumb. "It's actually a bit embarrassing."

"That's okay. I understand if you don't want to talk about it." I politely dismissed my question and closed the lid on the first aid kit.

"Ahh," he groaned, keeping me engaged in conversation. "I went out to see if I could get a present for my mom; her birthday is in a few weeks. I had some free time today, so I escaped from the hotel and went for a walk. I managed to go into one of the shops down the street, but couldn't find anything I wanted to buy."

He took a sip of beer, pausing to collect his thoughts. His eyes focused on the bar. "When I left the store, there were a handful of women waiting for pictures or autographs or something. I tried to be polite and walk away, but . . ." He let out a big sigh. "One girl grabbed me and tried to pull my shirt off. Then the chase started." His lips twisted in disgust. "I took off running and here I am. I feel like I just got mugged."

"It sounds to me like you did get mugged. Do you want me to call the police?"

"No," he said, shaking his head infinitesimally. "They were just excited fans."

I reached up to the top shelf for my unopened bottle of Johnnie Walker Blue, thinking that we both needed something special to calm us down.

"Would you like one?" I asked.

His eyes widened and he nodded enthusiastically.

"You have good taste," he complimented.

I briefly smiled and pushed a filled shot glass in his direction. He tapped his glass against mine before tossing it back.

"Do you mind if I ask you another question?" I asked tentatively.

"No, I don't mind. Please—ask." Ryan winced and puckered his lips from the after-burn of the whiskey. His expression was amusing.

"Well, I'm just curious why you're walking around without an escort. Don't you usually have bodyguards with you?"

"Yeah, most of the time," he shyly admitted. "I just really wanted to go for a walk by myself. It's beautiful outside today. I didn't think I needed security to do that, but I suppose I should rethink that, huh?" he said while examining the large rip in his T-shirt. "Damn. This was one of my favorites."

I couldn't help but nod in agreement with his statement; a shot of whiskey was burning my throat now. I refilled our glasses; it would take more than one to calm me down.

"Would you excuse me for a moment?" I asked politely. "I'll be right back."

I ran upstairs to get him a new T-shirt. There was a huge hole in his and I felt terrible for him. On my way through my apartment, I stopped to check my appearance in the mirror. *Great, my nipples are standing at attention. Guess I was in the cooler too long?* I tried to push them back in as I picked the clean T-shirt out of the laundry basket. It was still warm from when I took it out of the dryer this morning.

"Here. Please . . . take this," I said when I returned. I handed him my favorite oversized T-shirt. It was dark blue and soft from many washes. "Your T-shirt is really torn. You can't walk around looking like that. The bathroom is over there if you would like to change."

"Thanks. Thanks a lot." Ryan unfolded the shirt and looked at it, appearing very puzzled. "Wait, this shirt can't be yours. It's way too big. Is this your . . ."

I shook my head. "No, it's mine—well, it used to be my father's, but now it's a very comfortable sleep shirt." My admission made me shrug. "I just washed it. I'm sorry, it's all I have. You don't have to . . . I just thought . . ."

He smiled at me and pulled the shirt out of my reach. He wadded it up in his hand and departed for the restroom. The way he looked at me made me question whether he ever gets treated with kindness by strangers. My gesture seemed to take him by surprise.

When he returned, he held his hands out from his sides. His posture asked the unspoken question for me to give my opinion.

When I wore that shirt it fit me like a dress, but the soft cotton covered his physique like a second skin. I noticed the contours of his defined chest through the thin fabric and how the sleeves accentuated his muscular biceps.

I nodded and grinned. He looked gorgeous in my T-shirt.

"I think it fits you better," I murmured, noticing that the color made his blue eyes even more alluring.

"It's really soft, and it smells really good too." He had the collar pulled up to his nose. "Thank you."

"You're welcome." I smiled warmly. I was pleased that he no longer looked like a victim.

"So you live upstairs?"

I nodded; my eyes instinctively flashed up to the ceiling. I still couldn't look directly in his eyes. "My apartment is the entire second floor."

"Roommates?" he asked, as if expecting me to say yes.

"No, I live alone," I said quickly.

"Cats?"

I laughed lightly at his insinuation. "No. I'm allergic to them."

Ryan grinned. "Me too," he said. We tapped our glasses together and downed our second shot of whiskey.

"Would you like another beer?" I didn't want to assume.

He nodded and smiled. "Yes, please. If you don't mind."

While I was refilling his glass the keg kicked, sending a pop of foam all over my face, shirt, and hair. *Oh great, perfect timing.* I suppose by the way he laughed at me that he found it amusing.

"You have my kind of luck," he admitted.

"Ugh," I groaned, wiping myself off with a bar rag.

Ryan had a huge grin on his face. As much as I was embarrassed, his smile was quite contagious.

I reached down to pull the empty keg from the cooler and gasped slightly when I noticed he had come around the back of the bar. He was standing there staring at me again.

"Here, let me help you. It's the least I can do." He gently wiped some beer froth from my hair, then moved me out of the way to grab the empty keg. I felt flush—like my heart skipped a beat.

I noticed that when he was right next to me he sniffed me; he even leaned in to get a better whiff.

"Is that you that smells like . . . peaches?"

I looked at him out of the corner of my eye as I reflexively leaned away. I smelled my shirt to get a better understanding of what he was referring to.

"I guess so," I answered.

Ryan leaned over closer and smelled me again. I leaned farther away, almost tipping off-balance. His nostrils opened wider and a slight grin appeared on his lips.

"Peach-scented perfume?" he asked.

"No. Just soap and body lotion." *Why is this guy sniffing me?* "Do I smell bad?"

"No. Quite the opposite." He smiled and inhaled deeply through his nose, like he was sensing the most pleasing of all scents. He muttered something about it being a first under his breath. I didn't understand.

"So, you really own this place?" Ryan asked, carrying the empty keg to the back room for me.

"You sound surprised."

"Well, I'm not the best judge of a woman's age, but aren't you sort of young—I mean, you look about as old as I am and you own your own business."

His observation didn't bother me. I was used to having people make assumptions as to how I was able to afford a pub while only being twenty-seven.

"Well, my grandfather was the original Mitchell. Then when he passed away my dad took it over. My father died a little over a year ago; it's been mine ever since."

"Oh, I'm sorry—about your father," he corrected. "And your mom? Is she . . . ?"

"No," I murmured. "She died four years ago—right after I turned twenty-three."

"Wow. I'm sorry to hear that. So do you have any brothers or sisters?"

I just shook my head. "No." I shrugged, trying to appear content and cheerful. "Just me."

I hated the reminder that I was alone in this world. I wheeled the cart around to load up a new keg of beer as the sadness washed over me.

"Here, let me do that." Ryan placed his hand in the small of my back and gently moved me out of the way so he could take over loading the keg on the cart. I jumped ever so slightly when his fingers made contact with my body; I was surprised that he touched me.

We were so close that I could smell the scent emanating from his body; he had a slightly spicy but light and manly aroma. He smelled wonderful. I breathed in another whiff of him while I could, only I wasn't so obvious about it.

Ryan gave the keg a good shove to get it into the cooler under the taps. Why did I notice the muscles in his arms flex? I had to shake the thought from my head.

"Thank you." I smiled.

"Sure. No problem," he said happily.

"This bar is beautiful." He rubbed his hands across the mahogany rail as he returned to his seat. "You don't see craftsmanship like this anymore. The scrolling and detail is magnificent."

"My grandfather built it." I beamed. "Every time I look at it, it makes me smile. He put so much of himself into this place. All this woodwork you see was done by his hands. The booths, the wainscoting—he built it all."

Ryan stood up and walked toward the enormous wooden pillar that spanned from floor to ceiling.

"Your grandfather was a talented man." His fingers were busy tracing the intricate patterns carved in the dark oak post. "I really like the exposed red brick, too. This place reminds me of a pub I was in once when I filmed in Ireland. Has that authentic feel to it, you know?"

"Thanks." His compliment seemed very genuine and made me smile. "I always thought this place had that old-world charm too."

His gaze rolled over to the far end of the pub. "That's a pretty big stage. You have bands play here?"

"Yeah, just about every Friday and Saturday night. I've been thinking about doing open-mic nights during the week, too."

Ryan was distracted. "Yamaha," he said, drifting his fingers down the keys. "Your piano?"

"Yes." I nodded. For some unknown reason I followed him over to the stage. "That's my baby grand. It was a birthday gift from my grandfather."

"Cool. Looks like you have a pretty impressive sound system. Lighting and everything." His hand pointed and waved in the air.

Ryan's eyes flickered over to the opposite wall and he strolled away to investigate another part of the pub. Something else had captured his attention.

"What do you say to a game of pool?" he asked, raising an eyebrow at me as he stood in the brick archway that led into the poolroom.

"You want to shoot pool—with me?" I actually looked over my shoulder to see if he was talking to someone else, even though I knew full well there was no one else here.

"Sure. That is, if you're up to it. I haven't been able to play in a long time." His voice trailed; a hint of sadness etched his words.

I shook my head, wondering why he would want to spend any more time here than he had to. *Maybe he is just being polite?*

"I don't know," I whispered.

"Come on, please? Just one game. I'll even let you win."

"Why, don't you think I can beat you on my own?" *Does he think all girls suck at shooting pool, or is he just teasing me?*

"Well, I don't know. Are you really good? You'll probably kick my butt," he conceded. "But I think I'll take my chances. Come on, one game. I just need to get my mind on something else."

"Okay, one game." I nodded and proceeded to pick out a pool stick. He was rather irresistible when he pleaded like that.

"I'll rack, you can break," Ryan said, placing the billiard balls in the wooden triangle.

I leaned over the table in my breaking stance and cracked the stick into the cue ball, pocketing a striped ball.

"Huh, I think I'm in trouble," he chuckled.

I made the next shot, but missed the third. It was his turn.

"So you're a lefty?" he asked while he chalked the tip of his pool stick.

"No, not really. I'm ambidextrous," I shyly admitted.

"Ambidextrous?" He smiled. "Very interesting."

His reaction made me feel like I had to explain. "I'm mostly right-handed, but I shoot pool and throw with my left."

"I tried to write with my left hand once when I had my right arm in a sling, but it was nothing but scribble. Can you write with your left hand?" He motioned as if he were writing on paper.

"Yeah, but it feels awkward and I can only print. I think I would have been a lefty, but I remember the teachers in grade school forcing me to use my right hand instead. I was always slightly confused with which scissors to use."

He smiled at me again. After all these years, he was the first guy who'd ever noticed that about me.

"Sometimes I wish I could write with both of my hands. It would probably make autograph signing more tolerable." He smirked.

Ryan tried to make a bank shot but missed. His beer glass was almost empty, so I quickly walked over to the bar and tapped a pitcher of beer and got a glass for myself. I always shot pool better when I was relaxed, and I was anything but relaxed at this moment.

"May I ask what you did to get your arm in a sling?" I glanced up at him while lining up my next shot.

He smiled innocently and laughed. "It's a funny story, actually."

"I like funny stories." I shrugged a bit.

"Ahh, when I was around nine years old—my brother Nick was eleven—we had this bright idea to make a go-cart. We super-glued one of my mom's laundry baskets to a skateboard and a . . ."

I couldn't help but make a silly face at him.

"Wait, it gets better," he said with a laugh. "At first we just tied the basket to the back of my brother's bicycle and I, of course, got to ride in the back. But we couldn't get up enough speed. So we rolled the basket to the top of Twelfth Street hill. I climbed in and Nick gave me a shove. Did you know that you can't steer a laundry basket on a skateboard?"

I could picture him as a kid careening down a hill in a laundry basket. I started to laugh.

"That's how I got this scar right here." Ryan twisted his right arm to show me the mark on his elbow.

"Twenty stitches." He grinned proudly.

I shook my head and smiled, imagining him being an adventurous little daredevil when he was young.

"Hey, it sounded like a good idea at the time!"

I noticed another scar across his right forearm. "How did you get that one?" I pointed to the mark in question.

"Ahh, fishing accident." He laughed. "Nick again. Caught me with a hook once while we were fishing with our dad. I yelled, he yanked, and I got more stitches. To this day I stay far away from him when we're fishing. What about you?" he asked. "Got any good scar stories?"

"I have to think about that one for a minute. Wait, I have one—on my right knee."

"Well, you know you have to show it to me now," he teased.

I hesitantly pulled up the leg of my jeans to reveal the dime-sized circular scar on my kneecap. I was relieved that I had shaved my legs this morning.

"I don't remember if I was six or seven, but I got this the day my dad took the training wheels off my bike," I admitted. "I think there's a cinder or two still stuck in there." My finger pushed on the spot.

"Ha! It's a good story, but that's not a very good scar. It's barely noticeable," he added after rubbing his finger over the faint mark.

"Sorry, it's all I have. I usually go right for breaking bones instead of getting simple scars."

"How many?" he asked, taking his next shot.

"What? Broken bones? Two—left wrist and right ankle."

"And are there good stories that go along with the broken bones?" he asked, sounding hopeful.

"Right ankle isn't that exciting. I slipped and fell on some icy steps at college." I took a sip from my beer glass. "Left wrist, however, has a better punch line. Let's just say that's the day I learned that tequila and Rollerblading should never be used in the same sentence."

Ryan started laughing. "That's something I would have liked to see."

"What about you? Did you ever break any bones?"

He looked at me and nodded. "Quite a few, actually. Mostly fingers and toes, but I had my left arm broken once in high school. I was playing baseball and got taken out by the third baseman."

While he was telling me his story, I missed my shot; it was his turn.

"Thanks! Thanks a lot," he quipped. "You're killing me here. Do you think you could have at least left me a shot?"

I could tell he was just teasing me. He walked around the table looking for an angle as I had tucked the cue ball behind the eight ball.

I noticed that I was able to look at him now for more than two seconds at a time. I watched as the fingers of his left hand formed into a bridge while he was lining up to take his next shot. He had really long fingers. The muscles on his forearm flexed when he stroked the pool stick in his hand.

From my current angle, I took in the visions of his long legs and how the back pockets of his jeans curved on his shape. And when he leaned over the table, my blue T-shirt separated from his body, exposing some tight flesh on his stomach. I could see what the big draw was for his fans . . . and it wasn't his pool-playing skills.

"Eight ball in the corner pocket," I stated as I drew my stick back to make the shot that he had missed. With one precise movement, I tapped the cue ball and pocketed the eight.

"Good job." Ryan held his hand up and gave me a gentle high-five. I started to put my pool stick back on the wall when he interrupted me.

"Oh, no. You have to play me again." He handed the stick back to me. "I'm just warming up."

"Okay, one more," I agreed. "You can break this time."

When it was my turn again, I noticed that he stood right behind the pocket I was aiming for. I was trying to line up my shot, but it was difficult as he was shifting his weight back and forth from foot to foot.

"Um, can you move?" I asked, motioning with my hand.

"What? Am I bothering you?" He snickered.

"No. Well yeah, it's kind of annoying, actually." I lined back up for my shot, concentrating on the game. He moved a few feet away and then started twirling his pool stick back and forth. His movements were such a distraction that I missed an easy shot.

"Oh, good try," he complimented, although I could tell by his tone that he really wanted me to miss it.

Ryan was trying to make a long shot, so I moved to stand behind the pocket he was aiming for. I got into a comfortable stance, casually tugging my jeans down a bit farther on my hips, and slipped my fingers under my shirt to softly scratch my stomach.

His eyes toggled between trying to play pool and watching me scratch my fake itch. He let out a big breath and missed his shot.

"Oh, good try," I patronizingly complimented.

"I see." He laughed. "You don't play fair either."

I grinned and shrugged slightly; we both were busted trying to distract each other. He wrinkled his nose at me and made a funny face. It was actually quite adorable.

When I leaned down to make my next shot he stood directly behind the pocket again. This time he lifted the front of his T-shirt enough to fake a stomach scratch. I could see the hair on his stomach, which was visible above the top button of his jeans. One naughty little thought ran through my head, but despite that I made the shot anyway.

"Nice try. But the twirling of the pool stick was more of a distraction than *that* was."

I had to walk past him, and when I did he stuck the bottom of his pool stick between my feet, causing me to trip. He caught me with his free arm to keep me from falling.

"Ass!" I snickered.

"Sorry, I can't help it if you're falling for me," he said confidently.

"Pff, hardly," I muttered. I leaned my pool stick up on the wall.

"Come on. I'm sorry. I didn't mean it. Don't walk away," he pleaded.

"I'm just going to the ladies' room," I said over my shoulder. Ryan trotted up behind me.

"What, are you following me now?" I kidded.

"Hardly." He smiled a cocky grin at me and gave me an innocent little shove toward the ladies' room door.

A few moments later, we resumed game two and it was his turn to shoot.

"So, Taryn, tell me. Are you a fan of *Seaside*, too?" he asked, monitoring my reaction.

"No. I haven't seen it," I said calmly. It was the truth. I took a sip of my beer and contemplated refilling my glass.

"You haven't seen the movie? For real?" He was frozen in his spot, gaping at me like I had two heads growing out of my shoulders.

"No, I haven't." I shook my head. I guess he was amazed at that revelation; his open mouth turned up into a smile.

"Yeah right," he snorted and took a sip of his drink.

"What, do you think I'm lying to you?" I couldn't help but look him directly in the eyes.

"What about the *Seaside* books? Did you read any of them?"

"No, I haven't. Everyone I know has, though. I suppose that's why you're so popular these days?" I shrugged and finished my beer.

He twitched his lips into a smirk. "Yeah . . . I think you're lying to me." He scratched his forehead again.

His accusation irritated me; I didn't like being called a liar, but I remained amicable nonetheless. I got up from my seat and walked over to where he stood by the pool table. I stopped two feet in front of him and looked him directly in the eyes, making sure to hold his gaze before I spoke.

"I *honestly* have not seen your movie nor have I read the books. You can see in my eyes that I'm not lying. I don't know what else to say to make you believe me."

Ryan stood perfectly still, looking dumbfounded. After a few seconds, I broke our eye contact and walked over to the table where I had set the pitcher of beer. I filled my glass and looked to see where his glass was. *Might as well give him a refill, too.* I stepped toward him to top off his drink.

"What?" I asked carefully. He looked like he was in a trance. "Did I . . . say something wrong? I'm, I'm sorry I haven't seen your movie. I hope that didn't offend you."

"No. That's . . . perfectly okay," he said; a hint of a smile touched his face. I watched as he just about swallowed his entire glass of beer.

"So besides kicking butt on the pool table, what else do you like to do?" he asked after I officially won our second game.

"Lots of things," I quickly replied. I didn't know what to tell him. I was too busy wondering why he was still here hanging out with me. Surely he had more important things to do.

"Like?" he prodded.

"Well, I like anything that involves water . . . swimming, boating, things like that. During the summer, some of the local businesses here in Seaport have a softball league. Sometimes we play volleyball down at the beach. But unfortunately, since I took over running the pub I don't have as much free time as I used to." I shrugged. "I work a lot."

While I was busy talking, Ryan set up the table for game number three. I noticed that his demeanor had changed slightly. He was more at ease . . . relaxed . . . calm. It was as though a blanket of tension had been removed from his shoulders.

I was getting set to break at the table when he interrupted me.

"Quick, without thinking, what's your favorite movie of all time?"

I stood up a little too fast. The motion, along with several glasses of beer and shots of whiskey, affected my equilibrium.

"Um, um," I stammered while trying to figure out what my favorite movie of all time was. "I don't know if I have one particular favorite. I have a few, but it's hard to pick."

"Okay, well . . . what made the list?"

I sucked in a sharp breath between my teeth. "*Monty Python and the Holy Grail, Galaxy Quest*, anything from Pixar . . ." I rambled.

"I see. You like outlandish humor." He chuckled. He rattled off a bunch of funny lines from the Monty Python movie. It was obvious that he had seen the movie as many times as I did.

"Now go away or I shall taunt you a second time," we said in unison, both of us adding the French inflection to the movie line. It made me laugh out loud.

It was my turn to shoot again, and just as I was ready to make my shot, Ryan yelled another funny line from the movie. I couldn't stop laughing.

"Stop it!" I pleaded, wiping my eyes.

I tried to make my shot again when Ryan came up right next to me and said a line from a funny scene in *Galaxy Quest*.

"Is there air? You don't know." He sniffed the air. "Seems okay."

I was laughing so hard I couldn't breathe. "Stop!" I gasped.

I reached to give him a teasing nudge with my fingers. Ryan caught me by the wrist and gently pulled me in, folding my arm with his, until my hand was pressed against his shoulder.

"Okay, okay, okay," he said, cracking up with laughter.

I could feel the warmth of his chest on my fingertips. Even though we were bent into each other, laughing hysterically, my mind started reeling just from this innocent touch. I could not allow myself to have those thoughts about him, so I quickly pulled my hand away.

He continued making funny voices and quoting my favorite movies. I was laughing so hard that I lost the third game. I couldn't focus with the tears of laughter in my eyes.

"You cheat," I scolded him.

"Who, me?"

"Yeah, you, Mr. Innocent."

I was getting ready to take my next shot when he stood behind me. I looked over my shoulder; he made me nervous standing back there.

"What?" he asked with a grin, like he *wasn't* up to no-good.

I looked back at the table and tried to hit the ball when he grabbed the end of my pool stick.

"You suck," I teased him after barely hitting the cue ball.

"No, you suck. You missed the shot," he fired back at me.

I tried to crack him with the end of my pool stick but he quickly sprinted away, laughing.

Ryan leaned down to take his shot; he was just about to hit the cue ball when I faked a loud cough.

"Huh, um, you suck."

He miscued and didn't even hit another ball. The cue ball slowly rolled into the cushion. That's when he chased me around the table.

"That's it—you asked for it. Hey, where are you going? Like you could get away from me."

I made two laps around the table, laughing all the way.

Eight games of pool and a pitcher of beer later, we were tied—four games apiece. We were having a really, really good time. The whole time we played, his charm never faltered. Even though we teased each other, he still complimented me when I made good shots, he encouraged me with kind words when I had a difficult shot to make, and he smiled at me incessantly.

We carried on just like two longtime friends. Being around him was surprisingly easy. That whole celebrity persona slipped away and he was just—Ryan, a genuinely nice guy.

"All right, this one's the tie-breaker. Winner gets all the bragging rights," he said, playfully tapping me on my rear with the end of his pool stick. His face took on a serious expression as he lined up for his next shot.

"Can I ask you a question, Taryn?"

"Yeah sure, what?" I was curious about what he wanted to know.

"Well, I was sort of wondering if you're married or seeing someone. I don't know if I could handle having a jealous guy attack me today, too," he admitted.

"Um, no. I've never been married. And, you don't have to worry—there's no jealous boyfriend either," I answered quickly, trying to be light-hearted and reassuring about it.

After the words flew out of my mouth I wished I could have rephrased them. I stared down at the ground with embarrassment. *This is why I shouldn't drink beer—you get too honest with people, you idiot. He probably thinks you're some basket case that no man wants.*

But I rationalized that he had already been accosted once today; I was sure a bar fight would be the last thing he needed to deal with.

"You're not dating *anyone*?" He sounded sort of shocked.

Looking him in the eyes was like taking a shot of truth serum.

"No, no one," I answered honestly.

My mind flashed back to the last man I dated. How Thomas ("The Asshole," as he was referred to now) asked me to marry him, how he promised to love me forever, and how I gave the ring back after I found out that he had an insatiable appetite for random sex with strangers. He was the last entry on a short list of guys who'd smashed my heart into pieces.

"Hmm, that's good to know." Ryan nodded while leaning over to take his next shot on the pool table. "So why is that?"

"I suppose the right man hasn't walked through my door yet," I answered casually, trying to redeem myself.

In reality, men walked in and out of my door every day, but I'd been numb for so long I didn't even care to notice them. My need for self-preservation was stronger.

His eyes locked on mine as he purposely missed the last shot of the game.

"Guess I get all the bragging rights, then," I whispered after I sunk the last ball on the table. He congratulated me with another soft high-five.

I noticed him glance at his watch as he finished his drink. I assumed he was thinking about leaving, so I peeked behind the window blind to see if there were still people loitering on the sidewalk.

"Is the coast clear?" he asked, even though he knew my answer.

"No. There's still a crowd out there. I see guys with cameras and a lot of women."

"This is ridiculous," he sighed, and rubbed his eyes with his fingers.

"What's worse, the paparazzi or the T-shirt-ripping psychos?"

"They're about even," Ryan muttered. "Most of the fans are great, but some of them go to scary extremes—like today. And the paparazzi, well, they're relentless." His voice sounded so defeated.

"You really have no freedom or privacy, do you?" I said matter-of-factly as I glanced back at him.

"No," he whispered. "Not anymore."

He looked completely forlorn. I felt so bad for him. How could someone have everything and at the same time, have nothing at all? I had to fight back the urge to go over to him and wrap him in a big hug. I didn't know what else to say, besides, "I'm sorry."

He gave me a brief smile, but the anguish on his face was plain to see.

"They aren't going to leave until they're sure you're not in here, are they?" I didn't want to say this out loud, but it was a question that had to be asked.

"No." His eyes shot up to lock on mine.

"Well, you can't just walk out into *that*. No way." I envisioned him leaving through the front door and getting attacked again by the throng of screaming women.

"What choice do I have?" he sighed. "Even if I manage to get to the street . . ." his voice trailed in defeat.

My mind was plotting—how to gain him safe passage out of here. The thought of him getting accosted by that horde out there pissed me off.

"Let me go check the back door, see if the way is clear. Stay here, okay?"

Ryan didn't reply; the gleam of hope in his eyes was confirmation enough that he was willing to accept my help.

I peeked out the back door; the alley was empty. Where the heck would he go from here, though? My eyes searched the alley to be sure that there was no danger, and then I had a brilliant idea.

"Can someone pick you up?" I asked.

"Yeah." He nodded assuredly.

I reached for my cell phone.

"Maggie? Hi, it's Taryn. I need to ask you a favor. Well, you see, I have a very special guest inside my pub and he is in need of a safe exit. I mean, he's very well-known and, um, there are cameras and crazy women outside my bar. Yes, he's one of the boys from the movie."

My eyes shot up to him and I gave him my best crooked sorry-smile. "Can I send him through your shop . . . through your back door? No, he just needs to get to the street—safely. Okay, thanks, Maggie. You're the best."

I told Ryan, "Tell your driver to park directly in front of Maggie's Bakery on Fifth Street, between Elm and Mulberry Streets, and to call you when he is in position." Why did I all of a sudden feel like I was masterminding some great caper in a really bad thriller? "You'll be safe. Maggie is a nice, older lady. She won't even know who you are. She'll leave you alone."

I looked up to see him beaming at me—as if I were a lifesaver.

"The things we take for granted," he muttered.

"Hmm? What do you mean?" I wished he would explain.

"Nothing," he whispered, shaking his head as a twinge of a smile touched his lips. He pulled his phone from his pocket to call his driver.

Ten minutes later we said our goodbyes.

"Thank you, Taryn, for everything. I'm very sorry for putting you through this today."

"It's okay, Ryan. You don't need to apologize. It was nice to meet you."

"It was very nice to meet you, too. Huh, I can't remember the last time I felt this relaxed. It was nice feeling normal for once, even if it was only for a couple of hours. I had a *really* great time."

"I'm glad to hear that. I had a really great time too."

"Taryn, I hope I can trust you to keep our time together just between us—our secret." His eyes were pleading, and I knew that no one could ever be told about our encounter.

"Don't worry, Ryan," I assured him. I purposely looked him directly in the eyes so he'd know I was telling the truth. "Please know that you can trust me. It's as much my secret as it is yours. I swear I will never say a word about it to anyone. Never—I promise."

He held his hand out to shake mine, so I reflexively responded. I was all prepared for a friendly handshake, but instead he twisted my hand in his and ever so gently he kissed the back of my hand.

"See you," he said softly, still holding my fingers in his hand.

I felt my heart skip another beat as it flopped in my chest.

"See you," I managed to breathe out.

I walked him to the gray steel door in the kitchen and watched intently as he made it to the opposing door across the alleyway, completely unnoticed. Ryan paused in the open doorway and smiled at me one last time before disappearing into the bakery.

CHAPTER 3

Encounters

"DID I MISS something?" Marie asked. Her eyes looked me up and down as if I had the word "guilty" written all over my body.

"What do you mean?" I tried to sound oblivious to her accusation. I was not going to volunteer anything—I'd promised him.

She tilted her head over toward the window where two photographers stood on guard outside. I wanted so badly to run upstairs and dump a few buckets of water out of my second-story window to shoo them away.

"I have no idea. Maybe some of the famous wandered off the reservation," I replied flatly. "Did you cut up any limes yet?" I was searching for a new topic while keeping my fluttering heart in check; there was no way I was going to discuss the past few hours.

"Yeah, but we're almost out," she grumbled.

Eventually the paparazzi disappeared, obviously disappointed that they were not going to get the million-dollar shot of Ryan Christensen in my pub.

The rest of the night my mind lingered over the memories of the day. Ryan had been so charming, so kind, and funny. I felt such remorse for saying out loud that he was full of himself. I could not have been more wrong about a person.

His speckled blue eyes were so mesmerizing when he looked at me while kissing my hand. How strange I felt from this chance meeting! I allowed myself a brief smile before forcing my mind back on running my pub. I knew I'd never see him again; we came from two different worlds that weren't meant to coexist.

THE NEXT day I had some errands to run; I had put off grocery shopping long enough. I also had bands booked for Friday and Saturday nights, and that definitely meant that we would have much bigger crowds than normal. I completed my personal food shopping and then packed my cart with fresh lemons, limes, and oranges for the bar before heading to the checkout.

I picked the lane with the fewest people standing in line, thinking that would get me out of the store quicker. How foolish of me to assume that would be the case! The elderly lady in front of me began arguing with the cashier, and you know things are only going to get worse when the cashier calls someone for a price check. *Just my luck.*

I let my eyes glance over the front covers of the magazines that filled the end racks, trying to kill time. Most of the covers had delicious pictures of baked items surrounded by words like "low fat" and "diet" or photos of Hollywood actresses airbrushed to perfection. The absurdity of it all made me chuckle.

I studied the pictures of the Hollywood superstars that filled the front covers of the rest of the magazines until my eyes focused on a familiar face with piercing blue eyes. There he was—Ryan Christensen—a side note or feature on the cover of every gossip magazine on the rack.

I glanced over some of the titles around his pictures:

Seaside Star: Ryan—The Whole Truth
Ryan Christensen—Hottest Actor on the Planet!
SEASIDE'S Ryan Christensen and His Messy Love Triangle

As much as I despised those rag magazines, morbid curiosity got the better of me. I grabbed the first one with "The Whole Truth" advertised and thumbed through it until I came across Ryan's featured article. The pages were filled with glossy pictures of him trying to look inconspicuous in some club, pictures from the movie set, and photos of him posing.

There was no "truth" as the headline promised. All the words that surrounded his pictures were nothing more than speculated hints of scandal and allegations of his indiscretions.

As I scanned over the print, it appeared that I knew more "truth" facts about this man than this pathetic magazine did. During our time together Ryan had revealed a lot about himself—indirectly just through my observations, and directly through his stories.

I noticed Ryan rubbed his forehead a lot when he was stressed, how he cracked his knuckles out of habit, and how he chewed on the inside of his lip when he would ponder something.

My mind drifted over the four amazing hours we spent together yesterday. Those memories of Ryan were different from the visions plastered in the magazine. He was nice, down-to-earth, just like a regular guy.

For as kind and friendly as he was, I noticed other character traits that most people probably didn't see. Many people deem actors to be outspoken and gregarious, but Ryan was anything but that. He was shy but very playful, lousy at flirting, and a bit of an introvert . . . just like me.

But through his career decision, some good luck, and perhaps some incredible timing, Ryan's status was raised from normal guy to almost godlike overnight. Any chance he had at being a normal person was now destroyed by fame. That realization made me sad. I pitied him.

My lips pursed together as I read the caption under one of the pictures: "Ryan and Suzanne—making out on and off set." The words cast visions into my mind of him kissing every girl that presented an opportunity. He was desired by so many that he could have his pick.

My internal monologue started again. *He probably has a different girl in his bed every night, just like my ex-fiancé, Thomas.* The thought completely disgusted me. I shut the magazine and slapped it back on the rack.

BY FRIDAY night, I had replaced thoughts of Ryan Christensen with about thirty different mixed drink recipes. I was happy to see a decent-sized crowd enjoying the guitar player I'd hired. He was engaging the crowd with a good mix of popular tunes, and I couldn't stop myself from dancing behind the bar. *I'll have to book him again*, I thought to myself as I mixed two Jack and Cokes for a customer.

I caught sight of Pete, my weekend bouncer and longtime friend, as I scanned the crowd. He was six foot three, built like a linebacker, with a thick neck and a close-shaved goatee, and was partially blond but mostly bald. He was hard to miss. I wondered what was wrong to make him leave his post at the front door. I noticed he was escorting a young man with short brown hair and ripped jeans over to where I stood. The boy looked like he was an older teenager, but definitely not old enough to be in a bar.

"Taryn," Pete yelled over the music. "This kid says he has a delivery for you."

"Are you Taryn Mitchell?" the boy asked.

"Yes—that's me."

"I have a message for you," he said loudly as he handed me a white envelope.

I tore the envelope open; inside was a handwritten letter.

Taryn,

This nice kid in front of you is Jason. He's the son of one of our production assistants that I bribed to hand-deliver this note to you.

I had a wonderful time with you the other day and I'd really like to see you again.

If you'd like to see me, please write down your cell phone number so I can call you in private.

I hope you say YES.

Ryan

I had to read the note twice; it didn't sink in the first time. *Does this mean that he likes me? He wants to see . . . ME? Why? So I can be a third leg of some new love triangle? So he can get his rocks off with the local selection while he's in town?*

He was a super-celebrity and I wasn't—and as much as I wanted to see him again, I'm intelligent enough to know that nothing lasting could come from it.

I grabbed a pen from next to the cash register, bit the cap off with my teeth, and with all my strength and resolve I wrote NO on the back of a Mitchell's napkin. My heart was thumping from this ordinary but strangely painful action. He wasn't the first guy I'd denied, but he was definitely the first for a denial on a napkin via teenager messenger service.

Ryan Christensen was not long-term boyfriend material and I had no interest in having a one-night stand with anyone, regardless of how famous he was—so why even go through the motions? I could not put my heart on the line for this one.

I swallowed hard, folded the napkin, and handed it to the boy.

"Please give this to him, Jason," I muttered somberly. I was hoping not to regret this decision.

My eyes shot over to my trusty friend.

"Pete, please make sure this young man makes it safely to his car." I stood there and watched as the boy left through the front door with my reply in his hand while an old, familiar pain caused the fissure in my heart to crack a bit wider. It would be another long night devoid of love.

THE NEXT morning, the sounds of the birds chirping outside my window pulled me from my dreamless sleep. It was gray in my bedroom; not the bright, sunny yellow I had hoped to wake to. The weather seemed to match my sullen mood perfectly.

I took a deep breath and held it in my lungs for a moment before exhaling with force while a vision of Ryan appeared in my thoughts. I pushed my hair back off my forehead and tried to rub the sleep from my eyes. *Maybe if I press hard enough into my skull the vision will disappear?*

As I trudged my way down the hall to the bathroom, my thoughts flashed back to writing "no" on a napkin. Why did I do that? He'd asked for my phone number and I'd chickened out.

A split second later, rationality sunk in. He's not just another guy who has the potential to rip your heart out and hand it to you while it's still beating. He would be capable of *much* more damage than that.

But he wanted to see me again—so he must think that I'm attractive enough. After all, his last known speculated girlfriend was beautiful.

I took a long look at myself in the mirror, trying to see if I could agree with his assessment.

I pulled the hair tie from my ponytail and brushed out my long hair. My summer tan was faded, my bikini lines were just about gone, but I still had a bit of glow left on my face.

I turned the faucet on, splashing some cold water on my eyes. The more I rubbed, the bluer my eyes appeared.

"Not bad for a twenty-seven-year-old," I whispered out loud to the mirror.

But so what if he likes me—then what? Do I get to add a famous person to my short list of friends? Deep in my brain, doubt slipped out of its cage.

Despite Ryan's gesture, how could I ever compete with the many Hollywood starlets out there? All of them waiting in the shadows to bag their own leading man. With their designer clothes, designer hair, and high-gloss tans—not to mention their killer figures, silicone breasts, and filthy-rich bank accounts. Examples of them were listed conveniently in the supermarket tabloids, and they were all on the hunt for one of their own kind. Ryan Christensen was definitely on their eligible bachelor's list.

Then I wondered why I thought the famous, single actresses would be any different from me. They too had their fair share of stardom hell with losing their men to on-set hookups and wandering infidelity. Even the beautiful starlets were left brokenhearted.

And then my depressing thoughts got worse. Standing directly in line with the gorgeous actresses looking for husbands would be the legion of super-hot models looking for their own arm candy. *Ooh, look at me, I have Mr. Super-Hot Actor Man on my arm.*

If he weren't an actor and extremely famous at the moment, would any of these women *ever, ever* give him the time of day? *I think not.*

Heck, while I was making the list, why not add in all the eligible daughters of the rich and powerful . . . and top it off with several million regular women around the globe who would kill for a shot at Ryan Christensen.

That would be an awfully long line to stand in for one man.

Oh hell, what was the point? In a few weeks he'd be gone anyway. Off to another location to do his next movie with some totally sexy co-star he'd bond with, and in no time they would surely try to get into each other's pants.

Every day millions of people go off to work, but how many of them have to fake romances or stick their tongue in someone else's mouth for a living?

Honey, have a great day at work and I hope you get some good tongue action on set today! Oh, you're doing a love scene today with a hot, single actress? Good for you. Should I call the lawyer now or wait until you officially leave me for her?

How many actors' personal lives were ruined because of it?

I wondered if it would be possible for someone like Ryan to ever have a normal relationship. Maybe he would follow in the footsteps of so many others before him and just stick to brief relationships with a variety of actresses.

I thought about the majority of relationships among actors—only a handful of them were between actors and normal humans. The odds were stacked against me regardless.

I shook my fingers through my hair to toss the thoughts away. I was just deluding myself to think that this—whatever it was—could have ever amounted to anything.

Time to get back into the real world, Taryn. Men like that don't fall for ordinary people like you. I suddenly felt very insignificant all over again.

"WHY ARE you in such a bad mood?" Marie grumbled at me while she was making a drink. She knew me well enough to know that something was wrong.

I had spent the entire day beating myself up internally; by nine o'clock my internal struggle had reached the outside of my body.

I shook my head and tried to shrug her off. Best friend or not, there was no way I'd ever spill my secret to her; my private faux pas would become the public knowledge of everyone who stepped foot in the bar, because surely she would chastise me out loud for the rest of the night.

She leered at me, demanding an answer.

"Something didn't work out the way I had hoped." I figured that was good enough of an answer to give her. *I met a wonderful, quirky guy who could make me really happy but he's also extremely famous and could never be mine . . .*

"You want to talk about it?" Marie asked.

I knew she cared about me, but this was something I couldn't share.

"No," I replied softly. "Nothing to talk about. I'll be fine."

I was thankful that I had a large crowd of strangers mingling around my pub; there was enough of a commotion going on that I could stay distracted. One of my favorite local bands had just finished setting up their equipment on the stage and soon we would all be enjoying some rocking music. Pete held his usual position, perched on a stool inside the door, making sure to check everyone's ID and to collect a small cover charge for the band.

As I looked around, everything that was always stable and constant in my life was just as it should be. I accepted that my decision was a wise and healthy choice and stood firm in my resolve.

The evening progressed and Marie and I were dancing behind the bar as usual, mixing drinks and sliding glasses and bottles to our customers. The music was jamming, the crowd was thick, and my bad mood for the most part was lifted. Everyone was having a good time.

I was waiting on a customer when all of a sudden I felt a hand clamp tightly around my forearm and sharp fingernails dig into my skin.

"Marie! What are you doing?" I asked, looking down at her clenched hand. My eyes shot up to look at her face and I noticed she was turning white; her mouth was gaping open. I glanced down the bar in the direction of her petrified stare; I didn't know what the problem was.

"Marie?"

I scanned the crowd rapidly and then I saw him—Ryan Christensen—and a small group of people filtering through the crowd.

One of my regular customers, Dan, started smacking his hand repeatedly on the bar to get my attention. "Taryn, Pete wants to see you NOW!"

"Marie, let go!" I shouted, peeling her fingers off my arm. I ducked out the other end of the bar and made my way through the crowd to the front door. Pete was holding back a large crowd when I finally reached him.

"Taryn! What the hell was I supposed to do? I had to let him in—he paid."

"Pete, we can't let any more people in. We're at max now. All I need is the fire marshal to show up—they'll shut me down!" I yelled over the music.

"Well then *you* have to tell all of *them* that I can't let them in!" Pete pointed at the crowd that stretched all the way down the sidewalk.

"Pete, just close the door and sit on your stool in front of it. I'll get Dan to help you." I stepped outside onto the sidewalk and raised my voice to speak to the waiting crowd.

"I'm sorry, everyone, but we are at maximum capacity. If you'd like to come in, you will have to wait until other customers leave."

I rushed back into the bar and quickly located Dan.

"Oh, Dan, another thing . . ." I turned to take hold of his muscular arm. "If the crowd out there gets out of control, call the police, then come and get me immediately."

I hurried to get myself back behind the bar; in all the years we'd been in business we had never had a crowd this size before. Customers were two to three people deep at the bar. It was insane.

I spotted a burly man standing at the opposite end with money sticking out of his hand. His stance was somewhat intimidating. Marie was still dazed from seeing Ryan; she was having a hard time waiting on customers and remembering drink orders.

"Hi, what can I get you?" I asked the burly man. I figured he was personal security for the actors. He fit the look.

"Hi there," he said, smiling at me as he proceeded to rattle off a drink order.

I glanced around looking for Ryan; I knew he was in here somewhere. Our eyes locked when I found him; he was leaning on the far brick wall by the poolroom with his arms folded across his chest—staring at me with a slight grin. There was already a swarm of girls around him, but he didn't seem to be paying a lot of attention to them. He was talking to some guy instead.

As I was mixing their drink order, I noticed that two of the famous actresses from his movie were also in my pub. A few male patrons were trying to break through the bodyguard force field that surrounded them.

Ryan seemed to be having a good time. He had a big glass of beer in his hand and he was laughing and being quite social with his group, but not so much with the general public.

I felt weird from thinking about our first encounter and my rejection when he asked for my number. I was so nervous from seeing him again that I tried to ignore him, but it was hard. I could feel his presence all around me.

I was at the far end of the bar waiting on a customer when Marie nudged me with her elbow.

"He's sitting at the bar!" she squealed with excitement. She was squirming around so much I thought she was going to pee her pants.

"I tried to wait on him, but he said he wants to talk to you!" she babbled as she pointed a finger at me.

I flashed my eyes down the bar. He was sitting there casually with his arms folded, wearing a bit of a smirk, on the same stool he'd sat on the first time he was here. I continued to take care of my current customer before I made my approach. I wasn't going to rush.

I slowly walked toward him, taking care of several customers on my way, while my mind was flashing a million different thoughts. *Do I say hi? Should I pretend not to know him?* I wished I had another forty feet to walk, but I was out of floor.

"Hi!" Pathetic as it was, that was about all I could get myself to say.

"Hi back," he said, flashing a sexy smile. "How are you?"

"Surprised?" I shrugged. "And extremely busy, thanks to you." I tried to sound aloof.

"That's good, I guess." His eyes flickered over to the stage. "You have some great entertainment here tonight."

"Thanks. These guys are great. They play here a lot."

I felt myself smiling at him as we spoke, while my mind drifted over the memories of the last time he was here. No matter what, it was still easy to talk to him. That was, until I became aware that people were staring at us.

"So, can I get you a refill?" I asked, trying to be casual with him as if he were just another customer. I snapped right back into business mode.

Ryan quickly finished his beer and slid the empty glass toward me. As I walked over to the beer taps I glanced back at him; his eyes had followed me and he was smiling. I couldn't help but smirk back.

"What do I owe you?" He shoved his hand in his front pocket.

I shook my head again in disapproval. "Nothing, it's on the house; I know the owner." I shrugged. I was trying to be nonchalant.

"You don't have to do that, you know." He scowled at me.

I wrinkled my nose at him in response to his unhappy expression.

He mimicked me, until a smile cracked on his lips. "Thanks, . . . Taryn." Those piercing blue eyes of his quickened my pulse.

There were so many people at the bar, I had to tear myself away and wait on the next customer. People were shouting drink orders and waving money.

No sooner did I turn my eyes away when three women descended on him. They were giggling, gushing, flirting, and trying to get him to pose with them so they could capture their celebrity moment on their camera phones.

My lips curled in disgust. I was glad I'd made the decision that I did. There was too long of a line to get to that man. I attempted to ignore him again.

"What can I get you?" I asked the somewhat good-looking guy who was waiting for a drink. He mumbled something unintelligible; the music mixed with the hum of people talking and yelling made it almost impossible to hear.

I heard Ryan sneeze a couple of times in a row. My attention automatically shifted back to him. *I wonder if he's catching a cold?* I slid a few white cocktail napkins in front of him in case he needed a tissue. I wasn't looking as I set them down near his hand; I smiled when I felt his warm fingertips brush over mine.

"Sorry, I didn't get that." I cupped my other hand around the back of my ear so my latest customer would get the point. "What would you like?" I asked again.

"You're beautiful!" he shouted at me.

I grimaced at his words and his lame attempt to hit on me.

"Thanks," I replied flatly. "What can I get you?" I was getting impatient.

"How about your phone number?" he yelled back to me as he was almost lifting his body onto the bar. I noticed that after he spoke he looked back at his buddies so they could acknowledge his bravery.

I looked down and smiled as the embarrassment made me blush. My golden rule was not to date random customers, especially the ones who were assholes.

"Thanks. I'm very flattered," I replied with a halfhearted smile. "But sorry, the only thing you're going to get from this side of the bar is alcohol."

My eyes flickered back to Ryan, who was sitting there staring at me with a smug grin on his face.

"Oh, come on!" the young man pleaded with me. I just shook my head no.

A few men sitting at the bar teased the poor guy. "Ooh, shot down in flames. Ouch!"

I gave them a disapproving look.

"What do you want to drink?" I asked again, trying to be more cordial. In reality, he had ten seconds to reply before I was going to move on to the next customer.

"Three lagers," he finally yelled back.

Ten drink orders later, I was making a whiskey sour for a female customer when I noticed one of the actresses, Francesca LeRoux, descend upon Ryan. Francesca was young, leggy, superthin, with long, straight brown hair. She looked like a model. She was leaning on Ryan's shoulder with her arm around him, whispering in his ear.

I happened to be looking when she ran her fingers over Ryan's hair. He winced and tilted his head away from her touch. I could tell it bothered him. *Why does that bother me?* There was something about the way she touched him that irritated me.

A few moments later, Ryan moved back to the table with her to rejoin their group. He sat down in one of the side booths, but there were so many people around them that my view of him was obscured.

"What did he say to you?" Marie asked. She was going out of her mind with curiosity.

"I gave him a beer. He said 'thanks.'" I shrugged. "That's it."

"You had Ryan freakin' Christensen at your bar and you didn't talk to him?"

"Marie, what was I supposed to say?" I was not into having this conversation with her, so I walked away.

Ryan stayed at the table with his group, although I was trying not to keep tabs on his whereabouts. Three bulky security guards hovered around them, keeping the general population at bay. I saw a few women manage to squeak through and get an autograph, and I wished that they would just leave him alone.

I wondered if the way he ran his finger back and forth underneath his nose to scratch was another nervous tick, but he started to sneeze again. He had to be getting a cold.

As I was filling another drink order, my mind contemplated what the big deal was to get someone's signature on a piece of paper. Was it simply the act of stopping him from whatever he was doing to make him acknowledge another human being's presence?

I signed my name several times a day—mostly on checks to pay the bills—but it wasn't like the power company was on my doorstep flirting or screaming my name to get my signature.

I watched as he scribbled his name on the bottom of some girl's shirt. What would possess these girls to want him to write on their clothes with permanent marker?

I did notice one thing, though; some of the girls who stepped up to bug him ranged from quite pretty to extremely attractive, but they all seemed to be forms without faces to him. He didn't even really look at them. It was as if he, too, was in business mode.

"Hi!" shouted a male voice that snapped me out of my private thoughts.

I looked up to see a good-looking man wearing a suit jacket over a nicely pressed button-down shirt. Thick, dark hair . . . slight dimples in his cheeks . . . no wedding ring on the hand that rested on the bar.

"Hi. What can I get you?" My eyes adjusted to this new handsome man.

"What do you have on tap?" he asked, flashing an alluring smile at me.

I listed the ten different drafts and handed him a menu of available bottled beers just in case.

"Hmm, you've given me too many options. What do you recommend?"

"Well, that depends," I responded, "on whether you prefer a darker, full-bodied beer or a lighter, pale ale."

He leaned further onto the bar. "You're not making this easy for me. Why don't you pick one? I'm sure I'll like anything you choose."

I walked away smiling and grabbed a new glass along my way. I tapped one of the more popular ales and slid the glass across the bar to him.

"Mmm, that's good." He grinned and winked at me. "You have excellent taste."

His compliment made me laugh. He wasn't the first man to tell me that.

"My name is Mark. What's yours?"

"Taryn," I replied, wondering if he was going to pay for the beer I'd just served him.

"It's a pleasure to meet you, Taryn." Mark smiled and held out his hand to me.

I didn't want to be rude, so I shook it.

"Your hand is soft," Mark complimented.

"Thanks," I said warily, attempting to end our handshake.

Before I knew it, the slick man clamped his hand around mine, trapping my hand in his. I tugged back against his grip, but he was stronger than I was. My smile quickly faded, as I didn't like the hold he had on me.

"Did anyone ever tell you how beautiful you are?" he crooned. His free hand started petting my wrist and forearm in the same manner that you would pet a house cat. My stomach twisted in a knot.

I tried to pull my hand free, but he maintained his hold.

"Let go of my hand," I stated calmly, in an almost teasing fashion.

"I can't. Not until you tell me why I'm so drawn to you," Mark said, as if it were my fault that he couldn't control himself.

I tugged several times while he attempted to lamely flirt with me, but I could not break his grip.

"Let. Go. Of. My. Hand." I emphasized each word.

I looked over his shoulder, surprised to see Ryan standing right behind him. His beer was in one hand and the fingers of his other hand were tucked in his pocket; his narrowed eyes were fixed on mine. Next to him was one of his bodyguards.

"Oh Taryn." Mark flashed his best smile at me. "I can't let you go. Since you were so good at picking out a drink for me, I think you should pick out a restaurant for me to take you to."

"I don't think so," I replied coldly, tired of his game.

"Oh, come on, sweetie. Don't be like that." His tone made me wince. He trailed his presumptuous finger over my wrist.

Ryan looked at my new admirer and back at me; his face was showing his concern. I shook my head ever so slightly, hoping Ryan would heed my warning. I didn't want any trouble.

Two young women approached Ryan and attempted to get his attention. One of them grabbed his arm. Ryan immediately raised his elbow, obviously displeased with their forward behavior and intrusion. He almost spilled his beer. I could see he didn't like people touching him either.

I repeated myself, raising my annoyed voice at Mark. "Let go of my hand. That's three dollars for the beer."

"Come on—you should go out with me. We'll have a lot of fun, I promise." His tone dripped with coercion, but he finally released my hand.

"No. That will never happen. Three dollars, please."

Ryan held up his hand to the girls and I thought I heard him say, "please, not now" to them. His bodyguard immediately intervened.

"Just take a chance. I know you felt something just now when I held your hand. There was a connection there. Don't deny it," Mark pressed.

Ryan was glaring at him now. His anger was evident.

"Sorry. I didn't feel anything," I stated flatly, keeping all emotions out of my tone. This guy was beyond being an asshole.

"You hurt my feelings," Mark pathetically pouted.

Marie was watching me out of the corner of her eye too; we always looked out for each other. We had been friends since junior high, and we'd worked the bar together for so long, we had the creep signal down pat. I pulled the bar rag out of my back pocket and dropped it on the floor.

"Who's your new friend, Taryn?" Marie yelled over to me.

"Oh, this is Mark," I stated loudly as I pointed at him. "He wants to take me to dinner, but I just really want him to pay for his beer. It's such a dilemma."

Ryan chuckled ever so subtly.

My new admirer finally got the hint. He peeled three ones from his folded money, tossed it on the bar, and turned in a huff. He almost bumped into Ryan as he fled his spot at the bar.

Ryan smiled at me before raising his glass to take a sip of his drink. I flashed my eyes between Ryan and the open seat, hoping that he would get the hint. He didn't disappoint.

"Can I refresh your drink for you, sir?" I said in a proper yet joking tone as I snatched his glass off the bar.

He laughed slightly and nodded his head. I set his glass in the sink and tapped him a fresh beer in a new glass.

"Can I also interest you in doing a shot of one of the smoothest tequilas you'll ever have?" I set his new beer in front of him.

"Definitely interested," he stated directly, his piercing eyes locked on mine.

I reached up to the top shelf behind the bar and wrapped my fingers around a clear bottle with a round, silver stopper.

"What is that?" he asked, trying to read the bottle.

"Gran Patrón Platinum tequila." I poured two shots.

"Here's to . . . psychotic fans," I cheered, raising my shot glass in the air.

He tapped his glass against mine and we both tossed the shots back into our mouths.

Ryan reached in his pocket and pulled a wad of money out, but I shook my head at him.

"No. Put your money away," I whispered as I collected the empty shot glasses.

He frowned at me. Instinctively I scowled back. Then, like a two-year-old, he stuck his tongue out at me. I casually rubbed my middle finger across my eyebrow. We both started laughing.

When I glanced back up at him, Suzanne Strass, the other actress who'd followed him into the bar, was hovering around him. She whispered something in his ear; whatever she said made him roll his eyes and purse his lips. He didn't look happy with whatever she'd said.

Without saying a word, he got up and moved back to the table with his original group, where he stayed for the rest of the night. They had several additional rounds of drinks and seemed to all have a good time. I noticed Suzanne swaying back and forth to the music. Ryan sat facing in my direction, and every once in a while he'd stare at me until our eyes met.

Ryan's blue eyes were hypnotic and I couldn't help but smile every time one of us was caught staring. He was extremely handsome, but there was something else. He didn't hold himself in high regard; he just wanted to blend in.

His eyes held mine for an extra moment. He smiled at me, tilted his head slightly, and then proceeded to unbutton his top shirt. I was curious as to why he was undressing in my pub. I couldn't look away.

He patted his hand on his chest and stretched back. That's when I noticed he was wearing my blue T-shirt under everything else.

I chuckled to myself; no longer could I contain my big grin. He raised his eyebrows a couple of times and winked at me.

It was almost one o'clock in the morning when his group got up to leave. Ryan stood there watching me while he put his jacket on. He let out a sigh, then turned and headed for the door. And just like that, with no words, no goodbye, he was gone.

Fortunately when the celebrities left, so did most of the crowd. The pub was trashed. We'd gone through most of the bottles of beer I had stocked in the coolers as well as most of my liquor reserves. Bottles, glasses, and empty pitchers covered most of the tables.

"How freaking crazy was that?" Pete shouted as he helped collect the garbage.

Marie had tray after tray of dirty glasses lined up on the bar top, but despite the huge mess that awaited cleanup, she was still smiling from her celebrity encounter.

"I cannot believe that *they* came *here*!" she giggled. "I'm still jittery!"

I smiled at her. Ryan and his friends were just people who wanted to have a good time tonight too.

"One thing is for sure—Ryan Christensen couldn't take his eyes off of you," she teased me.

I groaned at her for pointing that out.

"And don't you roll your eyes at me either!" she reprimanded.

I let out a big sigh while visions of Ryan flashed through my mind. We did stare at each other a lot tonight.

Why did he try to protect me? I started washing dirty glasses trying not to think about it, but I was failing miserably.

CHAPTER 4

Games

"You made the paper," Tammy announced, tossing the Monday local section of the *Seaport Times* in front of me. My dear friend Pete was holding Tammy's other hand. He pulled out a chair so she could join me at the big, round table in the middle of the pub.

I was so glad when Pete put that engagement ring on Tammy's finger. He loved her so much and she surely made him happy. Tammy was a sweetheart and a great friend.

"We did?" I asked as I paged through the newspaper to find the article.

"Yep, you're on page two," she replied.

"Where?" I didn't see an article.

"There, the picture." Tammy pointed.

I studied the photo of people standing outside my front door. The caption read "Local night spot Mitchell's Pub had a long waiting line Saturday as visiting celebrities were reported to be inside."

"That's it?" Marie asked as she read over my shoulder. "No story?"

"Whatever. I'll take the free advertising," I joked. "And speaking of long lines . . . here, this is for you." I pulled two envelopes from my pocket and slid one to both Pete and Marie.

"What's this?" Pete asked, peering inside. He counted it out. "This is five hundred bucks!"

"Well, we had a monumental Saturday night and I wanted to share the profits with you. You both worked very hard and I wanted to say thank-you in more than words."

"Thanks!" they both said in unison.

Marie's husband, Gary, tried to grab the envelope from her.

"Hands off, mister!" she yelled, smacking his hand. "I busted my ass for this."

"Yeah, Gary. Keep your hands off that money," I scolded him. "Marie needs all of that. Maybe that way she'll be able to stay in the game longer tonight."

"Oh, I see," Pete bellowed. "You think you're going to win this money back tonight, do you?" He grinned at me.

"That's right. We're upping tonight's bets from quarters to dollars. And the sooner you shuffle the cards, the sooner I'll be rich," I teased him. "Marie . . . while you are over there, can you grab a bowl for the pretzels, pretty please?"

"So we're not playing for quarters?" Pete's face fell.

Tammy nudged him in the arm. "I'm pretty sure Taryn is joking."

Marie was digging in one of the cabinets behind the bar when the telephone rang. "Good evening, Mitchell's Pub."

I looked over at her, confused. "Don't answer that. We're closed, remember?"

"No, I'm sorry. We aren't open tonight. The pub will be open tomorrow at one o'clock. Sure, hold on a minute." Marie held the phone to her shoulder. "Taryn, phone call."

"Who is it?" I whispered.

She shrugged her shoulders, not bothering to ask. "I dunno."

"Hello?" I answered.

"Taryn? Hi, it's Ryan. How are you?"

"Good! And you?" *Why is he calling me?*

"I'm good. I was just wondering if you were open. Cal and I were looking for something to do and I thought about shooting pool," Ryan rambled.

"Well, actually I'm closed on Mondays," I said regretfully.

"Oh, what are you up to then?" he asked.

"I'm just hanging out with a few friends. On Mondays we play poker."

"Did you say poker?" It sounded as though he didn't believe me.

"Yeah," I laughed nervously. "We play every Monday."

"That sounds like fun."

I could hear another male voice in the background asking him to explain.

"Playing poker," Ryan said to someone else.

"Oh hell yeah!" the voice in the background replied loudly and enthusiastically.

"So I guess this is the part where I ask if you want to join us?" I snickered.

"I don't know. Are there a lot of people there?" he asked worriedly.

"No, just four of my friends. That's it."

"Just four? Do you mind if we come over?" He sounded hopeful. "We'd love to play; we need to get out of the hotel."

"No, I don't mind. That is, as long as you don't bring your psycho fans with you. By the way, we play for money."

Ryan laughed in my ear. "You'll have to sneak us in then. We can come through the alley."

"Hmm, sounds like you thought about this already," I accused him.

"Maybe," he shot back. "We'll be there in a half hour."

"Who was that?" Marie asked. Her eyes narrowed in on my face.

I sat back down at the big table and ran my finger around the rim of my beer glass.

"That was . . ." I took a deep breath. "Ryan."

"What? You mean like Ryan *Christensen*?" Marie just about shot out of her chair.

"Yep." I was fighting back a smile.

"And?" She glared at me.

"He and someone named Cal are going to be joining us tonight."

Tammy lurched onto the table, almost spilling her drink. "Cal? Cal Reynolds? You mean the actor Cal Reynolds who played Charles's brother Randolph in *Seaside*?"

"Who's Charles?" I asked.

"Charles! You don't know who Charles is?" Tammy shrilled at me.

I slid back farther in my seat and shook my head. She sort of scared me for a moment.

"Charles is the character that Ryan Christensen plays in *Seaside*!" Her expression made me feel stupid, like I was missing a big chunk of common knowledge.

"Okay, if you say so. He said Cal, so if that's the same Cal, then yes," I replied.

"NO freakin' way!" Tammy yelled. "*They* are coming *here*?"

"Calm down, Tammy. They were here Saturday night. Well, Ryan was but I don't think Cal was. Anyway, listen, it's no big deal, okay? They're just regular people." I tried to get her to come down from the clouds.

"You all have to be cool about this. I don't want to hear any of you gossiping about them being here, either. You have to promise. PROMISE!" I shook my finger at them. "They just want to play poker with us, so everyone just relax."

Marie's eyes were bulging. She knew I was holding back.

"All right, Taryn, spill it. What the *hell* is going on here? Ryan Christensen just showed up here randomly Saturday night, and now like it's no big deal that he's going to be joining us for poker?"

"I met him the other day," I reluctantly confessed with a sigh. "The boy that came in here Friday night had a message from Ryan. He sent him to ask for my cell number."

"That makes sense now," Pete replied.

"*What?*" I thought Marie's head was going to dislodge from her body. "He asked for your number?"

"Yes, all right?" I said a bit defensively. "But I didn't give it to him. I guess that's why he showed up here on Saturday."

Marie was shaking her head violently. "Ryan freakin' Christensen asked for your phone number and you *didn't* give it to him? Am I hearing this correctly?"

I just shrugged and rolled my eyes.

"Are you out of your mind?" Marie screamed at me while pulling on her own hair.

"I have my reasons."

"What? What reasons could you possibly have? One of the hottest guys on the planet wants your phone number, but you have reasons? This shit better not be about Thomas, because I'll kick your ass myself."

"No, this has nothing to do with Thomas. Ryan is a celebrity, for God's sake. He's only in town for a couple of weeks. What do you want me to do? Just lie down for him because he's famous?"

"I would," she said, but the look Gary gave her made her backtrack her comment. "I mean if I was *you,* I would."

"Well, you should know me better than that. You of all people." Her judgment of me hurt. "Look, he's a nice person, and if he wants to be friends while he's in town, I'm okay with that. But I'm not going to have my heart smashed again, by *anyone*. And I'm certainly not going to delude myself into thinking that he's going to pursue a relationship with me."

My own words stung. I stood up from the table and hurried to the bathroom. I did not want to continue this conversation. *Good enough for lust, but not good enough for love* flashed through my mind like a scrolling electric sign. Marie and Tammy followed me to the bathroom. The second Marie was through the door she pulled me into a hug.

"I'm sorry," she whispered in my ear. "I didn't mean to upset you."

"It's all right. I upset myself." I stared over her shoulder at the tiled wall as she squeezed me.

"Ryan is really, really nice. He's funny and kind and . . . he *is* the kind of guy I could easily fall for. But I can't. I will not allow myself to get caught up like that. He's a celebrity. He has girls standing in line for him."

I had to look away. Once again I found myself becoming interested in a man who was unobtainable.

"Oh, Taryn," Tammy said while rubbing my back, "he obviously likes you! Why else do you think he's coming around? Don't be so hard on yourself. You are a gorgeous, awesome woman. And you don't know what the future holds."

"I know why he's coming around," I said, knowing that he was a man with needs. "If he wants to be friends—fine, and if he wants to play poker—that's fine too. But please, please don't make a big deal about this, and don't pressure me about him either. You two are my best friends, and if you love me and care about me, then you will understand that I don't want to get used or hurt again. And I'm not interested in a one-night stand."

"Okay. We understand," Marie said, letting me go. "Ryan freakin' Christensen, huh?" She looked completely astonished. "Are you *sure* you don't want to have him just for one night and then tell us all about it and maybe take pictures?"

I smirked. "No, absolutely not."

"Hey, it was worth asking," she teased.

Twenty minutes later I met Ryan and Cal at the back door to the pub. They arrived in an ordinary SUV, and as soon as the car stopped, the two men leapt from the vehicle and darted into my open doorway.

"Hey you," Ryan greeted me with his crooked smile. "Taryn, this is Cal."

"Hi, Cal, it's nice to meet you," I said politely as I held out my hand. I had never seen him before, so there was no celebrity association in my mind when meeting him. He was just another regular person to me.

"Hi, Taryn. It's really nice to meet you too." Cal grinned widely at me, then flashed his eyes and raised his eyebrows at Ryan. I spotted the guy head-nod acknowledgment. "Ryan tells me you have a nice place here."

"Thank you," I replied. "Please, come on in, we're playing out in the pub."

Ryan and Cal followed me out of the kitchen. Cal gave Ryan a teasing shove. I guess I passed the friend test.

Everyone introduced themselves and my friends were somewhat contained in their emotions, although I can't deny they were starstruck. It's not every day you have famous people hanging out with you. I poured a beer for Ryan and Cal and danced my way to the large circular table where we would play.

"I love this song." Pete grabbed my hands and started to dance with me to the music playing over the sound system. We shuffled our feet for a few moments until he spun me under his arm in the direction of my usual poker seat.

"You two are crazy," Tammy squealed.

Ryan sat down next to me; he nudged me with his elbow before flashing me a smile.

"You know how to play Texas Hold'em? We play for money," I whispered to him.

He nodded at me and stuffed his hand in his front pocket, pulling out a wrinkled wad of mixed bills. I grinned at him. His casual disorganization amused me for some reason.

"Well, since you've made me extremely wealthy tonight, Taryn, give me two hundred in chips." Pete tossed his money across the table. "I'm feeling lucky," he said, rubbing his hands together briskly.

While I was counting out Pete's chips, Ryan was trying to straighten out his cash pile mess. He must have had almost a thousand on him; I saw several hundred-dollar bills when he organized them. Good thing those obsessed fans didn't reach into his pockets.

Pete was singing along with the song that was playing; he made me laugh with the way he bobbed his head back and forth.

"Hey Pete," Gary called across the table, "who sings this song?"

"Michael Bublé," Pete answered proudly, knowing that he had the right answer.

"Well maybe you should let him sing it instead? What do you say to that?"

"Wait for it . . . here comes the horns." As soon as the trumpets started playing, Pete chucked his two middle fingers at Gary with each beat.

I could see Tammy and Marie itching in their seats. Both of them kept gazing over at Cal and Ryan, like they were dying to ask them questions. Tammy started to open her mouth, glancing at me for my approval. I hoped my displeased expression would be enough to deter her. *Oh please don't ask them anything.*

Tammy held up her finger. "Just one?" she mouthed at me. "One tiny one?"

I let out a deep sigh and rolled my eyes to the ceiling.

Ryan looked at me, concerned. "What's wrong?"

"My girlfriends are dying to ask you questions . . . no doubt about your movie, but I wish that they would just leave you be," I said with humor while trying to let them know that I was a little annoyed.

"Can I ask you just one question about *Sea*—?" Tammy started.

"I knew it! I knew you wouldn't be able to resist." Pete laughed. "What is it about this freakin' movie that's like crack for you women?"

"I've been trying to figure that one out myself," Ryan admitted. He looked at me and smiled.

"Don't look at *me*. I have no idea," I defended.

"Yeah, you didn't even know who Charles was." Tammy laughed as she pointed at me.

Ryan was still grinning as his eyes locked on mine.

"I still don't know who Charles is," I admitted.

"I'll tell you what it is—all women love dangerous bad boys and that's what the movie is about," Tammy stated.

"Yeah, I guess there's something sexy about some guy who wants to kill you," Ryan muttered.

Just by his body language, I gathered that was not the first time he'd said those words out loud.

"Hey Marie, get me another beer or I'll kill you," Gary muttered. Marie smacked him hard in the arm.

"What? I'm just trying to be sexy for you," he pointed out, pushing his glasses back up his nose.

"What's your question, Tammy?" Ryan asked, still laughing from Gary's remark.

"I was wondering if the one scene from Book Two, where Charles finds Gwen bleeding in the cave, is going to be in the movie."

Marie moved to the edge of her chair. She obviously wanted to know the answer to that one too.

"Yes. It's a pretty significant scene. We've already filmed it," Ryan answered.

Marie and Tammy looked like they were going to explode from excitement. Pete was shaking his head; he thought the whole conversation was absurd.

"Oh Pete, you don't understand. Charles finds Gwen barely alive in a cave after she'd been shot. And he's supposed to kill her, but instead he takes his shirt off and wraps it around her to stop the bleeding. And then she looks at him and begs him to kill her so the pain would stop, but he says he loves her too much to let her die . . ." Tammy gushed like she was going to cry.

"And?" Pete asked. "Does she die?"

"Of course not! He," she pointed at Ryan, "saves her."

I glanced at Ryan; he was sitting forward in his chair with his head bowed. He appeared to be slightly uncomfortable with the conversation.

I leaned over to him, wrapped my arm around the back of his chair, and whispered in my worst British accent, "I see you've managed to get your shirt off."

Ryan looked over at me and laughed lightly. "It's a rock monster; it doesn't have any vulnerable spots." He grinned widely and leaned even closer to me, bumping his arm into mine.

Everyone else in the room was oblivious to our movie line references. It was as though we had our own secret language.

"And what about . . ." Tammy started again, but I cut her off with a wave of my hand.

"Please, Tammy," I pleaded while Ryan and I were still leaning close to each other. "Don't bug him."

Ryan quickly ran his finger under my chin, apparently pleased that I defended him. It felt like my skin burst into flames when he touched me.

"How long until you guys are finished here?" Pete interjected quickly.

"We'll be here for another six weeks and then we have a break around Thanksgiving," Ryan replied as he playfully kicked the back of my foot. His little tap made me smile.

"Cal, I understand you're married to KellyAnn Gael, is that right?" Tammy asked.

"Yes. We just had our sixth wedding anniversary." Cal nodded proudly.

"Is your wife here in Rhode Island with you?" Tammy continued.

"Not yet, but she's flying in on Saturday with our daughter, Cami. I just found a house for us to rent nearby."

"I remember watching your wife when she was on *Just Neighbors*. I loved that show. How old is your daughter?" Tammy asked.

"She's three—and quite a handful," Cal said. "I miss them."

"It must be hard when you're away from your family. But it's nice that she's coming out here to see you," Tammy said.

"Yeah, it's hard, but we make sure that the time and space that we're apart doesn't divide us," Cal said as he looked at Ryan and me.

With no one the wiser, Ryan stretched his leg and rested his foot so it was touching mine. As much as I wanted to move my foot, I couldn't. Why did he have to smell so damn good? I took a deep breath to clear out the haze he caused in my brain, straightened up in my chair, and moved my foot away.

We played poker for almost two hours, laughing, drinking, and picking on one another. Ryan and Cal were just two friends having a good time with the rest of us.

"Last round, and then I think we need to take a break," Pete announced as he dealt the cards.

I kicked Ryan back in the foot. He had kicked me too many times under the table when I wasn't paying attention and I owed him one.

Gary looked at his cards and folded immediately. "Couldn't you just deal me two good cards instead of that shit?" he ribbed Pete as he scratched his mustache.

I looked at my cards. Pete dealt me a ten and an ace—both hearts. "I raise four dollars," I said as I tossed in chips. I had two high cards in the same suit . . . not bad to start with.

Ryan peeked at his cards. "Call," he muttered. I felt his foot tap mine.

"Call," Cal said, tossing in his chips.

Pete was taking his good old time looking at his cards. While we waited, I stretched back in my chair and tapped Ryan in the back of his calf with the top of my foot, causing his leg to fly forward and his foot to slap on the floor. He peered at me through the corner of his eye and gave me a dirty look. His evil eye didn't last too long before the sultry grin appeared on his face.

Finally Pete counted off four dollars in chips and threw them into the pile in the center of the table.

"Fold," Tammy said, tossing in her cards.

"Me too," Marie huffed. "I'm keeping my chips."

Pete laid out the flop cards—another ten and two aces.

I had a beautiful full house—aces over tens. I noticed Pete frowning slightly as he sat back a bit in his chair. Pete always sat forward when he had a good hand. I could tell he had two lousy cards.

"I raise four," I said nonchalantly, casually tossing my chips to the center of the table. I didn't want to give away that I had an awesome hand.

Ryan was mangling a swizzle straw in his teeth. He glanced at me as he slid the straw around in his mouth. He played with his chips for a moment, and then scratched his eyebrow with his thumb. He was stalling.

"I see your four and raise you four," he replied with a challenge.

"Fold," Cal announced sadly. He tossed his cards and pressed back in his chair.

"Ah, I fold, too," Pete grumbled. I snickered to myself . . . I knew that was coming.

It was my turn again. I counted my chips; I had sixty dollars left and a strong full house. I was thinking about how Ryan scratched his eyebrow—was he nervous, or bluffing?

"I'm all in." I pushed all my chips toward the middle of the table.

Ryan's eyes narrowed on me and he had a serious expression on his face. His lips pursed and twitched a bit around the straw that wiggled in his mouth.

"How much was that?" he asked, nodding at my chips.

"Sixty," I replied.

He picked fifty-six dollars off his pile of chips and tossed them into the center. He still had chips left.

"Let's see what you got, sweetheart." He grinned, raising his eyebrows at me.

I flipped my ten and ace over. Ryan had two tens. We both had full houses, but my hand was higher. We looked at each other and smiled. It wasn't over yet.

Pete laid out the turn card. It was a useless nine of spades. I breathed a sigh of relief. I was still winning.

The last card, the river card, was a four of diamonds.

"Yes!" I said quietly.

Ryan chuckled, knowing that he just lost. He stretched back in his seat, and then ever so casually patted and rubbed my back as I pulled the chip pile to my chest. The sensation of his touch sent a twinge of electricity through my body.

Ryan squeezed my shoulders when we stood up to walk away from the table. His grip felt amazing on my achy muscles. It had been a long time since I'd let any man get close enough to touch me that way. I was starting to turn to putty under his fingers.

"Good play," he whispered his private compliment in my ear. I felt the warmth that emanated from his lips caress my skin. His chest pressed lightly into my back. A million tiny impulses fired through my body.

"I'm impressed. Remind me to take you to the casinos sometime," Ryan joked with me.

Cal and Gary walked over to the pool table and everyone else followed them. We all needed a short break and a stretch from sitting.

I quickly stepped behind the bar and grabbed a metal mixing cup, which I spun across my palm. I hadn't been in this good of a mood in a long time.

I'd just started pouring the vodka when Ryan joined me at the bar. "What are you making?"

"Mind Erasers." I smiled. "It's first-break shot time."

"Sounds good. I'll take two," he said, winking at me.

Ryan walked beside me as I carried a tray of shot glasses over to the poolroom.

"Don't you dare try and trip me," I joked with him after he gave me a nudge. I kicked the bottom of his foot as he was taking a step. He started laughing.

"This is a beautiful pool table, Taryn," Cal said. "Do you think we might be able to bring some people from the set here one night? I think everyone could use a relaxing, fun night like this." His eyes flashed over to Ryan. Ryan was nodding in agreement.

"I guess so." I looked over at Marie. "I suppose I can shut down one night for a private party."

"We'll cover your losses for a night if you'd be willing to do that for us," Cal said.

"You'll just have to let me know what night and we can arrange something," I replied.

Cal and Gary played a game of pool, and then Pete and Ryan played Cal and Gary as teams. Pete and Ryan dusted them. The guys got along great together.

"Are we going to play another round of poker or what?" Ryan asked as he was putting his pool stick back on the wall rack. "I'd like an opportunity to win some of my money back," he kidded me, giving me a finger poke in my stomach.

His eyes were absolutely mesmerizing as he looked at me.

"Good luck with that," I teased him and tugged on the straw in his mouth. Ryan clamped his teeth down hard on his straw and playfully snarled at me.

We all gathered back at the table to play the next round of poker. Everyone was concentrating on their cards; it was eerily quiet. Ryan and I had already pushed and kicked each other under the table a few times and we were both smiling at our secret.

Pete broke the silence first. "You know what I could eat right now?" he asked as he was stacking his chips.

"Pussy?" Gary answered immediately.

"Gary!" Marie yelped and smacked him in the arm.

Ryan was taking a sip from his glass; he just about spit his beer all over himself, breaking out in a laugh.

"What?" Gary flinched away from Marie. "He asked, I just answered. Sounds like a perfectly good thing to eat right now, right, guys?"

"You're driving him home." I pointed at Marie while laughing.

"Although I have to agree with Gary, I was actually thinking about those juicy steaks Taryn grilled for us a couple of weeks ago. They were delicious!" Pete ran his tongue over his lips.

"See? Pete has juicy meat on the brain," Gary teased.

"No, I think *you* have juicy meat on the brain," Marie groaned. She shot her elbow into his ribs.

I smiled and laughed with embarrassment. My friends were nuts.

"Ryan, do you like pus . . . steak?" Pete asked.

"Yeah." Ryan nodded and smiled shyly.

"You almost asked him if he . . . !" Gary was laughing hysterically as he pointed at Pete. He couldn't even finish his own sentence. He turned a few shades of red while coughing and trying to catch his breath.

Ryan looked down in embarrassment, but he was still grinning when he rolled his gaze over at me.

Pete ignored Gary's outburst. "Well, this girl here grills one hell of a steak," he stated proudly, pointing a finger at me.

"They *were* the best steaks I've ever had," Tammy agreed.

"What can I say?" I shrugged. "It's good that I get to use my college education."

"Where did you go to college?" Ryan asked conversationally.

"Brown, in Providence. Economics/Business—sirloin steak major," I declared.

"So are you going to grill me another steak soon, or what?" Pete wanted to get back to the point.

"Pete, you know I'll grill for you any day of the week." I love cooking for my friends.

"So where do you grill these wonderful steaks?" Ryan asked.

"On the roof." I laughed.

"No really." Ryan looked confused.

"On the roof," I repeated with a giggle. "The top of my building is flat. I have a garden patio up there. We have excellent summer parties, right, guys?" My friends all confirmed this. "You can see the ocean from up there, too," I continued.

"A steak does sound good right now," Cal agreed.

"Okay, let me ask this. How many people were you thinking about having here for this private party?" I asked Cal.

"Maybe ten or twelve?"

"And would you mind if my four friends here attend this gathering?" I asked.

"Sure, they're welcome. Absolutely," Cal confirmed.

"You tell me what night, and I'll grill steaks. How does that sound? Then everyone will be relaxed, happy, and well fed."

Ryan slid his foot under my leg. Our legs were touching now under the table and I was hyper-aware of his presence.

"We'll check everyone's schedule and get back to you. Is that all right?" Cal asked.

"Sure. Just so you know, I have entertainment booked for Friday and Saturday, but we can do a weeknight or Sunday if that suits you. Just give me enough notice so I can get the steaks."

We played for another hour; Marie started to yawn. "Are you ready? It's getting late." She grabbed Gary's arm and started to pull him up out of his chair.

"Oh man, been sitting too long . . . my hip hurts," Gary moaned. "Marie, you're going to have to get on top tonight." He grinned.

Ryan and I could not stop laughing.

Everyone started shaking hands and having those brief "it was nice to meet you—see you later" conversations. Cal used his cell phone to call for their driver. I was sad to see the night come to an end; it seemed to fly by so fast with Ryan here.

I walked my friends to the door and locked up behind them. Ryan and Cal would leave by the back door. Cal departed for the bathroom, leaving me all alone with Ryan. I started to clean up.

"I had a *really* great time tonight." Ryan smiled and set a few empty glasses on the bar. "Your friends are great."

"Thanks!" I smiled back. "I'm sorry about the questions, though."

Ryan shrugged his shoulders. "Don't worry about it."

"I'm glad everyone had fun," I said, even though I truly meant I was glad that *he* had fun.

"I'll call you when we figure out what night we can do this party gathering, okay? Um, so what number should I call?"

I stopped in my tracks and smiled to myself.

"What number would you like to call?" I asked, knowing what he was truly getting at. I just wanted him to say it.

"I'd like the number that I asked for, but I'm not sure I'm going to get it." He grinned at me as he took a new Mitchell's Pub napkin out of the holder and turned it over.

I took a deep breath and picked up the pen next to the register. I questioned my own actions as I wrote my cell phone number down. My friends were the only ones who had my cell number. I justified that he and I were becoming friends, too.

Ryan's smile was huge. "Thank you." He quickly snatched up the napkin and shoved it in his pocket.

I walked both of them to the back door and Cal thanked me for an excellent evening. He gave me an awkward hug before putting his coat on. Their car pulled up in the alley and Cal patted Ryan's arm before heading out the door.

Ryan looked down at me and smiled as he took a step closer. He wrapped his arms around my shoulders and pulled me in to give me a nice hug.

Sensations, long suppressed, rocketed through me when our bodies touched. His body pressed into mine when he hugged me tighter. I allowed myself a moment to appreciate his warmth, his scent, the feel of his back muscles on my hands, the enjoyment this hug gave me.

Ryan's hand gently cradled the back of my head, and his fingers slipped into my hair. He kissed me softly on my forehead; his lips lingered for an extra second or two before he released our embrace.

"I'll see you soon," he whispered softly, took a few steps back, and slipped out the back door.

CHAPTER 5

Connections

SO, DID HE try to kiss you last night?" Marie breathed in my ear.

"No." I shook my head, annoyed that she'd even asked. "You promised," I reminded her.

"Yeah, I know. I'm not pushing. I just wanted to know if that's the reason you're finally smiling. So he didn't try to kiss you?"

I opened a new case of bottled beer. "No. He didn't kiss me . . . on my lips." I trailed the last part of my sentence hoping she wouldn't catch it.

She started to jump up and down. "Come on! I'm dying here!"

"He gave me a hug, okay?" I quietly muttered. "And he sort of kissed my forehead." I shrugged it off and continued to put more bottles into the cooler. "Remember, you can't say anything to anyone about them being here. I'm not going to have my pub and my friends involved in any media circus. Got that? Not one word!"

She twisted her fingers over her lips and then cracked a cocky smile at me.

"I'm warning you! I'm pretty sure I can shove your entire body in this cooler. No one will find you in there!"

Marie ignored me and turned the TV channel in time to catch the seven o'clock entertainment news. Her excuse was to see if our pub made it to the television version of celebrity gossip, but I knew better. My attention was diverted to the screen when I heard his name mentioned.

"We got Ryan Christensen arriving at LAX this afternoon . . . ," some guy on TV said.

Ryan was filmed as he hurried through the airport. I was thankful that he had several security guards around him; the photographers and people bugging him for his autograph were relentless. I wondered if those leeches did nothing all day but lurk around the airport waiting for celebrities.

"What's he doing in L.A.?" Marie asked. She seemed just as surprised as I was.

"Shh, I want to hear this," I said.

Ryan's face toggled between a blank stare and moments of annoyance as the cameramen who chased him asked him stupid questions. He looked tired. They managed to film him signing an autograph or two before he jumped into an awaiting car at the curb.

I was surprised that he was on the West Coast. He hadn't mentioned anything last night about getting on a plane today—but then again, why would he?

It was soon after that when my phone buzzed in my pocket. My thumb hit the buttons to retrieve a new text message. To my amazement, *someone* sent me a beautiful picture of red and white flowers. I immediately smiled. I had never received virtual flowers before.

The text message read: "Greetings from LA"

Butterflies instantly fluttered in my stomach.

I texted him back. "Who is this?"

I didn't want to let on that I knew where he was.

I read his reply. "Knight who says Ni?"

I laughed out loud at Ryan's movie reference. "You r funny. Why r u in LA?"

"Interview n meeting with my agent n producer b back thurs"

"R u having fun?" I sent back.

A few moments later, he sent another message: "not really"

"Sorry to hear that," I replied, adding a sad-face emoticon.

"Can I call u later tonight?"

"Sure," I quickly typed.

IT WAS almost three in the morning when I crawled into bed. Since Ryan and his friends had been in the pub on Saturday my customer count seemed to rise. I laughed to myself considering most of the new crowd was female. As I lay there, I became quite absorbed in my thoughts of how pathetic some of his fans were. One girl was even wearing a T-shirt with Ryan's face on it tonight.

I wondered how Ryan felt about that. Most men would probably love the attention and get huge egos from it, but I couldn't see Ryan being into that at all. He was much too modest. I guessed things like that probably made him very uncomfortable.

Marie and I had hustled again tonight, and it was only a Tuesday. I was thinking about asking Tammy if she wanted to work weekends to help out while the celebrities were still in town. Once they were gone, things would go back to normal. But there were too many customers for just Marie and me to handle on our own. *Maybe I should hire some additional help? I could use a third bartender.*

I started to yawn; my eyelids were very heavy. I pulled my comforter higher over my shoulder, snuggling even deeper. I felt myself drifting when I was startled by my cell phone rattling on my nightstand. I looked at the number, but the screen showed "NO NUMBER."

"Hello?" I whispered. My voice definitely sounded groggy when I spoke.

"Hi. Sorry to call so late. Were you sleeping?" Ryan whispered.

"No . . . almost. How are you?" Another big yawn slipped out from my chest.

"I'm tired too. It's been a long day," he said glumly.

"What time is it there?" I glanced over at my alarm clock, but I was too out of it to do time zone math.

"It's almost midnight," he breathed out with a sigh.

"Thank you for the flowers," I whispered. "That was cute. You definitely took me by surprise."

He quietly laughed. "Good," he uttered. Considering he'd called me, his response was oddly brief.

"So what are you doing?" I could only imagine the glamorous movie-star stuff he must be up to.

"I'm in my hotel room. I just got back." By the way his cell phone crackled, it sounded like he was busy getting settled in.

"Hmm. Did you have a good day?" I murmured, trying to make conversation. I snuggled deeper into my blanket.

"It was all right, I guess. I'm glad it's over." Despite his response, the tone of his voice was off—*way* off. I could tell he was troubled.

"Ryan, what's wrong? Are you okay?" My eyes popped open and I sat up in bed, overwhelmed with concern about his well-being. "Something is wrong."

He sighed. "How can you tell?" He sounded surprised that I could read him like that.

"I just can. I can hear it in your voice."

"I'll be all right. Sometimes my life gets freaking insane. Today was one of those days." His voice trembled and he sniffed a few times. I could tell he was lying. He wasn't all right.

I took a deep breath, picturing him huddled up with his head between his arms again like that first day in my stairwell. "Do you want to talk about it?"

I listened as he blew air into his phone. "Ah, I don't know if talking about it will make a difference," he muttered.

He and I were so much alike. Now it was his turn to sit there feeling sorry for himself.

"Hmm. I have an idea. Why don't you crawl under your blanket and tell me all about it." For a moment I wished I could climb through the phone to comfort him.

He chuckled lightly. "Can you hold on a minute? I need to set the phone down."

"Sure," I whispered. I could hear that he was shifting around. I imagined him getting undressed . . . the light hairs on his stomach peeking above an elastic band. *I wonder what he looks like naked?*

He let out a big sigh, disrupting my thought.

"Are you better?" I asked.

"Much," he replied, but I didn't believe him.

I took in a deep breath and exhaled roughly. "You don't sound very convincing."

He laughed softly. I could just tell by his lack of answers that he was upset.

"Are you under your blanket yet?" I whispered seductively, hoping that might cheer him up.

"Yes," he snickered.

"Close your eyes . . . and relax. Just listen to my voice. Take a deep breath . . . Let it out . . . Just breathe." I wanted so desperately to take his worries away. The feelings were overpowering.

"You're lying on a soft blanket on a white sand beach. The sky above is a deep and cloudless blue . . ." I paused to let him soak the imagery in.

"The sun feels warm on your face . . . you can hear the sound of the ocean as the waves slowly roll in. You can feel the gentle breeze glide over your skin as it rustles through the trees . . . feel the stress leave your body . . . through your fingers . . . through your toes."

A soft "Mmm" slipped from his throat. "This is nice."

"Mmm, what's nice?" I breathed out.

"This . . . Feeling at peace . . . You."

"Hmm," I softly sighed into the phone, happy to know my words helped him relax.

"I wish I was there with you," he whispered.

"I wish you were here, too," I whispered softly.

After the words came out of my mouth, there was no taking them back but it didn't matter, I didn't want to take them back. My words came from my heart and not my head. Part of me hoped he really meant what he'd said.

RYAN CALLED me three times on Wednesday just to say hello and ask me how my day was going. I was completely floored that he called me so many times.

He had talked to Cal, and the plan was that the private gathering would be held next Sunday at the pub. The entire cast had been invited, but not everyone was expected to attend. The last head count was eight.

The third time Ryan called, it was midnight in L.A. and his obligations there were completed. He would be departing at noon out of LAX to Detroit, and then fly from Detroit to Providence. He'd be back in town Thursday evening. I laughed to myself that he felt the need to keep me up-to-date on his itinerary. I didn't even have to ask; he volunteered the information first. It was really kind of cute.

We were both snuggled in our beds as he filled me in on his day. He had an interview on a talk show and then a late meeting with some producer and his agent and manager about an upcoming movie project they wanted him to star in. Although Ryan wouldn't directly admit it, I got the impression that some of his career decisions were being made for him and that he was just supposed to agree with what they said.

Ryan's fame and popularity were so new and fresh that he was being swept away with it all. These movie moguls were all going to strike while the iron was hot. I didn't need to be part of his world to recognize that. Ryan was a new toy for them; his movie had made millions of dollars and it was easy to visualize the greed in Hollywood taking over like an evil succubus.

While I listened to his voice, I allowed my imagination to run free as I pictured what it would be like to have him lying next to me—so close that I could touch him, soothe him, protect him from the insanity. *Ugh! What am I thinking?* I had to stop myself from thinking those thoughts.

We talked for almost three hours; the birds were already starting to wake up and chirp outside my window. We started opening up to each other and our conversation became more personal. He told me that he grew up in a small town in western Pennsylvania and that his parents still lived in the same house to this day. How he once had a Jack Russell terrier named Bailey who used to dig holes in the yard.

I told him about the job offer I had accepted at a large brokerage firm in Manhattan, and why I had to turn it down when my father died suddenly. I was a week away from moving.

Ryan told me about the lead actress that he has to work with on these movies and how she sometimes behaved like a spoiled brat. He called her "BB," as all the tabloids referred to her as the British Bombshell, but she was better known as Suzanne Strass. She was a former child actress from London who recently turned twenty-one.

Even though they were friends, she sometimes annoyed the heck out of him, and it ticked him off that all the gossip magazines were spreading lies about them being romantically linked. She had tagged along with him the night he came into my pub.

Throughout our conversation, we laughed and teased. He was so easy to talk to. But he always seemed hesitant to talk about what was truly bothering him. I could sense there were underlying issues; however, he never went into details and I didn't want to pry. I could hear it in his voice that there were things that he wasn't sharing.

It was Thursday, early evening, when Marie flipped through the channels on the pub television. Ryan had given a brief interview with one of the evening entertainment news shows and it was being broadcast today.

It was strange watching him on television. Even though the voice was the same, the celebrity image on the screen was disconnected from the man I was trying so desperately not to fall for over the telephone. But some things were the same; he was charming and shy and slightly uncomfortable with all the attention during the interview. I noticed his nervous twitches and mannerisms when they asked questions that he was uncomfortable with. Still, he was humble and very adorable.

And then my heart lodged in my throat when I saw the additional footage of him being swept through a hysterical crowd by six bulky security guards. At one point I wasn't sure if he was even walking on his own or if the security team was carrying him.

The fans were reaching for him—holding cameras over their heads for the random chance that they might get his photo. Others were holding pictures of him hoping to get his autograph. A few women were crying and hyperventilating just from getting a glimpse of him.

The security team practically hurled him into the awaiting car; his fans were screaming and blocking his car in the road. Mobs of paparazzi were everywhere. I gripped the edge of the bar as my knees started to buckle. He was the prey being stalked by the wolves.

At that moment, I realized the magnitude of what he was sparing me from. It wasn't that he was the superstar adored by millions that made me weak. It was the feeling that I wanted to throw myself in their path to protect him that was most powerful.

An hour later my cell phone buzzed in my pocket. Ryan was texting me:

"Hi I'm back"

I quickly sent him a reply: "Hi r u ok?"

"Yeah why u ask?"

"Nothing glad to hear ur back safe." I couldn't tell him why I was worried.

"We r shootn night scenes gonna b a late one"

I smiled when I saw the sad smiley face. "dont work too hard have fun"

"I'll try to call u soon ok?"

"Ok"

I was relieved to know he was back in Rhode Island, away from that California craziness, although it appeared that some of that craziness followed him wherever he went.

We were very busy for a weeknight. It seemed that his huge female fan base that swarmed my pub had attracted a new selection of male customers—everyone was on the hunt, and the odds were better if you were a man.

"It's like freaking mating season," I yelled over to Marie.

She snorted at me. "I know! It's sick, isn't it?"

"I don't know if I should be appalled or thankful," I laughed back to her.

"I'm extremely thankful!" She bobbed her head back and forth and stuffed a few more dollars into our tip jar. "Go! Find a mate!" she teased me.

I wasn't opposed to finding someone and having love be a part of my life again, but every guy I came across was oddly the same. Lame approaches, cheap comments, scary aggressive behavior, or just not what I was longing for. At this point in my life I didn't feel the need to settle, nor have to make do with half of nothing.

It was after three a.m. again when I crawled into bed. My hands hurt from washing so many dirty glasses and empty beer pitchers, and it bothered me that I couldn't curl them underneath my chin like I normally did to sleep.

I never tried to buy into the fairy tales that most girls fell for, but for a moment I felt like I could really relate to Cinderella, being forced to clean up after all of the wicked and ungrateful.

I WAS still thinking about Cinderella periodically throughout the next day. I wondered why she never just snapped and told her evil stepmother and stepsisters to go to hell. Would things have been different for her if she had a baseball bat tucked up under her apron and didn't need Prince Charming to come and rescue her? *Why won't this sticky stuff come up off the bar? How hard do I need to scrub?*

"Hey, kiddo! How you doing tonight?" Pete asked, drumming his hands on the bar.

I was so lost in my own thoughts while scouring the top of the bar that his drumming startled me. My eyes focused in on his beaming face as I tried to shake my brain back into reality.

"I'm doing all right," I answered, forcing myself to smile.

"We should have a good Friday-night crowd tonight," he said enthusiastically. I smiled wider when he raised his eyebrows up and down at me. "Frank and the guys just pulled up. I'm going to see if they need a hand unloading."

Customers were filtering in while tonight's band set up their equipment. My head was slowly getting back into the game as my earlier distractions became replaced with juggling a multitude of drink orders.

As the evening progressed, the crowd grew thicker and the music became louder, and I found myself flowing and dancing behind the bar again. Tammy had agreed to work a few weekends, so I had her covering tables.

There were two men sitting at the bar that Marie felt I should be interested in. She kept nudging me in their direction, but I couldn't stop envisioning them having giant springs attached to their necks from the way their heads kept nodding at me.

"What's wrong with you?" Marie said as she put her arm around my shoulders. "That one in the baseball hat is cute. Go flirt with him."

I halfheartedly smiled and made a choking sound.

"Don't give me that shit!" she snapped. "You need to be brave and get back on the damn horse." Her hand cracked me on my backside.

Mr. Baseball Hat had just waved his empty glass at me when my phone vibrated in my pocket. My heart flipped in my chest.

"Hello?" I answered, very much knowing whose voice was going to respond. I had to cover my ear to hear him.

"Hi—how are you?" Ryan asked.

"I'm great! How are you?" I was genuinely happy to hear from him. Ryan was momentarily distracted by a side conversation. I heard him and another man exchanging words.

"Hey, man, how's it going?"

Why does that voice sound so familiar to me?

"It's going great," Ryan replied with a light chuckle.

"Good to see ya. Nah, just go on in," the male voice stated.

"Thanks. Hey, I'll see you later," Ryan said.

"I'm thirsty," Ryan said, answering my original question. "I'd really like a beer please."

I looked up to see that he was twenty feet in front of me, walking toward the bar. He had a big, sexy grin on his face as he slipped his phone into his jacket pocket.

Ryan was the center man in a pack of four other guys. I recognized Cal right away. One of the other men looked familiar—perhaps I'd seen him in a movie or something before but I didn't know who he was. The other two had to be private security—they looked like they could hurt someone.

"Hey, you!" Ryan greeted me with that smile that made my knees weak.

"Hi!" My tone was unintentionally a mixture of surprise and annoyance. I was very glad to see him, but now I'd have to deal with crowd control and his psychotic fans invading my pub. I looked behind him and sure enough, half a dozen giggling girls traipsed through the door.

Cal moved into the space next to Ryan. Obviously it was boys' night out.

"Taryn, this is Shane Richards," Ryan said as he waved his hand in Shane's direction. Shane was tall and overly thin, with unkempt brown hair. He looked like he should be in a rock band instead of being a movie star. Regardless, his smile was dazzling.

"What would you gentlemen like to drink this evening?" I tried to be cordial as more overly excited women came in. The second they saw Ryan and his friends, their demeanor turned to bubbling exuberance.

While the guys looked over my beer menu, the coyotes descended. Ryan was like a huge chick magnet, even though Shane and Cal were equally as handsome. In no time at all, the brave ones in the crowd tried to cozy up to the actors.

I tapped a beer for each of them and with every second that I had to watch all the overzealous girls flirting, I became more and more irritated. I placed the last beer on the bar when Ryan asked what he owed me.

I waved my hand. "Nothing. It's on me." I smiled.

My smile, however, quickly faded after seeing even more giggling women rush through my door. I hurried out from behind the bar; I was on a mission to stop the invasion.

"Pete, no more people get in," I inadvertently barked at him.

"Okay," he replied a tad defensively. "Sorry—are there too many people in there now?"

"No, but we've filled our quota of obsessive fans," I snapped as I eyed the girls who were waiting to pay the cover charge. "People need to get a freaking life," I mumbled to myself and stomped my way back to the bar.

Ryan and his friends were still standing by the bar, but now women surrounded them on all sides. *Tramp! Slut!* shouted in my brain as I stormed past them. Ryan's gaze followed me but I didn't look at him. I stepped back behind the bar and for a moment entertained the idea of smashing some girls with my baseball bat.

I purposely relocated myself as far away as possible from him and the gaggle of women, which landed me directly in front of Mr. Baseball Hat. I nudged Marie in Ryan's direction.

Fortunately, my pub was packed and I was hustling making one drink after another. I made a conscious effort not to look for him, even though it was hard. Occasionally I'd allow myself a quick peek, but I never let my eyes linger.

"Are you mad that he's here?" Marie whispered in my ear.

I shook my head while I prepared two vodka tonics.

"Well, you look mad." She laughed at me. "What's wrong?"

"I'm allergic to whores," I said under my breath.

"Oh, I see. Jealous, not mad," she said, correcting me.

I huffed out loud. "How am I supposed to compete with all of that?" I nodded at the crowd of women. "Ahh, it doesn't matter."

"You're fucked up," Marie snapped back at me while she was mixing a drink. "If you haven't realized it yet, he's in *your* bar. He's being nice to them, but he is *far* from flirting with any of them. He's too busy watching *you* to notice *them*."

I grimaced when she nudged me to speak privately.

"And another thing, if you're going to be jealous, then that means you like him more than you're willing to admit. This shit is a part of his life," she noted and waved her hands toward the wall of girls. "It comes with the territory, so you need to decide whether you can deal with that or not."

She stood right in front of me and grabbed my wrist.

"Taryn, you are so attractive and lovable. Everyone sees it. *He* sees it. But you are the only one who doesn't. You've let lowlifes like Thomas strip away your self-esteem. And it's pretty apparent that Ryan likes you, because he's not paying any attention to them."

I looked away from her to notice he *was* watching me. Just then, Mr. Baseball Hat waved his money in the air.

"I've got to wait on someone." I wiggled free from her grip.

"Do you need another one?" I asked.

"Hi. My name is Jesse. What's yours?" Mr. Baseball Hat asked.

"Taryn," I said with a forced smile.

"So, Taryn, do you work here every weekend?"

"Um, yes." *Here we go again . . . standard lame approach.*

"Do you know what the band's name is that's playing tonight?" he asked.

"They call themselves 'Being Frank.' Do you like them?" *How presumptuous of me; he's just trying to be friendly.*

"Yeah, they are really good. But seriously, tell me that guy doesn't look like Art Garfunkel."

His comment made me laugh. We all teased Frank because he *did* look like Art Garfunkel.

"You see it too, don't you?" Mr. Baseball Hat joked with me, laughing out loud. "It's the hair."

I nodded in agreement. My mind flashed back to Frank putting Pete in a headlock one night for that comment.

"I can't say that I disagree with you. Yes, he does look just like him." I laughed. "But whatever you do, don't make that comment to *him*!"

I was wiping the tear of laughter from my eye when I noticed Ryan sit down three bar stools away from my new admirer. Standing dutifully behind him was one of his bodyguards.

"So, Taryn, I was wondering if you'd like to go out with me sometime. Go have some fun. What do you think?" Mr. Baseball Hat choked out.

Something about the nervous look on his face was funny to me. A small chuckle accidentally escaped my throat. The poor guy looked slightly petrified yet he'd found a moment of bravery, and here I was being rude.

I quickly flashed my eyes over to Ryan. Ryan's body stiffened in his seat and I noticed his grip got tighter on his glass. It looked like he was holding his breath.

"I'm very flattered, Jesse. But I'm going to have to say no. Sorry." I was actually watching Ryan's reaction out of the corner of my eye.

Ryan let out a big sigh as his lips twitched into a smirk. I think he actually wanted to smile but fought the emotion. I didn't hide mine—I let the smile come out on my face.

"I figured you had a boyfriend anyway but it couldn't hurt to ask." Jesse shrugged.

Ryan finished his beer and slid his empty glass forward on the bar. "Excuse me, miss, can I get another beer, please?" he said with a confident smile.

I grabbed his empty glass and tapped him a fresh beer in a clean, frosted mug. I set the mug down and turned the handle so he'd be able to pick it right up in his hand. He slipped a ten-dollar bill on the bar and winked at me.

I let his money lie next to his glass and walked away; I had to wait on another customer and I had no intentions of accepting his money. I was wondering where Marie had disappeared to when I noticed that she was over by the stage, talking to Frank.

I watched as Ryan and his bodyguard walked back to the table to join his friends; a flock of women trailed behind him. I had to suppress my anger.

When the band finished their song, Frank started talking in the microphone. "Ladies and gentlemen, we have a very talented lady here with us tonight, and if you give her some encouragement, maybe we can convince her to come up here and play for you."

I looked up and scanned the crowd for the person he was talking about. I started to clap with everyone else.

"Taryn," Frank called out as he looked at me. "Why don't you come up here and play for these nice folks?"

My clapping hands stopped clapping. It felt like my hands were glued together.

"Oh, no." My head spun as the shock set in. "No!"

"Come on, Taryn! One song," Frank jeered. "Come on, everyone, let's give her a warm welcome."

"No." I was shaking my head so hard I was making myself dizzy. "No, I can't."

Marie grabbed my arm and forcefully pulled me out from behind the bar. "Go show 'em how special you are," she whispered in my ear, then gave me a shove toward the stage.

My heart was beating so hard in my chest that I felt like I could pass out. "Remind me to fire you after this," I griped at her.

The crowd clapped as I made my way to my piano. I was so embarrassed.

"What am I supposed to play?" I asked Frank.

"Whatever you want," he answered. "We'll try to back you."

I took a deep breath and adjusted my piano bench. It had been quite a while since I played in front of people, and now was not the best time for a panic attack.

I ran through the songs that I knew by heart. My eyes glanced across the crowded pub and I saw Ryan standing and watching me. As I thought of him, one particular song came to mind.

"Mmm, thank you." I adjusted the microphone to my lips and blew out a heavy sigh to get my nerves in check.

"This song is one of my all-time favorites, and I hope you like it. Ahm, it's called 'You've Got a Friend.'"

I placed my fingers on the keys, took a deep breath, and started to play.

The music flowed, and I miraculously remembered the lyrics and notes. I felt the strength and courage surge into me as my fingers danced over the keys.

As I played, I felt that every word, every note, was meant for Ryan and Ryan alone. I hoped that when he closed his eyes he did think of me, and if he needed me all he had to do was call out my name. There was no explanation for my overwhelming feelings; I was drawn to him like a moth to a flame.

For a brief moment, our eyes met from across the room. Ryan was the only one I wanted to look at. He had the most glorious smile on his face as he stood to watch me play. I pressed the keys with extra force, wishing that he could realize that this song was for him.

To my amazement, I received a standing ovation when I finished. I felt the heat rise to my cheeks as the embarrassment washed over me. I briefly covered my face with my hands. I looked over at Ryan again; he was still standing and clapping with a huge smile on his face, his head slowly shaking back and forth.

I politely thanked everyone and quickly turned the microphone off. There was no way I'd do another song. Pete was standing by the front door, clapping frantically. His cheers were definitely the loudest.

"Miss Taryn Mitchell, everyone!" Frank yelled into the microphone. I took a brief bow and quickly stepped off the stage.

It was hard to walk back to the bar through the thick crowd. Hands I didn't know touched me and patted me on the back, and people were in my face complimenting me. It was a very uncomfortable feeling, and for a moment I wondered if this was how Ryan felt all the time.

I walked right past him, even though he was smiling from ear to ear. I tried to return the smile, but I was too flustered to even look at him. He reached for me but I didn't stop. I was almost at a run when I ducked into my stairwell; I just needed a moment to calm down and get my nerves in check.

I only made it up four steps before crashing down to put my head in my hands. My heart was about to burst out of my chest and it was hard to breathe.

My eyes shot up when I heard my stairwell door open. Ryan slipped around the corner and shut the door quickly behind him. He was smiling and laughing lightly to himself as he stood there staring at me.

"Is this what it's like for you?" I asked, covering my heart with my hand to slow the pounding.

"Well, that depends," he said. "Are you referring to the extreme embarrassment or the full-out panic attacks?"

I just nodded and gasped in a few deep breaths of air.

"Either way . . . yeah." He nodded.

"Hey, come here." Ryan reached out to me, taking my hands in his. He pulled me into a nice hug, wrapping his strong arms gently around my shoulders.

"You were absolutely breathtaking up there," he whispered, reassuring me. "You have *nothing* to be embarrassed about."

His hand held my head to his chest and he softly kissed my hair; it felt confusingly natural to hold him. I clasped my hands together around his waist and pressed my face deeper into his chest. The soft scent of his skin was like an aphrodisiac, making me crave him even more.

I closed my eyes and felt my heart rate slowly coming down while he ran his hand over my back to soothe me.

"It's okay, sweetheart. Just breathe with me," he said softly.

CHAPTER 6

Respite

I HAVE OFF ON Sunday and Monday and I'd really like to see you . . . that is, if you don't already have plans with one of your admirers," Ryan teased. I noted the tone of sarcasm in his voice.

I smirked at him. Apparently I wasn't the only one slightly jealous. "Don't be ridiculous."

"Me?" He sounded shocked.

"Yeah, you. Like you have any room to talk."

He frowned at me.

"Well, anyway . . ." He leaned up on the stairwell wall. "I was wondering if you and I can go do something together."

I sat back down on the steps. As much as I wanted to refuse him and protect myself, I no longer had the will to do so. I couldn't deny this powerful attraction to him any longer. "What did you have in mind?"

"Anything," he breathed out desperately. "I just need to get away." He lightly tapped his head back into the wall.

"I don't have any plans," I willingly admitted. "Monday night is poker, but you already know that."

"Yeah, speaking of which, I'd like an opportunity to win some of my money back."

"Sure. I'd be happy to take all of your chips this time." I snickered.

A few moments of silence passed. I just stared at the scuff on my shoe, trying to calm myself and banish the confusion he was reaping in my mind. Ryan appeared deep in thought.

"Huh," he sighed. His eyes glanced up the stairs.

"What?" I looked over my shoulder to see what he was looking at.

"Nothing," he said, shaking his head. "I was just thinking about the last time I was in this stairwell. I was in a lot worse shape than you were a few minutes ago."

He made me laugh. "Perfect place for panic attacks then, huh?"

"I was actually thinking that it's more of a gateway to peace. Insanity out there . . ." He motioned to the door. "Respite in here," he stated firmly. "Are you ready for more insanity yet?" He reached out his hand and pulled me up from my step. "You can't hide in here forever."

I groaned. "No, I like respite better." A big sigh escaped my lungs. "I'm glad you came tonight."

"Me too," he said gently, looking me in my eyes. His fingers stroked my cheek. "Just think, I could have missed your stellar performance *and* your private panic attack all in one night."

"Don't be an ass." I attempted to poke him in the rib with my finger, but he caught my hand in his. The touch of his hand on mine did strange things to my heart.

"Come on, sweetheart." He motioned with his head, leading me to the door. "Insanity is waiting."

I slipped out the door first. Ryan stayed behind for a few minutes so we wouldn't cause too much of a stir appearing from the same place together.

One of his security team was standing guard right outside the stairwell door, doing a good job earning his keep.

I resumed my spot behind the bar and was greeted by Marie and Tammy, who were grinning from ear to ear.

"So am I fired or am I getting a raise?" Marie kidded.

"You were spectacular up there!" Tammy gushed. She gave me a quick hug.

I rolled my eyes, smiled at them both, and went back to business tending bar.

It was almost one thirty in the morning when my cell phone vibrated in my pocket; Ryan was texting me from the booth.

"too many eyes watching I will call u tomorrow"

"ok r u filming?" He was watching me type back to him.

"yeah all day n night too maybe til 1am?" He typed with a frown on his lips.

"I will b here," I typed.

"think about where to go Sunday please"

"I will"

"Promise?" He was staring at me now.

I looked over at him, smiled, and crossed my heart.

Ryan shoved his phone back into his coat.

I watched him head for the door; his security had him flanked. The second he stepped out into his personal rendition of insanity, I could hear women screaming and see the flash of cameras illuminating the dark street.

I SPENT a good portion of Saturday morning trying to come up with ideas of where to go on Sunday. It wasn't as though I could take him anywhere in public without causing a scene. I wondered what other celebrities did for fun. I'd seen plenty of pictures of famous stars out and about doing normal things like trying to get a lousy cup of coffee or having lunch. The simple fact that I saw pictures of them doing those ordinary things made me realize that there are few things they could do without being followed.

I remembered the words that Ryan had muttered under his breath that first day I met him: "the things we take for granted." I knew now what he meant. No longer could he simply walk out of a store or restaurant without being hounded for pictures or autographs.

Do celebrities ever get used to the insanity, or do they just develop a way of tuning it out? Ryan's fame was still fresh, and I knew that he didn't like all the attention.

I wanted to take him somewhere that he could just be himself. I laughed at myself, thinking that the only idea I had so far was for us to hide in my stairwell.

Hmm . . . someplace away from people; someplace where he could move around and yet remain unnoticed. Private . . . secluded . . . fun . . . safe. Then the idea struck me.

"Hi, Uncle Al, it's Taryn. How are you?" After a few moments of pleasantries, I got down to business. "Is anyone using Pappy's shack this weekend? I have a friend visiting me from out of town and I thought it would be a nice place to go for a day trip."

With my newfound brilliance, it was time to put the rest of the plan into action. There were supplies I would need to get and things to pack in the car. I made a list so I wouldn't forget anything and headed to the store.

Two hours later, I had all the items on my list and the trunk of my car packed with essentials. I was trying to get to the closet in the third bedroom when Ryan called.

"Hey, how are you?" I asked, groaning as I pushed a few heavy boxes out of my way.

"What are you up to?" He started laughing at the grunting noises I was making in the phone.

"Digging out my cooler. It's buried under some boxes."

"Cooler? What do you need that for?"

"I need it for tomorrow. Shoot!" I yelled as the phone slipped out from under my ear. It landed on the floor. "Hello?" I asked in a hurry. I hoped I hadn't hung up on him and was relieved when I heard him laugh.

"Sorry, phone slipped. Okay, you can stop laughing at me now."

"So where are *you* going tomorrow?" he asked. I loved his sarcastic sense of humor.

"Oh, that's a secret. You'll see when we get there," I teased.

"Secret? You're really not going to tell me where we're going?"

"Nope. It's a surprise. I'm pretty sure you'll like it, though." I laughed. "You'll just have to trust me."

"Uh-oh. Now I'm worried."

"Worried?" I tsked. "No worries. You'll be well hidden from the public. The place we are going to is . . . private. But we'll have to drive a few hours to get there."

"Now I'm intrigued." The excitement in his voice was noticeable.

"Oh, and you'll need warm, comfy clothes, because we'll be spending some time outside. Pack some extra clothes too, just in case." Visions of one of us falling in the lake crossed my mind.

"Now I'm really intrigued."

"Good. You'll have to tell me how, when, and where I can pick you up tomorrow."

"I was thinking about that," he sighed. "You know I can't just hop in your car at the hotel. Maybe you can pick me up at the set, but . . ." I could hear him breathe pretty hard.

"What?" I asked.

"I'm going to have to hide so I can get off the lot unnoticed." His voice was troubled.

"Hide? How? You want to hide in the trunk?" I joked, trying to lighten the concern in his tone.

"Ah, just bring a blanket. Damn, I hate this," he huffed.

"Ryan, it's all right. I understand. We'll do what we have to. It's no big deal."

He explained how to get in the catering entrance and that he'd leave my name with the gate security. It was the easiest way to get to him, but it was still tricky. Rumors were being leaked off the set all the time, and he was concerned that the paparazzi would follow us. His plan gave me another idea. There was one more phone call I had to make.

"Tammy, hey. I need a favor . . ."

EARLY SUNDAY morning I pulled up to the gate on the enclosed lot; it was a few minutes before nine o'clock. The entire location was penned in by a ten-foot privacy fence and cement block. It was very intimidating. The guard who greeted me had a pistol strapped to his hip.

"Hi. Taryn Mitchell. I have a delivery," I said to the guard. He looked over his clipboard of names. I had to show him my driver's license as proof of identity, and he made me open the back so he could look inside before letting me proceed.

"Go on." He waved and motioned to another security guard to move the barricade.

I parked next to a line of catering vehicles and noticed Ryan hanging out by one of the tents. There were people mingling all around, so I tried to blend in.

"Good morning, Mr. Christensen," I greeted him with a tip of my hat. A few people walked past us.

"Good morning," he said, flinching with confusion.

"Are you ready?" I mouthed to him.

He grabbed his bag and followed me along the rows of trucks and vans. I hit the key fob to unlock the doors, which made the lights flash.

"Nice van, Ms. Mitchell," he murmured at me.

"Bond, Taryn Bond," I muttered back to him.

Ryan jumped into the back of the van and I shut the door quickly behind him. The guards moved the barricades and I drove right past the waiting paparazzi completely unnoticed. Ryan laughed hysterically as we drove down the road.

"Where the *hell* did you get a catering van?" he asked, climbing into the front passenger seat.

"It's Tammy's." I removed the T&P Catering baseball cap off my head and shook out my hair. "She owns a catering business. Don't touch the pastries back there or she'll shoot you."

"Ms. Bond, you are truly amazing." He laughed.

I drove back to Pete and Tammy's house. Tammy and I exchanged car keys and Ryan thanked them both. "You two are the best," Ryan said.

"Have fun!" Pete tapped him on the arm. "Go enjoy yourself."

"Are you going to tell me where we're going, or is it still a secret?" Ryan nudged me with his elbow as I drove us out onto the highway.

I looked over at him and smiled. He was reading the road signs, trying to figure it out.

"Northwest," I answered.

He looked at me and just kept shaking his head. He was dying to know where we were going and I was holding out.

"And how long do we drive northwest?" he pried.

I glanced at the time on the dashboard. "Another hour and forty minutes."

Ryan spent a good portion of the trip chewing on his fingers. I noticed he was a fingernail biter.

"I like this car," he said as he closed his eyes. "Seats are really comfortable. Infiniti, right?"

"Yep. M45."

"Wake me up when we get there," he said brusquely.

"Oh, hell no!" I poked him in his side. He jumped and flinched away from me, laughing. "You have to stay awake."

We were about fifteen minutes away from our final destination when I pulled off into the parking lot of the local convenience store and gas station. This was the place where my family would stop before every trip to the cabin. I backed my car up to the tree line on the far end of the lot so Ryan would remain unnoticed.

"I want to get some coffee," I replied, answering the question on Ryan's face. "You want anything?"

"Yeah, would you get me a twenty-ouncer?" he asked, reaching in his pocket for money. I grimaced at his actions and ignored the money in his hand.

"Do you want anything in it? Cream, sugar?" I asked. I already had one leg out of the car.

"Yeah, make it a shade light and three sugars. Here, take this," he insisted, handing a twenty-dollar bill to me.

"Nah, I got it."

"Would you at least let me buy you a damn cup of coffee?" he pleaded. I could tell he was a little upset.

"Fine," I whispered and made a face at him. I didn't want to argue. I slipped the money from his fingers.

While I was paying for the coffees, I noticed that his picture was on the front of one of the gossip magazines. In the picture, behind him, was the front door to my pub. I grabbed the magazine and thumbed through it quickly to read what they had printed. Among the worthless drivel surrounding his pictures was a photo of him and the two actresses exiting my pub. I read the caption:

> Suzanne is growing closer to Ryan. The two have been spending a lot of alone time on and off the set, although they both deny that they are secretly dating. The two were spotted keeping each other company October 4 as they were caught leaving a local club after a late night of partying in downtown Seaport. "Ryan and Suzanne were very close all night and seemed happy," says an eyewitness.

I slapped the magazine shut and put it back on the rack. I knew the truth; he didn't pay much attention to Suzanne that night at all—he was too busy watching *me*, wearing *my* T-shirt, in *my* pub. I smiled widely; he was sitting in my car waiting for *me* that very moment.

"I got two sausage, egg, and cheese muffins," I said, handing his change and the bag over to him.

"Excellent! I'm hungry."

"I figured you might be. Hey, you need to share." I leered at him. He was already unwrapping the second sandwich while still eating the first.

"Here, take a bite," he snickered, even though he took another big bite of the muffin before holding it to my mouth.

I made the final turn on the last leg of our trip. The last few miles of road were bordered on both sides by tall pines and thick trees; the air was scented with the fresh perfume of the woods. The leaves were just starting to turn with fall's colors and they made beautiful hues on the windshield.

I turned onto the obscure drive to my grandfather's cabin and stopped to unlock the metal pipe gate that blocked cars from driving farther onto the property. Ryan slipped his sunglasses off; his eyes were wide with wonder.

"Welcome to my grandfather's fishing shack." I smiled at him as we drove up to the house.

"Shack? That isn't a shack," he declared, pointing to the house. He smiled in amazement.

Nestled comfortably in the woods was a log A-frame with a wooden deck that wrapped around the sides and past an enormous stone chimney. The front of the house was all windows that reflected the sun's rays breaking through the trees. Off the back of the house was a raised, screened-in porch that overlooked the lake.

"It's not that big. It only has two bedrooms," I answered his gaze. I parked the car in the stone-covered car pad right next to the stairs that led to the deck.

Ryan helped me carry the cooler up the steps to the front door. I gave him a quick tour of the house while I turned the power and water on.

"This is excellent," he said with an exultant grin on his face. I watched him wander around the room, touching and looking at everything.

"*That right there* is why I didn't want to ruin the surprise." I pointed at his smile. "After we get the car unpacked, I thought we might take the boat out on the lake . . . do a little fishing?" I waved the cup of night crawlers in the air.

"We're going fishing?" he asked, completely astonished. "You? You . . . fish?"

"Sure," I quipped. "That's why I brought you here. I thought we'd take the boat out on the lake."

We walked down the stone-covered drive to the one-car garage where the boat was stored. The boat was painted gunmetal silver, with black and red detail stripes and a dark gray interior.

"Nice!" Ryan said as he pushed the garage door up. "Seventeen-footer?"

"It belongs to my Uncle Al." I nodded. "It was my dad's and his, but . . . well . . . it was big enough for the two of them."

I climbed onto the big ATV that we needed to use to tow the boat down to the lake, but when I tried to start it the battery was obviously dead.

"Go get your car. We can jump-start it," he said confidently.

Ryan was enjoying himself, tinkering around with jumper cables and twisting the throttle on the ATV. He was like a kid in a candy store, so happy and relaxed. I loved how he was able to fix things. He reminded me of my father.

He backed the ATV up and I helped him hook the hitch to the boat trailer. I held his shoulders to steady myself as I climbed on the four-wheeler behind him. I took the liberty to give him a few extra squeezes to massage his tense muscles. I took his moaning as confirmation that he enjoyed my touch.

"Hold on tight." He patted and squeezed my thigh before twisting the throttle to set us in motion.

I rested my chin on his shoulder while the light breeze blew his hair onto my cheek. I nestled my frosty nose near his warm neck to add another delicious scent of him to my memory. I wished we had farther to drive so I could enjoy holding on to him like this longer, but it was a short distance between the garage and the lake.

The noontime sun was bright overhead. He backed the boat trailer into the water and helped me push the boat into the lake. We worked well as a team.

Ryan gave me a few teasing bumps when we walked back up the driveway to get our things. He just kept grinning and shaking his head at me.

We loaded up the boat with all the essentials—fishing gear, beer, and sandwiches—and Ryan started the little trolling motor to get us out on the water.

The air was still and it wasn't as cold as it had been the last few days. The lake was calm and reflected the trees and sky like a gigantic mirror. I tipped my sunglasses down to take in the sight of Ryan driving the boat. He was looking so good in his blue jeans and white thermal shirt with a brown coat. The grin on his face was one of heavenly bliss. I was thrilled that he was enjoying this mini-vacation.

"Head over toward those trees." I pointed. "That's my dad's lucky spot. He caught lots of fish over there."

"So how did you come up with the fishing idea?" he asked, casting his line out into the water.

"From you." I laughed lightly. I opted to put a lure on my line instead of one of the worms.

"Me? When did I ever tell you I love to fish?"

"The first day I met you. You showed me the scar where your brother hooked you in the arm."

He looked over at me and smiled. "You have a good memory for detail. I forgot about that. This was your dad's favorite spot? I can see why. It's beautiful out here."

I inhaled deeply, enjoying the soft scent of pine and fallen leaves. It was much different from the smell that emanated off the Atlantic.

Ryan stared at me for a moment, chewing on his lip. "Can I ask what happened?" he said hesitantly. "Your dad?"

I gasped slightly; just thinking about it hurt.

"The doctors told me he had a massive heart attack." I sniffed. "It was right after Labor Day last year. We weren't busy for some reason so dad told me to take the night off—said he'd lock up the bar for once." I grimaced from hearing his voice in my head. "When I came home I found him on the floor. I tried to do CPR on him until the ambulance came, but I was too late."

"I'm so sorry." Ryan looked at me apologetically.

"Thanks. It was really hard at first, but I've been dealing with it. I just try to remember all the good times."

"And . . . your mom?" He looked as if he shouldn't have asked.

I took another deep breath and held it in my lungs for a few seconds.

"My mom was hit by a car." I winced at the memory. "She was pushing a grocery cart through a parking lot when an elderly lady backed out of a parking space too fast and hit her. The impact shattered my mom's hip and severed her femoral artery. Doctors couldn't save her." I kept a careful hold on the memory so it wouldn't overpower me. Talking about my parents made it all seem fresh again.

Ryan stepped over to where I sat in the boat and gently rubbed my back. "I'm sorry. I can't imagine how hard that must be for you."

"It's hard, but you have to just go on, you know? You don't really know how much you miss something until it's gone," I said, looking in his eyes.

Ryan let his arm rest behind me. His presence was extremely comforting.

I felt the line on my fishing pole tug. "Hey, I think I got one!" I started to reel in my line. Ryan grabbed the net and leaned over the side to see what I'd caught.

"Nice!" he said enthusiastically, netting the largemouth bass that was on my hook. "He's got to be about ten inches." Ryan had to get the fish unhooked for me. "Good job!" He beamed.

I made a fish face at the poor fish before he released it back into the lake. "See ya, Mr. Bass."

"So tell me more about you," Ryan started.

"What do you want to know?"

"Everything," he stated emphatically.

As we fished he asked me a barrage of questions, and I found myself telling him my life's story. Some of his questions prompted questions of my own, and he didn't seem hesitant to tell me anything I wanted to know either.

"Actually, I was born in upstate New York," I told him, sniffing in some of the mountain air. "I grew up near Watkins Glen. Have you ever heard of it?"

"Sure," he replied. "I've even been there once. My dad took us there to see a race."

I smiled. "Our house was only four miles from the track."

"How long did you live there?"

"Until I was almost fourteen. We moved to Seaport when my grandfather got sick." I pulled my hair back from my shoulders.

"I thought you grew up in Seaport. I got the impression that your dad always ran the pub."

"No, my dad used to work for Corning. He was a VP there for a long time. But my grandfather had a stroke, so we moved here to take care of him. I think my dad loved his job, but when it all happened . . . I guess the timing was right for him to resign and slow down a little. Actually, he seemed happier when he took over running the pub."

"What about your mom? Did she work?"

I nodded and took a sip of my beer. "She worked in the admissions office at Ithaca College. I was planning on going to college there, but . . . things change, I guess. We moved here and Brown was closer. What about you? Did you go to college?"

Ryan smiled and looked slightly embarrassed. "I went to Pitt for two years."

"Pitt?" I repeated.

He nodded. "I *was* going for a degree in architecture," he said remorsefully. "I wanted to design houses and buildings. I love to draw."

"But you didn't finish?"

"I was living at home, going to school, and doing some local theater at the time. One of my acting coaches told me about this open audition in L.A., so I went, and soon after that I got my first major movie role. It's pretty much been a big blur since!" He chuckled. "I had to get an agent and a manager . . . and a lawyer!" He cast his line out into the water. "Sometimes I wonder how my life would have turned out if I'd stayed in college and didn't get on that plane to L.A."

"I'd like to believe that everything happens for a reason. If you hadn't gotten on that plane, then you probably wouldn't be sitting here in this boat on this lake right now."

"You're right." He beamed. "This would have been a shame to miss. I want to have a place just like this one day. A house on a lake surrounded by woods, dock for the boat, a big stone fireplace . . ."

"I miss the house we used to have near the Glen," I said. "That was near a lake too, kind of like this lake but smaller. It was a big, white farmhouse with a huge yard. We had a rope swing hanging from one of the big elm trees that would swing out over the lake; I remember we would start at the top of the embankment and run down this worn path and swing as hard as we could. It was a game to see who could swing out the farthest."

Ryan looked at me and grinned. "Sounds like you were a bit of a daredevil when you were younger."

I stretched my legs out straight, remembering how I used to jump off the rope swing.

"The best part of summer was when the grapes were ready to be picked. My dad built this huge arbor in our yard; it was covered in grapevines. I remember running out in the backyard first thing in the morning to pick the grapes that were covered in morning dew. Dad said that they were nature's wine," I reminisced. "Do you know how wine is made?"

"I know a little. I know more about drinking wine than how it's made, though. What about you?"

I nodded. "My family has co-owned a few wineries for a long time. I have a vested interest in three active wineries now."

"You do?" He was surprised.

I nodded again. "My parents invested a lot of money into some of the local wineries up around the Finger Lakes. We used to co-own five, but we sold our interests in one of them and two of the wineries merged. After my father died, I inherited all the shares. I'm a limited partner now, but I still get involved in the businesses sometimes. We've been great friends with the families that run the wineries—some of them I've known my whole life."

He winked at me. "Quite the businesswoman you are." I shrugged. "I like diversity. It makes for a steady income and good wine connections. I'm also a silent partner in Tammy's catering business; I stay silent and let it up to her to run it as she sees fit."

Ryan cast his line out again. "Isn't it hard to be in business with a friend?"

"No, not yet. Tammy and I have a legal business relationship. We're both partners in a limited liability corporation with signed agreements. I gave her the start-up capital. I wanted to help my friend, but I want to keep my friend no matter what happens. The business relationship is one thing, the long-standing friendship is another. She has the option to buy me out at any time."

"So let me get this straight. You own a bar, co-own a few wineries, and are a partner in a catering business? Did I get them all?"

"Well, there's the stained-glass business too," I murmured. "But that's more of a hobby now. Do you remember seeing the big glass 'Mitchell's Pub' sign hanging behind the bar?"

He nodded.

"I made that."

"You made that?" He sounded impressed.

"I made quite a few pieces for some of the local businesses. The bookstore next to my pub . . . I made their sign, too."

"I think I got one!" Ryan reeled in his line to find a small bass on his hook. "Did you like that worm? Did ya?" he asked the fish, like they were friends. It made me chuckle.

"So what about your parents?" I asked.

"My dad is a dentist," he said proudly. He parted his lips to show me his teeth. "This is all his handiwork." He motioned with his finger. "I had braces until I was sixteen."

"I bet that impressed the ladies," I teased.

"Yeah, got me *a lot* of dates. I was so happy when he finally took them off."

Ryan paused for a moment to take a swig of his beer. "My mom has been his office manager for forever. She pretty much runs the place. We always kid him that all he has to do is show up and tell people to say 'ahh.' Mom does the rest."

A minute or two passed and I had a vision of his dad's dental business being inundated with new patients. It made me laugh out loud.

"What's so funny?" he asked.

"I was just picturing your dad's waiting room being lined up with hundreds of new patients, all young and female! 'Oh, Dr. Christensen, I think I have a cavity. By the way, can you introduce me to your son?'"

"Hah! That's funny you said that. If someone new calls to make an appointment . . . if you're under forty and female, forget it. You're not getting in. My mom will hang up on you."

"Guess it's a good thing that I already have a dentist." I laughed. "I thought maybe they were grading the women for you. Only the ones with minimal amounts of plaque get your phone number."

He was laughing so hard he didn't even realize he had another fish on his line.

I set my pole down and retrieved the net. "Look at that!" I yelled. He had a huge fish on his hook. The poor thing was thrashing. Ryan had the biggest smile on his face; he was in his happy place.

"That's good eating right there." He held the fish up.

"No, no . . . catch and release," I reminded him.

We spent the entire afternoon fishing out on the lake. I learned some inside trade secrets of the movie industry and how he got hurt once doing some of his own stunts. He told me about all the stunts that he had to do for the *Seaside* movie and how each move was carefully choreographed. It was interesting to learn about green screens and how they sometimes filmed inside a huge building, but once the computer graphics and scenery were added it would appear that they were actually outside.

We lounged peacefully in the boat as we watched the hawks fly in the breeze. The setting sun changed the horizon to beautiful shades of orange and red, and the wind that blew across the water had a frosty chill.

Over the course of several hours we shared our stories, our thoughts, likes and dislikes, and hopes and dreams. We made each other laugh a lot. It was all so surreal.

"That was a lot of fun," Ryan said as he tied the boat to the dock. We walked up the path to the cabin and he took the fishing poles out of my hand.

"Thank you," he said softly. The smile on his face was genuine. He bumped his arm into mine, giving me a little nudge.

I was really happy that he enjoyed himself and that he caught more fish than I did. He didn't seem egotistical but he was still a man, and all men have their pride.

I felt a sudden urge to hold his hand as we walked to the house; his arm was almost touching mine. This would have been a perfect moment for it, but we didn't have that kind of relationship.

I wondered if we ever would. I could picture him all too clearly being a part of my life and me being a part of his. But the part of his life that I was imagining was this part, right now, a life of peace and togetherness—of normalcy. The kind of life that most people on the planet experienced.

In reality, Ryan's life was anything but normal now and that was hard to imagine. He was in constant turmoil, being hounded and chased. He had no privacy. His existence had to be shrouded in secrecy to keep intimate details from becoming public. What a trade he had to make for doing something he loved!

The entire time we were out on the lake, I'd wanted to ask him point blank why acting was worth it to him—worth the trade. *Was* there something in his ego that needed that brush of attention? Did he get a thrill out of pretending to be someone else, because that's what actors do—they get to live someone else's life for a while. But I couldn't do it. I couldn't ask. They were questions that remained unanswered.

The biggest question in my mind was whether peace and insanity could survive together in harmony.

CHAPTER 7

Revelations

"I'M FREEZING." MY teeth were chattering from being out on the lake. I turned the baseboard heaters on to warm up the cabin. "Ryan? Would you go get a couple of logs from the side of the house, please? I want to start a fire."

I grabbed the big steamer pot from under the counter, filled it with water, and set it on the stove. My stomach was making noises and it was getting close to dinnertime.

Ryan carried in an armful of logs and I helped him stack them next to the fireplace.

"The starter log stuff is in that box." I pointed to where he should look. I used some small branches to get the fire going.

"You're a real Girl Scout," he kidded and nudged me on the leg.

"Not really. I can't start a fire without a lighter or a match. I'd be in big trouble if I had to survive in the woods."

"I met the survivor guy from TV once," he said. "You know who I'm talking about?"

"Who? That guy who gets dropped off in the worst of places and then gets filmed while eating frogs and stuff?"

"Yeah. That guy." He nodded. "I met him at a party once. He was one bizarre dude. He had some really wild stories."

"You sort of look like the survivor man yourself." I laughed lightly. "You have bits of wood stuck all over your shirt." I picked some shards off of his sleeves while he plucked a few that were stuck to his chest. "Let's go outside and brush you off."

We stepped out onto the wooden deck and I immediately ran my hands over his arms to knock the dirt off. Instead of helping me Ryan just stood there, perfectly still, gazing at me while I dusted him.

I wondered for a moment if he was going to try to kiss me. We were so close; all I could think about was tasting him. He would only have to lean in a few inches. *I would succumb willingly . . .*

My hands slowed in their movements as I tried to be precise with removing the wood shards. My eyes were fixed on tracing the texture and contours of his shirt, since I couldn't look him directly in the eyes.

I thought about what his full lips might feel like on mine, how the skin on his muscular chest might feel under my hands. For a moment I could understand why those sick fans wanted to pull his shirt off. Now I thought about doing it too, and right after that, his shoes, his belt, his jeans . . .

I had to banish those thoughts. That line of thinking was way too dangerous.

"You should be able to get the rest," I muttered, quickly turning on my heels to hurry back into the cabin. *Don't do this to yourself, Taryn. You can't have him.*

I washed my hands thoroughly at the sink and unpacked some of the food from the cooler.

"What are you up to?" he asked when he joined me in the kitchen. I was rinsing the two enormous lobster tails I'd picked up at the seafood store.

Ryan peeked over my shoulder. "Mmm, lobster." He grinned, smacking his lips together. "Need help?"

I noticed that when he stood next to me, he was careful not to let our bodies touch. He kept a small but safe distance between us. I wondered if he did that on purpose.

Ryan sat down at the dinner table, in the same chair where my father always sat. The memory of that made me smile. I imagined my father being pleased with the man who now took his place at the table. Ryan and my father would have gotten along very well.

We had a lovely dinner together as the fire crackled behind us; the radio was playing soft music in the background. It was actually quite romantic.

A tinge of nervousness crept into my gut from being alone with him in a secluded cabin in the middle of the woods. *All alone . . . with him,* my mind repeated. *Bottle of wine . . . fireplace . . . bedroom just down the hallway.* I swallowed hard. Would he be expecting more? After all, I did bring him here. I'd pretty much set the stage for a convenient tryst.

"That was delicious, Taryn." Ryan stretched back in his chair, patting his stomach. "I'm stuffed."

I was glad he'd enjoyed it, but now the flow of panic was surging in like the tide. What was next? I had just started to smile at him when I felt queasy again. He helped me clear the table and I began washing the dishes when the wave of nausea hit.

"I don't feel so good." I rubbed my stomach and dashed for the bathroom.

I was gone for so long that Ryan had washed all the dishes and was kicked back on the couch by the fire.

"Are you all right?" he asked. I could hear the concern in his tone.

"No. I feel really sick."

"My stomach isn't feeling so hot, either."

I looked at him, surprised that his stomach was in knots, too. Apparently I wasn't the only one.

I had just sat down on the couch when I felt like I could vomit. I ran back to the bathroom just in time to make it to the toilet as dinner came back up . . . several times.

Ryan was pale when I came out of the bathroom; he hurried right past me and shut the door. I trudged down the hallway to the master bedroom so I could lie down; I was really feeling lousy. I turned the television on to drown out the sounds of Ryan getting sick.

"Whatever you do, don't go in there," he groaned as he lay down on the bed next to me. Even though he'd warned me, I couldn't wait. I darted for the bathroom again for round two of violent vomiting.

For the next several hours we took turns violating the bathroom. I hadn't been that sick in years.

"I just threw up air," I said as I curled back down on the bed next to him.

Ryan softly chuckled. "I threw up food I haven't even eaten yet."

His comment made me laugh.

"Do you think it was the lobster?" he asked, pulling the blanket up higher on his shoulder.

"I was wondering that myself." When I spoke, the words that came up my sore throat made me cough.

"But it was still partially frozen and I rinsed it. I was trying to think of what else we ate today. Maybe it was that breakfast sandwich? The sausage?"

"Could be. But we both got sick right away. I'm thinking tainted lobster—either that or it was the salad."

"My ribs are killing me." I winced as I rubbed my stomach. "But I don't feel like I need to be sick anymore, so that's a good thing."

"Me neither. I'm starting to feel a little better, actually."

"I'm so sorry," I pleaded with him. "Don't hate me."

"I don't hate you," he whispered sweetly, his fingers drifting across my forehead. He pulled the blanket up higher on my back to cover me up. "We're never buying any seafood again from wherever you bought that lobster, though, I can tell you that."

For as lousy as I felt and as sick as I just was, the fact that he said "we" sent a wave of elation through my soul.

Ryan was curled up in a ball and I could hear him start to breathe heavier. He had fallen asleep, so I turned the television off and closed my eyes. After that marathon session of nastiness, it wouldn't take me long to fall asleep either.

I knew I was dreaming when I couldn't see the ground that my feet were supposedly running on. I was trying to get through one of those mazes made out of tall hedges that you see sometimes in movies, and every turn I took was a dead end. I'd have to turn around and run down the same path that I just came from, all the while hearing Ryan calling my name and asking me to "come here, come here." I had to find him.

I ran down a long row of hedges and turned to the left where I thought his voice was coming from. As soon as I turned the corner, there was a mob of women, all wearing a picture of his face on their shirts, blocking my path. They started to laugh at me; some of them were cackling like witches.

Photographers stepped out of the shrubs and were taking pictures of me as I started to cry. I felt the twang of terror set in as one girl in the front row morphed into the likeness of Suzanne Strass. She grabbed me by the hair and pulled fiercely, bending me backward.

"He's mine, bitch!" she screamed in my face. "Not even in your dreams."

My eyes shot open from the sensation. Part of my long hair was trapped under Ryan's head. The sun was bright, so I assumed it was sometime after eight o'clock.

A shot of pain hit my ribs when I started to crawl out of bed; my stomach muscles were sore from throwing up so many times.

I went out to the living room and grabbed my bag so I could get freshened up. I desperately needed a shower; my hair was a mess and I *looked* like I'd spent the night vomiting.

The hot water felt good, and I noticed that I was feeling much better. I brushed my teeth to rid my mouth of the nasty taste and washed my body twice to rid my pores of illness. I couldn't get clean enough.

I put my jeans and a shirt on so I could go out to the living room again; my hairbrush was stuffed in my purse. Ryan came to the bedroom door and stopped to lean on the door frame.

"Are you finished in there?" he asked as a big yawn broke from his lips.

As he spoke, my eyes took in the sight of him. Sometime during the night he'd taken his jeans off. He was standing there in a white T-shirt and gray boxer briefs, and oh my, there it was, extreme morning wood.

HELLO! My brain shouted as my eyes traced the large bulge pushing out in his shorts.

He tilted his head and smirked when he realized that my eyes and thoughts were completely distracted. I think he actually meant for me to see that, because he didn't even attempt to move or hide it.

"Um, yeah, all yours," I muttered, embarrassed from being busted ogling his underwear. I turned and hurried out of his way, ignoring him when he chuckled.

While my brain was still tracing the outline of his morning friend, I grabbed my pack of birth control pills out of my purse and popped Monday's pill in my mouth. Even though it was only a placebo today, I still wanted to keep up with my daily routine. I couldn't have had sex this weekend even if I'd wanted to; that was probably another reason why I was feeling drained.

I had been on the pill since my first year of college, and the erotic vision that was in my mind right now was the exact reason why. Better to be safe than sorry, for I didn't want to have children without first being married, but I certainly wasn't going to keep my virginity intact until that happened.

"Taryn? Do you have an extra towel?" Ryan yelled from the bathroom.

"Yeah, hang on a sec." I pulled a fresh, white towel out from one of my bags.

He was partially hidden behind the bathroom door, although I could see that his shirt was now off. I tried not to look at him at all when I handed him the bath towel. I already had one huge image of him that was repeating in my mind.

I walked back to the living room wondering how many women have gotten an up-close-and-personal look at his package. I knew how many men I'd had sex with—I was still in the single digits for my total—high single digits, but nine is still under ten.

I figured with a body and a package like his, combined with endless opportunities from women throwing themselves at him, he probably took that thing out of his pants and showed it to as many women as possible. It was a frightening thought, and I secretly hoped my assumption was wrong.

I was putting the dishes away when he came out into the great room with nothing on except the towel wrapped around his waist. His left hand was gripping the two ends of the towel together; his other hand combed his wet hair back off his forehead.

"I need my bag," he muttered.

Holy shit! My brain shrieked again from the new sight of him. My eyes quickly took in his bare chest and arms, how they still glistened slightly from the water droplets that remained on his skin.

I gasped in a quick breath of air and turned away for the safer view of the kitchen sink. *Clean the sink—just clean the sink. Don't look.*

I could see his reflection in the kitchen window; he had his back turned to me as he opened the towel and rewrapped it around his waist. He stood there for a few moments, using both of his hands to comb through his wet hair.

Effin-A, he is HOT! Marie was right in her assessment. I was thankful that the metal sink was strong enough to endure my grip and hold me in place as I squeezed my legs together at the knees.

It had been far too long since I saw a mostly naked man, and this one was killing me with visions left and right. I think he realized that I was intentionally turned away from him because he sort of huffed, grabbed his bag, and headed back to the bedroom.

I had the kitchen all cleaned up when he came back to the island counter that separated the kitchen from the rest of the main room. He leaned on the island with his elbows right next to where I had my purse.

Shit! When I went to get him a towel, I'd forgotten to shove my pill pack back into my purse. Just as I turned to correct my mistake, his fingers picked it up. His look of curiosity was instantly replaced with a smirk when he realized what it was.

"You weren't supposed to see that," I murmured. I snatched the pack from his hand and shoved it back in my purse.

"What's the big deal?" he asked casually. "So you're on the pill. That's good to know." He smiled.

This was a conversation that I didn't want to have with him. "Are you finished in the bathroom? 'Cause if you are, I'd like to dry my hair quick."

"Yeah." He nodded. "Speaking of which, how are you feeling this morning?"

"I'm feeling better. My stomach muscles hurt, though. I feel like I did two hundred sit-ups. And you?"

"I'm feeling pretty good, actually." He stood straight and stretched. "Must have been the lobster. Are you up to taking the boat out again?" I could tell in his voice he was hoping.

"Yeah, sure. Just let me finish getting ready."

RYAN STEERED the boat back out on the lake and I was comfortable just lounging under a blanket. The bright sun warmed my face. I was feeling better, but still not one hundred percent. Being sick had made me overly tired.

Ryan was quiet as he repeatedly cast his line out in the water. A few times it appeared that he was going to say something to me, but then he'd turn away to shake his head ever so slightly.

"Aren't you going to fish today?" he asked finally.

"Maybe in a little while; I'm really comfortable just resting here."

He stared at me for a moment. "Are you sure you're feeling up to being out here?" he asked, truly sounding concerned.

"Yes. I'm actually quite content. I'm in a boat, out on a lake on a beautiful, sunny day. I don't have to be anywhere doing anything. No one is barking orders at me. I am thoroughly enjoying the simple pleasures in life." I smiled at him.

"Yes, this is very cool." He grinned in agreement.

"I was wondering something," he asked as he looked at me a moment later. "Do your friends know how we met?"

I was confused why he would ask that. I felt my eyebrows pull together when I pondered his question.

"What do you mean?" I needed him to clarify.

"My embarrassing run into your pub. Did you tell them about that?"

"No," I said quickly, confirming my trustworthiness. "I mean they know that you came into the bar, but none of them know under what circumstances. I'm sorry. I promised you that I would never say *anything*, but I had no choice but to tell them that you came in once before—it was the only way I could get past the questions so you could join us for poker. I swear the only thing I said was that you came in for a beer one afternoon. I didn't tell them anything else."

He looked at me funny. "That's okay. I just figured you were pretty close with your friends, that you would have told them about my run up your steps."

"No." I shook my head fiercely. "It's none of their business. Ryan, what happened to you was private. Besides, I made a promise to you that I would never say anything. I'll never break that promise."

He smiled sweetly at me before casting his line back out into the water.

I picked up my fishing pole and clipped a little bobber to the line. I didn't want him to feel like he was fishing alone, so I cast my line out and resumed my lounging position in the boat. If I caught a fish, the bobber would dip down into the water.

Two minutes later, I had a nibble and reeled in the first catch of the day. Another bass was on the line. Ryan took the fish off the hook for me. I was too bundled up to move that far.

"He's a tiny one!" Ryan said, examining the little fish up close. "Okay, that's two days in a row that you caught the first fish," he jeered.

"Jealous much?" I teased. "You'll catch the next five anyway."

"I'm about as jealous as you are," he said flatly. With a quick flick, he tossed my little fish back in the water.

"Taryn, I want you to promise me something." He looked at me until our eyes met. "I want you to promise that you won't believe anything you read or hear about me."

I opened my mouth to speak, even though I wasn't exactly sure what I was going to say.

"Just promise me," he insisted.

"I promise," I vowed.

"If you have any questions or you want to know something, you ask *me* first before you believe any of the trash, okay?" His face twisted in anguish.

"I will."

"Good." His expression relaxed slightly, but I could tell he was still deep in thought.

My mind flashed over the questions that were still nagging at me and I wondered if it was safe enough—if our friendship was strong enough—for me to ask. *Does* he have different women in his bed all the time? Was he dating or juggling several women right now? Was acting worth giving up his freedom?

I looked over at him as he sat peacefully fishing out on this beautiful lake. I knew he was living in some psychotic fishbowl, under constant scrutiny. Did I dare bring up any touchy subjects?

There was one question I felt I had the right to ask.

"Ryan?" I paused until he looked at me. "I do have one question. Since you've already asked me this question and I gave you an honest answer, I'd like to hear your honest answer, too."

His eyes narrowed with confusion.

"Are you . . . are you involved with anyone . . . now? I mean, I presume you're dating people." I was so nervous asking, I couldn't help but stammer over my words. But I needed to know if I was part of a collective. His face was expressionless, so I felt I had to continue.

"It's just . . . you asked me, the first day we met. I just wondered."

His expression changed from a blank stare to a slight grin. He looked me in the eyes.

"No," he said. "I'm not seeing anyone. And to answer the other question you're *not* asking, the answer is months—several months."

"Why is that?" I asked hesitantly.

He turned his gaze out toward the lake before answering. "How can I ever know if someone wants to be with the celebrity or if she's enamored with a character I've portrayed? The lines get blurred between what I am and who I am." He shook his head in disgust.

"Then there's the . . . fear of having intimate details appear in print. I already have enough to deal with when they print the lies." He started rubbing his forehead and I knew this was tough for him to talk about.

"I'm sorry," I whispered. "I—I shouldn't have asked."

"Why would you say that?" His brows pulled together as he looked at me.

"I feel bad for bringing it up. You have enough stress to deal with—you don't need me asking stupid questions."

"The fact that you're here, with me, gives you the right to know. This isn't just about me. Don't think for one second that I haven't considered how this affects you and your privacy.

"I've been seen in your pub twice. The paparazzi aren't stupid. I've tried to keep my reason for being there hidden, but I didn't do a very good job. Rumors about me staring at you have already been printed." He hung his head down and grabbed the bottle of soda that sat between his feet. "I don't care that they've printed that I was looking at you, but believe me, I do care that they leave you alone. Please tell me immediately if—"

"Ryan, how can you stand this?" I interrupted. "You are entitled to a life. You deserve to be happy. Is this career worth it?" I couldn't hold it in anymore.

He looked back out over the water. I could tell that he was torn.

"Yes and no," he answered. "I like doing what I do. I love being an actor. But the crazy bullshit that comes with it is something I didn't see coming. It's all become very overwhelming."

"I feel bad for you," I whispered.

He looked at me, confused.

"It's not right that you have to pay such a steep price for doing something you love. Especially since what you do is meant to be a gift to the public that torments you. You're an entertainer; you shouldn't have to hide, but I know why you have to. I know that they never leave you alone—that you're constantly hounded."

"That's an understatement," he muttered. "Taryn, I *really* like being around you, but I'm afraid that . . ." He paused to take a deep breath.

You're afraid that it can't continue. Don't be a coward, just say it. I knew it was coming eventually.

"You have to realize that being around me comes at a price for you, too. I need to know that you understand what you're getting yourself into, being with me."

Being with you? Well, that wasn't what I expected.

My thoughts were tangled just looking at him.

"I like being around you, too," I admitted softly. "We both know that I don't come from your world, but I have a fairly good understanding of how things are for you.

"Ryan, I'll do what I have to, to be part of that for you if you want me to. I'll deal with the craziness, because I know that comes along with being with . . ."

TARYN, you're slipping!

"Um, I mean, with being your friend," I corrected myself.

"You would do that for me?" he asked, questioning my loyalty.

"Yes," I answered without hesitation. "Yes, I will."

"And you'd deal with the paparazzi, and the fans, and the invasion of your privacy? Do you even know what you're saying yes to?" he asked as he scratched his head.

"You deal with it. Why is it so hard to believe that someone else would do the same for you?"

"It's a lot to ask of someone," he said, almost appearing guilty. His shoulders were hunched as he rubbed his forehead repeatedly. "A lot."

"Well, if you want me to be your friend then you have to give me the benefit of the doubt that I can handle it," I said bluntly.

"The media will dig for dirt on you. Is there anything I need to know before the rest of the world knows?" He eyed me intensely.

"There is nothing that I've been through that I'm ashamed of," I stated directly. "I've already told you a lot about me. I've never done drugs or been arrested. I've never posed nude or made embarrassing sex tapes, either." I chuckled lightly at my admission. "I don't have any skeletons in my closet."

My last comment caused him to smile briefly, but our moment of levity didn't last. He continued on with his warnings.

"You'll have to watch everything you do, everything you say. You'll be pressed for answers; they'll hound you for details." His lips curled up on his teeth from the thoughts. "They will provoke you with statements and allegations to get you to respond. You'll be followed and photographed. Can you handle that, too?" His tone was almost argumentative.

"Who are you trying to convince, me or you?" I spoke quietly. "Ryan, if you want me in your life . . . if you want us to be friends, then I'll deal with it. But it sounds like you're trying to talk one of us out of it."

"It's like inviting someone into your nightmares. It's not right for me to do that to you," he said ruefully.

"So what? You're not allowed to have friends or be close to anyone? Or have a good time and live your life? I'm sorry, but I'm not going to allow *them* to decide that for me or you." I wrapped my arms around my knees. "And if you think that I'm going to be scared away because of *them*—because of the bad stuff that you have to endure—then you have the wrong impression of me."

As I spoke, I suddenly became overwhelmed with mixed emotions. I was going through all this effort to try to be his friend, while deep inside I longed for so much more.

"I don't have that impression of you; that's another reason why we are here now." Ryan smiled at me and let out a big sigh.

Anger and disgust, directed solely at myself, crept up into my chest and burned my throat. *Why are we here now? Why am I even in this boat with you?*

I kept making mistakes, slips . . . one after another. *I can't fall in love with you. I can't allow myself to long for something that would never—could never be. I'm just kidding myself.*

The serene lake suddenly felt like shark-infested waters. I had to get out of this boat and back to safe ground—fast. I fought the urge to jump in the lake and swim for shore.

I looked at the time on my cell phone. "It's almost two o'clock. I should get you back. I'm sure you have things you have to do."

"Not really," he admitted, looking me in the eyes again. "I just assumed . . . it is poker night, isn't it?"

Despite my compounding fears, I couldn't help but revel in the fact that he was going to be with me tonight as well.

"I'm hungry," Ryan mentioned as we walked up to the cabin. "I'm starting to get a headache."

"We can stop for something on the way back. How does pizza sound?"

I DROVE us out onto the highway, and Ryan moved his arm to rest his hand on the top of the driver's seat. Every once and a while he would twist his finger into my hair on the top of my head. It made me shiver and smile.

"Does that tickle?" he asked.

"Yeah, it does!" I giggled, but he kept on doing it.

Every time I tried to reach for his finger, he'd move his hand away and chuckle. Our little game was fun.

About the ninth time, I managed to reach up fast enough with my right hand and flattened his hand on my head. He twisted his finger once more in my hair, under my hand.

"Okay, I'll stop then," he announced, and then he made a move that stunned me. He quickly gathered my hand in his and relocated our joined hands to rest on his thigh.

I glanced over at him in shock. I felt a slight rush when my heart skipped a beat; the sensation of his touch flooded my veins.

Ryan was staring intently at our joined hands; slowly he opened his grip and freed my hand but I didn't pull away—I didn't *want* to pull away even though I knew I should. My desire for him overpowered all logical reasoning. A small grin appeared on his lips.

After a few minutes, he repositioned my hand, setting it to rest palm down on his thigh. Ryan released me, then used his left hand to casually scratch his chin, all the while watching my hand on his leg.

I smiled, assuming this was another test. He paused to see if I'd pull my hand away. He was feeling me out to see how I'd react.

I left my hand where he set it. He placed his hand on top of mine and wove our fingers together. The smile on his face was breathtaking. He adjusted his seat to recline farther back, breathed out a contented sigh, and closed his eyes.

THE SUN was already setting when I pulled my car down the alley. I made sure that the passenger door would open to the back door of my pub so Ryan could get inside quickly.

I looked up and down the alley first; I was on the alert just in case there were paparazzi on the loose. I held the back door open while he darted from the car to the kitchen. It was a relief when Ryan was inside safely.

"Stay inside. I'll get the cooler and bags."

Ryan looked angry and helpless as he stood there. I could tell he wanted to walk out into the alley and pull the cooler from the trunk, but he couldn't. We could not afford to make any mistakes.

He started to breach the doorway to help me.

"Ryan, someone might see you! It's all right. I got it. Please, just back up." As soon as he could, he took the cooler out of my hands and slid it into the dark kitchen.

"Here, let me have those." He slipped his bag and mine from my shoulder. "Is that everything?"

"Just the pizza and our drinks, then that's it." I leaned back into the car and grabbed the pizza box off the backseat.

When I handed him the box, he was smiling devilishly at me.

"What?" I asked, dying to know why he was grinning.

"Nothing," he stated as he faked a swing to smack me on the butt.

"Okay—well, I'm going to park my car. You can lock this door—wait, let me turn on a light for you first. I'll come through the front."

I drove down the alley and parked my car in my normal spot in the lot on the corner of Mulberry. As I walked toward the pub, I noticed someone sitting in an old car across the street. I couldn't tell if it was a man or a woman, but I could see the dark outline of a person. *Don't get paranoid already*, I said to myself. I quickly unlocked the front door to my pub and hurried inside.

About a half hour later, Pete and Tammy arrived for poker. "Hey, kids!" Pete shouted. "Hey, Ryan. Good to see you, man."

"Hey, Pete." Ryan shook his hand. "How's it going?"

"I brought some dessert," Tammy giggled happily. She slid a tray of chocolate-dipped something-or-others onto the bar. "I thought we might sample these—let me know if it would be something good to serve on Sunday for the party."

I noticed the smug smile and wink she gave me when she thought no one else was looking.

"How's it going?" she asked me quietly.

"Good, real good," I said, even though at that very moment I was fighting off a wave of nausea.

"Did you have a good time up there?" she whispered in my ear.

I nodded and smiled. I didn't intend to share any details with anyone. Our weekend was ours and ours alone and I wanted Ryan to know that I wouldn't spill anything, even to my closest friends. Besides, he was watching me out of the corner of his eye.

I brought fresh mugs over to Ryan and Pete and poured them a beer from the pitcher.

"Thanks." Ryan smiled when I set his glass in front of him. A stick of pain shot into my stomach, causing me to hunch and wince.

"So, Ryan, how were they biting up at the lake?" Pete asked while waiting with an open hand for the beer I was pouring for him.

"Good! We both caught a lot. Although Taryn caught the first one on *both* days." He winked and quickly patted the back of my thigh.

"Yeah, but you still caught more than I did," I added. I wanted to give him his fair due.

I sat down in the chair next to Ryan and took a big sip of ginger ale. The slice of pizza that I'd eaten was sitting in my stomach like a rock. I contemplated resting my head on the table for a moment.

"Not drinking tonight, Taryn?" Pete asked, pointing at my glass of soda.

I suddenly felt light-headed. "No. I have a bit of an upset stomach."

Ryan leaned over and whispered, "Are you okay? You feeling sick again?"

"I'm fine," I lied, wincing from the new shot of pain that hit my abdomen.

"Were you sick?" Pete asked, questioning my condition.

I just stared at the table. I wasn't going to say anything; besides, I *was* feeling that I might be sick again—the saliva was pooling in my mouth.

Ryan patted my leg privately under the table and sighed.

"Both of us were really sick last night. We're not sure what made us sick, but we definitely had food poisoning, that's for sure," he explained, gently rubbing my back.

"Excuse me, please," I murmured, dashing for my stairs. I made it to my bathroom just in time to bring the pizza back up. My hands clenched the toilet seat as the stomach acid burned my throat.

"Taryn?" Ryan called out. "Are you all right?" I was brushing my teeth when he came around the corner. "Everything okay?"

I felt slightly dizzy when I motioned my reply. "No. I just got sick again. The pizza."

"Why don't you just cancel poker and go lie down? You're not going to have any fun if you're feeling lousy." Ryan stepped into the bathroom and pressed his hand against my forehead. "It feels like you're running a slight fever, too."

"I can't cancel on them. Why don't you just go down and play? Go have fun. Maybe I'll come down later if I feel better."

"No. I'm staying with you. I'll be right back." He was gone before I could even respond.

I went to my bedroom to change into comfy clothes. Resting on the couch sounded very appealing. Staying close to my bathroom was even more appealing. I had just pulled the quilt off the back of the couch and onto my lap when Ryan came back through my door.

"Pete called Marie and told her you weren't feeling well," he said while thumbing through his cell phone. "We exchanged cell numbers. I have Marie's number, too. I told Pete I'd call him later to let him know how you're doing."

"You didn't have to do that," I said. "All of you could have still played. I feel horrible for ruining your night and breaking Monday tradition."

"Don't be ridiculous. We wouldn't play without you. Here, I brought you a new glass of ginger ale. You should drink some water, too. We're *both* probably dehydrated." He set the glass down on the table. "I really don't need any beer in my stomach, either."

"Thank you," I said sincerely. "I think you're right about being dehydrated. That's probably why I feel so achy. I should drink some water." I pulled the quilt off my lap. "Would you like to see the rest of the place?"

I took him for a quick tour of my apartment. "This is the laundry room here and then these are the stairs that lead up to the roof." He followed me back down the hall to the kitchen.

"Wow, this is a really nice place you have. This kitchen is beautiful. I love the granite countertops and the cherry cabinets. Wine fridge and everything."

"Thanks. I just had it redone a few months ago. It used to be a horrible green color with white cabinets. It was really depressing. The bathroom is going to be my next project. Would you like some water?" I pulled glasses out of the cabinet for both of us.

While I was filling our glasses, I mentally questioned why he was so willing to hang out with a girl who'd just thrown up. Surely he had better things to do. But then he did intend to hang out with me all evening anyway to play poker, so I guessed it didn't make a difference to him how he spent those hours. I was just relieved that I had him here with me where he was protected from the insanity.

"Do you want to watch some TV?" he asked while kicking his sneakers off. My insides warmed, knowing he wanted to stay with me. He removed the throw pillow and nestled his body into the corner of the couch. "Here, why don't you lie down," he suggested as he placed the pillow next to his leg.

"No, that's okay. I'm fine." I sat down on the opposite end of the couch and curled my feet underneath me. I was afraid I might feel nauseous again if I lay down. His lips pulled together and he gave me a disappointed look.

Ryan wiggled his phone out of his pocket to listen to his voice mail. It sounded like he deleted thirty messages. Considering how in-demand he was, I was surprised that he didn't take any calls while we were fishing. Come to think of it, he hadn't taken any calls at all while he was with me.

His fingers tapped two more times before he held the phone up to his ear. "Hi, Dad," he said cheerfully. "What are you up to?"

I looked over at him and smiled. I was glad that he was the type of man who thought enough of his parents to call them. Ryan smiled back at me. It was impossible not to listen to his conversation since he was sitting three feet away, but I tried to appear distracted. While he talked, I flipped through the channels, looking for something to watch.

"You'll never guess what I did yesterday and today. I was fishing!"

He told his father all about the lake and the cabin and how relaxed he felt. It secretly delighted me to know he was happy and content.

While he was still on the phone, he asked, "Taryn, where's my bag?"

"They're still down in the kitchen."

He slipped out the apartment door and trotted down the steps. When he left, I figured he would have continued his conversation in private, but he just ran downstairs, grabbed our bags, and came back instantly to resume his position on the couch.

"Did you book a flight yet? I have to check my calendar." He started tapping the screen on his phone.

"Dad, just hang on a second. Okay," he said while touching through a calendar. "Mom's birthday is Friday the thirty-first. No, I'm scheduled to be on set. If you fly in Wednesday night then you can stay for the weekend." It was apparent by his tone that he was looking forward to seeing his parents.

While he talked, I wondered what his parents looked like. Did Ryan look like his mother or did he take after his father? The way he spoke to his dad made it clear that they had a great relationship.

"I have to work on the seventeenth. It's no big deal. We can celebrate my birthday when I come home for Thanksgiving. Okay, let me talk to Mom . . ."

I looked over at him when he indicated his birthday was coming up, apparently in November since he'd mentioned Thanksgiving. He'd be turning twenty-seven this year, too.

"Hi, Mom. How are you? I'm at a friend's place. *Her* name is Taryn." He winked at me. "It's a long story; I'll tell you later . . . because she's sitting right next to me, Mom. She's a sweetheart. You are going to love her."

I thought he might like some privacy and I was kind of hoping he might say more if I wasn't in the room, so I uncovered my legs quickly and went to the kitchen. I filled my glass up with water and searched through the pantry for something bland to eat. I had just found a box of crackers when Ryan came into the kitchen, still on his phone.

He started to rub his forehead. "It's getting worse, Mom. I can't go anywhere." I didn't need to hear her questions to know what they were.

I leaned my elbows on the counter and rested my head in my hands. I had a slight headache from being sick and not having any food in my system. The cabinet closest to the refrigerator was where I kept most of my medicine. I found the aspirin, but Ryan snatched the bottle right out of my hand.

"You shouldn't take these now. Mom, Taryn was going to take some aspirin but she shouldn't take them on an empty stomach."

I looked at him, puzzled.

"It could upset your stomach even worse," he said.

"We've both been sick, Mom. I think we had food poisoning last night but Taryn still isn't able to keep anything down. Can she take aspirin on an empty stomach? I didn't think so." He smirked.

I dropped my shoulders; I was doomed to deal with the pain. Ryan stepped closer and felt my forehead again. I guess my temperature was acceptable; he opened the box of crackers and tore open a sleeve for me. I was perfectly capable of opening the cracker box, but at the same time I loved that he was taking care of me. And here I thought that *he* was the one who needed taking care of.

"My mom says you should try and eat some toast and we should drink lots of water." He swept my hair off my shoulder with his finger, gazing at me again. "I'm *sure* you'll get to meet her when you visit, Mom." He smiled, appearing so happy. "I'll tell you all about her . . . *later*," he whispered.

Toast sounded good, but hearing him telling his mother that we'd get to meet each other one day completely stunned me.

"All right, Mom, I love you, too. I'll call you later tonight." He ended his call and popped a cracker in his mouth.

"Do you have a toaster?"

I opened the lower cabinet where it was stored.

"Why don't you go relax? I've got this." Ryan took hold of my shoulders and guided me toward the hall. I smiled on my way back to my living room. I could not believe that Ryan wanted to make toast for me. My heart suddenly felt very full.

"So what do your parents think of all this attention you've been getting?" I asked while we both munched on toast out on the couch.

"I guess they're overwhelmed. Their lives have changed, too, because of me. My mom and dad tell me that they're proud, you know, but they also let me know that they're concerned. My mom keeps telling me to keep my feet on the ground."

I nodded in concurrence. "You're going to have to always keep it in check. Just don't let the fame and notoriety turn you into someone you're not. Your parents love the son that they raised, not the celebrity you've become."

He looked at me funny and grinned. "Do you know that my mom said the same exact thing to me? And you're right," he answered dryly, "but you don't know how it is."

"No, I don't," I agreed in my softest voice. "And I'm not going to sit here and pretend that I have a clue as to what this is like for you. You'll have to explain it to me if you want me to understand."

He shook his head and shrugged. "When I'm on set working, things are great. I love it. But since I did *Seaside,* things have been crazy. The whole fan thing is . . . I don't know . . . incomprehensible. It's constant pressure to live up to the hype. Some days it squeezes harder than others." It was apparently difficult for him to find the words to talk about it.

"Well, just remember who you are, and try not to let *this* get bigger than that. The minute you stop being humble, you'll be in trouble."

He nodded his head in agreement.

"Ryan, you don't seem to be the type of person who got into acting because you have to feed your ego. You're apparently really good at it, and you love doing it. It's the career path you've chosen to follow, but it's not who you are in here," I said as I patted my own heart with my hand. "Just keep focused on the fact that it's your job and don't let it define you. You'll be okay."

"You sound like my mother," he said.

"No, I'm not trying to mother you," I defended quickly.

"No, no. That's not what I mean." He laughed. "I mean that you're saying the same things my mom has said to me. It's bizarre."

"Well, your mother is obviously a brilliant woman," I amended.

"She keeps telling me to be careful who I trust. Like I need the reminder." He rubbed his forehead again.

"Ryan, I have a pretty good idea why you have a hard time trusting people and why you have to question the validity of *everything* and *everyone*." I tilted my head until his eyes met mine.

"And I know I have to earn your trust—just like you have to earn mine. We're just two people trying to be friends. We both have a lot to risk. But I know your risk is much higher—it takes away your freedom and puts you in danger."

"I know. This business makes it hard to trust people. Then when trivial things like what I had for dinner becomes headline news, it really messes with my head."

"Well, I solemnly swear that I will not divulge that information to anyone. I'll take it all to my grave."

"Yeah, I guess you're pretty trustworthy. You wouldn't even tell your best friends that you puked your guts out last night," he teased.

"No," I corrected him. "I wouldn't tell my best friends that *you* puked *your* guts out last night."

"Speaking of puking . . . how are you feeling? Is the toast doing the trick?"

I nodded my head and took a sip of ginger ale. "I'm starting to feel better, thanks."

"Good," he said as he playfully tossed a pillow at me.

I faked like I was going to toss the pillow back at him, but instead I just set it down next to my leg.

His eyes flickered between looking at the pillow and looking at me. With a quick lunge, he curled his body up on the couch. It seemed as though he purposely fiddled with the pillow until it was in the perfect position under his head but mostly on my thigh. His feet hung out over the edge.

Our eyes met and I instantly felt his pull. I couldn't resist it any longer. Without even thinking, I softly ran my fingers through his hair. His eyes closed and he sighed as I touched him.

He took my other hand off his shoulder and laid it across his heart.

CHAPTER 8

Reflections

TAR—HURRY UP, THEY'RE going to replay it," Ryan yelled from the couch. I was refilling my water at the refrigerator in the kitchen.

"Watch this. Watch. The idiot is going to light the dynamite and then he doesn't run. I can't believe they are showing this on TV. Wait . . . it's going to blow him back like thirty feet. And boom!" he echoed.

I winced after seeing some moron fly through the air from sheer stupidity. I resumed my spot on the couch; Ryan adjusted the pillow on my thigh and pulled my hand back to his chest.

"I wonder how long he was in the hospital after that one," I said, leaning more of my body onto him so I could stroke his hair again. We were so comfortable together.

"This is the bad thing about television—three minutes of show and eight minutes of commercials," he groaned.

He was just about to change the channel when his phone chimed in his pocket. He looked at the number before accepting the call.

"Hey, Pete. Yeah, she's feeling better." His eyes looked up at me and his hand reached for my forehead.

"We were just watching *Mega Explosions*. You're watching it, too? Oh my God, did you see that guy? What an asshole! What did he *think* was gonna happen?"

While he was lying across my lap, I was secretly reveling in the fact that Ryan and Pete were getting along so well. I had always hoped that whoever I was with would get along with my friends. My ex-fiancé Thomas and Pete never saw eye-to-eye. There was always tension between them. I should have taken that as a warning sign right from the get-go, but I tried to make everyone happy while being quietly miserable inside.

But Ryan and Pete seemed to be in perfect synch right from the start. A huge smile crossed my lips.

"Here, Pete wants to talk to you." Ryan handed his phone to me.

"Hey, sweetie, how are you feeling?" Pete asked.

"I'm feeling better, thanks. I'm still achy though. Ryan made me toast and it helped to take my headache away."

"Oh, *Ryan* made you toast, did he?" he teased.

"Yes . . . and your point?" I snickered.

"Nothing. I'm just happy for ya. And I'm glad that you're feeling better. Tammy wants you to call her tomorrow. You two need to iron out the final menu for Sunday so we can get the food on order."

"Okay, I will. But I don't want any seafood from Shecky's. I'm pretty sure it was the lobster tails that made us sick last night. I got sick right after eating it. I mean it tasted all right, but within a half hour or so we were both violently ill." I looked down at Ryan and combed my fingers through his hair.

"I don't want any seafood from wherever those tails came from!" Ryan confirmed loud enough for Pete to hear.

"All right, I'll tell her that. Well, I'm sorry you weren't feeling good, but it sounds like you're on the mend, so . . . hey, can I talk to Ryan again?" Pete asked.

"Yeah, sure." I was momentarily surprised by his request.

"Yeah Pete, what's up?" Ryan sat up to talk. "Yeah, I am, why? They play at eight on Sunday; I was hoping to watch it." He started chewing on his fingernails again. "She is? Are you are freaking *kidding* me?" His eyes shot over to mine. The way he reacted made me wonder what they were talking about.

"Are you serious? Unbelievable!" He breathed out a long sigh. "That's . . . really good to know." He chuckled. "Thanks."

Ryan had a huge grin on his face as he shoved his phone back in his pocket. I was staring at him, hoping that he would let me in on the conversation.

"So, Taryn . . . Pete tells me that you are a big-time Pittsburgh Steelers fan. Is this true?"

"Oh, yeah. And a huge Pens fan, too." I nodded.

"You like ice hockey, too?" He looked at me like I was lying.

"I love hockey," I said with a big yawn, feeling sleepy and drained.

"You know I grew up near Pittsburgh, right?" he asked, waiting for my confirmation.

"No, I didn't. You only told me that you're from Pennsylvania, or 'Pee-Aye' as you call it. Oh wait, you did tell me that you attended Pitt." I yawned again. "So you like football too, I take it?"

He was just sitting there shaking his head in disbelief.

"What?" I asked.

"Nothing." He dismissed my stare, getting up to stretch.

I saw him glancing around, taking in the sights of my various belongings. He ran his fingers over my DVD collection and commented that I didn't have any of his movies.

"Sorry, not a fan." I shrugged, teasing him.

He leered at me.

"Wait a minute!" he said as he pulled a DVD from the shelf. "You do have a movie I was in!" He showed the cover to me. I honestly could not remember if he was in the movie or not.

"You weren't in that movie."

"Actually I am," he stressed. "My part was supposed to be bigger, but I got edited down to only four speaking lines. I'm in the mall scene."

Ryan started to reminisce about the beginnings of his acting career and how his life was almost normal back in those days. How he could go out in public and barely, if ever, be recognized.

"So how many movies have you been in?"

"This *Seaside* we're filming now will be my sixth; that's including the small role in this movie." He waved the DVD box in the air.

"First film was an indie flick called *Forever Wanting More*. It did so-so at the Sundance Film Festival, but now it's coming out on DVD—go figure. Then I played Ashby in *Watchtower*. I guess you could say that's the role that got my name out there."

"Wait, when did you go to California?"

"When I auditioned for *Watchtower*. I ended up sharing an apartment with Alan Schefler."

It didn't take Ryan long to see the blank look on my face.

"He's another actor I met when we started filming. Did you ever see *Watchtower*?"

"No," I said sheepishly, slightly embarrassed that I had never seen *any* of his movies, other than the one in which he'd had a tiny cameo.

He gave me a disapproving look. "Well, you didn't miss much. I died a horrible death in battle. Then I did *this* timeless piece." He put the DVD back on the shelf.

"While my scenes were being edited down to just about nothing, I started the first *Seaside*. I just wrapped on a film called *Reparation* a few weeks ago. Did you hear of that one yet?" he asked teasingly.

I felt guilty—that surely meant I must have *looked* guilty, too. "I've *heard* of *Watchtower* and *Seaside*—does that count?"

"I may have to deduct a few points," he said.

Ryan resumed perusing my music selection, occasionally slipping out a CD to look at it. He held up one of the jewel cases. "I wanted to buy this one."

"You can borrow it if you'd like. I have it on my iPod."

"Can I borrow this one too . . . and this one?" He started to make a pile in his hand.

I smiled and nodded at his choices, pleasantly surprised that we had the same taste in music.

"Cool . . . some new music for *my* iPhone." He grinned. "Wait, the CD is missing from this case."

"That one is in the player." I pointed to the shelf. "Take it out."

He nestled back into the couch and shoved eight of my CDs into his bag. Happiness fluttered inside me knowing he had a reason to come back.

He spent the next few minutes looking at me, then back at the TV, then back at me again—smiling the entire time. I wished I knew what he was thinking. He leaned over and grabbed the pillow, tucking it next to his leg.

"Why don't you lie down for a while? You should rest."

I was tired, and lying down sounded like a good idea. I grabbed the blanket, pulled it up over my shoulder, and stretched my legs out on the couch. Now that the urge to throw up was gone, it felt good to relax. Ryan rested his arm on top of mine.

We were watching some program about ghosts, but I could tell that Ryan was looking mostly at me. He curled his hand and softly brushed my cheek. It seemed that he was almost frightened to touch me; his hand seemed so hesitant. I didn't know whether he was testing himself or me.

I could feel his confidence grow as he ran his fingers through my hair. We were definitely becoming more than friends. I was so relaxed by his touch that it was hard to keep my eyes open.

Ryan's voice pulled me from the haze. He called someone to get a ride to the hotel. I wondered why he just didn't walk the short distance, but then it dawned on me why he couldn't.

"I'm gonna get going. I have to work tomorrow and so do you." He gathered his things and I walked him down to the back door.

"Thanks for taking me fishing. I had a great time."

"Me too."

"I'll call you tomorrow." He wrapped his arms around my shoulders and pulled me in for a nice hug. His hand held my face as he quickly kissed my cheek. He didn't linger. I was surprised that he didn't try to kiss me. It appeared that he was conflicted. I could relate . . . the line between just friends and something more was definitely blurred today.

"See you." I waved as he hopped into the waiting car.

That night I had the most beautiful dreams.

"ARE YOU feeling better today?" Marie asked when she came in at four p.m. to start her shift behind the bar, her eyes assessing my appearance.

"Yes, much," I replied. "I think I got food poisoning from the lobster. Either that or it was the bagged salad."

"Did Ryan get sick, too?" she wondered aloud.

"Yeah, we both were really sick, but he seemed to get over it quicker. I stopped for pizza on the way back from the cabin but after I ate a slice it just sat in my stomach like a brick. I'm sorry for last night . . . I didn't want them to cancel poker on my account."

"Don't apologize. You were sick. It happens. Besides, Gary and I had an awesome good time anyway, if ya know what I mean." She winked at me and held up three fingers.

"Three?" I gasped in amazement. "You or him?"

"Me, of course." She smiled and bobbed her head.

"That accomplishment deserves a high-five." I reached over to slap my hand into hers.

"So did you rack up any numbers yourself this weekend . . . all alone in the forest with Prince Charming?"

"No." I shook my head. "It's not like that. We just took the boat out on the lake."

"When are you going to see him again? I presume you *are* going to see him again?" she prodded.

"I don't know. He's working. I'm working. I guess I'll see him Sunday." I shrugged and continued to hustle behind the bar. "We didn't make any plans. Besides, he won't be sticking around here anyway. As soon as he's done filming, he'll be gone."

Thoughts of him leaving surged through my brain like wildfire and burned all the way down my throat and into my heart. This friendship with Ryan, these feelings growing inside of me for him, in reality all had an expiration date looming.

Even though I was mostly trying to enjoy the moment, the knowledge that the moments wouldn't last much longer was still overshadowing everything else.

I went about my day, but my heart felt like it was burning.

I had taken care of business—Tammy and I had finalized the dinner menu for Sunday.

I placed an advertisement in the local newspaper for a part-time weekend bartender and hung a "Help Wanted" sign that I'd made on my computer in the front window.

"Marie, I'm going to hire a part-time bartender," I said as I taped the sign on the glass. "I think we could use an extra set of hands on Fridays and Saturdays. It's getting to be too much for you and me to handle alone, and Tammy doesn't want to work every weekend."

"Sounds good to me. We've been getting slammed lately," she agreed.

"Yeah, just while the movie stuff is still going on. Once they all leave, we probably won't need the help, but I think it's too much for just the two of us."

Marie flipped the channels on the television until she got to the local news. It was mostly background noise to me until the reporter mentioned the words "*Seaside* movie."

"Over one hundred people had to be removed from the remote beach location where the second installment of the Seaside movie was being filmed today. Dedicated fans are desperate to get any glimpse of the film's all-star cast, including the movie's lead actor, Ryan Christensen.

"Local police were called to the scene after several individuals breached the

closed movie set and charged onto the beach. Police officers from at least two local municipalities were assisted by officers from the State Police to manage the crowd, and at this time two women have reportedly been taken into police custody.

"The women were stopped by on-set security and members of the production team as they attempted to reach Mr. Christensen and Ms. Strass while they were filming. Reports from eyewitnesses who were at the scene indicated that at least one of the women allegedly yelled obscenities and death threats at Ms. Strass, although it is unknown at this time the content of those threats."

The camera cut to four police officers who had two women in custody and were escorting them into the police station.

In an instant I was concerned for Ryan and his safety, but I fought back the urge to call him. Even though I had his number from all the text messages he sent, I didn't want to repeat past mistakes. I wasn't going to chase after any man. I made a pledge to myself at that moment that I wouldn't commit his phone number to my cell phone memory.

The fact that I cared and wanted to know how he was doing meant that I was already too attached to him. When he finally did leave Seaport, it would make it that much harder for me to cope.

I pulled my cell phone out of my pocket several times throughout the night just to make sure I didn't miss a call, but he never called as he'd said he would. I wondered what had happened to keep him from calling me. Maybe I was just misreading our connections or making them out to be more than what they really were. I truly hoped he wasn't busy making new connections with some other girl. *What am I doing?* I chastised myself. *I can't let my guard down. I need to stop this.*

I thought about the boyfriends that I'd had in the past and reviewed why none of those relationships ever lasted. I realized that I had made some typical girl mistakes with some of them . . . being too needy or too clingy, or just trying too damn hard to be what I thought they wanted me to be. I was too young at the time to truly understand what healthy relationships were all about.

Some of my relationships ended because after the sex, we realized that we had nothing else in common. There were no other threads to hold us in place.

I broke up with Tim when I realized that he wasn't what I wanted for my future. He was the type of guy who cared only about himself and his needs. I didn't need anyone to take care of me, but I did want someone to love me enough to try.

When I was with Dean, his broken heart became my mission to fix. He was a few years older than me and had already been married once and was going through a divorce. He also had a three-year-old son caught in the mix.

I really cared for his little boy. When I was around him I tried to be a good stand-in mother, until Dean reminded me one day that I *wasn't* his son's mother and that he had no intentions to ever have another child with anyone. That was when he stopped touching me.

My engagement with Thomas ended harshly, with bitter words and horrible accusations. I remembered all too clearly walking into his apartment to find him in bed with someone else. I'm pretty sure he planned it that way. He let me be the one to end the relationship so he wouldn't have to. Me barging in on him gave him one more reason to think his affairs were justified.

Even though I thought I was in love with these men at one time or another, I don't think I truly ever was. There was always something missing—that cosmic, soul-mate connection; the feeling that the two parts make a whole.

I didn't want someone who would have to force himself to love me or for me to pretend that I loved him back. I had always hoped that love would be mutually instinctual and natural—as easy as breathing.

I turned the light out on my nightstand when I'd had enough of thinking about my past failures.

One thing was for sure: Ryan had resurrected that one part of my heart that still clung to the hope of love's possibilities.

Later, I was dreaming about my father and wondered why he wasn't answering the phone. The telephone was on the table right next to his favorite chair in the living room where he was sitting. Was he sleeping in his chair? *Dad, answer the phone!*

I opened my eyes to realize that it was my cell phone that was ringing.

"Hello?" I answered, my voice sounding rough from just waking.

"Were you still sleeping?" Ryan asked.

"Yeah. What time is it?" I looked to my nightstand for the clock. It was eight forty-two.

"Quarter to nine. Do you want to go back to sleep?"

"No, that's okay. How are you?" I hoped he was safe.

"I'm all right. Sorry I didn't call you yesterday. I fell asleep in my trailer and it just got late. I thought you might have tried calling me."

"Oh, good. So you're all right?" I questioned, sitting up in bed.

"Yeah. Why?" He sounded confused.

"There was something on the news last night about some girls getting arrested? I was so worried about you." I couldn't control the magnitude of my concern.

"Why didn't you *call* me then?" he asked.

I didn't answer right away. I thought about what I was going to say. "Ryan, I don't want to bother you. You have enough to deal with."

"Huh. Taryn, you can call me anytime you want. Don't *ever* feel like you're bothering me. Just so you know, I turn my phone off when I'm filming, but as soon as I see I missed your call I'll call you back."

I shook my head in silence. Every time I'd initiated the telephone calls with guys in the past, eventually they would make me feel like I was pestering or smothering them. I had heard the words "I just need some space" mentioned before, and it was pretty much a guarantee that they would end up running in the opposite direction after that. Ryan would be leaving soon enough; I didn't want to give him one more reason to run faster.

"Taryn, are you still there?" He sounded annoyed.

"Yes, I'm still here."

"You didn't answer my question," he stated directly. "Are you *afraid* to call me?"

"I can't," I whispered. My reply was so truthful on many levels.

"What do you mean *you can't?*"

"I don't have your number." I hoped my lie sounded convincing.

"You're a bad liar, you know that? Good thing you're not an actress, 'cause you'd be out of work." He chuckled. "My number has been on every text I sent you. Huh, this is so strange. People I don't want to talk to call me all the time but the one person I really want to hear from is afraid to call me. The next time I see you, I'm going to program your phone. I may even put in my own ring tone just to irritate you."

"Is that a threat or a promise?" I tried to lighten the conversation.

"Oh, that's definitely a promise. Then you won't have any excuses," he snickered. "So let's practice today, shall we? I have to work the entire day. I'm scheduled to shoot until eleven o'clock but I have a dinner break around seven. I expect to hear my phone ring sometime between seven and seven thirty. That gives you a half-hour window of flexibility to call at your convenience. Now, answer this question truthfully. Do you still have my text messages or did you delete them all?"

"No, I still have them." I smiled.

"Then you, sweetheart, have no excuse . . . unless you just don't want to talk to me? Shit, I didn't consider that, but now that I'm thinking about it, I guess I should ask. Do *you* want to see me or not?"

I want to see you more than you could ever imagine. I took a deep breath. *Keep it light, Taryn.*

"We're friends, right? Why wouldn't I want to see you?"

"Phew," he breathed. "That's a relief. Good, so um, what did the news report have to say about what happened on set?"

"The reporter said that the police had to remove a hundred or so fans from the set and two women were arrested. Apparently one of them threatened Suzanne? Were you there when it happened?"

"Yeah, I was. We were shooting a scene on the beach but I was watching the playback reel when it happened. I heard someone yelling, but I had headphones on so I didn't hear what was said."

"The news didn't mention what was said either. Just that the one girl yelled some obscenities and threats at Suzanne. They showed footage of the two girls that were arrested."

"You're kidding me!" Ryan groaned.

"I hope you have extra security on hand, because some of these fans are terrifying," I urged. "Wanting pictures and autographs is one thing, but death threats are completely another."

"Yeah, I was told last night that there would be additional private security brought in while we're here." I could hear the anger enter into his tone. There was a loud rap on his door. "Hang on!" I heard him shout.

"Tar—I got to go. Are you going to call me tonight?"

"Yes. During your dinner break. I promise."

I was too awake to try to go back to sleep. The sound of his voice had already stimulated my blood. I wandered out to the living room, sat down at my desk, and turned my laptop on. I had to reconcile the cash register receipts and enter them into my log.

My e-mail was filled with thirty new messages, mostly from Uncle Al, who recently got his first computer after fifty-five years. Between him and a few other relatives, they were trying to corner the market on bad e-mail jokes.

There was one new message from Marie, with a tempting subject line:

From: "Marie Tannen" <cr8zy8@hotmail.com>
To: "Taryn Mitchell" <tmitch82@gmail.com>
Subject: Ryan in Seaside

You should watch this. This is one of the best scenes from his movie. And since you haven't seen it yet, you should at least know how good of an actor he is. This is why all the girls want him.

Inside was a link to a website to watch a video.

My index finger hovered over my mouse. *Do I want to see this or not?* My finger had a mind of its own and it clicked the button.

The video loaded. Ryan was lurking around some dark hallways in what appeared to be a dismal castle. He had a large, silver gun in his hand with a silencer attachment; his gun was raised and ready to fire. Suzanne was wearing some tattered clothes and she was pressed to his side as they slid down the dark wall. It was apparent that he was protecting her.

"I think they're all gone," Ryan said. "Gwen, what were you thinking coming here?"

Suzanne gazed up seductively into his eyes.

"How can I protect you? Tell me!" Ryan begged urgently.

"Just love me, Charles," Suzanne whispered.

He pressed her against the wall and kissed her passionately. The vision of him kissing another woman made me wince. She pushed him back, shoving him into the opposing wall while still kissing him.

Ryan's kiss was hungry. "If you love me like you say you do, you'll stay alive for me," he breathed out.

It was hard to watch him like this. It wasn't him . . . it wasn't the same man who made toast for me or felt my forehead. I struggled with the thought of seeing Ryan this way.

I had seen plenty of movies over the years, and the skill of the actors portraying the different characters was so amazing that you didn't realize that you were watching "acting." But every person who has ever been in a movie is still, at the end of the day, someone's son or daughter, a husband or a wife, a lover, a sister, a mother or father.

There was no denying that Ryan was extremely good-looking, and the character he portrayed on the screen was definitely sexy and appealing. But the character was make-believe. Charles didn't exist. He was created on paper. Ryan gave him life, but Ryan was not Charles.

Ryan was a guy from Pittsburgh who chewed on his fingernails and cared enough to prevent me from taking an aspirin on an empty stomach. That was the man I was falling for.

I made good on my promise to call him.

"Good evening, Mr. Christensen," I whispered seductively in the phone. "This is Stacy from housekeeping with your seven p.m. wake-up call." I figured I would mess with him.

"Well, hello Stacy," he snickered lightly. "Thank you for being prompt."

"Of course, sir. The management would like to know if you are enjoying your dinner this evening."

"Hmm, well, I can think of a few things that would improve the ambiance. Perhaps you could put your manager on the line so I can complain."

"Sure, one moment please . . ." I tried to change my sultry voice. "Hello, this is Megan, the night manager. I understand that you're very unhappy?"

"Hello, Megan. By the way, I really like this game. Yes, I am very unhappy. I'd like to know what you intend to do about it?"

"We could give you a cash refund or if you'd prefer, we could extend some complimentary poker chips to you?"

"Er, not acceptable. What else are you offering?"

"We are hosting an all-you-can-eat steak dinner this Sunday. Would you like a complimentary ticket?"

"I already have one. What else do you have?" he inquired.

"Did I mention that the dinner comes along with front-row seats to Sunday's game between the Steelers and the Giants?"

"Yes, and I'm looking forward to that," he stated with much enthusiasm. "But I'm unhappy *now.*" The whining in his voice was amusing.

"Well, sir, since your happiness is our number-one priority, why don't you tell me what would make you happy." I was momentarily relieved to lob the ball onto his side of the court.

"I can only think of one thing that would make me happy right now, and I don't believe that some girl named Megan could satisfy that. You wouldn't happen to have any Taryns there on staff, do you?" he asked.

I smiled. "Maybe."

"You really know how to make my day. Do you know that?" he asked. "I was not in the best of moods right before you called. Now I'm having a hard time remembering why I was in a bad mood at all."

"I'm glad. You want to talk about it?" I asked.

"Ah, I'm just a little stressed. It's been a long day. I'd like to leave here and relax on your couch but I can't. Since the weather is pretty decent outside, we can get some additional night shots done. And I really just want to wash this crap off my face, too!" he complained.

"What crap?"

"I have some stuff on to make it look like I have a cut lip. It itches. I really want to scratch it off."

"I'd like to see that. Were you supposed to be in a fight or something?" I asked. I was trying to imagine what he looked like.

"Do you want me to send you a picture? I can take one if you're that curious."

"Heck yeah! Is it just supposed to look like a cut or do you look like that idiot who didn't run away from the lit dynamite?"

"No." He laughed. "I was in a fistfight. You should see the other guy."

"Did you pummel him?" I was trying to picture Ryan fighting with someone.

"Let's just say two of them won't be bothering me anymore."

"That sounds like a movie line." I chuckled.

"It is," he said amusingly. "Can you name the movie it's from?"

I thought about his question for a moment. He even repeated the line for me and gave me another hint.

"*True Lies*," I answered enthusiastically, catching the inflection in his voice. "Bill Paxton says that to Jamie Lee Curtis when he takes credit for killing those guys in the mall bathroom."

"I can't believe you got that one!" He sounded proud. "So why is it that you know other movies by heart but you haven't seen any of my movies yet?"

I was surprised he'd asked me that question. "How will you ever know if I like Charles or just some guy named Ryan? Isn't it better this way?"

"Hah. You're right. From now on you are hereby banned from seeing any of my movies."

I knew he was kidding, but at the same time visions of me not being invited to any premieres flashed through my mind. I didn't want the fame or the red carpet; I just wanted to be by his side, holding his hand, loving him, and being proud of his accomplishments—whatever they might be.

Once again I was setting my hopes up for nothing, longing for a relationship that could never be. His inevitable departure date was still looming.

"Listen, Ryan, I have to go. Marie is all by herself behind the bar and we're kind of busy. It was nice talking to you." I had the sudden urge to flee.

"Okay. Um, I guess I'll talk to you later, then."

I don't think I even said goodbye. I shoved my phone into the front pocket of my jeans and hurried back behind the bar. The sooner I could get distracted, the better. I kept slipping up over and over again, letting my guard down with him and allowing myself to swim in dangerous waters.

A few minutes passed and my cell phone buzzed again. I opened the picture Ryan sent; he had a funny expression on his face while pointing to his fake cut lip. I couldn't help but laugh.

I tried to convince myself that I wouldn't get hurt if I kept this thing with him strictly platonic, but to do so I'd have to make sure that I didn't let him touch me anymore. No more holding hands or running my fingers through his soft hair, staring into his eyes. Hugging . . . that was dangerous too. Anything that involved physical contact must be off-limits. I even tried to force myself to have a dream where we were only friends, playing a game of softball with both of us on the Mitchell's Pub team, but even my subconscious betrayed me.

The following day I tried to banish the lingering memories of the hot and steamy dream I did have about him, where I tore the baseball uniform off his body . . .

"Hey, baby!" Marie greeted me as she started her shift Thursday night.

I dumped a new bucket of ice in the bin, thinking I should dump an entire bucket down my shirt, too. "Hey. I have some applicants coming in today. I'd like you to interview them too, since we both have to get along with whomever I hire."

"Sure. No problem," she said as she tucked her bar rag in her back pocket. "Did you hear from Mr. Wonderful?"

I smiled. "He called me three times today."

"Three?" She looked surprised.

"He wasn't in a lot of scenes, so he was bored," I muttered privately.

"Bored? Yeah, right! He's *definitely* crazy about you," Marie insisted.

Marie and I were handling a decent-sized crowd when our second applicant came into the bar. He was twenty-something, dressed like a normal human being, and he was early. Marie spent about twenty minutes with him before she returned to the bar.

"I like this one," she murmured to me in passing.

The young man's name was Cory. He was twenty-three, tall and beefy, with a short haircut and a dark brown goatee. He was taking business and computer courses at the local community college and needed rent money.

Halfway through the interview Ryan called me again. I looked at the time; he was on his dinner break.

"Hi, um, can I call you back?" I answered quickly. "I'm interviewing someone right now. I'll call you in a few minutes, okay?"

"No, that's okay. I have to get back on set in ten minutes and then I'm going out to eat with some of the cast. I just thought of something I wanted to tell you. I'll call you when I get to the hotel later," Ryan rambled and then hung up.

"Sorry about that," I apologized to Cory. Knowing Ryan, he just wanted to talk.

I escorted Cory out to the bar, and instead of leaving, he sat down on a bar stool. I liked the fact that he wanted to check out the atmosphere of the place. It showed he was interested in working here.

"I like him, too," I said to Marie. "If his references check out, maybe we can give him a trial run this weekend?"

"Yeah, sure." She nodded. "He knows his drinks and he seems like a nice guy. Something for all the females to look at?" she added. "Besides, two bitches behind the bar are enough."

CHAPTER 9

Gestures

I SPENT AN HOUR Friday afternoon calling Cory's references, even though I was pretty decided that I was going to hire him. Cory was willing to start tonight and that sounded perfect to me. I was wondering if Ryan was going to just show up again; surely we would get slammed with customers if he did.

I was tempted to call Ryan since he hadn't called me back last night. I wondered if he was waiting for me to call him—if it was a test. It didn't matter; I still wasn't going to sway from my rule not to chase him.

I had already given up hope of hearing from Ryan when I felt my phone vibrate in my pocket. I looked at the time; it was ten thirty.

"Marie, I'll be right back," I said as I ran for my stairwell.

"Hi," I answered, very much knowing whose voice was going to respond.

"Hi—how are you?" Ryan asked.

"I'm great. How are you?" I was definitely happy to hear from him.

"I'm good. I just left dinner. I really want to see you tonight."

"I really want to see you, too." *Damn, another slip.*

"Good," he said happily.

"Are you going to walk through my front door in two minutes?" I chuckled, attempting to cover up my mistake.

"Mike, stop right here. I'll see you tomorrow." It sounded like he had the phone away from his face, and then I heard a car door slam. I could hear his breathing rate pick up.

"Why does it sound like you're running?" I asked.

"Because I'm halfway down your alley," he breathed back.

I ran to the back door.

A few moments later a dark-cloaked figure slipped through my back door. The hood of his jacket was pulled way up to hide his face and he had his large messenger bag slung over his shoulder. His eyes met mine and he greeted me with a huge smile.

"Hey, you." He slipped his hand through his hair to knock his hood back. The lights in the kitchen made the reddish tinge in his dirty-blond hair even more noticeable.

"Hey, back," I said, matching his beaming smile with my own as he wrapped his arms around my shoulders to give me a quick hug.

"Brrr, it's cold out there." Ryan shivered slightly and stepped back to release me. "Um . . . so, how are you?"

"I'm good." I was smiling so hard my face started to hurt. He gave me a little wink. So much for not letting him hug me.

"You look . . . great," he complimented. He ran his eyes down my body; his fingers touched the edge of my shirt.

His eyes seemed to linger until the music playing in the pub distracted him.

"Sounds like you have another great band tonight." His head bobbed slightly with the music.

"Thanks! I have Far from Human playing." I gestured. "They're one of the better cover bands in town."

"They're really rocking," he said. "But I can't deal with a crowd tonight. I'd rather not have anyone know I'm here." I could see the concern in his eyes and I understood what he meant. "Do you mind if I hang out upstairs and wait until you're done?"

He smiled my favorite playful, smirky smile, which shattered most of my protective shell. The word "no" no longer seemed to exist in my vocabulary. I motioned with my head for him to follow me.

I squeezed through the kitchen door and opened the stairwell door, holding my hand out to him. Our eyes met as he gently placed his hand in mine, then I slipped him from one door to another completely unnoticed.

He took his bag off his shoulder and removed his jacket, making a small pile of his stuff on my living room floor.

Instinctively I walked over to my windows and pulled down the shades. I could only imagine the photographers scaling the walls to take pictures.

"How was your day?" I asked, trying to get back to friends mode.

"Busy. We filmed all day. I just got off the set and then a few of us went out for a quick bite to eat."

"No rest for the weary, huh?" I teased.

"No, not usually," he agreed. "But I was actually able to have a meal without fans screaming tonight."

"Did you use the ninja cloaking device?" I kidded.

"I told Cal what you said when we went to dinner tonight. He couldn't stop laughing." Ryan chuckled.

I laughed with him, remembering one of our sillier conversations from yesterday. "Were you on your way back to the hotel?"

"Yeah, but I decided to take a detour. Would have been nice to freshen up, though," he said as he rubbed his face.

"What? No cuts on your lip?" I was looking to see if he was still wearing any special-effects makeup.

"No." He grimaced at my comment. "But it's been a long day. Hey, do you mind if I take a shower?"

My mind went straight to Hell with the visions that instantly appeared in my thoughts.

"No, I don't mind." I tried to sound unaffected by his request. "You know your way around; make yourself at home." *Friends sometimes take showers at their friends' houses,* I justified.

Thinking about him being naked and wet in my apartment was too dangerous, especially with a crowded bar to attend to. I hurried down the hall to the bathroom and set out a fresh towel on the counter for him. My mind wandered as I tried not to envision him all soapy and wet in *my* shower.

I could all too clearly picture him standing in the stream of hot water as the soap lather gathered in the crevices of his muscular frame, washing him clean. *Do friends sometimes wash their friends? Naked, wet, hot sex in the shower . . . could I handle a "friends with benefits" relationship with him? Stop! Bar. Business to run. Focus, Taryn.*

"I have to run downstairs and make sure Marie is okay covering the bar. I have a new bartender working tonight. I'll be right back. Can I get you anything to drink while I'm down there?" Back to business mode.

"Yeah, no problem. Do what you have to do." He nodded at me. "Ah . . . if you can bring me back a beer, that would be great," he added.

"Do you have a preference?" I figured I'd ask.

Ryan smiled. "Surprise me."

After I'd settled things with Marie to cover the bar, I returned to him with a six-pack in one hand and a bottle of tequila in the other. He peeked up over some papers in his hand; a very sultry grin cracked on his lips as he shook his head at me in disbelief again.

"So what are you reading?" I handed a cold bottle of beer to him.

"I got a new script that my agent wants me to look over." He briefly held the papers up in the air. "It's called *Slipknot*."

I had never seen a movie script before and I was surprised to see it was a pretty thick packet.

"What's it about?" I asked, genuinely interested in knowing what types of movies he was being courted for.

"I've been told it's about a guy whose parents and sister are murdered and he has to uncover why it happened and who did it." He took a sip of his beer.

"Hmm, so it's a murder mystery? Is that something you'd be interested in doing?"

"I'm not sure. I have to read this whole thing and let my agent know if I'm interested by Tuesday, although it seems like *they've* already cast me for the part."

"This Tuesday?" I asked, surprised. "In four days you have to give them an answer? It looks like a lot to read in such a short time."

I didn't realize that some of these movie deals happened so quickly. "Talk about putting pressure on you. No wonder you're stressed."

His eyes flashed over to look at me. "Well, it's a studio film and they want to fast-track it."

I nodded, even though I wasn't sure what the heck he was talking about.

Ryan was staring at me. "You have no idea what I'm talking about, do you?" he laughed lightly.

I smiled, surprised he was able to read me like that.

"Okay, here's your lesson for today. Pay attention, because there will be a quiz." He held the script up. "You've heard of Paramount, I assume?"

I rolled my eyes.

"Okay . . . they are the 'studio.'" He gestured. "Without overcomplicating it, they've got the money. This film has already received a 'green light.' What do you do at a green light?"

"You go," I answered.

"Script . . . film has been pitched . . . money is there to back it . . . green light—go. With me so far?"

I hoped my look got the message across that I'm not an idiot.

"Now, this project is in preproduction. That's when the cast gets hired, budget is determined, and for this film I understand that Jonathan Follweiler is going to be directing. What it means for me are two things." Ryan counted on his fingers. "One, do I want to do it, and two, can I meet the production schedule dates. If I can't commit to being there, I can't do the film."

"So you still have the option to turn it down, right?" I asked.

"Yes. I haven't signed anything yet." He waved his hands. "And they need to make me an offer."

"Don't you have to audition first?" I tried to sound like I knew *something*.

"Not really . . . not anymore. All those screaming fans are like one huge résumé. I may have to screen test with potential actresses to see if the chemistry is there, but that's about it."

"Got it." I grinned.

"Good. Tomorrow we'll learn all about cinematography."

"Darn. I was hoping that tomorrow would be all about special effects." I pouted.

"Okay. Then as soon as I'm done reading this, I'll paint all your walls a lovely bright green and we can play with the CGI on your computer. How does that sound?"

"You'd better get reading then." I stood up to excuse myself. He startled me when he stood too.

"I have to get back to the pub and finish up the night; we're getting slammed down there. I even have Tammy helping out tonight. So are you going to be okay up here by yourself?"

He walked over to me and rubbed my arms up and down softly with his hands. "Don't worry about me."

"I feel really bad leaving you here like this," I uttered sadly, melting like butter under his touch.

"Tar, I know you have a business to run. I'm just glad that . . . well . . . I'm here. I'll be fine," he stressed. "I have excellent music to listen to and a fat script to read. That will definitely keep me out of trouble for a while." He winked at me.

I looked down at his feet. In all honesty, I really wanted to stay with him. "I still feel terrible, though."

Ryan's hand slid down my arm and he brushed his fingers over mine; his other hand lifted my chin until our eyes met.

"Don't. I'm looking forward to some peace and rest, actually. I'll see you when you get back."

I felt the jolt of electricity surge through my body when he touched me; I had to fight the new desires rapidly building in my heart.

"All right. I'll see you in three hours," I sighed.

"Before you go, I'd like your cell phone, please," he requested, holding out his hand. "I'm not going to check up on you. I just want to program it a little."

"I don't care. I have nothing to hide," I said. I pulled my cell out of my pocket and handed it to him. "Just don't give me an obnoxious ring tone."

"Don't worry. I'll take care if it. Now off you go. Back to work." He took hold of my shoulders and spun me toward the door.

I was glad we were busy tonight; it made the three hours go by fairly quickly, although I wished the band would have hurried more when they packed their instruments up.

I was so excited to finally lock the doors and get back upstairs to my very incredible guest that I ran up the steps to my apartment.

Ryan was lying on the couch, peacefully asleep. His long legs were stretched out and his bare feet hung off the edge. I was surprised to see he was wearing wire-rimmed glasses. He looked very studious and handsome.

I slowly removed the thick script that rested on his chest from underneath his folded hands and set it on the coffee table. He was so sound asleep that the motion didn't even make him stir. I grabbed the quilt that my grandmother made off the back of the love seat and covered him up.

I noticed his hair was still damp and unkempt from sleeping. I sat down on the wooden coffee table and took the sight of him into my memory. His lips were slightly parted as he breathed in his slumber and I hoped he was having peaceful dreams.

Goodnight, sweet prince, I thought to myself, taking one last look at him before I turned out the lights and headed for bed.

It was still dark in my bedroom when I woke, startled. I felt my bed jostle as Ryan carefully slid his body underneath my blankets.

Without saying a word, he snuggled up behind me and made himself comfortable on the spare pillow. I leaned back slightly to acknowledge him, resting my body against his chest. He curled up tighter behind me; I could feel that he was still fully dressed.

Ryan's hand skimmed down my arm. Very slowly, he slid his open hand on top of mine, lacing our fingers together. He let out a soft sigh when I closed my fingers around his.

However hard I tried to protect myself from getting hurt, it felt so right to lie here with him. Our bodies nested together perfectly—as if we were made for each other. It was apparent that he was just as affected by me as I was by him.

The sun started to rise and soft light filled my bedroom. I felt his arm pull me closer to his chest; his warm breath caressed my shoulder as he snuggled with me. His breathing returned to the sound of sleep, so I let myself drift back to my incredible dream.

I woke again when I felt him stir. His fingers flexed, gripping my hip. His fingertips circled to feel what I was wearing. His legs stretched and he lightly pressed himself into me when his brain received the message that I was only wearing panties and a T-shirt.

Dizzying arousal shot through my body from his touch. My mind quickly wandered with other visions of how his steely hands could grip my hips. New cravings for him were growing rapidly in my thoughts.

"Good morning," he whispered in my ear, sliding his hand across my stomach.

"Mmm, hi," was all I could say as our eyes met. He grinned at me and gently swept my hair off my forehead with his fingertips.

"Sorry I fell asleep on you last night. Why didn't you wake me when you got back?" He yawned.

"You were sleeping so peacefully, I didn't want to wake you."

He smiled that sexy grin at me—the one that makes my pulse race—while his fingers drifted over my skin and caressed my face.

The desire to lean into him and press my lips to his was so strong, and I didn't have the internal strength to fight it anymore. He appeared to be fighting the same urges, but that was a threshold of intimacy he didn't cross.

I rolled over to face him and nestled my cheek on his shoulder; my hands palmed his chest. I just wanted to touch him somehow, some way. He wrapped his arm over my shoulder so his hand could hold my head to his chest. My life would be perfect if I could wake up every day to this feeling.

Ryan nuzzled my hair and groaned. "I don't want to move, but I've got to get up." I watched his incredible body stroll out of my bedroom and heard the bathroom light click on.

After I was showered and dressed, I joined him in the kitchen. He was leaning against the counter with a coffee cup in his hand—another picture I committed to memory. His face lit up when I walked into the room; his reaction caught me off-guard. *Why is he so happy to see me? Me?*

Ryan looked so casual, standing there in a very familiar dark blue T-shirt, his jeans with the worn pockets hanging a bit on his hips. He hadn't put on any socks or shoes yet; his bare feet were holding him confidently in place. I never realized that seeing a man drinking a cup of coffee in my kitchen could be such a turn-on.

"Hey there." He flashed a big grin; his eyes looked me over. "I hope you don't mind but I made some coffee. Can I pour you a cup?"

"Yes, that would be very nice." I opened the refrigerator to get the milk.

"Here, let me get that," he said as he took the container from my hand.

I reached back into the refrigerator for the carton of eggs. I was hungry; I figured he must be hungry, too.

"Can I make you some breakfast?" I asked.

He smiled and nodded. "Breakfast sounds great."

The way we flowed together in the room was astonishing. I'd never felt so at peace with a man before in my life. Though we had only known each other for a short time, it felt as though we'd known each other all our lives. There was no stress or awkwardness between us. I think he felt it, too.

"What's on your schedule today?" I asked while buttering a piece of toast for him. His life seemed to be segmented by one appointment after another, and I highly doubted that he had much free time left today.

"I have to be back on set at ten." His eyes flickered up to meet mine.

I gave him a brief smile. I didn't want him to think that his schedule would upset me.

We discussed how to transfer him from my apartment to the set secretly. The plan was that I would drive him halfway to someplace obscure where he could transfer to a waiting car that would drive him to the set. His safety and my anonymity were the top priorities.

We spent our limited time left in my living room.

I saw his face brighten when he picked up my acoustic guitar, which was propped on a stand in the corner. He placed the guitar on his knee and gave it a quick strum. He surprised me by playing pretty well.

"I saw this on Monday when I was here but I didn't get a chance to ask you. Do you play, or is this just a decoration?" he wondered, looking at me over his shoulder.

"No, I play," I answered confidently, although I was far from a master. "I know a few songs. Sometimes I try to write my own music when the mood hits, but I'm not that good of a songwriter," I admitted.

He handed the guitar to me and gave me an encouraging nod. "Play something for me."

My heart rate picked up instantly as my nerves got the better of me. The pang of horror hit as I imagined making a total fool out of myself.

"Okay, no laughing. Promise."

"I'd never laugh at you." He crossed his heart with his fingers. "I promise."

"All right, let's see if you can name this tune." I played the first few notes.

"Easy. Pink Floyd," he said with a smile. "'Wish You Were Here.'"

I laughed when he made up his own lyrics. "No, that's not what he says." I gave him a teasing tap in the foot. I started the song over. Soon we were singing together.

When I finished, he slipped the guitar out of my hand and waved his fingers for my guitar pick. He gave me a quick wink and a grin and played a few chords.

"This is something I wrote," he said nonchalantly, adjusting the guitar on his leg. He started to play a beautiful melody. His song was intense; the lyrics resonated in my heart. While he sang to me, I felt myself falling deeper and deeper for him.

I stared at him in awe as he let himself slip into his music. My mind wandered into forbidden territory as I entertained illicit thoughts of tearing the guitar from his hands and climbing onto him to kiss him passionately. I imagined how his strong hands could hold my hips in place on his lap. How his tongue might feel on mine. I felt myself becoming extremely aroused just by thinking about it.

"What did you think?" he asked when he finished his song. The truth was that I was tingling in places where I hadn't tingled in a long time.

"It was . . . mesmerizing. I loved it."

A wide grin broke on his face.

While he returned my guitar to its stand, I took off for the solace of my bathroom. I locked the door behind me and leaned hard on the counter.

I had to get a grip on my emotions. He was too unreal. It would be so easy to fall madly, insanely, deeply in love with this man, and every second I spent with him was dragging me toward that point of no return. My heart was racing, the blood throbbed in my veins, and I felt slightly dizzy. *Breathe, Taryn. Don't do this to yourself! Stop it! When he leaves Seaport, you'll never hear from him again.*

I fought the war that was battling in my mind: do I allow myself to be carried away—to surrender completely and allow whatever happens to happen—or do I end it all now and avoid the devastating heartbreak that was inevitable? I knew that I would be completely incapable of having a casual fling with him, so that option was out. Even though I could not resolve my dilemma now, I knew that I'd soon have to make a choice.

When I returned to him, he was gathering his things together and it was time for us to go. I didn't want him to leave. I wanted to grab his hand and drag him back to my bedroom. My desire for him was leading the war.

But he had to go. He had obligations. Reluctantly, I grabbed my car keys and we headed for the door.

Ryan managed to hop from the back door into my waiting car unnoticed. We didn't talk very much on the way to meet his driver. I think he was too intrigued with how our secret exchange would turn out to hold any conversation. And my internal skirmish was still battling in my brain.

We met his driver in the empty rear parking lot belonging to one of the local textile manufacturers, where it would be difficult for anyone to see or hide to take photos. From there, his driver would take him to the location where they would be filming today.

He turned to me to say his departing words. His fingers reached out to touch my face and he thanked me for a wonderful morning.

"I'll call you later, okay?" he said as he pulled his hand away.

I smiled and nodded. It was the only response my confused brain was capable of.

He slipped out of my car and quickly hopped into the open door of the car that waited. All I could do was wave goodbye.

BY THE time I returned home, Pete was already there, busy unloading boxes from the van.

"I put all the steaks in the refrigerator and the liquor delivery is in the back," he said.

I stepped behind the bar to put the cash drawer in the register.

"Oh, and Tammy's got the rest of the catering under control. We got everything on the list, so we're good to go for the party tomorrow."

"Thanks, Pete. You and Tammy are the best. Did I give you enough money or do I still owe you?"

"The shrimp cost more than we figured, but we still came in under budget. I think there was about forty dollars left."

"Just keep it. Gas costs money, too. I'm just thankful I have friends like you two." I flashed him a big smile.

"So, what's up with you?" Pete asked.

I didn't know what to say or how to explain my mood.

"Hey, what's going on?" He came around to the back of the bar when I looked away. "I know you've been . . . in a different situation lately. You want to talk about it?"

When I looked him in the eye, I couldn't lie—completely. Pete was the closest thing I had to a brother in this world, and he knew me well enough to know something was wrong.

"I'm falling for him, Pete. I can't help it anymore. I tried to just be friends," I said. "But I want him. I've never wanted a man more, and now I'm worried that I'm just setting myself up for the biggest heartbreak of my life."

Pete wrapped me in his big bear hug. "You know, when Thomas pulled that crap on you, I wanted to kill him. You're too good of a person to accept anything less than the best in life. You deserve to be happy, Taryn. Not every guy is like Thomas. Granted, Ryan is, well . . . still he seems like a hell of a nice guy."

I knew Pete didn't want to say the words "famous" or "celebrity." I took a step back from him. Words like "celebrity" equaled "unobtainable" in my mind.

"You just have to give the poor guy a chance first. But sometimes you can also be your own worst enemy," Pete scolded. "If *you* never take chances, then of course you won't get hurt. But that's what life is all about, kiddo. Living through the good and bad, and—with any luck—having battle scars that heal."

"Pete, as soon as he finishes filming, he's gone. He is not going to stick around here." I sighed heavily at the one thought that brought me the most pain. "What am I supposed to do? Put my heart out there on a silver platter again and give it all away? How convenient that all the guys I seem to fall for own sharp knives."

Just then my phone vibrated in my pocket, startling me.

"Speaking of sharp knives."

"1 NEW MESSAGE" flashed on the screen. I read Ryan's text message and laughed to myself.

"I need duct tape."

"For what?" I texted back.

"Bb is throwing hissy fit again she hates her costume today"

I frowned and quickly typed: "can't u lock her in a trailer?"

"I wish"

"Is she coming tomorrow?" I asked.

"Yes sorry btw I slept great last night best night sleep in a long time"

My fingers quickly typed: "Liar"

"Truth!" popped up on my display. I smiled at his reply.

"C u tomorrow at 5?" I replied.

"U can c me tonight if u want?"

I couldn't text him back. I wanted to see him so bad, but the self-preservation portions of my heart and brain were screaming NO at me.

If I said, "Sure, come on over and hop in my bed again," would he deem me easy?

If I said, "No, because I really want a relationship and not a one-night stand," would he move on?

Why was I mentally torturing myself? *Remember, Taryn, he's going to be swirling out of your town and out of your life in a few weeks.*

Just because he is popular and well known, does that make him exempt from having to win my heart? Well, that's silly. *He cracks my will every time he is in the same room with me, so he really doesn't have to try too hard to win my affection.*

Maybe one day when I'm old and gray I can tell my story of how I had unbelievably insane sex with a movie star once? That would be something to tell the grandkids.

Maybe my name could be a sub-text blurb under his name on some Ryan Christensen website. *October—slept with foolish girl in Rhode Island before he met his movie-star wife and went on to have blue-eyed babies with her.*

I used to see everything so black or white. Once I made a decision, I stuck by it. But since this man entered my life, my whole being was disrupted and blurred in shades of gray-tinted what-if's.

One thing was for sure: if I gave in to him, I would want him again and again. There would not be a way to survive a one-time encounter with him. Ryan's foot touching my foot was enough of a gesture to make me want him. And when he held me this morning, his fingers twined with mine, his body pressed against me, making love to him was all I could think about.

"Taryn, are you okay?" Marie's voice snapped me back into the room. "Why are you sitting in the corner? Are you sick?"

"Just mentally torturing myself," I muttered.

"Oh, I see. And how's that going for ya?" she asked, cracking a grin at me.

"Not good. The angel and the devil are debating on whether I should cave or stand my ground."

"Finally! It took you long enough," she said excitedly. "And?"

I shrugged.

"You know what I think? I think you should stop all this nonsense and screw the shit out of him until he passes out from exhaustion. And when he wakes up, wash him and then screw the daylights out of him again!" She was beaming at me. "You'll have to feed him, of course, to keep his energy level up, but make sure you hide his clothes so he can't get dressed. Men can't run when they're naked."

I couldn't stop laughing. "Thanks! I needed that."

"Come on," she said while pulling me off the box in the corner. "Let's get you focused. It will be like training an athlete."

Our Saturday-night crowd was unusually light. I didn't have a band scheduled, so I'd presumed that we wouldn't have as many customers, but ever since Ryan had been to my place twice, every night seemed to be busy. I wondered why tonight was different. I noticed that the influx of extra women was missing. A few guys came in, but when they saw that the place was devoid of a hearty selection of prospects, they packed up and left.

"I thought we would be getting hammered by now," Marie huffed. "Where is the second wave of customers?"

One of the ladies sitting at the bar chimed in. "Ryan Christensen's whereabouts were posted on the Internet. My girlfriend called to tell me that the cast is eating at The Synful Grill. It has a new nightclub attached called Synergy. She said the bar is so packed that you can't even walk through the place."

"I've been there once," Cory said. "There's a ten-dollar cover charge just to get in. Drinks are really expensive, too. I'm sure there are lots of women there tonight."

Great! Apparently Ryan was occupying his time with other activities. I wondered if it was because I didn't reply to his last text about seeing him tonight. Would he move on that quickly? *Apparently . . .*

It was almost eleven o'clock when my phone rang instead of vibrating. I listened to my new ring tone, letting the song play out so I could hear the lyrics. My smile was huge.

"Hey you," Ryan breathed out. "Are you working hard?"

"No, not really. We're kind of dead, actually. What are you up to?" It was hard to hide my enthusiasm.

"I'm at some restaurant. We just finished eating."

"Wow. This late?" I looked at my watch. "It's almost eleven."

"Sorry I didn't call you earlier, but we had a director's meeting at eight and then it took a while for all our food to come out. The food pretty much sucked. It was disappointing," he said.

"I promise I'll feed you better tomorrow."

"Hmm, I'm looking forward to it."

I thought about the song that he chose to put on my phone, wondering if his feelings were that genuine. *I'm yours*, the lyrics said.

"I really like my new ring tone." I smiled. Despite his motives, he'd somehow managed to find my favorite song.

"Good. I'm glad," he sighed, sounding relieved.

"Pretty deep, though, don't you think?" I asked, prompting him to explain why he'd chosen *that* song.

"Maybe that was the intention," he retorted. "I wanted to get a message across so there's no confusion."

I swallowed hard, my subconscious fighting to protect me from getting crushed again.

"I love Jason Mraz," I continued, trying to stay on the lighter side. "He's one of my all-time favorites."

"I know. You have all of his CDs—minus the one that's in my possession," he said, laughing quickly.

I thought about how he'd held me this morning and how desperately I wanted him to hold me again . . . in his warm arms.

Could he be mine forever?

"So . . . am I to understand that you're *mine?*" I asked teasingly.

"I can be yours if you want me to be, Taryn," he whispered.

My breath hitched at his words. My pulse quickened and my fingers started to tremble.

"Is that your intention?" I asked, still skeptical.

Ryan cleared his throat. "My intention is to let you know where my heart is. The rest . . . the rest is up to you," he said softly.

I took another deep breath. My own heart was thumping in my chest now. "So . . . now what? Where do we go from here?"

"We give it a chance," Ryan declared quite convincingly.

CHAPTER 10

Possibilities

IT WAS ALMOST midnight when Ryan secretly entered through the back door of my pub. The lights were turned off, so the kitchen was dark when he arrived. He had his jacket hood pulled up over his head again and his trusty messenger bag was slung over his shoulder.

I had just locked the door behind him when he dropped his stuffed bag on the floor and slowly walked to stand in front of me.

"Hello," he whispered and gently smiled, bending slightly to give me a hug. Without hesitating, he slipped one hand around my waist; his other hand pressed higher on my back.

This hug was different—way different from his normal approach. He always hugged me around my shoulders; my arms would go around *his* waist.

His new stance surprised me and naturally forced my arms to wrap around his shoulders. My nose skimmed across his chest when he pulled me in. *God, he smells good!*

His fingertips pressed into my back as his lips softly kissed my forehead.

Fire burned through my veins; the touch of his lips on my skin sent a wave of arousal through my core. My hands responded instantly and instinctively, and without conscious intervention, I started to caress his neck.

The light from the bar peeked through the cracked kitchen door, illuminating his cheek in the darkness. My fingers reached to trace the light on his face. He looked down at me with smoldering eyes.

Slowly he leaned toward me and pressed his lips to mine. His first kisses were tender, pausing to rest his lips on mine (I suppose to measure my reaction), but my mouth encouraged him to proceed.

I felt his lips part as the soft tip of his tongue joined in with his kiss. His mouth was soft, wet, and completely hypnotic. Desire for him shot through every cell in my body, consuming my every thought.

He placed his warm hand on my neck to hold my face to his as he kissed me passionately.

My protective shell of self-preservation shattered into a million pieces as the entire outside world ceased to exist. Our lips moved together in perfect harmony as his tongue glided against mine.

His kissing was far better than I could have ever imagined. I tried like hell to remember why I had denied myself this type of pleasure for so long, but the heat from his ragged breath surged right into my head and melted my brain.

His hands were holding my face when he broke away from our kiss. He wrapped his arms around my body.

No, don't stop! What was left of my brain pleaded for him to keep kissing me.

"You don't know how long I've wanted to do that," Ryan whispered.

My heart was beating so fast, I wondered if he could feel it pounding through his jacket. I took a half step back and bumped into the counter behind me; I was quite light-headed. My hand was clenched on the front of his jacket when I staggered back; my grip pulled his body forward.

Like a lightning flash, he grabbed me under my arms and lifted me up onto the counter; his forcefulness turned me on even more.

My fingers wove into his hair and my legs wrapped around his hips; our lips expressed our mutual desire. He pressed himself into me; I could feel through his jeans that he was completely aroused. My mind raced, thinking about having him inside me.

His fingers clenched and clawed at the back pockets of my jeans, pulling me forward and bumping me into him. I envisioned him making love to me right here on this counter. By the way he rubbed into me, I was sure he was thinking the same thing. I softly moaned as the hunger turned to passion.

The intensity of our kissing calmed and slowed until our lips rested together. We both smiled.

"I don't remember. Did I even say hi?" Ryan whispered, joking with me.

"Yes. You had me at hello," I giggled on his lips.

He chuckled in my mouth.

"I think you have me confused with another famous actor," he said, kissing me in between laughs.

His mouth locked back on mine, convincing me that this amazing connection between us deserved a chance to grow.

Our hands had found each other's skin. His hands were under my shirt and midway up my back; one of my hands had skimmed down his neck and underneath the collar of his T-shirt.

I had his bottom lip between my teeth when thoughts of Marie walking in on our makeout session started to put a damper on my lust.

"You know . . . before we get busted . . ."

I slipped off the counter and into his arms.

Ryan gathered his bag from the floor. I was amused to see that he had to adjust his pants. His arousal was apparent.

I peeked out the door before attempting to sneak him from the kitchen to the stairwell. Most of the crowd had disappeared. There were only about twenty people left in the pub, but I still wanted to get him upstairs unnoticed.

Ryan had just slipped through the stairwell door when Marie came around the corner. She was looking for me and I was busted.

Her face broke into an exultant grin when she saw what I was up to. "Ryan?" she mouthed as she pointed to the door.

I shrugged. My shameful smile was enough of a confirmation for her.

"Glad to see you're taking my advice. Go on, I'll lock up. There are only a couple of people here. Pete and I will take care of it. Go, have a great night."

I was halfway up the steps when Marie called me back. I tossed my key to Ryan.

"I'll be right back," I said to him, nodding for him to go on without me. I trotted down the steps and almost ran right into Marie.

"You forgetting something?" she teased, holding out a chilled bottle of champagne.

Ryan had his coat off and was in the living room when I walked into my apartment.

"Gift from Marie." I handed the bottle to him. "She saw you. Sorry," I apologized. "Don't worry, she won't say anything."

"Do you want me to open this?" he asked, even though he'd already started to peel the foil off the top.

"Sure. Let me get some glasses."

He popped the cork and poured as I held the glasses. Ryan slipped one glass from my hand and held it up.

"To . . . possibilities." He tapped his glass gently into mine and flashed a sultry smile at me.

"What time do you think you'll be done tonight?" he asked, sipping his champagne.

"Actually, I've been given the rest of the night off. Marie and Pete will close tonight."

"Really? You're done for the night?" He sounded pleased.

"Yep. We weren't that busy for some reason. Guess there was some big commotion going on at the Synful Grill tonight—took most of my customers away."

He tilted his head to give me an annoyed look.

"The only reason I know that is because one of my customers received a message that you were there. She said your location was posted on the Internet."

"Unbelievable," he muttered. I could tell that upset him.

"Look, I'm sorry. I didn't mean to . . ."

He stopped me. "No, no, I'm not mad at you. It's just messed up. I can't even go out to eat without it being a huge pain in the ass. It's like having a stalker, only they travel in packs. I don't know why they even give a shit."

He started rubbing his face hard, so I tried to think of something that would get his mind off this path.

"Hey, would you help me a second?" I held out my hand to pull him up from his seat. He willingly followed me to the kitchen.

"Can you pull the other trays of steaks out of the fridge? I need to flip them." I had fifteen steaks marinating for our Sunday dinner.

"These steaks look awesome. What's in the juice?" he asked.

"Ah, that's a trade secret. I could tell you, but then I'd have to kill you!" I teased him. "I'm going to need help carrying these up to the roof tomorrow. Can I count on you to help me?"

"Absolutely," he replied, wincing at my thinking I needed to ask.

I could tell that his upset mood was slowly lifting. His gears were pretty easy to switch.

"The marinade is only the first part of the process. There's a whole grilling technique, too."

"Is that a trade secret too, or are you going to share that?"

"Truthfully, I stole the idea from an article in *Maxim* magazine."

"What are you doing reading *Maxim*? Looking for your picture?" He nudged me with his elbow.

"Yeah, right. My uncle got my dad a subscription for Christmas one year and there was an entire article on how to grill food." I shrugged. "So how do you like your steak? Are you a rare or well-done kind of guy?"

"Medium-well. I'm not crazy about seeing my food bleed." He shuddered.

"Me, too," I said, shocked that we had another thing in common.

When we finished in the kitchen, Ryan started to peruse my DVD collection. "Can we watch a movie? You have one that I'd like to see."

He kicked his shoes off and made himself comfortable on the couch. When I sat down next to him, he held his hand out to me.

"Hey, come here," he whispered. He repositioned his body so I was lying on his chest.

Ryan smiled at me and kissed my forehead softly. His finger gently raised my chin and he kissed me tenderly. I was surprised that he didn't try to make out with me again. Instead, after a few loving kisses, he just held me in his arms while we watched the movie.

I'd seen the movie he chose a few times before, so it was hard for me to really pay attention to it—especially since I was snuggled in his arms. Ryan was softly stroking my hair and my back and it made me very relaxed. I was so comfortable lying on him, I felt myself drifting.

"Taryn, wake up," Ryan whispered groggily. He shifted his body underneath me so he could sit up.

I rubbed my eyes and noticed the clock—it was a few minutes till two. Ryan slipped into the bathroom.

I waited for him to finish so I could take my turn.

"Do you mind if I stay?" he asked. "If not, I can always jog to the hotel. Hopefully the paparazzi are sleeping."

"It's pretty late," I whispered, not knowing how to convey my thoughts. I didn't want him to run anywhere.

We gazed at each other for a moment; I watched his mouth curl down in disappointment. I felt the same sadness thinking about him leaving. There was only one answer. "Stay," I whispered.

"Do you have an extra pillow?" His eyes flashed down the hallway to the living room. I guessed he was offering to sleep on the couch.

We stood there in the hallway leaning on opposing walls in silence, just staring at each other, waiting and gauging each other's reaction. He was trying to be a gentleman and not force his way into my bedroom without an invitation, but in my mind, the couch in the front room was too far of a distance between us. Things would be a lot different in my bedroom tonight from how they were last night, and we both knew it. The door to physical contact and sexual intimacy had been opened.

I held out my hand, craving for him to hold me in his arms the way he had this morning. Ryan gently smiled and placed just the tips of his fingers on mine. I curled his fingers into the palm of my hand and led him into my dark bedroom.

I turned on the little lamp that sits on my dresser to softly illuminate the room and quickly slipped into the bathroom to change. Ryan waited for me to return. He stood there, staring at me as he peeled his shirt off over his head. His chest and arms were strong and defined, and the light from the lamp made his skin glow.

I watched him open his jeans and take them off his long legs. He tried to lay his pants on my bedroom chair but he missed; some loose change pinged on the wooden floor when it fell out of his pockets. He quickly stripped his socks off and tossed them one by one to the floor.

Ryan slid into bed and adjusted the pillows until he was comfortable. We inched closer to each other and I hesitantly rested my hand on his bare chest. I wanted to let my fingers roam free, but my hand was inconveniently frozen in place.

He slid down the bed until our eyes were at the same level. We gazed into each other's eyes and he gently stroked my cheek; those unspoken words of the possibilities of what could happen next flowed between us.

His fingertips guided my face to his as he softly kissed my lips. His touch was so gentle it made me smile.

Slowly, sensually, our hands touched each other's bodies. Our fingertips lightly trailed over each other's skin, taking the liberty to explore uncharted territory.

His hand pressed in the small of my back as he pulled me closer; his kisses completely aroused me. Softly he bit and sucked my bottom lip into his mouth and I moaned from the pleasure.

I ran my hand down his back, pressing my fingertips into his skin to massage his muscular frame. I had wanted to feel his body for so long now and I was finally getting my wish.

His hand gripped my hip in response, sending another shock wave through my veins. I could feel his fingers tense and press into my hipbone as I ran my tongue over his luscious lips.

My fingers trailed down his chest to his stomach; his body quivered lightly under my touch. I could feel that he was completely aroused.

I was getting too carried away in the moment; a few minutes more of this and there'd be no turning back. Doubt, fear, crept into my thoughts, quelling ecstasy and desire. I placed my flat hand on his chest and lightly pushed back away from him; I needed a moment to catch my breath. I rubbed my eyes as the sensible person who lives in my brain spoke up.

"Taryn, I understand. I want you so bad, but I don't want to do anything you're not ready to do," Ryan whispered.

I had no will left. My body craved to feel him—all of him. My thoughts wrestled with that desire as all the warning bells went off in my head.

He wrapped his fingers around my wrist and moved my hand away from my eyes. "Talk to me. Tell me what's on your mind."

"I'm worried." I shrugged, trying like hell not to appear like an immature, neurotic mess. My words came out in a whisper.

"What are you worried about?"

I took a deep breath and sighed.

"I know you're not . . ." I murmured, stopping myself. "I don't do casual very well. Sex for me involves emotions and in reality . . . you're not going to be here for much longer." The words were difficult to say.

"Look at me, please. Look in my eyes," he softly pleaded.

I turned to gaze back at him. His eyes were captivating.

"If you haven't noticed, I'm pretty crazy about you. You're all I think about," he said as he brushed his fingertips on my cheek. "You're not the only one making an emotional investment here.

"I know why you're worried, Taryn." He took in a deep breath. "I'm not here to use you or to hurt you. You have to understand—it's not easy for me to have *any* kind of relationship, despite what people think. It's difficult for me to keep a private life or to trust anyone. One of my old girlfriends sold our relationship to the tabloids for money."

He looked away, wincing at the unpleasant memory. "After that, well, let's just say it's been a while since I've been this emotionally close with anyone."

He looked back into my eyes. "Believe me when I say that random one-nighters are not my style. That's all I need, for stuff like that to be in print, too."

"I guess we're two kindred spirits, then," I said.

"What do you mean?" He looked at me for an explanation.

"You don't trust women and I don't trust men."

"Huh," he breathed out. "So why don't you trust men?"

"I was . . . involved with someone a few months ago, too," I said hesitantly. I didn't want to accidentally say the scary word "engaged" out loud, fearing that Ryan might run if he thought I only had marriage on the brain. "Let's just say that one woman wasn't enough for him." I pursed my lips at the thought. "Anyway, sounds like we've both had our fair share of pain to deal with."

"Yeah, but the difference is that your heartaches aren't front-page news printed on the cover of millions of magazines," he huffed as he ran his fingers back through his hair. "And *you* don't need a publicist when you break up with someone."

I sat up on my elbow and rested my hand on his chest. "Ryan, I care about you, a lot. I guess that's why I'm hesitant to jump into this—because we both need to be able to trust each other. But I promise, no matter what happens between us, I will never, ever, betray you."

I stared into his deep blue eyes. "Inside here is compassion and tenderness, and I see a beautiful soul who deserves to be loved. I can only hope that you trust me enough now to believe me when I say I would *never* do anything to hurt you."

He rubbed my arm gently and then placed his hand on mine as it rested on his chest. A smile appeared on his face.

"I know." Ryan took a deep breath and looked me in the eyes. "My life has been turned upside down these last few years. I feel like I've been living this chaotic existence. But when I'm with you, I . . . I feel strangely at peace. I feel like I can trust you with my secrets. And you have something that no one else has. When I look at you," his eyes held my gaze, "you take my breath away."

His words momentarily took *my* breath away.

"Taryn, I'm fal . . ." He stopped to bite his lip and sighed, swallowing hard. "I care about you, too—so much more than I think you realize. I've been trying to take this slow for a reason, you know . . . trying not to rush it. But being with you is just so easy and natural, and I'm pretty sure you feel the same way."

"Yes, I do," I breathed out, amazed that we both felt so deeply for each other.

"I can't help the way I feel and I don't want to hold back these feelings any longer."

"Neither do I," I whispered.

Ryan gently smiled. "Taryn, every time I'm away from you, I can't wait to see you again. I just want to be with you." His fingers swept the hair out of my eyes.

At that moment, I felt every fiber of my soul want to take the huge leap of faith. I was already falling in love with him, and to hear his confession of his feelings made my decision easier. No matter what happened from this point forward, it was too late to worry or regret. My body hummed with desire for his touch.

I leaned over and softly kissed him. His fingers tangled in my hair and I felt his hunger for me. Gently, he rolled me onto my back; his eyes opened and locked onto mine.

"Are you sure? 'Cause I want you more than air right now," he sighed.

I reached up and pulled his face back to mine.

"Make love to me," I murmured on his lips. "Please," I begged.

Our mouths melted together. He wasn't in a hurry; he kissed me slowly, sensually. I could sense that he was going to make love to me, not just have sex with me.

Ryan slid his hand underneath my shirt as he kissed me. He pulled my shirt up and I helped him remove it from my body. Without taking his eyes off of me, he wadded my top up in his hands and tossed it across the room behind him.

He trailed his fingertips down my neck, stimulating my senses, slowly cupping my breast in his hand. A powerful jolt of arousal shocked into my belly as his lips moved from my mouth to my breast. My entire body tingled; could he possibly know how good that felt to me? My fingers combed through his hair and I pressed his face into my breast just a bit harder.

My eyes closed and I sank into the pure pleasure of his tongue on my skin. I ran my hands lightly from his hair to his shoulders, moaning from his touch.

I pulled his face back to mine, hungry for him. His hand slid down my back and his fingers entered the space between my skin and panties. A playful growl slipped up his throat when he squeezed my rear.

Ryan hooked the top of my panties with his thumb, peeling them away. I slowly wiggled, curling my legs onto his as he pulled them down and off my body. They also got tossed onto the floor. He ran his strong hand slowly over me, from my breast to my stomach; from my hip to my thigh.

He trailed his fingertips up the inside of my leg, driving me a bit closer to insanity. I gasped and shuddered under his touch. His long fingers toyed with me, stimulating all the right spots. I was so aroused I felt as though I could explode.

I slid my fingers under his waistband and used my forearm to push the cotton that separated us down on his hip. My hand clasped around him and stroked while he moaned in my mouth as we kissed.

He broke away from our mutual pleasure and removed his boxers. We lay there on our sides facing each other, completely free of clothing, as open and vulnerable as one could ever be with another human being.

Ryan reached up and carefully cupped my face in his hand. He didn't kiss me; he just rubbed his thumb on my cheek and over my lips as he gazed into my eyes for the longest time. A smile broke on his face and it made me smile back at him.

Slowly his body hovered over mine. His knees shifted on the bed and made my legs spread a bit wider, causing another wave of arousal to pulse into my veins.

He leaned down and softly kissed me. His kissing was slow, passionate, as if every touch of his lips were meant to convey a specific feeling.

I ran my fingers lightly over the arm that he used to steady his body as he placed himself inside me. I sucked in a sharp breath from the pleasurable pain that accompanied his penetration. I watched as he closed his eyes for a moment; he quietly moaned as he entered me.

His lips returned to kiss mine and he carefully pressed the weight of his body down on me. I opened my legs wider and wrapped them around his body; the desire to feel every inch of him was almost painful.

His eyes were fixed on mine as his hips slowly rolled. He kissed my lips and cheek softly while his hand held my rear off the bed. He was slow, intense, and precise. He sighed in my ear and I wrapped my arms tighter around his body.

"Oh, Tar. Oh God, you feel so good," he breathed out while he sucked my neck.

There was no awkwardness, no fear as he made love to me. Our bodies fit together like two lost puzzle pieces that were finally joined.

He rolled onto his back and pulled me on top of him. His hands assisted my movements while I lightly ran my fingers up and down his chest. His eyes were wide with pleasure.

I pressed my hands into the bed on either side of his head while I exerted more force.

He sucked in a sharp breath. "Oh, Tar," he moaned, softly kissing my chin. He wrapped his arm around my back, pulling me tightly to his chest. I felt his teeth gently bite into my shoulder while we moaned together.

"Lie down next to me," he whispered in my ear. I slipped off of him and rolled onto my side; he wrapped his arm under my thigh and entered me from behind.

"Oh, don't stop," I gasped. His fingers accompanied our union, finding just the right spot to send me over the edge. Ryan's mouth locked on mine, stopping me from screaming out loud from the mind-blowing orgasm that he was rocketing through my body.

As soon as I stopped quivering, he rolled me over onto my stomach. Our bodies were still connected when he pulled me up onto my knees.

I sucked in a few breaths through my clenched teeth as I felt his fingers and movements bringing on my second orgasm. I squeezed down on him, gripping him inside me, and I felt him shudder into me. He let out a long groan as we climaxed together.

Ryan lay back down next to me on the bed; our breathing was deep and labored. I heard him exhale with force as he ran his hand back through his hair. A trickle of sweat dripped down my neck and onto my pillow as I stared blissfully at the streaks of moonlight on my bedroom ceiling.

His hand slid over the sheet until his fingers found mine, taking my hand in his.

I breathed out all the air in my lungs, trying to get my heart to slow down. "Wow!" I giggled. I had no saliva left in my mouth.

He chuckled lightly. "You said it. That . . . was . . . wow!"

He rolled onto his side; our eyes met and we both smiled at each other.

Gently he wiped the hair off my forehead; his fingers trailed down my face and lifted my chin so he could kiss me again.

We lay there for a long time, arms and legs intertwined, staring intensely into each other's eyes. He softly placed tender kisses on my lips.

He let out a big yawn and then smiled. We were both exhausted and still reveling in the afterglow of our incredible orgasms. It was getting harder and harder to keep my eyes open. His yawns were contagious.

"Are you ready to go to sleep?" He kissed my nose.

I smiled and nodded slightly. "Mmmhmm."

I rolled over and leaned back against his bare chest. He pulled the sheet and blanket up over us and wrapped his long arm around me. I pulled his hand up to my lips and then wove my fingers through his.

"Good night, love," he whispered, kissing my bare shoulder.

All my muscles relaxed and I slowly drifted off to sleep, basking in the warmth and bliss of my most incredible dream. I felt his chest rise and fall as we breathed in and out together, peacefully floating on a cloud with him.

I thought I heard Ryan's voice softly say, "I love you." Although it was barely a whisper, the sound of his voice was so clear it snapped me back into consciousness.

My eyes instantly popped open. I felt his hot breath exhale forcefully onto my shoulder and his arm twitched, pulling me tighter to his chest. I listened to his breathing to see if he *was* sleeping. *Did he really just whisper that in my ear?* It sounded like he was already asleep. I closed my eyes, thinking I must be just imagining things.

THE CLOCK read 9:18 a.m. when I woke. Ryan's warm, naked body was nestled with mine. As much as I didn't want to move from my extremely comfortable spot, nature was calling.

I wiggled myself free from his arm and slid my body to the edge of the bed. I looked around on the floor for my clothes, not seeing them anywhere. I walked to his side of the bed. *Where the heck is my shirt?*

He rolled over to watch me hunt. "Good morning," he murmured happily.

I turned and smiled at him while I made a mental note to buy a robe the next time I went shopping.

"Good morning. Have you seen my shirt?" I asked with a smile.

"Yep. I know right where it is, but I can't tell you." He shook his head and combed his hair back with his fingers. He looked so damn sexy lying there naked in my bed.

I smirked at him. His T-shirt was on the floor, so I picked it up and slipped it over my head. The cotton held his delicious scent.

"Nice!" He grinned at me. "Hurry back."

Ryan took his turn in the bathroom while I put a pot of coffee on. Instead of joining me in the kitchen, he went back to bed.

I stopped in the doorway of my bedroom, leaning on the door frame while I took a moment to soak in the view. He was lying with his arms folded up under his head; the light from the window made his skin glisten.

My eyes traveled down his exposed body and I could see more clearly the light hairs that started at his chest and became more defined near his belly button. The bedsheet barely covered the rest of him, but I no longer needed to use my imagination.

He smiled at me and patted his hand on the empty space on the bed.

I grinned at him and slowly shook my head. I had another location in mind. His eyes narrowed on me with confusion. I giggled a little, stepped back out of view, and slipped his shirt off. I held the shirt up, waving it in the air so he could see it, and then dropped it to the floor. He was a smart man; I figured he'd get the hint.

I had just turned the water on in the shower when he slipped his hands around my waist. The hot water felt good on my aching muscles. It had been too long since I bent and stretched in the ways I did last night. I felt unbelievably relaxed as he rubbed my shoulders under the water stream.

We took turns washing each other. His hands lathered the shampoo in my hair as he pressed his fingertips on my scalp and neck. It was soothing and erotic at the same time. He was definitely enjoying running the soapy sponge over my body, making sure to wash every nook and cranny thoroughly.

My soapy hand washed him as his lips kissed me passionately. I let my mouth drink from the shower water on his chest before I knelt down in front of him. My eyes flickered up to watch his face express his pleasure.

His fingers tangled in my wet hair as I tightened my grip. I was so turned on just hearing him moan, I wanted to finish him off where he stood.

Ryan grabbed my wrists and stood me up. "Let's get out of here," he said.

I handed him a towel and wrapped another one around my body. He didn't bother to dry off. He dropped the towel on the floor and guided me back to the sink.

"Have a seat." He smirked, assisting me onto the bathroom counter.

He dropped to his knees and slid me to the edge; his hands pushed my thighs apart. I felt his tongue first, followed by a surge of pleasure. His fingers held me open as he buried his face into my body. He pressed my legs back farther. I ran my hands through his wet hair as he devoured me.

The heat inside my center reached its breaking point and I felt as though an explosion took place right in the core of my being. Each additional flick of his tongue sent shock wave after shock wave through my entire body out to the tips of my fingers and toes, and I shuddered from the ecstasy he unleashed on me. I swear I heard him chuckle ever so quietly as he kissed the inside of my thigh.

He stood up and placed himself inside me. Cool water dripped from his hair onto my chest and stomach as we moved together.

His arms held my legs apart, opening me wider. I watched his eyes squeeze shut; he was breathing hard through his open lips. Soft moans escaped from both of us.

"Ryan, let's go back to the bed," I gasped. I was sliding off the sink top. He lifted me up and carried me while our bodies stayed joined.

He lay me down on the edge of the bed and grabbed my ankles, placing them to rest on his shoulders. He rested his free hand on me; his thumb landed at just the right spot, causing me to suck in a sharp breath or two. *Damn, he is good!* I knew a second orgasm was coming soon.

"I'm close . . . in or out?" he asked between strokes.

"Oh God, don't stop," I moaned, squeezing down on him. I felt his teeth carefully bite into my ankle. "It's . . . k, stay in."

I almost stopped breathing while I let the internal climax have at me. My back arched reflexively; my hands clenched the bedsheet.

Ryan climaxed soon after I did and I felt his body shudder as he erupted inside me. A not-so-quiet groan rolled out of his throat.

CHAPTER 11

Grilled

SO I HAVE a question I've been meaning to ask you," I said as we took our second shower.

Ryan leaned into the stream of water, rinsing the soap off his shoulders. "What, babe?"

"How is it that you've been able to slip through my back door unnoticed by the paparazzi? I know they follow you everywhere, but somehow you've managed to hide from them."

He smiled. "It's complicated. Do you know what a shell game is?"

"Yeah," I said. "The coin or whatever is underneath one of three shells."

"Exactly," he confirmed. "Most of the time I switch cars. Like last night—we got driven back to the hotel, but then I slipped into a different car in the private parking deck and we drove out the public exit."

"Clever." I smiled and wrapped a towel around my body. "So, are the photographers going to follow the cast here today?"

"Probably. Too many people are coming here," he said while rubbing his towel over his hair. "Believe me, I thought about canceling this just to keep the extra attention away. But if the cast is coming here, we'll just say that we had a private cast party in your facility."

"You know you won't be able to leave with them tonight, right? It will be obvious if you're not with them when they arrive but if you're seen leaving . . ."

"I know, I thought about that . . . *after* I got here last night. I'm sorry."

"Nothing to be sorry about. Oh, wait. Does that mean I have to sleep with you *again* tonight?" I gave him a teasing shove and ran for the bedroom.

"I could make you suffer!" he yelled while chasing me. He caught me by the waist and swept me up in his arms. With a few quick movements he had me pinned to the bed.

"Promise? Don't toy with my emotions, Ryan Christensen," I giggled.

He leaned down and kissed me passionately again.

"Keep this up and we'll never get dressed," I murmured on his lips.

"Sounds like a plan," he chuckled, his eyes looking down at the new bulge pressing from behind his towel. "I'm quite sure I could toss you around this room for another hour or so."

"What time is it?" I asked. I couldn't see the clock on the nightstand.

He had to crane his neck to see the time. "Almost eleven thirty."

"Hmm, it *is* awfully early." I smiled and twined my fingers into his wet hair. "We have *several* hours to kill, actually."

He flashed his sexy grin at me and then placed his lips back on mine.

Ryan wasn't kidding when he said he could toss me around the bed for another hour. Our lovemaking this time had become even more adventurous as we learned each other's bodies.

"Holy shit," he gasped, crashing into a heap next to me on the bed.

I was still trying to catch my breath.

"I need . . . another shower . . . after that." He breathed out a lungful of air.

"Me, too." I wiped some sweat off of my forehead. My body was tingling all over from the incredible ecstasy he'd just unleashed on me—again.

"Put your hand on my chest," he requested.

I had trouble with this simple request. My hand slapped down on his skin.

"Ow!" he yelped.

"Sorry, can't feel my arms just yet."

"Feel that? You did that," he panted.

"What did I do?" I asked. My heart was pounding just as fast as his was.

He rolled over on his side and pulled me closer. His eyes locked on mine.

"You made my heart beat again," he said with a glorious smile. His lips softly kissed mine and I could feel all the passion that he meant to convey with each touch.

I gazed into his eyes and lightly brushed my fingertips across his face. Three little words flashed through my mind as I looked at him, but there was no way I'd say them out loud.

Ryan gathered my hand in his and folded my hand to his lips. I wondered if he had three little words in his mind too and if one day I might hear *him* say them out loud. At this moment it didn't matter; the way he looked at me was good enough.

I pressed his hand above my breast. "You did the same for me."

He kissed my fingertips and smiled.

"Come on . . . let's go get freshened up . . . again."

He took me by the hand and pulled me up off the bed.

"When do you have to be back on set?" I asked. I turned the tub water on and tested the temperature with my hand.

"I have to be in makeup at seven tomorrow. I have a fourteen-hour day scheduled," he muttered, placing our towels on the counter.

I wondered if I would drive him to our secret transfer place or if a driver would pick him up here in the morning. I'd save that question for later, for I didn't want to think at all about him leaving.

We climbed into the shower to wash again when Ryan's expression turned serious.

"Taryn, I want to be honest with you. There are some things you need to know before everyone shows up tonight."

My heart thumped in my chest, guessing that his honesty would reveal bad news. His timing was perfect, though—where could I go at this very moment? I was naked and standing in a stream of water.

I looked up into his eyes; if he was going to tell me something horrible, then he'd have to face me head on.

"I just want you to know that there's nothing going on between me and Suzanne, even though I spend a lot of time in *situations* with her where it seems like something could be going on."

"I don't know what you mean," I said as the water pelted me in the head.

"She's the lead in our movie, and I know you haven't seen it, but there are a lot of scenes where I have to kiss her—but it's just for the film. We have to be close, but I want you to know that I don't have those kinds of feelings for her." He stared at me intensely, monitoring my reaction.

I looked at him, confused. "What are you trying to say?"

"I think of her like a sister—a sometimes annoying sister. I'm concerned she might say something tonight that's out of line. And I just wanted you to know—from me—that there's nothing there."

"Okay. So if she says something to me I should just ignore her?"

"Just take it with a grain of salt. She might be cool, but I'm thinking she's going to say something stupid. If she says anything to you, just tell me, okay?" he said as he rinsed his face under the stream of water.

"Okay, I will. Are you finished, or do you need more time in here?" I was ready to turn the water off. I looked at him expecting an answer to my question, but fear struck me in the chest; his face was still troubled.

"There's something else you need to know," he continued. I felt the blood rush from my heart as he took hold of my hands.

"Francesca and I . . ." He looked down with guilt. The fear from not knowing what his confession would be knocked me for a loop. He looked me directly in the eyes when he spoke again. "It only happened once, and it was over a year ago."

I reached behind my back and turned the water off. I had to get a bearing on the admission he'd just made to me. I pushed the curtain open and was just about to step out of the tub when he gently grabbed my arm.

"Taryn, look at me. I swear it was only once . . . and after it happened I realized it was a big mistake. I want you to know that I don't have any feelings for her." His expression was sincere.

"Does she have feelings for you?" I asked. Disappointment coated my whisper.

"I don't know. Sometimes she says things . . . I know I should never have crossed that line with her." His hand lifted my chin so I'd look him in the eyes. "It doesn't matter. I don't care if she has feelings for me or not because I don't feel the same way. I never did. I never will."

I stepped out of the shower and wrapped a towel tightly around my body. I hoped the constriction of the towel could somehow keep my heart from cracking.

Ryan quickly wrapped a towel around his waist then grabbed my wrist, forcing me to look at him again.

"I'm sorry. I didn't mean to upset you like this, but I wanted you to know—directly from me—what the truth is. I'm telling you all of this because I don't want any secrets between us. She's coming here tonight, too, and I don't want our relationship to get . . ." He looked away to choose his words before looking back into my eyes.

"Taryn, I'm . . ." He paused to breathe out a deep sigh. "I only want you—just you. But I can't change the mistakes that I've made."

I had to make an instant decision. I could let the jealousy consume me and be angry, or I could thank my lucky stars that the man standing in front of me cared enough about me to tell me the truth.

I slowly reached my hand up to place it on his cheek. The water from his hair was dripping down his face. My heart skipped a beat from just touching him and I realized that my feelings for him were way too powerful to let his past change that. For the first time in my life, the man who was holding my heart in his hand was honest with me. It took a lot of courage for him to tell me what he was feeling.

"Thank you for being honest and for telling me." I smiled. Relief coursed into my heart when he took my hand in his and pressed my palm to his lips.

"Are you mad at me?" he asked carefully.

"No, I'm not mad. I'm not happy with the news, but we both have pasts. It's part of who we are. We've both made mistakes."

He took my face in his hands, staring into my eyes; his thumbs gently stroked my cheeks before he leaned in to softly kiss my lips.

I wrapped my hands around his ribs as he kissed me passionately. There were no cameras, no directors, no witnesses—just Ryan and me and our raw, unscripted emotions.

"We'd better get ready. We're going to have guests soon," I reminded him.

I started to comb my wet hair while doing everything possible to banish the visions of him and Francesca together.

As long as he was an actor, women would be coming at him from all angles and directions. But he was with *me* now, by his choice, and the feelings that he shared were real and as obvious as black and white, with no shades of gray.

Ryan slipped a new black T-shirt over his head; his jeans were hanging on his hips and the elastic waistband of his briefs was showing as he strung his leather belt through the loops.

I smiled, thinking that it took me three showers to get to this point in the day. My hair and makeup were finally done.

Oh my God, he is hot! I really just want to lie naked in bed with him all day.

"What?" he asked softly, noting my stare.

My eyes were still tracing the faint view of the exposed skin on his stomach.

"Tell me what you're thinking," he urged. I thought about it for a moment, then decided to be blatantly honest.

"I was just thinking about tearing your clothes off and crawling back under the covers."

He charged over to where I stood and wrapped his arms around me, lifting me off the floor. His aggressive approach made me laugh.

"I could rip your clothes off, too, but actually you are looking so incredibly sexy dressed." His eyes glanced down at my body.

I was in my favorite True Religion jeans—the ones that had cute leather lacing up the front, with a black tee and my black heeled boots.

"I could go back to sleep, though. You wore me out!" he snickered. "We'll just have to kick everyone out early."

I slipped my fingers into his hair and kissed him, appreciating that for this moment in time, he was mine . . . all mine.

IT WAS almost three thirty in the afternoon when Pete called to let me know that he and Tammy were out in the alley, getting ready to unload the food.

"Here, Taryn, take this box," Pete instructed. The back of Tammy's van was loaded.

"Something smells fantastic," Ryan said, taking the box from my hands. "Where do you want me to put this?"

"Just put everything on the counters for now. We need to set up tables," I replied. I couldn't help but smile at Ryan. He was smiling at me, too.

Ryan helped Pete set up a table for the food and then assisted in transferring all the food from the kitchen to the bar. It was apparent by the volume and variety of delectables that we were going to eat like kings and queens today.

Marie and Gary arrived soon after we started setting up. I had asked them to arrive early, for I wanted to make sure that my friends were safely inside before the cast arrived. My friends didn't need to be photographed today.

Tammy had set out linens to cover the buffet tables and I was in the process of opening one of them up when Ryan walked past me. He pinched me quickly on the butt cheek when he thought no one was looking.

"So . . . how's it going?" Marie grinned and raised her eyebrows. She noticed the way Ryan and I were beaming.

I glanced around to make sure we were alone before holding my hand up and spreading my five fingers out to her.

"*Five?*" she whispered in amazement.

I gave her a devilish grin and nodded my head.

"Did you take my advice and feed him well to keep his energy level up?"

"Oh, he ate *very* well this morning—several times. Wait, did you mean feed him food?" I teased.

"So what are you two ladies whispering about over here?" Ryan asked after he set another box on the table.

Marie and I looked at each other and just smiled; it was apparent on our faces that we were talking about—things.

Ryan wrapped his arms around my waist. "I guess our secret is out now?" he chuckled.

"What secret?" Marie's voice boomed. "It's so obvious the way you two are glowing around each other. The only thing missing are the words 'I had incredible sex' written on your foreheads." She motioned the words with her hand.

Ryan and I laughed as he squeezed me tighter. "It was beyond incredible," he whispered in my ear and kissed me on the neck.

Pete walked into the bar with another box of food, noting Ryan's hold on me. A not-so-nice word slipped from his lips.

Gary was right behind him, and when he saw us he started laughing.

"Looks like you owe me some money," he muttered.

"Doesn't mean anything," Pete snapped. He looked over at Marie; she twitched her lips and nodded her head to confirm his suspicions.

"Son of a . . . two more days . . . you couldn't hold off for two more days?" Pete busted on us.

I glared over at Marie.

"Don't look at me! You know how competitive those two are. It wasn't *my* idea."

Ryan released me and turned to Pete. "You bastards betting on us?" he asked jokingly.

"Yep," Pete replied. "And you cost me twenty bucks, you prick."

Ryan slipped his hand into his front pocket and peeled a twenty-dollar bill off of a small roll of cash.

"Here you go, Gary. Pete's loss was my gain." He laughed. "It was worth every penny."

Gary didn't hesitate. He snatched the bill out of Ryan's hand and stuffed it into his pocket. Marie teasingly nudged me.

"You know, Ryan, Gary is a Giants fan," Pete baited him.

"Oh, really?" Ryan asked, looking over at Gary.

"Ugh. Don't tell me you're a freaking Steelers fan, too," Gary groaned. "No wonder you and Taryn get along so well."

"What do you say to another bet?" Ryan's eyes narrowed on Gary. "I got another twenty in my pocket that says the Giants are going to get their asses handed to them tonight."

While the three of them discussed the terms of the wager, Tammy, Marie, and I finished setting up the buffet table.

"He fits in perfectly," Marie whispered in my ear. "Look at them. They're like long-lost college buddies."

"I know," I whispered back. The sight of the three of them getting along so well was heartwarming.

"Ryan freakin' Christensen!" Marie giggled as she gave me a shoulder hug. "So, tell me, is he packing or what?"

"What do you think?" I murmured.

She breathed out a rough sigh.

"Hey, no fantasizing about him," I warned. "You have your own. That one's mine. And try not to ask too many questions about their stupid movie, all right? They're just regular people."

Tammy set up an elaborate tiered cheese and veggie tray; she had hot and cold hors d'oeuvres, hot entrees to complement the steaks, shrimp and lobster bites, and several different little desserts and chocolate dipped what-nots.

I started to uncork a bottle of merlot while the guys discussed football trades and names of players. I never understood how men could remember all those details about sports, yet were incapable of remembering where they set their car keys or wallet.

Just like the other day when Ryan asked me where his messenger bag was. Did he really not remember where it was, or is there some primitive part of a man's brain that starts to shut down whenever a woman comes into his life?

Ryan was obviously hungry; he was popping food in his mouth between words. He had just shoved a big piece of cheese in his mouth when his cell phone rang. After a brief conversation, he met me at the bar.

"Cal and his wife are on their way. They're driving themselves. The rest of the group is coming separately; they were just picked up at the hotel. Cal told me that they are being followed by the paparazzi." Ryan's words sounded almost angry.

"I have to go start the grill; do you want to come up with me?" I asked, hoping he would follow.

He just nodded.

On our way through my apartment, we grabbed our coats. I presumed it would be cold outside. He playfully goosed my rear end all the way up the steps to the roof. I was getting the hint that he liked my butt.

I opened the rooftop door and turned to look at his reaction. His eyes instantly widened as he stepped outside.

"Oh my God, Taryn. This is incredible."

I'd had a good portion of the roof transformed into a nice patio. There was a huge, raised composite deck with an outdoor stone bar with a granite top. I had designed a corner-raised fireplace at one end of the patio; the end closer to the door contained the enormous stacked stone counter and stainless steel grill.

The entire patio area was covered by a wooden pergola roof; I had tried to train vines to grow up the pillars, but the October winds had dried up most of the leaves. Underneath the open lattice roof, I had attached tiny white lights to make the patio glow in the evening. Centered on the patio was a large teak table that seated twelve and directly above that, a wrought iron and glass candle chandelier. I turned the lights on for Ryan so he could see it sparkle in the setting sun.

"This is . . . beautiful," he proclaimed, appearing quite mesmerized by it all.

I smiled at him; I was glad that he thought so, too.

"You can really see the ocean from here," he sighed loudly.

I turned the gas on underneath the grill and lit the pilot. The burners popped to life with fire.

"It's not as cold as I thought it would be tonight. Do you think people might like to sit up here, too? I could start a fire."

"Yeah. I know I wouldn't mind hanging out up here for a little."

I pulled some wood out of the storage bin and stacked it in the fireplace. Ryan was standing at the edge of the deck with his fingers in his front pockets, looking out at the ocean and the setting sun. His face was beaming.

"I think this is my new favorite place in the world," he declared. "I thought your stairwell was the gateway to peace. This is the peace."

I stood next to him, enjoying the view of the colors over the ocean. I had seen the setting sun over the water a thousand times, but with Ryan standing next to me, it was as if I were seeing it for the first time. Ryan slipped his hand out of his pocket and took my hand in his. He lifted my hand to his lips, placing a soft kiss on my skin.

He leaned over to give me a kiss. Either he was a brilliant actor or he was falling for me, too. I hoped it was the latter.

I giggled lightly when he pulled my hand behind his back, causing me to get off balance and fall into him. He smiled at me and pressed his lips to mine. Ryan quickly let go of my hand and placed both of his hands on my neck, raising my face to his. His kiss was so passionate, I was totally lost in the feeling; so lost that I didn't hear the roof door open.

I did, however, hear someone when he cleared his throat. Pete had escorted Cal and his wife to the roof. Suzanne and Francesca were directly behind them. The second we realized we weren't alone, Ryan immediately let me go.

"My, aren't you two cozy already," Suzanne said in her British accent.

Ryan fired a dirty look in her direction. He ignored her and guided me over to Cal and his wife.

"Hey, Cal." Ryan shook his hand. "Taryn, I'd like to introduce you to Cal's wife, Kelly. Kelly, this is Taryn—Taryn Mitchell. She is the owner of this beautiful establishment."

I held out my hand to Kelly. I remembered seeing her many times on television, but she was even lovelier in person. She had straight blond hair, high cheekbones, and the type of smile that was infectious. I recalled she was only a year or two older than I was. We were about the same height and close to the same size, too.

"Hi, Kelly, it's very nice to meet you!"

"It's nice to meet you, too, Taryn." She gave me a nice hug. "Oh, wow. Cal, look at this view!" The sound of her voice was very familiar to me. I'd spent many years watching her show faithfully.

"Ryan and I were just appreciating the same thing before you arrived," I said to her. I felt Ryan's hand in the small of my back.

"This is magnificent, Taryn," Cal agreed. I saw him look at Ryan and smile.

Kelly walked to the fireplace; I could see that she wanted a closer look. "Cal, this is what we should put in the corner of our patio. I want this."

"It's quite easy to build," I explained. "I understand you have a young daughter? Something like this with the height would be safer for her. You can easily place a fire screen across the front."

Kelly and I continued our discussion about the grill and bar area. She was intrigued about the design.

"I actually sketched the design. I saw it in my head, the way I wanted it to be laid out, and then I had a local contractor build it all for me."

"It's beautiful. We'll have to bring you to California to design one for us. We just built a new home in Malibu."

It was easy to talk to Kelly. She was very open and pleasant, and was the type of person I could see myself being good friends with.

Out of the corner of my eye, I noticed Suzanne and Francesca slowly walking toward us. I didn't want to be rude to the rest of our guests so I smiled in their general direction. Ryan and Cal were having a conversation about something that happened with one of the cameras on the set the other day, and I noticed that Ryan barely acknowledged the other girls' presence.

I looked at the two actresses and gave them my best welcome smile.

"Hi." I held out my hand to Suzanne. "I'm Taryn. Welcome to my home." She barely took my fingers in hers and quickly shook my hand.

"I'm Suzanne," she mumbled.

I got the distinct impression that I was supposed to acknowledge that she was famous and I was expected to already know who she was.

"It's nice to meet you. And you must be Francesca," I stated warmly, holding my hand out to her.

"Yes," she said quickly, barely looking at me. Even though she'd only said one word, I could detect the French accent in her voice. She was as unpleasant to me as I had expected.

"I didn't have an opportunity to meet you both when you were in my pub, but I'm glad that you came today." There was no way I was going to be impolite, despite the less than warm reception I was getting in return.

I glanced over to Ryan, who gave me a smile and a nod. He was acknowledging my attempts at being cordial.

"Ladies, can I offer you a drink? We have a large variety of wines downstairs, or any other beverage you might prefer." I was hoping they might follow me down to the bar. I did not want to be carrying drinks up and down the stairs all night.

Much to my dismay, Suzanne wrapped her coat across her chest and plopped her ass down in one of the chairs. "I'll have a glass of white wine."

Francesca sat down next to her. My wishes for them to return to the bar were in vain. While I was running downstairs, I was going to make it worth the trip.

"Francesca, can I get you something to drink?" I asked nicely.

Before she responded, the rooftop door opened again and several new people joined us.

I recognized Shane Richards right away; he had come into the pub once before with Ryan and Cal. Next to him was a petite, twenty-something-looking woman with short blond hair and a lanky man with too much gel in his brown hair.

Ryan came to my side, and he was smiling at our new guests.

"Hey, everyone!" the young woman said. "Hey, Ryan!" She came right over to us.

I didn't know who she was, but it didn't matter. She was all aglow and looking like she wanted to have a good time, not like the other two who were glaring at me from their perches.

"Taryn, this is Kathleen Jarrett. She plays my wicked little assistant in our film." He smiled and gave her a teasing arm hug around her neck. "Kat, this is Taryn."

"Hey, Taryn," Kathleen greeted me. I held my hand out to her but instead she gave me a hug. "It's nice to finally meet you."

"It's nice to meet you, too," I said while hugging her back. I was curious as to what she meant by "finally"; I looked over at Ryan, slightly confused. He was just smiling.

"Ryan has told me a lot about you," she whispered in my ear. "I'm just so glad to see him happy."

"Taryn, this is Ben . . . Ben Harrison." Kathleen motioned to the man next to her.

"Hi Ben. It's nice to meet you." I held out my hand, but the way Kathleen was bobbing around, I wondered if she would pull us all in for a group hug. I was relieved when Ben shook my hand instead.

Ryan leaned over and whispered in my ear. "I'm allowed to tell you that they are *together*, even though their characters are mortal enemies. I told Kat that you're very trustworthy."

His eyes flashed to look at Kat, but she was just smiling and bouncing with happiness.

"They've been seeing each other for a while, but it's not public knowledge. They'd prefer if the public stays out of their private life."

"I completely understand," I replied. Apparently, Ryan had been sharing *his* private-life details with her. It didn't matter; she looked like she was trustworthy, too.

"Ryan, do you think we can get everyone back down into the pub for a minute? That way I can get everyone drinks and we can start eating soon." I was also thinking about my friends, who were noticeably absent from the rooftop gathering.

Ryan made an announcement and ushered everyone toward the door. I was relieved that he took charge. I didn't want to offend anyone, especially the two that were still glaring at me. The more they glared, the less I wanted to wait on them hand and foot.

Kelly and Kat stopped as we proceeded through my apartment.

"What do you guys think?" Ryan asked them, looking around.

"This is a really cool apartment," Kat said excitedly. "It's huge."

Ryan took them for a quick tour and stopped in my kitchen. I was surprised that it had made such an impression on him.

"Taryn designed it," he stated proudly.

I was glad that the rest of the group had gone downstairs. I could only imagine Suzanne rolling her eyes at Ryan's comments.

"I love the stove," Ryan added. "There are enough burners on this thing to make a meal for forty people."

"Maybe one day I'll know forty people to cook for," I joked. "Speaking of cooking . . . why don't we all go downstairs for a drink, and then I can get the steaks on the grill."

Suzanne and Francesca were sitting at the big, round table. I noticed that they were similarly dressed. Both had designer T-shirts on and their sneakers were the same, but in different colors. I wondered who was copying whom.

As I looked around at the cast, I could easily see whom Ryan got along with and who presented a challenge. I wondered, besides the obvious look of her, what attracted Ryan to Francesca. She looked like a model, but she seemed to have the personality of a rock. I didn't get the appeal; perhaps during a moment of weakness he was drunk or just so hard up that he wasn't looking for a hole with a personality.

Suzanne looked bored. Francesca, on the other hand, was sitting there taking mental notes. I could sense her wheels were turning. When Suzanne got up to use the restroom, Francesca trailed behind her.

I set out two bottles of opened wine on the end of the buffet table when I heard the two girls coming out of the bathroom.

"Didn't take him long to get some in this town," Suzanne said coldly. "Guess this one is the new flavor of the month." Her eyes looked me up and down when she noticed me standing there.

I didn't move. I just stood there with my arms crossed. The battle lines were being drawn right before my eyes and the evening was still young.

"Don't let them get to you," Kelly said as she made a small platter of finger foods behind me. "They're threatened by you," she mentioned casually.

"I don't understand," I whispered to her. "I don't even know them."

"You're taking Ryan off the eligible bachelors list and they're jealous. Those two have had issues with every girl he speaks to. Ryan is a nice guy; he talks to everybody."

Kelly took a moment to eat a seafood puff. "It's weird; they act like they have some kind of ownership over him. I'll be glad once this third movie is done; then we'll be rid of them." She smiled at me, like we were in on some secret joke together.

"I didn't know what I had done to offend them," I uttered.

"You captured Ryan's attention. That was enough." Kelly giggled.

After she sampled another bite of food, her expression turned serious. "So, how did you and Ryan meet?"

I wasn't prepared to answer that question. I didn't know what to say.

"I would prefer if you asked Ryan that question," I politely requested.

"Very good," she replied. "You're a quick learner." Kelly fired another question at me. "Are you dating him?"

"No. I'm not dating anyone," I responded. My answer wasn't altogether a lie. In reality, he had yet to take me on a date. Our relationship was anything but conventional.

"I like you. You're discreet. He made a good choice." Kelly put her hand on my shoulder. "Being involved with a celebrity has its own set of challenges. He needs to know that you can stand on your own while standing by his side. You need to be strong and not let the gossip and trivial actress egos get to you."

"Is this all a test?" I asked her point blank, my eyes looking around the room. I poured myself a glass of wine to calm my nerves.

"No, this is a party." She laughed at my worried look. "But it *is* a good start. You could consider this to be more like dipping your toes in the water."

We moved farther away from the buffet table to continue our discussion in private.

"I've known Ryan for almost two years now." Kelly smiled to herself, as though something she'd thought of amused her. "Let's just say he's very taken with you. I've never seen him like this with anyone."

I took a sip of wine and moved closer to her. I wanted to know what she knew.

"Taryn, he's very worried about you and how you'll cope with being in *our world*. Ryan is very sensitive. He's having a hard time coping himself. He's not comfortable with all the attention one garners as a celebrity." She paused to let Francesca pass us.

"You can't be the star of a major motion picture and *not* be in the spotlight, and this movie has surely thrown him into the spotlight! He's learning how to handle being famous. If you want to be in a relationship with him, you're going to have to learn with him."

She nodded her chin in his direction. "That right there is who he really is. But outside that door," her eyes flashed to my front door, "photographers are waiting on your sidewalk."

"I know. I wish they would leave all of you alone, especially him." Ryan and I were looking at each other from across the room. I wanted to run to him and wrap my arms around him in a protective embrace.

"I told him I would help." She smiled, noticing his glance. "I want to see him happy, and you seem to make him *very* happy." She patted me on the back.

Ryan made his way over to me; he was smiling that sexy grin the whole way.

"Hey," he whispered. "How are you ladies doing?"

"Oh, you know. We're just standing here talking about you." Kelly laughed lightly. She was fearless.

"I sort of figured," Ryan retorted, running his free hand over my upper arm.

I looked at him, amused. I had been so paranoid, avoiding saying things about him to my friends, but here he'd been talking about me to *his* friends all along. I surmised that he had shared his thoughts about me with a few people in this room.

"You have anything good to say?" he asked me.

I just smiled and shook my head to indicate my answer. "I'm sorry. I don't think we've ever met. Who are you?"

My words made Kelly laugh out loud. Ryan, on the other hand, pulled me in for a teasing headlock.

"I think I'll have to refresh your memory later," he growled in my ear.

"Promise?" I laughed.

"Cross my heart." He grinned.

I heard his stomach groan while he was wrestling with me. "I think I need to get those steaks on the grill," I said amid the laughter.

"Yes. I'm starving," Ryan agreed.

"Kelly, would you excuse me please? I look forward to talking more with you, but . . ." I patted Ryan's stomach. "Right now I need to prepare your meal."

Ryan followed me to my kitchen and, as promised, he helped me carry all the steaks up to the patio. I opened one of the stainless-steel drawers by the grill and retrieved my utensils and my large cast-iron kettle.

"See the hook over there in the fireplace? Would you hang this kettle there for me, please?"

"Sure, but you have to kiss me first." He smiled as he leaned over. His kiss was brief but persuasive.

When he stepped back to me, he wrapped his arms around my waist. "What's the timer for?" he whispered on my neck.

It was going to be difficult to grill fifteen steaks with his body pressed into my back like that. He swept my hair to one side, seductively kissing the nape of my neck.

"Grilling is a precision art," I giggled. Ryan's warm lips had found my earlobe.

"You know you're driving me insane," I whispered.

"No, I believe *you* are driving *me* insane," he uttered seductively.

"Are you here to learn or to distract me?" I grumbled.

"Sorry, sorry. Here to help." His hands let go of my hips.

I turned quickly to face him and wrapped my arms around his neck, kissing him passionately. He responded immediately, holding me in a tight embrace. Apparently he was hungrier for me more than the steak.

I had just slipped my hands into his back pockets when I heard the rooftop door slam and a female voice let out a groan. Ryan released me and I turned to see Suzanne and Francesca walking our way.

"Great," I murmured, loud enough for only Ryan to hear.

"Are you rehearsing again, Ryan?" Suzanne chided him as she slumped back down in one of the chairs at the table.

"I don't think so," he answered coldly. "But if you have a problem with it, you can go back downstairs."

"Oh, don't be so defensive. I just came up here to tell you that Cal is looking for you," Suzanne huffed while looking at her fingernails.

"Cal can wait. If he needs me, he knows *exactly* where to find me."

A smile broke on my lips. When the timer buzzed, I lifted the grill cover to flip the steaks.

"The trick is to grill the meat for three minutes on each side, then you let it rest for three minutes, and then you repeat the process." I looked up into his eyes. "Would you please bring the pot over from the fire? It should be hot now. Here, take this heavy glove so you don't burn yourself."

"Sure. No problem," he said cheerfully while sliding his hand across my rear.

I'm sure the sourpuss twins saw that gesture; I heard one of them scoff. I placed the first round of steaks in the hot iron pot and covered them with the lid. I had just set the second layer of steaks on the grill when Marie came through the door.

"Ryan, the guys are playing darts and they want you to even out the teams," she said. Her face was twisted in confusion as she looked at the two sitting at the table.

"Nah, I'm staying here with Taryn," he quickly replied.

I saw his eyes flicker over to Suzanne. I supposed he thought I needed his protection.

I touched his cheek. "It's okay. I have this." I smiled. "Go have fun with the boys. Marie will keep me company." I gave him my devilish grin to let him know I wouldn't be taking any of their crap.

"Are you sure?" he whispered. I knew he would stay if I asked him to.

"It's okay," I reassured him.

He leaned over to whisper in my ear. "Don't take any of their shit."

I smiled. He and I were on the same wavelength.

"I didn't intend to."

Marie was with me now; I had reason to just ignore them.

"That a girl. I'll see you in a bit." He gave me a quick kiss and a pat on the butt.

Ryan gave Marie a squeeze on her shoulder in passing. "Play nice, ladies," he said, looking back at the table.

"What's up with those two?" Marie whispered to me. She sat down on one of the counter stools.

I rolled my eyes.

"Did you meet Kelly and Kat?" I asked her.

"Yep." She nodded. "They are so cool. Tammy is down there with them now. Kat is really funny."

"I'm sorry I didn't get to introduce you to everyone. I've been distracted."

"No kidding." Marie giggled.

Suzanne started talking to Francesca; even though she was talking quietly, she apparently wanted me to hear what she was saying. She wasn't *that* quiet.

"You know the studio will be upset once they discover he's dating someone. It's all about how he's packaged. And as long as he's publicly single, his fan base will be higher and his movies will make more money. You don't think that they will allow him to be seen with her—I mean, she's not even famous. Won't take them long to put an end to it."

Even though she was appearing to be a mean and vindictive person, I wondered if there was any truth to her comment. Would the studio tell him who he could and could not date? Did he have to sign a contract or something that governed his personal life? I didn't know anything about the rules that came along with being famous.

"So, Taryn . . ." Suzanne chimed up, interrupting my private thoughts. "How did you and Ryan meet?"

I smiled briefly before turning around.

"I'm so surprised Ryan didn't tell you that story himself, Suzanne! Perhaps you should ask him how we met. He tells the story much better than I do."

"No, he didn't mention you at all," she retorted. "He's such a good actor *and* a good liar that I wouldn't believe anything he tells me anyway."

Marie's eyes shot up to look at me. She was instantly aware that this was a confrontation and not a casual conversation.

"I wouldn't know about his acting abilities. I've never seen any of his movies," I replied over my shoulder. "But when he looks at me I can tell he's being honest. He has no reason to *pretend* with me." I laughed quietly; only Marie could see me.

"Yes, well, enjoy it while it lasts. In a few more weeks he'll be leaving. Then what will you do?"

The smile on my lips quickly faded. The bitch had found my weak spot.

She noted my pause and used it to her advantage.

"You honestly didn't think he would stay *here*, did you?" she said condescendingly in her annoying accent.

When I didn't respond, she threw her next dagger.

"You did! How pathetic. You probably think what you have with him is special; like you are the first girl in this town that he has tried to sleep with. I hate to be the one to inform you but you aren't the first. My dear Ryan is *such* a talented actor. It's all the same, from town to town, how easily they all fall for him. He tells them what they want to hear so he can get laid. Pity how he leaves them all brokenhearted."

I had a sharp knife in one hand and a long tined fork in the other. The thought of stabbing her in *her* heart crossed my mind.

"Besides, we're leaving for Scotland soon, and he is contracted for movies immediately after that. He doesn't have time for a relationship. He'll be traveling the world, and you know the saying, 'out of sight, out of mind.' He'll think of you only until the next girl opens her legs."

Kelly's words about how I had to be strong flashed through my brain. Marie's words about this being a part of his life flashed after that. But I looked at Marie with desperation. I had no comeback for Suzanne's comment.

"Yes, we all know that Ryan has obligations, but I don't think that will be powerful enough to keep these two apart," Marie replied in my defense. "When I see how Ryan looks at you," she said to me, "I just know. That man is falling in love with you. You two are perfect for each other. You're his soul mate."

Temporary relief washed over me and a smile broke across my face.

"Soul mate?" Suzanne scoffed. "Oh, he *really* has done a number on all of you. He should get an Academy Award for that performance." She clapped. "You really have no idea how many women he has slept with, do you? And he made every one of them feel like she were his perfect match."

"You never know. Maybe Taryn *is* his perfect match. The way he holds her and kisses her, it's what his heart wants, not what the script says he's supposed to do," Marie fired back.

"Foolish American women. They are all the same," she said to Francesca. She rolled her gaze over to me. "Let me guess . . . he's been calling you and texting you? So typical for Ryan; that's how he gets them to fall for him. He probably uses the same lines on each of them, too.

"Ryan is an actor. He gets paid to fool people into believing he's something he's not. It's extremely difficult for people in our industry to have long-standing relationships, especially when they lie for a living."

I momentarily had a vision of tossing her off the edge of the roof.

"Ryan is a young man in his prime. He has no desire to settle, not when the world is laid out for him and he has all these opportunities. All the parties, all the women . . . they are just toys to him," she stated emphatically.

"His next movie starts filming in January. He'll be gone for months. After that we have hundreds of photo calls and junkets to promote *Day of Dawn*. We still don't know where we're going to film the third movie, but I can say with confidence that it won't be here."

Marie glared at her. "Other actors have relationships and get married all the time. I don't know why you think Ryan would be so different."

Suzanne sat up straight in her chair. "Married? Ryan? I don't think so. He isn't the marrying type. Besides, everyone knows that in the end, famous celebrities always marry celebrities."

"Not always," Marie argued. "Matt Damon looks quite happy. The way I see it, it's the relationships between actors that always end up in divorce."

"Yes, well, these momentary distractions could end up costing him his career. He's already been warned by the director to get focused," she said callously.

"Perhaps it was something on the set that was distracting him and taking away his focus?" I pointed out. "Maybe someone was having a bad costume day or was behaving like a spoiled brat? Or perhaps someone is still harboring feelings from something that happened *once* a long time ago? I'm sure those moments of irritation affect his performance as well." *Swallow that one, bitch!* I said to myself.

That was the final straw for her. She abruptly got up from her chair, shoving it back and out of her way with extra force. Francesca stood up two seconds later. The scowl on her face was evident, too.

"Don't overcook my steak," Suzanne huffed as she retreated for the door.

CHAPTER 12

Served

"WHAT THE HELL was that all about?" Marie asked the second Francesca slipped through the door.

"I'm not sure," I sighed. "I think Suzanne is in love with Ryan. At least she's acting like it. What the hell did I get myself into?"

Marie fluttered her fingers. "Don't worry about her. He obviously doesn't care about her."

I put the steaks back on the grill for their last cycle. As I poked them with the fork to move them around, I thought about Suzanne's statements. What *was* I going to do once Ryan left Seaport? I was caught up in the moment again with another guy who was leaving for good in a few weeks.

"Taryn, you look like you want to cry. Don't let those bitches get to you like that."

"Marie, she's right. They *are* leaving soon. He's got movies to make and he has to travel to many other places after this. How can it *possibly* work out?"

The smoke from the grill was making my eyes sting even worse. "Long-distance relationships never last."

"Don't think that!" she yelled at me. "He cares about you."

"So what? It doesn't matter how we feel about each other. He's going to have to leave eventually. Once he leaves, that will be it. This *relationship*, if that's even what it is, was doomed from the start." I felt the pain that precedes my tears crack into my chest.

"He's beyond famous. And once we're not around each other, temptation will be all around him. There are a million pretty women out there for him to choose from and I'm sure he'll form bonds with the next hot actress he has to work with." I had to breathe. Reality was setting in.

"I'm kidding myself to think he'll want to maintain a relationship with me. He'll never be able to stay faithful to me, and why should he? He's young, and single, and certainly not in a position in his life to settle down with someone. I'm nothing more than a stupid piece of ass."

I wiped my eyes. My eyeliner was noticeable on my finger. I felt the tear form and drip down my cheek.

Marie rushed around the grill and gave me a hug. I couldn't hold the tears in anymore thinking about losing him; they streamed down my face.

"What happened?" Ryan yelled, running over to where we stood.

Marie answered him. "That Suzanne is a bitch. She's lucky I didn't punch her."

"What did she say to you? Tell me!" He started to pull on my arm.

Marie let me go and I turned to take the steaks off the grill. I sniffed back my tears and tried to stifle the sobs that ebbed up my chest as I threw each steak in the pot. I couldn't look at him.

"Give me the fork," Marie ordered, relieving me of chef duty.

Ryan grabbed my upper arms and spun me around with force. "Taryn, sweetheart, what did she say to you? Tell me right now!"

I just shook my head. I couldn't stop the tears. I also didn't want to have this conversation with him while Marie was present.

"Marie, would you please take the steaks downstairs for me? Please? I need a moment," I muttered. Ryan was wiping my face with his fingers.

"Please, tell me what she said," he pleaded.

"She said a lot of things, Ryan. Mostly she reminded me *repeatedly* that you're leaving soon and you're not coming back here—and thinking about that hurts . . . so bad." I squeezed my eyes shut; fresh tears rolled down my face.

"She informed me that you're leaving for Scotland soon, and that you have many other movie commitments and so many other places in the world to be." I swallowed hard, trying to pull myself together. I didn't want him to see me crying over him. I wiped my cheek.

"Funny, I knew all along that you wouldn't be staying here. How could you possibly . . ."

"That bitch! I've just about had enough of her shit!" he yelled.

I didn't fully understand why he was mad at Suzanne.

"Don't blame her. She didn't say anything that I hadn't already considered. I just didn't need her to remind me today."

I looked away when I realized the day of reckoning was happening now.

"I should never have let myself get this attached," I said, chastising myself. I started to take a step back to walk away, but Ryan grabbed my arms again. I tried to squirm out of his hands but he tightened his grip.

"This is *exactly* why . . ." I didn't finish saying it out loud. My hands clenched into fists. In my mind, the inevitable heartbreak was already here, and I was furious with myself.

"Oh, God. Why did I let this happen? I'm so stupid. I should have *never, ever* . . ." Fresh air stuttered down my throat.

"Taryn?" Ryan's face twisted with confusion.

I knew he didn't understand why I was so distraught.

"I'm sorry, Ryan. I knew this moment would come eventually. That's why I tried to just stay friends. I don't want to put this on you. It's my problem."

"What are you saying?" He shook my arms.

I attempted to wipe my eyes, trying to find the internal strength to say the words. *I love you, but I can't keep you.*

"I'm saying we shouldn't see each other anymore. Then when you leave in a few weeks, no one gets hurt."

His mouth fell open. "What? No!" he shouted. "NO! Why are you doing this?"

"Ryan, we both know that you're leaving soon. Then what? We're going to try to have a long-distance relationship? I'm not *that* naïve." I wiped my face.

"The more time I spend with you, the harder it will be when you go. This relationship doesn't stand a chance and I know you know it. So why pretend that anything good can come from it?

"Let's just end this now instead of prolonging the inevitable. Then when you leave you're free to be with whomever you want to be with. No strings, no worries . . . no regrets." As hard as I tried to stick to my guns, tears were pouring uncontrollably down my face. I had to look away. "It's already too painful and I'm already too attached to you."

"Taryn, look at me," he pleaded. I noticed his voice crack.

I shrugged my shoulders, trying to escape from his hands. "I can't." My heart was breaking and I wanted to get away from the source of the pain.

"Please?" he begged.

"No. No," I said adamantly, my voice trembling uncontrollably. I tasted the salt from my tears as they dripped across my lips. I struggled in his hands, but he still wouldn't let go.

"No. It's all right." I swallowed hard. "You don't have to say anything. You don't owe me. Let's just go back to the party and when it's over we'll say our goodbyes."

My words burned in my throat and my heart crumbled to pieces. I had to let him go.

As much as I love you, you can never be mine.

His hands shook my arms.

"Please, just . . . let me go," I whispered between sobs.

"Taryn? No. No. Please, baby. Look at me. Look into my eyes. Please." It almost sounded like he was crying, too.

"Look at me!" he shouted.

The moment I looked up, new tears streamed down my face. I didn't want him to see me like this.

"I have no intention to walk away from you or let *any* amount of distance ruin this. Will it be difficult for us? Yes. Will it hurt me just as bad to be away from *you*? Yes."

Tears fell from Ryan's eyes.

"But one thing I know for sure . . ." He held my chin up to make sure I wouldn't look away. "I am falling in love with you."

My knees felt weak. I hadn't expected *that* response from him.

"With *you*, Taryn," he stressed, looking directly into my eyes. "I don't want *anyone* else—just you. And no matter where I am, wherever I go, you're the only one who is holding my heart."

He felt that I was no longer resisting, so he eased up on the grip he had on my arm. His grasp that once kept me from running away now held me up where I stood.

"We'll figure out a way to make it work. I promise," he solemnly vowed. "I have plenty of time between my schedules to come back here, and when I can't be here, I'll get you on a plane. No matter what, I'm not going to let you go." He stressed his last words.

"I'm falling in love with you, too," I confessed, looking up into his warm, blue eyes. "That's why it hurts so much."

He pulled me into a comforting embrace and crushed his lips on mine. I felt the weight of my uncertainties lift off my heart as I read his lips and the message his kiss conveyed. Knowing that he wanted me, hearing that he didn't want it to end, was exactly what I needed to move forward.

His kiss ended and he sighed heavily.

"Oh, sweetheart, don't worry. You're not gonna get rid of me that easily."

"That's good to know," I murmured against his chest.

Ryan hugged me, stroking his hand over my hair.

"I didn't know. I wasn't sure how long you and I . . ." I sniffed. "If this, between us, was only until you left Seaport."

"No. That was never my intention." He kissed my head.

"The way I feel about you, and after our incredible night and this morning . . ." I tossed my head back and took a moment to breathe.

"I don't know about you, but my feelings for you started way before *that*." He tried to joke.

"Mine, too," I admitted. "But Suzanne kept picking until she found my weakness." I sighed, collecting myself further.

"Ryan, I know you have obligations that will tear you away from here. Suzanne informed me of all of them, emphasizing how much you need your freedom. The thought of never seeing you again was excruciating. Allowing myself to fall madly in love with you and then having to let you go for good, I don't know if I could survive that."

Ryan softly kissed me. "I know how you feel. A few minutes ago when you broke up with me, I felt that same excruciating pain."

"I'm so sorry," I whispered, drowning in regret for hurting him.

"It's okay. I understand," he said while gently rocking me back and forth.

I wiped the moisture from my cheeks. "I'm sorry for falling apart."

"Stop apologizing. It's all right." He hugged me tighter. "Just don't ever break up with me again." He sounded truly rattled as he kissed my forehead.

"I swear I never will. The same goes for you," I muttered.

"I've already fallen for you, so you're stuck with me," Ryan assured me. "You know my parents are coming here in two weeks, and they are expecting to meet the woman I told them I'm falling in love with—you." He smiled and rubbed my cheek with his thumb. "I've already told my mom how crazy I am about you."

I nodded my head and smiled back. "I really want to meet your parents."

He kissed me again and rested his forehead on mine. "And I want you to meet them. I'm looking forward to introducing them to my *one and only* girlfriend."

I wondered if the other woman in his life knew where his heart was. "I think Suzanne is in love with you, too. She said some really hurtful things."

"Did you get her back?" He sounded hopeful.

"I got one good one in there. Marie got her a few times, too. It was like she wanted the challenge."

"I knew I shouldn't have left. That's why I didn't want to go downstairs."

"She would have gotten to me sooner or later. She seemed hell-bent on getting her point across."

He took my hand in his and held it to his lips. "Well, now you know *exactly* how I feel, so it doesn't matter what she or anyone else says. All right?"

I nodded in agreement.

"I told you I'm yours," he reminded. "I knew you didn't believe me! Do you believe me now?"

I felt silly for doubting him. "Yes." I laughed.

Ryan slipped his hand into my hair and held my face to his, kissing me passionately.

"Let's go get you freshened up," he suggested, rubbing his thumb under my eye. "You know, if you were on set right now, you'd have a team of makeup artists touching up your face."

"You speak from experience?" I asked while reapplying some eyeliner. I already knew his answer.

"Yes, it's true. I openly admit it. I wear makeup and lip color just about every day," he joked. "It's quite emasculating, although I do like the way my skin feels afterwards."

I could tell by his theatrical performance that he was trying to lift my spirits. Try as he might, I knew Suzanne was still down there, eagerly awaiting the result of her meddling.

"Wait, before we go, are you going to say anything to her?"

He sniffed. "I'm not sure yet. Do you want me to?"

"No," I quickly answered. Fear of another confrontation drove my response.

"Are you sure?"

I knew he would defend me if I asked him to.

"Yes, I'm sure. I think it would be best to just let it go."

"Then I won't say anything to her . . . here."

Ryan stopped at the bottom of my stairwell. He pulled me in and kissed me seductively. I couldn't help but smile.

"That's better." He grinned. Ryan took my hand in his and pushed the door open.

I noticed that everyone was sitting separated; actors were at one table and my friends were at another. Ryan set his plate down at the empty seat next to Pete. He pulled out a chair for me to sit down next to him.

"Tar, what would you like to drink?" Ryan asked, resting his hand on my back.

I attempted to get up and serve myself, but he leaned over me, holding me in place.

"A glass of wine, please?"

Marie was just about to take a bite of food when she flashed her eyes at me. She smiled at Ryan's actions.

"You okay?" she mouthed.

I nodded and smiled.

She let out a sigh of relief and shot a dirty look at Suzanne.

Pete stood up and held his glass in the air after Ryan took his seat. "I'd like to make a toast. To my lovely Tammy, for staying up until three a.m. making all this fabulous food, and to Taryn, for once again making the best steaks in Rhode Island. May we know how truly blessed we are having these ladies in our lives."

Pete leaned over and gave Tammy a nice kiss. He was so in love with her.

Ryan leaned over and whispered in my ear. "I am truly blessed." He kissed me tenderly.

Once everyone had finished eating and talking, Ryan and Pete were like the entertainment committee. Pete started a poker game with Kat, Ben, Shane, and Tammy. There was a lot of hooting and hollering coming from the big table. They were having a good time.

Ryan and I played pool with Cal and Gary. Marie and Kelly were busy talking up a storm at the corner table in the poolroom. Kelly was a huge celebrity advocate for breast cancer awareness and Marie had recently lost her favorite aunt to the disease. They were deep into their conversation.

The sourpuss twins were off on their own, text messaging and calling people. That was until Francesca got brave enough to separate herself from Suzanne and joined the poker game. Sure enough, Suzanne made her way over to the big table soon afterward. It was apparent that they were avoiding whatever room I was in.

Ryan never left my side, or should I say, my back. No matter where I stood, I could easily lean back and rest against him.

"Before I forget to tell you, I really like those boots," he whispered in my ear. "You're almost the perfect height." He pulled my hip back so I'd bump him and get his point.

"Do you want me to wear them later?" I teased.

"Would you?" he whispered seductively. "Every time you lean over the pool table, I just about go out of my mind."

I turned to him and looked him in the eyes. "Question . . . the first day, here, in the poolroom, were you looking down my shirt?" I whispered.

"Maybe, but only once or twice." He wet his lips and smiled. "I liked the lace that was on the edge of your bra. But what really got my attention was when you were leaning into the cooler. Those jeans you were wearing—yum." He took a deep, sultry breath. "Although the ones you're wearing now are definitely my new favorites. I'm looking forward to untying them with my teeth later."

"Just don't rip them. They were expensive."

He shrugged and scoffed. "I'll give you my credit card—go buy yourself a dozen more. Tearing those jeans off of you is worth every penny I have."

I dismissed his comment and continued our private conversation. "What about the distracting belly scratch? What did that do for you?"

He smiled bashfully while he chewed on his straw. "Do you really want me to answer that?"

"Yes."

He hesitated before answering. "I spent a few moments thinking about violating you on top of this pool table. Sort of the same thoughts I'm having right now, but now my thoughts are more from memory and less from imagination."

I heard something bump against the poolroom window, causing me to flinch. Since no one was near a window, it had to come from the outside.

"I think someone is trying to look in the window." I peered over Ryan's shoulder to see.

He grabbed my forearm and stopped me from getting any closer. "Don't," he warned. "Just ignore it."

"Ignore what? What's out there?"

"Paparazzi and fans. We've already been informed by our security."

"Do you have security outside?"

"Yes."

I tried to imagine it, picturing all their bodyguards and drivers just standing around outside in the cold . . . bored and hungry, waiting for the celebrities.

"Why didn't you invite the security guys inside? They could've at least had some food."

"No. Their job is to make sure we can relax and not worry about what they're worrying about."

"You're going to be seen leaving here no matter what," I said.

He ran his hand reassuringly over my arm. "Don't worry about it."

"But if you're photographed leaving in the morning?" I asked. I didn't care about me, I was worried about him.

He looked at me with a serious expression. "If I leave here tonight, the paparazzi might just think that I arrived first—alone—and that they missed me. If I leave in the morning, then the cat's out of the bag."

"What are you going to do?" It was his decision.

"I know what I should do. But what I *should* do is not what I want to do. If I leave in the morning, *they* are going to start following you." He motioned his head toward the window.

"What difference does it make? You've been here twice, and now there's a private party here. I'm sure the connection has been made."

"If I leave in the morning, that's it. It definitely begins. Are you ready for that?"

A few select words he'd said crossed through my mind: "I'm falling in love with you" and "girlfriend." Then I thought about the freedom that I take for granted every day. I would no longer walk around the Earth in complete anonymity.

"If you really meant all the words you said to me on the roof, then yes, I'm ready."

"Taryn, I just want to protect you. You know that, right?"

I nodded. I knew he didn't want me to be hounded. But how long could he, or would he, keep me a secret? I guess a little disappointment showed on my face.

"Well, we don't have to decide now. We still have a game to watch," Ryan said, giving me hope.

I turned the channel to *Sunday Night Football*. The familiar background music started to play and a few of the guys mimicked the tones.

"We're going to watch American football?" Suzanne whined.

Ryan turned and spoke over his shoulder. "We could call a car for you if you don't want to stay."

I smiled inside. He was being nice, but he really wanted to get rid of her.

"I can call for my own car, thank you," she snapped back. I was glad to see her use her cell phone.

I carried a fresh pitcher of beer over to the guys. They were all lined up at the table closest to the television.

"Gary, get your money ready," Ryan teased.

I filled Ryan's empty glass with beer. It looked tasty so I took a sip then handed it to him. He took a big gulp and handed the glass back to me.

"You get *your* money ready," Gary bantered back. "I already have one of your twenties in my wallet; just waiting for another one. Maybe you should give that twenty to Taryn to keep warm for me."

Ryan patted my leg. "Don't you worry about this twenty. It's nice and warm, and looking forward to having another twenty to be its friend."

He rested his arm on the back of my chair and whispered in my ear, "Let's do a shot."

"Preference?"

"How about that tequila we had that one time? Do you still have some?"

"Yeah. I think there's enough left in the bottle."

"Well, let's kill it. I'll give you money for a new bottle. That stuff was good."

Suzanne and Francesca put their coats on and then Suzanne announced their departure. Hardly anyone said goodbye to them. Kat yelled "see ya" very loud, but her tone was definitely more dismissive rather than a sincere goodbye.

I heard some screams coming from the waiting fans when they exited through the front door, but the screaming didn't last too long. Since the voices were female, the crowd outside was obviously waiting for actors, not actresses. My thoughts were that they were really waiting for one actor in particular to emerge.

I had known that the paparazzi were staked outside my building, but it was only when Suzanne and Francesca left that the number of them became apparent. The entire sidewalk and the full length of my exterior were illuminated by flashes from the cameras, completely lighting up the darkness outside my windows.

Once the two women were gone, it was as if everyone inside could breathe again. The men were getting loud, shouting at the football game, and the other women and I had to yell just so we could have a conversation.

My attention focused back on Ryan when I saw him talking on his cell phone. He didn't talk long, but whatever he heard pissed him off. He pounded his fist into the table. I watched as he leaned over and said something in Cal's ear. Cal just shook his head in disgust.

After everyone did a shot of tequila, I sat at the big round table with the ladies to play some cards. Kat was getting tipsy; she was so cute to watch as she giggled to herself.

"I'm glad the psycho twins finally left," Kelly announced. Her comment made me chuckle.

"Yeah, what's up with Suzanne?" Marie asked. "She's kind of like a bitch."

"That's an understatement," Kat laughed loudly.

"It's surprising; onscreen she and Ryan have such amazing chemistry. I thought she'd be nicer," Tammy said.

"That's because Ryan has the patience of a saint," Kat yelled in Ryan's direction. "We should call him Saint Ryan from now on."

Ryan looked over his shoulder and smirked at her.

"We all told him that if he'd just kill her already, we could go home. We even offered to bail him out of jail if he'd do it," Kat joked. "Right, Ryan? I'd bail you out of jail in a heartbeat, brother."

"That's why I check the clip in my gun before every scene." Ryan laughed. "I'm so paranoid that one of you are going to slip real bullets in there one day."

"And what about Francesca?" Tammy asked Kat. "She barely said a word to anyone."

"That's because Suzanne does the talking for both of them now. Sometimes we wonder if Fran is made out of wood and Suzanne has her hand up her ass making her mouth move," Kat said.

Ryan turned around, laughing hysterically at Kat's comment. He made a gesture as if he had a puppet on his hand.

"Francesca has issues," Kelly added. "At first she was really nice, but she developed this idolization of Suzanne, and then she became an evil clone." She lowered her voice. "Fran is infatuated with Ryan, or at least she was. I don't know anymore. We think since Suzanne was in a position to be close to Ryan, Fran started to mimic her—thinking it would attract Ryan's attention. It developed into this sickness."

"I'm still betting on the alien abduction theory myself," Kat added. "One more movie, and then we're finished with them. I am so not looking forward to having to hit the promo circuit with them again. It's going to be a freaking nightmare."

"Well, Suzanne said some harsh things to Taryn tonight," Marie added. "It's pretty obvious that she's got a thing for Ryan, too."

I looked down at the cards in my hand, displeased that she'd mentioned it.

"Taryn, she was a bitch to you. I wanted to punch her. Now when I see the next movie, I'm going to wish Charles would let her bleed to death in that cave."

I thought about Ryan having to go to work tomorrow. Would he say anything to Suzanne, or would he just ignore it for the sake of keeping his job? I presumed he would just keep his cool and do his scenes the best he could. It wasn't in his personality to invite confrontations.

I was glad he'd told me what he did when we were in the shower this morning. He was honest with me. I wondered if anyone else sitting at this table knew about his slip in judgment when he slept with Francesca. If they did, they certainly weren't going to bring it up in front of me. Kelly and Kat were above that.

I looked up at the television and saw that the Steelers had possession of the ball.

"Excuse me, ladies. I have to see this." I sat back down next to Ryan.

The quarterback had just thrown the ball for twenty yards and the Steelers' receiver was on his way to the goal. I stood up to cheer; Ryan stood up right behind me.

"Touchdown!" we both yelled. Ryan held his hands up in the air; I clapped my hands into his for a mutual high-five. The place kicker got the ball between the uprights for the extra point. Ryan gave me another high-five and a quick kiss. He was so happy, and seeing him happy made me even happier.

I noticed I was the only female even remotely interested in the game, but it didn't matter. I had everything my heart desired: great friends, new soon-to-be great friends, and the best man I ever could have wished for.

I stayed with Ryan until halftime. The Steelers were winning 21 to 7, Ryan was having a blast with the guys, and I was secretly entertaining thoughts of straddling him where he sat. The several drinks I had consumed further enhanced my naughty thoughts. I was feeling buzzed and completely aroused.

"Play me a song," Ryan whispered in my ear.

I looked at him like he was crazy.

"What do mean, play you a song?" I grinned and looked him in the eyes.

"On your piano. Play something."

"Why don't you play *me* a song?" I challenged. "My guitar is just up those steps." I pointed to the door.

"Oh no! I asked you first. Come on, just one." He stood up and pulled me off my chair, practically carrying me like a football over to my piano.

I lifted the cover off the keys and stared at them. I had no idea what to play. I played a few notes, hoping that a song would come to me while remembering all the songbooks I used to have.

I started to play a few notes and Ryan's face lit up.

"Journey?" he asked.

I nodded and began to sing.

Soon I had a gathering around my piano, all of us trying to remember the words. It was amusing to hear my friends sing off-key. Our rendition of "Don't Stop Believin'" ended horribly, since I couldn't remember all of the lyrics.

"How about this one?" I played a few notes.

It was karaoke night in Mitchell's Pub.

"Play that song you played that night," Ryan requested coyly. "Please?"

At his urging, I played "You've Got a Friend" again. This time I wasn't nervous.

Cal took Kelly in his arms and started to dance with her. It was such a beautiful sight. Pete twirled Tammy under his arm, and Ryan leaned across the top of my piano, smiling at me.

I sang to him and him alone.

We were all having a good time singing and laughing, until the police sirens sounded and the red and blue lights flashed in front of my pub. I immediately hopped up off my piano bench.

"Pete!" I yelled.

"I'm on it," Pete answered as he trotted out the front door.

I stood near the door waiting for him to return. It seemed to take him forever. I wanted to look out the window to see what was going on, but Ryan stopped me. Eventually Pete came back in but he wasn't alone; two police officers were with him.

"Pete, what's going on?" I asked, nervous. It had been a long time since I had cops show up at my pub. Usually they came after someone started a fight outside, but I had no idea why they were here now.

"Good evening, Miss," one of the policemen addressed me as he looked around at my guests.

"Good evening, Officer," I replied. "I'm Taryn Mitchell. I'm the owner here. What is going on?" Ryan stood dutifully behind me.

"We received a complaint about a crowd blocking the street traffic," the policeman said.

"As you can see, we are holding a private affair for our visiting guests." I looked at Ryan and Cal. Seaport was not a large community; I presumed that the dozen or so police officers we had on staff all knew that celebrities were in town.

The policeman looked at Ryan and nodded his greeting. "Mr. Christensen."

"Good evening, Officer," Ryan replied. He was standing with his arms folded across his chest. "My apologies for the crowd. Unfortunately there isn't much we can do about it."

"We will make sure that the street is clear. There are too many pedestrians on the sidewalk. We'll request that they disband, but they will surely regroup once we leave," the officer said.

"We appreciate your help," Ryan responded.

"Yes, thank you," Cal added.

"Would you like me to call in a request for a police escort when you leave?" the officer asked.

"I'm not sure. We have private security with us this evening," Ryan answered.

"Yes, we spoke to them outside," the officer said. "They are trying their best to keep it orderly, but we understand there is only so much they can do."

"We should be fine. Thanks for the offer." Ryan reached out to shake the officer's hand.

My heart rate was accelerated, but Ryan seemed to maintain his cool. Pete escorted the police out the door; hundreds of camera flashes lit up the darkness the moment the door opened.

I noticed that Ryan turned to walk away; I presumed he didn't want to be seen when the front door opened. He sat down in his seat in front of the television and started rubbing his forehead. His body language confirmed my suspicions.

I stood behind him and started rubbing his shoulders. I knew he was bothered by the mayhem outside and I wanted to take his mind off of it. How much pressure could one man take before he would crack?

Ryan leaned his head back and closed his eyes. "That feels good," he murmured.

I was trying not to get angry with the crowd outside for ruining our evening. I kissed his forehead, trying to soothe him. I didn't need to be able to read his mind to know the thoughts that tormented him.

Our guests stayed until the football game was over, but soon after that everyone proceeded to gather their things. Gary reluctantly handed over twenty dollars to Ryan, and Ryan graciously accepted it.

"I'm going to go back to the hotel with the rest of them," Ryan said. The sadness was evident in his eyes. "I really want to stay with you, but I think it's best if I go." His eyes flickered to my windows. "I have to be on set anyway early in the morning."

I wrapped my arms around his waist as he hugged me. "I don't want you to go. But I understand why you feel you must."

"Tar, they know I'm in here. Suzanne told the crowd on her way out," he whispered in my ear. "I want to make sure that all of our friends get out of here safely, and I'm not ready for the paparazzi to start stalking you, too."

Ryan turned to Pete. "Pete, Tammy, what do I owe you? Do you have a bill for the catering?"

Tammy looked sideways at Pete; she didn't know what to say.

"Ah, Ryan, Taryn paid us already," Pete replied.

"How much was the bill?" Ryan asked me.

"It wasn't that much. Don't worry about it." I couldn't help but feel a little sad that he wasn't staying.

"That's not what I asked." He sort of laughed, but I could tell he was annoyed. "How much was it?"

I just ignored him and started cleaning up.

"Why won't you tell me?"

"You know, Ryan, I thought you were smarter than that," Marie commented while piling up dirty glasses on the bar. "Taryn doesn't want you for your money."

I turned to her and grimaced.

"Besides," she continued with a laugh, "she's not hurting for cash, that's for sure."

I knew she was trying to make a point to Ryan, but I still gave her a displeased look. My wealth was something I didn't like to flaunt.

Ryan pressed his body into my back. "Sooner or later you're going to have to get used to letting me pay for things, you know that?" he whispered. "There's no way I'm going to allow anyone to think I'm taking advantage of you—you included."

"There's only one thing I need." I placed my hand on his heart. "The rest is just details."

"I'm not going to argue with you tonight, but this conversation is far from over." He smiled lightly and kissed me.

Several of their security team came inside the bar. Ryan had collected his things from upstairs, and he walked me over to the steps to my apartment so we could have a private moment in my stairwell.

"Thank you for doing all of this. You were a lovely hostess. Everyone had a great time." He leaned and gave me a very passionate goodbye kiss. "I'll call you tomorrow. I don't know if I'll be able to make it for poker—it all depends on when we finish."

I nodded and kissed him again.

We all said our goodbyes at the front door; I hugged everyone before they left and they warmly hugged me back. I'd made some very good new friends today.

Pete and Tammy were staying behind to pack up the leftover food while Marie and Gary helped me clean up.

Two security men walked out the door first; Cal and Kelly led the pack, Kat and Ben were behind them, and Ryan and Shane were sandwiched between three other bodyguards.

The screams from the awaiting crowd were ear-piercing and quite frightening. I took a few steps back, ducking behind Pete while we all watched the camera flashes light up the night sky.

CHAPTER 13

Windows

IT WAS CLOSE to one thirty in the morning when I crawled into bed. The memories of the last few days swirled in my mind in segmented but vivid pictures. I thought about the most important memory—Ryan's admission that he was falling in love with me, and how I'd admitted that I was falling in love with him. It was a huge relief to know that our feelings were mutual and I could now let my feelings for him run free.

I could see that it might be difficult to maintain a healthy relationship with him, but would it really be so different from having a relationship with any other man? No matter whom I got involved with, it would take patience and understanding for love to survive—two qualities that I knew Ryan possessed.

Being in his world, the world of public fame, would take some getting used to. But I was more than willing, after today, to get going on that next part of my life. I could easily see myself by his side, supporting him in his adventures. But by the same token, I did not want to repeat past mistakes; in particular, the mistake of giving up who I was to be with a man.

I thought of what I might have to give up in order to be with Ryan. Would I have to sell the bar? Maybe I could keep it and have someone else run it for me. I would still want to maintain control to ensure that the Mitchell name remained untarnished.

Maybe Ryan would want to live in California like Cal and Kelly. He said that my rooftop was his new favorite place in the world, but would it be his favorite place forever? Would I want to stay in this same apartment forever, too?

When I was engaged to Thomas, it was expected that we would stay in my apartment above the bar. That was the plan, considering Thomas wasn't coming into the relationship with much to offer. But I had always hoped for more—perhaps a nice farmhouse on a secluded piece of property with mature trees large enough to hold a tree house. A place where my children could run free and play with the family dog. Somewhere I could grow a garden and plant flowers.

What about my friends? Would I have to say goodbye to the friends I'd had for most of my life? My parents were gone; I had no siblings, no real ties to Seaport other than the fact that this was where I called "home." It was my safe haven in a world of uncertainty.

Ryan's presence in my life had generated a whole new list of questions for me to ponder. I wanted a life with a partner in it, and Ryan was appearing to be as close to perfect for me as one man could ever be. He was a guy's guy, rugged and manly, but he was also loving and tender. He wasn't selfish, like Tim, and he wasn't opposed to love, like Dean. And most importantly, one lady seemed to be more than enough.

I loved the way he took charge of situations, too. The way he'd spoken to the police this evening—it actually turned me on. He wasn't the type to take a backseat to anyone. He was strong and could handle himself, and he had demonstrated on more than one occasion that he wanted to take care of me. His actions were natural—as instinctual as breathing.

The more I thought about it, the more I decided that whatever path life would take me on would be worth it, as long as Ryan was by my side.

I nestled under my covers; a smile crossed my lips when Ryan's voice uttering the words "I'm falling in love with you" echoed in my mind. I let sleep take me under with that being my last thought.

I just about leapt out of my skin when my alarm system went off. A surge of adrenaline coursed through my veins, and I ran to my bedroom door and locked it. I looked at the clock; it was almost five. Not more than thirty seconds passed before the alarm company called my cell phone.

"Hello, this is Taryn Mitchell," I breathed into the phone.

"Ms. Mitchell, this is Jeff from Shield Security; we have indications of a breach in your building. Are you in the building?"

"Yes," I stammered.

"Are you secured?" he asked.

"Yes, I've locked myself in my bedroom." My heart was pounding; the alarms were blaring.

"Sensors are indicating a window on your first floor. We have alerted local authorities. The police have been dispatched; their ETA is four minutes. I will stay on the line with you until authorities arrive. Are you in need of medical assistance?"

"No. I'm fine. Scared, but fine." I was trembling as I put some clothing on.

"Ms. Mitchell, the police have arrived. They are unable to get inside."

I unlocked my door and crept out into the hallway. I could hear the police banging on the front door.

"I'm going downstairs to let them in," I informed him.

As soon as I opened the front door, the police quickly escorted me out of my building so they could do a sweep for an intruder. I was shaking like a leaf when they sat me inside a patrol car.

Another patrol car came speeding down Fourth Street, red and blue lights blazing. I believe every cop on duty in Seaport was there. After what seemed like an eternity, an officer came to the car. I recognized him as the same officer who'd come into my pub when Ryan and our guests were here.

"Miss, my name is Officer Carlton," he said.

"Yes, Officer. You were here earlier."

"Yes ma'am. We've searched your facility for intruders. No one is inside. It appears that a large rock has been thrown through your front window. There are no other signs of forced entry."

I just nodded. I was freezing and scared shitless.

"Is there someone you can contact to help you? You will need to board up your window. We are going to take pictures of the scene first and I'll need to take a statement from you."

I still had my cell phone in my hand.

"Pete?" my voice cracked.

Pete and Tammy arrived about thirty minutes after I called.

"Tammy!" Relief washed over me as I hugged her.

"Taryn, are you okay? What happened?" she asked.

I repeated my story. Shattered glass was all over the table and booth, and the impact took down one of my neon bar signs.

"In all the years we've had this pub, this is the first time we've ever had any vandalism. I don't understand." I shook my head. I tried to imagine why someone would hurl a rock through my window. For a brief moment, I wondered if it was some obsessed fan that did it.

Tammy and I held the sheets of plywood in place while Pete boarded up the window. The sun was starting to rise; in another hour or so I'd be able to call a contractor to come fix the glass. I also needed to get the insurance company involved. *All this hassle for what? I hope that whoever threw the rock got whatever was bugging them out of their system.*

Tammy stayed with me while Pete went to work. I felt horrible for getting him out of bed so early. He'd only had four hours of sleep, if that.

"What would be the motivation for someone to do this?" I asked, pouring shattered glass into the plastic garbage can.

"I don't know. It's so senseless and juvenile," Tammy muttered.

"Do you think I was targeted?" I wondered.

"I hope not. Are you thinking it was a fan or something like that?"

Apparently I wasn't the only one to have that thought. I nodded my head in agreement.

Ryan's fans were obsessed; I wouldn't put it past one of them to do something like this. After all, the first day I met him, one of his fans had gone beyond admiration and moved toward assault.

"Well, at least I know that the security system is working. The security company called me within seconds of the alarm going off."

After we finished cleaning up, I gave Tammy a ride home. We'd made it only four feet outside my building before the paparazzi descended on us and the cameras started to click. There were eight or nine of them, and they already knew my name.

I concentrated on the keys in my hand and the cracks in the sidewalk as we hurried to my car. Just like Ryan had warned, they started prompting me with questions.

"How's Ryan? Are you his girlfriend? Taryn, to your left—look to your left. What was the occasion for the party? What happened to your window? Are you and Ryan Christensen dating? Taryn, look over here. You're beautiful—I can see why he likes you."

I unlocked the car doors and Tammy and I jumped in as fast as we could. The photographers were still taking pictures as I backed out of my parking space.

"Oh my God, Taryn. I'm freaking shaking," Tammy stuttered as I drove down Mulberry Street. Her hands *were* trembling.

I was shaken as well, but not as much as I thought I would be. Maybe because I had mentally prepared myself for this, it didn't affect me as severely as I'd imagined it would. The thought of Ryan being proud of how I'd just handled myself with the paparazzi flashed through my thoughts.

I dropped Tammy off at home and returned to my parking spot a block away from my pub. The paparazzi had mostly disbanded, but there were still three of them lingering by my door. I didn't smile at them or acknowledge their presence; they were blood-sucking leeches in my book.

I locked myself inside and waited for the insurance adjuster to arrive. I thought about calling Ryan but resisted. It didn't matter; he called me anyway. I refrained from telling him about the window while he was still on set filming. He needed to focus, and I certainly didn't want to add another piece of stress to his life. I decided to wait to tell him about the window until he was back at his hotel.

After a few phone calls, poker night was cancelled. Everyone seemed fine with staying home, although Tammy and Marie both offered to come stay with me. I thanked them but declined. I was fine playing my guitar by myself.

"Are you still playing poker?" Ryan asked when he called at eight o'clock. I was surprised that he was in a good mood, considering he was on set for almost thirteen hours.

"No, we're not. Everyone decided to stay home."

"Everyone still tired?" he asked, slightly chuckling.

"Well, sort of. I didn't want to tell you earlier while you were filming, but someone hurled a rock through my front window at five o'clock this morning."

"What?" he bellowed. "Which window—upstairs or downstairs?"

"Downstairs. It was the middle window, with the Mitchell's logo. The whole window shattered into pieces."

"Are you okay?" I could hear his concern.

"Yeah, I'm fine. I was scared to death when my alarms went off, but the security company called the police right away. So I had the cops here . . . again," I sighed. "The officer who came earlier was the same one who took my statement."

"I should have stayed," he said.

"It's okay. I called Pete. He and Tammy came right over. Pete boarded up the window with a couple of sheets of plywood and Tammy helped me sweep up the glass." I rubbed my eyes and yawned. "I called my insurance company and a glass contractor. The glass will get replaced on Wednesday."

"Tar, I'm sorry," he whispered.

"Nothing for you to be sorry about," I quickly replied.

"If I would have been there, I could have boarded the window myself," he said with authority.

As much as I wanted to believe he sincerely meant what he said, I couldn't picture him out there at six in the morning boarding up my smashed window. The paparazzi would have had a field day with that scenario. But I knew he meant well.

"I still would have had to call Pete. I don't have any plywood lying around. Pete is working on his house—I knew he had a few sheets on hand."

"I've got to call Pete and thank him. He's a good man and a good friend."

I was pleased that Ryan said that. It made me happy that he considered Pete his friend, too.

"Did you pay him for the plywood?" Ryan asked.

"No. Shoot. I didn't even think to offer. Now I feel bad. It was so early when it happened and I wasn't thinking. But I will, now that you mentioned it."

"No. I'll take care of it. I'll call him tomorrow."

"Why would you do that? It was my window that was smashed."

"Taryn, just let me do this. I'm a little mad that you didn't tell me earlier."

I sighed. "I didn't tell you because you need to stay focused while you're working. Besides, I figured you had enough on your plate dealing with Suzanne. I could just tell in your voice when you called earlier that she was giving you a hard time."

"She was," he chuckled. "Fortunately, she can be quite professional when the cameras are rolling."

"Did you say anything to her about yesterday?" I asked, wondering if he'd confronted her.

"No," he admitted. "Tar, I didn't want to start anything. I hope you're okay with that."

"Yeah, I'm perfectly fine with it, actually. It's not worth the tension."

"That's what I thought. Besides, you know how I feel about you," he whispered.

I smiled. "Yeah, I suppose I do."

"Speaking of which . . . what are you up to?"

"I'm just sitting here playing my guitar and listening to music," I said as I played a few chords.

"Want some company?"

"Race you to the back door?" I joked.

He never even said goodbye. I heard a faint click when he hung up on me.

I waited by the back door for him. The Lexington Hotel was only three blocks away. I smiled when I saw him finally turn the corner.

"Phew," he sighed. "I'm out of shape." His breathing was slightly labored from jogging. "I had to take the long way because the paparazzi are camped out by the hotel."

"Which way did you go?" I asked.

"I snuck out the door by the swimming pool and went down the boardwalk a block. I told one of the hotel workers that I wanted to go for a jog, so he gave me a key to get back through the door to the indoor pool." He grinned, showing me the key. "Only cost me one autographed poster."

I laughed. "I wondered what took you so long."

"Hug me, I'm all sweaty," Ryan joked, wrapping his arms around me.

He tossed his jacket onto the living room chair and immediately picked up my guitar. "So, what were you playing?"

"Nothing, really."

He started to play a little bluesy tune. "I miss my guitar. I wish I had it with me, but I had it sent to my mom and dad's after the last press tour. I'm always afraid it's going to get damaged or stolen."

"Why don't you have your parents send it out here?" I suggested.

"I thought about it, but it can stay with the rest of my stuff. All my worldly possessions are in boxes in my parents' basement."

"I remember you telling me that you used to have an apartment out in L.A. So you don't have a place there anymore?"

"No. I packed up all my stuff before I started filming the first *Seaside*. I figured I'd be on location for seven, eight months . . . between filming *Seaside* and then *Reparation* right after that, what was the point to keep it all there? Besides, I have no desire to live in California anymore. I was planning on moving back to the East Coast anyway. I told you that, didn't I?"

I was glad to hear him say that he wanted to live on this side of the country again.

"Yeah, you did." I nodded.

"Hey, isn't there supposed to be a music store around here somewhere? One of the PAs said he saw a sign on one of the buildings nearby."

"There used to be, but it has been closed for a while now. There's a big music store about thirty minutes away, though. Why? You want to go there sometime?"

"I was thinking I'd just buy a new guitar," he said casually. "One of these days, if I can ever get there." He grinned. "Or I can just steal this one from you." He strummed my guitar with more force. "It has a great sound."

"I have a better idea—why don't we just keep it here where it's safe and you can visit it whenever you'd like. How does that sound?" I joked.

He wrinkled his nose at me.

"So, what's a PA?"

"Oh, it's short for production assistant," he said, as if I was supposed to know what their job was.

"And they do what?"

"All sorts of things." He shrugged.

"That clears it up perfectly," I said sarcastically.

"They work for the ADs." He grinned, knowing he was messing with me.

"Oh. So they must NBC the BFFs on HBO with LOLs, right?"

He started laughing hard. "Exactly!"

"Got it. It's all clear as mud now."

"Okay," he retreated. "Are you ready for your next lesson, Ms. Mitchell?"

He stopped playing my guitar for a moment. "AD stands for 'assistant director.' They're responsible for stuff like the shooting schedule—you know, what we're doing for the day. They also track our daily progress, making sure that we're keeping up with the overall production schedule. Some of the ADs make sure the cast and crew is where they're supposed to be—stuff like that. The PAs, or production assistants, really do all sorts of stuff. Some work with the film crew; others are running stuff around the set, delivering paperwork or telling me to get out of my trailer. I couldn't even begin to tell you how many ADs and PAs we have on this film—loads."

"So when is the quiz?" I asked jokingly. "I'd like some advance warning so I have time to study first."

"Soon. Very soon," he said, strumming over the strings to croon his words. "I haven't decided whether it will be oral or written, though." I definitely picked up on his hints.

The more he continued to play my guitar, the more I was willing to go along with just about anything he suggested. I liked the little facial expressions he made when he played—how his eyes would scrunch closed or his lips would twitch to the beat.

My eyes traveled down the tendon in his neck; how tasty it looked connecting to his collarbone! His gray T-shirt obscured the rest of the view. I just about lost my mind when he licked his own lips.

"Here you go," he said, handing me the guitar. "Your turn."

I was so dazed by my own thoughts that I just sat there like a lump for a few seconds.

"What?" he asked, looking at me funny. I knew I was supposed to reach for the guitar, but my arms didn't respond.

"Here . . . play," he kindly urged.

When I regained the use of my limbs, I played a favorite song of mine, but my fingers messed up. I tried to start over, getting the chords right the second time.

Ryan wrapped his fingers around the neck of my guitar and removed it from my lap. He carried it over to its stand. Talk about a subtle hint. I guessed I'd really butchered the song.

"I'm sorry," I muttered, abashed by his actions. "Was I *that* bad?"

He shook his head and pulled me up from the couch by my hands. Without saying a word, he scooped me up in his arms and kissed me as he carried me down the hallway.

IT WAS still dark in my bedroom when Ryan's cell phone alarm beeped. I felt him stir, rolling over to stop its chime. I opened my sleepy eyes and looked at the time; my alarm clock displayed 5:30.

Ryan let out a groan and sat up on the edge of the bed, retrieving his clothing from the floor.

I ran my fingertips down his spine to let him know I was awake.

"Morning, sweetheart," he uttered quietly. He leaned back against me and kissed my lips softly, sweeping my hair off my cheek.

I brushed my hand over his defined chest.

"I have to get going," he said with a frown.

"I know," I whispered, saddened by the thought.

I turned the security alarm off and peered both ways down the darkened alleyway. Each end of the narrow road was illuminated by streetlights. It appeared that the entire town, including the birds, was still sleeping. "I don't see anyone out there. The coast looks clear."

"Okay. I'll call you later." He hugged and kissed me goodbye.

I crawled back into bed and pulled his pillow to my chest, enjoying the soft scent of his cologne that still lingered on the pillowcase.

"YOU'RE WHISTLING," Marie said as she tapped a pitcher of beer for a waiting customer.

"Sorry. I'll stop," I apologized, fearing it was annoying. "That will be two dollars, sir." I smiled at the older gentleman that I'd just served.

Marie's eyes glared at me. "Whistling? Extremely good mood? He was here last night, wasn't he?"

I couldn't hide my smile. "Maybe."

"No wonder you turned me down when I offered to come over." She nudged me in the shoulder.

"It wasn't planned, believe me."

"When he calls, ask him what he did with all the cobwebs that were growing between your legs. We need to make more hats for the needy," she said dryly. "Or did he call you already today?"

I smirked, secretly acknowledging that I'd spoken to him at lunchtime and again mid-afternoon.

Marie grabbed my elbow and uttered her words privately. "If you screw this relationship up, I swear I will kill you myself."

"Believe me, I'm trying not to," I said, returning to washing a few dirty glasses in the sink.

"So are you seeing him later? I could close for you if we're not that busy."

I wished I could take her up on that, but Ryan had other obligations.

"He's catching the red-eye to Newark tonight. He has an interview and a dinner meeting in Manhattan tomorrow."

Marie gave me a questioning look.

"He's doing a little press for his last film," I explained.

I saw the light bulb go off in her head. "Oh, *Reparation,* right?"

I laughed lightly at the absurdity of her knowing so many details about my boyfriend's life.

Ryan, of course, called me later that evening.

"So, are you all packed for your trip?" I asked.

"Almost. I'm packing right now. I wish I didn't have to go to Manhattan, but at least it's a short flight from here. You found my schedule, right?"

I smiled. Ryan cared for me to the point that he wanted me to know his entire schedule, and this was the second time he'd asked me if I had it.

"Yes, I posted it on the refrigerator. Hopefully you can slip through the airport unnoticed."

"That's the plan."

I grabbed his schedule to review it again. Wednesday morning he had an appearance on an early morning show at seven. At one p.m. he had a photo shoot, and then last on his agenda was a dinner meeting with his manager and some producer later that evening.

He had an early flight back to Rhode Island on Thursday morning.

"This schedule says you have to be back on set on Thursday. Jeez, did they even factor in a bathroom break here anywhere?" I groaned. I wondered how he could stand living such a hectic life.

He laughed. "No. I have to hold it."

"According to this schedule, it looks like you can go to the bathroom on Saturday around eight p.m."

"I'll have to reschedule that. I'm hoping to have other plans," Ryan stated, as if we were having a business meeting.

"The interview on Wednesday is really early in the morning," he groaned. "That's going to be the killer."

"Do you know what questions they're going to ask, or do they just spring them on you?" I inquired. I pictured him having to answer on the fly and how nerve-wracking it must be to come up with coherent replies.

"Sometimes they give you an idea of what they're going to ask, but most of the time it's just unscripted banter. Every one of these interviews is pretty much the same. Tell us about the movie, what's it about, how does it feel to be playing that character. It's all quite mundane."

"That is, until they ask you those uncomfortable, personal questions," I joked. "I noticed you rub your forehead when you don't like the question."

"I do what?"

"You rub your forehead. When you get uncomfortable or upset, you rub your forehead. You probably don't even realize you're doing it." I couldn't help but tease him.

"'So tell us, Ryan . . .'" I started, using my best fake talk-show host voice. "'All the women in the audience want to know what type of underwear you're wearing right now.' Or . . . 'Everyone wants to know if you are dating someone.' You squirm in your chair and then you rub your forehead. It's your *tell*."

"My what?" he laughed.

"Your tell, you know? Like when you're playing poker? It's that unconscious movement or action that lets everyone know you're bluffing."

"Oh, *tell*. Yeah, I know what that means. Great, now I'm *really* going to be self-conscious onstage. Not only do I have to worry about the stupid questions and my mumbling answers, I'll be worrying about touching my face and giving my secrets away."

"I'm sorry, I didn't mean to make it worse." It was hard to plead and suppress a laugh at the same time.

"I suppose I need a new gesture, then, huh?"

"Why don't you rub your middle finger across your eyebrow if you don't like his question? That ought to be good for ratings."

He was laughing too hard to reply.

"See, you like my ideas." I laughed with him.

"Yeah, I do. But I also recall you did the same gesture to me once."

"Well, pick another one, then. But you'll have to let me know what your new gesture is so I can watch for it."

"Let me think about that for a minute. There are so many subtle movements I could make that no one would notice. I like this. It's so evil. Okay, let me think . . .

"All right, I got one. I'll scratch my chin if I really want to tell him to go to hell. How does that sound?"

I laughed. "Sounds good. No one will even notice. So what does rubbing your forehead and scratching your chin at the same time mean?"

"Don't be a smart-ass," he bantered back. "And if he asks me if I have a girlfriend, of course I have to deny it to keep my private life a secret, but how about I'll touch my nose with my finger so you know I'm lying?"

I felt my heart skip a beat when he said the word *girlfriend*.

"So, you have a girlfriend? Do I know her?" I asked, fooling with him.

"Don't make me hang up on you," he threatened.

"No, I really want to know. Is she hot?"

"No, she's not hot." He paused before changing his tone. "I'd say she's more . . . irresistibly beautiful and incredibly sexy than hot. And I'm insanely crazy about her, so watch what you say."

"Wow," I breathed out as I felt my face flush. "Good thing I don't know her. I'm getting really jealous."

"Well, if you really feel the need to confront her, go look in the mirror. I'll wait."

I didn't know what to say. I was completely astonished. My mouth was hanging open like a fish out of water.

"Why, Ms. Mitchell, are you speechless?" he teased.

"Yes. Completely."

"Good. Now while you're stunned into silence, I'm gonna get going. I want to try and sleep for two hours before I have to fly."

"Okay, have fun, and be careful in New York."

"I'll try. I have off Sunday and Monday, if I read the schedule right," he yawned. "I'm freaking tired. It won't take me long to fall asleep, even though I don't have my favorite pillow to wrap my arm around. But this weekend, I'm really looking forward to fixing that! I'll call you from New York when I get a break, okay? Good night, sweetheart. Pleasant dreams."

THE SUN'S rays were just starting to beam through my window when my alarm clock chimed. 6:55 A.M. flashed in large red numbers as my eyes adjusted to the light. Part of me wanted to hit the snooze button and enjoy ten more minutes of sleep, but the other part wanted desperately to see him again.

I felt I needed to connect with his celebrity life. I wanted to know what his life was like when he wasn't walking around barefoot in my apartment. If I was going to love him honestly, fully, and completely, I had to know all the facets of who he was and embrace them all equally.

I curled up on the couch and rapidly flipped through the channels until I found the right network for the morning show. I frowned when I had to endure several minutes of commercials.

As tired as I was, I could only imagine that Ryan was just as tired, if not more. I had the luxury of just waking up and lounging in my pajamas. He, no doubt, had already been up for an hour or so and was probably stuck in some makeup chair, having a team of stylists fuss over his wardrobe and hair while powdering his face to hide his sheen.

You poor bastard, I thought to myself as a smile broke on my face. *You're probably squirming in the chair right now.*

Of course they waited until the last ten minutes of the show to bring him out. The other forty minutes were coated in teasing pictures, video clips, and a few hundred "later on in the show" lead-ins.

Ryan smiled and waved to the audience as he made his way to the open chair on the stage. He was so freaking handsome in a dark tweed jacket over a dark gray button-down shirt that hung out over his pants. He had stubble growing on his face and he grimaced when the female audience screamed for him. A few women yelled "I love you" as he was taking his seat, and just as if on cue, he rubbed his forehead.

The host rolled right into asking those standard questions about his latest movie, and I laughed when he asked Ryan to tell everyone what the movie is about. He shook his head as he smiled and I could, as clear as a bell, hear the comments that were being made in his subconscious. He was right—every one of these talk shows was identical.

It was after the first commercial break when the host got to the million-dollar question—was he dating anyone. I flew off the couch and stood right in front of the TV, dying to know how he would handle answering.

Ryan's eyes looked down for a second and he chuckled a bit to himself. As he looked up at the camera he shook his head and stated with a dead-on poker face, "No, I'm not seeing anyone. I really don't have time to even talk to anyone."

And then he did it. With a cocky smirk on his lips, he raised his right hand and rubbed his fingers down his nose. His fingers then completed the motion by rubbing and scratching his chin.

I broke out into my own private hysterics.

It was still early in the morning when Ryan called. He had finished the interview with just enough spare time before having to head to another studio to have his picture taken repeatedly.

"What are you doing now?" I asked while lounging in bed.

"Being photographed and filmed while walking down the sidewalk," he groaned. "It is exciting news, you know, that I can walk in a straight line. *Damn . . .*" he breathed out.

"What?" I froze.

"Ahh, I just dropped the papers I had in my hand. Great, they're taking pictures of me picking crap up off the sidewalk. . . . Yeah, hi, thanks, just one day."

I could hear the crowd around him asking questions and he was giving them quick answers. People were asking for his autograph over and over again and to take their picture with him.

"You've been here since two a.m.? You're crazy!" I heard him say to a female fan. "Tar—hang on a second."

"Ryan, Ryan, can I get a picture with you too?" "Ryan, over here!" It sounded like he was getting mobbed.

I heard what sounded like his security team instructing the crowd to back up and give Mr. Christensen some space. "No, you already got one from him," I heard a man's voice say.

"Why do you want me to sign this? It will ruin it," Ryan asked some fan. I heard a girl's voice begging him.

"Okay, you already got two autographs," the unknown male voice asserted again.

Eventually I heard a car door slam and he breathed out a sigh of relief.

"Marla, would you please hand me that soda. Thanks. . . . All right, now I can talk again. Sorry. This is unbelievable," he muttered. "Are you still there?"

"Yeah, I'm still here."

"I can't believe that girl wanted me to sign her violin! I should have said no."

I heard a woman's voice in the background talking to Ryan.

"Hey, it's not my problem if that's not her violin. And if it's damaged now, that's not my fault. Can I refuse to sign stuff if it's not a picture or a book or something?"

I couldn't make out the woman's response.

"Can you imagine what David would say to me if he got a bill for a violin? 'Your client ruined my Stradivarius.'"

I scrambled for something to say. "Hey, did you ever get a birthday gift for your mom?" I asked, remembering the circumstances that led to the day we first met.

"No. Shit . . . thanks for reminding me. I completely forgot."

"Well, while you're in New York, I'm sure you can find something nice there. Either that or you can find something when you get back."

"It doesn't matter. What should I get her?"

"Anything a man would hate to have to pick out on his own?" I joked. "I don't know . . . jewelry, perfume, a new purse? What do you think she'd appreciate?"

"Jewelry," he replied. "I've never gotten my mom perfume. I'm allergic to most of them. Let me take care of this now while I'm thinking of it. I have a dinner meeting at seven. I'll call you after that."

"Okay. Have fun." I was sad to hang up with him.

Later that evening, Marie flipped through the channels on the TV until she found the evening entertainment news. My attention was captured when, in the first minute of the show, they ran over the highlights of what was to come in tonight's episode and Ryan's picture was flashed on the screen.

I turned up the volume when his story was featured.

"Tonight's exclusive: Ryan takes on New York. The hot young star was spotted today as he was leaving the Good Morning America *show in Manhattan. The busy actor was caught multitasking, talking on his cell phone while signing autographs for fans. When asked how long he'd be in Manhattan, the sexy star replied 'just one day.' Ryan is in town to promote his latest film,* Reparation, *due to be released in April.*

"Later today he was spotted entering The Diamond Exchange on trendy Park Avenue, where he reportedly purchased several gifts. Look out, ladies! There's no denying his onscreen chemistry and reported hookups with his leading ladies. Rumors have been circulating that he's romantically involved with Suzanne Strass, who is starring again with Ryan on the second installment in the Seaside *franchise. Insiders have reported that the two have been quite friendly between takes. Perhaps things are getting steamy between them off-camera? We will keep you posted as this story develops."*

There he was—captured in moving pictures on my television. I noticed a tall, thin woman with short black hair hovering around Ryan while he signed autographs, and then I saw him sign the violin. I presumed the woman was Marla. She got into the sedan with him.

The world wanted any tidbit of news on his life, and he was recorded while on the phone that very moment, talking to me. A big grin flashed across my lips. Oh, how I loved my little secret!

"What are you smiling about?" Marie asked, breaking in on my private reverie.

"He was on the phone with me when that was filmed." I smiled, nodding to the television.

It was appalling how the gossip and news shows embellished flat-out lies about him and his co-stars. No wonder he had to be so careful. Any slip was fodder for the media, which was spread like wildfire and believed by millions.

I had *my* reasons for being hesitant, but now I had another reminder why he had to be hesitant, too. He was a constant moving target.

CHAPTER 14

Date

"SO WHAT ARE you up to?" Ryan asked when he called me on his lunch break on Friday.

"I'm . . . shopping." My tone was definitely mischievous.

He laughed lightly. "You sound like you're up to no good."

"Maybe. I'm hoping I have a date this weekend and I wanted to get something nice to wear. Hey, you're a guy. Let me ask you . . . do guys like really short dresses, or will a new pair of jeans work?"

"That depends. Where is your date taking you?" he snickered in my ear.

"Nowhere. He's kind of shy and *very* private. I'm happy to just stay home and keep him warm and safe. Maybe spoil him a little? I could probably get away with a little tank top and stilettos, but I'd really like to impress him. Do you have any suggestions?" I was thoroughly enjoying toying with him.

"How about a very small towel? I know most guys like when women wear towels. Something about the convenience of it that's appealing—you always have a place to dry your hands."

"Towels? Hmm." He'd definitely caught me off-guard with that one, but I was glad he was playing along.

"Oh look—Victoria's Secret is having a towel sale today. Imagine that. So in your expert opinion, what *color* towels do men prefer?"

"Color isn't important. The less snaps and fasteners the better. Towels should not be complicated," he said casually.

"You have a good point. This man I'm hoping to see lives a very hectic life. I'd hate to add to his stress level with additional complications. Maybe I'll just buy this snapless black towel here. Top it off with some thigh-high nylons, a thong perhaps, although panties are optional . . . and heels. How does that sound?"

"So what night is this date? I don't want to call you at an inconvenient time." I heard him laugh under his breath.

"I'm not sure," I replied. "He's a very busy man. But I'm going to get a variety of towels just in case he's dirty and needs to be washed. I'm thinking that might help reduce his stress level."

"You realize I'm due back on set in like twenty minutes? Do you have any idea of the damage you have caused?" he growled at me. "I have half a mind to leave here and break down your back door, but I'm afraid I can't go anywhere in public in my current state."

"I'm sorry. Did I *raise* your stress level?" I asked. "I just want to be clear about your current state."

"Very much so," he confirmed.

"Then I guess we're even." My fingers drifted over several lacy bras, imagining his reaction to seeing me wear something like this.

"Even? Tell me when I inflicted this kind of pain on you without finishing you off."

I thought about the first time he made my body tingle. "The morning when you played your song on my guitar. I definitely, definitely had an unsatisfied moment there."

"Really? Interesting. I would not have guessed that. It's good to know, though. You sort of had the same effect on me the other night," Ryan admitted.

"When?" I asked, surprised.

"Monday night when you played. Why do you think I took the guitar out of your hand so quickly? I couldn't think straight anymore." He laughed.

"I almost tore the guitar out of *your* hands that same night. I was thinking about chewing on your neck," I whispered seductively.

"Okay, so you have to talk about something else because I am *not* in good shape right now," he groaned.

"That's debatable."

"Stop," he pleaded.

I tried to come up with benign conversation. It was difficult, as I was walking through a lingerie store filled with naughty, frilly things.

"You sound exhausted," I breathed.

"I am. It's been a long day already and we're filming night scenes tonight."

"Crash in your trailer for a while," I suggested.

"You read my mind," he said. "Sometime between three and seven I'm turning my phone off to sleep."

I spent quite a few dollars on silk, satin, and lace in different hues. It had been a long time since I'd felt inclined to, for lack of a better term, dress to impress, so I got carried away while shopping—for him. My mind wandered over our conversation, and picturing that he was aroused because of it provided a lot of incentive to buy even more.

I also spent more than I would have liked to on two simple but tastefully adorable cocktail dresses: one was black satin sheathed in black lace and another in a unique shade of sapphire blue, just in case. My wardrobe seriously lacked formal wear, as there was never an occasion to get dressed up, nor had I ever entertained thoughts of going out in public with a man like Ryan. I also thought about meeting his parents. That would definitely be an occasion to look my best. I bought myself a lot of new things so I'd have new wardrobe options.

That night, Marie flipped the television back to the entertainment news, much to the dismay of several of my male customers who were enjoying watching the sports highlights. My heart sank when I heard tonight's headlines.

"Ryan's steamy Manhattan hookup" was all I needed to hear to send my emotions into a downward spiral. Pictures of him dressed in a suit with his arm around some girl were flashed all over the screen. She was young, attractive, and there, with him, in pictures. I was feeling the extreme burn of jealousy roll through me as my phone rang.

"Hi. What?" I answered. My voice definitely sounded perturbed.

"Taryn? What's wrong?" he asked. "Are you okay?"

"No, not really," I grumbled.

"Why? What's going on?"

"Marie turned on *Celebrity Tonight*," I muttered.

"I should have warned you."

"It doesn't matter." The damage was already done.

"Yes, it does matter," he breathed out. "You can't believe anything you see or hear about me. Please. You promised. The girl in the picture is the daughter of the producer. I told you he brought her to dinner."

"No, Ryan—stop. Just stop . . . please," I whispered.

He breathed out a heavy sigh. "Then why are you so upset?" he asked point blank.

I just huffed in frustration.

"You asked me to trust you. That goes both ways."

"Ryan, stop. That's not why I'm mad. I just hate how the media embellishes the truth with lies. I wish they wouldn't say that kind of stuff about you," I sighed. I couldn't bring myself to tell him the true reason I was upset.

He laughed softly. "Tar, you know it's not true."

I knew why he didn't want me exposed, but at the same time I wanted to be by his side, supporting him. Maybe if the world knew he had a girlfriend they wouldn't speak lies. Maybe if it was *me* in those pictures . . . maybe if he just announced on the morning show that he was dating someone instead of denying it . . .

"I know it's not true. I'm trying. It's hard not to be a little jealous when you're pictured on TV with someone else," I murmured.

"Well, if you're done being upset," he said, unruffled, "I was wondering if you might like to put on one of your new dresses tomorrow night."

SATURDAY COULD not come fast enough. I made arrangements with Marie and Pete to take care of things at the pub and I was glad that I didn't have entertainment booked for the evening. Cory was working tonight with Marie, so the bar was covered.

Ryan had offered to send a car for me, but I didn't want to have to explain it or raise anyone's suspicions—especially the paparazzi's. I gathered that he wanted our evening to start off with a certain level of class, but he sided with me to keep it more secretive. We agreed that I would drive to meet him at the same parking lot behind the textile mill where I had once dropped him off, and we would go from there.

I slipped on my new blue dress over a matching blue strapless lace and silk bra and panties. The dress had delicate straps with rhinestone details where the straps met the satin top, which accentuated my curves. I decided against nylons and opted for bare legs and high heels. It was cold outside; my dress would be hidden for a while under a dress coat until we got to wherever we were going. My big reveal would have to wait. Our destination was dinner, but I had no idea where. That, too, was a secret.

When I arrived at the lot, there was a black sedan with tinted windows waiting for me. As I parked my car, a man I did not know came to my door and opened it for me.

"Good evening, Ms. Mitchell. My name is Richard. Mr. Christensen has requested that I keep your car secured until you return." He held out his hand for me as I exited my car.

"May I have your car keys, please? Your car will be delivered here upon your return," he assured me. "This way, please." He motioned for me to follow him to the sedan.

Richard held the sedan door open, and as I peered inside, the backseat was empty—all except for one long-stemmed red rose. My eyes flashed back to Richard; I was completely confused and I hoped he would give me an explanation. He smiled and motioned with his hand for me to get in the car.

There were two men sitting in the front seat: the driver and a larger man who I assumed was security, although he was dressed in a suit.

"Good evening, Ms. Mitchell," the burly man greeted me. "My name is Anthony. I will be escorting you safely to your destination tonight."

"Good evening, Anthony," I replied. "It's nice to meet you." My mind wandered with thoughts of where I could possibly end up tonight. *Where are they taking me?*

We drove south along the coast for almost an hour until the car turned toward the ocean. The sedan entered a marina and stopped along the docks, where several large yachts were moored. It was then that I realized for our first official date, Ryan had chartered a yacht. *Unbelievable!* I thought to myself as my personal bodyguard opened my door.

"This way, please, Ms. Mitchell."

We passed several huge yachts; they seemed to get bigger and bigger as we approached. I watched carefully where I stepped, for I was navigating the wooden dock in high heels and I was afraid to get a heel caught between the planks.

Anthony directed me to a slip, where we turned to board a stately yacht named the *Day Dreamer*. It was beyond magnificent. The rows of windows were black as night and reflected the waves that rolled into the docks. My heart was pounding with nervous excitement. I hadn't even seen him yet, and this was already by far the best date I'd ever been on in my life.

I crossed over the gangway to board the boat and as my eyes lifted I saw

Ryan standing there in the moonlight, waiting for me. He reached out his hand to take mine; he had the most beautiful grin on his face.

"Hey you," he sighed, then softly kissed me. I just smiled and shook my head at him in disbelief.

"What do you think?" he asked with a smirk on his face.

"This is unbelievable," I breathed out. "I'm speechless."

"Let's go in where it's warm." He led me by the hand through the ornate glass doors. Inside the closed cabin the lights were slightly dimmed, casting a beautiful hue on the marble and glass interior. The parlor was more elaborate than any five-star hotel could ever hope to be.

The tapestries and décor were all shades of brown and rust—so warm and inviting. Lush floral arrangements of roses and lilies adorned the tables and the air was perfumed with their scent. Soft, relaxing music played over the sound system.

"Can I take your coat?" Ryan asked, stepping behind me.

I slowly unfastened the buttons; his hands slipped the wool off my bare shoulders. He handed my coat to an awaiting steward, who disappeared quickly from the room.

I did a slow turn to face him.

"You are absolutely stunning," Ryan said softly.

He was wearing a dark suit and a white button-down shirt. It was the first time I'd seen him dressed up. He was freshly shaven and wearing that cologne that always intoxicated me.

"You're quite breathtaking yourself." I smiled back at him.

He ushered me toward the center of the yacht, where a magnificent staircase led to the upper and lower decks. Gilded mirrors and artwork hung from the walls. We passed an ornate bar and a small galley on our way toward the bow of the yacht.

The front salon was decorated in hues of blue and beige, with two semicircular sofas dominating the central area. The entire room was clad in windows allowing a panoramic view of the moonlit ocean.

Overlooking the bow was a magnificent mahogany dining table set elegantly with two place settings. Real silver, crystal stemware, white china, with an exquisitely tall bouquet of fresh flowers in the center; it was all too perfect.

"Good evening, sir. The captain would like to know if you are ready to depart?" one of the ship's stewards asked Ryan.

"Yes, please," he graciously replied.

The ship's engines hummed to life and I could see the crew pulling in the ropes that secured us to the docks. I walked over to the window to get a closer look as we departed the slip. The moon was almost full; fluffy clouds dotted the night sky, occasionally obscuring the moon from view. We would have a perfect night to be out on the ocean.

Ryan stood behind me; his hands rested on my waist as he softly kissed my bare shoulder.

"So, what do you think?" he whispered in my ear.

It was hard to form coherent words. "Very impressive for a first date."

"It's not our first date. If I recall correctly, *you* took *me* out on a boat for our first date," Ryan uttered. "Do you have any idea of how much I wanted to kiss you when we were out on the lake?"

"I was thinking about kissing you when we were on the deck, actually," I quietly confessed.

"I almost kissed you then, too," he admitted.

"Why didn't you?" I wondered, looking up into his eyes.

"I hesitated and you ran off." Ryan sighed, appearing regretful.

In a matter of moments, we were out on the open sea. The moon shone in the sky like a beacon illuminating our way.

"I really like your dress," he murmured. His hand swept my hair to the side so he could softly kiss my neck. I felt his tongue, then his teeth, brush and graze on my skin. My desire for him could no longer be contained.

I turned in his arms; our eyes met and our lips found each other's. His strong hands pressed me closer to his chest. He kissed me passionately. My fingers tangled in the back of his hair as the intensity of our kissing consumed me.

Slowly I slid my hands down the front of his shirt, across his waist, until my fingers found the back pockets of his pants. A soft moan escaped his mouth as I tensed my hands in his pockets; his warm hands held my face to his.

His kiss became soft and slower. I could spend an eternity kissing this man. Ryan pulled me into a warm embrace before releasing my lips from his. He had a smug grin on his face.

Our moment was interrupted when the steward came back in the room. "Excuse me, sir. Dinner will be ready in about fifteen minutes. Shall I bring you a bottle of champagne or would you prefer wine?"

Ryan glanced down at me. "Do you want champagne or wine before dinner?"

"You choose," I replied. I wanted him to make the decision.

"We'll have the champagne," he answered.

Ryan and I toured the yacht before dinner; we wandered down the stairs to take in the sights of the lower deck. Dark, rich woods and designer wallpaper covered the hallways that led to the staterooms. We took turns peeking into the various rooms; each room was decorated in different patterns and colors.

My eyes mischievously glanced at the door to the master suite, hoping to encourage him to steal away with me for a moment. He laughed before stating, "Tempting, so *very* tempting, but our dinner will get cold."

Our fabulous dinner was served in courses, and I was quite full after the prime rib. Everything was delicious; it felt like we ate for two hours. Dessert would have to wait.

After our plates were cleared, an older man wearing a tuxedo joined us in the salon. He sat at the baby grand piano that graced the port side and proceeded to play.

Ryan stood up and held out his hand. "Dance with me," he whispered.

He took me in his arms and placed my hand in his as he slowly turned us on the floor. His hand gently caressed the small of my back; he rested our entwined hands on his chest.

I whispered in his ear, "Thank you for the best date of my life."

He didn't comment. He just raised his eyebrows a bit and smiled at me.

I closed my eyes as our cheeks touched and rested together. Our bodies swayed to the music. And every so often, his lips would reach mine.

It was almost midnight when the ship approached the docks. As we disembarked the yacht, I noticed that the marina looked totally different. Anthony was waiting to escort us safely to our limousine.

When we drove out of the marina I noted that the name on the sign was different; this was not the same marina where I'd boarded the yacht, and we were headed northeast. Ryan gathered my hand in his as we sat in silence.

"Shell game?" I murmured.

Ryan just smiled and raised my hand to his lips.

I placed our hands on my lap and he started to draw random patterns on the inside of my thigh with his fingertips. I was smoldering in my own skin.

The limo pulled into the empty parking lot and I could see my car waiting with Richard standing guard. When we were at a complete stop, the driver and Anthony exited. I had anticipated my door to open a moment later, but it didn't. I glanced back at Ryan; he looked absolutely adorable sitting there smiling at me.

"I hope you had a good time tonight." He grinned confidently.

My hand was already gripping the door handle to let myself out. I was confused—was this the good night, goodbye time?

"What?" he asked, obviously noting my expression.

"I didn't realize that this was the end of our evening," I said, adding a hint of playful disappointment to my tone. "I thought . . ." I looked away. "I guess I thought wrong."

"I don't want it to be the end of our evening, but I don't want to assume either," he spoke softly.

"I thought I was the one assuming." I gently smiled. "Let's go." I motioned. "Drive us home."

As we exited the car, Ryan stopped to remove his bags from the trunk of the sedan. He gave me an impish grin as he shrugged. He was like the little boy caught with his hand in the cookie jar.

I felt a little self-conscious myself, considering there were three witnesses to our indiscretion. Ryan didn't seem to care. He relieved Richard of my car keys without a second thought and opened the passenger door for me.

"Pull down the alley," I instructed. "Then you can hop out."

"Son-of-a . . ." Ryan growled. The headlights of my car illuminated the alley, shining light on the photographers hovering around my back door. He quickly threw my car into reverse and backed out into the street. He drove down the street in front of my pub; paparazzi were staked out there as well.

He sped past them, barely pausing at the stop sign.

My eyes were focused on the anger on his face. "Ryan, just pull over," I said slowly.

He drove another few blocks and pulled into the parking lot of the local grocery store. He lightly pounded his fists into my steering wheel.

"Ryan, I'm ready for this, if you're ready to be seen with me."

He looked over at me; some of the anger left his expression. "Cat's gonna be out of the bag."

"They already suspect. They're back there waiting at my doors. I've been followed and photographed all week."

"I know," he said. "I've seen the pictures. You're all over the tabloid sites."

"They took my picture when I left tonight, too," I said with regret.

I looked down at my hands. Thoughts of him not wanting to be officially seen with me crossed my mind. After all, I was a commoner, a "nobody" in his world of fame. My insecurities started to surface when he didn't speak.

"It's okay. Just drive to your hotel. I'll drive myself home." Disappointment coated my words. My perfect date was quickly turning sour, even though deep down inside I understood. "Then you'll be safe."

"I'm not worried about that. I'm worried about *you*. Your life is going to turn chaotic, just like mine. The paparazzi are relentless. I feel like I'm throwing you to the lions."

"You're not throwing me, Ryan. I go willingly . . . if you truly want me by your side. But still, I understand why."

He took my hand in his, gently tugging my arm to get me to look at him again.

"They are going to hound you."

"So what?" I countered. "They've already started."

"That doesn't bother you?" His eyes scrunched together, assessing.

"They are annoying, but really, if something like that bothered me enough, I wouldn't be sitting in this car with you right now. The question is—does that bother *you*?" I uttered, barely above a whisper.

"Yeah, it does. But not for the reason you might be thinking," he retorted. "I'm afraid to take away your freedom."

He made it sound like he was sentencing me to solitary confinement. I just didn't see it that way.

I shook my head to disagree. "I thought you might be ashamed to be seen with me," I whispered.

"Ashamed?" He looked at me like I was being absurd. "Is that what you think? That I'll be *ashamed* if our relationship becomes public?"

I silently nodded my head.

He slapped the gear shift into drive and squealed the tires as he turned the car around.

Ryan parked in my spot in the lot. Photographers descended on us before we even got out of the car.

"Wait, let me get my bags first and then I'll get your door," he instructed.

We were followed all the way down the street as we hurried to the front door of my pub. The lights from the camera flashes in the dark were blinding and disorienting. It was like staring into strobe lights. I made the mistake of looking up at one of them when we crossed the street. Their intrusive questions never stopped either.

While I fumbled to get my key in the lock, one of the groupies asked Ryan for his autograph, to which he nicely obliged. I was surprised that several men wanted his autograph, too. They were prepared with glossy prints of him in hand. I recalled Ryan referring to them as "autographers" once.

I couldn't get the door opened fast enough. Ryan and I hurried through the door and he shut it with force to lock the insanity out. I started to panic slightly when I couldn't see the keypad properly to turn the alarm off. I had to blink repeatedly until I finally punched the code in. Then I set the alarm again to be *sure* to keep the insanity out.

"I'm seeing spots." It was hard to navigate through the darkness.

He chuckled lightly. "Me, too. No matter how many times . . . one of them still gets me in the eyes."

Ryan helped me with my coat, which he tossed onto the living room chair.

"I'm sorry for the way I reacted," he said, looking at me with apologetic eyes. "You need to realize that I only want to protect you."

"I know. I want to protect you, too," I whispered.

I slid my hands into the space between his shirt and jacket, skimming my fingers up over his shoulders. I didn't care that we'd just been hounded by photographers; I wanted to feel his skin on mine.

I combed my fingers into his hair; our kissing was intense and passionate.

The fingers of both his hands caressed the space between my shoulders. I could hear the metal teeth separate as he slowly unzipped my dress.

He raked his fingers across my back, peeling the dress from my body. I felt the satin when it landed around my ankles.

His eyes took in the sight of me as I stepped out of my dress. I presumed he liked the look of the matching silken lace ensemble I was wearing underneath—that paired with my high heels. His head swayed and his breath was rough before his open mouth locked onto mine.

I unbuttoned his shirt while he kicked his shoes off and opened his belt. My fingers slid over his bare chest, pulling his tucked shirt out of his pants. He shuddered ever so slightly under my touch.

In one quick movement he leaned down, catching my waist with his shoulder. His arm wrapped around my legs to hold me in place. I giggled as he quickly carried me down the dark hallway to my bedroom.

WE SPENT most of the day lounging in bed. In between the marathon sex sessions and a nap, we managed to shower. We even had breakfast in bed.

"So how do you deal with it?" I asked. I pulled the sheet up over my shoulder.

"Deal with what?" He looked over at me.

"Everything. The demanding schedule, the obsessed fans, the photographers, and still manage to make movies."

He laughed quietly. "I honestly don't know. Sometimes it feels like I'm having an out-of-body experience."

"Come on! Tell me!" I rested my hand on his bare chest.

He rolled his eyes a bit. "You have a schedule to follow, right? Every day you get up and you either go to work or you have other things you need to accomplish."

"Yeah, but I don't have people screaming at me."

"That's not true," he insisted. "I've seen people bark orders at you many times. '*I want sixty mixed drinks and forty pitchers of beer.*'"

"It's not the same." I disagreed with his comparison.

"How is it so different? You run a business, and with that comes dedication and responsibility. You have to be in front of people, some of whom you don't like, or don't know. But yet you smile and play your part. They expect something from you, and you have to deliver. If you truly think about it, we all are acting in one way or another."

I nodded; he had a point.

"Take for instance my brother. He has to travel a lot for his job. He's gone at least one week out of every month for a career that he doesn't like very much. He has to get on a plane and leave his wife, Janelle, and their baby girl, Sarah, all the time. Yet he *acts* out his part; he puts a smile on his face and he goes to work every day. That's what he does for a living.

"Acting is something that I really like doing. It's kind of easy for me to slip into another character and it's fun to explore what it's like to be someone else. And it's far from boring, that's for sure. If I had to sit behind a desk every day, I think I would kill myself. But for some people, sitting behind a desk is a dream job. To each his own, you know?"

"But what about the pressure?"

"What about it? Every job has its pressure. My pressure is just magnified because it's publicized. All the directors out there want to make quality films that earn millions of dollars at the box offices. That's what they get measured by. I get measured by my acting abilities and my public draw. The bigger those numbers are, the bigger my paycheck is! If you don't have an atmosphere downstairs that pulls in customers, your sales are down and you don't make money."

"I know all about metrics. Economics/Business degree, remember?" I replied. "I guess I'm just worried that the pressure might be too much for you one of these days."

He thought about my comment for a moment. "Do you remember how you felt after you sang onstage in front of all those people?"

"Yes."

"And how did you feel?"

"Petrified that I made an ass out of myself."

He smiled at me. "Okay, and when you played the same song in front of people last weekend, some of whom you barely knew, how did you feel then?"

"It was easier. I wasn't worried at all."

"And why was that?"

"Because I knew I could do it, for one."

"You had confidence. I guess it's the same for me. The more I get to act, the more confidence I have in *my* abilities."

"Yeah, but you could have all the confidence in the world and still cave to the pressure," I stressed.

"Yeah, I know. And I feel it some days. *You* know that. But I also have a million reasons to deal with it—millions." He smiled.

"So it all comes down to money?" I questioned.

"Well, we all have to earn a living somehow. My mom is the one who told me to join the drama club and my dad is the one who told me to get a job. I'm blaming them."

His comment made me laugh.

"You know how many years most people have to work to earn what I make in six months? One movie . . . millions."

"Yeah, but there's a difference between being comfortable and being greedy. Are you hoping to be one of those mega-rich mega-stars one day? You know—the ones who only have one name now? Brad? Tom?"

A tinge of fright struck me when I wondered if he would end up ditching me down the road so he could be the other half of a mega-couple. I had a comfortable amount in the bank, but I was far from mega.

"I'm looking to ride this as long as I can. Who knows, maybe one day I won't want to do this anymore. There are other ways for me to be artistic. Sometimes I look at my brother and envy him for what he has—a normal life and a family. That's one of the many reasons why I'm here with you now. You're my peace in all this insanity."

"Oh, I see. I'm just a piece for you," I accused jokingly.

"That's not what I meant and you know it." He tickled me.

"So what is it about acting that you love so much?" I wondered.

He rested his head on his hand and looked at me seriously. "You want to know why I like being an actor? It's actually a lot of fun. Okay, imagine this . . . next time you pour a beer, I want you to look like you're furious. Hold that look on your face—make sure you look at *that* camera—then walk five feet to your mark and hand the customer his beer. Wait until he takes a drink and then say your lines. It's that complicated."

"What are my lines?" I asked.

"Oh, you really want to pretend? Okay." He sat up on his elbow. "Your lines are 'I thought about killing you for a long time, Joe. Today I finally get my wish.'"

"What's my motivation?" I questioned, trying to get in the mind-set.

"Joe killed your partner . . . I don't know. Think about something that pisses you off."

I sat up and wrapped the sheet around my body. It was hard to pretend and be naked at the same time.

"Hey, what are you doing?" Ryan asked while trying to tug the sheet out of my hands. "I like that view."

I playfully slapped his hand away. "I have to focus."

"The script says that this is a nude scene," he insisted, pulling the sheet off of me. "Just ignore the cameras," he teased.

I rolled my eyes. Fighting him was a lost cause.

I thought about confronting the idiot who smashed my window with a rock—how I'd like to smash a rock through that person's window. I looked at Ryan and proceeded to glare at him.

"I thought about killing you for a long time now, Joe," I said coolly. "I'm just glad today is the day I finally get my wish. That wasn't beer you just drank. It was poison. If you tell me where he is, I just might give you the antidote."

Ryan flashed a big grin at me. "That was pretty good. I liked the improv."

I just continued glaring at him, hoping he would play along. His happy expression disappeared when I kept giving him the dirty look.

He pretended to pop something in his mouth.

"You forget, Peaches, that my agency developed that poison. Sorry to disappoint you, but I won't be dying today. You, on the other hand . . ." He sprang up and pinned me to the bed. His body straddled mine; his hands held my wrists to the mattress. His aggressive acting actually turned me on.

"I just might be inclined to let you live," he said persuasively. "But it all depends on what you're willing to do for your country."

"I'll never give in to you, Joe!" I said with conviction and squirmed under his grip. "You may be strong enough to take my body, but my heart belongs to Ryan."

He leaned down and kissed me passionately. I didn't know if we were still playing or if he was serious, but his kiss was definitely serious. He released my wrists and I tangled my fingers into his hair as his tongue swirled with mine.

"I thought your heart belongs to Ryan?" he snickered.

"It does. As does the rest of my body."

"Hmm." He smiled his glorious smile at me. "That's good to know. Now flip over so I can carve my initials back here."

I let out a shriek as he grabbed my rear.

CHAPTER 15

Dinner

"WE NEED TO get out of bed and get dressed," Ryan said, noting the time.

"Are you insane?" I asked. "I thought the plan was to stay in bed *all* day?" I was surprised that he wanted to go somewhere. Him of all people.

"We can't. We have dinner plans tonight." He was smiling in a way that worried me.

"We do?" I was confused. He hadn't mentioned having dinner plans all day. Thoughts of another yacht trip came to mind.

"Yep. I've been invited to Cal and Kelly's for dinner and I told them I would drag you along," he said while pulling on my hand to drag me out of bed.

"But, but . . ." I whined. I really wanted to stay in bed and avoid the photographers that were lurking about.

"I promise, we'll stay in bed all day tomorrow if it makes you happy." I noted the sarcasm in his voice.

"Oh yeah, like that wouldn't make you happy, too." I gave him a light shove. He grabbed me around the waist and moved me out of the way so he could dart out the doorway first, laughing on his way to the bathroom.

I had just slipped a white tank top over my head when Ryan came back into the bedroom.

"Nice!" he said. "Pants optional this evening?"

"Not wearing pants tonight." I put on a charcoal-gray sweater dress over my tank. The dress came down mid-thigh and had a deep V-shaped neckline and an attached hood. It was another new addition to my wardrobe.

I zipped up my black suede high-heeled boots to finish off the look.

Ryan gave me an odd look.

"Is this okay?" I asked anxiously, worried that he didn't approve. I knew the paparazzi were waiting outside to take our picture.

"Very much so." He nodded. "You look adorable. Very sexy."

Ryan dressed in his signature style, layering a long-sleeved steel-gray collared shirt over a white T-shirt and jeans. We sort of matched.

"Wait—before we go, I have something that would go great with your outfit." He unzipped his bag. He deliberated for a moment, making sure he had the right package before handing me a gorgeous gift bag.

"Here, this is for you. I got you a little something when I was in New York." His face showed his anticipation.

"Ryan!" I gazed at him lovingly, surprised that he'd bought me a present.

"Go on. Open it," he urged.

I peeked inside the bag; nestled in the pretty tissue paper was a black jewelry box. He stared at me expectantly as I lifted the lid off the box.

Inside was a silver necklace with two diamond-encrusted hearts twined together, one inside the other. I looked at him, bewildered.

"Ryan, oh my God. This is absolutely beautiful," I whispered, touching the pendant with the tip of my finger.

"I noticed you like to wear silver instead of gold, so I opted for white gold. Here, let me help you put it on." He took the delicate chain out of the box.

I lifted my hair so he could attach the clasp. While he struggled with the delicate chain, my nervousness made my heart beat faster. I felt his hands rest on my shoulders when he was finished. He pressed his chest into my back.

"Do you like it?" he whispered seductively in my ear. I felt his warm breath on my skin as he trailed the tip of his nose down my neck.

"I love it," I sighed, tilting my head even farther to enjoy his nuzzle. "You shouldn't have." His gesture had taken me completely by surprise. I turned in his arms.

He smiled at me and slightly shrugged his shoulders. "I wanted to. You look beautiful wearing my heart."

"Thank you." I reached to kiss him.

He picked the bag back up off the bed and handed it to me. "There's one more thing inside."

I looked at him, perplexed. I reached inside the bag and found another black jewelry box in the tissue paper. This one was smaller. I felt all the color rush from my face.

I opened the lid slowly. I gasped as my eyes took in the sight of spectacular diamond earrings, set in white gold as well. From the post, a diamond baguette led the way to where a diamond solitaire dangled below. The diamonds were at least a carat each.

"This is too much," I breathed out. I was suddenly feeling very lightheaded. "I can't accept these."

"Don't you like them?" His face twisted with concern.

"They're beautiful." I gazed at them, watching the diamonds sparkle in the light. "But I can't accept these. It's too much. You shouldn't have spent . . ." I could only imagine how expensive earrings like these were.

His fingers covered my lips. "If you like them, put them on. They're yours."

I stared at the box, unable to move my fingers. Dinner on the yacht, diamonds . . . it was too much. This man standing in front of me was not here because he was rich or famous. The only gift I wanted from him was the one thing that his money and fame could never buy—to be my one true love forever.

I snapped the box shut and handed it to him. "I can't. One present was more than enough. Please." I shook the box for him to take it out of my hand.

"Would you like something else? I could exchange them for a bracelet or something. Just tell me." He was trying to be accommodating.

"No." I gently smiled. "I don't want anything else. Please. This pendant was more than enough."

He looked confused as his eyes toggled between questioning me and looking at the little black box in his hand.

He shrugged and became slightly irritated. "I'm not going to even pretend that I understand this." He set the little box on my dresser.

We were instantly photographed the moment I opened the front door. Ryan and I hurried down the street to my car; we practically ran. I wished I had a closer parking spot, but my building was very close to the beach and most of the buildings didn't take parking into account.

Ryan had my car keys in his hand, and every so often I felt his fingers touch my back when I wasn't walking fast enough. As we crossed the street, we were surrounded by almost thirty people. We had photographers and fans filming us, blinding us with flashes of light. The cameras clicked nonstop.

Mixed in the crowd were several men begging him to sign glossy photos and a few obsessive female fans. They just hounded him. One girl with curly brown hair grabbed the sleeve of Ryan's jacket, pulling him off-balance.

"Hey! Please don't touch me," Ryan yelled, yanking his arm away. "Come on, this is not cool."

Everyone begged for photographs and autographs. "Ryan, Ryan, over here"—the words were chanted over and over again by the assorted intrusive menaces that plagued us.

I looked up to see the faces of some of his fans; they were mostly young women—twenty-somethings—but there were a few older women there as well. Even though he was with me, it didn't matter. It was as if I weren't even there to them. In some twisted way, I was actually glad the photographers were surrounding us; they provided a barrier between us and his female admirers.

I looked up at the parking lot long enough to see my car, but something was horribly wrong: white, red, and hot pink stood out against the stark black paint. When we got close enough, I was relieved but now angry; my car was covered with love notes, cards, and all sorts of paper. Notes to Ryan were stuck in the door handles and under the windshield wipers. My windshield was covered with crap. I quickly cleared the passenger side while Ryan grabbed handfuls of paper from the driver side, tossing it all to the ground.

I hopped into the car as fast as I could and locked the door behind me. The crowd was terrifying. The same girl who'd grabbed his arm pressed her hands on the driver-side window yelling "I love you" at Ryan. I noticed she had a big gap in between her front teeth. These people were scary and sick.

Ryan looked over his shoulder to back my car out of the spot, but we were surrounded by people on all sides. I tried to cover my eyes with my hand to block the camera flashes; the photographers were relentless.

"I should have called for security," he muttered under his breath. "This is fucking ridiculous. Move, already!"

He continued to inch back out of the parking spot until the crowd finally parted enough for him to back up all the way.

Even as we drove out of the lot, photographers ran alongside the car, continuing to take our picture. Ryan got my car out on the road and hit the gas pedal; my tires squealed from the power. He looked as if we'd just robbed a bank; his expression was a combination of panic, frustration, and anger.

"Are you all right?" he almost yelled at me.

"I'm fine," I stated calmly, looking over at him. "How are *you?*"

He shook his head and let out a big lungful of air. "Unfuckingbelievable."

This is exactly what I was referring to this morning in bed. How can he stand to deal with this craziness all the time? Today was certainly not the first day something like this happened to him. At what point do you tell yourself that the money and fame aren't worth it? Even though I was thinking it, I didn't say a word to him about it. I knew he was beside himself; it was clear that the turmoil was wreaking havoc on his brain.

"How do I get on the interstate from here?" he asked excitedly.

"Turn right in three lights." I tried to remain calm. "Do you have their address?"

Ryan locked up my brakes and made a quick right turn through one of the neighborhoods. I grabbed the seat with one hand and the door armrest with the other as he wove my car through the streets.

"We're being followed," he growled. "Don't let me hit any dead-end streets."

My heart was pounding and I was petrified.

"Taryn!" Ryan shouted. "Where to?"

"Left," I breathed.

He handed me a slip of paper that he took from his coat pocket. "That's where we need to end up. Direct me."

"Turn right at the gas station. Down there, get on the 103. See the sign?"

Ryan nodded. His lips were pursed tightly together. I could tell he was seething.

"Ryan, it's okay. There's no one behind us," I said quietly, patting his leg with my hand. As soon as I said it, a large SUV turned the same corner.

"Wrong!" he shouted, making a right turn through a red light.

"Make a left and then a right and get on the 103. It's a highway."

I felt the car accelerate even faster.

"Ryan . . ." I breathed and slid my hand onto his leg. We were going almost ninety miles per hour.

"I'm just trying to put some distance between us," he muttered. His tone was still irritated.

I looked over my shoulder and out the rear window. "Are we still being followed?"

"I don't know if I lost them, but I'm not taking any chances."

I entered the address into the navigation system; soon the computer was giving him driving directions. He let out a big breath of air; I noticed he'd calmed down a little. He dropped the speedometer down to seventy-five.

"You okay, babe?" I asked.

"Yeah, I'm okay." He smiled at me briefly and then patted my thigh.

During the next ten minutes of complete silence, I thought about all the crap we'd removed from my car and how it was just lying there in the parking lot. Even though I didn't want to know what his fans had to say in the notes, the fact that they were strewn all around my monthly rental space bothered me.

"Ryan, when we get back tonight, I need to pick up all that paper in the parking lot. That lot doesn't belong to me; I have to pay a monthly fee to park there and I can't leave my spot all littered like that."

He nodded at me. "I'll take care of it." With one call, he made arrangements to have Jason clean it up.

"Thank you," I whispered.

He loosened his grip on the steering wheel. "Did you talk to Marie about covering the bar while my parents are visiting?"

"Not yet," I replied. I had been putting that conversation off.

"Tar, please. Can't you take a couple of days off?" he pleaded. "I finally have a normal weekend and I really want you to be with me."

"What were you planning on doing?" I asked, wondering how I could be in two places at once.

"I don't know," he answered. "I was sort of hoping that you might have some ideas. I want to take us all out to dinner Friday night, though—someplace *very* nice for my mom's birthday. Do you have any suggestions of where we can take them?"

"I know a few nice restaurants."

"Just one request . . . some place outside of Seaport," he added.

"Have they ever been to Boston? It's not too far of a drive from here. There are some things we can do in Providence, too," I suggested, thinking it would be easy to take day trips and still work the bar at night.

"I know what I'd *like* to do this weekend." His tone was mischievous.

"And what would that be?"

"I'd love to take my parents up to the lake." He looked over at me and raised his eyebrows. "I'd love to take my dad out on the boat. Can we do that?" He was so excited.

"Ryan, it's Halloween. I have bands scheduled. It's one of my biggest weekends of the year. Let me see if I can rearrange coverage for the pub first, okay?"

We drove up the coast for almost a half hour, then turned into a gated beachside community. I was relieved to see the security guard on duty and a huge metal gate blocking the rest of the world from entering. I'd never known we had gated communities so close.

The homes were typical three-story beach houses, all placed very close together. The house that Cal and Kelly had rented was only three homes away from the beach. "This must be really neat in the summertime." I smiled over at Ryan.

"Yeah, too bad it's October," he said in agreement. I was glad to see that he was almost himself again.

He opened my car door and held my hand as we walked up the sidewalk to the front door.

"Hey guys, come on in!" Cal greeted us and took our coats.

Behind him, the most adorable little girl with long blond hair came running down the hallway. She hid behind her daddy's legs.

I peeked behind Cal and smiled at the little cutie. "Hi," I said softly, crouching down to her level. "You must be Cami."

She giggled at me and hid her face. "Cami, are you being shy?" Cal asked, tickling her head.

"Hi!" Kelly said as she joined us at the door. "Glad you could make it." She gave me a big hug.

"Thank you so much for inviting us." I returned her hug.

"Whyin!" Cami pointed at Ryan. Slowly she came out from behind Cal's legs.

"Come here, you!" Ryan scooped her up and kissed her on her cheeks before spinning her around in his arms to tickle her belly. Her giggles were precious. They obviously knew each other very well.

We walked through the front entryway and down the hall to the large family room that bordered the enormous kitchen. Something smelled wonderful. The house was decorated in shades of white, blue, and beige with hints of seashells and starfish; typical for a beach rental home.

"How was your ride over?" Cal asked Ryan.

Ryan set Cami down and looked at me before answering. "It was a bit crazy, but we made it. Taryn's car was covered with notes." He looked at me like he was guilty of something.

"You're kidding!" Cal said. "How the . . ."

"The pop were waiting for us when we got back from the marina last night—they were at both doors. And then when we left to come here, the fans were waiting as well. The paparazzi even chased us for a couple of miles."

Cal shot a quick glance at me. "How'd she do?" he whispered to Ryan, but I overheard.

"She did great. I was the one who flipped out."

Even though I was interested in their conversation, I was distracted by a pair of big blue eyes and a naked Barbie doll staring at me.

"Is that a Barbie doll?" I asked Cami.

"Uh-huh, wanna see?" She held the doll out to me.

"Hello, Barbie, my name is Taryn. It's very nice to meet you."

Cami giggled. "Her name not Barbie. Her name Dora."

"Dora? What a pretty name! It's nice to meet you, Dora. Dora, Dora, Dora, the Explorer," I sang, making Cami giggle at me again.

"How do you know the Dora song?" Kelly asked as Cami ran back down the hallway.

"There's not much else on at two o'clock in the afternoon. Sometimes I'd rather watch cartoons than the other choices."

Two minutes later, Cami came running back with another naked Barbie in her other hand. "Here, you be Beauty and I'll be Dora."

I took the Barbie into my hands and danced her around on my leg.

"Cami, don't be a pest," Kelly announced from the kitchen.

"Come on, Cami, let's take our dollies on an adventure." I danced the doll over to the kitchen counter where several large chairs were poised. "So, Beauty, does Mommy need help in the kitchen?"

"No thank you, Beauty. Dinner is almost ready," Kelly replied. "Does Taryn need a glass of wine yet?"

I answered with a wink and a nod.

"What about G.I. Joe over there? Do you and Malibu Ken need drinks?" Kelly teased.

I pulled out one of the chairs and my little friend was right by my side. "Would you like to sit on my lap? We can play dollies up here."

Cami just nodded her head at me like she was in a trance.

We played with the two dolls on the counter. "You know, Cami, when I was your age I loved playing with Barbies, too. I would sit in my room for hours, building houses and taking my Barbie for a ride in her car."

"You did?"

"Uh-huh! But my Barbie had clothes. What happened to your clothes, Dora?"

"Dora gonna take a bath," she told me, matter-of-factly. "And then, and then, and then, and then, she gonna brush her teef. See? Like dis. Open wide." Cami opened her mouth.

While the adorable little girl was showing me her teeth, a little squeaker of a toot slipped out of her bottom. "Oops!" she giggled.

"Did you sit on a mouse?" I asked her.

"No, I farted," she announced to everyone.

I couldn't stop laughing. Cal took her off my lap.

"Say you're sorry to Taryn," he said in between laughing.

"Sorry," she said in her beautiful little voice.

"That's okay, sweetie."

"Come on. Let's see if some little girl needs to go potty." Cal led her down the hallway.

Ryan stood behind me, rubbing my shoulders and laughing that I got tooted on.

"She got me good once. You remember that, Kelly? When we were filming the first movie, I had her sitting on my lap and I was tickling her and she peed all over me."

"Ryan, that was so funny, *none* of us could ever forget. And believe me, it's a rite of passage once you become a parent. I don't think there's a mom or dad on the planet that hasn't gotten peed, pooped, or puked on."

"Well, your daughter peed on me, and my baby niece Sarah has power puked on me already . . . guess there's only one more rite of passage then for me, huh?" Ryan laughed.

"It's not official until it's your own child." Kelly corrected Ryan's assumption.

"You mean all these other times don't count?" he whined.

Cami came running down the hall and ran right to my leg. I lifted her up and sat her back on my lap. "Are you all better now?"

She nodded her head. "I pooped."

"On the potty like a big girl?" I asked. Ryan stuck his head over my shoulder to get in on the conversation.

"Uh-huh. And, and, and my daddy . . . he wiped my bottom."

"He did? What a good daddy!" I said excitedly.

"Wanna see my toys?"

"We're going to eat dinner first, Cami," Kelly said as she took the little girl off my lap. "Sorry about this. I couldn't find anyone to babysit her."

I waved a hand and smiled. "Don't worry about it."

We all took our seats at the dinner table. Cami insisted on sitting next to me. She was my new best friend.

"We'll have fun later, I promise," I said to Cami. "But first we have to put some yummy food in our bellies. Then maybe you can show me your toys."

"Ooh, pwetty!" Cami had my new necklace in her hand. "Hearts. Can I have it?"

"Cami, no. That's not yours," Kelly reprimanded her.

"I think it's pretty, too," I whispered to Cami. "I like the way it sparkles."

I looked over to Ryan and smiled. He was grinning at me again.

Cal and Kelly covered the table with a variety of gourmet foods that smelled divine. They were almost too pretty to eat.

"Kelly, everything is delicious." I complimented her while trying a taste of each selection.

"Thanks! Cal and I took some cooking lessons from a friend of ours who's a chef. Usually we just have macaroni and cheese out of the box, but it's nice to cook like this every once in a while."

Cami didn't eat; she wanted a peanut butter sandwich instead, but she wasn't going to get one.

I scooped up some food on her fork and pretended I was going to eat it. She opened her mouth for me and I got her to eat a forkful.

"That was a good bite! My turn." I tried a piece of juicy prime rib.

"Cami's turn again." I didn't care that the three other adults at the table were staring at me. My game was getting the little girl to eat her supper.

"Taryn, I think we need to take you home with us. She hasn't eaten like this in, well, I can't remember the last time she had such an appetite." Kelly looked astounded.

"Sorry, can't let you do that," Ryan interjected. "We're staying on the East Coast, where things are normal."

The bite of food I had in my mouth suddenly became very hard to chew. Had I just heard that correctly? I wished I could spit the food into my napkin so I could breathe, but I couldn't be rude. I took a big sip of wine to wet the food; hopefully that would help me swallow it. I really wanted to gasp in a few deep breaths of air. *We . . . are staying . . . East Coast . . . We . . . Holy shit.*

"More!" Cami shouted at me, snapping my attention back to the table. She had her little mouth opened wide, just like a baby bird. I shoveled another pile into her mouth.

After that comment, I couldn't eat anymore. I was in a freaking daze thinking about *us* . . . East Coast . . . children . . . rites of passages . . . little blue-eyed babies . . .

Once we were all finished eating, I helped Kelly clear the table while the men took Cami into the family room to keep her busy. I was scraping a plate into the garbage can when Kelly asked me, "Are you okay?"

I blinked a few times, wrapping my thoughts around her words. "Yeah, why?"

"You just got real quiet. I was wondering if it was because of what Ryan said?"

I smiled. "Kelly, every time he says *we* . . ." I took a deep breath.

She smiled back at me and whispered, "Feels good to be in love, doesn't it."

"Yes, it does."

Later, we all sat back at the dinner table and talked; Cami was sitting on my lap and we were both coloring in a book with crayons. I was having a blast, trying to get the different shades of purple to blend on the petals of the flower I was coloring.

"Is that your masterpiece?" Ryan teased Cami.

"Whyin, don't touch," she scolded him.

"Another good thing about Pennsylvania—that's where they make crayons," Ryan stated.

"And Yuengling Lager, too," I added.

"Philly cheesesteaks," Ryan continued.

"Will Smith is from Philadelphia," Cal contributed.

"Pittsburgh Steelers and the Pens," Ryan and I added together. We held our fists up and tapped our knuckles together.

"I'm taking you to a hockey game. I'll check to see when the Pens are playing at home and we are going," he said to me.

"Won't have to twist my arm to get me to go." I smiled at him.

"Hey." Cami patted me on the cheek to get my attention.

"Taryn," I said my name.

"Tawyn," she repeated. "You color the gwass too. Use dis gween."

"Can I color, too?" Ryan asked.

"No," Cami fired quickly. "Me and Tawyn coloring. You wait your turn."

I started to laugh. Kids are so brutally honest.

Ryan pretended to sniff and acted like he was starting to cry.

"I think you hurt Ryan's feelings," I whispered in her ear.

Cami looked up at Ryan and pouted. "Whyin, don't cwy." She set her crayon down. "I hold you." She leaned over to him and he pulled her out of my arms.

My heart melted watching him hug her, while my thoughts wandered to picture him holding our child one day. He would make a great father.

I slid the coloring book and crayons in front of him so he could have his turn. She plopped down on his lap and picked her red crayon back up in her little hand. I couldn't stop smiling.

It was almost nine o'clock and way past Cami's bedtime when Kelly announced that she had to say good night to everyone. She was so quiet sitting on Ryan's lap, minding her own business and just coloring, that you barely realized she was there.

She started to cry when Kelly picked her up. Ryan gave her a little kiss on the cheek. I had to give her a hug; she demanded it.

"Good night, sweet princess. I'll see you soon, I promise," I whispered to her. She kissed me on my cheek.

"I think I'm going to have to call Mike tonight before we leave," Ryan said to Cal. He rubbed his forehead. I knew it bothered him to think about calling for personal security.

I placed my hand on his arm. "Why don't we just do a drive-by to see how bad it is first? If the crowd is too large I'm calling the police. We have laws about loitering and I'm far from happy that my place was vandalized."

"I heard about that," Cal said. "Sorry to hear your window was broken."

"Thanks. Fortunately I was able to get the window replaced immediately. The logo will be added back on the glass this week. One thing is for sure: no matter where I live, my house is going to have a security system. Just knowing I have that makes it easier to sleep at night."

"Oh, yes, it's a must," Cal agreed. "We have an intricate system wired in our new place in Malibu. Motion sensors and yard sensors; we have so many sensors that I don't even know what half of them do. Ryan, you're going to need that *and* a bunch of mean rottweilers around your house."

"I have to get the house first," Ryan admitted. "I've been living out of a suitcase for so long now, I don't know what it's like to be home."

"You should think about getting a place. You're not going to be on the go forever," Cal advised.

I noticed Ryan's eyes flicker up to me and then he looked back at the coloring book, spinning it under his fingers. "I've been thinking about it a lot, but I'm not sure *where* I want to settle just yet."

"By a lake," I murmured, putting the crayons back into the box.

"With a boat dock." He smiled to himself.

"Surrounded by woods," I added.

"Maybe grow some grapes." I felt his foot tap mine under the table.

"Watch the leaves change colors from the deck." I tapped him back.

"Big farmhouse . . . or maybe a really cool log home?" he mused, raising an eyebrow at me.

I shrugged. Either style suited me. "Stone fireplace in the living room." I slid the coloring book out from under his fingers and paged through it like a magazine.

"Maybe one in the master bedroom, too?" he questioned, chewing on his thumb. "By the enormous tiled shower?"

"With the nonslip bathroom countertop?" I couldn't hide my smile any longer.

Ryan grinned from ear to ear. "Big glass doors that open to the patio."

"With another fireplace?"

"Right next to the gas-grill outdoor kitchen," he affirmed.

Cal looked like he was watching a tennis match. "Sounds like you two have all the details worked out. Now you just need to pick the colors and the location." He laughed.

"Cami is in bed." Kelly sat back down at the table; her eyes glanced over all our faces. "Why is everyone smiling?"

"Ryan and Taryn just designed their dream home, I think. And it sounds like they have most of the details covered, which is good." He tapped Ryan in the arm. "It will save you a lot of arguments down the line, believe me."

"What was that supposed to mean? We didn't argue *that* much when we built our house."

Cal countered her comment with a few eye rolls.

As much as I wanted to fantasize about it, in reality Ryan and I hadn't known each other long enough to talk about this kind of stuff. The last thing I wanted to do was get my hopes up. *Protect self,* my subconscious told me. *Think about something else . . . but what? Need a new topic. Please, someone think of something else to say.*

I started to count backward from one hundred in my mind, hoping that would help. Visions of waking up in Ryan's arms every morning in our beautiful lakeside home broke right through my number counting.

I felt the chain of my new necklace catch on my hair, sending a pinch of pain down my neck. I adjusted the chain to untangle it, ripping a few hairs from my head in the process. I picked the pendant up in my hand and looked at it again: two beautiful hearts twined into one.

"That's a very beautiful necklace you're wearing," Kelly said.

"Thank you." My smile quickly flashed over to Ryan.

"Are those real diamonds?" she asked upon closer inspection.

I looked at Ryan, perplexed. I'd never asked if they were diamonds; I'd just assumed.

Kelly noticed my gaze over at Ryan. A smile cracked on her face. "A gift?"

Ryan's lips twitched and he nodded in confirmation.

"You have very good taste, Ryan."

"Thank you. I was glad she liked it."

"I love it," I corrected.

"I got her diamond earrings, too, but she won't wear them."

I sighed. "One very expensive present was more than enough." My eyes locked on the coloring book; I wasn't used to having a man buy me jewelry, or anything else for that matter.

I heard Ryan scoff. "Get used to it," he stated directly.

Kelly patted me on the arm. I think for a moment she understood.

"No, I'll never get used to it," I whispered out. "I will always appreciate your kindness and generosity, and never take it for granted." I hoped he could see the truth of those words in my eyes.

"Do you have a sister, Taryn? Because I have a brother who's single," Cal joked.

"No, I'm sorry Cal, I don't." I didn't understand why he said that. Were all women perceived as gold diggers?

I jumped slightly when I felt someone touch my rear. I looked behind me to see Cami in her pajamas with a stuffed bunny under her arm.

"I thought you were sleeping?" I said to her, pulling her onto my lap.

"Cami! It's bedtime, young lady." Kelly was upset.

"Tawyn, you weed to me?" She rubbed her eye with her little hand. Her soft plea warmed my heart.

"Sure." I stood up, but Kelly tried to relieve me of her. "It's okay. Can I put her to bed?"

She was so light to carry—such a petite little thing. I could see why she had a hard time staying asleep; her bedroom was obviously not *her* bedroom. There were nets, shells, and sea horses hanging from the corner. This was nothing more than a strange guest room in a rental beach house, not a room for a little princess.

I read her *The Little Mermaid* under the soft light of her night-light, using my best voices to pretend to be the different characters. She liked my Ariel voice the best. I watched as her little mouth formed into gentle O's when she yawned. Her big blue eyes were getting heavy. I closed the book and softly stroked her long, blond ringlets while quietly singing a few lullabies.

Ryan popped his head around the door, watching me as I sat on the floor singing to the little girl. Her eyes closed, and in an instant she was sound asleep. I stared at her for a few moments; she was absolutely adorable.

Ryan was blocking the doorway; his body was backlit by the little night-light in the wall outside Cami's room. I looked at him and smiled.

He stepped in front of me and slid his hand around my waist, drawing me into his chest. His other hand slowly slipped across my jaw and stopped at the back of my neck; with the slightest bit of force he pulled me in for a kiss.

This kissing was different. Maybe it was my perception, but it wasn't the "slide my tongue around in your mouth I'm so hot for you" kind of kiss. It was more tender, personal, and loving.

When we returned to the dining room, Kelly was leaning over the table, slicing some kind of chocolate dessert coated with a white whipped topping. "Is our daughter finally sleeping?"

"Yes, she's sound asleep."

"Taryn sang to her." Ryan took my hand in his under the table.

"Well, I think you two are going to make wonderful parents one day—

when you're ready. Cami really surprised me tonight. She never goes off with people she's unfamiliar with. But you," Kelly mused and slid a piece of pie in front of me, "she loved you instantly."

Her comment made me smile. I was quite taken with the little girl myself. I felt Ryan's hand squeeze mine.

"She's absolutely adorable, Kelly. One day, perhaps." *Change the subject, Taryn.*

"Kelly, I've been meaning to ask you a question. When you were on *Just Neighbors* there was a character—his name was Kip?"

"Yes, Kip. That was Jesse Oberly who played him."

"What ever happened to him? I was surprised when he was killed off. I'm sorry for bringing it up, but when I see you, I think of him and wonder why he died on the show. Did he make someone angry and get fired?"

"No, Jesse left on his own. Actually, I just spoke to him and his wife a couple of weeks ago. He has a ranch in Tennessee now where he breeds and trains racehorses. He's never been happier. One day he had a meeting with the producer and said he wanted out. He'd only signed on for one season, and when his contract was fulfilled, the writers had his character die. More drama that way."

"Why did he want to leave? His character was so popular," I asked, sampling my slice of pie.

"He wasn't happy. He was a brilliant actor; very natural in front of the cameras. But he didn't like all the attention or the invasion of his privacy. Kind of reminds me of someone else we know?" She looked at Ryan.

"Kelly, they post on the Internet where I'm having dinner, for God's sake. The attention I can handle; the obsessive crap is something altogether different," Ryan defended himself.

"No, I understand. When my show first aired, our cast went through something similar. We were followed and reported on, and of course they said we were all sleeping with each other, too. I think in one week it was reported that I slept with four different actors from the show. While I was in the makeup trailer, supposedly I was getting lucky at the same time. One of the magazines reported that I had a weeklong affair with this one actor when in reality I was at home with the flu. Cal knows. We had just started seeing each other."

"So how do the magazines get away with printing all the lies? Can't you sue or something?" I asked.

"I wish. It's the lies that sell the magazines," Kelly uttered sadly. "The bigger the lie, the more money they make. And if they get some racy pictures, too, that could turn a hefty profit for the photographer."

"We had our picture taken a lot tonight," I murmured. Ryan squeezed my hand again.

"Just be prepared, sweetheart. Those pictures of us are going to be all over the tabloids, Internet, you name it. There are going to be outlandish captions under those pictures, too, like when we both cleared off your windshield? If you moved your arm too fast to sweep one of the papers off, they'll print that you were having a jealous fit." He rubbed his forehead. "Just don't read them."

He looked me in the eyes. "Remember what I told you when we were fishing? You can't believe anything you hear, read, or see. If something needs to be clarified for the public, I have a publicist."

"Can I ask a stupid question? Are you even allowed to have a girlfriend while doing these *Seaside* movies?"

Ryan looked at me as if I were crazy. "*What?*"

"Are you under some contract or anything that says you're not allowed to be seen in public with a girlfriend?"

"No." He shook his head and squinted at me. "Where would you get an idea like that?"

"Something Suzanne said." I shrugged.

"What did she say?"

"She said that the studio executives will be upset once they discover you're seeing me—that they wouldn't allow it."

Ryan abruptly sat forward; the legs of his chair squeaked on the tiled floor. "She said *what?*" His eyes were wide.

"Exactly what I just said, and also that if you stay single, your fan base will be higher and your movies will make more money. But if the public knows you're involved with someone, you may lose fans, your movies won't make as much money, and the studio executives won't allow that to happen."

"Is this another reason why you were so upset last Sunday? Because of these lies?" Ryan asked.

"Well, it was part of it. Suzanne made it seem like some studio executive was going to break us up first."

Kelly gasped.

"That's completely absurd," he muttered. "They can't do that." He looked at Cal for reassurance. Cal didn't say a word; his head was swaying back and forth in disbelief.

"So what other lies did she tell you?" Ryan's angered look frightened me.

I looked down at the table, hoping to dismiss this entire conversation, but he squeezed my hand again.

"Taryn, what else did she say?"

I took a deep breath and looked at Cal and Kelly. I didn't want to say it in front of them. "I'll tell you later," I said quietly to Ryan.

"No, I want to know now."

"I always said that girl was trouble," Kelly interjected.

"She basically called you a womanizer, but in many more words," I whispered.

"What? She called me *what?*" His eyes scrunched up in confusion. "What is that supposed to mean?"

I stared at my dessert plate. "She said that you sleep with different women in every town. You tell them what they want to hear so you can get some, and you leave a trail of broken hearts behind you."

I locked my eyes on his. "She also said that you lie to women to make them feel like they're your perfect match—that you're a talented actor and a gifted liar and I was just another fool to fall for it. 'Stupid American girls . . .' Then she said that once you leave to do your next movie and find your next conquest, you'll forget all about me."

Cal started to laugh. Apparently my comment was amusing to him.

"Oh my God! No way!" Kelly shouted. "Taryn, that's such a lie. Ryan is the complete opposite of that."

Ryan's face turned red. "She's a fucking piece of work, that girl. Why didn't you tell me all of this before?" He was definitely angry.

"Because I was scared and I didn't want to cause problems for you." I hid my eyes under my hand. "I even thought that if I let you go, then you wouldn't feel obligated and somehow you'd be better off. You have enough stress to deal with without me ruining your career. The last thing I want is to be another name on your stress list."

"No wonder you were crying so hard. I went downstairs for fifteen minutes; when I left you with Marie everything was fine, and when I came back, you were falling to pieces and breaking up with me. It all makes sense now."

"You tried to break up with him at the party?" Kelly shrieked in horror.

Ryan nodded at her and then glanced back to me.

"I'm going to rip her throat out when I see her," he spit through his teeth.

Thoughts of his career and his movie being jeopardized because of me flashed through my mind.

"That's why I didn't tell you," I muttered, feeling guilty.

"Taryn," he started.

"Ryan, you have a multimillion-dollar movie riding on the fact that you have to get along with her. And there's a third movie that you are under contract to finish. I don't want to be the catalyst to dissension."

"She's right, Ryan," Kelly agreed. "As much as I despise that girl, you do have contractual obligations. And having you blow up at her in front of everyone would not be a good idea."

"Why is she doing this to me?" His fingers clenched his hair. "We *used* to get along so well."

"She obviously wants to keep other women away from you, so either she's in love with you or . . ." Then it dawned on me. "Or she's fending off the competition for a friend."

He looked at me and it clicked. "Francesca," he murmured.

His eyes flashed over to Cal and Kelly, who were both staring back in surprise.

"She knows about my slip with Francesca. I'm not keeping any secrets from Taryn. And just so you believe me, Taryn . . ." He looked over at Cal. "Cal, would you please tell Taryn when, where, and why."

"That's not necessary," I interjected.

Cal cleared his throat. "Well, I don't know about the why, Ryan; only you can answer that one. But it's been over a year now since . . . then."

Cal focused on me. "We were in Maine filming the first movie. I remember it clearly like it was yesterday." Something he recalled seemed to trouble him.

"Ryan had his first traumatic fan encounter. He seemed completely overwhelmed. Fans were everywhere screaming. We went into a club and some girl grabbed him around the neck. Her boyfriend either tried to pull her off of Ryan or he took a swing at him—I'm not sure, but Ryan ended up getting punched in the face." The thought made his lips curl in disgust. "Anyway, we tried to calm him down; he spent a few hours in the corner tossing back shots of whiskey."

"Fran was always sniffing around his trailer; it was no secret that she had a crush on him," Kelly added.

"But for the longest time, he just ignored her. Personally," Cal added to Ryan, "I think you were homesick and freaked out."

"A lot of both, actually." Ryan grimaced.

The way Ryan spoke, I imagined he was quite lonely when he gave in to Francesca.

"After that one time, Fran started to act strange. Things have been weird ever since. And since we've gotten back to filming the second movie, the two girls have been inseparable," Cal told me.

"Who was the girl that sold the story to the tabloid?" Kelly asked Ryan.

"That was the girl I was seeing from the theater back home. You met her once when we shot the scenes in Acadia, remember? She came to Maine that one time." Ryan fisted his hair. "Who knows, maybe the bitch sisters got to her, too? Ah, it doesn't matter. She was more concerned about hooking up with my agent and getting me to make calls for her than she was about our relationship." He shrugged the thought from his mind.

"I'm going to have to deal with this," Ryan muttered. He chewed his lip, pondering.

"Ryan, just let it go," I advised. "Anything you do is going to make things worse. Just do your movies, play your part. A few years from now this will all be behind you."

"Yeah, you're right." He gave me a brief smile and squeezed my hand.

I was glad he agreed. Suzanne seemed to have more than enough reasons to despise me.

CHAPTER 16

Fused

RYAN HELD MY hand as he drove us home; our arms rested on the center console.

"I really like driving this car," he commented. "It handles great."

"You *look* like you enjoy driving this car. And I'm enjoying getting driven around for once. I'm so used to driving that I never get to really look at the scenery."

"We need to get the windows tinted darker, though. That way the photographers can't get too many daytime driving shots of you," he grumbled.

I'd never given any consideration to thoughts like that, although I'd never had to worry about having my picture taken, either. Still, I loved hearing him say "we."

He adjusted his grip on the steering wheel. "I never get to drive. I'm always jumping in the backseat of cars instead."

"Or hurled into the backseat of cars," I added.

He looked over at me quickly. "Hurled?"

"I saw you on television once. You were getting carried through a crowd by a few big security guys. It looked like they just tossed you into the car."

"When was that?" he asked.

"When you were in L.A. a couple of weeks ago. I panicked when I saw how they manhandled you." I felt his hand squeeze mine tighter. "Your car was completely surrounded by screaming fans; they were pounding on your windows. I worried for a moment that they were going to break through the glass. That was the night when you first called me, wasn't it?"

"Yes." He raised my hand to his lips. "And that was the night you calmed me down. I remember crawling under the blankets to talk to you."

"I remember wishing that you weren't on the other side of the country," I whispered.

"Guess we both got our wish." He grinned.

He turned onto Mulberry Street; we were only a block away and I had my cell phone in hand, ready to call the police. Parked across the street from the pub were some SUVs, a van, and a few cars. There were a few photographers on the sidewalk, but not the large crowd I had feared.

Ryan looked up and down the street. "Ready to make a run for it?"

I was relieved to see my parking spot free of love notes and trash. "Make sure you pay Jason well," I requested quietly.

Ryan kept me on the inside of his arm, close to the buildings instead of the street. We sprint-walked down the sidewalk. It didn't take long for the paparazzi to wake up and start clicking.

A few photographers jumped out of the vans, clicking their cameras fiercely. I just focused on the lines on the sidewalk and the distance from my feet to the door.

For one second I let my eyes glance up to check for danger; that's when I noticed the curly-haired, gap-toothed girl running toward us. She had things in her hands, no doubt a picture or two for Ryan to sign.

I thought it peculiar; most girls travel in packs. You would rarely see one without a fellow girlfriend tagging along . . . just like Suzanne and Francesca. But this girl seemed to be alone.

People were yelling "Ryan, Ryan," and even a few times yelled "Ms. Mitchell" or "Taryn" to get me to look, but I copied Ryan's stance and kept my focus on getting to the door. Some of the photographers were trying to be nice, asking us if we'd enjoyed our evening. Ryan didn't answer. He tucked his chin down to his chest and I felt his grip on my waist get tighter. I had my key ready in my right hand.

The curly-haired girl reached us before we got to my door. She almost lunged at Ryan, and I gasped at her forward behavior. He instinctively raised his right arm to block her and turned his body in my direction. I could feel his panic level matching mine.

"Whoa, whoa!" he cautioned her.

She started babbling about how much she loves his movies and his acting abilities. He graciously slipped the marker out of her hand and scribbled his autograph inside her book, trying to be cordial. A few other annoying men and women stepped up to get autographs, too, and Ryan signed his name as quickly as he could.

I grimaced as I stuck my key in the door; I hoped that their pathetic day was complete now that they'd disturbed him and gotten his signature on a picture. I twisted the key in the lock and grabbed the sleeve of his jacket with my other hand, pulling him through my doorway.

We walked up my apartment steps in silence, both of us slightly traumatized by the rush that followed the simple act of coming home from a nice dinner with friends. I turned on only one light in my living room; I could imagine all the people down on the sidewalk staring up at my windows, analyzing the shadows in my apartment. *I wonder if these shades are opaque enough? Do I need heavy curtains, too?*

I hung our coats up in the closet.

"Ryan, do you have your phone or is it in your coat?" I patted his pockets to feel for it. He was staring off at one of the closed windows, deep in thought. My words pulled his attention back to me. I smiled at him, but his mind was a million miles away.

I went into the kitchen and pulled a two-year-old bottle of ice wine out of the wine fridge—my favorite. I poured two glasses; I figured he could use a nightcap and I wanted him to try one of the wines from our vineyards. He was sitting in the single chair in the living room; his head was in his hands.

I crouched down in front of him, drawing his eyes to look at me. "Hey, are you okay?" I handed the glass to him.

"I guess I'm just tired," he murmured. I didn't buy it. He was troubled again, and I was wise enough now to know why. Several ideas of how to distract him danced through my mind.

I hurried down the hallway with my newly formed plan. I would need a few things and a few minutes alone. After taking a thorough moment to freshen up in the bathroom, I locked my bedroom door and changed my clothes.

This will take his mind off his worries, I thought to myself as I buckled the dainty leather shoe strap around my ankle. Once I was complete, I made my approach down the dark hallway, stopping just where the light met the darkness. Ryan looked up and gasped.

"You like?" I asked, turning slightly for him to get a new view of the alluring black undergarments I was barely wearing.

He sprang out of the chair like someone set him on fire and crossed the distance between us in three strides. I combed his hair back with my fingers and softly bit his earlobe in my teeth.

"Want to go violate me on a pool table?" I whispered in his ear before pulling his lips to mine.

THE SOUND of people yelling at each other startled me from my sleep. My head jumped off the pillow as my eyes tried to focus in the morning light.

"Huh, what's wrong?" Ryan mumbled, still mostly asleep.

I suppose I woke him when I flinched. I heard truck brakes squeal and doors slam; the noises were coming from the alley.

I crept over to the window on my tiptoes; the wood floor was cold. Outside, there were several men with cameras arguing with the driver of one of the delivery trucks, but I couldn't see the entire alley from this angle as part of the fire escape was in the way. I pulled the blind back another half inch to get a better view.

"Honey, put some clothes on first if you're going to peek out the windows," Ryan muttered. He was rubbing his eyes with his fingers.

I grabbed one of his T-shirts from his open bag on the floor and slipped it over my head. The cotton held his scent, and although I liked his manly smell, this shirt desperately needed to be washed.

"What's happening out there?" he asked. I was still trying to figure it out.

"There are a few photographers arguing with a delivery truck driver." I observed arms being raised over heads; it seemed that the alleyway discussion was getting heated. "There are cars parked in the alley; I guess the truck can't get through. They can't park there."

It was apparent that the paparazzi were camping out by my doors, waiting for any sign of Ryan Christensen. I thought about calling the police but I didn't need to; a cruiser had just turned down the alley.

"The cops are here now." Two police officers exited the car and I noticed that they both had their hands hovering over their guns. Arms continued to wave in the air as both parties argued their sides to the cops. "I guess the paparazzi can't read the 'No Parking' signs."

"Arrest them all!" Ryan boomed, curling his hand underneath his face on the pillow.

His comment made me smile.

"Baby, come back to bed," he whined.

I looked at him, then looked at the doorway; I decided I might as well hit the bathroom while I was up. He saw my hesitation and decided to race me. If he hadn't bumped me into the hallway wall I would have won, but he let me go ahead of him anyway. While I made a pot of coffee, I heard the shower turn on.

I pulled the shower curtain back far enough to get a view. We had no boundaries anymore. I watched the water and soap bubbles glide down his body. Damn, he was hot.

"You want to join me?" he asked, scrubbing the shampoo in his hair.

I thought about it for a minute. Even though we both fit in the tub, one person was always left in the cold end of the shower and I wanted to spend some extra time primping.

"I'll wait until you're finished."

He held out his hand. "I can't wait that long. Get in here."

I stepped over the edge of the tub.

"It would probably be better if there were two showerheads in here, huh?" he asked as if he could read my mind. I nodded in agreement.

"When were you planning on starting the bathroom remodel?"

I hadn't really thought about it until he asked. "I don't know. I need to finish the design first. I only have rough sketches."

"The hotel I stayed in when I was out in L.A had a huge tiled shower. It even had a power console for all the features." He motioned down the wall with his hand. "I've never seen a shower so complicated. There were jets in the walls, removable shower wands, and a big showerhead in the center."

"It probably had a steam setting, too," I added.

"So what do you think of that idea?"

"Sounds expensive. I don't think I could afford that," I said, rubbing my hands across his soapy chest. "Besides, there's not enough square footage in this bathroom to hold that large of a shower."

"I wish you would stop worrying about stuff like that." His warm eyes glistened as he looked at me. "And I'm not talking about putting something like that in *this* bathroom."

His hand reached out and grabbed my butt, pulling me toward him. He slipped his fingers over my neck and placed a lingering, persuasive kiss on my lips. I think I got the message he was trying to convey, but I still was not going to make any assumptions.

"Do you have any idea how incredibly sexy you are?" he asked. I groaned softly at his flattering remark.

"That's funny . . . I was thinking the same exact thing about you."

His lips turned down and he rolled his eyes.

"See, you feel the same way about those kinds of compliments." I poured shampoo in my hand.

"By the way, thank you for last night." He smirked. "I guess I need to apologize for tearing your panties to shreds. I don't know what came over me."

I smiled, remembering fondly his exuberance when he ripped the small seam on my sheer underwear and ran his palm up my spine to bend me over the pool table.

"I'll give you my card so you can replace them," he murmured.

"That's okay. You don't have to do that; I have more. Don't worry about it." I was concentrating extra hard on not cutting my leg with the razor.

"Why are you so damn opposed to letting me buy you things?"

I shrugged, wishing he'd drop it. "I'm not used to having someone want to buy me things, Ryan. I never really had that in other relationships. I always had to take care of myself."

In actuality it was always *me* who was the one who gave things to the boy instead of the other way around. All of the boyfriends I'd had in the past were barely getting by on their own, let alone had enough money to buy gifts for me.

"Well, I'm not like that, Taryn." I knew he was generous and meant well.

"Ryan, I have never been nor will I ever be the type of woman who expects things or takes advantage of people. If you want to buy me something, I can't stop you. But I don't expect you to, either. And I'm certainly not going to take your credit card and go on a shopping spree."

"Then answer this; why did you pay Tammy and Pete for the catering? Do you think I'm the type of person who wants to take advantage of you?" His tone was definitely leaning toward anger.

I was starting to wonder if this was our first argument . . . over money, of all things. I found myself becoming frustrated with the whole topic.

"Maybe I want to take care of you just as much as you want to take care of me. Did you ever think of that? Why did you buy me diamond earrings and a necklace? It's the same question."

I turned the water off and he handed a towel to me.

"I got you those things because I wanted to. I was in a jewelry store and you were the only person I was thinking of." His tone was soft.

"And I paid Tammy because I wanted to treat you to a nice dinner party with all of *our* friends. *You* were the only person *I* was thinking about."

"Then why won't you accept the earrings, if it's my way of taking care of you?"

"Because they were expensive and unnecessary. I told you, there's only one gift I hope to have from you." I placed my fingers on his chest. "And if you're unsure of what that is, it's right underneath my hand."

"You already have that," he whispered.

"Then I have everything I need." I rose up on my toes to kiss him.

I dried my hair in the bathroom and assumed he'd still be in the bedroom when I finished, but he wasn't there. I found him in the kitchen; he was digging in the refrigerator, still wearing a towel.

"Are pants optional today?" I teased, wondering if he wanted to spend the day in bed again. I took two coffee cups out of the cabinet and poured a cup for each of us.

He smiled innocently. "I'm actually out of clean clothes. Do you think I can use your washer?"

Ryan dumped his entire bag, minus his suit, into my washing machine. Typical guy—not bothering to separate whites and darks. I pulled everything back out of the washer and made two piles.

"I wish I had the rest of my clothes from the hotel; that all needs to be washed, too."

"Can anyone pick it up for you?" I asked.

Three phone calls later, he made arrangements with Jason and the hotel to retrieve his things. Jason was going to deliver his bags, but not for a couple of hours. I was looking forward to seeing Jason to thank him for cleaning up my parking space.

I went into the spare room to see if I could find something for Ryan to wear; I knew I still had a few boxes of my dad's clothing that I hadn't gotten around to taking to the Goodwill. Ryan followed me as I hunted.

"There are some sweatpants in this box. Everything is clean."

He checked the tag on a gray pair of sweatpants and slipped them on. My father was bigger than Ryan, but not by much. I found some cotton shirts in another box.

I tossed a black T-shirt to him.

"All this was your dad's?"

I nodded and moved a box away from my collection of stained glass. I didn't want the box to fall and break anything.

"This is as soft as that blue shirt you gave me. Fits, too! Are you getting rid of all this stuff?"

"I was going to donate it. You're welcome to take anything you want."

"Are you sure? You don't mind?"

"No, I don't mind." I smiled. Ryan's presence made the loss of my father a lot more bearable.

"Cool. My clothes seem to keep disappearing from the hotel. I'm wondering if Jason is even going to find anything left to bring over here."

I laughed. "I heard about that. Guess someone is selling your stuff on the Internet, eh?"

He smirked at me. "That's why I don't bother buying a lot of expensive stuff."

He had made a small pile of clothing that he apparently wanted to have. Even though he was a celebrity, he certainly didn't act like one. That was one more trait about him that I adored.

While he was still rummaging through the T-shirt box, I paged through one of my stained-glass books. I thought that since he'd invited me to his mother's birthday, I might make her a gift. I didn't want to go empty-handed; I wasn't raised that way.

"Does your mom like stained glass?" I found a nice picture frame that I could make for her.

"I guess." He was still busy digging in another large box of stuff. "Cool! Thermal shirts. Taryn, this one still has tags on it." He put it on his pile. "Why do you ask?"

"I think I'm going to make her something for her birthday. Do you think she might like this?" I showed him the picture.

"That's really nice. But you don't have to do that. I already got her a present. It can be from both of us." My heart skipped another beat when he said the word "us" again.

"Thanks, but that's from you. I was thinking that I'd like to give her something personal from me."

I selected a piece of textured, clear glass and held it up to the light.

I sat down at my table with the pattern and began to trace out the different-sized rectangular shapes I would need, while Ryan was still digging through the boxes of clothes. I grabbed my glass cutter and began to cut along the lines I'd traced.

"That looks like fun. Can I try?" he asked hesitantly, but I could hear the desire in his voice. I couldn't help but grin at him. None of my past boyfriends had ever taken an interest in watching me work—again, Ryan was a first.

"Sure! Have a seat." I held his hand on top of the cutter and guided his hand until he had a feel for the amount of pressure he needed to apply.

"How am I doing?" he asked, concentrated on cutting the glass.

"You're doing great! Just cut it past the line a little farther so that the creases overlap; that will make for a cleaner break."

It was hard watching him work while he was chewing on his bottom lip like that.

"Job well done, Mr. Christensen," I complimented him when he'd finished. "Next step, the grinder."

"Ooh . . . the *grinder*," he said in a low, sexy voice. "Kind of sounds like what you did to me last night."

"Maybe if you ask nicely I'll do the same to you later tonight." I gave the front of his sweatpants a little tug.

"You are my most favorite person in the whole wide world. You know that, right?"

"Here, put these safety goggles on." I giggled. "Pieces of glass will fly all over; you have to protect your eyes."

"This is just like high school shop class," he chuckled, slipping the less-than-attractive glasses on his face.

I turned the grinder on and this time he stayed behind me with his hand on top of mine, gliding each piece around the bit until it was smooth. I was trying my best to concentrate on smoothing the sharp edges of the glass in my hand, but he was making it quite difficult with his lips so close to my ear.

I stopped after grinding a few pieces. "You want to give it a try on your own?"

"You trust me with your power tools?"

"It's either the grinder or foiling the edges." I pointed. "Take your pick."

"Man!" He patted his chest. "Man use power tool. Man get more coffee first." He turned the machine off. "Woman want more coffee, too?"

"Woman get man breakfast," I laughed, grabbing the back of his sweats to expose his bare bottom.

After fixing us some food, I took a bite of my bagel and watched as he stood at the grinder.

"Are you having fun over there?" I asked.

He looked back at me and smiled. "Yeah, I am. This is pretty cool. I'm in the zone."

Once all the pieces were foiled, I laid out the pattern and handed him the flux.

Have you ever soldered before?" I asked.

"Yeah, but not like that." He nodded at my work.

"Here, like this." I showed him what I needed him to do. I started soldering the pieces together.

"Give it a try." I let him have my seat. Surprisingly, he did a great job. Within two hours, our work of art was complete.

He held the frame up toward the light. "My mom's going to *love* this!"

I walked off to the bedroom to get changed, since Jason would be delivering Ryan's bags soon and I was barely dressed. I slipped on a pair of jeans, layered on another shirt, and headed back to the living room.

Ryan was leaning on the wall by the front windows with a cup of coffee in his hand, peering down at the street. His face was troubled again.

I stepped next to him to see what he was looking at, but he blocked me with his chest.

"Don't," he murmured. "No sense in both of us being upset."

I looked him in the eyes, my expression pleading. His lips pursed together and he muttered one word. "Fans."

"How many?"

"Lots."

I took his free hand in mine. "Come on, I'll make you some fresh coffee."

We sat quietly at the little wooden kitchen table. I knew he was completely absorbed in thinking about the crowd outside. He wore his emotions on his sleeve.

I rubbed the top of his hand. "What is it about the fans that upsets you so much?"

He looked away in disgust. He spent almost a whole minute shaking his head, breathing hard, and rubbing his hand across his forehead. Finally he looked me in the eyes.

"They absolutely terrify me," he whispered.

I squeezed his hand in reassurance.

"I have this horrible feeling like one of them is just going to go too far one day. Some of their behavior borders on the delusional. They scream at me . . . they say that they love me." He looked pained. "How can they even say that?"

I put my cup down on the table. I wanted him to finally let it all out and I wasn't going to be distracted by anything.

"So I made a stupid movie once. Big deal! Thousands of actors make movies every damn day. I'm a person, just like any other guy." He paused to scratch his eyebrows.

"I am followed everywhere I go. Everything I do is scrutinized to the nth degree. And then I have to deal with *that*?" He waved toward the front of my apartment.

"What do they expect? Are they waiting down there for me to pick one of them out of the crowd? 'Now serving number forty-eight?' Do these women actually think that if they stand on your sidewalk long enough they might get a date with me? It's psychotic.

"I had to have my cell number changed so many times I can't count anymore. These girls leave notes and letters on everything—my car, the front steps to the hotel, your car . . . you name it. For what? Does Mindy or Cindy think that just because she wrote on a piece of paper that she's the perfect woman for me I'd be inclined to call her? What is *wrong* with all of them?

"You saw how many notes covered your car yesterday. For the sake of argument, let's say that there were forty separate notes. That means there are forty women out there who are deluded enough to think that their sparkle paper is going to attract me to call them."

I saw his lip tremble as other thoughts ran through his mind.

"Forty . . . compounded by the thousands; you saw how they just grabbed, putting their hands on me, trying to tear my clothes. Any one of them capable of . . ." he huffed.

He placed his other hand on top of mine. "And now, what I fear most is that I've involved *you* in the insanity. Rocks being thrown through *your* windows . . . If anything ever happened to you I'd never forgive myself." He choked on these last words. His eyes squeezed together and he tilted his face toward the floor, sniffing.

I stood up immediately and reached my arms around his shoulders to hold him. He wrapped his arms around my waist and pulled me to his lap. I held his head to my chest and let him release his pain. I felt each one of his tears as they saturated my shirt.

I could only imagine how long he'd been holding it all in. How many months had he suffered in silence, hiding this misery from everyone, including himself. Never wanting anyone to see how vulnerable his fans had made him.

I lightly rubbed his neck and shoulders while placing kisses on his forehead. I wanted nothing else in the world but to soothe him and take his misery away.

"It's okay," I whispered. "I'm here. I will *never* let them hurt you."

His fingers pressed into my skin, clutching my shirt in his hands as he finally broke down from all the stress. Tears trickled down my cheeks too from seeing how anguished he was.

I kissed his head and pulled him in tighter. We held onto each other while our fears and insecurities got the better of us. A new bond between us formed instantly, a connection built on emotional support and trust.

He looked up at me; his eyes were puffy and red and filled with the remains of his sadness. I gently rubbed my thumbs under his eyes to wipe away the last of the moisture. I gave him a soft kiss.

"Taryn Mitchell," he said, looking me in the eyes. "I love you. With all my heart."

I felt all the blood rush from my body and surge back into my chest. All this time I'd waited for a man to say those words to me and mean it, and now I was hearing them from the one person I had truly hoped would say them.

I gazed into his eyes and said what was in my heart. It was as easy and natural as breathing.

"I love you, too—more than anything in this world."

CHAPTER 17

Moved

I WAS STILL SMILING when I trotted downstairs to let Jason in. Ryan waited deeper inside the pub to avoid being photographed when I opened the front door. I kissed him one more time before leaving him standing near the edge of the bar.

It had been a good hour or so since Ryan spoke those three little words that made my heart sing, and I was still glowing. I didn't care how bad my face hurt from wearing this grin; I was completely, one hundred and fifty percent in love with him.

Jason was surrounded by people as he waited for me to let him in. He had a friend with him—another boy who looked to be in his late teens, with shaggy brown hair and a few blemishes on his face.

"Hey, Jason," Ryan's voice echoed mine. The boy had a garment bag slung over his shoulder and was wheeling a large suitcase behind him. His friend had a large duffle bag hanging off his shoulder and was carrying a large box in his hands.

"Hey, Ry," Jason said, parking the suitcase and extending a hand to shake Ryan's. "This is my friend Shawn."

"Guys, this is my girlfriend, Taryn," Ryan said proudly, putting his arm around my shoulder.

We gathered up his things and carried them upstairs. Ryan set his large suitcase on the bed and unzipped it. All his clothes were just shoved into one big heap. I noticed the name on the luggage tag wasn't Ryan's—his tag read "Shell-B Enterprises," with a Los Angeles address.

Ryan carried most of his stuff into the laundry room and then joined the two boys, who were already making themselves at home on my furniture.

A few seconds later, Ryan came back into the bedroom. "I want to give them some money," he told me. He kissed me quickly after returning his wallet to the nightstand.

"Hey," I called out, stopping him before he got too far. "I have that new video game system, if you guys want to play. It's all in the large drawer below the TV. There's a sports disk and a ninja fighting game."

Ryan's face lit up with happiness.

I pulled the zipper open on his duffle bag and dumped it out on the bedroom floor. A moment of shock struck me when I saw the strip of condoms and an empty condom wrapper mingled in his stuff. I picked up the empty wrapper—the inside was dry. Seven wrappers were still intact.

I ran over the facts that I had so far. One, Ryan had slept with Francesca, but that was over a year ago. Two, he was supposedly in a relationship with a wanna-be actress he knew from Pittsburgh, but that was *before* the Francesca incident. Three, his last known girlfriend dumped him over the summer; and four, Kelly had said that Ryan was the opposite of what Suzanne had accused him of being. Ryan had said to me once that it had been months. Months of what, though? Not having sex? Not dating anyone?

I tried to remember the exact question I asked him while we were fishing—was he seeing someone. He said no, and to answer the question I wasn't asking—months. The question that remained in my mind was: who was the lucky recipient of the used condom?

The front of his suitcase was lumpy, so I unzipped it and pulled out the contents. There were a few boarding-pass stubs and luggage receipts mixed in with some used napkins and empty gum wrappers. Mixed in that were a few pairs of dirty socks. I slid my hand back inside the large pocket to make sure I had gotten everything when I felt my fingers bump into something stiff.

In my hand was an ordinary greeting card with the words "I Miss You" printed on the front above a picture of a setting sun. I opened the card; inside was a picture of Ryan cuddling with an actress I recognized immediately, Lauren Delaney. Long, silky brown hair, with a stunning face and figure—it made me cringe to think he was with her once. Inside the card was a handwritten sentiment:

Here's something for you to think about
while we're apart!
Love, Lauren

I stuck my hand back into the large pocket to see if there was an envelope, but the pocket was empty. I flipped the picture over; there was the answer I was looking for—February 9th of this year. I laughed to myself at the irony; that was right around the same time I found Thomas in bed with that girl.

I quickly shoved the card and picture back down in the pocket and stuffed the ticket stubs and paper remnants on top of it. Even though I could hear Ryan with Jason and Shawn out in the living room, the last thing I wanted to do was get caught rummaging through his things.

I picked up the strip of condoms and shoved them back in his empty duffle bag.

That action led to another thought—every time Ryan made love to me, not once did he use protection. He never even attempted to put a condom on—ever. He knew I was taking birth control pills, yet he was still taking chances. He'd obviously used condoms before with other women—but why not with me? Why was I different?

Our lovemaking had always been spontaneous and unrestricted, and we certainly didn't hold a lot of conversations during our moments to talk about birth control or swap medical records. Why did neither one of us seem concerned with whether or not I got pregnant?

"Tar, where are you going?" Ryan asked as I opened my apartment door.

I looked at him with the thoughts of unprotected lovemaking still in my mind.

"I'm going to see if the mail came," I quickly answered. He sprang to my side in a few quick steps.

"You're not going outside, are you?" he muttered under his breath.

"No. Mail slot is in the front door. The mail gets delivered at three thirty."

"Phew," he sighed. "Please don't go out unless you absolutely must. There are too many fans out there right now."

Inside my door, I saw a larger pile of mail than normal. Lying on top of my mail were cards simply addressed to Ryan Christensen. I shook my head in disbelief.

He smiled quickly at me when I returned, then resumed his actions with the controller. He and Jason were playing the ninja game; both of them were swinging and punching their controllers in the air. It was slightly amusing watching them play.

"This is like a freaking workout," Ryan groaned.

I sorted through the mail: electric bill, two credit card solicitations, a new clothing magazine, and a few other random pieces of junk mail were mixed in with his fan mail.

I held up the envelopes that were addressed to Ryan and waved them in the air.

"What's that?" he asked, swinging his arm to kill the pretend bad guy on the television screen.

"Ryan Christensen fan mail," I announced.

"You're kidding." He scoffed. "Just throw them in the trash."

I was dying of curiosity to see what his fans were writing to him about. "Can I open one?"

He grimaced. "Why the hell would you want to do that? Tar, you really don't want to see that. Just throw them away." He laughed. "Good hit, Jay!"

I figured he really didn't care, so I ripped open the top envelope. Inside was a card with hearts drawn on it, and the girl who'd sent it even conveniently enclosed her picture with a phone number. He was right; these women were beyond delusional.

"What do you think, honey? Is that psychotic fan the one for me?" He laughed, eyeing me as I looked at the girl's picture.

"Maybe. She looks sort of desperate," I teased.

"Can I see?" Jason reached for the picture. "Dude, look at this chick!" He handed the picture to Shawn.

"Damn!" Shawn choked. "She's a two-bagger."

Ryan started laughing. "Okay, let me see." He put the game on pause and pulled the picture out of Shawn's hand.

"What's a two-bagger?" I asked.

Jason was laughing too hard to respond.

"A two-bagger is where the chick is so ugly that you both have to wear bags over your head. That way if her bag falls off while you're doing her, you don't get blinded by the ugly," Shawn explained.

"Are there any more pictures?" Jason asked.

I pulled the envelopes out of the trash can and opened them one by one. I didn't bother to pull the cards out; I just looked inside for pictures.

There were four pictures altogether. One of the fans was gracious enough to show her breasts. I handed them all over to the boys. I looked in the last envelope to make sure I hadn't missed an enclosure when I noticed that a picture of some girl was glued to the inside of the card.

Oh my God. I gasped and pulled the entire card out of the envelope. There she was, the curly-haired, gap-toothed, psycho fan. The card was covered in glossy snippets of Ryan's face that she'd obviously cut out of many different magazines. She had included her face in some of the pictures next to his, replacing Suzanne's face with her own. Scribbled all around the pictures were "I Love You" and "I Love Charles" sentiments. Her name was Angel.

Visions of this wacko taking the time to cut out Ryan's face and glue each piece to this card freaked me out. It felt hard to swallow. I couldn't get the card out of my hand quick enough; my fingers fumbled it into the garbage can and I ran to the bathroom to wash my hands. Fear and panic struck me; this was beyond admiration, and this particular psycho fan was just outside my front door.

I was shaking slightly as I folded the clothing that I'd gathered from the dryer. I could clearly see why Ryan was terrified. For a moment, I was terrified, too. I placed his clean clothes on the bed while my emotions did a slow boil. How dare they, all of them, do this to him . . . to us!

I grabbed my cell phone and marched to the front window. There were so many people down on the street, you would have thought we were having a street fair.

"Yes, this is Taryn Mitchell. I'm calling from 114 South Fourth Street, Mitchell's Pub. I'd like to report a large crowd blocking street traffic. There are also a lot of people loitering in front of my business. I'd like them to be told to leave. Thank you."

Ryan chuckled to himself. "Calling the cops doesn't help, but if it made you feel better, then I guess it's worth a try."

"How about a high-pressure fire hose?" I muttered, peeking out behind the blind.

"I can get you some stink bombs," Jason offered. Ryan grimaced at him. "No, I'm serious. The special-effects trailer is loaded with cool shit."

Jason's comment about the movie set reminded me of another phone call I had to make. I called Cory.

Not only did I want him to cover my absence while Ryan's parents were in town, but having a man working in the bar suddenly sounded very reassuring.

"Dude, we're gonna roll," Jason said on his way to the door, slapping his hand into Ryan's.

I led them down the stairs so I could turn the alarm off once again.

"Jason, thank you so much for all your help. I truly appreciate it."

"No problem." Jason smiled back at me. "I'm glad to see it all worked out for him." He motioned his head back to Ryan.

As the boys left, I could see a few police officers moving everyone along. I was thankful that the police made the vans across the street move, too. They were at metered parking spots; unfortunately after six p.m., the parking meters were no longer valid.

I returned to my laundry detail; Ryan helped fold some of his clothes. I moved the shirts he'd picked out of the boxes from the washer to the dryer.

"Taryn, we need to talk," he said, leading me back to the bedroom.

I had no idea what he wanted to talk about. He sat me down on the bed.

"I was wondering how you felt about me staying here. Wherever I am, that follows." He tilted his head toward the living room. "I'm worried about how it affects you and, well, your business."

I shrugged his comment off. I was more concerned about his safety than mine.

"Ryan, I'm fine with you staying here. I guess I just overreacted a bit when I saw how your fans terrorize you. It angered me. At least when you're here, I can protect you.

"To be honest, I love having your arms around me at night and waking up next to you in the morning. After all, isn't that what it's about anyway—two people, in love, together?"

He picked my hand up in his and smiled. "Yeah, it is. But unfortunately the fans and the paparazzi—they follow," he reminded.

"I know, and I don't care. I do care about you, though." I looked directly into his eyes.

"Hmm," he lightly purred, apparently pleased by my comment. "So you're okay with this?"

"Yeah." I smiled and nodded.

He took a deep breath. "Then how would you feel if I told you I wanted to stay here more? Maybe even *every* night?"

I swallowed while the exhilaration from his question flooded my heart and circled confusion in my brain.

"What?" I breathed out. "Are you saying you want to move in with me?" My sheer surprise came out as a whisper.

"Well, I was just thinking that when I'm done working, instead of going to the hotel, I could come here. This is where I want to be anyway. What do you think?" he asked hesitantly, biting his bottom lip.

I took a deep breath, gathering my words before I spoke. *Was he even allowed to do something like this while under contract to film?* I had to ask. "I think . . ."

His cell phone rang on the nightstand. "Shit, hold that thought . . ." He looked at the number and took the call.

"David, hey. I'm doing great. Yeah, I have a minute." Ryan covered his phone with his hand. "My manager," he whispered to me.

His face morphed from an elated smile to a look of disgust in an instant.

"No, I didn't move out of the hotel. I don't know why they called you. I just had all my things retrieved so I could wash my clothes, that's all," he sighed.

I watched Ryan start to rub his forehead. He walked out of the bedroom but he didn't go far; I could still hear every word clearly.

"I've been staying at Taryn's," I heard him confess.

Apparently his manager knew about me.

"I'll take my chances. You know, David, I just don't give a shit anymore. I am so sick and tired of hiding and having every fucking detail of my life become public knowledge." Ryan's voice became louder, distressed.

"I'm done with being locked up in some hotel like a prisoner. I'm sick of it! It's been like this for over two years. I'm going out of my mind. I want to have a normal relationship with someone for once. . . .

"Yeah, I guess you're right. I'm no longer allowed to have a personal life," he responded defensively. "I wish someone would have told me that I'm not allowed to have a fucking life at all, because I sure don't remember seeing *that* clause in any of my contracts."

I stood there, motionless, listening to him shout in the hallway. My pulse quickened and my hands started to tremble, knowing I was the reason for his defensiveness.

"Fine, then if that's the case, inform the studio that I'll pay for my own security. Do that, 'cause I'm not living in lockdown anymore. I can't . . . deal with it."

After a pause, he sighed. "Why? So I can have more of my clothes mysteriously disappear? I'll do my own laundry. I don't want strangers touching my clothing—it creeps me out. . . .

"I'm pretty sure she knows what she's gotten herself into. The paparazzi have been on to her for weeks, and that was before we were seen together publicly. . . .

"I don't care what the media says about me. The only person I'm worried about, the only person I care about, is Taryn. . . .

"Don't worry about me. I'm staying focused. They're getting a quality performance." Ryan was irritated. "I've seen all the dailies—they look great. Kenneth hasn't said a word to me about it; I would hope the director would tell *me* if he had concerns! . . .

"Are you kidding me? If they want to *discuss* things with me, then they can come here. No, you listen to me, David. I'll fucking walk away before I let anyone dictate my life. I'm pretty sure I can live quite comfortably on the twenty million I already have in the bank. . . .

"I'm the one trying to be a professional here. She's probably pissed that she can't just knock on my hotel room door to get my attention anymore.

"If the third movie sucks, then I suggest they start pointing their finger in the proper direction. I'm regretting ever signing on for this project. Yeah, I know, David. All right."

I dumped the clean load of white laundry onto the bed—a reflex to make it *look* like I hadn't been listening intently. He stopped in the doorway and leaned on the frame with his arms folded across his chest.

I didn't say anything. I knew he was upset. I think he sensed I was, too. How else could I be?

"I know you heard my conversation," he said softly.

"I'm making things difficult for you," I whispered, fighting back my tears of guilt.

"No," he said, shaking his head in disagreement. "You're the only thing that's keeping me sane."

"I don't see how that's possible," I said somberly, diverting my attention to separating the laundry.

Ryan stepped to my side and took his socks out of my clenched hands.

"Do you love me?" he asked emphatically, his eyes piercing. His fingers lifted my chin. "I mean really *love* me?"

"Yes! Yes I do," I stated, looking directly into his eyes. "With all of my heart."

A smile touched his lips.

"You know that my life is anything but normal. So I'm going to ask you one more time. Are you sure you're okay with this—me staying here with you?"

"Are you allowed to stay here?" I half expected him to say no. "Will *they* allow it?"

"I'm a grown man. I'll do what I want." He rubbed my arms.

"You're breaching your contract," I said, assuming it was in the fine print somewhere.

"They are required to pay me and assure my safety and comfort. I'm not going to let them own me. Taryn, I want to be with you, if you'll have me."

His mesmerizing blue eyes stared straight into my soul, searching for my reaction.

"I'll make some room so you have a place for your things." I kept my tone low.

"Taryn, that's not what I asked." He snatched me gently by the wrist.

Overwhelming guilt was rolling in on me now.

"Ryan, I want you here more than you can ever imagine. But I also know that there are reasons why you're kept hidden and guarded in your hotel room. I'm afraid that if you stay here, then everything the studio has arranged for you will be jeopardized. You already have enough stress because of me."

"Because of you? Are you serious? Why do you keep saying that?"

I shrugged, wondering why it wasn't blatantly obvious to him the way it was to me. "The trouble with Suzanne, and now with your manager and the studio people . . . not to mention the things that the tabloids will print about you being with me. That surely is going to cause problems for you. I don't want to damage your career, Ryan."

He laughed at the absurdity. "You are *not* the cause of my stress. And all the press about our relationship is doing the opposite of damaging my career, so please stop thinking that way. Sweetheart, you are the only thing keeping me from jumping off the roof."

I rolled my eyes.

"I don't care about any of that. And I'll hire my own security team if it ever comes down to it." He shrugged. "Regardless, that's not for you to worry about."

I looked at him, surprised. "Despite what you say, I *will* worry about it. Anything that troubles you troubles me."

He sighed heavily.

"Taryn, I think you realize by now that being involved with me comes at a hefty price. I told you before it was difficult for me to have any kind of relationship, and all of this bullshit is why. I hope and pray that in a year or so when I'm done with this trilogy and move on to other projects, this craziness will die down. But right now, it is what it is. Security teams, secrets, lies, hiding, insane schedule—it comes with the territory. It's my life."

He took my hand in his. "My crazy life is going to become your crazy life. It's happening already. Are you willing to put up with all the craziness and nonsense and love me anyway?"

I did not hesitate with my reply. "Yes, absolutely," I breathed out. "What about you? Are you willing to do the same? Put up with all the nonsense to keep loving me?"

"Absolutely. Without question." He grinned.

Ryan's warm hand brushed across my neck, pulling me in for a kiss.

IT WAS almost seven o'clock when Pete called to inform me that they were parking almost two blocks away since my street was quite busy.

Ryan and I waited in the dark bar for our friends. I didn't want to turn the lights on and give the paparazzi any reason to wake up prematurely. Ryan looked adorable in my dad's gray flannel shirt with a fresh white T-shirt underneath. He called his bodyguard Mike and made arrangements to get picked up in the morning. I was elated knowing that he was definitely staying with me tonight.

I stood by the door, waiting for their knock, although I didn't need to wait—the moment they paused at my door the cameras started to flash.

"Hurry, come in." I waved, trying to hide as best I could behind most of the door.

It angered me that the paparazzi were taking pictures of *anyone* who entered my pub. A twinge of panic ebbed up my spine thinking about how things would be tomorrow, when I had to unlock the doors to let the public inside.

Pete was balancing three pizza boxes in front of him. "All right, where's the fucking president?" he called out.

I turned the lights on and Pete nodded to Ryan, who was leaning on the bar.

"Oh, hey, Ryan," Pete boomed. "You see the president around here?"

"Only presidents here are in my pocket, Pete." Ryan shook his hand.

"Rumor has it that Brad Pitt is visiting," Marie joked on her way in. "Oh, it's just you, Ryan. Somebody should go out there and tell them that Brad isn't in the building. What a freaking disappointment."

"Nice to see you too, Marie." He squeezed her shoulders and pretended to choke her.

"Gary, good to see you, man." Ryan shook Gary's hand.

"Hey, Ryan. Ready to lose big tonight?" Gary teased.

Tammy gave me a hug with one arm; she had a cake pan with a lid on it in her other hand. She gave Ryan a one-arm hug, too. "I made a new dessert I'd like everyone to try."

Pete placed the pizzas on our big, center table. The aroma of melted mozzarella and tomato sauce filled the room and everyone was mentioning how hungry they were. I tapped a pitcher of beer and we all took our familiar seats to eat and drink.

Ryan grabbed a slice and stood up from the table.

"Pete, can I talk to you a minute?" He motioned with his head for Pete to follow him. The two of them disappeared into the kitchen. I wondered what that was all about.

"Taryn, there are a lot of people out there." Marie nodded toward the door. She looked over her shoulder to see where Ryan was. "How long has the crowd been there?"

"Since yesterday. Ryan and I went to Cal and Kelly's for dinner. His fans coated my car with love notes, too."

"How can he stand that?" Tammy asked, shuddering from the thought.

"It's difficult. Those girls out there are all wacko! One of them grabbed his arm when we were speed-walking to my car. I was actually relieved that we were surrounded by the photographers; it was like they created a circle around us to keep the girls out."

"I know, I saw the pictures," Marie said. "Tar, you're on the freaking Internet. Just search for his name and the pictures they took come right up. You looked great, by the way. I liked the gray sweater dress with your leather jacket and black boots."

For a moment everything went dim. I felt like I might pass out from hearing the confirmation that my picture was now on the Internet, forever associated with Ryan Christensen.

Ryan and Pete walked out of the kitchen; they were both laughing at something, although Pete looked a little worried.

I squinted at Ryan and gave him a questioning nod. He leaned over and spoke quietly in my ear.

"I gave Pete a few bucks for the plywood and I paid him for the pizzas. And I thanked him for being a great friend and for taking care of the window and everything."

I squeezed his leg. Ryan was truly a good man, down to the core.

After we finished eating, we started our usual game of poker.

"How's your business doing, Tammy?" Ryan asked somewhat overcasually, tossing his cards into the center of the table.

"Good! It's hard to keep up, though, trying to make all the food in our kitchen at home. Hopefully I'll get a few more jobs and then we might be able to afford to look for a shop somewhere."

"Why don't you let her use your kitchen, Tar?" Ryan suggested. "You have that huge kitchen back there that you don't use."

I recalled conversations I'd had with Pete about that and the reasons why it never happened. I was also wise enough to sense I was being set up. "I've thought about that before, Ryan, but the kitchen as it stands isn't fit for cooking and baking. New gas lines need to be run and all the appliances need to be replaced. Even the copper piping needs to be removed and replaced. It's an expensive disaster back there. That's why I don't serve food in the bar."

"Well, why don't you look into it and see how much it would cost?"

I shook my head, wondering why he cared and hoping he would let it go.

"What?" he asked.

I leaned over and whispered in his ear. "Please drop it. I can't. I already have one huge loan I'm paying on for the renovations I did to the poolroom, stage, and sound system. I can't afford it."

"I'm sure we can figure something out," he said privately in my ear.

"Figure what out?"

He tapped me in the foot and scratched his nose.

Several rounds of poker later, I was losing big-time. My game was off tonight; I had a hard time reading everyone's tells. Ryan smiled devilishly every time he won more of my chips.

"A few more hands like this and you'll have to ante with clothing," Ryan slyly suggested, kicking me in the foot.

"I'm not drunk enough for strip poker," I muttered.

Ryan abruptly sat up and joked, "Where's the tequila?"

"Not so fast! I still have a few chips left," I said.

"Yeah, but not for long," he teased. "All you have to do is ask. I'll be glad to loan you a few chips. We can even call it a favor if you'd like."

I smirked at him.

"Speaking of favors . . ." Ryan continued, making his general announcement. "I have a favor to ask of all of you." He looked around the table at my friends. "My parents are coming to town this Wednesday and they'll be staying here until Monday. We want to take them to dinner and spend as much time as possible with them." He smiled at me. "I was hoping you'd let me steal Taryn away for the entire weekend. Do you guys think you could handle a few days without her?"

I glowered at the table. I could not believe he'd just done that. He didn't even give me an opportunity. I suppose he thought that I would chicken out.

"Of course!" Marie answered immediately.

I knew exactly what she was thinking just by the way she looked at me. It was a combination of "Oh my God" and "Holy shit" followed by a lot of high-pitched, excited screams. This was a big step—Ryan freakin' Christensen was introducing me to his parents.

I hadn't even told her that he was sort of staying with me. That round of screaming would have to wait.

I had serious doubts whether or not they could handle Halloween weekend on their own. This was a big occasion for Mitchell's Pub, and I felt guilty as sin for sticking them with it.

"I have bands booked for Friday and Saturday. Cory will be working every night this week, too." I looked at Marie and sighed. She smiled and winked at me.

"I can help out," Tammy added. She was also grinning excitedly at me.

"Are you guys sure? I really feel bad . . ." I started my apology but Marie cut me short.

"Taryn! It's okay! We can handle it. Pete will keep a head count. We'll just make sure that we don't overcrowd the place, that's all," Marie confirmed. "Besides, we can always post a sign out front that says he went away for the weekend so don't bother looking for him in here." She pointed at Ryan.

"If you think it will help." Ryan winked.

Pete cleared his throat. "Well, as long as we're sharing good news, Tammy and I have an announcement to make."

For some reason when he said this, I wasn't surprised. I knew something was up. All night Pete and Tammy had been gazing lovingly at each other, as if they were protecting some deep, dark secret.

"Tammy and I have officially set a date for our wedding."

"We're getting married on Saturday, September fourth," Tammy gushed, looking into Pete's eyes.

I noticed Ryan fidget in his chair. The air that he breathed out of his nose was audible, but a little smirk appeared on his lips. I wondered which word did him in.

Was it the word "married" or "wedding" that caused him to squirm?

CHAPTER 18

New

My hand stretched to hit the snooze button. It was way too early to be awake, but Ryan had obligations—he had to get in the shower and go be a movie star.

"Ten more minutes," he groaned, nestling his face against the back of my head. My eyes closed and I drifted right back to sleep, but the buzzer on the alarm clock wouldn't allow it to last.

"Babe, it's five thirty. Your car will be here in a few minutes." I rubbed his back to wake him.

"Mmm," he moaned. "That feels nice."

His cell phone rang, forcing him to reach for it. "Morning, Mike. Yeah, I'm up." He got out of bed, rubbed his eyes, and looked out the bedroom window. "The alley looks clear. See you soon."

I smiled to myself while I made him a cup of coffee. I was so in love with the man who woke up next to me and was now in the shower getting ready for his day.

I thought about how different things were since the first time he spent the night. How I'd wrestled with the thoughts of not allowing myself to get hurt again versus the burning desire to love again.

"I have a twelve-hour day scheduled. I'll call you when I'm on my way," he said as he dried himself with a towel. "What's on your agenda today?"

"I have to drop off the deposit at the bank and I was going to do some grocery shopping. I'm almost out of coffee and there's really no food in this place."

"While you're at the store, would you pick up a couple of things for me? I'd really like some sort of soap that doesn't smell like fruit." He sniffed the skin on his arm. "Just pick out something for me, please? Oh, and make sure you keep your cell phone with you at all times, just in case."

In the kitchen, he wrote a short list on a piece of paper. "Here's some money. It's all the cash I have left on me after losing to Gary last night." He pulled a random mix of bills from his pocket and laid it on the table. "Use it."

We waited by the back door in the pub kitchen for his driver. I punched in the numbers to shut the alarm off. "The code is 283091, and then you hit this button here."

He repeated the number. "You may have to remind me; I don't know if I'll remember it."

"It's my birthday but in reverse . . . remember? Nineteenth of March in eighty-two. You should at least remember the year." I nudged him.

"I remember when your birthday is," he droned kiddingly. "Do you remember mine?"

"November seventeenth." I grinned. "Three more weeks."

His driver honked once and he kissed me goodbye. "Got to go. I'll call you later." The annoying cameras started clicking the moment he stepped one foot out the door.

By the time I'd reached the apartment door, I heard my cell phone playing Ryan's ring tone.

"I forgot something," he said, sounding a bit regretful.

I hurried to the kitchen. "You need me to add something to your list?" I already had the pen in my hand.

"No. I forgot to tell you that I love you."

My heart skipped another beat just hearing him say those words. "I love you, too," I whispered.

I plunked down in the kitchen chair and took a moment to revel in his words; his grocery list was still in my hand. I scanned over the items he'd requested—typical items that you use every day: shampoo, razors, body soap, and contact lens solution. I chuckled when I read "man-scented shave cream." Poor guy. All the products I had in my bathroom were definitely scented for women.

I did an inventory of the things I had on hand in the pantry and added a lot to his list. The last item he had noted was raisin bran cereal. His needs were simple.

I turned my computer on to check the balance of my accounts before going shopping, just so I knew how carried away I could get. I pressed the icon to open up my Internet connection; the second my finger clicked, my mind flashed to Marie telling me I was on the Internet.

Search: **Ryan Christensen**

I hesitated before hitting Enter on my keyboard. My pinky finger hit the key anyway.

It was like opening up the floodgates to Hell. There were over 62 million different hits for websites with his name. At the top of the page were several items listed under "News results."

Ryan Christensen's steamy nights in Seaport
Ryan and Suzanne—their devastating breakup
Trouble in Paradise! Split could ruin the next *Seaside*
It's Over!—Ryan moves on
Ryan's New Love

I clicked the last selection and was redirected to some gossip news website in the UK. There was a picture of Ryan and me as we were coming back from Cal and Kelly's. I could tell when it was taken by which side of my body was facing the buildings. I read the article.

Ryan's New Love

Ryan Christensen and Suzanne Strass may play star-crossed lovers onscreen, but fate has something else in mind for these two actors in real life. Ryan has ended his almost two-year relationship with Suzanne and is reportedly dating local Seaport, Rhode Island business owner Taryn Mitchell.

"Ryan met Taryn several weeks ago and is completely smitten," says an insider. Ryan, 26, and Taryn, a 27-year-old New York native, have been turning up the heat on their relationship. Ryan has been seen entering and exiting her apartment at all hours of the day and night and has spent several all-nighters with the attractive blonde.

It was also reported that Ryan had all of his things removed from his private suite at the Lexington Hotel on Monday, where he had been staying while on location, and had them delivered to Ms. Mitchell's apartment. His reps have neither confirmed nor denied the relationship.

"Ryan has been disappearing a lot lately and has been spending less time with his co-stars," says another insider, although last week we reported that almost the entire cast spent several hours together at a private party hosted by Ms. Mitchell herself.

"Suzanne and Francesca left the party early and both appeared quite distraught. That's the day Ryan let Suzanne know there was someone else in his life now."

I scrubbed my fingers through my hair. Even though the relationship rumors between Ryan and Suzanne were completely false, there was still a lot of truth mingled in the article. God, most of this happened less than twenty-four hours ago and it was already in print! No wonder his manager called yesterday. I clicked on another link.

Split could spell disaster for the *Seaside* movie series.

Timing could not have been worse for Ryan and Suzanne's relationship to fall apart—Charles and Gwen's relationship in the third installment of *Seaside* is elevated to new intimate levels and is *the* primary focus of the story. "Everyone is worried that their off-screen relationship will have damaging effects on their onscreen chemistry. If there is tension between the two of them it will certainly show in the film. The smallest of changes can really destroy their amazing chemistry," says a *Seaside* insider.

I spent the next hour searching him on the Internet. I was shocked to see how many photos there were of Ryan, including thousands of pictures of him and Suzanne together. There were even a few fan-made websites devoted to worshipping his every move; one included almost a day-by-day blog of his life.

I found that there were photos of me on several of the tabloid websites as well. Someone had taken several pictures of me walking down the sidewalk alone; there were also pictures posted of Tammy and me taken the day my window was smashed. There were a lot of pictures of Ryan and me from the night we went to Cal's.

The general consensus indicated that I was nothing more than a homewrecker, the reason why Ryan and Suzanne were being ripped apart. I could all too clearly imagine the die-hard *Seaside* fans coming after me to burn me at the stake.

How convenient for me that they were already out on my sidewalk!

I thought about having to leave the apartment to go grocery shopping and panic welled in my veins. Would the paparazzi follow me into the grocery store to report on what type of body soap I pick out for Ryan? Most of the pictures of celebrities I'd seen showed them outside, although the inside of airports seemed fair game; could they follow me inside the grocery store?

I looked out my front window; most of the street seemed clear, except for the normal traffic. Maybe Ryan was seen leaving this morning and the paparazzi and obsessed fans followed him?

I took a shower and spent extra time fixing my hair and makeup, just in case. I took my time, fighting the urge to stay holed up in my apartment instead of going outside . . . out *there*. I could understand why Ryan hid in his hotel room.

I put on my best jeans and my low black ankle boots with the chunky two-inch heel—just in case I needed to run—and my black leather jacket and sunglasses. I counted the money Ryan had left for me—one hundred and twenty dollars—and put it in my purse. Grocery list, purse, bank deposit, keys, cell phone . . . bravery? Where did I leave my guts? *Don't let them decide for you; you can do this.*

I paused by the back door, fixed the alarm, took a deep breath, and stepped out into the alley. That's when the cameras began to click. About five paparazzi followed me, asking me questions the entire way down the alley. I didn't answer; I kept my focus on getting to my car. At one point I found that I was almost able to tune out their questions by thinking about something else.

I made sure to look as if the love notes that were stuffed under my windshield wiper for Ryan didn't bother me. I even think I smiled once. I patted them into a nice pile and placed them on the passenger seat.

Did these freaking women actually think that his girlfriend would be considerate enough to pass their love notes on to him? Surely they had to know this was my car and not his!

Maybe they hoped that if we ever got into a fight, he might pick the first love note in the pile and go running to their arms? That these notes were somehow entry tickets to the Ryan Christensen lottery and the lucky winner would be chosen randomly from the stack? What the hell was in all of their heads?

I knew exactly why he'd broken down yesterday; these people were loose on the streets. My mind flashed back to the old zombie movies and I pictured that Ryan and I were the only ones not turned into monsters—yet.

I took a moment to program my music selection. *Ah, there it is*—I knew I had it, "Zombie" by The Cranberries. I smiled, turned the volume up, and put my car into reverse. *Take a picture of that.*

Since I had a large amount of cash on me from my profits at the bar, the bank was the first stop on my agenda. I stood in the small bank line waiting for the next available teller; my options narrowed when one of the two tellers working placed her "Window Closed" sign on the countertop. Just my luck I would have to do my banking with someone I went to high school with, Michele Weeks—another downside to living in a small town.

She noticed me standing in line and suddenly she was smiling at me from ear to ear. *Great.* This girl never said more than two words to me all through high school and now she was grinning at me like we were long-lost friends. Why *would* she talk to me back in those days? I wasn't part of that crowd; I hung out with the normal kids who *didn't* think they were better than everyone else.

Back then she was the head cheerleader, dating one of the three most popular guys in school, who just happened to get her pregnant right after graduation. Now she was the head teller at my bank. I laughed inside; funny how she always had the term "head" associated with her name.

"Hi, Taryn!" she greeted me with excitement. "How are you?"

Like you really care.

"Good, thanks. Deposit please," I said, sliding the rubber-banded stack of cash and my deposit slip toward her.

She took my money below the counter and typed onto her computer. She was still smiling and looking me over, and I knew at any moment she was going to ask her burning question.

"Taryn, please tell me. Is it true?" she whispered her plea to me. Her eyes scanned back and forth for eavesdroppers. "Are you really dating Ryan Christensen?"

Wonderful, another freaking nosey fan. A few smart-ass answers ripped through my brain, such as "No, he's just living with me and having as much sex as one man is humanly capable of without dehydrating," but I kept my composure and stared at her blankly.

"Come on!" she urged. "I won't say anything."

"That's good to know." I leaned into the counter a few inches farther, my eyes glanced from side to side to pique her interest, and then I dropped the bomb. "Neither will I."

Her smile morphed into a frown in an instant, and she shifted her focus to angrily count my deposit. She slid the receipt toward me.

"Have a nice day," she droned. I could tell she didn't really mean it.

I decided to drive out of Seaport and into the next town to do my grocery shopping. Why? I didn't know. Something about putting distance between me and the zombies, perhaps?

I drove past one of the large hardware store chains and another thought dawned on me. I turned around and parked in the large lot. I wanted to get copies of my keys made so I could give Ryan his own set. I hoped he'd get a better understanding of just how much I wanted him with me.

I was just on my way into the Super CostMart when Ryan called.

"Hey, you. What are you doing?" he asked.

"I'm on a top-secret mission," I joked as I set my purse in an empty wire cart. I stopped for a moment; it felt like I had something stuck to my shoe. I crossed my foot up on my knee to take a closer look. That's when I noticed the older Plymouth drive slowly past me. It almost stopped right next to where I stood.

"Oh my God," I breathed out, ripping the gum off my heel. I dashed with the cart toward the doors.

"What?" He panicked with me.

It looked like the curly-haired, gap-toothed girl, but I wasn't absolutely sure. Whoever it was had large sunglasses on. There was no sense in making him worry unnecessarily.

"I had some gum stuck to the bottom of my shoe."

"Oh, you scared me for a minute," he said. "Hey, do they sell socks in the grocery store? I just ripped another pair."

"I don't know about the grocery store, but I'm walking into the Super CostMart right now. Can I buy them here, or do famous movie stars require expensive designer socks?" I teased him.

"Let me ask Cal," he joked. "Just get me some plain white crew socks, preferably ones without holes in them. You know the kind that I wear."

"Anything else?" I asked.

"Duct tape and a shovel?"

I sighed. I could only imagine the hell Suzanne was putting him through on set. "How bad is she today?"

"She's being difficult," he muttered. "Taryn, you know I'm making this movie, right? So please don't be jealous when I tell you this, but we had to do a kissing scene this morning and she complained that I had coffee breath and made a big freaking ordeal of it. It was embarrassing."

I knew how he felt about her; jealousy was low on my list of emotions. "Ryan, I know it's pretend. She's nothing for me to be jealous over. I'm more worried about your relationship with the director. Did you get it filmed?"

"Yeah. We had to do several takes until the playback looked good enough to be believable. Kenneth was happy with the fourth take. If you remember, pick up a bunch of spearmint gum, too. Then I have something to take the bad taste of *her* out of my mouth."

I had to banish the thoughts of them kissing. "How long are you going to be on set today?"

"The call sheet says till seven for me, but you never know. We shot two scenes already. I was just going over my lines for the next one, which is coming up in about fifteen minutes." He yawned. "Fortunately she's not in that scene. I should be there close to seven, eight at the latest."

"I'll leave the back door unlocked for you; hopefully there won't be too many hairy leeches back there waiting."

"Did you smile for the cameras this morning yourself?" he uttered with amusement.

"Wasn't too bad. I made sure to smile when I retrieved today's selection of love notes off my car though. I kept them in a nice pile in case you need bathroom reading later."

"I was hoping for softer toilet paper than that," he laughed.

By this time, I had walked through the store and was staring at a wide variety of men's socks. I tossed three packs of socks into the cart. "I'm getting you three bags; all of your holey socks are going in the garbage tonight."

"Hey, pick up a bag of nacho chips and some salsa. I've been hungry for some Mexican food lately."

"You want tacos for dinner tonight?" I figured that sounded good, too.

"Promise? Don't toy with my emotions, Ms. Mitchell."

"You're bad. I'll see you tonight. I have to go pick out some manly scented stuff for my boyfriend now." It warmed my insides to say that word again—out loud.

"Okay, Peaches." He laughed.

I snapped my phone shut and turned the corner into the soap aisle. Our conversation had me smiling. I found the men's body soap section and started opening and sniffing all the bottles. I smiled to myself, taking the mental picture of Ryan naked, wet, and all soapy into my mind. It was one hell of a private thought.

He'd asked for new razors, so I wheeled my cart down the next aisle to check that item off the list. I was looking over the different brands of men's shaving cream when I saw her out of the corner of my eye—the curly-haired, gap-toothed girl. She was at the end of the same aisle, pretending to be looking at some product on the shelf while watching what I was doing. I felt a jolt of terror sting into my spine. It *was* her I saw in the parking lot!

Don't panic, we're in a public place. Maybe it's just a coincidence.

I selected the rest of Ryan's toiletries and hurried away to the shampoo aisle. I was on a mission to get what I came for and then go hide in another part of the store.

By the time I was finished shopping, my cart was loaded to the brim; I was no longer shopping for one. Even though I was mostly focused on my list, I still nervously looked over my shoulder every now and then. Was the curly-haired girl following me? I was slightly relieved that I never saw her again.

The cart was heavy and hard to push through the parking lot. The front wheel was wobbling, and I had to use two hands to keep it going in a straight line.

Sounds of tires squealing on the macadam captured my attention; instinctively I looked for the source of the noise. That's when I saw the old blue Plymouth coming straight at me from the end of the line of cars.

Thoughts of me dying in a parking lot, just like my mother, flashed through my mind.

Some deep-down impulse forced me to release the grocery cart and leave it where it was; my body jumped in between two parked cars. If the psycho bitch was going to take me out, she'd have to take a few cars out with me. But instead, she drove right past me. She didn't even glance in my direction.

I watched as she drove off out of the parking lot. She hadn't aimed for me at all. I felt quite silly for letting my imagination get away like that. I shook my head to get my mind back to the task at hand, and pushed my cart to the trunk of my car to transfer my bags.

When I pulled down my alley, the paparazzi were there, waiting for me. *I wish they would stop taking my picture and help me,* I thought to myself as the cameras clicked around me. *Wow, exciting news . . . Ryan Christensen's girlfriend grocery shops! Stop the damn presses!*

People are starving all around the globe, the pollutants we pump into the air are destroying the ozone, the world economy is in the toilet, yet the most exciting news at this moment was to capture me digitally as I unloaded my groceries.

I transferred all the bags from the trunk to the kitchen and then drove off to park my car. I hit the key fob to lock my car doors and was just about to cross Mulberry Street when I saw the old blue Plymouth turn the corner two blocks away. *She keeps this shit up and I'm getting a restraining order.*

I hurried down the alley; again in a strange way I was actually relieved that there were other people around, even if they were the pesky paparazzi. They only wanted to take my picture; somehow they were not threatening. And now that I had seen them several days in a row, their faces were becoming familiar to me.

One photographer I recognized was a small Italian-looking man with short, peppered dark gray hair and a scruffy beard. He was the nicest of them all so far. He didn't ask annoying questions; he just asked me how my day was going. I wondered if some of these leeches actually had a heart when it came to their chosen profession.

Another one of the photographers was taller, maybe six-two or six-three, with a well-pronounced nose and dark, olive skin. He also was somewhat nice, complimenting me on my clothing all the time. Today he liked my jacket. I pondered when the fact that I didn't always wear designer clothes would come into play.

As I unlocked my back door, the short Italian man wished me a blessed evening. "Thank you, sir. You, too," I replied with a cheerful smile.

After I'd carried all the groceries upstairs and had most of them put away, I called Tammy.

"Hey, I need you to ask Tony a question for me." Tammy's brother was a police officer in Providence. "I think I have a fan problem. Can you ask him what the criteria are for getting a restraining order?"

Tammy gasped. "Is it that bad already?"

"I don't know. This one girl just keeps showing up. I'm not sure if it was a coincidence or not, but I just saw her in CostMart over in South Hampton. And she just drove down the street after I unloaded my car. I'm a bit freaked out, actually."

"I'll ask him. Maybe you should consider not opening the bar by yourself? Can you wait until someone else is there with you?"

She had a point. "That's a good suggestion. I can wait until Cory gets here. He'll be in at four. It's not like I make a hell of a lot of money in the afternoon anyway."

"Rather be safe than sorry," Tammy said.

"You're right. Please ask Tony for me; see if he has any suggestions."

I put all the groceries away, then placed a small pack of hamburger meat in a skillet on the stove. I thought I'd start dinner now so when Ryan got home, we could eat together.

Home? Wait . . . did my brain just say "home"? I walked around my apartment, observing that there were little bits of Ryan in *every* room. All his clothing was stowed away in my bedroom, pants from yesterday lying on my chair, his expensive watch and cuff links were on my dresser next to his bottle of cologne, a new script and a book were sitting out on the coffee table, and his toothbrush was hanging in the bathroom next to mine.

Blending my life with his seemed so effortless. I tried to recall how and when it all happened.

It was almost four o'clock—time to turn the bar lights on and open for business. I was comforted knowing that Cory would be here soon. I turned the television on for background noise and adjusted my business hours sign to reflect the new opening time.

I had expected to see Cory as the first person through my door, but instead a few female patrons came in—no doubt here for sightings of Ryan Christensen. The three girls sat down at the bar; they looked quite young.

"Good evening, ladies," I greeted them. "What can I get you?"

One of them was sort of glaring at me; I didn't care for the vibe she was emanating.

"I'll have a rum and Coke," she said.

"Sure. May I see some identification first, please?" I asked politely. *If you're not twenty-one, you're not staying.*

One of them was barely twenty-one and the other two were twenty-two years old; all three of the girls were from Massachusetts, which was a forty-minute drive from here just to the border.

I was so relieved to see Cory walk through the door that I couldn't suppress my smile. One of the girls whipped her head around to see who I was smiling at.

"Hey, boss. Sorry I'm a few minutes late," Cory apologized. In actuality he was only four minutes late. Certainly not a big deal, especially since I had changed his schedule from part-time to almost full-time.

"No worries, Cory. I'm just happy you could work." I patted him on his shoulder. Secretly I was thanking my lucky stars that I wasn't working alone.

"Limes?" Cory asked, looking around. I hadn't cut any yet.

"I'll go get some," I said cheerfully, trotting back to the kitchen.

I had several limes and lemons in my hand when I came through the kitchen door. At that very moment, the curly-haired, gap-toothed girl walked through the front door of my pub. I sucked in a quick breath from the shock, almost dumping my armful of fruit on the floor. I scurried behind the bar, getting as close to Cory and my baseball bat as I possibly could.

I knew her name was Angel, but she was turning out to be more like the devil in my book. She looked around the inside of the pub before hesitantly making her way to the far end of the bar. I was glad she sat at the opposite end of the long bar from where the kitchen would be visible. Ryan would be coming through the back door eventually.

She reached into her little clutch purse and I felt the adrenaline start to release into my bloodstream. This girl absolutely terrified me; there was no way of knowing what she had hidden in that purse. I kept some distance between us until I could be sure of what she was up to. Eventually she placed some money on the bar and folded her hands on top of it.

Slowly I made my approach. "Good evening. What can I get you?"

"I'll have a whiskey sour," she whispered. It was weird; she never made eye contact.

"May I see some ID, please?" I wanted to know who she was and where she came from.

She reached back into that ominous little bag of hers and pulled out a small wallet. Her fingers fumbled for her driver's license.

ANGELICA STAUNTON, DOB 2/17/1978
943 S. BRIDGE ST, Apt 12C
BROOKLYN, NY

She was thirty-one years old and a long way from home. Now I at least had more information to give to Tammy's brother. I hoped I could get him to do a background search on this wacko.

I made the drink that she'd requested and tried to be as cordial as possible when I set it in front of her. I purposely mixed her drink light; no sense fueling her psychosis with extra alcohol.

Marie came in at five to start her shift. She made a face when she saw that most of the patrons in the pub were female. Cory was already trying to charm three of the girls at the bar. They seemed to like him, too. Cory was a good-looking guy—tall, well-kept, with nice arms and a flirtatious smile. I hoped he was a good distraction.

Marie held her purse up in the air and shook her keys, indicating she was going to lock up her belongings in the office. I completely understood her reasons; the bar was starting to look like the setting for a Stalkers Anonymous meeting. Sure enough, about a dozen or so young women came into the pub. The trail of tramps didn't end. All of the fans that had been waiting outside were now *inside* my pub.

"What the fu—!" Marie gasped. "Where the hell did they all come from?"

"The street, where else?" I breathed back.

"Taryn!" She shook her head at me. "This is effed up! What are we going to do?"

I had no idea what to say to her. I was also worried about serving minors accidentally. We had this size of a crowd only on weekends, and life was manageable when Pete carded everyone *before* they stepped foot into the bar.

"They all need to be carded and labeled somehow," I said. "Cory, card *everyone* before you serve them. I'm going to see if I still have those paper wristbands."

I hurried to the office and dug through my dad's old desk. I found the pack of wristbands, but the glue on them was so old that they didn't stick together anymore. In another drawer I found a stamp pad and a date stamper. That would have to do.

I went table by table, checking driver's licenses. I was glad that I did, because a few patrons turned out to be underage. They were requested to leave immediately. It felt good to kick a few of Ryan's fans out.

Women packed my bar; it was indescribable. All ages, shapes, and sizes forced their way in. For what? For the hopes of getting a glimpse of *my boyfriend?* The man who loved *me* with all his heart? It reminded me of the time his car was surrounded out in L.A. by screaming, hysterical fans. My mood instantly morphed from stressed to pissed.

Marie approached a table of four women who were just sitting in anticipation. "If you're not going to order something you have to leave!" I heard her tell them. "No, water is not an order. We serve alcohol here. This is a bar."

She slapped her serving tray on top of the bar. I could see she was just as pissed as I was. "This is freaking ridiculous, Taryn."

"I know. I don't know what to do," I muttered in defeat. "I don't know what I *can* do, besides stand up on this bar and tell them all that he's not here."

I really wanted to tell them all that he was mine and they were delusional, crazy bitches, and maybe end my rant with an "everyone get the hell out," but I couldn't.

I was so busy carding people that I completely lost track of the time. My pocket started singing to me.

"Hi," I breathed out, running for cover in the kitchen.

"Hey, everything all right?" Ryan asked.

"No. My bar is inundated with female fans. I don't know what to do." I felt a panic attack coming on. "If they see you," I gasped. It was getting harder to breathe.

"Shit, I was afraid of this. Okay, just stay calm. I'll fix this. Do you trust me?"

"Yes," I replied.

"Take care of your business. Stay out in the bar. Things will be a little hectic, but once they get what they came for they'll leave." He was in business mode.

I nervously paced behind the bar, mixing drink orders to occupy my brain. I had no idea what he was talking about, and I had had just about my fill of dirty looks for one night. I knew what each one of them was thinking—*why her?* What was so special about me that caught his attention? I even heard a few of them say that I wasn't pretty enough to be his girlfriend. I felt as though the neighbor's dog had snuck into my house and peed all over my carpets just for spite.

A black sedan pulled up out front and parked. I saw Ryan's bodyguard open his car door and they walked to the front door of the pub. The moment Ryan's foot hit the carpeting, the women started to scream. My shoulders instantly hunched up and I covered my ears with my hands to muffle the sounds. Cameras were clicking everywhere. Girls even stood up on some of my chairs.

Ryan smiled and waved to the adoring fans while his guardian ushered him safely into the poolroom. I noticed one of the paparazzi also followed them. Just then my cell phone played my favorite tune.

"I didn't know what else to do. Don't be mad," he whispered. "I love you."

"Ladies, ladies," his bodyguard, Mike, called out. "Mr. Christensen will be signing autographs and providing photo opportunities for one hour. One photo per guest only, please."

"It's brilliant! I love you, too," I answered him.

In an instant, a line formed. Actually, the line started forming before Mike even spoke. I looked at my watch—it was almost seven. I filled a large glass with soda and took it over to the poolroom.

"Ms. Mitchell," Mike greeted me with a partial smile. He had his bulky arms folded across his chest to look even more intimidating.

"Hi, Mike. Would you please give this to him for me? Can I get you something to drink, too?"

Mike shook his head.

Marie, Cory, and I stood behind the bar, just watching. I noticed how none of the other paparazzi entered my bar, but some other menace did—a reporter.

A well-dressed lady sat at the bar, smiling at me. I glanced down the bar to notice that the gap-toothed psycho fan was anxiously standing in line.

"Ms. Mitchell, Sheila Moore from the Celeb Entertainment Network. I was wondering if I might ask you a few questions?" She flashed her shiny, white teeth at me.

"I have no comment," I answered quickly. "No interviews."

"Just one question, honey," she goaded me. There was only one person on this planet that called me "honey" and she was not it.

"No," I said firmly. "Please leave now."

"You know, that attitude is not very good for his career." She smiled her fake smile at me. I wasn't falling for her tricks. As if answering her probing questions *would* be good for his career!

She eyed Marie and I could see the little hamster on the wheel in her brain churn another revolution.

"No, you cannot interview any of my employees, either," I said sharply. "Now I would prefer if you left." Her eye daggers were confirmation enough of her unhappiness. I really didn't care. I barely spoke to my closest confidants about my relationship; she was crazy to think I'd spill any details to her.

My attention was diverted when new customers came into the pub. Thankfully it was some of my regular male customers. They were obviously happy seeing the large selection of women. The guys quickly punched numbers into their cell phones; it was the modern-day version of sending smoke signals to the other tribesmen.

Ryan's little plan seemed to be working. As the women got their meet-and-greet satisfied, they exited right out the door. The crowd was thinning. Marie nodded her head in response to seeing some of the girls leave.

It irked me to hear some of the comments these women were making about Ryan. Most were gushing about their encounter with him—how hot he was, how they'd like to "do him," as they put it.

Two young women sat at the bar in front of me, talking about his hair and his dreamy eyes, and how they couldn't believe how lucky they got tonight to be at the right place at the right time.

I was washing a few dirty glasses when one of the girls expressed her next observation out loud. She presumed that since Ryan was here without Suzanne, they must not be a couple like everyone thought. And since he was out prowling the streets of Seaport (and slumming with the locals), he must be looking for a good time. She felt her odds of getting him had just increased. She even came up with a few lines to let him know he could have her. She decided that her "want to come back to my place and have sex?" line was the winner.

A few weeks ago statements like that would have drifted in one ear and right out the other, not affecting me the slightest bit. But now I felt the burn rip right through my heart. The red-tailed beast called Anger welled in me. These women talked about him as if he were a thing, an object, a possession to be had. And the thing they desired was the man that I loved.

Marie studied my facial expression for two seconds before concluding that I was almost at the end of my rope.

"Go take a walk. Cory and I have this." She steered me along by my shoulders.

"I'm going to see how he's doing, then I'm going up to have dinner with him. I'll be back a little later." I couldn't hide the anger any longer.

He had just about ten minutes left until his hour of people pleasing was over, and there were still about fifteen women in line. Mike smiled at me and moved slightly so I could look in on Ryan. Two girls were chatting up a storm with him, tossing their hair, smiling, and flirting. It made me sick. Ryan was standing there with his arms folded across his chest, trying to be nice. When he saw me he grinned, ran his finger down his nose, and scratched his chin. It made me laugh.

Two girls to go until curly-haired, gap-toothed Angelica would get her turn. She was definitely looking me up and down, just like the rest of them. I adjusted my shirt, ran my hands over my butt, and smirked. *Look at that, ladies—it's his favorite part.*

Ryan was growing anxious to get this over with; he waved at Mike to let the next one in. Two girls went together to meet him. They were beside themselves—it was like meeting God to them.

Ryan moved away from the table when the two girls left. He stretched and walked over to where I stood.

"Hey you." He smiled and privately drifted his fingers over mine.

"Hey back."

He yawned. "I am so done with this. How many more are left?"

I roughly counted. "Twelve. Just finish with them; maybe they'll leave you alone now."

He wrinkled his nose and winced. "I'm so hungry. I'm getting a headache."

"Then make it quick. Dinner is ready when you are." I tugged on the bottom of his shirt.

Angelica was getting nervous in line; she was shifting her weight from foot to foot. Ryan saw she was next and whispered something into his bodyguard's ear. Mike unfortunately let Angelica pass. She clutched her little purse in her hand, making me really nervous. I watched her every move, ready to pounce if she tried anything.

She said a few gushing words to Ryan and then started to open her purse. I saw the edge of something silver in her hand; adrenaline coursed through my veins. I was just about to push Mike aside and tackle her when she pulled out a silver camera. Ryan posed with her quickly; now I understood why the photographer was invited along. She looked at the camera and asked for one more picture to be taken, but the photographer told her no and moved her along.

Angelica looked distraught when she walked out of the poolroom. I thought she was going to stay inside the bar, so it surprised me when she left the building. *Good riddance, psycho.*

Several new girls got in line, and now the new total was closer to twenty.

"Mike, he's had enough," I whispered. "Two more and that's it. He has a headache and he has dinner waiting."

"Okay, Taryn." He turned to the ladies. "You two and then we are done. No more."

I watched as the bad news was whispered down the line. Quite a few of them let out loud "aws," but I didn't care. He'd served his fans enough today. Ryan patted Mike's shoulder when he was finished. "Thanks, man, I owe you one."

"No problem, Ryan. I'll see you at six. Go get some rest."

Ryan smiled and waved briefly to the ladies who were still waiting in line; their cameras clicked like crazy. He turned his back to the waiting fans and quickly darted through our stairwell door.

CHAPTER 19

Entrances

I LOVE YOU FOR getting me real soda," Ryan said enthusiastically. The can hissed when he cracked the pull-tab. "So how was your day, honey?"

I turned and shoved a taco chip in his mouth, stifling his sarcasm. He smiled and cracked me hard on the butt.

"I got a birthday card for your mom. It's on the table."

He grabbed another chip and dipped it in the salsa. "Oh, cool. I completely forgot to get her one." He read the card quietly to himself. "Aw, she's going to get all mushy on me after she reads this."

Ryan wrapped his arms around my waist, hugging me from behind. "Thank you," he whispered, kissing me on the neck.

I turned in his arms and slid my hands over his shoulders; I was waiting for my proper hello and was relieved I didn't have to wait a second longer. He tasted salty and tangy, just like taco chips. It made me hungrier, but not for food.

"Thank you for defusing your legion of followers," I said warmly. "I really appreciate what you did, and I was surprised to see how many of them left once they got a chance to meet you."

He crunched into his taco. "Mmm. Just like I imagined it would taste. I was *so* hungry for this; I was thinking about it all day." He had apparently moved on mentally from his previous business mode.

"I got you a present today." I pulled my purse off the back of my chair. "Here."

"Keys?" he asked with a mouthful of food, and then it dawned on him what they were.

"Back kitchen door is silver and the gold one is the apartment door. Now you have your own set." I tried to hide my smile as I bit into my dinner.

He quickly leaned over the table and gave me a kiss. "Thanks. So what else did you do today?" he asked.

"My bank teller wanted to know if I'm really dating you," I snickered.

He looked surprised. "What did you say?"

"I told her that we weren't dating; I said we're just having unbelievably incredible hot sex with each other instead." I figured that would make him laugh.

"You did not say that!"

"Oh, and I also told her how sweet and considerate you are and how you always make sure I have a mind-blowing orgasm first. I thought that would make her day."

He smiled at me while he chewed.

"She didn't seem too happy when I dropped my pants to show her your autograph. I could tell by the way she slapped my deposit receipt down and told me to 'have a nice day' through her teeth that she wasn't pleased."

"Now I know you're full of shit."

I smiled back at him. "She told me she could keep a secret and I told her so could I," I informed him. "And how was *your* day, honey?"

"I killed Suzanne several times today. I thought after I stabbed her mentally with a big knife that she'd die, but that bitch kept on getting back up! So I got the pickax and slammed it into her forehead, you know, right here?" He pointed. "But she wouldn't stay down."

"Babe, did you not learn anything from me? Did you try the poison?"

"Poison?" he scoffed. "Takes too long and I wasn't in the mood to wait. I put real silver bullets in my gun. She took twelve in the chest." He shoved the last bite of his taco into his mouth.

"And? Did that do it finally?"

"I wish. I don't believe there is any way to kill the anti-Christ," he laughed.

After we were finished eating, he helped me clean up the kitchen and put food away. I was glad that he didn't expect me to be his servant or housekeeper. He took a few extra minutes to inspect the inside of the refrigerator, checking out all the items I'd gathered at the store.

"Look in the pantry, too. I hope I got the right chocolate chip cookies. You weren't specific."

"Ah, look at this," he said excitedly. "Just like home." Ryan ripped open the cookie bag, shoving one in his mouth and palming one for later. "Did you have enough money?"

"Your contribution was about half," I said. I started washing the dishes.

"Liar," he breathed in my ear. Ryan turned the sink water on for me so I could rinse a plate.

I smiled. He was right, I was fibbing. I'd spent almost four hundred today getting all this stuff.

"Maybe we can *bang* out the finer details later? Come to some mutual agreement?" I wondered aloud.

"You want to negotiate the terms of our contract?"

"Contract?" I questioned. "I didn't realize I was under contract."

"Well, of course you are. I've already signed on the dotted line back here." He brushed my rear with his long fingers. "I'm locked in. It's an iron-clad contract, by the way."

"Question. Is there a no-competition clause written in this contract?"

"Absolutely. There *is* no competition, either. None." He took the wet plate from my hand to dry it.

"I'm not sure. There was quite a line forming today. All of them *so willing* to negotiate."

Ryan's eyes narrowed on me. "Tar, in all seriousness . . . Did that, what happened tonight, bother you? Tell me the truth."

"No," I answered immediately. "The fan appreciation didn't bother me at all. What bothered me were some of the comments that were made. I mean, I think it's public knowledge why you're holding court in my pub and why they all knew they could find you here. But when these girls are sitting on the other side of *my* bar, talking about wanting to have sex with you *right* in front of me, it's a little aggravating. It's sort of like a slap in the face," I admitted. "I don't know how to explain it."

"I understand. I'd feel the same way if a bunch of guys were talking about you that way. But since *Seaside*, I've come to realize that this world is full of cruel, ruthless people—all ready to knock you down the minute you show the slightest bit of weakness."

Ryan rubbed my arms. "I at least have a few years under my belt dealing with it. I know it's all new to you and it's going to affect you in many ways, just like it's affected me. We need to be strong together. It's you and me against the world, babe."

"That sounds like it's from a movie," I joked.

"Probably. But it doesn't mean we can't use the same line in our story." He softly kissed my lips.

"Are you going back to work?" He'd started digging in his bag when he asked.

"Yeah. I told Marie I was going to have dinner with you and that I'd be back. What's that?" He had a few blue colored papers in his hand.

"It's tomorrow's call sheet. It's like an agenda. What scenes we're going to shoot, times, my lines . . . all of that fun stuff. I was going to go"—he motioned over his shoulder—"read." He smiled impishly.

"Do you want your love letters, too?" I teased, knowing where he was headed.

"Don't you have a pub to run?" he groaned. His phone started to play some really cool music. I could make out the words "home, home."

"My dad," he answered my look.

"Hey, Dad, what's up?" His smile disappeared. "What do you mean they cancelled your flight? Oh, so when are you coming, then? Wait, let me write that down." He motioned for a pen. I introduced him to the junk drawer.

Ryan wrote down *Flight 1560 Newark 10:30 a.m.* "I won't be able to make it 'cause I'm scheduled to be on set. You don't need a rental car—just take a shuttle over to the hotel. . . . Well, I was going to come to the airport to get you but I can't do ten thirty, Dad. No, I haven't been staying at the hotel." He took a deep breath and looked at me.

"I've been staying with Taryn. She's willing to put up with me." He smiled as he spoke. "Yes, she is a wonderful woman. You'll see.

"Dad, you and mom only need to stay at the Lexington Thursday and Friday . . . because we're taking you somewhere for the weekend."

I flagged his attention. "I can pick them up at the airport," I mouthed.

He held one finger up for me to wait. "Dad, hang on."

"I can pick them up if they need a ride to the hotel. I don't think there's a shuttle from Providence all the way to Seaport."

He covered his phone with his hand. "I was going to see if I could get one of the limo drivers to go get them. Hang on," he groaned.

"What, Dad? . . . I was going to see if I could get one of the set drivers to come get you, but Taryn just offered to pick you up. No, she owns her own business, remember?" He talked over his phone to me. "Are you sure you don't mind getting my parents at the airport?"

"No, I don't mind," I answered him.

"Lexington Hotel, Dad. That's where you'll be staying," Ryan informed his father.

"Why don't your parents just stay here?" I suggested.

"Here?" As he contemplated the invitation, a dent formed in his brow.

"Guest room?" I pointed toward the hallway.

Ryan couldn't wait any longer; he hurried out of the kitchen and darted into the bathroom with his phone, so I headed for my pub.

Most of the fanatics had vacated the pub by the time I returned. The crowd was thin and very manageable for Marie and Cory. There were maybe twenty women still lingering in the bar.

"That was a smart thing Ryan did," Marie said. "After you both went upstairs, most of the women left. Look out front."

I walked closer to the windows and looked outside. The sidewalks were surprisingly empty. There were a few greasy paparazzi still loitering, but the horde of women was gone. Apparently, it was known that Ryan Christensen was *in* for the evening.

"So what are your thoughts about managing the bar in my absence?" I wanted to make sure Marie was okay with me taking off for a few days, especially considering what happened tonight with his fans.

"Tar, you haven't had a vacation in years. This is a huge step. Go, have fun with him and his parents. Who knows, maybe you'll come back married or something wonderful like that."

"Yeah, like that will happen," I kidded. "But in all honesty, I have been thinking about stuff like that. This place has been my whole life. Now—not so much, you know."

"Your priorities have changed," she stated.

"Yeah, I'll say," I nervously admitted.

Marie pointed to the ceiling. "His schedule is so different. He's going to expect you to travel and be with him wherever he is. And I tell ya, if I was you, I'd follow him *anywhere*!"

I smirked at her.

"That's not what I mean. Well, it is what I mean, but that's beside the point. Before I knew him, I had this mental picture of him as a celebrity. But he's more than that, I know that now. That's why you're head-over-heels in love with him. He's just a really great guy. And it seems like he's ready to settle down with someone. He's not playing the field, that's for sure."

"Yeah, I'd have to agree . . . considering he sort of moved in with me yesterday," I muttered, bracing myself for her reaction.

"What?" Marie gasped.

"We had his clothes delivered so we could get his laundry done and, well, he asked me if he could stay with me." I took another deep breath, anticipating her elation. "All of his stuff is upstairs now. That's why he's up there. He wants to stay here."

"Are you freaking kidding me?" She beamed in amazement and then pulled me in for a congratulatory hug while jumping up and down.

"No. I'd never kid about that," I whispered as we hugged. "That's why I have a lot to think about, because *this pub* is what *I* do for a living."

"It's not all you do," she reminded me.

"I know, but it's *my* primary income. I don't want to be solely dependent on my husband's income, even if he isn't the one I end up marrying. I want to have a strong, equal part in this relationship. And I'm not going to repeat my mistakes and give up who I am."

"You've been a shrewd businesswoman so far. I'm sure you'll make smart choices."

My pocket started to play Ryan's ring tone.

"Hey, what's up? . . . No, I'm not knocking on the door. Let me check." I held the phone to my ear and rushed over to my stairwell. I was instantly pissed when I saw two girls at the top of my steps, giggling and knocking on my apartment door.

"Whoa! What the hell do you think you're doing?" I shouted, surprised to see them up there. They both looked at me as if I were disturbing them.

"This is Ryan Christensen's apartment, right?" One of the tramps sneered at me.

"No, that's *my* home and private property. Get the hell away from my door!"

"Jeez, what's your problem?" one of them sniped. I was so tempted to run up the steps and come back down dragging her by the hair. "He's in there, isn't he?" she giggled, like she was in on the secret.

"It doesn't matter who is on the other side of that door. What gives you the right to think you could just barge on up there?" I snapped my phone shut. I'd just hung up on Ryan, but it didn't matter; I knew he could hear me screaming at them through the door.

"Relax. We just wanted to meet him; party a little." The other girl shook her boobs at me.

Marie was standing behind me with my baseball bat in hand. I flipped my phone open again.

"You have two seconds to get down here before I call the police. ONE . . ." Fortunately, I didn't have to count to two. "Collect your things and leave, now!"

"Bitch," the one girl mumbled on her way past me. I could not believe she had the audacity to call me a name!

"Excuse me?" I snapped. "Step foot in my bar again and I'll have you arrested for trespassing." I slammed the door behind them. I turned to walk back to the bar, still fueled by the encounter.

"Who's next?" I said to Marie, but loud enough for the rest of the lingering women to hear. I was so mad I could have thrown them all out.

"I need to get a lock," I muttered, standing in front of my stairwell door. But what good would that do? Just one more key and one more speed bump to getting Ryan upstairs unnoticed. I walked into the kitchen and stared at the wall behind the useless counter. I tapped on the drywall, thinking about how I could move the entrance to my apartment. I hoped to one day have a simple home in the woods with my prince; no longer did I think about living above the bar for the rest of my life. If I ever wanted to rent the apartment out, the tenant would be bound to enter and exit during bar business hours.

I flipped open my cell phone and called Pete. Home renovation was what he did for a living and I knew he would have some suggestions. I unlocked my apartment door just as Pete answered. Ryan was relaxing on the couch, blue papers in one hand, television remote in the other, stripped down to comfy sweats and a T-shirt.

I sat down next to him and he put his arm around my shoulders when I finished my phone call. I leaned my head on his chest.

"Taryn, this obviously isn't a good idea. Maybe I should just stay at the hotel."

I felt my happiness drain right out of my heart. "NO. Absolutely unacceptable."

"I knew this was gonna happen but I let it happen anyway. Me being here is causing a lot of trouble for you and your pub."

He was feeling remorseful. I could hear it.

"Ryan, it doesn't matter where you are. Like you said, this stuff follows." I sat up and looked him in the eyes. "I want a life with you, if you truly want a life with me. Your fans caught me off-guard today, but I can promise you it won't happen again. I'll be better prepared next time. I want you here with me, where I can protect you from the nonsense."

"Who's going to protect *you*? Isn't that *my* job?" He glared at me.

"And what? Your solution is to stay away from me to protect me?" It wasn't meant to be a question.

"*I* brought all of this to your fucking doorstep, Taryn! I did this!" Ryan argued, stabbing himself in the chest with his finger.

"So what? You think I didn't know that stuff like this could happen? I'm not some naïve little girl who's starstruck and oblivious, Ryan. There is no way I'm going to allow you to feel guilty about shit you have no control over. I have to learn how to deal with your fame, too, and I will."

Ryan slumped back, defeated.

"Do *you* really love me, or was that something that accidentally slipped out?" I asked.

His eyes narrowed. "I meant every word, every time I've said it. *I love you.*"

"Then it's you and me against the world, and we don't deviate from that course. That's our story, remember?"

He tossed his blue papers onto the coffee table and reached for me, hugging me tightly.

Pete and Tammy arrived fifteen minutes later. Pete had his toolbox in one hand and his tape measure attached to his belt.

Ryan greeted them when he slipped into the kitchen. We talked about how we could seal off the original door that opened into the pub and relocate the door to open into the kitchen. It was the quickest fix.

"But that means if I ever try to rent the apartment out, the tenants would have to come through the kitchen to get in. Ahh, I'm not so sure I like this. What would keep them from going right out into the bar?" I said, pushing the kitchen swing door with my fingers.

"That certainly is a problem," Pete added. "These old buildings were never meant to be businesses; they were all homes. And if we seal off the kitchen, then you'll have safety violations for not having an emergency exit."

I looked around the kitchen. There was just no good way of relocating the stairwell. Pete and Ryan ran back upstairs to deliberate. I could hear them tapping on the inside of the stairwell wall.

"I spoke to my brother," Tammy whispered. "Does Ryan know about the restraining order?"

"No." I shook my head. "I'd like to keep it that way for now." I didn't want to add any more stress to Ryan's life. "What did you find out?"

"He said you could get one if you feel she is stalking you. But you'd have to go to the police and then file papers at the courthouse. You'd also have to appear in court. It didn't sound simple."

"Nothing's ever simple. I did get her name today, though," I said proudly. "She came into the bar earlier and I carded her."

"No way!" Tammy said in surprise.

"On Monday she slipped a card for him through my mail slot and she signed it 'Angel,' and when I carded her, her license said her name was Angelica. Angelica Staunton, all the way from Brooklyn."

"Write her name down for me. I'll see if Tony can run a background check on her."

I had just slipped the paper with her name on it to Tammy when Pete and Ryan came back into the kitchen.

"Tar, I think we've solved your problem," Pete boomed happily. "Here, look at this."

Pete was smiling at Ryan as if they'd just solved world hunger.

"What's this line?" I asked, looking at their drawing.

"That's a new wall. Ryan, let's measure it. What you got?"

"Thirty-two and a half," Ryan said.

"That's going to be a long-ass wall! It's going to go straight to the back wall there." Pete pointed. "You'll have a separate outside entrance from the alley and then we can cut a door here in the middle so you don't have to go outside to get up to your apartment. One day if you decide you want to block it off, it's an easy fix."

Pete tapped his finger on the drawing. "The stairs would stop there, and then I'll put in two steps to reach the floor. You'll only end up losing four feet. That counter there would have to go.

"Ryan, hold the tape measure again. See, you were right. We wouldn't even have to move the back door; it's fine where it is. The new wall will come here—six inches away from the frame."

Pete's metal tape measure snapped back in the casing. "Taking out the brick wall will be a pain, but it's doable. You'll need a new steel door . . . and a construction permit."

"This is brilliant." I was quite excited. "Pete, you're so freaking smart."

"Don't look at me—it's his design." He pointed a thumb at Ryan.

"At least my two years at Pitt weren't a total waste," Ryan said confidently, twitching his head like it was no big deal.

I secretly added one more trait that I loved about him to my list.

"Ryan, can I get you to redraw this rough sketch? Then I can attach it to the construction permit application," Pete asked.

"Yeah, sure. No problem. Tammy, how big of an oven would you need back here? I guess this stove has to go, too; it looks like a fire hazard."

"Ryan, I can't get a permit for that until I update the fire suppression system for over the stoves," I muttered privately. "All the water lines need to be replaced. That alone is over twenty grand."

He wrapped his arm around my shoulders and whispered in my ear. "Let's figure out what it will cost and we'll talk about it."

It sort of bothered me that he was so willing to part with his money. He reminded me of some kid who had twenty dollars burning a hole in his pocket.

Pete and Tammy left shortly after Ryan gave him a new sketch of the construction, and Cory and Marie were well in control of the bar, so I stayed in my apartment with Ryan.

"So, Ms. Mitchell, since we've come to new agreements, are you ready to renegotiate the terms of your contract?" Ryan raised a questioning brow, smirking hopefully on our way to the bedroom.

"That all depends on what you're offering."

"How about two for the price of one on Tuesdays?" he snickered, pushing the door closed with his fingers.

RYAN WAS so sound asleep he didn't even budge the first time the alarm clock chimed. He was lying flat on his back, spread out on the bed in the same position he'd been after our incredible night. I figured I'd give him a few more minutes, so I went out to the kitchen to start a pot of coffee.

"Ouch," I muttered, walking to the door with a slight limp; my hip was hurting from how he'd maneuvered me last night. I smiled inside, remembering how I got in this much pain.

"Babe, time to wake up," I said when I'd returned. I rubbed my hand across his chest.

Our morning felt like it could quickly become routine. While he showered, I made Ryan's coffee—poured in one of those Styrofoam to-go cups that look like they were bought at the convenience store, and then brushed my teeth while he informed me of his schedule.

We were just like any other normal couple getting ready to go to work. I set out a new pack of gum next to his keys and organized his blue papers so he wouldn't forget them. His cell phone was plugged into the charger, so I readied that for him too.

"You are the best assistant I could ever have hoped for." He wrapped his arms around my waist and kissed me goodbye at the back door. "I love you. I'll call you later."

I trudged up my steps, now wide-awake in the wee hours of the morning. Bored, I turned my computer on with the original excuse of checking on my bank statements, but instead I searched his name.

After I checked his one fan-made blog site, I returned to the news results.

Today's headlines showed the following:

Ryan Christensen autograph signing
Fans make Ryan's new love jealous!

"What the . . . ?" I clicked on the link that referred to my jealousy.

Beware, ladies! Fans make Ryan's new girlfriend see Red!

Fans lined up inside his new hangout, the rustic Mitchell's Pub in Seaport, RI, to see their favorite star as he held an impromptu meet-and-greet Tuesday night. A few lucky ladies who happened to be at the right place at the right time got to meet the sexy actor as he posed for pictures and signed autographs for his die-hard fans.

A few ladies who happened to be there when he arrived shortly before 7:00 p.m. said that he was happy and friendly as he greeted his fans.

"We only had to wait for twenty minutes, so it wasn't too bad. It was worth every second!" one lady reported. Other women who waited over an hour reported that Ryan's supposed new love, bar owner Taryn Mitch-

> ell, was furious as she watched him sign autographs. "She told women to get out and then she yelled at everyone inside—we just laughed."
>
> But a friend of the actor isn't surprised, reporting that Ryan's new girlfriend seems like the jealous, controlling type. It won't take him long to get tired of her. She even tells him who he can hang out with. He has cut off most of his friends from the set and is only allowed to socialize with her friends. Ryan doesn't stay on set any longer than he has to. He's always sneaking off to check in with her when he is there. It's like he has to tell her everything he's doing.
>
> Another insider reports that Ryan has been completely controlled by Taryn. She's even insisting that he move in with her, pushing the relationship into fast-forward. "His luggage was removed from the hotel on Monday."

I felt like I might pass out. This report took everything out of context, and now the entire world would think I was a controlling hell-bitch!

Would he ever get tired of me, like the story said? Did he want someone tending to his needs, or would he think I was crowding him one day? I remembered what happened when I dated Dean. He didn't want someone to take care of him. Every time I tried to be a doting girlfriend, he pulled farther and farther away.

Was I already ruining this relationship? Had I stepped onto the wrong path without even knowing it? I didn't think I was controlling him. Was I? Would he think that I was trying to smother/mother him by setting out his phone, keys, and a pack of gum? I considered that maybe I shouldn't do that anymore.

Ten minutes ago I'd been blissfully happy and now I was a complete and utter mess inside. I curled up under my quilt on the couch and tried to distract myself with television. It didn't help; my mind raced, and a few tears of uncertainty and insecurity dripped down onto the pillow.

Why do I hear music playing? I pondered in my dream. I suddenly woke, hearing my cell phone play in the kitchen. I was a little disoriented. How long had I been sleeping? I looked at the clock on the DVD player—it was a few minutes before ten.

I tossed the quilt off my legs and plodded to the kitchen. My cell phone showed two missed calls—both from Ryan.

I called him back immediately.

"Are you okay?" he asked loudly.

"Yeah, I'm fine. I fell asleep on the couch. I'm sorry, I didn't hear the phone ring."

He breathed out a heavy sigh. "I got worried when you didn't answer."

"I'm fine," I repeated, rubbing my eyes. "How's your day going?"

"It's tolerable. We just took a break. Hey, I was wondering if you could do me a favor? Cal told me about a restaurant someplace outside of Providence called Sabatini's or Salatini's, something like that. I tried to find it on the Net but I can't locate it."

"Let me look." I bumped the mouse on my computer to get the screen saver to clear. The cause of my mental breakdown earlier was still on the screen. "I'm searching for Italian restaurants Providence," I said. I paged through the results.

"La Scalatini? Does that sound like it?" I clicked on the link to their website.

"Can you make reservations for Friday night for my mom's birthday? What time do you think? Eight thirty or nine?"

"Let's shoot for nine; then we have extra time in case we need it," I replied.

"Sounds good. Put it under your last name. Are you going out today?"

"No. I have things I want to do around here." I thought about cleaning the apartment and finishing the laundry. "I have to wash our dirty bed sheets," I snickered.

"Yeah, you did make a mess of things last night," he teased.

"I had help," I giggled.

"I actually think I sprained my hip."

"*You?* I've been limping around here all morning," I admitted.

"Have you really? Huh, that's too funny. And here I thought I was the only one hurting. Guess we put a hurting on each other," he growled. "Cal asked me why I was moving so slow."

"You were asleep about five minutes afterwards . . . in the same position." I laughed.

"You wore me out with all of that good loving. I have to stop thinking about it. I'll see you around seven. I love you."

"I love you, too."

I smiled as I tore the sheets off *our* bed and carried the pile to the laundry room. I heard my phone ring again, but it wasn't his ring tone.

"Hey, Marie, what's up?"

"Taryn?" I could tell by her voice that she had been crying.

"Marie, what's wrong?" I panicked.

"Gary's mom died this morning."

"Oh my God, Marie. I'm so sorry." An old memory of me calling Marie to tell her my mom had died flashed through my mind. "What happened?"

"She must have had a stroke in bed last night. Gary's dad couldn't wake her. And we just saw them a few weeks ago."

"How's Gary?"

"He's a mess." She sniffed. "First time I've ever seen him cry. He's already called off work and, well, it's the other reason I'm calling. Please don't be mad," she pleaded, "but he got us tickets to fly to Tampa tomorrow. He wants to be there—help make arrangements with his dad. We're flying out at eight twenty in the morning."

"No, I completely understand. Don't worry at all."

"Tar, we're going to be gone for a couple of days. I don't think we'll be back until Monday or Tuesday. I hate to do this to you."

"Marie, don't worry about it. Family is first, always first. Is there anything I can do? Do you need anything?"

"No. Just your understanding and love, that's all we need. I really hate this. I know you wanted to spend the weekend with his family; I feel like I'm sticking you. I feel horrible. I'm so sorry."

"Marie. Please. It's okay. I'll figure something out. Just give Gary and his family our condolences."

I turned the washing machine on and added the soap. *Shit*. What was I going to do now? I had just unloaded the dryer when my phone rang again. All of a sudden I was popular.

"Hi, Pete," I answered glumly.

"You okay?" Pete asked.

"Yeah. No. I just got off the phone with Marie. Gary's mom passed away this morning."

After a few minutes of filling him in on what little information I had, he got to the reason for his call. He had calculated the cost of the materials to do the stairwell remodel. The steel door alone was several hundred; combined with drywall and wood studs, it came to almost two thousand dollars. That didn't include his labor.

Pete figured once he got the work permit Thursday morning he could start later that day, but it would be loud with all the banging and he'd have to cut through the brick wall to make the new outside door.

"I can start the demo of the drywall tonight and get that out of the way. Tammy is going to be busy making food for a luncheon she's catering tomorrow anyway. Oh, and before I forget to tell you, she booked a party for Saturday, so she can't work Friday and Saturday nights," he said.

That put the icing on my cake. I was hoping that Tammy would be able to lend a hand to manage the crowd, but now that option was gone, too.

I snapped my phone shut and sat for a while. I couldn't handle the crowds on my own. I was already looking forward to a weekend off with Ryan and his parents. I had just made dinner reservations for Friday. His parents had already cancelled their hotel stay. *Damn.*

I let out a big sigh. I couldn't cancel on Ryan nor jeopardize meeting his parents for the first time. I wandered around the apartment, trying to figure out what to do.

I was leaning on the washing machine when I thought I heard someone scream, instantly grabbing my attention.

"No freaking way," I groaned, looking out my front window. I could clearly see the line of girls forming on my sidewalk. They were waiting for me to open, and it was obvious that they weren't here to drink. The line was so long, there must have been forty or more of them.

I hurried down my steps to get a better look at the situation. I peeked through the blinds, shocked at what I saw. Girls were leaning on my walls; some were sitting on the sidewalk. I looked in the other direction to confirm that the line started at my door. *Un-freaking-believable!*

Right then I made my final decision. I walked to the kitchen to get a piece of cardboard. In my office, I grabbed a fat, black Magic Marker and wrote in big letters:

MITCHELL'S PUB WILL BE CLOSED FOR CONSTRUCTION UNTIL FURTHER NOTICE

I could hear the anger from the waiting crowd when I put the sign in my window. They certainly let me know how they felt about it, but I ignored them and went back upstairs. I had phone calls to make and bands to cancel. There went my Halloween weekend income.

"I'm on my way," Ryan said when he called from his car. "How's the crowd? Everything all right there?"

"There is no crowd. Most of the girls left after I put the 'closed' sign in the window, although a couple of them pounded on my door," I sighed.

"Closed? Taryn, what's—"

"I had no choice," I said. "Gary's mom died this morning. He and Marie are leaving for Tampa tomorrow morning to be with his dad. Marie is staying home with him tonight; he's pretty distraught."

"Jeez, why didn't you call me?"

"For what, Ryan? To give you bad news while you're having a stressful day as it is? I figured I'd fill you in when you got here."

"What about Cory? Isn't he supposed to work tonight?"

"I cancelled him. I cancelled the bands I had scheduled to play this weekend, too. Actually, I've been on the phone most of the afternoon, it seems. Oh, and Pete called. He's coming here tonight to start tearing down the drywall on the steps. That was another reason—Tammy has catering jobs this weekend, so she can't work, either."

"We just turned into the alley. I guess I get to try out my new keys. I'll see you in a minute."

A few minutes later he sprinted up the steps and through the apartment door. "Tar?" he yelled down the hallway.

"Kitchen."

"Hey, you." Ryan hugged and kissed me. "Are you okay?" His fingers drifted down my cheek.

"Yeah, just a bit out of sorts I, guess." He kissed my forehead when I looked down at his feet.

"I'm sorry you had a crappy day." Ryan hugged me so tightly it kind of hurt.

Deep inside, I was marveling that he actually cared what kind of day I had. He was the first in my history of dating to show that emotion.

He sniffed the air. "What smells so good?"

"Pork chops?" I pointed a finger at the glass dish that I'd just taken out of the oven. "Pete is on his way; I figured I'd make him some supper, too, since Tammy is busy baking for tomorrow."

"Tar, what's wrong? I can tell you're sad."

"I'm thinking about Gary. I just have a lot on my mind." I set out three dinner plates on the kitchen table, trying to suppress the memory of my own mother's funeral by trying to figure out what account I was going to move money from to cover Pete's costs.

Ryan filled three glasses with ice and water. "Did Pete call you with an estimate today?"

"Yeah."

"And?" He sounded perturbed.

"He said two grand for the materials; that didn't include his labor."

"That's not bad. I thought it would be more."

Easy for him to say . . . I was trying to figure out how I was going to manage taking a thirteen-thousand-dollar hit this weekend. If I put off the stairwell remodel, then I'd only be down ten thousand in income, minus having to pay for two bands that weren't going to play. It made me edgy to lose that much income from the bar. Halloween was one of my biggest cash nights.

As soon as Pete arrived, we had dinner.

He must have been starving. "That was delicious, Taryn," he complimented. He scraped his plate with his fork. "I've forgotten what it's like to eat home-cooked meals. Tammy only cooks for other people now."

"It was delicious. Thanks for cooking." Ryan smiled and gave me a quick kiss. He brought his dirty plate to the sink and rinsed it off. "Are you ready to tear down some drywall, Pete?"

"What? You helping?"

"Hell yeah. I'm hoping you have an extra sledgehammer, 'cause I have some pent-up Suzanne aggression to get rid of. Oh, and before I forget . . ."

Ryan trotted back to the bedroom and returned with his checkbook. He dug in the junk drawer for a pen.

"What are you doing?" I asked.

"Writing Pete a check."

"For what?"

"The renovations." He looked at me like I was missing the obvious.

"No, I can't let you do that," I stated directly. "My building . . . it's my responsibility."

"Who said anything about you paying for it? I'm paying Pete." He wrinkled his nose at me.

"No! I can't let you do that," I stated firmly.

"I don't really care what you say. I'm paying for the construction and that's that. End of discussion," he said sternly.

Pete was smiling at him for some reason.

"That's way too much, Ryan. No! I can't let you pay for it."

"Taryn, please don't argue with me." He looked back at his checkbook and continued writing. "Pete, I'd appreciate if you would contact the security company and get a separate system added to the new doors. I'd like a sensor put on the roof door as well."

"Okay, will do." I presumed Pete could see the tension growing in the kitchen. He pulled the keys from his pocket. "I'm going to go get my tools. I'll see you downstairs."

Frustration coated with anger started to well up inside me as I washed the dishes. Ryan stood behind me, placing his hands on the edge of the sink counter to keep me from moving away.

"I know you're pissed at me," he whispered in my ear. "But if I wasn't here with you this fix wouldn't be happening. It's because of me that we're doing this. And when I'm not here, I want to know that you're safe. So please try not to be mad at me for long." He nuzzled his face next to mine.

"Besides, I still owe you for the chocolate chip cookies." He swept my hair to the side. "And the card you got for my mom . . . and all of the other stuff you bought for me." He drifted his lips down my neck.

"And the cake I see you're going to bake since all of the ingredients are lying out on the counter. I'm guessing that's for *my* mom?" Ryan wrapped his arms around me. "I take care of you, you take care of me. That was the deal you signed last night."

I leaned back against him and turned my head to look up into his eyes.

"I love you," he said, softly kissing my lips before departing for the door.

An hour had gone by and after I took the cake out of the oven, I went to check on the guys to see how much progress they had made. The hammering had stopped, so I presumed they were finished with the demolition.

I could not believe how different the view was from the top landing with one of the stairwell walls removed. Sandwiched between the layers of drywall was an old layer of plaster and thin strips of wood. I picked at a loose piece of drywall that hung from the corner, trying to even out the jagged line they had made at the top of the landing.

"Taryn amazes me," I heard Ryan say. My body became rigid after hearing my name mentioned. I held my breath in my lungs so I wouldn't make a sound.

"I can't believe how obstinate she gets when I offer to do anything nice for her. I bought her earrings, but she refuses to wear them. She said I spent too much money. I guess I have to take them back to the jewelry store." He sighed. "I thought it was genetically impossible for women to turn down jewelry, but not her."

"She's one of a kind. But then again, I think you already know that," Pete replied.

"I've never met anyone like her. First girl I've gone out with that hasn't wanted *anything* from me. I'm not quite sure how to react. Has she always been like this?"

"Yeah," Pete answered him. "As long as I've known her, she's always been a giver, not a taker. Taryn has helped us out so many times over the years; that's why I'm here whenever she needs me. I could do something nice for her every day and it wouldn't be enough."

He laughed lightly. "Just like tonight. I come here to try and do some work, pay her back somehow, and yet she's up there cooking dinner to make sure we're taken care of. And it's not just me now—I'm talking about you, too. She'd go out of her mind if you didn't get a hot meal in your stomach."

"I *want* to take care of her, believe me. But she fights me when I try. I'm not sure what to do." Ryan sounded defeated.

"Here," Pete said. I heard the hiss of a cap being twisted off a bottle of beer.

"I don't know what to tell ya, Ryan. She just needs to be loved. You know, real love. She was hurt really bad a few months ago; I thought she'd never let another man touch her again."

"What do you mean? What happened?"

"Ahh, don't say anything to Taryn, but she was dating this guy . . . I couldn't stand him, actually," Pete admitted. "He was an asshole. I used to think she put up with his crap because it took her mind off of dealing with the pain of losing her pop . . . I don't know. We all suspected he was cheating on her, but when she'd confront him about it he'd always have an excuse. Then he'd turn it around on her, making her feel like shit for even saying something. I thought she'd had just about enough of him, and then one day out of the blue the son of a bitch has an epiphany; tells her he loves her and wants to marry her—even got her a piece-of-shit ring."

"Then what happened?" Ryan said.

I heard Pete clear his throat. He had lowered his voice to the point that it was almost hard to hear him. "She went over to his apartment one afternoon and caught him in bed screwing some girl. That was that. She finally saw it with her own eyes. Took all that I had within me not to go over there and crush his fucking skull."

"She said something about some guy and how one woman wasn't enough. Now I understand. She never told me she was engaged, though."

"Does it matter?" Pete asked.

"No. Not one bit. I just don't know why she didn't mention it to me."

"Well, it's pretty obvious to me. You're not just *some guy*, Ryan. You've got girls lining up all around the world for you. You don't think something like that isn't going to make *whatever* girl you're with a bit insecure? Taryn is up there just hanging on by a thread, waiting for you to bolt the minute you find someone else. Tell you the truth, we're all kind of preparing for that day."

"I can tell you that *that* isn't gonna happen. That woman up there is mine. I'm never going to let her go. In my mind, there is no one else," Ryan declared.

I felt a slight rush in my chest and gasped from hearing him say that.

"Well, I hope what you say is true. I mean, you've only known her for a couple of weeks," Pete said, a hint of doubt etched in his voice.

I heard a glass bottle clink on the counter.

"You want to know why she's fighting you?" Pete asked somewhat harshly. "Because she is smart enough to know that the day will come when you're not here every day. You've got more opportunities than most men could ever dream of to meet women. You don't even have to *try* to get laid—there's a whole selection waiting and willing right out there on *her* sidewalk!

"Taryn is an intelligent, attractive woman. Let me tell ya, she's not without opportunities of her own. You should see how many guys drool over her every day."

"I know. I've seen plenty of them hit on her," Ryan admitted.

"Yeah, they do. But she's not like that—she never was. And when some dirtbag from Seaport didn't think enough of her not to cheat on her, what's to say you won't do the same?" Pete asked. "When you're out there doing your thing and some hot model climbs on your lap and sticks her tits in your face . . . you gonna be able to resist that?

"This is *her* life here, Ryan. This is *her* stability. It's the only thing she can count on in this world. She struggled and suffered for every bit of it. And you come in here, taking that over. When you break up with her, every time she looks at that new wall or that new door . . .

"Ah, just do us all a favor—if you aren't one hundred percent in love with Taryn and ready to make a life with her, then stop. Don't do what you're doing. Please don't hurt her like that."

"Pete, I don't want to take anything over or hurt her," Ryan said somberly. "I want to share everything I have with her. My life, my money . . . I want her to be the mother of my children one day."

I flinched back from the shock of hearing his admission.

I heard Ryan sigh loudly. "Pete, I know you don't know me that well but believe me, I'm done with the meaningless shit. I've been crazy about Taryn since the first . . ."

Since the first what? I leaned closer to the wall to hear him.

"Huh. I just realized something. She has been taking care of me since the first day that I met her. Not even—from the first ten seconds of me setting foot in this place. Knowing Taryn, she probably never told you the real story of how we met.

"She stopped the fans that were chasing me. She shut this whole place down for me, and here she is . . . doing it again. No wonder she's so sad today. I'm messing with her safety net. Oh fuck, how do I fix this?"

"I don't know," Pete muttered. "Marry her? Never leave her for some Hollywood slut? What kind of answer are you looking for?"

"Pete, I'm so in love with her and I've told her that already. I've never felt this way before, about anyone. I know what I want. I want a life with *her*."

"I know, Ryan. I can tell just by the way you look at her." Pete sighed heavily. "Oh, man, well, just treat her right, 'cause I'd hate like hell to have to break that nice jaw of yours if you ever break her heart."

CHAPTER 20

Insight

I'LL BE FILMING when you pick my parents up, so I'll call you when I get a break," Ryan said, rubbing the shampoo in my hair.

I leaned back to rinse under the water. "I thought I'd take them to lunch near the set; there's a really nice restaurant down by the pier."

"Just so you know . . . my dad is going to insist on paying for lunch. It will offend him if you argue." He looked at me with a knowing smirk on his lips.

"Like father, like son?" I asked jokingly, rubbing the soap bubbles on his chest.

"Exactly. But when we take them to dinner tomorrow, he'll pass the check to me—just watch. Hey, do you want to bring them to the set this afternoon instead? I'd really like you to see what I do for a living, since you won't watch any of my movies."

"I don't know," I murmured. "Won't that cause problems with you-know-who?"

Ryan grimaced at me. "I don't care. I want my girlfriend . . . my love," he looked me in the eyes, "to know what I do and where I go every day. I *want* you to trust me. I *need* you to trust me, Taryn."

"Are you sure it won't disturb you or ruin your performance? I don't want to mmm—"

His wet mouth was locked on mine, stopping my words in midstream.

"Please." He kissed me again softly, resting his forehead on mine. "I need you to understand what I do. I need you to see that when I'm on set, I'm an actor. That what I do is pretend. My lips, my heart, *and* my body . . . they belong to you."

I looked up at him and nodded. After eavesdropping on his conversation with Pete, I knew he wanted me to trust him.

"Do I have to make a poster and scream 'Ryan, Ryan'?" I kidded.

"Hah!" He laughed. "The only time I want to hear you scream my name is when I'm making love to you. Although you did call me God the other night. That's acceptable, too." He leaned down and gave me another kiss.

I put on my nice dark trouser jeans and white long-sleeved cotton top, with my brown suede zip jacket and a soft green scarf wrapped around my neck. I wanted to look nice the first time I met his parents, and I was nervous since I was meeting them alone.

We had agreed that I would bring his parents to see him in action tomorrow. Ryan showed me a picture of his mom and dad to help me recognize them easier, although I must admit it was hard to commit a picture flashed at me to memory. Both of his parents were in their upper fifties in age, but still looked quite vibrant and youthful. At least I knew that they would be seeking me out in the airport, too.

I was, of course, photographed walking down the sidewalk to my car. I opted for leaving by the front door, since most of the paparazzi were now loitering by my back door. I allowed my eyes to scan the area for any signs of the old blue Plymouth, and I was relieved that Angelica Staunton's car was nowhere to be seen. There were, however, a few love notes stuck to my car. I collected them and shoved them into the center console.

I kept checking my rearview mirror for any signs of photographers following me as I drove to the airport. I was relieved that I didn't see any.

My nerves were getting the better of me as I stood in the open entrance to the airport; my stomach was filled with butterflies. Dads were always easier to win over; I knew from experience that it was always the mothers that were the challenge.

It was almost ten thirty when a new stream of passengers started to pass by. Their flight from Newark actually landed a few minutes early.

"Taryn?" A lovely woman politely approached me. His mother was just as I had pictured. She was about an inch shorter than me, five-five-ish, thin but softly padded by well-earned years. Her reddish-brown hair was long and thick on the top but cut short to her neck. I recognized her instantly; Ryan had his mother's features and most definitely her eyes.

"Yes! Mrs. Christensen. It's so nice to meet you!" We gave each other a hug.

"Oh, it's so nice to meet you too, dear. Please, call me Ellen. This is Ryan's father, Bill."

I instinctively reached out my hand to shake his, but he pulled me in for an awkward hug. "It's so nice to meet you, sir."

"It's nice to finally meet you too, young lady," Bill said with a huge grin on his face.

Ryan's father was tall, just like Ryan, but with another thirty or so pounds of weight. I could see bits of his father in Ryan, too. Bill's face was rounder and clean-shaven, and he wore rectangular wire-rimmed glasses. Ryan had inherited his hair color from his father, although Bill's hair had tinges of gray mingled in it. I pictured Ryan taking on his father's looks one day.

"So this must be the Infiniti my son keeps telling me about," Bill said from the passenger seat. I smiled as he ran his fingers over the dash.

"Ryan likes to drive it, and to be honest, I rather enjoy it when he does. He's a great driver," I stated proudly.

"We have his car in our garage back home. It was the first thing he bought when he cashed in his first big paycheck. Come to think of it, that car is the only thing he bought. I'm going to have to remind him that he can afford his own garage now. Then my car doesn't have to sit in the driveway."

"You will do no such thing, Bill," Ellen reprimanded him. "At least we know that we can get him to come home every once in a while, even if it is to visit his car."

"Our son tells us that you've never seen any of his movies. Is that really true?" Bill asked.

"Yes, sir, it's true." I nodded my head. "I've never seen him act before. He wants us to come to the set tomorrow, so I suppose I'll get to see him perform for the first time then."

Ellen laughed out loud. "I believe you're the only woman on the planet who hasn't seen his movies."

"To be honest, I think it's better that way," I justified.

Ryan's ring tone began to play on my cell phone. I knew he was going to be on edge until his parents were safely in my care. His behaviors were becoming so predictable.

I drove down the coast to a nice restaurant that jutted out over the ocean. We had a lovely view of the Atlantic from our window table.

Ryan's parents were very nice and friendly toward me. I had expected to be grilled with questions, but Ryan had apparently filled them in with a lot of details, so our conversation was more validation of the things they already knew.

I told them about attending Brown University and my career goals at that time, and my current involvements with the vineyards and the pub. His parents asked a lot of questions about the vineyard businesses and the details of co-ownership, and I was happy to tell them what I knew.

His father was keen on knowing as much as he could about diversifying his holdings and investment opportunities other than the standard retirement plans. We had a long conversation just on that subject alone.

It was apparent throughout the conversation that his father was worried about Ryan's money and making sure it was properly invested. I told them that I felt Ryan was looking to expand into other areas of opportunity but I didn't go into specifics. I certainly didn't want them to know how willing he was to dump his money into refurbishing the kitchen in my pub.

The last thing I wanted was for his parents to think I was only after their famous son's money. I tried to inadvertently express how I was doing financially so they would be at ease knowing that I'm a smart businesswoman all on my own and I have my own money in the bank.

They told me stories about Ryan and how he liked to draw pictures of houses when he was younger. His parents always thought that he'd become an architect one day. Even when he was a child, everything he drew or built had to be symmetrical. Block buildings, Tinkertoys, Legos—everything was always designed evenly.

Ellen recalled how Ryan's modeling career started—she took Ryan to get his picture taken when he was three years old and the photographer suggested that she take him to one of the local modeling agencies. Soon after that, Ryan was pictured in national clothing store fliers modeling children's clothing. His pictures were even used in a few parenting magazines. She promised to show them to me one day. I was sure that would embarrass Ryan to no end.

It was late in his high school years when he became active in the drama club. His mother said he was a natural on the stage. I loved listening to her stories—to hear the pride in her voice when she spoke of him.

They also spoke a lot about their other son, Nick, and his wife, Janelle, and how they met at work and fell madly in love. They had been married three years now and had their first daughter, Sarah, almost ten months ago. His parents were very easy to talk to, and I had the same feeling talking to them as I did when I first met Ryan.

Just as Ryan had predicted, his father snatched up the restaurant bill even before the waitress set it on the table. I held out my hand, for I really did want to treat them to lunch, but his father waved for me to put my hand down and strung a few no, no, no's along as he reached for his wallet. I dropped it, so as to not offend him.

I took them for a brief drive around the area, showing them the only two spots where I knew Ryan had filmed. I spared them the details about the two women who were arrested storming onto the movie set when they filmed on the beach. I figured they, too, had enough to worry about.

I drove down my street, showing them the front of my building while also secretly assessing how many fans and paparazzi were staked out. I drove down the alley, despite having paparazzi lurking there as well. Ryan's father quickly unloaded their luggage from my trunk.

I was surprised to see that he knew the little Italian photographer. "Jimmy? Jimmy Pop? Are you still chasing my son?" Bill asked.

"Oh, Mr. Christensen, oi!" Jimmy said in his thick accent, tossing his cigarette butt into the alley. "Mrs. Christensen! You look so lovely! Oh, my, my. What a blessed day. How are you?"

"We're well. We're here visiting our son. You guys aren't bothering him too much, are you?" Bill teased.

"Oh, no, no. Well, you know, it's a job. I miss when your boy works in nice, warm places. This cold weather, it's no good for my hands. Oh, the pain," Jimmy said, rubbing his arthritic fingers.

While we stood there talking to Jimmy, other photographers took our picture. Ryan's parents didn't seem to be fazed by it.

"Your son . . . he has a lovely girl here. Look, look, how pretty. Oh, makes my heart happy." Jimmy patted his chest. "She not like those others." He waved a crooked finger in the air. "She's very nice."

"Thank you, sir. That's very kind." I smiled at him.

"See? She call me sir. No other one call me sir. They all say, 'Jimmy, you go away.'"

I noticed how Jimmy's pants seemed to be two sizes too big. The front of his pants puckered where his belt cinched up the extra fabric. He was looking malnourished.

"Jimmy, are you hungry? I have half of a sandwich here that I didn't touch. Would you like it?" I handed him the Styrofoam box.

"You give me food?" He looked inside to see the half of the chicken club wrap I hadn't eaten and an unopened bag of chips.

I nodded. "You put that in your belly. I'm going to take Ryan's parents in now. They've had a long trip."

"Bless you, Miss Taryn. Bless you!"

I quickly moved my car to the lot and noticed the old, blue Plymouth parked on the opposite corner of Mulberry Street. Angelica was sitting in her car again. Just seeing her, knowing that she was doing nothing with her life other than stalking us, sent a chill of fright down my spine. I hurried down the alley to my back door to flee Psycho Girl's view.

"I'm sorry for the disarray, but I'm remodeling. Please come in." I walked them into the main bar area and turned on the dimmer lights. I turned the billiard room light on too so they could see the entire pub.

Bill walked over to the pool table. "So this is where it happened?" He tapped his fingers on the felt, looking at me for confirmation.

My cheeks suddenly became flushed and a wave of panic coursed through my chest. How much did Ryan share with his father? Did he tell his dad about ripping my panties off and bending me over the pool table? Bill was standing in almost the same exact spot.

I looked at him like a deer caught in headlights.

"Where he met you?" his father continued.

Oh, thank God.

"Yes," I breathed out. "He came through that door, and . . ." I opened my hands.

"Ryan told us how the girls were chasing him," Ellen added. She knew I was keeping the details out.

"Speaking of girls . . ." I walked over to my front door and retrieved today's pile of love letters. There were at least thirty today.

"You get a lot of mail," Ellen commented.

"It's not my mail. These are all for your son. His admirers have started to leave their love notes in my mail slot. They cover my car with letters, too. These girls must think he has a real open-minded girlfriend or something."

"Let me see, please." Bill reached for a sample. I willingly handed him the pile.

He tore one of the envelopes open. This one happened to have a picture of a naked girl in it. I could tell by the way his eyes bugged out in his face.

"They know no boundaries," I muttered. "A few days ago, I caught two of them trying to break into my apartment to see him."

"Ellen, it's getting worse. We have to talk to him." His father was very displeased with whatever he saw in the next few envelopes.

I helped carry their luggage upstairs to my apartment. Bill and Ellen appeared amazed when they saw the lovely conditions their son was living in. They showered me with compliments. I had spent extra time cleaning and preparing for their arrival last night to make sure they would be pleased.

"Can I interest you in a glass of wine from one of our wineries?" I took them into the kitchen. His mother's eyes lit up and a huge smile appeared on her face as she entered. I did have a cool kitchen.

"Taryn, this is magnificent! Bill, look at this stove. I *want* this stove," she insisted.

I pulled out a new bottle of chablis and uncorked it. I was in the mood for white wine. Just then, I heard Ryan run up the steps.

Ryan dropped his keys off on the entry table by the door and he had a box under his arm when he came into the kitchen. He hugged his father first, since he was still standing. His mom stood up from the table and gave her son a big squeeze and a kiss.

"Oh, it's so good to see you," she gushed, rocking him back and forth where he stood. It was such a heartwarming reunion.

As soon as she released him, Ryan came over to me and pulled me in for a nice, respectful hello kiss.

"Hi, honey. How's everyone doing?" He looked around at all of us to make sure we were getting along. His mother told him about the nice restaurant where we had lunch and how she enjoyed the view of the ocean. I poured four glasses of wine and handed them out.

"Taryn, this is delicious," his father commented, swirling the wine around in his glass.

"Here, check these out." Ryan handed the box over to me. Inside were all different styles of sunglasses. "Some sunglass company wants me to wear their shades. They sent a whole box for me *and* my lady."

I rolled my eyes at him.

"For real. Look at the letter. 'Mr. Christensen, we are honored to provide you with our Fall collection of Sun Jammer Eyewear. We have provided you with styles to suit men as well as a selection of women's eyewear for your favorite lady.' See? 'Favorite lady,' right there in black type." He poked me in the belly on his way to the pantry. Ryan opened the door and removed the bag of chocolate chip cookies.

"Oh no, you have *her* feeding your fix now?" Ellen scolded.

We took his parents on a tour of the apartment and we put our coats back on to visit the roof patio. Bill and Ellen appeared speechless—up until the point that Ellen stated she wanted to redo their entire backyard to look like my roof.

I knew Ryan was starving; he was starting to pick at anything he could readily shove in his mouth when we returned to the kitchen. I turned the oven on and pulled out the ingredients I had set aside to make chicken Cordon Bleu. I pounded the chicken breasts flat while Ryan nabbed a few layers of the sliced cheese. He was too hungry to be of any use.

"So what do you say, son? Want to lose to your old man in a game of pool?" His father gave him a nudge.

While the men played downstairs, I prepared dinner. His mother watched over what I was doing.

"I never thought to put that in with the bread crumbs," she commented. She helped coat the rolled chicken and was amazed by my deviations from the normal recipe. I liked to be creative when I cooked.

Later that evening, we gathered at the oval wooden dining table that was off to the side of my living room. I hadn't sat at that table for a meal in a very long time. It felt nice to eat as a family again.

"Taryn, this is fabulous," Ellen complimented.

Ryan kicked his foot into mine under the table and winked at me. "I told you she was taking excellent care of me." He grinned.

"So are you two going to tell us where we are going this weekend, or are you going to keep your mother and me in suspense?"

Ryan looked at me and smirked. "Should we tell them, or make them suffer like you made me suffer that day?"

I stabbed a few green beans on my plate. "I think we should tell them."

"We are taking you to Taryn's family cabin at the lake, where *we* are going fishing." He motioned to his father with his fingers. "And you two ladies can go shopping till your feet fall off."

Our evening with his parents slowly came to a close. Ryan had to be back on set early in the morning, and his parents were tired from their flight.

I quickly slipped into my bedroom to get my pillow and carried it out to the living room.

Ryan looked at me in utter confusion. He picked my pillow up and started to carry it away. "Babe, I thought we were going to bed?" He yawned.

"No," I whispered. "Please leave it here. I'm going to sleep out here on the couch."

"Why?" he asked, completely perplexed.

"Your parents," I whispered again.

"What about my parents?"

"Out of respect!" I quietly stated the obvious.

"What are you talking about?" I wished he would keep his voice down.

"Ryan, I'm not going to sleep with you in front of them," I whispered.

"Are you kidding me?" Just as he spoke, his mother stepped up behind him.

"What are you two whispering about?" she asked.

"I'm not quite sure, Mom. For some reason Taryn thinks she has to sleep on the couch."

I was thoroughly embarrassed now and had to explain myself.

"I don't want to disrespect you, that's all. It's fine," I politely informed. "I don't mind sleeping out here." I tried to yank my pillow out of Ryan's hand but he wouldn't let it go.

Ellen looked confused, and then I saw the light of understanding turn on above her head.

"Oh, sweetie, that's not necessary." She walked over to me and gave me a big hug. "I appreciate your consideration, but Bill and I are not *that* old-fashioned." She gently laughed in my ear. "This is your home."

Ellen touched Ryan's cheek while she was rocking me. "You stay with Ryan in your room," she said tenderly. "Oh, how I would have loved to have met your parents." She kissed me on the cheek.

"Why did you think you had to sleep out on the couch?" Ryan asked privately in our bedroom. He pulled our comforter up over my shoulder.

I shrugged, slightly self-conscious. "I just don't want your parents to have the wrong impression of me, that's all. I wasn't raised that way."

"Oh, you don't have to worry about that. You've already made a good impression on my parents today," Ryan whispered, inching his way down the bed until our eyes were level. "My dad talked my ear off when we played pool. He was rambling on about how intelligent you are and how I could learn a thing or two about money management from you."

"I'm glad they like me; relieved, actually. It's very important that they approve." I shifted to be closer to him, gently rubbing his neck while we talked.

"Oh, they approve all right. You've won them over, that's for sure." He brushed my hair back. "Do you have *any* idea how much I love you?"

"No," I whispered, egging him on. "How much?"

"Let me show you," he whispered. He softly kissed my lips, once, twice, before his wet mouth moved with mine.

I WAS up and out of bed before everyone else so I could spend some extra time showering and getting ready. I was already slightly jittery thinking about going on my first major-motion-picture movie set. Never in my wildest dreams did I ever think about doing what I would be doing today.

"Are you excited?" Ryan asked, pulling my heart necklace out from behind my shirt while we waited by the back door.

"Nervous." I half-smiled. My stomach was in knots.

It was still dark outside when our car arrived. It was too early for the paparazzi to be up. Ryan's day usually started before the sun came up. I was relieved knowing that his parents would be with me throughout this experience.

We briefly paused at the security gate and then proceeded to drive farther onto the lot. The limo wove through several rows of trailers and other trucks before stopping by a long, white trailer.

"Here, you'll need these." Ryan handed us badges on long cotton cords to identify that we were permitted on set.

He had his blue papers rolled up in his hand.

"I have to go to makeup and get my face done. Tar, come with me." Ryan took me by the hand. "Mom, Dad . . . I'll see you over there." He pointed to the direction of where he'd be filming.

His bodyguard, Mike, and another man escorted us to a long trailer. Inside were several beautician chairs and a complete makeup counter with mirrors. The second we were through the door, several people started to attend to Ryan. He had barely a moment to introduce me to the special-effects makeup team. The people I met were polite, but they had a job to do and little time to do it. Everyone was in a rush.

First, Ryan had to change into his wardrobe; he had to wear dark pants and a white button-down cotton shirt that was pre-speckled with what looked like blood. Then he was covered in a cotton shawl and several makeup artists went right to work on him.

He just sat there while they covered him in creams and pigments, using sponges and brushes and all sorts of items I had never seen before. One of the makeup artists, an older Asian woman wearing thick-rimmed red glasses with her long ebony hair pulled back into a ponytail, started brushing purple pigment below Ryan's left eye. By the time they were done with him, he looked like he was on the losing end of a fistfight, down to the dried fake blood coming out of his nostril.

He smiled and winked at me. "I look pretty rough, huh?"

Even though I'd just watched them transform him into this bloodied mess, I almost wanted to cry seeing him looking so beat up. Instead, I smiled and nodded in agreement.

"Pete said he'd do this to my face if I ever broke your heart. Guess I'd better not do that, then."

I was glad to know that he was totally unaware of my eavesdropping during his conversation with Pete. I rolled my eyes at his comment, pretending to have heard it for the first time.

Another male assistant was chattering back and forth over a handheld radio. "Ryan, they're ready for you over on set nine."

Moments later, we were whisked away on the back of an ordinary golf cart, Mike dutifully by his side. Once we'd stopped, Ryan quickly spoke into my ear.

"You're going to see some stunts today and, at the end of this scene I have to . . . kiss . . ." His face twisted in disgust. "Her."

We walked onto the set; I had to blink several times to realize that this ornate castle hall was actually built inside an ordinary warehouse.

"Jake, please send someone for my parents. I want them here with Taryn," Ryan requested. Then he said to me, "You should be okay here. No heckling!" He kissed my forehead before rushing away.

I was hiding off to the side of the one wall, trying to stay out of the way. Thick black electrical cords twisted and twined all over the floors. There were bright lights, scaffolding, and all kinds of gadgets everywhere. I was petrified that I might accidentally bump something expensive or someone important. People were hustling all around me. Some were wearing headphones or carrying a piece of technical equipment. Clipboards, cameras, lighting adjustments—it seemed like chaos all around.

I felt a hand touch my back and realized that Ryan's mom was next to me now.

"Overwhelming, isn't it?" she asked. I was in a daze watching it all unfold around me.

A woman wearing headphones around her neck approached us. "Hi! Welcome! You may want to move over there to get a better view. Come with me."

I looked around for Ryan; he was standing with several men and they were all moving their arms in the air, looking like they were discussing how Ryan should throw his punch. It appeared to be a rehearsal before they filmed the scene. An older man, short and almost bald, wearing headphones around his neck and carrying some device that looked like a small telescope, stepped over to talk to Ryan.

"That's the director," his dad said.

Ryan spent a good amount of time nodding and discussing how he was supposed to move.

"I think that guy to Ryan's left is the stunt coordinator."

I was glad his father was standing behind me explaining things. I had no idea who any of these people were.

I heard someone yell "quiet on the set." I tried not to breathe.

I watched a man hold the clapper board out in front of the camera.

Ryan took his position in the fake room. I could see his image on three small video screens near the director.

"Rolling!" someone else yelled.

"Action!" the director called out.

Ryan took a few steps and then was attacked by a man in a cloak. Ryan threw a right hook, and a cord pulled the man he punched back onto a pile of foam.

Was that it? Everyone was mingling around on the set again. I looked at his father. "Did they just film that?"

Bill smiled at me. "I think so."

Ryan had to get back into position, and then he fought the same man again. It took them almost an hour to film this one particular scene. They shot it from so many different angles.

The only time I knew that they weren't filming was when the makeup artist was touching up Ryan's face. I was constantly wondering how everyone knew what was going on. Either you had a job where you had to run around and scramble or your job was to stand around and look important.

"Hey, girl! I heard you were here." Kat gave me a hug.

"Hey, Kat! Oh, it's good to see you." I was relieved to see another familiar face in this chaos.

"Hi, Ellen, Bill! Here to see your boy in action, huh? What's he doing now?" Kat looked around to see where Ryan was. "Oh, great. Make way for the queen."

I saw Suzanne walk through another entrance. Of course, she glanced over and saw that I was standing there. Her eyes opened wider.

"You're going to be cool with this, right?" Kat bumped my arm. "He has to, um, kiss her now. Yuck. You don't have to look if you think it might bother you."

In reality, I wanted to see this. I needed to have this experience of seeing him . . . act. "I'll be all right," I murmured.

Suzanne seemed unfazed that I was there; actually, she seemed to be in a good mood. She was laughing and sort of carrying on with Ryan. He laughed, too, at whatever she said. It was a relief to know that their relationship wasn't totally ruined because of me.

After what seemed to be an extraordinary long time, they finally got into their positions to film the scene. Ryan's eyes locked on mine for a moment; it seemed like he was trying to send me a message telepathically. I knew what was coming next.

I was too far away to hear the dialogue that they exchanged, but the scene involved Ryan still being bruised and bloodied. He grabbed the upper part of Suzanne's arms and they seemed to fight each other. She wasn't supposed to like the grip he had on her. She reached up to slap him in the face and he grabbed her by the wrist. I remembered how, when we played pool that very first day, I tried to teasingly nudge him and he caught me the same way in midair around *my* wrist.

With his other hand he grabbed her around the back of her neck and forcefully pulled her in for a kiss. After a brief second of her fighting it, she surrendered to his lips.

I took a deep breath through my nose while he kissed her. It was harder than I thought it would be to see the man I was in love with kiss another woman. I knew it was pretend, but the burn of jealousy still pulsed through me. I unconsciously curled my fingers into fists by my sides; my fingernails dug into my palms. Ryan's mother placed her hand on my shoulder as reassurance that it was going to be all right.

When I couldn't take it anymore, I looked down to the ground, then turned my gaze to the opposite wall. Something struck me as odd—why was that man over there taking pictures of Ryan kissing Suzanne? He didn't use a flash on his camera.

"How are you doing?" Kat whispered to me. I could hear the tension and concern in her tone.

Suzanne really played it up; my presence was encouraging her Oscar-worthy performance for sure.

"I want to peel her off of him and set her on fire, but I'll get through it."

The director yelled, "Cut."

Kat laughed, amused by my comment. "It will get easier with time. You at least have the satisfaction of knowing that he's hating this part of his job."

"Is he really?" I wasn't so sure by the looks of it.

"See, Ellen? Taryn wants to crack Suzanne in half. This girl is definitely in love with your son." Kat wistfully danced in place.

"I don't want to crack anyone," I quickly replied. I didn't want his parents to think I was obsessive or controlling.

Ryan and Suzanne's kissing scene had halted and the director was talking to both of them. They nodded at him as he gave his direction. Apparently they had to do it again. I watched as they ran through their dialogue again, he had her by the arms again, and once again he grabbed her by the back of the neck. This time she fought him a little longer before surrendering.

The second time wasn't as bad as the first, although it still bothered me to see Ryan kissing someone else. My mind scanned over all the various movies I had seen in my lifetime and all the kisses that were exchanged on film. All those kisses had to look believable to sell the feel of the movie. I thought about one of my favorite actors and how he had to kiss the actress in one of his movies. Yet at night he went home to his lovely wife and their children.

I can do this, I told myself. *His lips belong to me—he even told me so. It's just pretend; I'm his—he's mine.*

I was in mid-discussion with Kat and his parents about some of the background story to this movie when Ryan slipped his hands around my waist. I wasn't expecting it, so I jumped slightly from his touch.

"What did you think?" he whispered in my ear.

"I think you looked pretty tough fighting that guy. I thought you actually punched him! It looked real from this angle." I giggled as he held his hands to my stomach.

"That's movie magic," he snickered.

"I think you have a cool job," I murmured back to him.

"And what about the other part?" Ryan asked tentatively. He whispered his words on my neck.

I knew what he was referring to—kissing the . . . Suzanne.

"First time was very difficult, but the second, um, take? That was slightly easier. She seemed to put more effort into it, though, probably because I'm here."

"I have to agree. Her performance was definitely for your benefit," he said. "Maybe you should be here every day? Did you see how nice she was to me?"

We took a walk around the area and Ryan showed us his trailer. It was really nice inside; like a mini apartment on wheels. He made sure to show me the large bed in the back where he napped sometimes when he wasn't needed on set. The bedroom had a large television built into the wall, and his refrigerator was stocked with his favorite soda.

I was in Ryan's trailer when Tammy called.

"Taryn, my brother called me. He has some information on that girl. You may want to go to the police. Taryn, she's not well."

Ryan was watching me; his eyebrows were pulled together in confusion, trying to figure out my conversation.

"Can you be more specific?" I asked.

"You have to realize that Tony isn't supposed to do this kind of stuff. You can't tell anyone, especially when you talk to the police, okay?"

I was instantly concerned when she said that. I had a lot of questions I wanted to ask her, but since I had an audience, I had to be cryptic.

"I understand. Please . . . go on."

"I'm going to read you the report he gave me. Angelica Staunton, age thirty-one, former addresses are Bridgeport, New Jersey, Brooklyn, New York, and there's one address on her in Los Angeles. She's been arrested three times: once for prostitution in New York and twice for other offenses in California. Taryn, ten years ago she had a restraining order put out on her. When she was in L.A. she was accused of stalking another celebrity.

Her second arrest was for a violation of a court order. Her third arrest was for breaking and entering—she was found at three in the morning, bathing naked in the swimming pool at the celebrity's home. I can't tell you the celebrity's name because Tony wouldn't give that to me."

I took a deep breath through my nose and squeezed my eyes shut. This girl was now stalking my boyfriend.

I stepped into the bedroom area of Ryan's trailer. "Has she ever done physical harm?" I whispered.

"There's nothing in the report other than her making threats, but she's definitely a stalker. I wouldn't take my chances."

"Thanks, Tammy. I owe you one."

"What's going on?" Ryan asked.

"Nothing." I halfheartedly smiled. "I'll tell you later." I ran my finger down my nose so he would know I was lying.

After lunch we drove to another location offsite. Ryan had his face touched up; more purple pigment was added under his eye. He told me that the entire movie was shot out of sequence. He explained to me why they did that. I'd never known that movies were filmed that way; I'd always thought that they were filmed as the movie progressed, just like a stage play.

We drove to an ordinary house by the beach, which would be his next location for filming. As we drove down the street, we were inundated with scores of female fans of all ages, shapes, and sizes, all screaming for their favorite actor.

We were ushered inside quickly. Ryan waited behind. The minute he stepped out of the car, the fans screamed. I watched him from the doorway; his bodyguards shielded him as they moved him from the car to the house. Ryan barely acknowledged the crowd. Somehow the paparazzi knew where to find him and we were all photographed exiting the limo, but the cameras clicked double-time when he was in view. My love was constantly under the microscope.

Ryan had some pretty intense lines that he had to say in the scenes that were filmed in the house. Each of his lines was expertly delivered. For the first time since I met him, he was different. He wasn't Ryan—he was Charles. He truly amazed me. I could see why his fans adored him. But despite his professional demeanor and his superb acting skills, I adored him for different reasons.

I was actually tired from spending an entire day in his world. I think it was all the standing around and doing nothing but watching that tired me out. I was used to running around and keeping active to do my job; his work was more mentally tiring than anything. I grinned at him as he joked with the crew. Even though it was serious business to film, everyone was having fun and being very supportive.

On our way home down Mulberry Street I spotted her, Angelica, sitting in her blue Plymouth across the street from the parking lot where I park my car.

I unconsciously gripped Ryan's arm and gasped.

"What?" He looked to see my expression of terror. "Tar, honey?"

"Nothing. I'll tell you later." Instinctively, I slumped down in the seat to get my head below window level.

Pete was still inside the pub kitchen when we arrived, hammering away. The old counter was gone and he had the new wall partially built already. I was shocked to see how far he had gotten.

Ryan and his parents started talking with Pete about construction stuff; I was a little distraught, so I headed upstairs. It didn't take me long to crawl onto the bed.

"Tar, are you tired?" Ryan asked, finding me in the bedroom. He shoved his pillow under his arm. "So what was that all about in the car earlier? Why did you grab my arm like that?"

"She was sitting in her freaking car again," I muttered into my pillow.

"Who? What are you talking about?"

"Angel. Or Angelica Staunton, as she's really known." I looked at him with fear in my eyes. "Curly-haired, gap-toothed girl? I think she's been following you . . . and me. She followed me to CostMart the other day. She was in the bar that day you signed autographs, and now once again she's just sitting in her car on Mulberry Street. Honey, she scares the hell out of me."

Two seconds later he pulled his phone out and made a call. When he hung up, he told me, "My manager says we should go to the police and file a complaint."

Ryan sat back down on the bed. "Taryn, I'm not mad, but you have to promise me that you'll tell me immediately if anyone is following you or scaring you. You know that these girls are . . . well—you know. Just promise you'll tell me right away," he insisted.

I nodded. "I promise."

• • •

RYAN LOOKED handsome in his black pants and white button-down shirt. I put on my new black cocktail dress and adjusted the empire-waist satin sash.

He took the little black box off my dresser and held it open, reminding me of the diamond earrings I'd been avoiding.

"Please. Humor me," he insisted.

I hesitated and took a deep breath. I was holding the twined hearts pendant in my fingers as it rested on my neck.

"I'm not taking them back, so you might as well wear them!" He put the box in my hand. "Listen, they are a gift, from my heart to you. You do nice and thoughtful things for me; I do nice and thoughtful things for you. Equal partners," he stressed.

I couldn't argue, even though I felt awkward for accepting them.

The restaurant was very accommodating, even blocking off an entire room for us to dine in private. Several customers gasped when Ryan walked through the main dining area, and I noticed it was the ladies who immediately recognized him. Mike and our driver, who was also a bodyguard, blocked the entrance to our section of the restaurant so no one would bother us during our dinner.

"Mom." Ryan raised his glass to offer a toast. "To the best mother in the world! Happy birthday!" He leaned over to her and gave her a hug and kiss. "We have gifts for you, but I thought it best to save those until later when you can open them in private."

I knew that people were watching; any of them were capable of reporting the details of our evening to the tabloids. I was catching on to Ryan's hesitations and the reasons behind each of his actions. We could not help but be paranoid.

"Taryn made you a birthday cake. After dinner we'll go back to our place."

A wave of elation surged through me when he said "our place" to his parents.

"I hope you like chocolate," I said in happy response.

We were about an hour into our dinner when a new wave of female patrons entered the restaurant. We could hear their giggling and commotion from our private room.

"Guess the word's out." Ryan smirked. I couldn't tell whether he was bothered by it or in some way liked the attention.

"That's something your mother and I wanted to talk to you about, son. We're very concerned about all these fans and their behavior."

Ryan opened his mouth to speak, but his father cut him off.

"Now before you start reassuring me that you have it all under control, I saw some of those letters that these girls are leaving for you in Taryn's door, and I must say that their forward behavior is alarming." Bill rubbed his forehead, just like Ryan does when he's stressed.

"You know your mother and I will support you in your decisions, but when your decisions put you and your family in danger, well, I have to speak my mind about that."

"Anyone who is in the public eye has fans, Dad." Ryan tried to dismiss his father's concern. "I don't think you and Mom are in any danger."

"I realize that, son, but these fans of yours are leaving their perverted notes for you in this young lady's front door." Bill motioned his hand in my direction. "I see how much you care for her, so I'm including her in our family when I speak."

"I know." Ryan rubbed his forehead now. "I'm having extra alarms put on her apartment and I'm thinking about hiring personal security to watch over her when I can't." He looked at me; his expression waited for my reaction. I sighed and held my tongue.

"Son, this is exactly what I'm talking about! Your brother, your mother and me, we don't need bodyguards to go to work every day. There's a reason why you have these men surrounding you, protecting you. If there was no danger, then you wouldn't need protection! You know we are proud of you and we want you to be successful, but not if it's going to put you in harm's way." Bill shook his head fiercely.

My mind immediately flashed to Angelica sitting in her car, watching our every move. Waiting for . . . what? An opportunity? To find a weak spot in our armor?

"Dad, no one is going to hurt us," Ryan said quite confidently. Funny how two hours ago he made phone calls about our gap-toothed stalker. I squeezed his thigh with my hand. I didn't care for him lying like that to his parents, either.

"I won't let anything happen to you." He patted my hand to reassure me.

"I just wish you would give some thought to what else you could do with your life that doesn't affect your safety. We'd be just as proud of you if you did something else," Bill asserted.

"I know. I've been thinking about it, actually. Taryn's been giving me some good ideas." He winked at me.

I had no idea what he was referring to.

"But that will have to wait. You know I've signed a few contracts to do other movies. I can't back out now."

I wasn't so sure that Ryan wanted to back out of anything even if he could. He really loved being an actor and he was really good at it! He was able to slip into a completely different persona and actually convince the outside world that he was someone else.

"And what are your thoughts on of all of this, Taryn?" his father asked.

I took a moment to gather my thoughts. "I think that Ryan is truly passionate about being an actor, and it's what he wants to do for a career. I've seen today with my own eyes that he is a brilliant actor. If, one day, he doesn't want to do this anymore, well then, it will have to be his decision. I'll support him with whatever choices he makes."

My eyes shifted from addressing his father to looking at Ryan. There were too many people roaming around the restaurant, so I kept my voice low. "You know how I feel about you. I want you to be happy no matter what you do for a living. We'll deal with whatever life throws our way."

He smiled, squeezing my hand privately under the table.

Leaving the restaurant reminded me of seeing the red-carpet interviews on television.

Mike flanked Ryan; Ryan had his hand in the small of my back, guiding me along.

Word had obviously gotten out that Ryan was in the restaurant. His fans were lined up on both sides of the walkway outside. A few girls who looked like they had yet to reach puberty were mixed in with all the teenagers and women who were there to get a glimpse of Ryan Christensen. Oh, how they screamed for him!

Fear struck me once again as our car turned the final corner to deliver us home. Angelica's car was still parked on the side street, just a short distance from my car. I squeezed Ryan's hand tightly several times to get his attention. When he looked at me, I nodded in the direction of the old blue Plymouth. His lips curled, ready to utter the "F" word. He held his anger inside.

"When we come back from the cabin, I'll take care of that," he muttered privately in my ear so his parents wouldn't hear.

"I think she's sleeping in her car," I whispered back to him.

The paparazzi were lined up in the alley behind my bar; I guess they realized by now that this was Ryan's main entry/exit point. I stepped out of the car first with Mike, and immediately the cameras started to flash. It was hard to get the key in the door while being blinded by the flashes.

Once we were upstairs, we gave Ryan's mom her birthday gifts.

"This one is from Ryan." I handed her the bag with the jewelry in it. Ryan frowned at me, apparently for saying that it was just from him.

She opened the bag and removed a small, black box. Inside were gold and diamond earrings in a channel setting. Elegant and tasteful, just as I would have expected for his mother. She, too, stated that they were too much.

I looked at Ryan and smirked. Obviously I wasn't the only one who thought his gifts to be a bit extravagant.

I handed her a larger gift bag. "This one is from both of us. Careful, it's heavy."

"What did you two buy?" she questioned, feeling the weight of the bag.

"We didn't buy anything, Mom. We *made* that."

I smiled, remembering that day fondly. She removed the tissue paper that surrounded the frame.

"Oh my! This is absolutely beautiful!" Her face lit up, looking at the frame in the light. "You *made* this?"

"Ryan cut and ground all of the glass and even did most of the soldering," I stated proudly, wrapping my arm around his waist.

He put his arm around my shoulder. "I had an excellent teacher."

"I can't believe you made this!" Ellen rose from the couch and hugged us both. "Thank you!" she said as she kissed us one at a time. "I love it! I absolutely love it! Now maybe I could get you two to pose so I can take a picture of you while you're all dressed up. That way I'll have the perfect picture to put in this beautiful frame."

This was one photo I didn't mind posing for.

THE NEXT morning, I hurried down the alley to get my car, much to Ryan's dislike, but I wanted to move the car closer to the back door. I didn't want to haul all our bags down the street and give the photographers even more fuel for their tabloid lies. It was bad enough that the paparazzi followed me down the alley.

We packed the trunk, and Ryan smiled briefly when I handed him the keys. I knew that gripping the steering wheel and pressing the gas pedal in my car would make him happy. He got some sort of elation from driving.

"White van just pulled behind us," I informed Ryan while we waited at a red traffic light two blocks away from the pub.

"Don't worry, I'll lose them." He thoroughly enjoyed testing the limits of my car on the open highway.

Ryan's driving got us to the cabin in an hour and a half. We had lost the pursuing photographers within the first ten minutes of our trip.

His parents were pleasantly shocked to see our final destination. His father kept patting him on the back and smiling, although neither of us owned the property he was being congratulated for.

After everyone was situated, Ryan and I took the boat out of the garage so he and his father could go fishing. I rode on the back of the four-wheeler with him, nestling my nose into his neck that was no longer unfamiliar territory. This time our relationship was completely different from the last time we were here. I remembered wondering if we would ever be a couple and here we were, a couple.

"Taryn, this place is magnificent," Ellen said, wrapping her arm around my shoulder. We stood on the embankment overlooking the lake. The weather was chilly but sunny, with perfect blue skies.

"One day," Ryan said happily. "Right, Taryn?"

I shrugged my reply, hoping, but still not banking on anything. Not this soon, anyway. I wondered why Ryan felt so sure so soon. Is there really such a thing as love at first sight, or was he trying to convince himself that this was what he wanted? I didn't want to second-guess my feelings, though, for I was truly, madly in love with him.

"One day what?" his mom asked.

"Have a place like this." Ryan beamed. "Bigger house, but on a lake."

"What bigger house?" Bill inquired, placing his hand on Ryan's shoulder.

"Just talking about having a house of my own one day, Dad. I can't live in hotels forever."

"Good. You should buy a home of your own. Don't throw your money away renting some place. A house is a good investment. After all, you certainly can afford it now, son."

"I want to design it myself, though. Well, not completely on my own." He wrapped his arm around my shoulder. "I know this talented woman—she designed an awesome kitchen and the most amazing rooftop patio I've ever seen. I think I'll ask her how big of a closet she wants. Put in a whole art studio room just for making stained glass?"

I smiled at him, but inside I was freaking out. We'd been together for only a month, and already I was going to be designing a house with him? Was he serious? He looked serious. He surely sounded serious.

"So, what are you ladies going to do today?" Ryan asked, hugging me from behind at the edge of the water. His mother walked away to speak to his father; they headed toward the dock. I really think she just wanted to give us a moment of privacy.

"I think we're going to the outlet mall today. I want to stop at the one antique store. I haven't been there in years. Maybe we'll do that tomorrow, though."

He partially released me to reach into his front pocket. Then I felt him stuff something into the right front pocket of my jeans.

"That's a thousand," he whispered in my ear. "I want you to spend it on anything your heart desires."

I slouched in his arms, my body language showing my displeasure of his gesture. "Ryan."

"Taryn, please. Go have fun with my mom. Enjoy yourself."

"Did your father shove a thousand dollars in your mom's pocket, too?" I softly asked.

"I honestly don't know," he admitted. "My parents have been married for thirty-four years and they share everything, money included." He sighed in my ear. "And my father didn't recently cash another five-million-dollar paycheck with another eight million coming."

I pinched my eyes closed. "I don't want your money, Ryan." I felt horrible for allowing it.

"I know," he murmured on my neck, stopping my hand from leaving my pocket. "Consider this practice for the next thirty-four years."

"Well, if or when the thirty-four years officially starts, we can have this conversation again," I said gently. I pulled the money out of my pocket and tried to hand it back to him, but he wouldn't take it.

"So are you telling me we have to be married before I can even attempt to spoil you and share what I have?" he groaned.

"No. It's just . . . that's a lot of money, Ryan."

He snickered in my ear. "No, that's not a lot of money. That's not even enough to buy a pair of shoes in Beverly Hills."

I rolled my eyes, even though he didn't see my reaction.

"If you love me like you say you do, then what's the problem? I want to make you happy."

I knew exactly where he was going with this. His chest was pressed to my back, his arms held me in position, and next he was going to try to trip me up in words.

"I do love you. I love that you want to take care of me. But this . . ." I held the money up, "does not equal happiness or love." I knew he wanted to treat me well, but part of me felt like he was trying to buy my affection.

He wrapped his left arm across my chest. "Taryn, I know you're a self-sufficient, independent woman and I love that about you. And loving you means that *I want* to take care of you—physically, emotionally, *and* financially. If I wanted to piss you off today I would have shoved a hundred grand in your pocket," he growled in my ear.

I slumped in his arm.

"Yours, mine, ours . . ." He shoved the bills deeper into my pocket with his long fingers. "Didn't you say once it was just details? That *this* is what matters?" He patted his right hand over my heart.

I leaned my head back on his shoulder and nodded reluctantly in defeat. I had to agree with him; after all, he did volley my own words back at me.

"Your parents took care of each other. My parents take care of each other. You've been taking care of me—just let me try to take care of you." He trailed the tip of his nose up and down my neck, knowing how much it makes my will crumble. "Please?"

His lips brushed my skin. "Go have fun with my mom. Buy yourself some new clothes or shoes or some fruity-soapy stuff. Whatever makes you happy," he uttered persuasively in my ear. He released me, confidently knowing that he had just reduced me to a pile of rubble.

I drove to the outlet mall first; there were enough stores there to keep us busy for an entire day. The money Ryan had shoved in my pocket felt like it weighed eighty pounds; maybe it was my guilt for accepting it that weighed that much.

I instantly felt better about spending his money when the first thing I bought was three new pairs of jeans for him. After seeing all the items that constituted his wardrobe, he needed some new pants. His mother shook her head at me when I pulled some of the cash out of my pocket.

She waited until we were out of the store to reprimand me.

"I know Ryan wanted you to spend that money on yourself, not on him." Her expression was tender and disapproving at the same time.

"He desperately needs new jeans. Believe it or not, he only has a few pair. A lot of his clothing was stolen from the hotel." I quickly justified my actions.

"You truly *are* as selfless as he said you are." She pulled me by the elbow into a trendy clothing store.

I found a few articles of clothing that I liked. His mother was pleased that I had finally selected things for myself.

I didn't think I had enough of Ryan's cash left in my pocket, so I grabbed my bank card out of my wallet. The teenage girl behind the counter was looking at me strangely as she examined my card for a signature.

"Taryn!" His mother's reproachful tone caught me by surprise.

"Holy cow!" the girl behind the counter blurted. "You're Taryn! Taryn Mitchell!"

"Do I know you?"

"You're dating Ryan Christensen, right?"

I looked at his mother. I didn't know where else to look.

"It *is* you! Oh my God! Is *he* here, too?" Her eyes scanned the store.

"No, dear, he's not." His mother answered her question. "May I have that card, please? We're going to pay with cash instead."

The cashier was smiling frantically at me. "You are so freaking lucky! He is so hot. I saw *Seaside* like thirty times already. Oh my God! Wait until I tell my friends that I met you!" She jumped around like someone was electrocuting her.

"Wait, are you Ryan Christensen's mom? Oh my God, oh my God! Do you both mind if I take your picture? Please?" She was already pulling her cell phone out of her pocket.

"You want to take our picture?" I asked, totally confused by her frantic behavior. *Why would she want our picture? We aren't the ones who are famous.* Ellen wrapped her arm around my waist and we both quickly smiled for the picture. It was over in a second.

Ellen handed my bank card back to me and tapped me in the pocket to use the cash instead. I shook my head no but she tapped me harder in the leg. It was as if Ryan had his own private watchdog monitoring me. Reluctantly I used the cash.

I held the door open for her when we left the store. "That was weird."

"Was that your first time, dear?"

"First time?" *First time for what? Spending his money?*

"To be recognized, without Ryan being with you?" Ellen said.

"By a stranger, yes." I swallowed hard from the excitement.

She laughed softly. "I never deny it when people ask if he's my son. But I'm sure you know that I never say anything beyond that! After a while you'll get used to it, that and the cameras."

"I wish you would have let me use my card to pay for the clothing. It bothers me to spend his money," I grumbled.

Ellen smiled and slipped her hand around the inside of my elbow. "Do you know that you are the first girl he has introduced us to in over five years?"

"Really? I find that hard to believe," I said, completely astonished. I thought maybe her memory was fading. "Surely you met the girl he was dating when the first *Seaside* movie started filming? Wasn't she from Pittsburgh?"

"What girl from Pittsburgh?" Ellen asked.

"The girl he was dating from the amateur theater? He said she visited him in Maine when he was there filming."

"Oh, yes, I remember now. That one . . . her name was Brooke. She was the girl who tried to use him to further her acting career. We did meet her once, but that was when he was in a stage play with her back in Pittsburgh. She ended up moving to California and she hunted him down. He told us about her, but we never met her when they were together. She made quite a mess for him in the papers, too, with her lies," she said, slipping her purse strap back over her shoulder.

"No, the last girl he introduced us to was the girl he was dating his second year in college. Her name was Mandy, but they broke up when he started performing with the theater troupe. Actually, she broke up with him, come to think of it. That's right . . . she left him for someone else. Anyway, I hung up on her when she called the house after *Seaside* premiered. All of a sudden he was good enough for her again."

"But I'm sure he's dated a lot of women since then?" I stated the obvious.

"Oh, well, yes, I suppose he's dated quite a few. But that was all before he became well-known." The expression on her face turned to sadness.

"He lived in California for a while and he met a lot of girls. I heard all about them—well, at least the ones he told me about, but we never met any of them. All users and takers, if you ask me. He was pretty serious with this one girl he met in Los Angeles, but that ended quickly when she forged one of his checks to pay for a boob job."

She shook her head; the memory seemed to anger her. "But since *Seaside* premiered, it's been tough for him. Ryan dated this actress a few months ago, but she broke it off with him so she could date another actor. The papers sure had a field day with that one, too."

I wondered if she knew about Lauren, or was she referring to someone else? She left me no time to ask.

"But you, my dear, he can't stop talking about you. You have captured his heart. As his mother, I see he is at a different stage of his life now. He's finally growing up. I think he is realizing that his dreams of being a famous actor come along with a lot of pain and heartache."

"He and I have had quite a few talks about that," I admitted. "And honestly, I think things would be fine if the media just left him alone. I just wish I knew how to protect him without making things worse."

"Well, maybe you won't have to. He told me several times that he's not sure if this is what he wants to do for the rest of his life. I think other priorities are presenting themselves since he has met you. He just about gave up hope finding someone who would love him for *him*. Do you know what I'm trying to say? He's already told me that you're the one he wants to . . ."

"There they are!" We heard several young women shout, interrupting our conversation. The girls were walking fast down the sidewalk toward us with smiles on their faces.

"Is he here? Where is he?" one of the girls asked exuberantly. Her eyes were desperately searching the store windows.

"That *is* her! And his mother!" Another girl was almost running down the walkway. She had a cell phone up to her ear.

"Ellen, let's go." I grabbed her arm and we dashed out into the parking lot.

What did he tell her? I'm the one he wants to what? So much for knowing; now his fans were chasing us.

CHAPTER 21

Decisions

WE STOPPED AT the grocery store on the way back to the cabin. I'd convinced Ryan's mom that it would be easier to cook than to go out and have his whereabouts known to the public. I wanted the cabin and surrounding area to be our safe haven, if such a place could exist for us. Having his mother and me recognized was bad enough.

While we were in the checkout line, I noticed that *my* face, along with Ryan's, was now on the front cover of two gossip magazines. A large photo of us covered the entire front of one of them. I recognized that it was a photo of us taken on our way to Cal and Kelly's. The large headline announced: "Gone Public! Ryan's new love."

There was my face and his, less than two feet away from where I stood. I slipped my sunglasses out of my purse and put them on. I nudged his mother; she had already noticed the pictures herself. She took a deep breath and sighed. I could tell she was disgusted.

I wanted to pick up the magazine and see what else it had to say but I fought off the urge. I knew it would upset me if they printed lies. Besides, I didn't need to read a magazine to tell me what was happening in my life. I was living it.

Ryan and his father were still out on the lake fishing when we returned. I could see them from the back of the cabin. We waved to each other when he saw me on the embankment.

Ellen and I unloaded the car and spread the food out on the kitchen island. She was specific with the items we purchased at the store; she wanted to show me how she makes Ryan's favorite meal.

"He asks for this every time he comes home," she said while browning beef tips on the stove.

Ryan and his father carried their fishing poles and gear into the house, and Ryan gave me a quick kiss before going to wash up.

"Mom, what are you making?" he asked, even though I think he knew what she was up to. "Is that what I think it is?"

"Your mom is showing me the secret family recipe." I uncorked one of the bottles of wine that I had packed.

Ryan warned me, "Now you know you can never divulge this information to anyone. This recipe was my grandmother's. It can only be passed down."

"I'm under contract, remember? Sworn to secrecy." I twisted my fingers over my lips.

We were enjoying the bottle of wine when Ryan decided to check his messages. He turned his cell phone on and soon looked perturbed.

"Twenty missed calls," he groaned. He scanned through his messages, deleting one after the other.

"Holy shit!" he said excitedly. "Tar—pen, paper." He was grasping at the air.

"You know that script I read a few weeks ago? They want me for the lead," he said confidently. Ryan grabbed me by the waist and spun me around in the air. He was elated.

"Honey, that's fantastic!" I hugged him as he twirled me in a circle. Just as I had suspected all along, these studios and movie moguls were all going to strike while Ryan was hot. His parents were thrilled.

Ryan called his agent. "Hey, Aaron. I'm taking some time off with my family this weekend," he said.

Ryan's mouth hung open as he wrote the number nine on the paper and drew circles around it several times. "Hell yeah, I'm in! David assured me that I could make the schedule dates. I'll see you in L.A. in a couple of weeks." He ended his call and looked around at all of us.

"They're offering me nine million to do *Slipknot*," Ryan said proudly.

"My God, Son! This is truly a weekend full of celebrations." His father pulled him in for a hug and a manly pat on the back. I was so happy for him, for his success, for the joy this news brought to him.

I walked outside for some wood to start a fire. Ryan, of course, followed me. I had two logs in my arms when Ryan stopped me with his body. He took the logs out of my arms and set them on the ground. He was holding his phone to his ear.

"Hey, David. Yes, I got the call from Follweiler. I already talked to Aaron. I'm clear on the dates in April, right? . . . Thanks, David. It's *great* news! All right, I'll talk to you soon.

"I want you here when I make this next call," he said, touching my cheek. "Stay."

"Mr. Follweiler, it's Ryan Christensen. . . . Yes, sir. I just got your message. Thank you for this opportunity! I'm looking forward to working with you, too. It's an honor." Ryan was ecstatic.

"I'm still in Rhode Island; we're almost wrapped on the second film, and then I'll be in Scotland for ten days in the beginning of December for final scenes. . . . No, I'm living in Rhode Island now. Yes, that's correct, with Ms. Mitchell. No, she's not an actress. No, she's not a model, either." Ryan laughed briefly.

"Oh? Yes, of course!" Ryan glanced up at me with a surprised look on his face. "We'd love to meet you for dinner. I'll be in L.A. the third week of December for the *Seaside* wrap party.

"I have the script. Yes, sir, I'll call your office on Monday to coordinate a meeting. Thank you *so* much!" He beamed at me.

"Mr. Follweiler has invited *us* to dinner."

I couldn't believe that some director knew Ryan's personal business. Hollywood was worse than the NSA. There were no secrets.

After our delicious meal, we decided to play a game of cards. We were drinking wine and had a nice fire burning in the fireplace. Everything was peaceful.

"Mom, did you have fun today?" Ryan asked.

"I was clothes shopping, honey." She winked at him. "Taryn was recognized by a young cashier. The girl knew that she's dating you. She even asked us to pose for a picture."

"Her picture is plastered all over the Internet with me, Mom. You know how it is. This week she'll be in every gossip magazine in print. I was worried how it would affect her, but she seems to be handling it very well." I noted the sound of pride in his voice. It made me smile.

"Just as long as you don't *read* the garbage they print with the pictures, we'll be fine." He kicked my foot so I'd get the point.

"I hate to break it to you, son, but the two of you are already on the cover of the magazines. There's a big picture of you and Taryn on the cover of the *Weekly Reporter*. We saw it at the store today." Ellen's expression was a mix of unhappiness and pride.

"Your mom and I also got chased by some of your fans at the outlet. Either I was recognized or that cashier called some friends. I think they were hoping that we would lead them to you, but we gave them the slip," I told him.

"Welcome to my world." He frowned. "So, what did you buy today?"

"She bought you new jeans," Ellen quickly tattled on me.

I saw him look over at me, even though my eyes were still staring at my cards. I knew I was going to get scolded, so I held my index finger up and stopped him in his tracks.

"Ah, before you complain, I'd just like to say that I've personally washed all the pants that you own, and you were desperately in need of a non-ripped pair. I only got you three pair—and one is just like those old favorites you're wearing right now with the button fly."

"Please tell me you bought yourself something," he groaned, obviously displeased that I'd spent his money on him.

"Yes, I did. I got a couple of new shirts and some pants. Thank you for buying them." I leaned over and gave him a quick kiss.

"Thank you for thinking of me, too."

"Well, I can't have my boyfriend walking around with his underwear showing through the holes in his back pockets. The color and style of your underwear needs to remain a closely guarded family secret," I snickered.

His mom started laughing at me. "Why are all these fans so desperate to know what kind of underwear you have on? They ask you that question every time you get interviewed."

"He's a movie star. All women have fantasies about what their favorite actor looks like . . . somewhat naked," I answered.

"All women?" Ryan questioned, raising an eyebrow at me.

I looked at him, knowing exactly what he meant. "I'm sure you have your fantasy list, too. But I don't want to know who's on that list in case you ever have to work with one of them."

"Who's on *your* list?" he goaded.

"Just one. Ryan Christensen. He's *so* dreamy!"

His parents were laughing hysterically at my comment. "I think you've met your match, son," his father bellowed.

Ryan made a special effort to model his underwear around the guest room when we all departed for bed. He was trying to get my attention.

"I wish I would have brought the script with me. I'm going to need to run lines. Do you think you'd like to help me do that when we get home? Follweiler wants me to screen test with a few actresses out in L.A."

Ryan crawled under the covers and I snuggled up against him. "Sure. I'd be happy to help, although I don't know how good I'll be at it. I mean, I'm not an actress."

"You don't have to be, although Follweiler thought you were. It's no big deal, babe. You just need to read the lines." He yawned. His eyes examined my face. "What's wrong?"

My worry must have been showing.

"I don't know. I guess I feel at a disadvantage that I'm not that familiar with all this acting stuff. Sometimes I feel inadequate."

"It will come. You'll end up knowing more about it than I do one day." Ryan twisted my hair in his fingers.

I shrugged as he held me.

"What's really bothering you?" he asked, concerned.

I sighed heavily, unsure of whether I should tell him.

He tilted his head, waiting.

"Actors . . . actresses. You usually don't hear about actors and tavern owners," I whispered. I figured it was a safe start.

Ryan frowned at me. "Taryn, I really like that you're *not* an actress. I like being able to separate my personal life from the craziness. I think it's a big part of why I'm so attracted to you. You make me feel normal. I can just . . . be myself." He rubbed my arm. "So don't let that worry you."

He slipped his arm out from underneath me and rested his head on his hand.

"The fact that you're a smart and savvy business owner is definitely, *definitely* more appealing to me." His eyes departed from my face and followed his finger as it trailed down my chest.

"Your parents are in the next room," I reminded him. His fingertip was tickling the skin underneath my lace bra.

"So?"

"You tend to be loud," I teased.

"Me? I don't think so. Let me show you how quiet I can be."

It was silent in our room, all except for the sounds of our rough and labored breathing from our passionate kisses.

Ryan's hand slipped the strap off my shoulder. "Let's take this bra off," he whispered on my lips.

I rolled slightly to allow his hands to reach, but a faint noise in the background was distracting me.

"Shh." I held my finger up for him to wait. "Do you hear that?"

"Hear what?" he whispered, trying to open the clasp.

"Wait. I hear something." I jumped out of bed and tiptoed to the door.

Then I heard what I'd thought I heard originally. I waved to Ryan to join me. A huge smile broke on my lips.

We stood there quietly listening to the steady rhythm of the thumping noise until we heard his mother moan.

Ryan sprinted back to bed and ducked under the blankets. "Oh my God!"

"What? So your parents are getting some. Must be something in the mountain air that inspired them!"

I crawled back into bed. "Are you still feeling inspired, too?" I figured since his parents were being so open-minded . . .

"No!" he fired quickly and shuddered from the thought. "How the hell am I supposed to look at them tomorrow? That's *my* mom and dad!"

"Well at least you know that when you get to be your father's age, you'll still be . . . um . . . active." I giggled.

Ryan covered his eyes with his hands. "They're my parents, Taryn! They're not supposed to . . . I don't want to think about them doing that kind of stuff."

"Just as much as they don't want to think about *you* doing that kind of stuff?" I shouldn't have teased him. "Oh, honey. Do you want to watch some television?"

"I'm gonna need fucking therapy after this weekend," he muttered.

He was totally freaked out and our moment was now ruined by his mental torment. There was no way he was going to sleep tonight, either. I knew him well enough to know how he dwells on things.

Time to create a distraction. I got out of bed and started to change.

"Where are you going?" he asked.

"Beach," I answered coyly, pulling his sweatshirt down over my naked body.

• • •

"GOOD MORNING," I greeted Ryan's mother in the kitchen. She was primped, with all her hair sprayed into permanent position. Not a single hair was out of place. She returned my smile with one of her own. We both had our secret reasons for smiling; mine just wasn't as loud as hers was last night.

I had a hard time looking at his father, though, with a straight face. Visuals of Bill getting all up in Ellen last night was almost comical. The four of us stood in the kitchen in uncomfortable silence; eyes glanced back and forth from face to face over cups of coffee. Ryan looked like he was in pain. I couldn't stand the silence any longer.

"Ellen, there are a few antiques stores I was thinking about going to today while the men are out on the lake. How does that sound?"

"Sounds wonderful! We can go wherever you want." I think she would have been content to go anywhere that involved looking at stuff on shelves.

I patted Ryan's stomach. "I'm going to make some breakfast first so you have fuel in your tank to catch all those fish today."

He smiled and gave me a soft kiss.

It didn't take long to drive to the big, red barn filled with local antiques. I was relieved that Ellen and I got along so well. She wasn't the probing, busybody type; not like some of the mothers of my past boyfriends.

Along the way, we talked about what she does to manage Bill's dental office; it sounded a lot like what I have to do to manage the bar, minus dealing with all the insurance claims. It was comforting to know that we could relate to each other beyond the fact that I was dating her son.

Being around Ellen was like having a mother and a friend all wrapped up in one. She reminded me of just how much I missed having my mom around.

"I want to get Ryan a birthday present while we're here, but I never know what to buy him anymore. He's been traveling so much; anything we buy him just ends up in our basement," Ellen said, flipping over the price tag on an old dry sink.

"I know. I was thinking about what I could get him, too. His birthday is less than three weeks away. He had mentioned about getting hockey tickets, but I'm not sure what his schedule is like. I only seem to know week by week what he's up to."

A thought amused her. "Ryan told us you're a Pittsburgh fan. It's like Heaven made you just for him."

I laughed uncomfortably at her comment. "I don't know about that, but I'm glad you think so. I truly do love your son. I just want to make him happy."

"Hearing you say that thrills me beyond words." She squeezed me quickly around the shoulders with her free arm. "I was so worried that he'd end up with the wrong girl one day. I'm so relieved that he's made the perfect choice. And to tell you the truth, I'm glad your picture is on the cover of those magazines with him. It kills me every time I hear the media pairing him up with that Suzanne."

"I gather you don't like her," I said, hoping she'd explain why she felt that way.

"No, not really. I've tried to warm up to her but . . ." Ellen shuddered. "She only cares about herself. She thinks the world revolves around her."

Ellen looked at me intensely. "I don't know if you know this yet or not, but she has a *thing* for my son. Ryan, thank God, doesn't feel the same way. I was so worried that he might fall for someone like her, though, considering how many actresses he gets to meet and has to work with. I feared that one of them might end up being my daughter-in-law one day."

My mind drifted from her comments. I could easily see myself being his wife and the mother of his children, just like a normal husband and wife, but as the wife of a movie star, what would I do to keep myself busy and productive? Would I live out of a suitcase, too, following him around the globe? Living off him like some pathetic freeloader? Was I even movie-star wife material?

What could I do for a living to assure I was a contributing partner in a globe-trotting marriage? Heck, I'd struggled with the decision of closing the bar this weekend. How the hell would I be able to have a long-standing relationship with a man who is never in one place for very long?

Another movie, another distant location, another sexy lead actress for sure. While I was distracted picking out tile patterns for the bathroom, could some well-known vixen get to be the recipient of the next condom in his pack?

No matter which way I envisioned it, all paths ended up with me losing him. The world was unfolding on a silver platter to him, just like Suzanne had said. The parties to come . . . all the women . . . temptation all around.

Inside I was a partial wreck.

"Taryn? Are you all right?" Ellen noticed my mental absence.

Unconsciously I shook my head. I wasn't all right. My internal monologue came pouring out of my quivering lips.

"At first I didn't want to get involved with your son *because* he was a celebrity. Then we just spent time together and I got to know him for who he truly is. That's who I fell in love with. I hope you believe me when I tell you that I'm not with him because he's famous. And I don't want his money, either.

"He's a beautiful, caring, loving person and I love him so much. I've never felt this way about anyone. And I know he loves me. But I'm so scared. There are so many women out there, all desiring him. It's not like we're going to have a normal life, ever. It's hard enough to have a normal relationship, let alone have your relationship be analyzed and ripped apart by the world.

"He's always going to be traveling and away for months at a time. What do I do? What if I'm not enough? What if we're not strong enough?" My chest started to feel tight. I had been holding all these thoughts in for so long, never talking about them with anyone—not even my closest friends—and now they all came bubbling to the surface.

His mother moved to face me and looked me right in the eyes.

"Taryn, I don't think you give yourself enough credit. I have never heard Ryan talk about another girl the way he does about you. He didn't think it would ever be possible to find true love after he became famous, and he has found that in you. You!" She said in a stern voice as she tugged at my wrist.

"Let him love you, Taryn. That's all he wants. I know this can be stressful, having such a public relationship, but you need to stay true to each other and you will work through all of your fears. The two of you will figure it out. And don't be afraid to talk to him about anything, either. You have to be open with each other if you want *any* marriage to survive." Ellen touched my cheek.

"I know. I am trying. I love him with all my heart."

"Oh, sweetie. It will all work out. You'll see." She gave me a very comforting hug. "Ryan will make sure of it."

"Thank you," I breathed in her ear, hugging his mother like she was my own.

"You're welcome. Anytime you need to talk, I'll always be here for you."

Although it was easier said than done to confront these feelings, I felt at ease with her. My connection with her made me miss my mother even more.

"I guess Ryan will still be here when it's his birthday," Ellen said. "I'd better find him something, then, while we're here."

"I was thinking about having a small birthday party for him at my pub. Do you think some of his old friends from home might be interested in coming to Rhode Island?"

"You could always ask. He's lost touch with a lot of his friends. He always checks in with Matt and Scott when he comes home. Other than that, I really don't know who his friends are now. You'll have to get their phone numbers from Ryan."

I thought about how I would do that. I certainly wouldn't ask him for their numbers; that would ruin any possible surprise. I'd have to be sneaky.

"I thought he was coming home for Thanksgiving, or did that change?" Ellen asked.

"I'm sorry. I don't know. He didn't say anything to me." My words cast other thoughts through my head.

"That's when he always gets together with the boys. Every year they drive to Potter County to go deer hunting."

I thought about last Thanksgiving and feeling like an oddball at Pete and Tammy's table. I was glad that they'd convinced me to come over; I had thanked them but declined several times until Thomas ditched me at the last minute.

Thanksgiving was always a big production for my mother. She'd make a huge turkey and all the fixings. All the relatives would gather and we'd eat too much.

As we grew older, my cousins had families of their own and everyone scattered in their separate directions. After my parents died and I turned down one too many invitations, my phone stopped ringing at the holidays. Large family get-togethers seemed to be a thing of the past.

Ryan had not mentioned his Thanksgiving plans to me, but I had hoped—or, more accurately, assumed—that we would be together, especially after the conversation I'd just had with his mother. If not, I'd be alone once again.

Maybe Ryan would want to spend the holiday alone with his family before traveling to finish filming *Seaside?* Thanksgiving I could deal with, but another Christmas by myself . . . that would be painful.

Last year, Thomas conveniently picked a fight with me two weeks before Christmas and we temporarily broke up. I still think it was because he didn't want to have to buy me a gift.

My mind was wandering when my eyes noticed an old Gibson acoustic guitar tucked away in the back corner of the antiques shop. I picked it up and gave it a strum; it had a great sound. I handed the cashier my bank card and five hundred and ninety dollars later, walked out with Ryan's birthday present.

After a full day of roaming through stores, we'd both had our fill of shopping. I turned the car in the direction of the cabin. Ryan and his father were busy doing something by the edge of the lake.

"What are you up to?" I asked. Ryan was squatting down and had a big boning knife in his hand. He was gutting a fish.

"Look at this bass! I couldn't throw this one back. Taryn—supper. Supper—Taryn." He was trying to be funny with the poor fish's dismembered head.

"We should cook that outside on the fire pit." I pointed in the direction. "Good job, man," I said in my playful cavewoman voice. I gave him a congratulatory squeeze on his shoulders.

"Man catch fish for woman," he stated proudly.

I started a fire in the large, circular fire pit and sat down in one of the wooden chairs that surrounded it. The sun was starting to set and the fire felt nice and warm on my hands. Ryan put the metal grate over the hot coals, and soon his catch of the day was cooking.

"Taryn, how much property does your family own here?" Ryan asked.

"I think it's almost three acres. Why?"

"Who owns that property over there? There's nothing but a little shack house on it." Ryan pointed to the east side of the lake.

"I don't know. I've never seen anyone there. Deeds are public records; I'm sure it would be easy to find out."

"I love this lake," he said; the tone of adoration was evident. "I spent all day out there designing a house in my head."

He looked over to me. "Tell me, if you could pick a place, where would you want to live?"

"I don't know, but by a lake sounds perfect," I answered truthfully.

"I wonder if I could buy that land over there?" Ryan pointed. "What?" he questioned my stare.

I was surprised by his comment. "I just assumed you would want to live closer to your parents—somewhere in Pennsylvania."

"How's the fish doing?" Bill asked, taking the seat next to me.

"It's cooking, Dad." Ryan pushed the tinfoil pack closer to the center. He was not going to be distracted from his train of thought.

"Honey, it doesn't matter to me. As long as I'm close to an airport I can live anywhere, but I'm not going any farther west than Pittsburgh. What these people pay for homes in California is crazy. I could build a ten-thousand-square-foot house here for the same amount of what you'd pay for a one-bedroom apartment in L.A."

"Ryan, are you planning on coming home for Thanksgiving?" Ellen interrupted.

"I was planning on it," he answered, turning his attention to her. "I want Taryn to meet Nick and Janelle, and I want to take her to Mellon Arena for a hockey game. I have to ask David to check on game dates and tickets."

Ryan looked back at me, resuming our original conversation. "The only decision you need to make is what to do with the bar. If you still want to manage it, then we have to live closer to the coast."

"Pull that back to the edge, son. It's going to burn there," Bill instructed.

While Ryan was distracted, I stood up from my chair.

"Excuse me, please," I murmured. I pulled my car keys out of my coat pocket as I crossed the lawn.

Ryan trotted up behind me. "Tar, what's up? Are you going somewhere?"

Part of me wanted to get the guitar out of the car; the other part did not want to have to think about selling the bar in order to keep a boyfriend. "No. I'm not going anywhere," I said.

"I thought maybe I upset you. Did I?" He took hold of my arm, stopping me from taking the next five steps that would put me at my car door.

"No. I'm not upset. I'm . . ." I sighed. "I'm not really ready to make those kinds of decisions, Ryan."

"I understand. I'm sorry. I know . . . I'm rushing you."

"Yeah, a little," I said. "I need some processing time. I thought we'd stay in the apartment a while longer. You know, start there." Frustration coated my words. I think I even huffed. I felt like everything was in fast-forward and at any moment, the proverbial carpet would get yanked out from underneath my feet.

Ryan looked conflicted by my reaction. "Come on, let's go for a walk."

He took me by the hand and led me toward the dock. We sat down on the long bench in the shadow of the cabin lights.

"Taryn, since I've met you, I've been thinking a lot about the future." He scratched his forehead before looking me in the eyes again. "I can't help it."

Ryan picked up my hand and twined our fingers together.

"When I was out there on the lake today, all I could think about was building a house right over there in that clearing. I could see it all in my head. A big log-sided home with a private gated entrance. A boat dock over there jutting out on the water. A small boat house to keep a boat in.

"But all those thoughts *include you*. I'm not thinking about me anymore, I'm thinking about us. And maybe I'm rushing those thoughts, but I know what I want.

"I understand if you're not ready for all of that just yet, but I want to know if you can picture it, too. Is that something you want?"

I looked in his eyes when I spoke. "Yes, very much so."

He let out a big sigh and smiled. "That's good to know. Then *we're* on the same page.

"But . . . last night when we were talking out on the beach, you sort of clammed up on me," he sighed. "Before we go on . . . well, I just want to make sure that we want the same things."

"I'm pretty sure we do," I said softly.

"Then why did you get distant on me last night?"

I thought about what his mother said to me this afternoon. I had to stop fearing that he'd run away if I talked about my feelings openly with him.

Ryan squeezed my hand to get my attention.

I took a deep breath and looked at him.

"Ryan, I've heard the words 'I love you' before, and every time I believed them they just turned out to be nothing more than words. I need more time to know that I can rely on you when you tell me you love me. I haven't had the best of luck in relationships."

"Me neither," he interjected.

"Then why are we rushing it?"

Ryan stared down at his feet, rubbing his sneaker over the knot in the wooden plank. He pursed his lips and shrugged.

"I don't know," he said. "I guess I'm just ready to get on with the next chapter of my life. I've been living like a nomad for the last two years. It's really starting to get to me."

I knew he was lonely and terribly isolated by this sudden, overwhelming fame. I had been surviving in loneliness for months myself.

"Last night you said some things." I wiggled uncomfortably on the bench, measuring my words. "I need to know that it's truly *me* that you want, and not just the idea of a life with *someone like me* that's driving you."

Ryan rolled his gaze back to me. He stared at my face for a moment before he spoke. I felt as if I were missing some obvious point.

"Taryn, it *is* you that I want." He laughed lightly, implying I was being silly again. "*You* are the reason I'm even thinking about all of these things. I just want to be sure that *we* are heading in the same direction, that's all."

I thought about several different directions we could actually head. I didn't want to assume.

"Well, since you've mentioned words like *married* before, I guess I don't need to feel frightened to bring it up."

"No, you don't," he confirmed gently.

"Children?"

"That, too," he said with a soft smile.

"If those are the things that you want, too, then I'd say we are heading in the same direction." I looked him in the eyes.

Ryan nodded.

"Then let's just let it grow naturally," I softly pleaded.

"Okay," he whispered, agreeing with me.

A light breeze blew across the water, sending a chill through my body. I shivered, wishing we were having this conversation in front of the fire pit.

"Are you cold?" Ryan asked, wrapping his arm around me. He rubbed my arm to warm me.

My teeth chattered together as I sniffed in some chilly air. "Just a little."

Ryan was still deep in thought. His brow was furrowed—a telltale sign that he was mulling over something. I snuggled deeper into his hug and waited.

"I've been thinking about what you said," he answered my glance. "I know it's easy to toss the phrase 'I love you' around. I've said that line out loud a couple of times myself." He twined our fingers together again.

"And I'm sure girls have said the same to you," I said.

"Yeah." His eyes brightened and he laughed lightly. "Can I tell you something? Promise me you won't laugh."

I crossed my heart with my fingers. "I promise."

"You know that first night when we stayed together here in the cabin? As sick as we were, there was no place on Earth I would rather have been than here with you."

I smiled at his statement. "I'd say we got to know each other on very intimate levels that night."

"I know. But it made me realize something . . . it made me realize how comfortable I am with you. And then that first night I stayed with you in your bed, when I woke up in the morning holding you, I thought 'this is the woman I want to wake up to for the rest of my life.' I knew that before I even kissed you for the first time.

"Every time I get angry or upset, you have this magical way of bringing me back to Earth. I don't know how you do it, but somehow you manage to keep me sane."

"You do the same for me, you know," I added.

"That's good to know." He shot me his sexy smirk.

Ryan lifted my hand to his lips. "So when I say those words to you, *that* is what I truly mean. You need to realize that who you are, right now, is exactly what I want and need."

My heart had never felt so full. I looked into his eyes. "No fair . . . you stole all of my lines."

"Ryan, Taryn! Dinner is ready." His mother shouted from the deck.

Ryan looked at me. I shook my head quickly; I wasn't finished with our conversation.

"Start without us!" Ryan yelled back.

"So what else is on your mind?" he asked.

I stared up at the stars, watching the flashing lights of an airplane as it passed through the nighttime sky. It was a good distraction while my mind sorted through the various insecurities that had been plaguing me lately. I was unsure if any of them were conversations I wanted to get into right now.

He squeezed me again. "If my memory serves me correctly, it was right after I mentioned filming *Slipknot* when you shut down on me last night."

My head bowed instinctively and I sighed.

"I'm scared, Ryan," I said slowly. "You're going to be on location more than you'll be home—wherever home may be. Separation, growing apart . . ." I winced. "It's going to be hard, and I'm afraid if we force our relationship to be at stages where it hasn't grown naturally, well . . ."

I looked him in the eyes. "What happens when you're filming and you have to do some love scenes with another woman? What if her kiss is what you feel you're missing out on? On-set romances happen all the time—some by accident. You know as well as I do that it happens. I can't get it out of my head that all actors end up falling for actresses. What if a bar owner from Rhode Island isn't enough?"

"Honey, there's a big difference between kissing you and faking it for film," he laughed. "I'm getting cast in a lot of romantic movies, and it's going to be unavoidable. Everyone wants to see romance. But it's not real. It's not this. What you and I have . . . this is real. You'll just have to trust me."

"Well, these are all the things that I'm thinking about. It's not easy for me to trust men," I whispered.

"I know. I have to prove that I'm not like the others. It's all right. I can do that," he said, giving me an elbow nudge. "How about if I call you every fifteen minutes to remind you that I'm madly in love with you? Will that work?"

I rolled my eyes and laughed.

"I can wear one of those iron chastity belts if it will make you feel better."

"Would you?" I kidded back.

"I'll have to get you another chain so you can wear the key as a necklace."

I smirked. "I don't want you to think that I'm some insecure mess. It's just that, well, this stuff happens, and . . ."

"What about letting Marie run the pub?" he quickly suggested.

Great . . . he found another one of my issues.

"Ryan, the pub is *my* source of income. Marie isn't opposed to taking care of things so I can travel, but honestly, with or without you, I need to maintain my own sense of stability. I'm not going to sit back and do nothing while having a high time spending your money. That's not me. I've got to hold my own in this relationship."

Ryan crossed his ankle up on his knee.

"Did you give any more thought to leasing out the kitchen to Tammy? Then that's even more income for you. Even if Tammy doesn't use it, you can lease it out to someone else."

"That's going to take a lot of money, Ryan. More than I can afford to spend right now. And I know what you're going to say."

"Twenty grand, Taryn, is not a big deal. I still think that's a lot more than what it should cost just to replace the plumbing. We can make it legal if you want so you don't have to worry. Or I could just take it out in trade." He pulled me by my shoulder to bump me into his chest.

I sighed.

"Listen, Taryn, I'm not going anywhere. So I have to travel when I film. So what. Like I said, we'll travel together from time to time, and then I have a few weeks off here and there. If I promise to . . . slow down, will you promise to quit worrying?"

I nodded.

"Say it," he taunted.

"I promise," I said, laughing lightly at his urging.

"Okay . . . and I promise, too." Ryan's fingers lifted my chin.

I gazed lovingly into his eyes. Those eyes, so blue, filled to the brim with passion and conviction, were absolutely mesmerizing. We were drawn together by an invisible magnetism that reached all the way to the core of my being.

"I love you, Taryn Lynn Mitchell," he said with a smile.

"I love you, too, Ryan William Christensen."

Although I thought I had been in love before with other men, never did those three little words mean so much to me as they did at this moment with this man. The feelings that flowed between us were natural and effortless, as easy as breathing.

While he was kissing me, I heard his stomach growl loudly. "We'd better get inside for dinner." I pulled him by the hands.

"You know, when you walked away with your keys I thought you were planning on speeding off in your car."

"No." I laughed. "I actually got you a birthday present today. There's no way I can get it home without you seeing it, so I thought I'd just give it to you now." I unlocked the car and he let go of my hand.

"I got it at the antiques store down the road. I hope you like it."

"Wow! Look at this! It's an old Gibson." His fingers strummed over the strings, but his cell phone buzzing in his pocket distracted him. "Ahh, I just turned the damn thing on and already it's ringing.

"Hello? Who is this? Oh . . . what?" Ryan was short with whoever was on the other end. He turned his shoulder away from me, dropping his voice to a whisper. "I thought I made things perfectly clear the last time we had this conversation. I told you . . . things have changed. So stop calling me," he said quite callously.

He turned his phone off and walked a few feet away before noticing that I wasn't following him. He held his hand out to me and waited until I caught up, silently towing me toward the house.

"Are you two all right?" Ellen asked when we entered the kitchen.

"Yeah, Mom. Taryn and I had some things to discuss that were more important than dinner." He picked a piece of fish off the plate and shoved it in his mouth. "See this?" he whispered in my ear. "Family, peace, no screaming fans, no security, home-cooked meals, normalcy. This is what I want. This is what I miss."

"I'm glad to hear that," I said. "Because it's the only way I know."

After dinner, I grabbed some blankets and with two open bottles of wine, we made our way out to the backyard. Ryan and his father threw more logs on the fire, setting a nice blaze in the fire pit. Millions of stars dotted the clear sky.

I took Ryan's guitar and softly played a few chords.

"What are you playing?" Ryan asked.

"Nothing . . . I just had some lyrics in my head."

We took turns playing, each of us adding to the melody.

We were trying to come up with words that rhymed. After an hour, we had written part of a song . . . our song.

"When is your next movie going to start filming, son?" Bill asked.

Ryan stopped playing. "Rehearsals start January third. I'll be filming in Miami for almost three months," he said as he looked over at me.

"What's the movie called?" Bill continued.

"It's called *Thousand Miles*. It's already been scheduled to be released by next November, I guess right around Thanksgiving again."

"What's the movie about?" his mother asked, filling her wineglass.

"It's a drama about an FBI agent," he pointed to himself, "who volunteers to drive his best friend's sister to see her fiancé, who lives in the Florida

Keys. It turns out that the fiancé is a serial rapist who's on the run. My character is falling in love with her the entire trip."

"Who are you going to be working with on this film?" Ellen asked. "Any other big names we might know?"

"The only other part that I know that's been cast is the lead actress. I'll be working with Lauren. Lauren Delaney," he quickly added.

The sip of wine I was taking instantly burned my throat. *Lauren? Like, ex-girlfriend Lauren?*

The way he said her name gave me the impression that he expected his mother to know who he was talking about.

Instantaneously, my eyes shot over to his mother to see her reaction. Her expression was a dead giveaway; the mix of shock and panic was evident.

CHAPTER 22

Protected

WE DROVE DIRECTLY to the airport from the cabin. Even though we were two hours northwest of Seaport, we were only forty-five minutes west of Providence. Ryan made sure to mention that out loud.

Since it was known that the airport in Providence was the entry/exit point for our visiting celebrities, several paparazzi were on guard . . . waiting for any celebrity to pop up on their radar. Ryan knew what was waiting for us, so we said most of our verbal goodbyes in the car on the way.

The paparazzi landed on us like flies, ruining the last few moments we had together with his parents. We gave his parents quick hugs and kisses while they retrieved their bags from the trunk; the camera flashes were disorienting and annoying.

The final proof that Ryan Christensen's new girlfriend spent the weekend with his parents was being captured digitally on stills and video. *Wonderful—more fodder for the gossip magazines.* I felt like swinging Ellen's suitcase around in a circle to see how many paparazzi I could knock out.

Ryan was getting angrier by the minute. I was relieved that TSA agents came right over to the car to assist us. As much as we wanted to spend a few extra minutes with his parents, we couldn't dawdle.

Having my picture taken was a lot more tolerable than the invasive questions and comments that spewed out of the paparazzi.

Ryan and I jumped back in the car and as soon as the main traffic lane was clear, we drove off.

"When we go to my parents' for Thanksgiving, we'll need security," he muttered, moving over into the proper lane to get us out of the airport. "I'll have a car drop us off."

The moment we pulled into the alley, the paparazzi came running. We quickly unloaded the rest of our bags and his new guitar into the kitchen while the cameras clicked.

We were asked questions upon questions about our weekend. Did we have fun? Where did we go? Did we have a nice visit with his parents?

Mingled in there were the stupid questions; one guy actually asked us what we thought about the president's stimulus package. Then he asked us if we'd heard the news about the latest celebrity who volunteered to be on that television dance show. Why the heck would we answer or respond to questions like that?

Some of their questions were down right aggravating. One of the photographers asked Ryan if Suzanne knew that I'd met his parents, and how does she feel about that? Did it make her jealous? I wanted to tell them all to go to Hell, but I kept focused on getting the car emptied.

"New door is in," Ryan said. He was straining to keep his mind on other things and he tried to get me to focus with him.

I saw that we had a new steel door installed a few feet away from the existing kitchen door. We were so distracted by the paparazzi that I didn't even have time to see all the progress Pete made on the new wall inside.

We drove down the alley and crossed over Mulberry Street into the open parking lot. We were just about parked when Ryan abruptly slammed on the brakes and put the car in reverse.

"Ryan? What's wrong?"

It took me no time at all to follow his stare. There she was—Angelica—sitting in her freaking blue Plymouth parked catty-corner to the lot on Mulberry Street. Ryan gunned the engine and drove back out onto the street.

"Blue Gran Fury. We're going to take care of this shit right now. Which way to the police station?"

Ten minutes later we walked into the Seaport Police Station. The officer informed us that they would investigate the matter, but we had to go to the county courthouse to apply for a protection-from-abuse order. That was not handled by the police.

We walked swiftly down the sidewalk to the courthouse doors. Ryan was wearing dark sunglasses and tried to look inconspicuous, but he couldn't go anywhere without being recognized. Two flustered women stopped us on the sidewalk and asked him for his autograph. Ryan momentarily slipped into his people-pleasing mode and even stood and waited for these two annoyances to find something for him to write on. He was so gracious.

We took the elevator up to the third floor of the courthouse and found the office that was supposed to help us. Fortunately, the office was empty—all except for the two women who worked there. One was an older woman with bleached blond hair sitting at a tan metal desk, busy typing away on a computer. She looked up at us for a second and then quickly returned to what she was doing. We didn't even qualify as a distraction.

The other woman sitting behind the counter, however, who was younger than the first, recognized Ryan immediately. I could tell—she looked up and blinked rapidly in astonishment. Her mouth popped open and for a moment I thought she was going to scream.

It's amazing how quickly people jump for you when you're a celebrity. I never knew the power that came with it until moments like these happened. Ryan could have asked the lady behind the counter to eat road kill and she probably would have obliged. If you could bottle Ryan's fame and charm into one container, you'd have the recipe for a lethal weapon. We completed the paperwork in no time, and within minutes we met with the judge.

"I had her investigated," I informed the judge. Ryan was surprised by this revelation but maintained his composure. I squeezed his hand.

"There's a restraining order against her in the state of California for stalking another celebrity. She was also charged with breaking and entering into the celebrity's home. She has physically placed her hands on Mr. Christensen on our way into our home, and she has been sleeping in her car outside our place of business, which is also where our home is. She has followed me all the way to South Hampton and repeatedly leaves messages for him on our vehicle and in our mail."

A temporary restraining order was granted immediately, and, after one brief three-minute telephone conversation between Ryan and the judge's fourteen-year-old daughter (who happened to be a huge Ryan Christensen fan), we received the rest of the royal treatment.

We were informed that a deputy sheriff would serve the order to Angelica. A hearing for the permanent restraining order was scheduled for next Wednesday. Ryan and I would both have to appear for the hearing. We left the courthouse armed with two copies of the order—one for each of us—and we even received a police escort home.

Ryan parked my car in the lot and we sat and watched as two police cruisers descended on Angelica, blocking her from leaving the spot where she was parked, while the deputy served her the order.

"What's happening?" I asked out loud. One police officer had removed her from her car and she was being handcuffed.

"I don't know," Ryan answered. "Looks like she is getting arrested."

The paparazzi had a field day taking her picture and ours as we waited in the car. She was placed in the backseat of one of the police cars while two officers searched her Plymouth.

The photographers, autographers, filmers, and fans swarmed around us. Ryan and I hurried for the back door of the pub.

I closed the steel kitchen door behind us and punched in the security code. Ryan had turned the light on, illuminating the new wall and door that spanned the length of the kitchen.

"Wow!" I breathed out. The new thirty-foot wall was definitely a distraction from my thoughts. I noticed Pete had even painted the new wall white.

"This looks really good," Ryan beamed.

I was glad to see that the new interior door had a lock on it, but Ryan was able to open it. Mounted on the wall inside the hallway was a new light switch. Next to it, a keypad for the new security system glowed in the dark. Pete had even installed an ornate wooden railing where the original wall used to be.

Ryan pulled the note that was taped next to the keypad off the wall. "Call security co. to program new code—new keys are on kitchen counter upstairs," he read aloud.

"It's one o'clock out on the West Coast. Don't forget you have to call Follweiler's office today." I tossed my car keys onto the kitchen table.

"Thanks for reminding me. What would I do without you?" He kissed me quickly.

"I don't know? Forget shit?" I teased him.

He gave me a light shove. "Call the security company; get us hooked up. I'll call Follweiler."

We went our separate ways to make our phone calls. I programmed the new code into the panel to activate it. Ryan had made our dinner plans with Mr. Follweiler's assistant and when he came back into the kitchen, he was on the phone with his agent.

It was almost humorous how many phone calls we both made. Ryan was due back on set first thing in the morning; he called Mike to arrange safe transportation. I called Marie to check in on how they were holding up. They had just gotten home a half hour ago and cancelled on playing poker tonight.

Ryan was on the phone with Pete, yapping away on everything from construction to fishing.

My last call was to Cory to see if he'd be able to start at four, since I had no valid reason not to be open tomorrow. I was glad that he was willing to work any hours I was able to give him. I even hired his roommate, Trevor, over the phone. I needed someone to card people at the door during the week. I wasn't going to allow what happened last Tuesday to repeat itself.

I ran downstairs to the get the mail and removed my makeshift cardboard CLOSED sign from the window. There was a huge pile of mail on my pub floor. There were also a FedEx package and several boxes sitting on the bar. I opened a garbage bag and stuffed it with all the mail and deliveries so I could carry it upstairs.

"Ryan?" I called out, setting the bag on the floor.

"Bathroom!" he yelled. I knew him and his daily routine well enough to know that at this time of the day, he'd be gone for a while.

I grabbed his cell phone off the kitchen table and quickly toggled through his stored numbers, looking for listings for Matt and Scott. He had quite a few girls' names in his phone, which bothered me to see. Amy, Brandy, Cheryl, Gina, Heather; the list went on and on. The twinge of jealously worsened when I passed Lauren Delaney's cell number.

I was hoping that he wouldn't want or need to call any of those numbers ever again. It would be so easy for me to delete them all, but that would be wrong. Back to the task at hand . . . there were a few choices for the name Scott, but only one listing for Matt. I quickly wrote his number down on a piece of paper and shoved it in my purse.

I looked at the FedEx package. It was overnighted from California and addressed to William Bailey, c/o Mitchell's Pub. I noticed that Pete wrote a note on the back to let us know he'd signed for the package.

"Do you know a William Bailey?" I asked, handing the package to Ryan.

"Yep. That's me."

I must have looked confused.

"What's my middle name?" he asked.

"William."

"What *was* my dog's name?"

"Bailey." It made sense now. "Okay, I get the connection, but why the alias? What's that about?"

"It's my secret name. Well, one of them," he admitted. "I can't use my real name on anything. If fans or whoever see 'Ryan Christensen' printed on something, it disappears or becomes public knowledge. It's also one of the names I use when I check into hotels and stuff."

"I noticed your luggage had 'Shell-B Enterprises' on it. Is that an alias, too?"

"Yeah, well, that's my company name," he sighed, scratching his forehead. "You have no idea the lengths people go through to dig up private information." He pulled out his wallet and showed me his credit card.

"This has my real name on it 'cause that's who I am, but see—underneath my name—there's my company name. My credit card bills, my cell phone number, are all listed under my company name. It's the way things have to be to keep records private. If my luggage gets lost, no one knows it's mine. My bags would get shipped to California to my manager."

"Oh, that makes sense," I said, but still curious. "Shell-B? Where did that come from?"

He laughed. "That's a mixture of a couple of things. First of all it was my dream car, which I now own. Sitting in my dad's garage is a 2008 Shelby GT500 KR. Blue with silver stripes. Two hundred and eight original miles on her. The other reason for the name, well, do you remember our conversation about the shell game?"

I nodded, remembering that time in the shower fondly.

"Why not make finding me a shell game, too?" His face glowed with his secret. "Whenever you travel now, you'll have a fake name on your luggage. We'll have to take a look at what you have your name on. People can hack into shit on the Internet like you wouldn't believe."

I was twirling my cell phone under my fingers while we were talking. I was curious about something completely different from what we were talking about. I punched a few buttons and waited.

Ryan's phone started to play. The music was familiar, but I didn't know the artist.

"Why are you calling me?" He laughed.

"Just curious," I admitted. "That's my ring tone? Who is that?"

He twitched his lips and smiled. "It's an oldie. Did you ever hear of Cream?"

I nodded. He picked his phone up but I stopped him.

"No, wait! Just let it play. I want to hear it. 'Sunshine of Your Love?' Is that the name of the song?"

"Yep. It's a cool song, but I never get to hear it, 'cause somebody you and I know has issues about calling me." He gently kicked my foot under the table.

Ryan ripped open the tab on the FedEx package and pulled out three packs of paper. Each pack was an inch or two thick.

"What's all that?" I asked while I dumped the mail out of the garbage bag onto the table.

"Scripts. More scripts. What the hell is all of *that?*" he yelled.

I gasped when I saw multiple four-by-six glossy pictures of Ryan and our stalker, Angelica, from the day that he posed with her in my pub. There were also glossy pictures of Ryan alone, mostly side shots of him entering through the back door of the pub. The scariest of all the photos was a picture of Ryan and me walking down the sidewalk. Angel had scribbled out my face with a black felt-tip pen and drawn a target on my chest. I almost passed out at the table.

I flipped one of the pictures over and read the back.

"You're always on my mind. Love Angel."

I desperately separated all the pictures from the pile of mail. Ryan's eyes grew wider and his face turned white. Each picture had a handwritten message:

"I love you! Angel"

"Why are you avoiding me? Call me please?"

"She'll never love you as much as I do!"

"Yours forever-Ryan and Angel"

"Please call me!"

"Wherever you go, I'll always be there. Love Angel"

"We belong together"

And the picture of me with the bull's-eye had three words written on the back . . .

BANG! YOU'RE DEAD!

Ryan's face still showed his horror and his fingers were unsteady as he started to open up one of the boxes addressed to him. I heard him gasp in shock again. Inside the box was a brown plush teddy bear that had a big gash down the front of its chest, and some of the white stuffing was sticking out. There was tape across the opening. The note inside the box read "I'm brokenhearted without you."

The other boxes had the same handwriting on them. Ryan didn't touch them. He shoved everything back into the garbage bag.

I was shaking, but I still had my mental faculties. "Ryan, don't throw any of that away. We'll need all of it for court."

In total there were four packages, seventeen pictures, three threatening letters, and nine greeting cards from her. She even included what appeared to be drops of blood in one of the cards.

Ryan quickly called his manager. "David, I want private security immediately for Taryn. I want someone posted inside her business during working hours and I want someone to escort her anywhere she has to go when I'm not with her. I'll also be hiring a lawyer out here in Rhode Island."

The only thing preventing us from both screaming was the knowledge that she was in police custody at that very moment.

THE NEXT morning, our schedule quickly shifted back to our normal routine, and I promised Ryan that I wouldn't leave the building. I handed him a to-go cup of coffee and kissed him goodbye in the hallway. Mike shielded Ryan as he climbed into the backseat of the car sent to deliver him safely to the set, and the paparazzi were waiting to take his picture the minute he stepped out the door.

I was mentally preparing to open the pub back up for business and reviewing the precautions I needed to get in place before I unlocked the front door. Despite all the terrifying circumstances from yesterday, I also had a top-secret birthday party to plan.

"Hi, is this Matt?" I asked hesitantly, staring at the piece of paper that contained the phone number I'd stolen from Ryan's cell.

"Yeah? Who's this?" he replied.

"My name is Taryn. Taryn Mitchell. Do you know who I am?" I didn't know if Ryan's friends kept tabs on the news.

"No. Should I?" he asked defensively.

"How can I say this without you hanging up on me. Are you near a computer?"

"What?" Matt questioned.

"Do you have access to a computer?" I asked again.

"Yeah. I'm sitting in front of one. Why?" he asked.

"Please go on the Internet and search my name." I spelled my full name for him so he'd get it right.

"Aw, come on. Can't you people just leave him alone?" Matt groaned.

I knew by his response that he'd found me.

"Matt, please, just listen to me. It's really Taryn Mitchell calling you. Your longtime friend Ryan is living with me in Rhode Island."

"Bullshit," he replied.

"No, for real. I am telling you the truth."

"I'm not convinced, but I'm glad to see Ry's got a smoking-hot girlfriend."

"Thanks. I'll take that as a compliment."

I remembered a funny story Ryan told me about Matt. "Okay, how is this for convincing? Sitting under a car cover in his dad's garage is a 2008 Shelby GT500, blue with silver stripes. You beg him every time you see him to let you drive it but he won't let you because you have a habit of flipping cars. You're the only guy he knows that could flip their mom's station wagon."

"Hah!" He laughed out loud. "Is he there? Let me talk to him!"

"You believe me now?" I chuckled. "No, he's not. He is on set." I explained that I wanted him and Scott to come to the surprise party.

I called Kelly next. I needed a devious plan to get the entire cast to my place for Ryan's birthday. She said she'd get word to the director through Cal.

The last call I made, which I'd purposely saved for last, was to a lawyer in Providence.

"I have to be on set at that time, so you'll have to go to the lawyer without me," Ryan said when he called me at lunchtime. "Unless you can change the appointment to another time when I can go?"

"No, that's okay. I can go by myself. I'll take care of it. The lawyer said that both of us don't need to be there."

"You won't be going anywhere by yourself," he stated with authority. "The security company is sending someone over now. They told me somebody should be there this afternoon. I'll see you tonight."

A few moments later the pub doorbell rang. I ran downstairs expecting to find an older, father-type bodyguard, but instead there was a FedEx deliveryman at my door. He handed me a letter-size package addressed to Taryn L. Mitchell. It was from a bank in Sioux Falls, South Dakota.

I tore open the zip tape; inside was another envelope that contained a new platinum credit card with *Taryn L. Mitchell, Shell-B Enterprises* embossed on it. My face twisted in anger as I tossed the package onto the kitchen table. Ryan and I would definitely have a discussion about this one when he got home.

It was almost two o'clock when my doorbell rang again. This time there was an unbelievably gorgeous young man standing at my door. He was wearing a black leather jacket, blue jeans, and silver-rimmed Oakley sunglasses. He had Heath Ledger's face and Vin Diesel's body, with sandy blond hair. I was tempted to rub my eyes. Part of my brain was already burning in Hell.

"Good afternoon, Ms. Mitchell? I'm Kyle Trent, Protection Services." He held his hand out to greet me.

"Hi. It's nice to meet you. Come in. Please, call me Taryn." I swallowed hard when he unzipped his jacket. The scent of his leather jacket and cologne permeated the air. I noticed that his chest was chiseled underneath his fitted black T-shirt and he was wearing a concealed pistol under his right armpit. *Why couldn't the security company send me an old guy? Holy shit, he's young and gorgeous! This is not good.*

We sat at the large table in the middle of the pub to have our first meeting. Kyle told me that he was a third-degree black belt, a weapons specialist, and a trainer within his agency. I tried to stay engaged in the conversation, but my mind kept on wandering. I found myself staring at his lips.

I informed him of my current situation, filling him in on the necessary details about the celebrity I was dating and our unwanted stalker. I showed him a picture of Angelica.

Kyle was very easy to talk to. He told me that he lives just on the other side of Providence in a small town in Massachusetts, so it didn't take him very long to drive here.

He did an inspection of the pub, familiarizing himself with the layout, security systems, and exits. We ended with a tour of the apartment.

It felt awkward—almost like I was committing a sin—to have Kyle in my apartment. Ryan had hired him, so it wasn't as though I'd found this totally gorgeous man on my own and invited him up for a cup of coffee, but something still gnawed at my gut. It could only be guilt that tormented me;

guilt for allowing my eyes to look at another man. I had to get him out of my apartment—fast.

Several female fans were already waiting outside on my sidewalk, but I wasn't going to open until Cory and his roommate, Trevor, showed up. I introduced the guys to my new bodyguard and filled them in on why Kyle was hired. Cory looked at me oddly and then shook his head. I wondered if he was worried about our stalker, but soon the meaning behind his attitude became more evident when he hand-carried three new cases of beer out to the bar, flexing his arm muscles along the way.

Trevor took a seat at the front door to ID everyone who came into the pub. Sure enough, half a dozen girls walked into the bar. It upset me to see that Ryan's fans just didn't know when to quit.

Marie stopped abruptly and gasped when she saw my new bodyguard for the first time. "You are so screwed," she whispered at me in passing.

Her eyes flickered over at Kyle, who was sitting at the edge of the bar, keeping watch like a hawk.

"I know. Ryan is not going to be happy when he sees him," I whispered.

"How old is he?" Marie asked.

"He told me he's twenty-nine," I said.

"Married?"

I shook my head no.

It was a few minutes after nine when my cell phone played Ryan's ring tone in my pocket. "He's home now," I said to Marie.

Ryan, of course, wanted to meet my new protector. We all met downstairs in the pub kitchen. Just as I had suspected, Ryan morphed from being happy to be home to jealous and pissed in an instant.

I hugged and kissed Ryan quickly when he came through the door. I purposely did this in front of Kyle with the intent of sending a message to both men exactly where my loyalties lie. I tucked my fingers into Ryan's back pocket and held on to him the whole time that we talked to Kyle.

After our meeting, I took Ryan by the hand and we went upstairs to have dinner together in our apartment. He was quiet . . . too quiet, and I knew him well enough to know why. I stood up and repositioned myself on his lap, straddling him to get his full attention. That made a smile appear on his lips.

I took his face in my hands and kissed him sensually on his cheek. "How was your day?"

"It was all right," he muttered.

I knew he was lying. I gave him a smirk to let him know I wasn't buying it.

He pursed his lips. "I kept messing up my lines. I had a hard time concentrating today." He shook his head in disgust.

My hands massaged his shoulders. "Today is over. Put it behind you. Things will be better tomorrow, you'll see," I whispered in his ear.

He gave me a brief smile, his shoulders slumped in defeat. He ran his warm hands over my back.

I found myself getting aroused by trying to get *him* in a better mood. I nibbled his ear. He let out a pleasurable moan.

His hands slid forward over my ribs; his thumbs rubbed over my breasts. My body instantly tingled from his touch.

"Mr. Christensen," I murmured on his lips, "your presence is requested in the bedroom."

He smiled before locking his lips to mine.

Twenty minutes later I resumed my position behind the bar with a smug smile on my face. When I'd left Ryan, he still had his jeans wrapped around his left ankle and he was lying flat on his back on the bed.

I was pleasantly surprised when Ryan came down to the pub a little while later. He was wearing my tattered Mitchell's Pub baseball hat and a satisfied grin. It pleased me to see him wearing another one of my possessions.

He took a seat next to Kyle and never took his eyes off me for the rest of the night. Kyle stopped every girl that stepped up to Ryan and politely asked them to leave Mr. Christensen alone. He also shooed away every girl that was brave enough to approach him. I had a new appreciation for my bodyguard. So did Ryan.

THE NEXT morning, Kyle arrived exactly as scheduled to drive me to the lawyer. He placed the box of evidence Ryan and I had gathered from our stalker in the trunk of the car before escorting me out of the pub safely. I felt his hand press in my lower back as he held the car door open for me. His cologne was soft and masculine, and wrapped my head in confusing thoughts. The paparazzi thoroughly loved the new image in their lenses.

Once I was finished meeting with our new lawyer, Kyle drove me back to the pub and escorted me into the building. The paparazzi were relentless with their aggravating questions, although I think it was apparent to them that Kyle was a bodyguard by the way he shielded me.

Kyle did a safety sweep of the pub, the bathrooms, and my apartment before leaving me alone for the afternoon. He would return before four o'clock, when I opened to the public.

After Ryan came home and we'd had dinner together, I resumed my spot behind the bar. Ryan eventually came downstairs into the pub and sat next to Kyle. My bodyguard was excellent at keeping the unwanted women at bay. Finally, Ryan was able to just hang out and drink a beer while watching sports on the big screen . . . just like a normal person. That still didn't stop women from taking pictures of him with their camera phones.

Ryan was in mid-sentence, telling me a funny story about what Kat did on set this morning, when I noticed a group of women walk into the bar. One particular woman stood out—the one with kinky-curly hair and eyes like the devil.

"Oh my God, Ryan!" I gasped. "She just walked in! Run!" I ordered.

"Kyle! That's her!" Ryan breathed out as he stood up; his haste caused his bar stool to tip back and tangle in his legs. Ryan's body stumbled backward into mine. I caught him ineptly in my arms as his off-balance body weight pushed me back into the wall. We both looked on in terror as Angelica made her approach.

She was heading straight for Ryan and me; her eyes never left us. Her skin was sallow and the dark circles under her eyes made her look even more menacing in the dimmed pub lighting. She was on a mission and nothing was going to stop her.

Kyle moved so fast that it was hard to discern his actions. With one precise strike, he placed her in an arm- and headlock; a split second later she was facedown on the ground. With expert movements, he had her hands restrained behind her back.

"Ryan! Why are you doing this to me?" Angelica cried and screamed. "I love you!" she yelled. "That bitch has brainwashed you! I'm gonna kill her!"

My fingers trembled as I pulled my cell phone out of my pocket and dialed 911.

RYAN WAS granted the morning off from filming on the day of the court hearing. He put on his suit jacket, and I wore my nice dress pants and a cream-colored sweater underneath my black suede coat. I knew we'd be photographed and filmed relentlessly. Ryan's manager arranged to have a security team escort us in and out of the courthouse.

Ryan and I scurried into the large, black SUV that waited for us in the alleyway. Kyle and Mike, our bodyguards, shielded us as we climbed into the vehicle. Directly behind our car was another black SUV with additional security guards. Ryan's publicist, Marla, was already seated in the other car.

Reporters, photographers, and fans were lined up outside the courthouse when we arrived. People were shouting and screaming at our car. It was pure chaos.

"Once team two is in place we will exit," Mike informed us from the front seat. He pushed his communication earpiece deeper into his ear.

I was sandwiched in the backseat between Ryan and Kyle. Despite how safe I should have felt sitting between these two men, I couldn't stop myself from trembling.

Kyle sighed, then patted and rubbed my forearm to reassure me.

Ryan glared at Kyle's gesture. He gathered one of my shaking hands in his and raised it to his lips.

"It will be okay, babe," Ryan whispered, pulling me closer. "We'll get through this."

Reporters attempted to interview us as we exited the car. Ryan and I kept our attention focused on getting through the courthouse doors. Court officers and private security surrounded us as we entered the building. Mike and Kyle, minus their firearms, escorted us to courtroom number three. Not only was Kyle protecting me, today he would also be a witness.

Ryan and I were seated at a large wooden table that faced the raised dark oak bench where the judge would sit. Our attorney was already seated; the box of scary evidence was sitting on the floor next to him.

Cory and Marie were seated in the first row behind us. They, too, were witnesses to Angelica's threats.

Sitting at the other table across from us was Angelica's attorney. Our lawyer leaned over and informed us that she would be using the public defender's office to represent her case today.

One male and one female police officer escorted Angelica into the courtroom. She was wearing an orange prison outfit and her arms were handcuffed to a chain that wrapped around her waist. Her ankles were shackled. She didn't look at us when she entered.

Angelica's hair was disheveled, sticking out in all directions. The circles under her eyes were deep and purple, making the starkness of her yellow skin even more pronounced.

"All rise!" the court clerk announced. "Court is now in session. The honorable Judge Brian Keller presiding."

The court proceedings were long and tedious. Our attorney had to present each letter, picture, and package separately, and one-by-one they were all entered in as evidence. I even provided a copy of the picture of Angelica grabbing Ryan's arm when we went to Cal and Kelly's. That picture of her attack was in every magazine and splattered all over the Internet news.

Our attorney informed us that he had to present every piece of evidence carefully so that Angelica's actions would be deemed a credible threat to our safety.

Each one of our witnesses was called upon to testify that they had indeed heard Angelica threaten to kill me.

Her public defender tried to cross-examine our witnesses, but it did her case no good to do so.

Our attorney played the 911 audiotape of my call to police the night she came into the pub. I shuddered, listening to my panicked voice begging for the police to come immediately and Angelica's rant in the background as she threatened to slice me into pieces. I choked back tears while the nightmare of that evening replayed in my thoughts. Ryan squeezed my hand tightly under the table.

We sat and listened as each of her letters was read out loud to the judge. The content of the letters was equally disturbing. This deluded woman actually thought she was rescuing Ryan from the sluts who were ruining his career and stealing his love away from her.

The judge questioned Angelica directly, asking her to explain her behavior.

She looked at Ryan, but he looked away.

"He hid messages in his movie for me. He knew I was smart enough to figure them out. He didn't want the others to know that he was in love with me," she said quietly. "I just want to protect him, but she made him leave for three days so she could brainwash him." Angelica pointed at me. "She's afraid he's going to leave her for me. That's why she crawled into his head, like a worm, and turned him against me."

It was hard to breathe while she spoke. This girl was *the* poster child for modern-day horror movies. She was the reason nightmares existed.

The judge deliberated with the lawyers and then delivered his verdict. A permanent no-contact restraining order was granted and put in effect immediately. Angelica was informed that it meant that she could not mail, e-mail, call, text, or send anything. Any attempt to contact either one of us, or interfere with us or any member of our families, our friends, and fellow employees, would be deemed a violation of the order. She was instructed to remain no less than five hundred yards, or roughly a quarter of a mile, away from us at all times. The judge also ordered that she be subjected to a psychiatric evaluation. Another hearing would be scheduled to sentence her for the violation of the temporary restraining order.

"Is that it?" I softly asked our lawyer.

"Yes. She'll be incarcerated for a while," he replied. "I will represent you when she is sentenced for the PFA violation. You don't need to be present for that. I'm sure this was traumatic enough for you."

Ryan and I received new copies of the permanent restraining order, and with that our day in court was over. Our last hurdle was still ahead of us . . . getting through the gauntlet of reporters and paparazzi that waited outside the courthouse doors.

CHAPTER 23

Celebration

"DO WE HAVE to be quiet?" Ryan's friend Scott asked out loud.

"No. He would be suspicious if the bar was quiet," I said.

I was glad that we had a separate entrance from the back door to our apartment now. Ryan would never see everyone gathered in the pub until I brought him downstairs. He also would have no reason to look in the guest room and accidentally see his friends' suitcases.

Tammy had prepared a lavish buffet of food and desserts, and everyone was snacking on the variety of hors d'oeuvres scattered around the bar. All our friends were here, waiting for the guest of honor to arrive.

I went upstairs to wait for Ryan and was relieved when he finally came through the door. I called Marie quickly to let her know that Ryan was in the building.

"Hey, babe," he said glumly, giving me an unenthusiastic kiss. I knew why he was sad, but I couldn't ruin the surprise.

"What's wrong? Are you in a bad mood?" I asked, even though I knew he'd be like this.

"Sort of. Actually, I'm pissed. I thought these people were my friends. Cal and Kelly are going to meet us at the restaurant, but everyone else had plans or excuses. Even Kat blew me off."

"I'm sorry." I tried to seem sympathetic.

"Yeah, but . . . ah, it doesn't matter." He threw his keys onto the kitchen the table. I could tell his feelings were hurt. "Tomorrow is our last day of filming. Everyone is going to be leaving. I just thought that we could all get together before . . ."

I stepped over to him and wrapped my arms around his waist. "I promise that you will have a good time tonight. When we get back from dinner, I have a special birthday surprise for you. You'll just have to trust me." I grinned at him. "Come on . . . let's go do a few shots before Mike comes back. I'm planning on getting you all liquored up on your birthday."

He reluctantly followed me downstairs, grumbling the whole way about how his wacko fans were going to scream when they saw him in the pub. We no longer had our Ryan Christensen fan buffer working for us; Ryan had dismissed Kyle from being my bodyguard as soon as the court proceedings were over and Angelica was locked up.

I ignored his bellyaching and dialed Pete's number. That was the signal that Ryan was on his way.

"Why do I smell food?" he asked when we stepped into the pub kitchen. I smiled, got behind him, and pushed his hips so he would go through the swing door into the pub.

"Surprise! Happy birthday!" everyone yelled.

Ryan's face lit up when he saw all his friends that he thought didn't care about him gathered and waiting. Most of the production crew was there as well.

"Okay. You got me," Ryan admitted. "No wonder everyone had other plans tonight." He went from person to person, giving out handshakes and hugs. Eventually he noticed his longtime friends Matt and Scott standing by the bar.

"Holy shit!" Ryan yelled, giving Matt a manly handshake and hug. "What the . . . ? When the hell did you guys get here?"

Ryan's reaction was exactly how I hoped it would be. He was elated and totally taken by surprise.

"We got here this morning," Matt said. "Your lovely girlfriend over there picked us up at the airport."

"Aw man, it's good to see ya!" Ryan was hugging Scott now.

I stepped over to Ryan and he wrapped his arm around my shoulder.

"I can't believe you did all of this!" He gave me a big kiss.

"Happy birthday, honey!" I beamed.

"How long are you guys going to be in town?" Ryan asked Matt.

"We leave on Sunday."

"This is too much. I can't believe this. Where are you staying? Tar, where are they staying?"

"We're staying with you." Scott punched him in the arm. "That way we don't have to drive anywhere to get loaded."

Ryan looked at me, apparently to get confirmation that Scott was telling the truth.

"Matt and Laura are going to stay in the guest room and Scott is going to couch surf. Their bags are already upstairs. I didn't see the need for them to stay at a hotel." I shrugged.

Ryan wrapped his arms around my shoulders to give me a hug. "Thank you," he whispered in my ear. "I love you so much!"

"Come on, birthday boy. Everyone's been waiting for you. It's time to get this party started!" I tugged his hand to follow me.

"Cory! Fill 'em up!" I motioned to the stack of champagne glasses sitting on the bar.

"Wait. I can't get too wasted tonight. We have final scenes tomorrow," Ryan said.

"Did you hear that, Kenneth?" Cal shouted to the director of their movie. "Ryan doesn't want to get too drunk tonight because he has to work tomorrow."

Kenneth smiled and laughed out loud. "Actually, Ryan, I have a big confession to make. We—ahh—wrapped today. Tomorrow's call sheet that you have, it's a fake. You're the only one who didn't know that today was the last day on location here."

"What?" Ryan looked totally confused. "So all that crap about the wardrobe and then you sent me to the makeup trailer—that was all bullshit?"

Kenneth grinned and nodded.

"I spent two hours sitting in that chair! Two hours while Mia painted me!" Ryan yelled in jest.

I started laughing and pointed over to the poolroom, where Mia, the makeup artist who'd stalled him, was standing.

"Hey, I had to get you off the set somehow." Kenneth laughed.

"Were you in on this, too?" Ryan looked at me. His eyes questioned my participation.

"In on it?" Kenneth questioned, laughing heartily. "She orchestrated it."

"Hey, I'm not taking all the credit," I protested. "I had a lot of willing accomplices. Everyone standing in this room was in on it."

Cory and I handed out champagne glasses to everyone.

Pete tapped a spoon on his glass to get everyone's attention. He raised his glass in the air to make a toast.

"Here's to Ryan . . . a great man and a great friend! May you be blessed with great health! No, wait," he paused. "I don't think you need that. You are pretty healthy." He squeezed Ryan's biceps. His eyes scrunched together to ponder his next statement.

"Well, then, how about . . . To Ryan, may you be blessed with great wealth! No, come to think of it, you are pretty filthy-stinkin' rich, too."

Ryan started to chuckle. He looked slightly embarrassed.

"I've got it . . . I've got it. Ryan, for your birthday, may you be blessed with the love of a great woman! Wait! Shit! You already have that, too!" Pete pointed a finger at me.

"Well, what the hell?" Pete whined, faking his disgust.

Everyone laughed at Pete's toast.

Pete looked at the many faces in the pub, waved his glass in the air, and said, "To Ryan, may you get so drunk tonight that you puke all over yourself, you lucky bastard!"

"Here, here!" Our friends raised their glasses.

Ryan took me by the hand and we mingled with our guests. He was anxious to talk with Matt and Scott, since he rarely got to see them.

"Ryan, this is my girlfriend, Laura," Matt said.

Laura reached out and shook Ryan's hand. I was curious to see how she would react, and I was so relieved when she maintained her composure. The last thing I wanted was a giggling fan sleeping in the room next to ours tonight.

"Man, where are all the single women?" Scott was looking around the pub. "You call this a party?" he teased Ryan.

"Laura, why don't you come with me? We'll let the boys catch up." I patted Ryan on his back and headed over toward my friends.

"So, you're really dating Ryan Christensen, huh?" Laura asked. I'd misjudged . . . maybe she was a fan after all?

"So, you're really dating his best friend, huh?" I smiled at her.

"Yeah, I guess I am," Laura realized aloud.

"Did you see his movie?" I asked, half expecting her answer.

"Yep," she nodded and continued quietly, "but between you and me, I don't get what all the excitement is about."

I couldn't help but laugh.

"What's so funny?" Kelly asked.

I kept Laura's comment to myself and introduced her to everyone instead.

"Ryan said you're coming out to L.A. with him in December," Kelly said happily. "We'll have so much fun!"

"Kelly . . ." I motioned with my head so I could speak to her privately. "I need to get a dress for the party. Do you think you can help me find something appropriate before you leave for California?" I thought about the one and only formal-wear shop that I knew of, which was halfway between Seaport and Providence. That would be my hunting grounds.

"Why don't we shop for a dress when you come out to L.A.? What better place to find a designer dress," Kelly retorted.

"I don't need a designer dress, I just want to look nice."

"You'll be photographed on the arm of Ryan Christensen. You *need* a designer dress," she insisted. "Don't worry, I'll make sure you look absolutely gorgeous."

I glanced over toward the bar and noticed a pack of guys around Ryan. They were all doing shots.

"Ben, Kenneth . . . get over here!" Ryan yelled exuberantly.

"He *is* going to puke tonight if he keeps that up." Marie laughed.

"He won't be alone." I raised my eyebrows, nodding my head in Ryan's direction. "*All* of our men are over there doing shots. Good thing none of them are driving tonight."

"Where did you get the cute bartender, Taryn?" Kat asked.

My eyes flashed back over to the bar. "That's Cory. I hired him to work weekends, although it's turning out to be almost a full-time job for him now. Marie and I thought Ryan's fans would appreciate looking at something other than us. And to tell you the truth, it's comforting to have a man working here. The scary fan adoration hasn't stopped."

"Speaking of scary, where are the psycho twins?" Marie asked, noting that Suzanne and Francesca were absent.

"Don't know, don't really care," I admitted.

"We should get everyone eating," Tammy advised. I helped her uncover all of the hot chafing dishes. Soon a long line formed for hot food.

Ryan butted in line behind me. He wrapped one arm across my chest and whispered in my ear, "Thank you for my party. You really got me good." His free hand patted my rear.

Mike, Ryan's personal guard, walked up to us while we were in line.

"Guess you're not driving us to dinner tonight, you lying S.O.B.!" Ryan teased.

"Not tonight. I'm just a guest. But I do need to talk to you." His tone became serious. "I just got a call from Suzanne's driver; she and Francesca are on their way. And just so you know, they spent some quality time in the hotel bar before requesting to be driven here."

Ryan dropped his forehead onto my shoulder. I knew he was stuck in a no-win situation.

I tenderly patted his hand that rested on my chest. "That's all right. They can come—after all, they were invited. Things are different now, and this is sort of a wrap party, too."

Ryan breathed out hard on my neck. I could smell the whiskey and beer mixed in with his anxiety.

While Ryan and I made our plates of food, thoughts of Mike's dedicated service to him filled my mind. "Ryan, what's Mike's last name?"

"Murphy."

"Who does he work for?"

Ryan piled some shrimp on his plate. "He works for a company called PSG. I think it stands for Protection Services Group or something like that. The studio hired them. Why do you ask?"

"Is this the first time he's working for you?"

"Yeah. He was assigned to me when we got here. It's the same company Kyle works for. I guess they're global or something."

We sat down at the table to eat. He looked at me, waiting for me to continue.

"He is just really dedicated to you. And you seem to have a great relationship with him. I was just wondering how long he's been protecting you."

"It's funny you mention that. I've already talked to Mike about working for me." Ryan patted me on my thigh and shrugged. "Everywhere I go, I get new people hovering around me. It's hard to feel safe when you don't know or trust the people who are supposed to protect you. I wish I didn't need it." He rubbed his forehead.

"Well, I like the way Mike takes care of you. It would make me feel better to know someone like that was guarding you full time."

"Yeah, I agree." Ryan stroked my hair. "I'll see what I can do about it."

Frank and the rest of the Being Frank band started their first set on the stage. I had the volume on the sound system turned down so the music would still rock but we wouldn't need to yell at each other to hold a conversation.

"You even hired a band?" Ryan asked in between taking bites of food. He kept shaking his head.

I smiled at him while I was still chewing. "Happy birthday, honey!"

"And you gave me shit when I bought you earrings." He pursed his lips. "And then you go and do something like this." He looked at me with a serious expression, even though I knew he was teasing. "I'm gonna buy you really big freaking diamonds now, just to piss you off."

His absurd comment made me roll my eyes. I placed my hand on his cheek and gave him a quick kiss. "Don't you dare! I don't want big freaking diamonds. I just want you."

Ryan abruptly pulled my chair closer and straddled his legs around it. He was gazing at me intently, so I put my fork down and gave him my full attention. He slid his hand across my back and took my chin in his fingers. His eyes flashed to look at my lips before he kissed me.

"I love you," he murmured. "Never doubt that."

"Happy birthday, Ryan!" Suzanne shouted, rudely interrupting our moment. She was slurring her words while she tried to awkwardly hug him. "We weren't sure if we were going to make it here tonight."

Ryan barely turned around to thank Suzanne and Francesca for coming. He nicely suggested they get some food instead of drinking.

"Hey, who's the hot blonde?" Scott asked Ryan in passing.

"You like that?" Ryan teased him. "Go, have at it. Best of luck to ya." Scott eagerly ran off in Suzanne's direction.

I laughed, watching Scott follow Suzanne like a desperate dog. I was still mulling over his reaction toward Suzanne when I noticed Kyle standing by the door. He was talking to Mike and he already had a beer in his hand. I was surprised that I'd missed his arrival. I hadn't expected him to show up.

Ryan did a double take when he turned to see what I was looking at.

"What's Kyle doing here?" The way Ryan said it, I knew he was irritated by Kyle's presence.

"I invited him," I said. My words sounded more like a confession.

Ryan glared at me.

"I've been planning your party for a few weeks, hon," I admitted. "I invited him when he was still working for us."

"Hey, Ryan, happy birthday." Kyle held out his hand. I could see the hint of a challenge by his gesture.

"Kyle," Ryan said flatly and shook his hand. I watched as both of them put extra effort into how hard they squeezed each other's hand.

"Taryn, do you think I could talk to you for a sec?" Kyle motioned for me to follow.

"Where are you going?" Ryan asked, glowering at me.

"I don't know. He wants to talk to me. I'm going over there," I replied, wondering what his new biting tone was all about.

"Hey," Kyle breathed out. "So, how are you?"

"I'm good, thanks." I tried to be friendly without appearing overly excited to see him. "How are you?"

"I'm fine. I've just been thinking about you. I've been a little worried about you, actually. We really didn't get to talk much after the court hearing." Kyle's eyes flashed over to Ryan, who was leaning on the bar staring at us.

"I was hoping that the incident and the court proceedings didn't shake you up too much. So, you've been doing all right since then?" he asked, focusing all of his attention back to me.

Kyle was ignoring Ryan's glare. I, however, could feel Ryan's eyes burning holes in my back. I knew Ryan was a little intimidated by Kyle, but he still he had no reason to be so jealous.

"I'm fine," I said casually. "It was quite a traumatic experience, but I'm glad to say that I haven't had any nightmares from it. Thanks again for being there. I felt very safe when you were around," I said, trying to give him a compliment. "I appreciate you protecting Ryan and me."

"Yeah, sure. It's my job," he said with a dismissive tone. "Any other fans causing problems for you?"

"No, but the bar business has surely picked up," I willingly admitted. "I have a doorman on post every night now."

Kyle laughed. "Yeah, the sidewalk out there is filled with disappointment. The fans are heartbroken that you're closed to the public tonight."

"Are there a lot out there?" I craned my neck to see if bodies were visible on the other side of my front window.

"Pretty many. They're holding their Obsession Club group meeting," he snorted.

"Great! Next thing you know, they'll be organizing fund-raisers and selling raffle tickets."

"I wonder if they'll be selling cookies?" Kyle joked. "I really like those chocolate mint ones. They're good to dip in milk."

"I guess they can count on your support then, huh?" I teased. "You're probably good for two or three boxes, right?"

"Sure. Why not? I mean, it seems like a *worthwhile* cause." He grinned.

I frowned at his tiny dig at Ryan.

"That band up there is really rocking," Kyle said enthusiastically. He was tapping his fingers on his beer bottle. "This is a really nice party you put together."

"Thanks. It was a little tricky, but I guess I pulled it off." I glanced around at the large gathering. My pub was packed; everyone seemed to be having a good time.

"You know, *my* birthday is in April. Feel free to throw me a party like this." Kyle bumped me with his elbow as he took a sip of his beer.

"So are you here with a date?" I asked, looking around for a stray woman.

"No," he said uncomfortably. "Why are you looking at me like that?"

"I was just wondering why someone like you doesn't have a girlfriend, that's all."

He looked at me as if my question were ridiculous.

"Don't make that face at me," I teased. "So?"

"I don't know," Kyle groaned. "Maybe I'm too shy?"

I scoffed. "Yeah, right. I don't think that's a problem for you."

"Maybe I'm too picky," he added, taking another sip of his beer. "It's hard to find the complete package these days."

"Well, write down your list of requirements; I'm sure there is a girl or two out there on the sidewalk that comes close," I jeered.

"Nah. I don't have to walk that far to find what I've been looking for," he stated directly as he looked me in the eyes.

I was just about to make a witty comeback when Kyle's smile vanished.

I felt a hand slip around my elbow; Ryan was reclaiming me.

"Taryn . . . Honey, there are some people I want to introduce you to, if you're finished with your conversation here?" The tone of his comment clearly indicated I was to end my conversation—now.

I was enjoying talking to Kyle, but apparently Ryan's tolerance had reached its limit.

"I guess I'll talk to you later," Kyle said, slightly irritated. He tried to appear unaffected by Ryan's attitude, but the anger and resentment were evident.

"Excuse me, Kyle. Please, enjoy the party." I gently smiled, trying to hide my embarrassment.

Ryan took my hand and pulled me along through the crowd. He was towing me toward the poolroom, but I yanked him toward the empty space by the kitchen door instead.

"What?" Ryan's tone was curt.

"What's the problem?" I asked sweetly, curbing the anger that was starting to swell. It was time for us to have *this* discussion. I let it go when he'd first dismissed Kyle from our security detail, but this jealous attitude needed to stop.

"What do you mean?" His eyes scrunched together, looking at me like he didn't understand my question.

"I was just talking to him. I don't understand why you're being like this," I whispered, thinking he didn't trust me.

"I don't like the way he looks at you, all right?" he growled.

"I don't get it. How does he look at me, Ryan?" He was being ridiculous.

He scoffed at me, like I was missing the point. "What? You don't see it? I'm *pretty* sure you know when you're getting hit on, Taryn."

I rolled my eyes. "Please," I chided.

"I just don't want you to accidentally give him the wrong impression, that's all," he said calmly.

I sighed. "Ryan, I love you. There is no reason for you to distrust me."

"I trust you, but I don't trust *him*." Ryan nodded his chin in Kyle's direction.

When I looked over my shoulder, Kyle had a cocky smile on his face and he raised his beer bottle in the air to acknowledge us.

"You worry over nothing," I groaned. "Now can we go back to having a good time?"

"Yeah, I guess," Ryan muttered. "I'm sorry."

"Just shut up and kiss me, you fool," I teased, slipping my fingers over the edge of the front pockets of his jeans.

"There he is!" Tammy shouted. She hurried over to where we stood. She grabbed one of Ryan's arms; Marie forcefully removed his other arm from around my waist.

"Time to blow out your candles, birthday boy!" Marie announced as they hauled him off to the food table. Tammy had baked an enormous birthday cake and we all sang to Ryan before he blew the candles out.

Everyone was having a great time; people were dancing, shooting pool, and playing darts. Ryan's friends were attempting to get him wasted, but he reached a point where he refused to do any more shots.

I did the proper girlfriend thing and stayed away from Kyle as much as possible, even though he did try to talk to me several times.

I noticed that Suzanne and Francesca sat at the bar all night. Cory was leaning across the bar, flirting tough with Francesca. He even got away with touching her hair a few times. She was smiling and pretending to be shy, but she was definitely engaging Cory's advances.

Scott and Suzanne were hitting it off tremendously. She was touching him, squeezing his arm muscles, and laughing at everything he said. Despite outward appearances, she still knew where Ryan was at all times.

It was getting late and many of our guests had already left.

"Do you mind if I take off?" Cory asked, his eyes sliding over in Francesca's direction. Suzanne and Scott were practically wrestling with each other; they couldn't keep their hands to themselves. Francesca stood by the door, waiting impatiently and staring at Cory while he talked to me.

"They invited us back to their hotel," he admitted.

For some reason, I wasn't too surprised.

"Go ahead. Have fun. Wait, are you driving?" I asked.

"Yeah, it's okay though, I stopped drinking a while ago. I want to remember every detail of the next couple of hours, if you know what I mean!" Cory smiled smugly and flashed his eyes back to Francesca. "I'll bring Ryan's buddy back tomorrow."

"Hey, where are they going?" Ryan stopped dead in his tracks and wheeled around when he noticed Scott leaving. Scott didn't even acknowledge Ryan; he was completely focused on other things.

Slowly the rest of our guests departed, and it was almost three in the morning when I turned off the lights. I planned to clean up the bar in the morning. I had more important things to take care of.

Matt and Laura were stowed away comfortably in the guest room. I closed our bedroom door and smiled in disbelief.

My birthday boy was sprawled out on our bed, wearing nothing but his birthday suit and a slightly drunken grin . . . waiting for his birthday present.

CHAPTER 24

Sobering

WHAT THE HELL happened to Scott last night?" Matt asked, stuffing another piece of bacon in his mouth. Laura was taking her turn in the shower.

"He left with Suzanne," Ryan answered. "Maybe she won't be so bitchy now." He chuckled to himself.

"Hopefully, Cory gave Fran someone *new* to think about, too." I winked.

Ryan smiled at me over his cup of coffee.

Once everyone was showered, dressed, and fed, I went downstairs to clean up the pub. I was clearing off the tables when Ryan popped through the door. He started to gather the garbage.

"What can we do to help?" Laura asked. I was thankful that I had willing hands to help clean up the remains of Ryan's birthday party.

"I still can't believe you did this," Ryan said, kissing me on one of his trips past. "How long have you been conspiring behind my back?" he asked.

"A couple of weeks. Your friends were more than willing to be in on the surprise."

"Matt told me you made him look you up on the Internet," Ryan teased.

"Yeah. He didn't believe you had a girlfriend." I poked him in the stomach and went to answer the doorbell.

"Hey. There they are!" Ryan's voice boomed when he saw Cory and Scott walk through the front door.

"Man! What the hell is it with all the photographers and chicks out there?" Scott motioned with his thumb, pointing to the door. "Don't they ever go home?"

"No. They live here now. They're like zombies that don't die when the sun comes up." I laughed at my own comment.

"So how was your night, Scott?" Ryan gave him a teasing nudge in the arm.

Scott's eyes narrowed. "What do you think? I made her fucking night . . . several times," he boasted. "She's a screamer, that girl."

He held up a small, white plastic bag in his hand. "Good thing we stopped at the drugstore on our way back. I'm planning on making her scream again tonight."

Ryan's face puckered up. He grabbed Scott's arm and hauled him off into the poolroom. I didn't care much for Suzanne, but she was Ryan's co-star and a celebrity—she had no privacy either. There were enough rumors and scandals floating around in the media about the *Seaside* cast already. Suzanne's indiscretions didn't need to be added to the pile. I was sure that Ryan was going to tell him the same thing.

"Francesca and Suzanne are planning on coming here tonight," Cory quietly informed me. "I hope you don't mind."

I shrugged and shook my head. It didn't bother me, as long as Fran wasn't here to see Ryan. But I was wise enough to know things like this could have powerful ripple effects.

"Cory, I'm not going to tell you what you can and cannot do, but you *do* realize that Fran is a celebrity. I hope you keep your private activities with her private and discreet. Understand?"

"Yeah, I understand. I know what I've gotten myself into. Don't worry, I'm not going to be like that guy and announce stuff to the world." He nodded his head in Scott's direction. "Francesca is sweet and I'd never do that to her. But I would like to see her again. And she wants to see me too, so . . ." Cory shrugged.

"Just keep it private. That's all I ask. We're *all* under the microscope now," I stressed my point.

"I will. Hey, sorry I can't stay to help clean up. I've got to get some sleep. I'll see you at four," Cory said, putting his sunglasses back on. "Oh, and before I forget, I already talked to my roommate. He'll cover the door tonight."

"Did Cory leave?" Ryan asked me a few moments later.

I nodded.

"Damn. I wanted to talk to him, too."

I whispered to Ryan. "I talked to him. I reminded him to keep his personal business private and discreet. You may want to talk with Matt and Laura about confidentiality as well."

"I already did." A tiny smile cracked on his lips.

The early afternoon flew by quickly. It took us several hours to clean up the mess, and I mopped all the floors and even cleaned the bathrooms. Ryan suggested several times that I hire a company to clean the bar every day, but I was used to taking care of the grunt work on my own.

Scott passed out in the guest room upstairs; I guessed he hadn't slept much last night either. Ryan, Matt, and Laura were lounging in the living room, watching television. I logged on to the Internet.

"What are you doing, Tar?" Ryan's tone indicated his disappointment.

"Checking up on things."

"Why are you looking?" he groaned, concerned.

I flashed my eyes up to him and kept my reply quiet. "Because your public image is *my* concern, too. Before I forget to tell you, Francesca and Suzanne are coming tonight. We're going to need security in the bar. Do you want Mike here?"

Ryan didn't answer. He just walked away.

I clicked a link and was directed to a gossip magazine's website. The headline "Ryan Christensen's Love Affairs" caught my attention. The site had side-by-side pictures of Ryan and Suzanne kissing, Ryan and me walking down the sidewalk, and Ryan and that girl from the Manhattan dinner meeting. The story pretty much accused him of being a reckless playboy. The words "plays the field" were included in the article.

I clicked another link and was now viewing pictures of Ryan kissing, smiling, leaning on, and holding Suzanne. The caption stated that their love affair was still going strong.

I hit the back button and clicked on another link—this one described my new bodyguard, Kyle, being the new man in my life and how Ryan was furious and jealous. There was a picture of Kyle and me entering the back door of my pub together. The article posted a random picture of Ryan looking angry next to it. All meant to generate shock, I supposed. The story made it sound like I was cheating on Ryan.

The last click I made showed a picture of Ryan and Suzanne snuggling in a bed. It looked like they were both naked, although you could only see Suzanne's bare shoulders. Most of Ryan's naked torso was exposed.

I jumped when Ryan popped his head next to mine.

"Turn it off before I throw the damn laptop out the window." He whispered his angry threat in my ear.

I quickly closed the Internet connection. Ryan grabbed me by my wrist and pulled me out of the chair. We hurried down the hallway to our bedroom.

He shoved the door closed behind him with extra force and glared at me.

"How long have you been surfing the Web like that?" he growled between his gritted teeth.

I didn't answer. His anger caught me off-guard.

"Why the hell are you looking up shit on the Internet? Do you need more reasons in your head not to trust me?"

"Please keep your voice down. We have guests, remember? I'm sorry," I whispered. I felt terrible that I'd upset him.

"I am trying so damn hard to make sure our relationship stays on track, knowing full well that we have more obstacles than most. And then I see you doing that shit! What the fuck, Taryn?"

I didn't know how to fully explain my actions. "I was curious to see what the public was being told." I was so ashamed, my words were barely audible. "I'm sorry. I won't do it again."

"What else do you need to know? This is our life, right here! It's happening right now! I am standing in this room with you. I'm not out there in those pictures. I don't give a damn what the public is being told!"

"What if the situation was reversed and the magazines were printing stories that I'm some whore who's screwing three different guys at once. You don't think that would concern *you*?" I asked.

"But you're not! And I certainly am not doing what they accuse me of. I have no control over what trash they print."

"Yes, you do." I thought about several ways he could get the point across to the world that he was a one-woman kind of man, that he in fact was currently involved with just one woman, but he'd have to make that move on his own.

"How?" Ryan barked.

I chickened out and bit my tongue. "I thought you had a publicist," I stated calmly.

He scoffed. "If all those *Seaside* fans want to fantasize that I'm actually living the shit that's filmed, that me and Suzanne are some star-crossed lovers, what am I supposed to do about it? Put out a public statement that they're all deluded?" He threw his hands up in the air.

"And that picture of me and that girl from New York, that little picture is going to still pop up years from now. Those trash magazines are going to say that I'm cheating on you with her one day."

He took a deep breath. "You have to realize that some of that shit is printed specifically to generate public reaction. They will post pictures of me and Suzanne just to keep the public interested in the film. They will print shit just to keep my career controversial and fresh. I may be asked to do stuff that might upset you just to pique public interest. It's all part of the game."

He sat down on the bed, facing me. "Taryn, our relationship has to be built on trust. That stuff is just going to tear it down."

I looked down at my hands. He was right; my behavior was incorrigible, but I wasn't alone there.

He took my hand and pressed it to his chest. "This . . . this is real."

"So if your PR team asks you to screw some actress to pique public interest, is that what you're willing do to keep your career controversial? I just want to be clear on how far you're willing to go."

His tone was angry and sarcastic. "Yes, Taryn. I'm going to throw away our relationship, forget that I'm in love with you, and screw every woman that throws her legs up in the air. Is that what you want to hear? Is that what you need to believe that I truly am? Just like your ex-fiancé? That I'm no different from every other asshole who has ever cheated on you?"

I looked away and winced from the sting of his words. That was a low blow, but in a way I deserved it. Pain cracked in my chest and the tears of shame formed in my eyes.

He stood up from the bed and knelt down on the floor in front of me.

"I'm not them, Tar. I don't know what else to do to make you have faith in me. Why don't you trust me?"

"I *do* trust you," I muttered, wiping the tear from my cheek. "This whole conversation has nothing to do with trust. There are just so many other influences out there. It's hard to keep up with it all." I looked him in the eyes.

"Ryan, your life *is* public. I *want* to know what's being said about you. I want to protect you from all the daggers that are flying in your direction. Shield you from the lies." I picked a tissue out of the box on the nightstand and wiped my face.

"You can't protect me from it—you're way outnumbered," he said, defeated.

I took a deep breath. "It's more than that. The other reason I look is, sometimes I feel like I'm living with two people . . . the man I'm in love with and some other guy I barely know. The photo shoots, premieres, public appearances, magazine spreads, interviews—all of that is in here, too." I pressed my hand back on his chest. "I look so I can understand it all; so I can be connected and in love with *all* of you."

Ryan rubbed his face and sighed. "I didn't see it that way. I'm sorry I yelled at you," he whispered, staring solemnly into my eyes.

I sniffed back my tears and acknowledged his apology with a nod.

"I don't want your mind to get clouded with the lies, Taryn. That's all." He picked up my hand, wrapping it in his. "It's so easy for fabricated stories to appear believable. They even merge pictures and try to pass them off as real."

"Regardless, Ryan, all those *real* pictures of you, all those poses, stills, and magazine spreads, those are all little bits and pieces of you—of who you are, of things you've been through, things you've experienced. All of that is a side of you that I don't know. In a way, it helps me understand you."

He breathed out another sigh and tapped our gathered hands into his forehead. He looked up into my eyes.

"I think this is the part where I apologize and we kiss and make up," he suggested softly.

I fidgeted a bit, still wiping the remnants of tears from my cheeks. "I think this is the part where we realize that we still have a lot to learn about each other. That it takes a lot more than physical love to keep people together."

He stood up in front of me, pulling me up off the bed by my hands.

"You're right," he agreed. "I'm so sorry for blowing up at you."

"I'm sorry for giving you a reason to do so, but I hope you see the reasons why I look and don't get upset with me if I do it again."

He shook his head, exhaling harshly. "You're going to see stuff and think it's true. I really wish you wouldn't."

I spent the next few hours trying to look happy in front of our guests, careful not to let on that I was still mulling over the heated discussion he and I had.

Suzanne and Francesca showed up later in the evening; tonight was their last night in Seaport. Both of them had flights to catch the next day. Scott was trying to pump Suzanne full with shots—I suppose to loosen her up again—however, she continued to watch every move that Ryan made.

She would flirt with Scott and then check to see if Ryan saw it. Unfortunately for her, Ryan had other things on his mind that he was worrying about—fans.

It didn't take long for word to get out that Ryan Christensen was in Mitchell's Pub again. Girls started to arrive in droves. Cory's friend Trevor was working the door for me, and after a while I had him stop allowing people in; we were crowded enough with obsessive females.

Ryan was doing his best to just deal with it all. I could see he was trying to have fun and blend in and not worry about the extra attention he was getting, but he had to work at it.

Suzanne did not like it at all when Scott left her side to become Ryan's wingman. Just standing in close proximity to Ryan provided Scott with a hearty selection of new women to talk to. It didn't take her long to slip her way in between Ryan and Scott.

"Taryn?"

I heard my name called out. It was a female voice—French accent. Francesca waved her fingers at me.

"Yes, Francesca?" I asked, trying to be polite.

"Can I speak to you privately?" Her eyes scanned tentatively for my reaction.

Ryan, of course, noticed us walking toward the kitchen door. I gestured my confusion, silently answering his questioning stare.

"I just want to apologize to you," she said. "I have treated you badly and unfairly, and I'm very sorry." She sounded sincere.

"It's all right," I responded, trying to sound just as sincere. "Don't worry about it."

"You probably know that I have liked Ryan for a long time, but I know that he does not feel the same way about me as I do him." Her admission made her stare at the floor.

"He deserves to be happy and I can see he is in love with you." Her lips curled into a brief smile. "I can only hope that I, too, will have that happiness one day."

"You will," I assured her.

"I was wondering . . . has Cory said anything to you about me?"

Her question perplexed me for a moment. I felt like we were young teenagers talking about our boy crushes and she was searching for insider information.

"I think it's safe to say that he likes you," I told her, feeling suddenly like an older sister.

"I like him, too, very much. He is so nice and sweet and handsome, but . . ." She stopped to ponder.

"But what?" I asked.

She twitched, almost afraid to continue. She didn't need to.

"You're afraid of what the public will think," I stated, pointing out the obvious.

She looked at me and nodded.

"How does he make you feel?" I questioned, knowing there was more.

Francesca smiled gloriously and pressed her hands to her heart.

"You deserve to be happy, too. And the choice is really yours. Cory is very ambitious, but he will still put your needs ahead of his own and treat you like gold. He's just beginning to find his career direction. And he will be successful at it. But then there's always the alternative choice . . . you could get involved with some young, rich guy who constantly thinks that the *next* girl he hooks up with is going to be even better than you." I waited until she looked at me again.

"Francesca, I'm terrified about what the public thinks of me," I admitted. "I know people all around the world feel that he could do better than me, but better how? Someone with more money . . . more fame? Are those the things that truly matter when it comes to loving someone completely and knowing that good, bad, or otherwise, that person will love you just as much in return?"

"No," she agreed.

"Then go be happy."

I let Cory leave early that night.

RYAN WAS busy attempting to cook dinner when I joined him in the kitchen late Sunday night. His friends had left in morning for their flight back to Pittsburgh, and after five days with house guests we were finally alone. Even though Ryan was sad to see his friends go, he knew he would be seeing them in a few days when we traveled to his parents' home for Thanksgiving.

"Smells good," I complimented. "Need help?"

"Nope." He grinned at me. "I got it all under control."

I laughed under my breath on my way to the bedroom. He was only making hamburgers and boxed macaroni and cheese, but the kitchen counter was a total mess. I grabbed the stack of scripts from his nightstand and carried them back to the kitchen.

"Did you finish reading this one?" I glanced at the title on the front cover. "*Behind the Words?*"

He looked over his shoulder and sneered. "No. I couldn't finish it. It was stupid. I'm not going to portray a homophobic writer who wants a sex change."

"I still think you should pursue this one . . . *The Isletin Solution*. This one has Oscar potential."

"I was going to read that one next. Was it good?" he asked, licking his thumb. "You're finished with it, right?"

"Yeah, I finished it last night after you fell asleep. It was excellent."

"What's it about?"

"It's the story of two Canadian doctors who discovered insulin and forged the way for the treatment of diabetes. You would be perfect for the lead role of Charles Herbert Best. He was a physiologist and chemist," I said, flipping through the script. "It's based on a true story. It's written from Best's point of view, even though he wasn't the lead scientist in the discovery."

"Great. Another Charles character," he groaned.

"Ah, so what. You're already used to people calling you Charles," I teased.

"How do you know all of that stuff about the characters? Is it written in the script?"

"No. I researched some of it on the Net. I was curious."

"So you think it's a good role for me?" he asked, wiping his wet hands on the dish towel that hung over his shoulder.

"I think it's a perfect role for you. You'd be able to show a wider range of emotions with this character. There are a lot of heart-wrenching scenes. They did their research on dogs, and one of the dogs that he was really attached to dies."

"Sounds sad. You really think it has Oscar potential?" He narrowed his eyes on the script.

"Yeah, I do. The story is very compelling, and you'd play a hero instead of an action star. I visualized you in the role the whole time I read it. It's a tear-jerker. This is the type of role that wins awards."

"Since when did you get so knowledgeable about films and awards?" he asked in a teasing fashion.

"Since I started dating this hot movie star who's getting cast into all these romantic popcorn films. I've just been doing research on acting and stuff," I admitted.

"Well then, move that one to the top of the stack. I'll talk to Aaron and David . . . see what they think."

"You don't want to read it first?" I was surprised that he was just going to take my word for it.

"I trust you." He smiled.

"Did you read this one . . . *The Only Way*?" I asked, peering at it inquisitively. "I haven't seen this script before."

"Yeah, I read through it last week. It was couriered to the set. I really liked that one, but Aaron told me that they already signed Chase Westwood, so that one is out."

"And what are your thoughts about *Bottle of Red*?" I removed the script from the stack. It was the first one that I had read.

"Lame," he answered dryly.

"I agree. O—U—T out."

"*Sacred Mountain*?" I continued, panning through the pile.

"What was that one about again?" he asked in between taste-testing dinner on the stove.

"Secret UFO base in the mountains."

"Oh, yeah. That one was heavy sci-fi. What did you think of it?" he asked, almost sounding hopeful.

I pursed my lips and sneered.

"What's that reaction about?" he countered.

"Aliens?" I think I rolled my eyes. "That would be a huge diversion from the roles you've been taking. Is that something that interests you?"

He shrugged. He seemed unsure of his direction.

"Ryan, what's your goal here? I mean when you dreamt of being an actor, what kind of actor did you want to be?"

"Brando," he stated with admiration. "I wanted to be Marlon Brando. The Godfather, you know? I can't tell you how many times I looked at myself in the mirror while trying to imitate him. He was the reason I wanted to get up on stage and act."

Ryan sat down at the table with me. "When I did the first *Seaside,* I was thinking about Gary Cooper—how he would have delivered it. I can only hope to be in that league as an actor one day. That would be the ultimate."

"Well, then, there's your direction. If that's the perception you want people to have when they think of you as an actor, then you need to position yourself correctly in the right roles. Isn't that something your agent and manager should be helping you with? I mean some of these scripts . . . well, they aren't going to get you there."

"They're just trying to get me jobs so I make a name for myself. It's tough. You've got to take what you can get sometimes," he responded.

"I don't know about that. By the looks of it, I think you could afford to be a little more choosey." I patted the nine scripts under my hand. "Perhaps if you needed a paycheck you could consider some of these, but I think that if you want your dreams to come true then you need to point yourself in their direction." I held up the script for *The Isletin Solution.*

He smirked. "Yeah, you're right. Hey, after dinner we need to run lines for *Slipknot* again."

I smiled at the thought. I really enjoyed helping and watching him get into character.

I tried to "act" when I read the lines instead of just reading from the script, to the point that Ryan started coaching me when we rehearsed together. We rehearsed so often that I was starting to memorize the lines of dialogue of the other characters and the feelings they were intending to portray in each scene.

Ryan did have a cool job. It was oddly liberating "pretending" and feeling permitted to have different emotions and reactions from your own. I could see why he loves what he does for a living.

The lead female role had a lot of dialogue. She was a medical student and avid rock climber who rescues Ryan's character out on a mountain. What I liked most about her was that she didn't take a lot of crap from anyone.

It was very eye-opening, making me acutely aware of my own personality.

CHAPTER 25

Thanks

YOU TWO WAIT in here. Give me a minute. Let me get your bags out first, then I'll get you into the terminal," Mike said, leaning over the front seat to speak to us.

There must have been almost fifty photographers, fans, and the simply curious gawking out on the sidewalk by the doors for departing flights.

"This is fucking crazy," Ryan muttered. He had his back turned to the car door, but the photographers ran to the other side of the car trying to get shots of him. It was hard to see in through the dark tinted windows.

"I hate airports," he said. "Are you ready for this?"

I nodded, despite the fact that I was a nervous wreck.

Airport security was waiting outside now; they were trying to move people away from the doors to the terminal. Mike opened the car door and Ryan slipped out. His foot wasn't even on the ground yet when the frenzy began.

"Ryan! Ryan! Can you sign this?" People were yelling at him repeatedly.

"Ryan, over here!" The cameras flashed nonstop.

"Can I take my picture with you?" some girl asked sweetly.

My poor Ryan didn't know which way to turn. Mike and our driver flanked him on both sides while he signed a few autographs. Some of these people had glossy photos of his movie character in hand, and it amazed me that they were so prepared for our arrival.

Ryan scribbled his signature quickly with a borrowed pen while Mike used his arm and hands to block people from getting too close. I noticed he avoided the men with professional prints and signed his autograph for the fans instead. He posed and smiled for almost twenty photos.

I removed my backpack from the trunk of the car, slung it over my shoulder, and readied my small carry-on suitcase. The paparazzi swarmed like angry bees, fighting among themselves for better position. Mike finally handed Ryan his messenger bag and duffle bag and then asked the crowd to back up.

I felt so helpless. These "people," for lack of a better term, had us surrounded. I grabbed the back of Ryan's jacket, fearing I might get left behind in the mayhem.

Ryan felt his jacket tug and glanced back at me to confirm I was the one doing the tugging. I tried not to look at the photographers, even though I knew my picture was being taken over and over again.

Ryan grabbed my hand and we hurried into the terminal. Mike was by his side; Ryan had me in tow. Airport security had us surrounded now. Never in my life had such a simple task like getting on a plane been so frightening!

"Ryan! So is it official? Are you and Ms. Mitchell an exclusive item?" some paparazzo asked. Ryan didn't answer.

"Is it true that you and Taryn are living together?" another photographer asked while running alongside us.

Ryan still didn't answer. He had that familiar look on his face; the one he wore when he was sick of all this shit but tried to look indifferent.

"Come on, guys. That's enough," Mike said to the paparazzi who were walking backward, taking our picture and filming us.

"Mr. Christensen, this way," an airport security officer called out. We followed him through a separate opening in the barriers so we could get in line to go through the scanners. We were ushered to a small counter where Ryan showed our boarding passes to the waiting TSA agent, who verified that we had seats on an outbound flight.

"Go first, honey," Ryan whispered and nudged me ahead. He was looking down at the ground most of the time. I glanced briefly over his shoulder and noticed that the paparazzi were filming us removing our coats and shoes. Fortunately, Mike was blocking them from getting too much footage of Ryan.

I grabbed a gray plastic tray and tossed my coat and shoes into the bin. I pushed my backpack and small suitcase down the rollers until it met the rubber belt that fed into the scanner. Ryan was still checking his pockets for loose change. I smiled at him; he always had random amounts of money stuffed in his pockets.

I waited for Ryan and Mike to clear through the metal detector. Airport security escorted us, and instead of leading us toward the gate, they ushered us through a plain white security door.

"Where are we going?" I whispered to Ryan.

"We're early. We're going to the VIP lounge."

I had never been in a VIP lounge before. It was beautiful! The large room had a high ceiling and was segregated into smaller sections, divided by walls and full-length semi-sheer curtains. The walls were tiled in dark gray slate with stainless-steel accents. Each wall had four flat-screen TVs mounted across it, all broadcasting a different news channel.

In front of every TV was a cozy decorative chair and table for travelers to sit and relax. There was even a side room with free beverages and a small food buffet.

Ryan pulled out his phone and turned it on, scanning through his messages and calendar. I, however, was still in a slight daze from getting into the airport. This chaos was obviously old-hat for Ryan.

I can't tell you how many times I flew in and out of this airport and never knew that such a room existed. I stood by the large glass window, watching the planes take off and land, trying to get my heart rate to stabilize.

Ryan came over and stood behind me, placing his hands on my shoulders. "How are you doing?" he whispered.

I looked up at him and nodded. "I'm doing fine." I tried to sound convincing, but deep down I was still rattled.

"Ten more minutes and we'll head out for our flight," he said, opening his bag to retrieve my Mitchell's Pub baseball cap. It made me smile when he winked and put the cap on his head.

"I've noticed you've been avoiding those autographers lately," I said, questioning him.

Ryan nodded. "They make money off of my signature. I'm sick of it."

A man in a suit, wearing a TSA security ID badge, came into the lounge for us. We were escorted down a long hallway and through another plain white door that dumped us near our gate.

All the other passengers on our flight to Newark were already boarded. Ryan, Mike, and I took our seats up in first class. I made Ryan sit in the window seat. People were already stretching their necks to see him.

The flight to Newark Airport was quick, and after we landed, the airline staff assisted us in exiting the plane.

Airport security had us surrounded as we walked to our next gate. Mike escorted us to the gate, then turned to say goodbye. He was headed to South Carolina to see family.

"Have a good holiday, Mike." Ryan patted him on the arm and shook his hand.

"You too, Ryan. Taryn." Mike gave me a hug.

"Happy Thanksgiving, Mike. Thank you for everything." I hugged him warmly.

"I'll see you in a week." Mike tapped Ryan on the shoulder. "Don't eat too much turkey!"

TSA agents and airport security walked us to our departing flight bound for Pittsburgh. Three teenage girls ran after us, begging for Ryan's attention. Ryan graciously stopped to take a picture with them . . . forever smiling . . . forever pleasing his fans.

When we landed, we were again escorted by airport security toward the exit. As we hurried through the terminal, people were pulling out cameras and cell phones to capture the sight of Ryan Christensen walking through the airport.

I felt Ryan's hand squeeze mine tighter when we caught sight of his mom and dad standing there waiting for us. All four of us were smiling, happy to see each other again. Sure enough, a few paparazzi were waiting outside the airport doors.

The afternoon sun was starting to dip in the sky as we approached Ryan's hometown. He pointed out 12th Street, showing me the infamous hill where he'd taken the maiden voyage in the laundry basket.

Ryan edged closer to the car door; his hand was reaching for the handle. I could see the excitement in his eyes and the overwhelming anticipation he was feeling for being home.

I'd tried to visualize the neighborhood Ryan grew up in when he talked about it, but no verbal description could compare to seeing it with my own eyes. The tree-lined street was beautifully tinted with autumn's colored leaves, many of which were already in piles on the ground.

The houses on his parents' street were situated fairly far apart. Each home was set back from the street and had a large front yard with plenty of grass to mow.

We turned onto a long driveway that was lined with trees and simple but tasteful landscaping. Ryan let out a sigh.

His childhood home was beautiful: an impressive two-story red brick Colonial with a large front porch.

We parked in front of the two-car garage that entered into the side of the house. His father pressed the garage door opener that hung from his visor. It was apparent that the family was used to entering their house through the garage.

Ryan didn't even make it to the kitchen door—he had to pull the gray car cover up off the front end of his Shelby. The car was a beautiful shade of sapphire blue, with two silver racing stripes from bumper to bumper. It surely was impressive.

"I've been running it every once and a while. She should start right up," his father informed him.

Ryan bunched the car cover up in a pile in the corner of the garage.

"Don't just leave it there! Fold it up!" Bill reprimanded him.

"I will, Dad. Just give me a minute to say hello." Ryan beamed at his car. "Hello, baby." He touched the fender lovingly. "Did you miss me?"

I couldn't help but smile at Ryan. Boys and their toys! He reached into a cabinet mounted on the wall and pulled out the car keys, unlocking the doors to his precious vehicle.

He was already hopping in the driver's seat when his father yelled at him again. "Aren't you even going to invite Taryn into the house first?"

"I just want to make sure she starts."

I held up my hand to his father and tried to dismiss his anger. "It's all right. Let him start his car. He won't be able to think of anything else until he does." I set my backpack down on the ground next to my suitcase.

A turn of the ignition and his car roared to life. The smile on his face was so huge it was as if he'd died and gone to Heaven.

"Hop in. Let's go for a ride!" he yelled over to me.

I ran for the passenger door.

I slipped down into the black leather bucket seat and snapped on my seat belt. Ryan revved the engine and the car vibrated and purred beneath us. His long fingers wrapped around the gear shift with white-knuckled anticipation.

He, of course, had to squeal the tires when he pulled out onto his street, causing the rear end to fishtail a bit. Look out neighbors, the crazy Christensen kid is back in town!

He drove out on some long back roads lined with farms and cornfields, driving too fast most of the time. He made a left turn and mashed his foot down on the gas, shifting forcefully through all the gears. At one point we were slightly airborne over a little knoll in the road. His driving was dangerous and exciting. I knew he'd been looking forward to this adrenaline rush more than anything.

Ryan from Pittsburgh was home.

"Did you have fun?" Ellen asked when we came through the kitchen door with our bags. She was busy making dinner. "Ryan, take your bags upstairs," she ordered.

Bill was sitting in a dark brown recliner in the family room that was off of the kitchen. He was reading the newspaper and peeking over the top of it to occasionally watch television. It made me smile, fondly remembering my own father sitting in his favorite chair reading the newspaper.

I followed Ryan up the tan carpeted stairs to his room. He smiled at me as he pushed the last door on the right open with his shoulder. His old room had one four-paned window centered on the wall that overlooked the front yard. He flipped on the bedroom light, illuminating the lamp that sat on the single nightstand next to the bed. The light cast a shadow on the plain beige walls and new tan carpeting.

He had a dark oak desk with an old computer and printer sitting on it. On top of his tall wooden dresser were two baseball trophies and a small decorative lamp. And in the corner of his room stood a wooden coat rack, long empty of coats and clothing.

A tinge of sadness flowed into my chest. His room, the room he'd spent all of his youth growing up in, was obviously cleansed of most of his things. He didn't have an apartment, a house, or even an old bedroom that was *his* anymore. All the fragments of his existence were boxed up and put aside or forgotten.

I understood why he was dying to get in his car the moment we arrived. That car was the only thing that was his . . . truly his. More importantly, I now knew why he'd moved in with me so quickly and was rushing the thoughts of building a house by a lake. My love was desperately craving a home . . . a connection . . . a safe haven to call his own—for he had nothing in this world but a suitcase and another lonely destination.

I dropped my bag off my shoulder and grabbed the front of his jacket with both of my hands. I wanted him to feel the depth of my love for him through my lips. I was desperate for him to realize that he was no longer alone in this world; that as long as I had a breath still left in my lungs I would provide him shelter and be his safe haven in all this uncertainty.

He slipped his fingers underneath my jacket and pushed it back over my shoulders. His coat came off next. He walked backward to the bed, pulling me down with him. We kicked our shoes off and twined our clothed bodies together, passionately kissing each other.

"I love you," I murmured on his lips, staring directly into his open eyes when I said it.

"I love you, too," he breathed back.

I rested my head on his chest, listening to his heartbeat while he softly stroked my hair. He kissed my head several times and wrapped his arms around me tighter, conveying his own message of love back to me.

All too soon, our unspoken conversation was interrupted by his mother's voice. She was yelling up the stairs that Nick and Janelle were here.

"Hey, brother!" Ryan greeted Nick with a hug. I stayed off to the side, smiling and waiting to be introduced.

Ryan and his brother had similar features, but Nick took after their father more than Ryan did. Nick had darker brown hair and was just an inch or two shorter than Ryan in stature, but close your eyes and you couldn't tell which one was speaking. The similarity of their voices was uncanny.

Ryan hugged Janelle next, kissing her on her cheek.

"Hey, movie star!" she kidded him. "How are you doing?"

Janelle was just a little shorter than I was, and she was adorable. She had highlighted light brown hair, which was straight and cut blunt at her shoulders. She wore trendy black-framed glasses and had a captivating smile.

"Nick, Janelle, this is Taryn." Ryan beamed.

Nick pulled me in instantly for a big hug. "It's so nice to meet you. Welcome to the family," he whispered in my ear.

"Thank you. It's nice to meet you, too."

Janelle and I hugged next. She, too, welcomed me to the family. Ryan had already captured their daughter, Sarah, in his arms. The baby started to cry.

"She hasn't seen you in six months, Ryan," Janelle said, taking the baby from him. Poor Sarah was still crying.

"How old is she?" I asked.

"Ten months."

"She's beautiful!" I tugged gently on her lacy outfit. "Look at the pretty flowers on your dress."

The baby stopped crying and looked at me.

"Hi, Sarah! It's so nice to meet you! You look so pretty in your little dress."

The baby smiled at me. Janelle looked at the baby then looked at me, smiling, too.

"Can I hold you so Mommy can take her coat off?"

Janelle leaned the baby toward me and I lifted her into my arms.

"Hi, there! Do you want to go for a walk?" I paced around the living room with Sarah. She started to babble at me, telling me a big story, and I answered her with sweet comments of my own.

I took her little coat off while she cooed at me.

"Say hi, Uncle Ryan." I waved her little hand at him. Ryan was forever smiling at me.

"Where's my little peanut?" Bill asked for his granddaughter. "Come to Grandpa!" He took the little girl out of my arms.

Sarah didn't like it; she started to cry again.

We all moved into the family room, and Janelle set up a little play area on a blanket on the floor for her daughter.

Sarah was still crying while being passed around from person to person. Ryan tried holding her again, but she didn't want any of it. Her little face was turning red. I sat next to him on the couch and started talking to Sarah. I was glad she stopped crying so Ryan could enjoy holding her.

"What is it with you and kids?" Ryan asked me. "You're like a freaking drug to them."

His comment was absurd. I rolled my eyes and dismissed his question.

"See? Watch." He held the baby away from me and she started to cry. He moved the baby next to me and she stopped. He repeated his little test and she cried when he held her away. The third time he did it, Sarah cried in both places.

"There goes that theory," I kidded him.

"What are you doing to my poor child?" Janelle yelled.

"Experimenting," Ryan replied. "Every time we're around kids, they're drawn to Taryn like a freaking magnet. Watch."

I thought he was making a big deal out of nothing.

He held Sarah away from me; she was still crying. Then he put Sarah on my lap. I stood her up on my legs and held her to my chest. Sarah grasped my heart necklace in her tiny fingers.

Ryan grinned at me smugly when she stopped crying. He held his hands out. "See what I mean?"

"It's not me, it's this necklace," I said. "Maybe it has special powers."

"No, I think it's you."

Sarah was busy playing with my necklace. Her little face puckered up with frustration when she couldn't get my pendant in her mouth. I made a funny face back at her, which caused my nose to tickle. That's when I caught the scent of something else. I held her little bottom closer to my nose to confirm my suspicions.

"I'm not a drug, Ryan, I'm a laxative." I stood up with the little girl to get her changed.

"Did she poop?" Nick snorted when he asked.

"Yep. Constipated children seek me out wherever I go." I laughed.

"Bet Ry was a bit constipated when he stumbled onto you," Nick joked.

"I was definitely backed up, that's for sure," Ryan mumbled under his breath, adjusting the waist of his jeans. "But I sat on Taryn's lap for a few minutes and then I felt better." Ryan grinned at him devilishly and Nick cracked up laughing.

I smirked at Ryan's comment.

"What?" he questioned my reaction.

I handed Sarah to him. "Here, go do another rite of passage," I suggested jokingly.

"What? Do you want me to change her? I don't care." He was all cool and confident.

"She's eating solid foods now, Ry. Sure you won't gag?" Nick asked.

"Give her to me," Janelle instructed. "I'll take her upstairs. We don't want the superstar to get his hands dirty."

"You punks don't think I'm up for the challenge?" Ryan questioned assertively.

"Ten bucks says you gag," Nick taunted. "What do you say, Dad? You want in on this bet?"

Bill reached into his pocket, searching for money.

"I'll take that bet," Ryan retorted. "Both of you!" He pointed.

The entire family followed Ryan upstairs to Nick's old bedroom. Janelle placed a pad down on the bed and readied a new diaper. The rest of us stood around watching. All eyes were on Ryan, waiting for his reaction.

He undressed Sarah down to her diaper and had to ham it up by cracking his knuckles and wiggling his fingers.

"I should get the camera," Nick mused.

"Nicholas!" Ellen scolded.

"What? Do you know how much money I could get for one picture of the movie star changing a poopy diaper?"

Janelle and I started laughing.

"Not as much money as you could get for a pair of his dirty underwear on eBay," I mumbled.

"You both suck! You know that?" Ryan was peeling back the tape on the diaper and had to stop because we were teasing him.

"Taryn," Nick whispered, "gather up some of my brother's ass-stained shorts and sell them quick so we can all go to Hawaii for Christmas."

"You're a dick!" Ryan looked directly at his brother. We were all laughing. "You can all just shut the hell up and get your money out."

Janelle slapped a few wet-wipes in Ryan's hand.

"Okay, I'm going in," Ryan announced.

"Is that what you say to all your women?" Nick teased.

Ryan was laughing so hard he couldn't breathe.

"Boys!" Ellen yelled. "Poor Sarah is waiting. Change her diaper already."

"Nick, go get the scuba gear." Ryan had tears coming out of his eyes.

"Forceps, lantern, flame thrower . . ." Nick spit out his words with laughter.

"Move, I'll do it." Janelle was getting impatient.

"No! I got this!" Ryan gasped between laughs, trying to pull himself back together.

He hesitantly pulled the diaper back, briefly exposing the green explosion that awaited cleanup.

"Oh!" Nick shouted loudly.

"Damn, baby! What are they feeding you?" Ryan teased.

"Beer and eggs with a side of peas, obviously." Nick laughed.

Janelle dove right in, cleaning up her daughter.

"Now stop. I can get it." Ryan elbowed her out of the way. "They sell these baby wipes by the truckload, right?"

"Yeah. We buy that stuff by the pallet," Nick volleyed, laughing. "We don't mess around with the single tubs anymore."

"You could always take her outside and hit her ass with the hose," Ryan suggested.

"Nah, we save that for when she's got the shit smeared all the way up her back," Nick answered.

"I'll take you both outside and hit you with the hose," Janelle warned. I couldn't stop laughing at their banter.

Ryan had the baby all cleaned up and was wrestling with the new diaper when he told his dad and brother to pay up. He handed Sarah off to Janelle.

I was standing with my arms folded when Ryan sauntered over to me. "Next one of those is all yours." He cracked me hard on the butt.

"Go wash your hands. It's time for dinner," Ellen ordered.

We were gathered at the dinner table when Nick started in on me.

"Taryn, Mom tells me you haven't seen any of my brother's movies." Nick leered at me.

"I think I'm the only one on the planet who hasn't," I joked. "He thought I was lying when I told him that."

Ryan kicked me under the table, so I kicked him back. I clipped him right in the ankle by accident and he winced from the pain. He pinched me in retaliation.

"We should watch it tonight. Break her in." Nick pointed his dinner fork at me.

"You can do whatever you want, but I'm not watching it," Ryan stated firmly.

"What do you say, Taryn? You want to watch *Seaside?*" Nick asked. "See what a big-time actor he is?"

Ryan scoffed at his comment.

"No, that's okay." I knew that it would make Ryan uncomfortable. "Maybe some other time."

"You should watch it. It's really good!" Janelle added. "I've read all the books, too. Then you'll know why all the women worship him," she said teasingly.

I looked over at Ryan and smiled. I knew why they worshipped him, but their reasons were completely different from my own.

"I'll watch it sometime, but not tonight. Besides, Nick, Ryan tells me that you're a lousy poker player. I was curious to see if he was right." I felt Ryan squeeze my thigh.

After we cleared dinner away, we started playing cards. Ryan was right; Nick couldn't bluff his way out of a paper bag if his life depended on it. Needless to say, the poker game didn't last too long before egos got in the way.

Next, we played a board game, which was a lot more fun. I haven't laughed that hard in a long time. I think I fit right in with Ryan's family and their teasing, although Nick seemed harsh on his brother sometimes.

Little Sarah was hungry and needed a bottle.

"Give her here," Ryan requested, removing Sarah from her grandmother's arms.

The visions of him holding and feeding her added one more reason for worshipping him to my private list.

It was close to midnight when we finally crawled into bed together. I was tired from the flight and the delicious dinner that filled my stomach. Ryan's bed was only a full-size, not quite as roomy as the queen-sized bed we shared at home. *Hmm . . . at home* . . . the thought of those words made me smile.

Ryan's body molded around mine, keeping me snuggled and warm in my comfortable cocoon. My back rested on his chest as it did every night.

Ryan huffed in my ear. He was grouchy and restless.

"What's wrong?" I whispered.

"I can't sleep." He tugged on my T-shirt. "Can you take this off? I need to feel your skin."

I hesitated. At home we always slept naked, but we weren't at home.

"Don't worry, my mom won't come in here."

I took my top off and tossed it to the floor.

"Ah, that's better," he snickered. "This is sort of exciting. Might get busted by the parents having a naked girl in my bed."

I giggled softly when he squeezed me. I understood what he was talking about. I felt like a teenager breaking the house rules.

"We'll have to be quiet, then," I whispered flirtatiously.

He rubbed his stubbly chin on my shoulder before opening his mouth to playfully bite me. It made me giggle again.

"I love it when you bite me."

He twined our fingers together.

"I know," he whispered. "And it also drives you crazy when I run my nose down your neck."

"Yes," I confirmed. "And it drives you insane when I bite your earlobe."

I turned over to face him.

"My parents think I'm sleeping over at Jenny's house tonight. Are you sure your parents are sleeping?"

He smiled and laughed softly, growling when he palmed my rear in his hand.

"Maybe tomorrow night we can go parking in that fancy car of yours," I teased.

"I'll have to do you on the hood," he groaned seductively. "We can't go parking in the Shelby tomorrow. We have a limo taking us to a hockey game, remember? How about this? If I promise to respect you in the morning, will you give me your virginity tonight?"

"Is it going to hurt?" I shyly asked, batting my eyes.

"I'll be very gentle, I promise."

THE SOUND of Ryan's mom clanging pots and pans down in the kitchen woke me up. I had promised her I'd help, since she planned to cook a feast, so I quickly got dressed and joined her.

"Ellen, this pie is ready to go in the oven." I slid the glass pie dish out of my way and wiped the flour off of the recipe card. "What's next?"

She handed me another recipe card.

"This is Ryan's favorite," she whispered.

"What's Ryan's favorite?" Ryan asked. He was sitting at the dining table with his legs stretched out, scanning through his cell phone.

"Pumpkin roll?" I answered.

He looked up and smiled. "Put extra filling in it, please."

Ellen stood next to me. "You'll have to double the recipe for the cream cheese filling. I think I have enough of everything."

I was reading the recipe card when I heard Ryan huff. He proceeded to text someone.

"Everything all right?" I asked.

"Come here. I want to show you something."

He handed his phone to me and I read his reply.

"Flattered but not interested very happy w someone"

I looked at him, confused.

"Hit send," he instructed. I did what he told me to do.

"What is this about?"

He slipped the phone out of my hand and tapped the screen a few times before handing it back to me. There was another text message.

"Hi! Next time ur in LA want to go out? Promise u will have good time all night guaranteed!"

I felt my lips curl in disgust after reading that. I handed his phone back to him. "Who's that from? Anyone you even know?"

He tapped another button and showed me the name of the very famous actress who'd sent that message. I was shocked.

I looked at him and shook my head.

"Don't get mad," he cautioned. "I'm not interested in that. And you saw the exact message I sent back." He took a sip of his coffee. "Besides, sleeping with her would be like sleeping with half of Los Angeles. Yuck." He shuddered and stuck out his tongue, trying to be funny.

"How many of those offers do you get a day?" I asked.

"Don't worry about it. All you need to know is how I reply."

"How many?" I asked again.

"How many guys ask *you* out each day?" he sharply retorted. "I'd say we're just about tied."

I stood at the sink, washing some of the dirty dishes while hoping that the overwhelming jealousy would burn away my other insecurities. He had met thousands of women, dated well-known actresses in the past, traveled the entire globe and visited exotic locations . . . why he would want to settle for just one woman when he could have so many was beyond me.

I thought about what I would do if the situation were reversed. If I had his opportunities, would I be out there playing the field or would I want a relationship with one person? Well, that was an easy question to answer. Of course I'd want a meaningful relationship with one man. But men are different creatures.

I peered at him through the corner of my eye. He was sitting at the wooden dining table drinking his coffee while trying to do the crossword puzzle in the newspaper. The famous celebrity who'd just won three awards for his acting skills was just sitting there in a wrinkled T-shirt and sweatpants. His bare feet were scrunched up on his toes, bouncing his heels up and down as he chewed on the tip of the pen.

He had no idea of the damage he'd just caused in my brain. That little text message felt like just another nail in my coffin. He wasn't interested in that one, but what would happen if he got another offer he simply couldn't refuse?

Ryan was beyond jealous of Kyle, hence why Kyle was dismissed from being my bodyguard so quickly. How easy it was for Ryan to eliminate the true competition with a simple phone call! Despite how attractive and sweet Kyle was, I used my brain to recognize that my attraction to him was superficial.

Men, however, don't always think with the brain that sits between their ears. All too often it's the little brain in their pants that takes over. Would Ryan's love for me stop him dead in his tracks before he listened to the devil that lived in his pants?

"Shoot," Ellen grumbled.

I quickly turned my head in her direction. Her butt was sticking up in the air while she rummaged through the refrigerator.

"I don't have enough cream cheese," she groaned.

I tried to shake off my other thoughts.

"What are you going to do with the turkey? I think it's just about completely thawed." I poked it with my finger. She had it sitting in the other sink.

"There's no room in the fridge," she announced. "I don't know."

"You should soak it overnight in brine and ice. That will make it nice and juicy tomorrow."

She looked at me, perplexed. "Brine?"

Ryan escorted me to his dad's office so I could print out a recipe from the Web. I really think he wanted to make sure I didn't Internet surf while I had the chance.

"Here's the recipe." I handed it to Ellen.

"I have to run to the store. I don't have some of these things." She sounded stressed. "Janelle is bringing Sarah over soon. You two will have to watch her for me."

About twenty minutes later, Janelle came through the door with Sarah in one arm and a diaper bag containing an arsenal of baby supplies in the other. She was running late for an appointment.

Ryan was on the floor playing with Sarah when Janelle darted out the door. He was helping Sarah stack up little wooden alphabet blocks. She was concentrating so hard; her angelic face showed her determination.

I couldn't help myself; the sight of him playing with the baby overwhelmed me. I shut the mixer off and joined them on the floor. Ryan patted me on the thigh a few times before clamping his hand down on my leg.

"What do you say? Think you want one or two of these someday?" he mused, twisting his finger into Sarah's ringlets.

"I think you already know my answer." I smiled.

Ryan grinned widely. "Two would be cool."

"I'm surprised, though," I continued. "Someone in your position . . . I would have thought that having kids would be the last thing on your list."

"Why would you say that?"

I was surprised that he questioned me. "I don't know . . . you're young. You're a famous celebrity. You travel the world."

He rolled his eyes at me.

"Sometimes I'm surprised that you even want a girlfriend. Why have one when you could have so many."

Ryan rolled onto his back and groaned. "Not this conversation again. I thought we were beyond this?"

I took a deep breath and sighed. "Ryan, you're only twenty-seven. And you know damn well you can get any girl you want whenever you want. Hell, they even text their offers to you. There are women all around the globe who would pay to have sex with you. Before you talk to me about having children, are you *sure* you're done sowing your wild oats?"

He covered his eyes with his hand. "I can't believe you're asking me this," he muttered.

"You're a guy! That's what guys do. Fast cars, fast women. I don't want you to wake up next to me when I'm all pregnant and have regrets." I teasingly squeezed the inside of his leg.

He started laughing. "How much money do you think I could make from all these women who want to have sex with me?"

"Billions!" I quickly replied.

"Really? Help me drag a mattress out into the front yard. You can sell lemonade and I'll just fuck people all day," he cackled.

The baby crawled over to Ryan and whacked him in the head with a wooden block.

"Ow!" He rubbed his forehead. "You're right, Sarah. That was a bad idea. Uncle Ryan's junk will fall off if I did that all day."

She crawled onto his chest and slapped him a few times in the face.

"Hey! Why are you beating me up? Huh? Do I have a potty mouth? Go beat up Aunt Taryn—she's the one who's being silly." He picked her up in his hands and pressed her up into the air.

Ryan sat Sarah on the floor and rolled to his side.

"Sarah?" He whispered a whole bunch of nonsense in her ear. "Tell her!"

Ryan used his finger to make Sarah's bottom lip move. His voice changed to a high pitch. "Uncle Ryan says he's done sowing, so you can just chill."

He whispered in her ear again. "Uncle Ryan says you have to be married first before you have babies. And I stink, so you should change me."

"Give her to me," I said, reaching out for her.

I lay Sarah on the floor between my legs and grabbed the diaper bag. Ryan turned on the television, stopping on a channel just in time to hear some announcer say his name.

"Today on CTV . . . We got Ryan Christensen in the airport in Providence with his new girlfriend."

Large graphics streamed across the screen and the announcer's voice came back. Different embarrassing pictures of Ryan were flashed between the verbal comments. "Keep your panties on, *Seaside* fans! Just when you thought you saw it all—Ryan Christensen eats—Ryan Christensen picks his nose—Ryan Christensen sits in a car—we bring you . . .

The camera panned to a young, male reporter. "We caught him feeling himself up."

Video of Ryan patting his front and back jeans pockets when we were in the airport in Providence was shown on the screen.

"What's up with this guy?" the show host asked.

"I don't know, but our camera guy caught him feeling himself up before he went through the metal detectors," the young guy answered.

"Feeling himself up?" the host questioned.

"Yeah, he was searching his pockets and stuff. I mean, what idiot goes to the airport with change in their pockets!"

The video of Ryan patting his pockets now included me in the shot.

"Do we know who the girl is? Is she an actress?" The host circled my picture on his video screen.

"Her name is Taryn Mitchell. She owns a bar or something in Rhode Island."

They showed old, random photos of Ryan with different drinks in his hand, pretty much accusing him of having a drinking problem.

"Wow, that's impressive. Are *all* the girls in Hollywood dead?" the host sneered.

Everyone on the television screen laughed.

"I'm sure his fans hate her," one woman commented.

A clip from an old black-and-white movie was shown. All the townspeople had torches and pitchforks.

Another girl chimed in. "She's a lot prettier than Suzanne Strass, I think."

"Yeah, and she can help him turn into another celebrity alcoholic," some other man bantered.

"Our camera guy asked him if they're officially a couple but he didn't say anything. He's dragging her through the airport by the hand. I mean, isn't it obvious? I don't know why he just doesn't admit it. She's not his wardrobe consultant, that's for sure."

The picture refocused on me, on my face, and then zoomed in on Ryan holding my fingers as we walked through the airport. Sound bites of women crying were added in. The segment ended with repeat shots of Ryan feeling his back pockets and one more close-up of him shoving his hand in his front pocket. They even threw in sound effects of women moaning when Ryan patted himself down.

I let out a sigh and lifted Sarah up so I could fix her yellow tights over her new diaper. I gave her a few kisses on her forehead while she played with my heart necklace.

Ryan turned the television off and threw the remote onto the couch behind me. He looked like he'd just got punched in the stomach.

I reached out to him. We were both upset from seeing that garbage on TV. Ryan slowly moved to sit next to me on the floor. We leaned back on the couch and looked at each other. Ryan rested his arm behind me, combing his fingers through my hair; his other hand gently rubbed through Sarah's little brown curls. He sighed heavily and I knew he was agitated.

I leaned over and kissed his lips, just to let him know that everything would be all right. His fingers tensed and pressed into my scalp, holding my kiss tenderly to his. His lips were troubled.

I wondered which one of us would crack from the bullshit first.

I spent the rest of the afternoon helping his mom in the kitchen. She was preparing a feast for Thanksgiving and I wondered just exactly who she thought was going to eat all of it. I handled making the brine for the turkey. Ellen watched me intently as I mixed the concoction.

I was standing at the sink when Ryan came up behind me, holding me in place again with his long arms. He brushed my hair off my shoulder and drifted the tip of his nose up and down my neck. I tried to keep the volume of my moan turned down.

"As much as it warms my heart to see my son happy and in love, get the hell away from my helper," Ellen ordered.

"You've had her long enough, Mom. We've got to go get ready for the game. Our car will be here in an hour."

Soon after Nick and Janelle arrived, the sleek black stretch limousine pulled into the driveway. The four of us were going to the game together; Ryan's parents were watching Sarah for the evening.

"You should come home more often," Nick teased Ryan, noting that the limo was fully stocked with beer, liquor, and two bottles of champagne. Janelle was preoccupied; eventually she pulled a magazine out of her purse.

"Here, I thought you two might want to keep this one," she teased and tossed the glossy paper onto Ryan's lap.

Ryan took a sip from the champagne bottle he and I were sharing and narrowed his eyes on the cover. He handed me the bottle and turned the little light on above his head so he could get a better look.

Ryan and I were on the cover—the entire cover. We were both dressed up and it was apparent to me that the photo was taken on the night we took his parents to dinner. The caption below our bodies read "Ryan's in love!" Next to our photo were several side notes under the bold letters "Ryan Christensen shows off new girlfriend." The additions informed the world that he was living with me in our "Love nest in RI" and that he had introduced me to his parents.

"Well, at least it's a nice picture of us," Ryan stated indifferently.

"The story isn't bad, either," Janelle added. "I thought it was something you might want to keep, you know." She looked unsure.

Ryan handed it to me with a smirky grin on his lips. "I'm sure you want to read it."

I set the magazine down next to me on the seat and took another sip of champagne from the bottle. I could only imagine the horrible things that were said about me in there. It would only take seeing one negative comment about either one of us to send me into my own downward spiral.

Ryan gave me a perplexed look. He presumed I would have ripped the magazine open immediately, dying to know what was written.

"I'm not reading that now. I'd rather not cry my eyes out before a hockey game," I said.

"Why?" Janelle asked. "It's not bad. Really."

I disagreed. "I just know there are lies printed in it. There always are. I've been blamed for breaking him and Suzanne up, for causing rifts on set between the actors. They print that I'm keeping him from seeing all of his friends. I even lost out on the national poll on which girl the public would rather see him with. Suzanne won with seventy-two percent."

I rubbed my cheek, trying to keep from getting upset.

"Well, there's nothing like that in this one," Janelle said.

"I'm sure there is," I muttered, pushing the magazine farther away. It was the paper version of poison to me. "Every one of these writers seems to have the need to get at least one good dig in. I don't understand why they feel I'm not good enough."

"Honey! Who gives a shit what they write?" Ryan said. "I sure don't."

"Let me see it," Nick asked. "I'll tell you whether or not it's safe to read."

He quickly thumbed through the magazine, stopping to flash us the large interior picture of Ryan and me walking down my sidewalk, obviously ignoring the paparazzi.

"Oh my God!" Nick looked over the top of the magazine. "It says here that you forced my brother to learn how to make stained-glass picture frames. Is this true?" He looked horrified.

Ryan laughed at his brother's antics.

"I have to admit, that one is true." I nodded.

"Does it say anything about her being mostly naked when she subjected me to a day of arts and crafts and power tools?" Ryan asked. All of a sudden his interest was piqued. "Are there pictures, too, 'cause I *want* those."

"No, no pictures like that," Nick said. He resumed reading.

"What's this? You . . ." He gasped, holding his shaky fingers in front of his mouth to emphasize his fright. "You baked a birthday cake—and then you had the audacity to make my parents eat it?" His voice changed to a high pitch to sound like he was crying, and he cringed. "How *could* you?"

Ryan gave me a teasing shove. "Yeah, Taryn! How *could* you?"

I hung my head down. "I'm sorry. I have no excuse for my actions," I whispered.

"No champagne for you!" Ryan took the bottle from my hand.

"She even begged us to come to some birthday party in Rhode Island. We're lucky I was traveling last week, or else she would have subjected Janelle and me to more of these horrors." Nick focused back on the magazine.

Then, Nick made me jump slightly when he gasped loudly. "Tell the limo driver to stop. We have to kick Taryn out. It says right here she's just using my brother for sex."

Ryan sat up quickly. "That's true! She forces me to . . ." He covered his eyes with the champagne bottle and pretended to cry, slumping back into the seat. "All the time!" he wailed. "And she beats me, too. She says 'you get naked and get in that bed or I'll give you something to *really* cry about, mister.' I mean, I'm only human. I'm not a machine."

"Janelle beats me all the time," Nick cried. "I feel so used."

"You wish!" she laughed.

"I don't know about you, Janelle, but if I have to pick up his dirty socks and underwear, I want something in return," I said.

"I know," she agreed. "The Christensen scent sure doesn't smell like roses."

"Hey, we take pride in our scent," Ryan argued.

"If your fans only knew . . ." I replied. "Maybe they wouldn't be standing so close to our doors."

"I thought your fans were too busy kissing their *Seaside* pillowcases to travel all the way to Rhode Island," Janelle teased.

"Go ahead and laugh, Janelle. I'm laughing all the way to the bank."

"Pillowcases?" I questioned. I had no idea what she was talking about.

"And bedsheets. Now girls all around the globe can sleep with Charles at night." Janelle laughed.

"I dry humped *my* Charles pillow just last night," Nick mocked, making obscene gestures.

Ryan threw the champagne cork at him. I gathered Ryan didn't like that last dig, because he threw the cork with some force. Nick flinched away, smiling.

"I used the real Ryan Christensen as a sex toy last night," I whispered in Ryan's direction, trying to keep him in a good mood.

Ryan gave me a high-five and winked at me. "Damn straight! And then I sprayed you with my personal scent to keep the other animals away."

Our limo drove past the main entrance to the arena, but the driver didn't stop. Maybe he didn't know where to drop us? We ended up stopping in the back of the arena near a few large buses. The driver opened Ryan's door and we headed toward a private entrance. Ryan took me by the hand; I drew in a deep breath and followed him toward the back door. Ryan Christensen would never again enter through the front doors of any place like a regular person.

Two arena employees were waiting for us. We were escorted into an elevator that took us to the upper deck where all the private suites were located.

"Whose suite is this?" Nick asked.

"The bank I deal with has it rented for the season," Ryan answered. "They gave up four of their tickets for us, but we won't be alone. There are eight other tickets for this suite. All these suites are completely booked. This is as private as I could get." I watched as he rubbed his forehead.

"So we're party crashing? That's cool." Nick belched and cracked open a beer.

The suite was fully stocked with beer and wine, and there was a hot buffet of food already laid out on a long table. Ryan and Nick dove right in, helping themselves to the assortment of dishes and snacks. The two brothers were already partially drunk, so I was glad that Ryan was getting some food in his stomach.

I looked out the large glass window that overlooked the arena. On the other side of the glass were twelve private seats. The suite door opened, causing a flash of light to reflect off of the window. I instinctively turned around to see who was entering. What a big mistake that was!

Four giggling girls came through the door. They just about burst out into hysterics when they saw Ryan Christensen was truly in the suite. My eyes quickly flashed over to Ryan; I noticed he stopped chewing the wad of food that was crammed in his mouth for a brief second while his lips pursed together in annoyance.

Janelle subtly elbowed me and we both chuckled lightly. The girls were all decked out in short skirts and low-cut tops. One even had her copy of *Seaside* in hand. Ryan quickly darted away from the buffet table and positioned himself between Nick and me. No matter where we went, Ryan could not escape his fans.

* * *

THE FOLLOWING afternoon, Ryan's family gathered in the kitchen, readying Thanksgiving dinner.

"Honey, where do you want me to set this?" Bill asked. He was lifting the enormous turkey out of the oven.

Ellen pointed to an obvious empty space on the stove, slightly irritated that she had to give him direction.

Memories of my dad asking *my* mom the same question flashed in my mind. My dad was helpless, too. I turned my attention back to scooping sweet potatoes into a serving bowl. Janelle was softly humming songs to herself while she set the dinner table.

"Hey, honey . . . where is Sarah's bottle?" Nick yelled from the brown recliner in the family room.

When Nick yelled, I instinctively looked over. His voice sounded so much like Ryan's it was hard to tell the difference.

Ryan came sauntering into the kitchen wearing one of the new pairs of jeans that I got for him. For some reason, that thought made me warm inside. I noticed he was looking around the family room for something.

"Hey, honey? Do you know where my sneakers are?" Ryan asked, momentarily distracted by the television. My head naturally turned to answer him.

Instead of replying, I broke out in laughter. I held onto the counter as my hilarious internal thoughts cracked me up. Everyone stopped what they were doing to look at me, wondering just what the heck was wrong with me.

"There are too many honeys in this room!" I breathed out in jest, answering Ryan's glance. That term of endearment must have been engrained in all of them. It was also apparent that *all* the Christensen males were now incapable of independent thought and action.

"Every time someone yells 'Honey' I turn around."

I'd asked for it. I was bombarded with repeated "Honeys" from all three of them.

Ryan started our first Thanksgiving dinner playfully kicking me under the table. We were both smirking when he slipped his leg under mine so our legs were resting together.

"Did you guys have fun last night?" Bill asked, passing the bowl of stuffing to me.

I opened my mouth to speak, but Nick was quicker.

"It was all right, up until Ryan's fans showed up in the suite," Nick interjected curtly, poking his butter knife at Ryan. "Superstar had to sign his autograph and pose for pictures and everything with his little girlfriends." His snide tone was evident. "'Ooh, I want a picture. No, pose with me!'" Nick teased in a forced high-pitch voice.

Ryan slapped some mashed potatoes on his plate. The serving spoon clanged loudly when it made contact with the china; the noise made me flinch. The scowl on Ryan's face was evident. Instead of Nick being thankful that Ryan had provided an entire evening of first-class entertainment—free of charge to him and his wife—he saw the opportunity to give his brother a cheap shot and took it.

"How the heck did that happen?" Bill questioned. He looked over at Ryan. "I thought you had a private suite?"

Ryan shrugged. "It *was* a private suite, Dad, but there were still eight other ticket holders. One of the girls' fathers was some senior VP at the bank that has it rented for the season. She brought friends."

Bill's face pulled down in a frown.

"It's humbling, you know. I mean, most actors would kill to have my problems. This is what all actors strive for. A-list movies, A-list parts . . . not having to go to audition after audition only to be turned down or passed over. I should count my blessings; after all, it is Thanksgiving." Ryan took a moment to eat some food. "Besides, I'm getting used to all of the unwanted attention." He looked right over at Nick when he said it. "It used to really bother me, but I'm finding that I can just tune it out and ignore it."

I picked up on his little dig back to his own brother. Sibling rivalry was alive and well right here at this dinner table.

"Fleury made some incredible saves last night and Crosby scored two of the three goals," I said to their father, hoping to break the tension that was starting to build between the two brothers. Ryan's left hand slipped over my shoulder and he smiled at me. "I've been a Pens fan all my life, and that was the first time I got to see them play live on home ice. I had so much fun. Thank you again for taking me," I gushed, hoping Nick would get the message to appreciate his brother.

"Mom, this turkey is really delicious," Nick complimented. "Everything is really tasty this year."

"Don't thank me, thank your brother," Ellen stated between bites. She paused to chew.

Nick quickly tossed his next jab. "Why? Did Ryan open his fat wallet and hire a professional chef to cook for us this year?"

I noticed Janelle smacked him in the leg under the table. I was wondering if this was Nick's normal behavior or if he was going above and beyond to be an asshole.

"No, Nicholas." Ellen broke out her corrective mother tone. "But your brother did bring Taryn home with him. She's the one who cooked most of this delicious food, including the turkey you're enjoying."

Ryan set the gravy boat down. "Who knows, Nick. Maybe next year we could have Thanksgiving at my multimillion-dollar completely pretentious house," Ryan snarled. "I'm sure Taryn will be gracious enough to spend an entire day cooking for my family again. And, by the way, the next time you feel inclined to dry-hump your 'Charles' pillow, imagine ten percent of all the royalties going into your daughter's trust fund before you get yourself off. By the time she's two, she'll be worth ten times more than you."

"Okay, that's enough," Bill reprimanded, trying to tell his sons to knock it off.

"I'm just teasing him, Dad. I don't know why the superstar is getting all sensitive," Nick said.

Ryan set his dinner fork down and pushed his chair back, audibly noting his departure from the table. His fingers touched my chin. "Honey, I need some air. I'll be back."

"Son, sit back down," Bill somberly requested, but Ryan didn't listen. He grabbed his coat and keys and stormed out the kitchen door.

I folded my hands on my lap when I heard the Shelby squeal out of the garage.

"Taryn, I'm sorry," Nick uttered, trying to sound sincere.

I stared at him for a moment. "Thank you, Nick. But I'm not the one you should be apologizing to."

"I can't help it if he can't take a joke!" Nick laughed uncomfortably, stuffing more food in his mouth as though his insults were no big deal.

I sat there in shock. I couldn't believe how a member of Ryan's own immediate family, his only brother that he looked up to, could be so callous and cruel. After all the crap that Ryan had to put up with being an actor, coming home to his family should be a relief for him, not another source of pain. I looked at their parents before I turned my attention back to Nick. I couldn't hold my thoughts any longer.

"Before you chastise your brother, Nick, you should know how much he envies you."

"Envies me?" Nick scoffed.

"Yes, you," I stated calmly. "You have things in your life that you take for granted every day—freedom, anonymity, privacy, security. Things your brother no longer has. His success that you tease him about comes at a very steep price, but I thought you knew that already." I glared at him.

"You also have things he desires—a home, a wife, a child—normalcy. You know what your brother has?" I tilted my head, making sure to hold his eye contact.

"He has acute paranoia from deranged stalkers and fans coming after him, public humiliation on a global scale when they print lies about him in forty different languages, negative criticism about everything he tries to do, and constant scrutiny by everyone—even from his big brother that he adores." I counted them off on my fingers. "But surely you must know that already. So if you feel inclined to let him know how remorseful you are, perhaps you should think of that before you apologize."

Nick looked completely dumbfounded. He was sitting there with his mouth hanging open.

"Would you excuse me, please?" I whispered at Ryan's mother before rising from the dinner table. "I'm going to make sure he's all right." I grabbed my coat from the closet and called Ryan's cell.

"Honey, come back for me. I want to go for a ride, too. I'll be waiting outside."

CHAPTER 26

Tests

CALL ME ONCE you're in the limo, okay?" Ryan sighed. "Just so I know you made it home safely."

I could see the sadness clearly in his expression. It matched my own. We both knew it would be almost three weeks until we saw each other again, and the last minutes we had together were flying by. He turned his Shelby onto the main road that led into the airport.

"I will." I sniffed, trying not to cry. I didn't want to leave, but I had to get back to running my pub. Ryan was planning to spend some well-earned time away with his friends Matt and Scott and his brother before leaving for Scotland. The four men were going hunting. He and his brother also had some making-up to do.

"You know you really didn't need to do this . . . Marie or Pete could have picked me up," I muttered.

"Taryn," he groaned, looking over at me. "You know why. I don't like that you're flying home alone, either."

I stared out my window, thinking that he worried too much. Our stalker was incarcerated and most of the *Seaside* fans had left town once the filming wrapped. The reasons to be frightened and paranoid were gone.

"I'll be all right. You should stop worrying," I whispered.

He shook his head at me; his lips frowned at my words.

All too soon, we were parked in front of the doors for departing flights.

I leaned across the center console and kissed him. I had to turn my Mitchell's Pub baseball hat on his head so the visor would be out of my way.

"I love you," I uttered, missing him already.

"I love you, too. I'll see you in L.A. on the sixteenth." He took my face in his hands and kissed me again. "It's going to feel like forever," he whispered, resting his forehead on mine.

I turned to look at him one last time before walking into the airport . . . alone. No security, no police escort, no one taking my picture, no one shouting my name or his. I stood in line to go through baggage screening and security completely unnoticed. The airport was busy with holiday travelers, but none of those travelers even looked twice at me.

I sat in the waiting area right outside my gate, not hidden away in some VIP lounge. There was no reason to hide. It dawned on me that my heart rate was . . . normal. My heart wasn't pounding in my chest the way it was when we first started this trip. Fear was pleasantly absent from my blood. A young woman approached me. She gently smiled before asking if the seat next to me was taken. I smiled slightly to myself; I didn't even make a blip on her radar.

The only difference between this flight home and any other flight I'd ever taken was that I was flying first class instead of sitting in the economy seats in the back of the plane. Flying first class definitely had its perks, but the flights were so short that it didn't really matter what seat I had to sit in to get home. I said a little prayer of thanks when my plane finally landed in Providence. I was not a fan of flying.

I pulled the handle out on my little suitcase, adjusted my backpack on my shoulder, and followed the other passengers toward the exit. I looked around at the people waiting for family and loved ones to arrive, wishing I were being greeted by familiar faces, too. Instead, some stranger would be taking me home. That thought made me feel even lonelier. I'd fought the impulse to call Marie so many times to ask her to pick me up, only because I knew Ryan was paying for this ride home out of his pocket. Besides, he'd insisted on a security escort. *Which one of these strangers is my driver?*

I noticed his face first before I read the little sign that he held in front of his body, which had "Mitchell" written on it. I squeezed my eyes shut for a moment; fate certainly had a wicked sense of humor.

He smiled at me, but it wasn't one of those "I'm smiling because I have to be nice to you" smiles; it was more of a smirk—as if he were committing a crime by standing there holding my name on a card. I stopped in front of him and took a deep breath before I found the guts to say hello.

"Welcome home," Kyle said smugly. "Can I take your luggage for you, Ms. Mitchell?"

He carried my suitcase and ushered me out to the car, which was another surprise. I had expected the typical black sedan or an SUV; even a stretch limo wouldn't have been as shocking. Instead he had his own personal car waiting . . . a nice little two-door silver Audi.

"Did you have a nice holiday?" Kyle asked. I sensed he was just trying to make polite small-talk.

"Yes, I did. Thank you for asking." I chuckled lightly to myself, trying to ignore how cute he looked. "But the bigger question is, why are you the one who is taking me home?" I was already in trouble just being in this car.

He smiled, knowing I wanted him to explain. He hit the gas pedal to get us out of the airport faster.

"I saw the pickup request on the assignment log and I volunteered," he confessed. "I just wanted to see how you were doing." He looked over at me and shrugged. "Why, is your *boyfriend* going to be mad?"

The way he said it, I could tell that he didn't care whether Ryan was going to be angry or not. He almost sounded as though he welcomed the challenge.

I stared out the car window, watching familiar road signs flash by. "Probably," I said. "When I tell him."

Kyle glanced over quickly. "Then save yourself the argument and don't tell him."

"I have to tell him. Just in case someone took our picture. His PR team will have to be informed."

"Wow!" He sounded astonished. "You really have gone Hollywood, haven't you?"

His comment raised my pulse slightly. "Why do you say that? Because I happen to be involved with someone whose life is constantly under public scrutiny? Because I don't want to give him one more reason to be hurt—that makes me Hollywood?"

"Hey, look, Taryn, I didn't mean to upset you. It's just that you don't seem like the type of woman who would put herself out there to be scrutinized like that. But who am I to judge? Maybe you like having your picture plastered all over those magazines in the grocery store. What do I know?" he muttered, looking over his shoulder to change lanes on the highway.

I huffed. "I could definitely do without the lies that they print."

He laughed lightly. "I can't be sure, but I'm willing to bet those were all things you never had to worry about with other guys *before him*."

I thought about his statement, backtracking through my history of failed relationships. "Lies have followed every relationship I've ever been in." My admission made me frown. "Even the ones fabricated by the gossip magazines."

"I don't know. I thought the stories about our alleged love affair were rather amusing and eloquently written," Kyle said comically. "I suppose that's why he got rid of me so quickly."

"You'd be correct in your assumption," I whispered.

"So are you tired of all the lies yet?" he asked, shifting his car to accelerate past a few tractor-trailers.

I stared at him. "What kind of question is that?"

His eyes flashed over to look at me before turning his attention back to the road and driving.

"I think you can do better. I think you deserve better." The tendons in his hand flexed when he tightened his grip on the steering wheel.

"Better than what?" I asked. If he was going to pass judgment, he'd have to defend his opinion.

"Better than being put in harm's way. Better than subjecting yourself to public ridicule. Better than allowing the media to use you like a punching bag." He glared over at me. "Do you want me to go on? Because I can make a long list."

I focused on the landscape outside my window while trying to subdue the burning feeling in my chest.

"No," I muttered coldly. "I get your point." My cell phone started to play in my purse. It was Ryan's ring tone.

"Hi," I answered, happy to hear from him, but annoyed that he couldn't wait for me to call him.

"Where are you?" Ryan demanded.

"I'm in the car. We just left the airport," I lied. Kyle looked at me and smirked, indicating that he caught my fib to Ryan.

"Oh, why didn't you call me? I've been worried!"

"I just got in the car. I was going to call you but you beat me to it." I tried to be quiet, but Kyle was sitting less than ten inches away from me. There was no way to keep this conversation private. I rubbed my face with my free hand. I was getting a sinus headache from this entire experience.

"Well, I just wanted to make sure you landed safely and that there was a car waiting for you to take you home, that's all."

I knew Ryan cared, but he was also getting a bit controlling.

"Yeah, there was a driver waiting," I whispered. I heard Kyle chuckle. "Everything is fine."

"You don't sound fine," he pressed. "What's wrong?"

My love knew me well enough to call me out on a lie. "Nothing. My sinuses hurt—must be from the flight. How about I call you when I get dropped off at home? Is that okay? Then we can talk."

Kyle started laughing out loud when I snapped my cell phone shut. "Mr. Christensen checking up on you?" he teased.

I gave him a dirty look. "He's concerned, that's all. Besides, he cares enough to make sure I'm taken care of."

"Sounds to me like he's getting a little possessive."

"Maybe he feels that I'm worth possessing," I fired back.

Kyle fidgeted in his seat. "Yeah, he's right. I can't fault him for that one."

He drove down the alley, stopping by the back doors of my building. For the first time in a long time there were no paparazzi, no fans, no one near my doors. The relief I felt was refreshing. Kyle carried my suitcase into the hallway; there was no way I'd allow him in the apartment.

"Thanks, but I can carry it. Please just set it down." I rubbed my cheek again. My face was starting to hurt for some reason. "Thank you for the ride home."

"Yeah, sure—no problem. Ahh, so, are you going to be open tonight?" he asked.

"Yes. That's why I came home. I still have a business to run." I looked at my watch, noting that I had three hours to rest before starting another long night behind the bar.

I walked him out into the alley, hoping to send him on his way quicker. Kyle pushed the trunk of his car closed and smiled.

He held his arms open, silently asking for a hug goodbye. My body responded without me even thinking about it, dragging me unconsciously into the danger zone.

"It was nice seeing you again." He grinned, locking his eyes on mine. "I'll see you soon."

I towed my suitcase into the bedroom and dropped everything, including my coat, on the floor. Our bed looked so soft and inviting, and the desire to lie down for a few minutes was overwhelming. I snuggled up on my pillow and pulled Ryan's pillow to my chest, catching his familiar scent and wishing he were lying next to me. *I'll just close my eyes for a minute . . .*

My head sprang off the pillow when I heard my cell phone.

"Taryn! What's going on?" Ryan shouted. "Where are you?"

"Shit. What time is it?" I looked over at my clock. It was a quarter of four. I sat up quickly; my head felt like it weighed forty pounds and my throat burned. "I fell asleep on our bed," I murmured. "I'm sorry I didn't call."

He was irritated. "You couldn't call me quick before you laid down?"

"I said I'm sorry," I repeated forcefully through my sore throat. "I think I'm getting a cold. My nose is all blocked up. I feel awful."

"You sound sick, babe. I'm sorry. I was just worried."

"I have fifteen minutes to pull myself together before I have to open," I groaned. That's when my sneezing fit started.

Marie was already behind the bar when I went downstairs. Cory came in a few moments later. Both of them would be working Friday night; I had a band scheduled to play. Marie's grin twisted to a concerned stare when she spotted the wad of tissues in my hand. I wasn't in the bar for more than a few minutes before she turned me by the shoulders and sent me packing for my apartment.

"I'll wait to hear about your trip when you're not contagious. We got this," she insisted. "Cory and I will be all right. Go, and take your germs with you."

I curled up on my couch with a box of tissues and my quilt and drifted back to sleep.

I woke up when the band started playing down in the pub. The reverb from the sound system made my pictures vibrate on the wall.

"How are things going?" I asked Marie. It hurt to swallow. I looked around at the crowd in the pub. Pete waved to me from his stool by the front door.

Her eyes stealthily slid back and forth. "*Kyle* is in the poolroom shooting pool," she said. "What the heck is he doing here? He already asked for you once."

I rubbed my face with both of my hands. "He drove me home from the airport."

"What?" she yelled. "How the hell did that happen?"

"He saw the pickup assignment and volunteered. I'm in so much trouble."

She looked at me, trying to ascertain why I thought I was in trouble.

"I didn't tell Ryan . . . yet. He's going to be so pissed."

"Did something happen between you two? I mean, you and Kyle?" she corrected.

"No, there's nothing going on." I looked over my shoulder to see if I could spot him in the poolroom. Our eyes accidentally made contact and I watched him set his pool stick up against the wall and head in my direction.

"Hey, Taryn. What's wrong? Are you okay?" Kyle asked.

I shook my head. "No, I have a cold."

Other thoughts ran through my head, such as how much I wished Ryan were here so I didn't have to try and explain all of this over a cell phone. The crowd in the bar was definitely manageable, but I started washing dirty drink glasses anyway. Cory looked at me like I was crazy—little did he know I was using it as an excuse to get away from gorgeous Kyle.

"Boss, what are you doing?" Cory grumbled, dropping the bottle of house whiskey back in the tray.

Marie grabbed my arm and hauled me away from the sink. "Go back upstairs. This is all under control. You're sick. You need to go rest," she ordered, loud enough for Kyle to hear.

Kyle waved his fingers in the air to say goodbye but I ignored him and kept on walking. The way I felt was odd. Kyle was a professional bodyguard; his presence should have made me feel safe and secure, but instead I felt the complete opposite of that. His presence around me was surprisingly dangerous.

IT WAS almost noon on Saturday when my doorbell rang, rousing me from my comfortable resting spot on the couch. I pulled my hair back in a hair tie and grabbed a few tissues along my way.

Kyle was standing in my alley with a large, brown paper bag in his arms. "Hey, how are you feeling?" he asked.

Oh, God, why are you torturing me?

"Worse, actually," I squeaked.

He held out the grocery bag. "I got you some supplies," he said happily. "Thought you might need some of this stuff."

He followed me up to my apartment and set the bag on my coffee table.

"Tissues, nighttime cold medicine, daytime cold medicine, cough drops, and a whole container of chicken noodle soup from my favorite corner deli." He pulled each item out of the bag. "Oh, and some crackers."

"Thanks, but you shouldn't have," I muttered. Little did he know how many facets that one statement had. I knew for a fact that he'd had to drive over an hour to get here. It wasn't as if Kyle lived right up the street. He was definitely going out of his way to see me.

"Would you like some soup now?" he asked, testing the temperature of the container with his hand. "It's still slightly warm."

I nodded and started to stand up. Some hot soup sounded appealing for my sore throat.

"Sit down," he insisted. "I'm pretty sure I can figure out how to use your microwave."

My eyes traveled to watch his incredible body and his nice ass walk toward my kitchen. I covered my eyes and rubbed my face to banish the thoughts. I had to get him out of my apartment—as soon as possible. Then another thought flashed through my mind. This wasn't just *my* apartment anymore. This apartment was a home that I chose to share with Ryan, a home where we were living together in happiness and where no other man should be standing.

"Careful, it may be too hot now," Kyle cautioned, handing a mug of soup to me.

"Thanks," my voice strained as I set the cup down on the table. "Kyle? I appreciate all of this, but why . . . why are you here?"

"What, we're not allowed to be friends?" he quickly replied.

I thought about his question for a moment and replied with one of my own. "If your girlfriend was traveling out of town for work, do you think she'd appreciate another woman being in her home while she was gone?"

"What does that have to do with us being friends?" he countered.

As sick as I felt, I still wasn't falling for his bullshit. "I don't think you're here because you want to just be friends."

"You think I have some ulterior motive?" Kyle questioned my glare.

"Please," I squeaked. "Don't question my intelligence." I wiped my snotty nose with a tissue, hoping that would discourage his thoughts even more.

"All right. To tell you the truth, when I saw that you were flying home alone I thought that maybe you and pretty-boy broke up."

"Do not call him that."

Kyle drew in a deep breath. "You've got to admit that being with him definitely has its drawbacks."

His little digs at Ryan really irritated me.

"Oh, and I suppose things would be a lot better for me if I were dating someone else? Someone like you perhaps?" I hoped my tone was sarcastic enough.

"Your life would be a hell of a lot more private, that's for sure. No cameras, no photographers, no fanatics." He tossed a pack of crackers over to me.

"Wait. Let me see if I got this straight. So instead of being with someone like Ryan, who is trying to do everything possible to shield me from danger, you're saying I'd be better off with someone like you, who willingly risks his own life every day to put himself in front of danger to protect complete strangers. Is that right?"

He looked away, and then a little cocky smile appeared on his lips. "You've at least thought about it. That's a good start. And I would protect you a hell of a lot better than he would. Besides, being with me doesn't come with risk."

"Don't be so sure of yourself. You are the one who's forcing me to compare the two of you. And to tell you the truth, there is no comparison." I got up from the couch, irritated now by his presence.

"Kyle, I appreciate the soup and the kindness, but we can't be friends."

He crossed his foot up on his knee, getting even more comfortable in the chair. "Why not?"

"Because you don't want just a friendship," I scornfully stated the obvious. "Kyle, I love Ryan. I have committed my heart to him." I picked up Kyle's coat. "I'm sorry, but I think it's time for you to leave now."

"That's a shame. You'll never know what could have been." I noticed he didn't even attempt to get up. "You're not married to the guy, and I don't see a ring on your finger, so the way I see it, you're still available."

"Available? Did you not just hear what I said?" I was no longer just irritated; I was starting to get angry now.

"I heard you," he muttered. "I also know that it won't be long before he screws up and cheats on you. They *all* do eventually. He's not the first actor I've had to watch over. You'd be surprised to know the great lengths they go through to keep their little affairs hidden. Even the married ones screw around."

"And you'd be totally different from that. You'd *never* cheat on me." I laughed mockingly.

"No, I wouldn't. And if you were with me, I'd only take local assignments so I wouldn't have to travel and be away from you," he continued. "There would be no reason for you to ever doubt me."

"I have no reason to doubt Ryan, either. You're a man, he's a man; either it's in your nature to cheat or it's not." My throat felt like I'd been swallowing razor blades and I was starting to run a fever again. It was time for him to go.

"And I can tell you, Kyle, that it's not in my nature to cheat, either. I love Ryan. That's all you need to know. Now if you don't mind, I'd really like to rest." I shook his coat in my hand so he'd get the message.

He stopped to look at me before taking his coat from my hand. "I'll be watching and waiting. You're an intelligent woman. You'll come to your senses soon enough."

His assuredness was getting a bit creepy.

I was glad when he finally left. I watched him walk halfway down the alley to make sure he was leaving before locking up and setting the alarm.

Back in my apartment, I picked up my cell and hit the first entry in my phone book. It was time to come clean with Ryan.

BY MONDAY my cold had morphed into something altogether more atrocious and wicked. The pain in my sinuses and chest was almost unbearable and I could not stop coughing. My ribs and stomach muscles hurt badly from all the hacking, and it was getting harder and harder to breathe. Marie helped me into her car, which was parked by the back door. I was relieved just knowing I would be seeing a doctor today.

"I told Ryan about Kyle," I whispered between coughing up lung tissue.

Marie looked at me, waiting for my further explanation.

"He was livid." I wiped my nose. "But then after he calmed down he was glad that I told him. He doesn't know everything, though. I spared him some of the details."

"What details?" she asked, patting me on the back as I coughed severely.

I shrugged, not knowing how to say it. "Kyle pretty much said that I'd be better off with him instead of being with Ryan."

"No! He didn't! What the hell else did he say?"

"He said I should consider dating him instead. That he'd be better for me. He also brought me soup." I coughed out my last words.

"Soup?" She laughed. "Oh, he's good. What did you say to him then?"

"I told him I love Ryan and that he should leave. He sort of worried me a bit at the end. Like he didn't want to take 'no' for an answer."

Marie stayed in the waiting room while I went in to see my doctor. He informed me that I had a sinus infection and bronchitis. For as terrible as I felt, I was wondering if there weren't a few other lung infection terms missing from his diagnosis.

We stopped at the local pharmacy, where I got a multitude of antibiotics, nasal spray, and an inhaler. I mistakenly glanced over the front of *Celebrity Weekly* while standing in line at the checkout. The cover of the magazine had a byline that stated distance was tearing Ryan and me apart. He'd just left for Scotland this morning; how could we be split apart already?

"Why are you buying that shit?" Marie scowled. "As if you aren't in bad enough shape already, you need to torment yourself more?"

"I'm not buying it." I coughed violently into my sleeve. "I hate the media. Why do they do this?" I showed her the cover.

I had no intentions to spend even a penny on that crap. It was lies like these that enticed people to buy the garbage in the first place. And every time someone bought one of those magazines, it allowed some idiot to keep his job as a purveyor of lies and gave another idiot incentive to exist as an intruding photographer. Every dime spent on those rag magazines perpetuated the nonsense.

That's when Marie informed me that a photographer approached her the other day and offered her two thousand dollars if she'd get him pictures of the inside of my apartment. These leeches were now going after my friends. Of course Marie declined, but it was apparent that the magazines wanted to get their hands on actual photos of our "love nest," as they put it. Now I was even more paranoid about having anyone in my apartment.

Ryan called me every day while he was in Scotland, even if it was for only five minutes. He tried to describe the landscape and architecture so I could visualize the experience he was having; he even sent me a few cell phone pictures, but I still wished I were there with him to experience it firsthand.

It didn't take long for pictures of the cast in Scotland to surface on the

Internet. Ryan's fan site was quite reliable with the latest selection of candid photos. Tongues around the globe were sent wagging once the photos of Ryan and Suzanne's "love scene" were leaked. Even Kat called me to make sure I wasn't going to go ballistic from seeing the scandalous photos.

For some reason, the lies about Ryan and Suzanne's rekindled romance didn't bother me as much as it did when I'd first met him. I guess I knew both of them well enough to know that Ryan didn't have any romantic feelings for her despite how often his lips had to touch hers. I knew Ryan harbored deep resentment for Suzanne and her antics. She had wronged him too many times in the past for him to ever let go of his grudge, let alone ever love her.

I did, however, worry about Suzanne. Many of the little stunts she pulled pointed to her being madly in love with him. I was on to her little game; after all, I, too, was once young and foolish. She didn't try to break us up for Francesca's benefit—I was wrong with that assumption. Her comments and evil tongue had only one beneficiary. After her little failed tryst with Ryan's friend Scott, she'd made comments indicating that she had hoped that if his friends thought she was good enough to sleep with, maybe he would feel the same way. Unfortunately for Suzanne, her actions had the opposite effect on Ryan.

The media sure had fun with all these rumors and lies. According to the reports, Ryan was back with Suzanne, Suzanne reportedly told me to stay away from her man, our relationship was over, and I was having a secret affair with my former bodyguard behind Ryan's back. It was beyond ridiculous.

"YOU FEELING up to getting out of the house today?" Marie asked, interrupting my private viewing of several old Ryan Christensen interviews on the computer. I clicked the video pause button and gave her a bit more of my attention. I'd been holed up in my apartment for an entire week.

"Tammy wants to take us to lunch. We have to stop at the jewelry store and then we need to go look at bridesmaid dresses," she rambled through the telephone.

I was feeling a lot better, and getting out into the fresh air did sound appealing. I was also hoping to squash some of the new worries that had mysteriously cropped up in my brain.

Marie and Tammy had been acting, I don't know—strange toward me for the last couple of days. I couldn't pinpoint the specifics; I could just sense it. Maybe it was the new way they both awkwardly smiled at me that caused me to feel weird?

I had been really ill and I was extremely thankful that my two best friends were there for me, but I couldn't help but worry that they were getting tired of me and my new life of drama.

"Tammy, your wedding band is beautiful!" I gushed, watching the diamonds sparkle in the light. She handed a check to the sales clerk.

"Thanks!" Tammy glowed. "Only six more payments and it's mine."

"Hey, Taryn, come look at this one," Marie called out. She was looking at emerald rings.

"How much is that ring right there?" Marie pointed to a very gaudy ring.

The saleswoman took it out of the case and checked the tag. "This one is three thousand."

My eyes bugged out. It was an ugly ring for three thousand dollars. Marie tried to put it on her finger, but it wouldn't go past her knuckle without a good shove.

"Here Tar, you have tiny fingers. Model it."

I slipped it on my right hand and held it out to her. It was the kind of stacked setting that would take a layer of skin off anyone you brushed up against accidentally.

Marie played with the ring on my finger, checking the look of it from several angles. I was surprised that she even liked this style of jewelry.

She held my hand out to the sales clerk. "So, what do you think? Does it fit her?"

"She would need to be sized," the woman answered, twisting it freely on my finger. "You could probably go down a half size smaller."

I took it off immediately and handed it back to the clerk. I didn't want anyone to think I was interested in buying this ugly ring.

"This ring is tiny. What size is it?" Marie placed it back on her finger.

"It's a six," the woman droned. "It's the standard stock size."

"There you go, Taryn. Your next job could be a hand model since all of these would fit you," Marie teased.

I thought about modeling my middle finger for her.

"How small is her finger?" Marie asked.

The saleswoman slid a few metal rings around my finger. "You would wear a five and a half."

"Are both hands the same size? I heard one hand is always bigger," Marie said.

The woman measured my other hand. "They're the same."

"Try that one on." Marie pointed to another ring. The woman handed me an opal and emerald disaster.

"You know you'll have to start working your fingers out more if you're going to be interviewing for all those hand jobs." Tammy snorted at her own joke.

"I'm sure Ryan would be happy to help there." Marie laughed. "Come on, let's get out of here and go try on some really ugly taffeta dresses now. We got what we needed."

"Speaking of dresses . . ." I said and opened my purse to retrieve my cell phone. There was another very important affair that required a very special dress closer than Tammy's wedding on my calendar.

"I can't believe you have KellyAnn Gael's number and you can just call her to talk about dresses like it's no big deal," Marie teased. "Who else do you have in there now? Drew? Gwyneth? Demi?" She grabbed for my phone just as her own phone started to ring.

"Hi, Cheryl," Marie muttered awkwardly. "Hey, can I call you back? I'm out with my friends Taryn and Tammy right now." She groaned. "Okay, well . . . um, let me think. How about if I call you at *five thirty*? Five thirty," she repeated.

"Gary's sister," Marie answered my questioning stare. "She's being a real pain in the ass lately."

CHAPTER 27

Hollywood

IT WAS STILL dark outside when Tammy drove me to the airport the following Tuesday morning. My flight out would put me on the West Coast at one o'clock in the afternoon, leaving me plenty of time to be entertained by Kelly. Ryan had told me to make sure I packed light, since it was a lot warmer in Los Angeles, and to bring my new Shell-B Enterprises credit card as well to check into the hotel. He wouldn't be landing at LAX until almost nine o'clock at night on his return from Scotland. It would take him three different flights to reach California.

The sun was bright when I walked through the terminal at LAX. I smiled to myself when I went almost unnoticed by the leeches with cameras. My hunch was correct; there were paparazzi staked out at this airport twenty-four hours a day, seven days a week. My reverie quickly faded when I realized that Ryan would have a different fate when he landed tonight. He would be tired and annoyed by the unwanted attention from the paparazzi. Surely they would not let him go unnoticed.

There were quite a few drivers waiting for arriving passengers near the exit. My eyes quickly scanned the names on the cards that each one of them was holding, but I did not see my name. I looked again. Surely I must have missed it the first time. I reread each card looking for Ryan's name. That's when I saw "Bailey" written on a card. Underneath it was Shell-B Enterprises. A smile broke on my face when the driver asked if I was Mrs. Bailey. *Not yet, but maybe one day?*

I definitely felt like an outsider in this foreign land called Los Angeles . . . palm trees and expensive cars were on every street. The hotel where we would be staying was beyond anything I had ever experienced as well. It exuded wealth.

"Good afternoon. I'd like to check in, please," I said to the man behind the marble counter.

"Your name?"

"Bailey?"

He typed into his computer. "Card, please," he requested.

Panic welled in my chest. I had no identification with Bailey on it. I handed him my driver's license and wondered how long it would take Kelly to drive here and rescue me when this guy kicked me out of the lobby for false impersonation.

He handed it back to me with a smile. "I need your credit card, please, for verification," he corrected.

The key card he handed me in return didn't unlock just any old hotel room. That wouldn't be Ryan's style for treating me well. This room was a huge suite dressed in shades of burgundy and cream with a rich mahogany wood floor. Elegant wooden doors separated the grand living room from the bedroom, and there were two separate sets of French doors that opened up to the private balcony. The suite even had its own dining room.

I set my bag down on the billowy beige and burgundy striped duvet that covered the king-size canopy bed and sighed out loud. Mr. Christensen would surely be treated like a king in this bed later.

I turned on the light in the bathroom and was surprised to see a plasma television mounted on the wall, in perfect view from the large soaking tub. And then there it was—the final touch—the glass-encased shower with the shower panel of many pleasures. I had to give him credit; he was a simple man with simple needs, but when it came to providing luxury, he surely did it right.

Kelly picked me up at the hotel an hour later and proceeded to take me to the swankiest stores in L.A.

"Two things before we go in there," Kelly announced, parking her car. "One, you're going to go into sticker shock, so don't look at the price tags, and two, Ryan said you have a fifty-grand credit limit on your card, so we have to behave."

"Fifty thousand?" I felt faint. I reached for the air-conditioning dial in her car and turned it up. She laughed at me.

"There's no way in hell I'm spending . . ." I had to swallow. My throat felt tight. "I don't care *how* much money he has."

"Relax," she told me. "We won't spend all of it."

"I just need a dress for the party and something nice to wear for our dinner meeting with Mr. Follweiler. That's it. I even brought my black heels from home."

She spent the next several hours dressing me like one of her daughter's Barbie dolls.

"Kelly, four thousand dollars for two dresses?" I whispered nervously in her ear. Apparently these prices were no big deal to anyone living on this side of the country.

"We're going to take all of this," Kelly informed the girl behind the counter. She had stacked up the jeans and tops and even the totally sexy black leather ankle boots that I fell in love with. "Oh, and the Dior handbag as well." She piled that on top.

"Kelly!" I gritted through my teeth. Everything that I'd said I loved was on the pile. The purse alone was over a thousand dollars.

"No," I stated adamantly to the cashier. "Only the two dresses and these shoes. I don't want to buy any of these other things."

Kelly smiled and then whispered privately in my ear. "You are going to be photographed the entire week. You need to look the part. This isn't some wanna-be actor we're talking about here. The public expects his girlfriend to be stylish and sexy."

I turned around and spoke quietly. "I don't care. I'm not spending his money on things that are unnecessary." I pushed the extra items to the side.

"Can you give us a minute?" Kelly asked the cashier, pulling my arm for me to follow her. "Taryn, he told me to make sure you get whatever you want."

"All I want are these two dresses and the shoes," I informed the cashier.

"Your total comes to four thousand seven hundred and ninety," she announced.

I swallowed hard as I handed her my Shell-B credit card.

It was almost eleven o'clock when Ryan finally came through the door of our suite. He'd barely stepped four feet inside when I wrapped my arms around him. He dropped all his belongings on the floor and grabbed hold of me. It felt like everything that had been wrong was put back to right the moment his lips touched mine.

• • •

"LOOKS LIKE you had fun yesterday," Ryan said, nodding his chin at the garment bags hanging on the door. I couldn't believe how much I missed waking up in his arms.

"I wouldn't necessarily call it fun," I breathed out on his neck, hiding my eyes in his hair.

Ryan lifted up the bedsheet and looked down at our bodies.

"Okay, now I'm really worried. I have thoroughly checked, and I know you're a girl. You have all the proper girl parts." He ran his hand down over my rear, causing me to fidget. "I thought all women love to shop. What's going on?"

I turned away, reluctant to have another conversation about my aversion to spending his money. "I don't know. I mean, I had a lot of fun with Kelly. It's just, well, I feel guilty."

"Guilty? Why, did you rob the store?" His eyes pulled me back, forcing me to tell the truth.

"I just wanted to get a nice dress. I didn't think it would cost so much. I'm only going to wear it for a few hours."

"How much did you spend?" he asked, sounding reproachful.

I looked up at him with one guilty eye. "In total?" I swallowed hard. "Four thousand eight hundred? I got two dresses and new shoes to wear, one for dinner tonight and another for the party Saturday."

He shook his head and scowled at me. "What were you thinking?"

"I know. I told Kelly it was too much, but she told me that your girlfriend has to look stylish," I confessed. "I should have tried to find something more affordable back home, but it's too late now. I'll pay you back, I promise."

"No. That's okay. I guess I'll have to do another movie or something. It's either that or we'll have to drag the mattress out into the front yard again." He sounded all disgruntled and then he rolled his body on top of mine.

"Tar, you're going to have to get used to dressing up when I do public appearances, award shows, and premieres. You know that, right?"

I nodded.

"Dresses and stuff aren't cheap. But if you feel that strongly about spending my money, you could always work off your debt," he said slyly, softly kissing my lips. "I must warn you, though; I may ask you to do things that you might find disgusting and perverse." His devilish grin made my heart race.

"Nah, that's okay. Let me get my purse and I'll write you a check." I teasingly tried to wiggle out from underneath him.

"I don't take personal checks." He pinned me with his long arms, pretending that he was going to take a big bite out of my exposed breast. "Besides, I was hoping to subject you to fifty years of hard labor."

"Does this mean we have to renegotiate our terms again?" I whined, locking my ankles together over his rear.

"Absolutely. Now roll over so I can change the fine print on our contract. I just have to get my eraser out down here," he joked.

Our morning together passed by so quickly, and now he was off again.

"I'll see you around six," Ryan said, kissing me goodbye in the privacy of our room. "Listen, just have fun and enjoy yourself this afternoon with Kelly. And don't ask how much, all right? Just put it on the card—*my* card, not your card," he corrected. "After the screen tests, I have to pick up my new suits and then I'll meet you here."

I kissed him goodbye and frowned when he slipped from my hands.

Kelly saw to it that I had the works done at the spa that she took me to. I was scrubbed, massaged, and purified. I had never felt so relaxed in all my life. My skin glowed. After the manicure and pedicure I had my hair cut and styled. I felt fabulous.

"Just so you know, when we get back to the room I'm tearing that dress off your body," Ryan informed me in the car on our way to the restaurant.

I rolled my eyes.

"I'm serious!" He took my hand and rubbed it down the front of his pants. "Feel that? That's from just thinking about it."

"You need to focus." I nudged him. "Titles of Jonathan Follweiler films . . . go."

He rambled three titles; I listed twelve more from memory.

"I printed out all his work," I said, unfolding the papers I had in my purse.

"Let's see, television credits . . . director and producer of *City Pulse*, director of *Original Stories of Trouble* and *13 Lies*—all of which are current projects. He has never received an Academy Award, but he was nominated in 2004 for two—Best Picture and Best Directing for *The Wandering Road*. Oh, and his film *Safe Distance* grossed two hundred million."

I flipped the paper to the next sheet. "Last project was the film *Nefarious Hearts*, which premiered back in May."

I proceeded to quiz Ryan all the way to the restaurant. Again the cameras clicked the minute we stepped out of the limo, but our bodyguard moved us quickly into the building.

It was quite intimidating being the only female at a table of four very powerful men. I took the first seat next to Mr. Follweiler; he looked the least intimidating and most friendly out of the selection.

Even though I received a warm welcome, I couldn't help but feel as though they expected me to be a brainless bimbo, the stereotypical famous-actor girlfriend that was just arm-candy. Their conversations conveniently omitted me from participating, so I sat quietly and observed. I noticed that none of them even bothered to ask for a response from me.

Ryan tried to be accommodating by smiling in my direction every once in a while, but he looked just as uncomfortable as I felt. I'd had a feeling that this was going to happen, so I kept a few aces up my sleeve just in case.

Ryan's agent, Aaron, was just what I'd expected: forceful, powerful, quite arrogant, and a know-it-all. He knew everyone in this town and was definitely one of its strongest players. I sensed when he looked at Ryan that he saw nothing more than a juicy cash cow in front of him. Ryan was the meat behind his creative manipulations. Ryan's manager, David, on the other hand, spent a great deal of time adjusting his Rolex on his wrist and checking out the short skirts and big breasts that passed by every twelve seconds.

I noticed a lull in the conversation and took advantage of it.

"Mr. Follweiler, I just want to congratulate you." My words came out nervously as I spoke quietly to him. "I read that your film *Nefarious Hearts* might get several Academy nods, including Best Picture. How very exciting!" I smiled politely.

"Thank you! I'm exceptionally proud of that film." He adjusted his position to face me. "Did you have an opportunity to see it?" He raised an eyebrow.

"Yes, sir, I did. Although I must apologize that I was only able to see it once it was released on DVD. I'm sorry I didn't contribute to your opening numbers, but regardless, I thought it was fabulous."

He smiled at me and shifted his weight to lean in my direction, setting his glass of bourbon down to place an inquisitive finger near his mouth. "So tell me dear, what was it about the film that you really liked?"

Ryan squirmed in his chair. I could feel his paranoia, but I was prepared with witty small talk. I sensed right away that this was his test; Jonathan was calling me out to see if I had really seen the film or if I was lying through my teeth.

"I was very intrigued by the character development—how all the principal characters were introduced in flashbacks? That was very inventive. It really captured my attention. I must admit that I was taken with the main character, Giles, right away. Oh, the conflicted feelings that he evoked in me! I didn't know if I wanted to love him or despise him." I politely chuckled. "But in the end, of course, I couldn't help but root for him. And that's why your film was recognized by the Academy. I thought Gerard did a phenomenal job in the role as well."

Little did anyone at this table know, I had just watched the movie two weeks ago while I was still recovering from bronchitis, and I had read several published reviews to obtain the bullshit that just rolled out of my mouth. The movie actually confused the heck out of me at some points.

Jonathan nodded his head and smiled widely at me. We continued to have a discussion on the film's cast, until his head and attention tilted in Ryan's direction. "And you, Ryan? Did you by chance get to see my last work?"

Ryan kicked me in the foot as he straightened up in his seat and adjusted his shirt collar. I looked over at him lovingly, knowing full well he had not seen the film nor prepared for this meeting. David looked away, pretending to be distracted.

"Ryan?" I beamed. "Would you mind if I told him the story?" I ran the tip of my finger down my nose, then gently rubbed my painted fingernails under my chin.

Ryan cleared his throat nervously and then acknowledged my secret gesture. "By all means." He motioned with his hand for me to continue.

I looked back at Jonathan, pretending to fondly remember my tall tale.

"It was just at the point when Grant admitted to Giles that he was a thief and an accidental murderer when Ryan and I had our first heated film debate." I smiled at Ryan. I could clearly see in the way he narrowed his eyes at me that he was dying to know where I was going with this.

"Ryan was of the opinion that Grant's revelation would be deemed as the ultimate betrayal to his brother and that in the end, brother would turn on brother. But I disagreed. There was something in the way Giles was so meticulous in his personal habits as a child that I just knew that the two brothers would unite in the end.

"By the way, Mr. Christensen, I do believe you still owe me a bottle of wine for losing that bet," I teased.

"I believe I owe you an entire vineyard by now, sweetheart." I felt Ryan's hand slide onto mine.

"You must be very intuitive to have guessed the outcome. Bravo!" Jonathan paused to take another sip of his bourbon. "So, tell me, what does your intuition tell you about *Slipknot*? Ryan told me you've been running lines with him, so I assume you've read the script in its entirety?"

I took a deep breath. "Yes, sir . . . many times," I said.

"Well, then? What does your intuition tell you?"

"It has action and suspense along with a healthy dose of romance. Isn't that a film trifecta?" I stated the obvious.

Jonathan shifted in his seat. "Do you feel the story is Oscar worthy?" he asked, eagerly awaiting my reply.

"She isn't qualified to answer that question, Jon," Aaron callously interrupted.

"He is right. I can't answer that," I admitted adamantly.

Jonathan raised a hand to stop us both. "My question has nothing to do with qualifications," he dismissed. "I want to know your gut feeling."

"Jonathan! Really! We know it's going to be phenomenal." David looked around at everyone, laughing confidently. "Why wouldn't it get an Oscar nomination. I mean . . ."

"Now, David, let the lady speak!" Jonathan ordered. "Taryn? Please, go on."

"Honestly? For Best Picture?" I hesitated and took a big gulp of wine from my glass. I could feel Aaron mentally yelling at me to shut up, and David appeared ready to vault over the table to cap my mouth, but I was asked a direct question.

I thought about all the research I'd done on the Oscars when I wondered what kind of role Ryan could play to garner a Best Actor in a Leading Role nod and recalled that all Best Pictures seemed to have one thing in common.

"I don't think so, sir. Will the film gross millions? Absolutely—especially with a strong lead actor like Ryan. And with your brilliance and vision it will *definitely* be a hit. But I think the script as it stands is missing that epic overtone that is required of Best Picture awards. The story is compelling, but the main character is a mystery solver—not a hero."

Aaron tossed his fork onto his plate, noting his disapproval. I held my eyes closed for a few seconds and internally bashed myself for opening up my big lipstick-covered mouth. *Maybe arm-candy, dumb bimbo would have been a safer approach after all?*

Jonathan leaned over and spoke directly to Ryan. "Where did you say you found this amazing woman again?"

"On the *East* Coast." Ryan chuckled. "Why? You planning to steal her from me?"

"Perhaps, if you're not careful. I can't tell you how refreshing it is to have an honest conversation with someone." Jonathan smiled and patted my hand. "That's a quality that this business is seriously lacking."

His warm eyes glinted at me. "Relax, my dear. I had the same exact feelings about the script. I've already discussed some rewrites." Jonathan continued, chuckling to himself. "Now on to the business at hand. Let's discuss making a film."

I slid back into my chair while my nerves twisted into knots. The urge to get on a plane and run for home was overwhelming.

Once the limo driver had returned us to the private garage entrance to our hotel, Ryan and I practically ran from the elevator to our room. He pressed me into the door and kissed me passionately, shutting the rest of the crazy world out behind us.

Just as Ryan had forewarned, he almost tore my dress off, struggling impatiently with the zipper. We aggressively removed each other's clothing, undressing right there in the entryway of our suite like some sex-starved, horny teenagers. Our bodies joined together, testing out the sturdiness of the living room furniture, the coffee table, and even the polished mahogany dining table before twining into one on the freshly made canopy bed.

The next morning we barely had time to swallow our room-service breakfast before having to be on the move again. I thought we were going to be able to spend some time together alone, but that was an unfulfilled wish.

Riding in the backseat of another chauffeured sedan, we passed the famous Hollywood sign on the hillside as we drove to the studio where Ryan was to attend a magazine photo shoot.

David, Ryan's manager, was forever twisting his expensive watch on his wrist. "Did you read those scripts that Aaron sent you?"

"Yeah, I did," Ryan answered, scanning his cell phone messages again.

"*Sacred Mountain*, Ryan. That's your next big hit."

"I'm not interested in sci-fi right now, David. I told you that I want to pursue *The Isletin Solution*. You and Aaron are supposed to be working on that."

David's lips pursed. "I don't know why you have that script stuck in your head. People are not going to line up at the theaters to see Ryan Christensen playing some med student from the 1940s who does medical trials on dogs."

"It was the 1920s—1921 to be exact," I interjected.

David shot me a dirty look. "What did you say?" he asked, annoyed by my interruption.

"It happened in 1921. You said the 1940s," my seemingly uncontrollable big mouth replied.

"Whatever. It doesn't matter," he said tersely, quickly turning his attention back to Ryan. "You'll be better off doing *Sacred Mountain*. You need another project lined up, and this one has a big budget—big action with a big studio to back it—not to mention a big paycheck for you!"

Ryan looked over at me, trying to gauge my opinion before he gave his response. I scratched my chin repeatedly.

"A sci-fi film, David? Really?" His nose wrinkled.

"Yes, Ryan. Really. You need to line up a project after the third *Seaside* and this one is it. I'm telling you—this one is all yours. Aaron and I already spoke to Stevens at Universal. All you have to do is say yes and we can seal this deal. But the time is now, Ryan. He wants you to lock in, so let's lock it in." David's enthusiasm was apparent.

"I don't know. I've read the script and the story is weak. I'd rather do films that are more meaningful and memorable—character driven. Are people going to run to the theaters to see me frolic around with little gray aliens? I don't think so. I'll quit acting before I do shitty films. Besides, Taryn read *Isletin* and she feels it would be a better role for me."

I gasped from the surprise. Why did Ryan have to mention my name? He said it so nonchalantly and then simply returned to being distracted with his phone. David instantly glared at me and I could feel his disdain. I wanted to defend myself but I kept my mouth shut instead this time. This was between Ryan and his manager.

"*Isletin* isn't a studio film," David groaned. "It's an indie project at best, which is career suicide. That's why none of the major studios want to pick it up." He made sure to look directly at me when he said that. "You need big action blockbuster now. You have to keep this energy rolling."

"I'm already signed on for three films next year. Besides, I want to try and have a life somehow in between it all." Ryan picked up my hand and wove our fingers together. David's disapproving eyes stealthily followed this gesture.

"Ryan, let me give you some advice. You haven't been in the business long enough to pass up opportunities like this. And forget about slowing down. You slow down now and your career is over in this town. *Sacred Mountain* is a money project and the producer is even willing to wait until you're done shooting the third *Seaside*. You need to jump on this project and forget about the script that has no backing."

Ryan took a deep breath; his indecision was starting to show. I squeezed his hand in mine to get his attention. When he glanced over at me, I rubbed my forehead and then scratched my chin. He would not make his mark as a serious dramatic actor with a story line like the one in *Sacred Mountain*. It was beyond cheesy.

"Let me think about it," Ryan replied. "I want to talk it over with Taryn."

Marla Sullivan, his publicist, was already at the studio waiting when we arrived. Ryan was scheduled to give a brief interview after the photo shoot; Marla was there to mind his tongue and make sure his image was captured correctly.

I was under the impression that this shoot was just a magazine spread and an interview of Ryan; however, that assumption was quickly bashed when I saw Suzanne in the makeup chair. For the next seven hours, I watched Ryan and Suzanne make numerous wardrobe changes as they posed together over and over again.

Suzanne, of course, played up her most fortunate position. She was reveling in the fact that it was she in these photos with Ryan and not me. In between shots, a team of makeup artists tended to her and made her smoky eyes even more alluring.

I was able to take a few relaxing breaths when Ryan posed alone. He looked uncomfortable from time to time, cracking jokes and occasionally making funny faces to help pass the time.

I remembered the last time I had my picture taken professionally; it was when I graduated from Brown. It was one of those memories that I tried to suppress in the darkest corners of my brain.

I winced, recalling that fateful day when I was waiting for my mother to come home from grocery shopping so we could go pick up my pictures from the photographer. That was the day she died. If only I had gone shopping with her instead of giving her a hard time, I could have prevented it.

"Are you okay?" Ryan asked during a break.

"Yeah." I nodded. "Just deep in thought."

"David wants an answer." He looked unsure.

"What are you going to tell him?"

"What should I tell him?" he countered.

"It's your decision, honey. I'll support any choice you make."

He gave me a disgusted look. "I want your opinion."

I took a deep breath. "Ryan, all of your idols have done a wide variety of films. Some were memorable, some were a paycheck, and some were a disaster. But you said it yourself . . . it's those decisions that could make or break a career.

"You have three projects coming up, all films destined to be box office hits, but they could be your stepping stones to even greater things. You know as well as I do that *you* are in a unique position to really direct your career. But you choose. Don't let them choose for you.

"You're signed on for *Thousand Miles,* with *Slipknot* scheduled right after that. Then you have the press tour, junkets, and premieres for *Reparation* in the beginning of April and *Seaside Two* in July. Rehearsals for the third *Seaside* start in September. You have nothing on the docket after that, and if Universal is willing to wait . . ."

Ryan nodded.

"But Ryan, it's not just a matter of schedule and whether you're available or not. Is *Sacred Mountain* the type of film you want to be associated with? My opinion is that it doesn't have a story line that will make you shine and stand out as a powerful leading man. I mean, would Leonardo DiCaprio do it?"

Ryan shook his head quickly. "I don't think so."

"Well then? You and UFOs will make money. You and UFOs will not garner awards or make you a well-respected, well-rounded actor. Dreams only come true if you point yourself in their direction."

I watched his expression change when he comprehended.

I was surprised that his manager and his agent were pushing the sci-fi movie on him. Ryan had never taken a role like that before, and although I could see the importance of showing his acting range by portraying different characters, the lead in *Sacred Mountain* seemed to be a huge deviation from what he had been doing.

While we dressed in our evening wear for the wrap party, I couldn't help but bring the subject up again. Ryan was very open to discussing the pros and cons of the role. I wanted to make sure that the decision he made was well thought out and that my influence didn't hinder him from accepting a worthwhile role.

"Wait to be escorted," Marla informed Ryan when we pulled up to the grand hotel where the *Seaside* wrap party would be taking place. Her authoritative tone snapped me out of my private thoughts.

"I know," Ryan mumbled, clearly knowing what was expected of him.

Marla edged her body closer to Ryan so she would be able to exit the car right behind him. Ryan's door opened and several formidable security men surrounded him immediately. Four men quickly escorted him across the street where the paparazzi and hundreds of fans were waiting.

The camera lights and photo flashes lit up the nighttime sky. I sat there completely helpless, watching Ryan become blinded as the volume of excited screams became deafening.

I slid across the leather seat to exit the car at the curb, but Marla was blocking my way. Once Ryan was safely across the street, I was allowed to get out of the car. "This way, miss," some man in a suit ordered.

I was removed from the car and was allowed to watch the mayhem unfold across the street from a discreet spot near the hotel entrance. People were screaming and shouting at Ryan for his autograph and for pictures. "Ryan, Ryan, over here, Ryan!" Hundreds of cameras flashed like strobe lights in his eyes while he willingly subjected himself to the call of fame. He signed autograph after autograph and posed with every person who had a camera.

Marla and David, his "handlers," hovered dutifully behind Ryan while he played his part. I wanted so badly to run across the street and drag him away from all of that insanity. He was a person, but he was being treated like public property. Everyone wanted a piece of him and I doubted there were enough pieces of him left to go around.

After almost ten minutes, Ryan was finally escorted back across the street by his security team. He was immediately ushered to a carpeted area where the press was waiting.

Ryan wasn't alone on the carpet; several of his cast mates were also giving interviews. Ben and Cal both tapped him in the arm when he passed by. I stood off to the side while Ryan posed and spoke to reporters; he appeared to be in his uncomfortable business mode again. I didn't know whether to be proud or concerned for him.

"You look gorgeous," Kelly whispered in my ear. I turned around to see her standing behind me.

"Oh, Kelly!" I hugged her, relieved that I wasn't standing alone anymore. "You look fabulous, too."

Suzanne's limo pulled up to the curb and she was immediately escorted to the carpet where Ryan and the guys were standing. She didn't hesitate stepping over to Ryan's side.

"I'll see you inside." Kelly patted my arm as Cal whisked her away. I watched as they posed as a couple for the paparazzi.

I stood there by myself again, placed off to the side and out of the way by one of Ryan's handlers. They had me hiding inconspicuously next to some topiary in the dark, where I could feel like an idiot privately in my three-thousand-dollar outfit. I definitely felt out of place.

"Good evening, Taryn," David greeted me in the shadows.

I was momentarily stunned by his sudden friendliness. He'd been a lot more standoffish toward me yesterday. His wandering eyes glanced over my body and his creepy demeanor sent a twinge of revulsion through me.

"Good evening, David," I said politely, even though his eyes were stuck at viewing my cleavage.

"So . . . *you're* the one giving Ryan bad career advice," he surmised, laughing every so slightly. "I was wondering who was filling his head with nonsense. Now I know."

I glared at him; his moment of niceties was blatantly over.

"Well, we obviously have a difference of opinion on what's considered bad career advice, David."

"You could say that again," he said arrogantly. "And you certainly are imposing your opinions freely on him."

Great, another confrontation. Apparently he was still bitter that I'd infringed on his territory.

"He and I talked about the scripts, that's all. Ryan is a grown man. *He* makes his own career decisions," I retorted. I was watching Ryan from a distance while he spoke to a reporter.

"He used to make his own decisions, but that doesn't seem to be the case lately," David stated curtly. "Oh, by the way, that was a real risky move you made at dinner the other night—speaking to Follweiler like that. Perhaps you should consider leaving the career management activities to those of us whose job it is to do so. Okay, sweetheart? Your job is to just look pretty on his arm."

What nerve this jerk had! I didn't know whether I wanted to slap him in the face or knee him in the crotch. Instead, words flew out of my mouth.

"You know, David, you are so far away from having a clue that I'm surprised there's even air for you to breathe there. You did nothing to prep Ryan for that meeting and then you left him hanging out to dry when Jonathan asked him about seeing his film. The way I see it, I kept that meeting going and saved Ryan from being embarrassed and humiliated. So instead of bashing me, perhaps you should consider thanking me."

I caught movement out of the corner of my eye. Ryan was walking toward us.

"We can go in now, honey. I'm done out here." Ryan took me by the waist.

"David, I've made my final decision. No aliens," Ryan said firmly. "I've read both scripts and I agree with Taryn. She's got great instincts, and she feels *Isletin* is going to be a hit and a high point in my career. I agree with her. You're *my* manager. I want you to push Aaron for it."

"Ryan! There's no money there," David objected. "You're making a huge mistake."

"Then that's my problem. By next fall I'll have over fifty million in the bank. Maybe I'll get involved in producing the film, or I can retire and grow grapes, but it will be my decision. Please, just do what I ask."

"Ryan!" David tried to stop him. "You're going to take advice from your bartender girlfriend?"

Ryan turned and glared at him. "Just do what I ask, David, or I'll find someone else who will."

CHAPTER 28

Holidays

"IT'S SO GOOD to be home," Ryan sighed, dropping his duffle bag and suitcase on the floor. He flopped backward onto our bed and smiled.

"Mmm," he moaned, shoving his nose into his pillow. I crawled on all fours to join him, glowing in the fact that he felt my apartment was his home, too. It was certainly a home with him in it.

"I know we just got off of two planes, but what are we doing for Christmas? Do you want to fly out to Pittsburgh and see your mom and dad or not?" I wanted him to make a final decision so I could make travel arrangements. Christmas was just five days away.

Ryan groaned loudly. "As much as I love my mom and dad, I don't want to fly anywhere. I only have two weeks off."

"Well, you could always put your family on a plane and have them come out here," I suggested.

He wrinkled his nose. "No. We have to go or I'll never hear the end of it. You know what I really want to do for Christmas?" He wrapped me in his arms, pulling me close. "I want to go cut down a big evergreen and have my first real Christmas tree. My parents put up the same fake tree every year. I've never had a real tree, even when I lived on my own."

I smiled and softly kissed his lips. Being normal sounded wonderful.

The next morning, we borrowed Pete's pickup truck to go get a tree.

"Here are the directions Pete wrote down." Ryan handed me a piece of paper. "After I get on the highway, where do I go from there?"

I flipped the paper around, noting that we'd just passed a place that had cut trees for sale. But Ryan wanted the experience of cutting his own Christmas tree down.

"Go five more traffic lights and then turn left. We need to get lights and a tree stand, too. There's a store there."

Ryan put the truck into park and I saw the panic start to well up on his face. "I can't go in there," he whispered.

"Sure you can," I softly replied. "It's a small mom-and-pop hardware shop. See? They have Christmas lights and stuff."

He shook his head, indicating that he was staying put.

"It will be okay. Not everyone on the planet knows who you are." I tried to ease his worry. "Besides, you haven't shaved in a couple of days . . . it's almost like a disguise. If anything happens, we'll run for it. I promise." I held out my hand.

Hardly anyone was in the store except for two older gentlemen who worked there and a nice older lady who wrapped each of the glass ornaments I picked out. The gentleman with the dark gray hair spent over ten minutes telling us which tree stand would be better for a live tree and how Ryan should brace it so the tree doesn't fall over. The man had no idea who Ryan was; in his book we were just ordinary customers.

Ryan was grinning from ear to ear when we walked back to the truck with our bags. He was able to go into a store like a regular person and buy lights for his Christmas tree without anyone taking his picture or asking for an autograph. I was glad; such a simple task that people take for granted every day brought such joy to him.

The best part was wandering around a huge tree farm looking for our perfect first tree.

He spent a few extra minutes shaking the loose pine needles off our beautiful tree out in the alley before dragging it up our steps.

"This is wonderful," he announced, glancing up and down the alleyway. "Look, honey! No paparazzi!"

Ryan bolted the tree in place by the front window. He stood there with a big grin on his face, marveling at his handiwork. I had the stereo on in the background, playing all the traditional Christmas songs to set the mood while we decorated our first tree . . . together.

ON CHRISTMAS EVE, we went to Pete and Tammy's house for dinner. It was so nice to see Ryan relaxed and happy. When we returned to the apartment later that night, I realized that both of our blood pressures were normal for once. No one had chased us down the sidewalk taking our picture while asking us ridiculous questions or pestered him for his autograph.

"Do you want to open your gifts now, or wait until the morning?" Ryan asked, tossing my car keys onto the kitchen table. The glint of hopefulness was evident in his eyes.

"You can open two presents," I told him, knowing that he would be completely distracted by the first gift I planned to have him open. "The rest have to wait until the morning." I picked a specific box off his pile of gifts and handed it to him.

"Okay, then you get to open two." He crawled around the side of the tree and picked up one of the smaller boxes he had wrapped. "You first."

Inside the box was an exquisite silver bracelet with a Celtic knot design woven around several brilliant garnets. Ryan had done the majority of his Christmas shopping when he was in Scotland. Everything that he bought on his trip or ordered over the Internet was shipped to Mitchell's Pub.

"Ryan, this is beautiful! Thank you so much!" I put the bracelet on and then leaned in to give him a kiss.

He tore the paper off his package. His eyes opened wide when his fingers lifted the silk stockings from the box.

"I hope these are intended for you to wear." He smirked. "I don't think this sheer item is my size." He gingerly picked the rest of the outfit from the tissue paper and held it up. "You are definitely trying to kill me." He laughed. "Do I dare ask when you plan on, um, wearing this?"

"Now," I answered nonchalantly. "That's the second gift you get to rip open tonight."

I relieved him of the box and softly bit his earlobe. "I'll meet you under the tree in a few minutes."

The living room was dark, all except for the soft white lights that sparkled between the branches of our Christmas tree. Ryan was lying on his side on the quilt he laid on the floor, stripped down to his black boxer briefs. I had a bottle of champagne and two glasses in my hands as I made my approach.

He sat up immediately when I came into view. I did a slow turn to show him the full picture.

"Oh wow, thank you, Santa," he breathed out.

By the time he was done unwrapping me, my outfit lay in shreds.

It was in the wee hours of the morning when Ryan chuckled lightly in my ear. The sound of his laughter instantly woke me up. I was unsure if he was still sleeping or if he was waiting for me to awaken.

The moisture in his mouth made some popping noises and then it sounded like he moaned. Not a painful moan—this sound was one of pleasure. I wondered what he was dreaming about.

The sky outside was just starting to change with the light of the rising sun. I looked at the alarm clock; it was almost seven—way too early to be up.

His arm jerked suddenly; his hand cupped my bare breast and he moaned again.

Is he sleeping? As if on cue, he started to softly snore. He was dreaming and squeezing my breast in his sleep!

I rolled in his arms to face him. Ryan woke with a start, looking at me through his cracked eyelids. He groaned and rolled over onto his back.

"Sorry, babe," he mumbled, pulling the sheets up on our bodies.

I nestled my cheek on his chest, receiving a warm, welcoming arm to hold me there. In an instant, he was asleep again. I, however, was wide-awake and wondering about his dream.

I kissed his bare chest; my mischievous tongue took the liberty to taste him. I slid my open hand down his side, stopping in the muscular dent on his hip. His eyes were still closed, but his lips turned up into a smile. A soft purr slipped from his throat.

My hand found a new destination and with a few strokes, he and I were on the same page. I was hungry, hungry with desire to pleasure him; determined to make his dreams come true. With a faint giggle, I disappeared under the bedsheet. My lips found him in the dark; satisfaction washed over me when I heard the air stutter down his throat. His long fingers tangled in my hair.

It didn't take long for the comforter and sheet to land on the floor after being pushed out of the way. We rolled and twisted together as one; our bodies twined into a myriad of different positions. Our lovemaking under the tree last night was full of passion, although my outfit definitely brought out a different side of him. He was more forceful, aggressive, slightly overexcited.

This encounter in the dim light of dawn was the opposite—it was the total experience of getting to the destination rather than hurrying to the destination itself.

His powerful hands pressed into my skin; his strong arms wrapped around my body as he made love to me. We were free to enjoy each other, silently reading subtle movements, tender kisses, and playful bites.

My body tingled from his expert touch; the pleasure he unleashed on me rippled through my core.

His thrusts became quicker, more powerful, as he heightened my orgasm further. I knew he was climaxing; I could feel his release inside me. His clenched fingers left impressions in my hips and he groaned from the gratification of his discharge.

He held me in his warm embrace. "I love you—with all of my heart," Ryan whispered passionately, gazing at me while sweeping my hair back from my face.

I slipped my hand into his hair, pulling him in for another kiss. "I love you, too, more than anything in this world," I said softly, getting lost in the depths of his sparkling blue eyes.

RYAN CARRIED his cup of coffee out to the living room and sat with his legs crossed on the floor by the tree. He was so eager to open Christmas gifts, the anticipation was getting to him.

"I hope you model those later." He raised his eyebrows devilishly. I tore open the small box that contained a few pairs of red plaid undies.

"Only if you promise to model these." I tossed a wrapped package in his direction, knowing that they contained several pairs of new boxers.

"I think that can be arranged." He winked at me.

He opened up the computer software I got for his laptop next. "What's this?" he asked, reading the front of the box.

"It's for writing and recording your own music. Open that one." I pointed to another package.

"You plug the microphone into the USB port and you can play your guitar and record it. I was sort of hoping you'd finish our song that we started up at the cabin."

He grinned.

"Something for you to mess with while you have a few minutes of downtime?" I suggested.

I opened the thin, flimsy package he handed to me next. Inside were brochures and worn pictures cut from magazines. I looked at him, completely puzzled.

"I've been saving those pictures for a long time now," he told me. "Those are all the places in the world that I want to see. I thought maybe you could pick one and we could take a nice vacation."

I flipped through pictures of the Great Wall of China, the Eiffel Tower, and several other well-known wonders of the world, only to stop at a picture where the water was a beautiful shade of teal blue and the sky was a deep azure. I didn't need to go farther than that. I showed him the photo.

"Bora Bora." He beamed happily. "Is that where you want to go?"

I nodded and grinned widely, imagining the two of us on the beach in the picture.

"Done. Tahiti, here we come," he announced joyfully. "I was actually hoping you'd pick that one. We can stay in one of those huts that are out over the water." He tore open the wrapping on a new bottle of his favorite cologne.

I opened up the box that was shipped from California. Inside was a chocolate-brown Dior leather handbag. I smirked at Ryan.

"Kelly said you really liked it, so . . ." He shrugged.

We were surrounded by shreds of Christmas wrapping paper, like two little children on Christmas morning. Ryan had plenty of new toys, video games, and software to keep him occupied.

"Last two." He grinned as he trotted back to the living room from the bedroom. The two gifts he had in his hand were not under the tree. He handed me another flat package and a small box. I felt the adrenaline when it released into my bloodstream.

"I'm really surprised you didn't ask any questions when I took your car the other day." His eyes narrowed on me. "Most women would have nagged until they got an acceptable answer, but then again, you're not like most women, are you?"

"You told me you had some business to take care of. I just assumed you were going shopping."

"I did have business to take care of and I guess you could consider that shopping." He nodded at the items in my hand. "Open the flat one first."

I peeled the tape back on the paper, taking my time to breathe. My heart was pounding for some reason. He placed his hand on mine to stop me for a moment.

"This is a gift for *both* of us," he informed specifically, waiting for my confirmation. Once I acknowledged his message, he withdrew his hand so I could continue.

I looked at the words printed on the paper, only to flash my eyes quickly back on him.

"Ryan, what . . . ?" I tried to absorb what I was looking at.

"That's the property deed to the twelve acres of land right next to your grandfather's cabin. It's officially ours."

"How? When?" I was so shocked I couldn't form a complete sentence. "Twelve?"

"I have people," he said comically. "Besides, you're not the only one in this house that is sneaky. I can plot behind your back too, you know."

I smirked at him. "What? Did you buy the whole lake?"

"No." He laughed. "Just most of the east side of it. I tried to buy the whole thing." He shrugged innocently. "I'm currently in negotiations to buy the five acres next to ours down by your dad's lucky fishing spot. We'll see if the owners sell or not. If they do, we'll own half of the property that surrounds the east side of the lake."

"Well, I guess it's a good thing that I got you that 3-D architect software. At least I know you'll have the motivation to use it now. No wonder you laughed when you opened it." I nudged him.

I still had the other little package resting in my hand. Inside the red and green Santa paper was a box . . . a ring box.

My eyes shot up to look at him; he was smiling at me.

I looked down at the box, almost petrified to open it. Hundreds of thoughts ran through my mind all at once.

"Open it," he encouraged.

It was hard to swallow. *Is he doing this now? Is now the moment that he's going to ask me? Holy shit. Before I open this box, what am I going to say? Am I going to say yes to his question? Yes! Of course I'm going to say yes! Why wouldn't I? Look at him—so adorable, smiling at me like that. So caring and thoughtful. You have no idea how much I love you, Ryan Christensen. Yes! My answer is yes!*

I carefully opened the lid to the white box. The hinge was quite stiff; I had to use extra force to separate it. My eyes adjusted as I took in the sight of the ring nestled inside.

A slight gasp of air stuttered down my throat as my thoughts readjusted to a new response.

Inside was a beautiful silver ring with a huge oval garnet surrounded by an intricate Celtic knot on each side of the setting.

"It's beautiful!" I sighed. "Thank you!" It matched the Celtic bracelet he'd given me last night and the earrings and necklace I unwrapped this morning.

Ryan took the ring out of the box and held my right hand. "It's sterling. I had it inscribed. It says 'My heart is yours.'"

After he showed me the inscription, he slid the ring onto my right-hand ring finger. It fit perfectly. My hand shook slightly.

"I said that the property is for *our* future, and I mean that. Even if it's just to put a vacation home there. No decisions have to be made now. And when we're both ready, I intend to put a few rings on this hand." Ryan raised my fingers to his mouth and softly kissed my left hand.

IN A blur, the ten days Ryan had off had dwindled down to three. We spent two days in Pittsburgh with his family and almost an entire day was spent just flying back and forth. It was slightly easier to move through the airports if people didn't expect him to be there, but we were still stopped by a few fans that spotted him.

All I knew was that the precious moments I had with Ryan were quickly ticking away.

New Year's Eve had arrived and my pub was packed. A few die-hard fans traveled to the little town of Seaport after it was published in the media that Ryan was spending the holidays in his secret love nest in Rhode Island.

Ryan had hired Mike to be his personal guard full-time, and I felt better knowing that Mike was in the bar with Ryan for our evening celebration. Cory's friend Trevor was tending the door and my friends were providing an extra buffer around Ryan, just in case.

The band onstage was jamming and Marie, Cory, and I were hustling behind the bar. I looked over at Ryan and smiled. He was sitting in his spot at the bar wearing my Mitchell's Pub cap; Mike sat on one side, Pete on the other, and Gary was sitting next to Pete. The guys were drinking and talking and just having a great time.

I was so happy to see Ryan relaxed, and I grinned whenever he laughed hysterically at their conversations. I was grateful to the crowd, too; for the most part his fans just admired him from afar. A few women managed to sneak in to talk to him, but he didn't seem to mind the conversation. The minute a fan stepped up to him, the other three guys intervened. Needless to say, no woman was able to hang around Ryan for very long.

I had just grabbed two bottles of beer out of the cooler, only to look up and see Kyle standing on the other side of the bar. I gasped, slightly startled that he was here.

"Can I get one of those, miss?" he asked, nodding at the bottles in my hand.

"Sure, I'll be right with you," I unconsciously responded with a smile, tending to my current customer. I looked over at Ryan knowing he was going to be pissed that Kyle was here. Ryan was laughing heartily until he noticed my expression. His unspoken words of concern instantly turned to anger when he eyed Kyle at the opposite end of the bar. Ryan stiffened in his chair and stared Kyle down.

I slid a bottle over to Kyle, who had wedged his body conveniently between two ladies to get to the bar.

"I see pretty-boy is happy to see me," Kyle sneered, taking a long swig of his beer.

"Don't start, Kyle," I warned and hurried out from behind the bar.

"Come here, please." I dragged him by the sleeve of his leather jacket to speak to him privately. "I want to know, right now, if you have any weapons on you," I said, knowing that he had a permit to carry concealed firearms.

He took another swig of his beer and patted the space under his right arm. "I never leave home without it!" he stated proudly.

"And you felt the need to bring that into my pub for what reason?" I asked directly.

"Never know when I'm going to need it," he reasoned. "I'm not breaking any laws. Besides, by the looks of it, there are enough of his fans in here—any one of them could be a psychotic stalker," he said eerily.

"Hey, Kyle. How's it going?" Mike greeted him with a pat on the shoulder, expressing more concern than friendliness.

"Just enjoying a beer on New Year's Eve, Mike. And you?"

"Making sure things stay peaceful and calm around here." Mike patted him again, gripping Kyle's collarbone in his hand so he would get the hint.

"Mike, I was just going to ask Kyle if he would mind taking his firearm back out to his car. I would feel a lot better if I knew there weren't any guns in my pub tonight."

Kyle finished his beer in one big gulp and set the empty bottle down forcefully on a table filled with patrons. "I'll remove mine if you remove yours," he arrogantly challenged Mike.

"I'm pretty sure you don't want things to go down this way tonight, Kyle. Taryn asked you to leave your piece outside. It's a simple request."

"Fine, I'll leave," Kyle said. "Don't want to upset pretty-boy tonight."

"Kyle, I didn't say you had to leave. I just don't want you armed while you're drinking in my pub, that's all."

"Come on . . . let's take this outside," Mike calmly suggested, loosely gripping Kyle's arm.

"Get your fucking hand off of me," Kyle responded angrily, shoving Mike's hand away.

Ryan was at my side in an instant, taking the shortcut behind the bar to reach me.

"What's up, Kyle?" he asked coldly. He stepped in front of me, protectively pushing me back with his arm.

"Do we have a problem here?" Pete muscled his way in through the crowd. Gary was right behind him. Cory raced out from behind the bar to back up Ryan.

Kyle smirked, almost analyzing whether he'd be quick enough to take down all five men on his own. Part of my brain considered that he probably could, and I didn't like those odds.

"Listen! Everyone just calm down," I ordered, elbowing my way back in between Ryan and Kyle. "Kyle, you are more than welcome to stay, enjoy the band, and have a good time—just like everyone else. I just don't want people who are *not* working for me to be carrying weapons inside my bar. Go out to your car, lock up whatever toys you have on you, and come back inside. Okay?" I wanted to defuse the situation as quickly as possible.

"Okay," Kyle conceded, drawing in a breath through his nose. "Taryn, come for a walk with me—please?"

"Oh hell no!" Ryan snapped, blocking me with his arm again.

Kyle scoffed at Ryan's reaction. "Is your name Taryn?" he jeered.

"You're not going anywhere with my girlfriend," Ryan snarled.

"And why is that, Ryan? Are you afraid that I'm going to tell her? Afraid she might find out that she *wasn't* the first girl you nailed in this town?" Kyle said mockingly.

"You don't know shit!" Ryan raised his angry voice.

"Oh, I don't? So I guess you never told her about the little hottie you've been screwing on your movie set?"

"You need to shut the fuck up before I shut you up," Ryan threatened, stepping even closer to Kyle. Mike put his hand on Ryan's chest, giving him a heedful warning.

"So are you going to deny it now? Go ahead. Lie to her some more, *Ryan,*" Kyle taunted.

I looked up at Ryan, begging for an explanation. His face was turning red, coated with anger.

"Are you cheating on me?" The question flew from my brain and right out my mouth.

"No! Absolutely not! Never!" Ryan looked me directly in the eyes and squared his shoulders. "What he's referring to happened before I met you."

"So it happened?" I squeaked.

"Yeah, so what?" he muttered. "What happened before you and I got together is in the past, but since our friend here has an agenda, I guess my past actions need to be explained. For the record, *Kyle,* I slept with one girl one time and that was *before* I even met Taryn, so you might want to get your facts straight."

Ryan quickly turned his attention back to me, locking his eyes on mine. "I've never been unfaithful to you—*never.*" His words were urgent, direct.

I inched around Ryan's side. "Kyle, why are you doing this?" I demanded.

"You deserve better," he said emphatically, almost pleading with me. "Better than the lies he offers."

"What the hell is your problem? You think by coming in here and making a scene it's going to make me want to choose you instead of him? Like maybe if you get him out of the picture you'd have a snowball's chance in hell with me?"

"Huh. You believe him?" Kyle countered.

Memories of every beautiful moment I had spent with Ryan flashed in fast-forward through my mind. We'd been through too much for me to doubt him. "Yes. Yes, I do."

"Man, you *are* a good actor. He'll do it again, Taryn. They all do," Kyle yelled over the music. His attempt to convince me to agree with him goaded Ryan even further.

Ryan had reached his limit. That last comment made him snap. He raised his hands, lunging for Kyle's throat. Pete and Mike instantly intervened, quickly blocking Ryan from making contact.

"Kyle, you need to leave—now!" I scowled at him. "Get out of my bar."

"Don't you *ever* come near her again. You got me?" Ryan flipped out in a fit of rage. Pete grabbed hold of Ryan's arm; Mike was gripping the front of his shirt.

Kyle just stood there, appearing unaffected, hoping that he'd get a chance to take Ryan down.

"I said get out!" I stepped in between them, staring straight at Kyle.

I'd had enough. My customers were watching the action unfold, waiting to see if Ryan Christensen, the famous actor, was going to get into a fistfight. I turned and walked away, completely disgusted, and headed for my stairwell.

Ryan was at a run when he hit the first three steps to our apartment. He stopped abruptly when he saw me sitting on the top landing. He leaned up against the wall and let out a big sigh.

He tried to maintain his temper as his words came out through his clenched teeth. "I'm going to ask, and I want the truth. Did anything . . . *ever* . . . happen between you and that asshole?"

I scoffed, shocked that he would even question my fidelity. But then again, I really wasn't surprised. Ryan and I both had trust issues.

"No. Nothing . . . never." I stared directly into his eyes.

"Not even a kiss?" he growled.

"*Never*," I whispered adamantly. "I hugged him goodbye once when he dropped me off from the airport at Thanksgiving, and I told you about that." I put my head in my hand. "I suppose even that was a mistake," I mumbled.

Ryan finished the climb up the steps and sat down next to me on the landing. We sat there in silence, both trying to calm down.

"I think it's safe to say that neither one of us was a virgin when we met," Ryan muttered. "I've never asked you about the guys that you were with before me, because hearing about it would just make me crazy. And you've never asked, so I figure the same goes for you. What difference does it make who we slept with before? We both have pasts."

I nodded in agreement, knowing he was right.

Ryan drew in a deep breath. "The first week I was here I hooked up with one of the PAs," he admitted. "I messed around with her a couple of t—"

"Ryan, stop," I interrupted, trying not to visualize this new girl as being the lucky recipient of the missing condom.

He looked at me, confused by my order.

"Don't lie to me," I whispered.

"I'm not," he confirmed.

"You told Kyle one girl, one time. You just slipped and said a couple. What's the truth?" I breathed in desperation.

"Can't you see he's trying to rip us apart?" he said, almost pleading with me.

"He and a million other folks," I corrected.

"Tar, I don't have to explain myself to Kyle, but I am being truthful with you. So I had sex with some girl—twice—before I even knew you," he stressed. "It was nothing. It meant nothing. And I ended it. I swear to God, from the moment I met you, I have not touched, been with, or even looked at another woman. Suzanne doesn't count." He laughed lightly, then collected himself. "I've been completely faithful to you."

I stared at my feet, trying to keep hold of my emotions.

"When we were out on the lake, you said it had been months since . . . I just assumed that meant sex," I confessed.

Ryan exhaled loudly.

"Taryn, when we were out on the lake, I was already falling madly in love with you. And I didn't lie; it had been months since I had a girlfriend." He collected my hand in his. "When I got to town here, I was . . . lonely. I took advantage of an opportunity," he admitted.

I thought about why lovers lie to each other—feelings and egos are such fragile things.

"Do you have any more secrets, or is this the last of them?" I asked.

Ryan thought for a moment. "I lost my virginity to Kelsey Bowman when I was sixteen," he confessed.

I smiled and nudged him in the leg.

"Do you want to know how it happened?"

I laughed uncomfortably. "No!"

"What about you? Are you keeping any secrets from me?" he asked cautiously.

I looked him directly in his eyes. "No."

He twisted my garnet ring to align it on my finger. "Do you remember what I told you Christmas morning when I put this ring on your finger? Honey, there is no one else. There hasn't been anyone else. I'm in love with you, Tar."

As I watched the last minute of the year count down, I resolved that his past and mine needed to stay there . . . in the past.

Ryan grabbed the belt loop on my jeans and pulled me off to the privacy of the dark kitchen. His arm wrapped around my waist; together we were ushering in a new year, a new chapter to our lives.

"Ten, nine, eight . . ." he counted backward on my lips. I couldn't help but be giddy at our closeness; my arms wrapped around his neck tighter, holding him fast to my body.

"Happy New Year, honey," he whispered, his warm mouth kissing me passionately.

The bar was completely crowded, but at that moment in the darkness we were the only two people on the planet.

OUR DAYS together turned to just hours and then to mere minutes; Ryan was leaving for Florida to start filming his next movie.

"Call me once you get settled in," I requested, trying to keep my extreme sadness at his departure under control. I turned my car ignition off.

His gentle hand rubbed my cheek. "I will. Don't be sad. I'll see you in three weeks, I promise." Ryan looked over his shoulder nervously, expecting that at any moment photographers could rush up to my car.

"Three weeks." I nodded. "I think I can make it."

"You could always quit your night job and come stay with me," he teased.

"I'm working on it."

"I know. I'll see you on the twenty-second. Keep your calendar open," he reminded me.

Mike was already standing behind my car with their luggage, waiting patiently.

"You'd better go. Kiss me already."

"I love you," he whispered.

"I love you more."

"Doubt that." He leaned and kissed me again.

"Oh, I forgot to tell you," he said quickly; one of his long legs was already out of my car. "There's a crew coming tomorrow morning to start demolition on the pub kitchen."

"What?" I asked, slightly louder than I had intended. "Wait, we only just got the estimate."

"I know. I hired them."

Ryan hopped out of the car before I had a chance to argue. "So if you want to yell at me, you'll have to call me later and do it over the phone."

"Ryan!" I whined.

"Sorry, I can't hear you," he mouthed on the other side of the closed passenger door. He looked at me intently through the glass window, grinning.

I read his lips when he silently said, "I love you," placing his palm on the window to say goodbye.

I smirked and watched his sexy butt dash off toward the terminal.

CHAPTER 29

Options

WOW, THEY'RE REALLY making progress," Pete commented, assessing day four of the kitchen remodel. "It's going to be beautiful once it's finished."

I nodded, watching the crew install the new stainless-steel ovens.

"So I take it you've forgiven him?" he asked, slightly distracted by watching the installers struggle with the appliances.

I suppose my reactions and behaviors were completely predictable.

"I was never mad at him, Pete. And now that this kitchen is finally getting done, I'm actually quite relieved. I guess I'll have to just get used to his generosity."

"Now, there's a good idea." Pete staggered slightly, giving me a teasing bump. "You know most decent men have it ingrained in them to take care of their family. He just wants to be the provider, that's all."

I sighed heavily as Pete's words sunk in. "I know."

"You know he's going to marry you, especially now since you're the proud parents of twin kitchen sinks." He winked.

"Yeah, right." I elbowed him in the arm for teasing me. "Are you taking bets?"

"Yep. How about a grand?" he suggested, pretending to reach for his wallet.

"Pass. Just keep your money. I may need to borrow some to pay him back for all of this."

"Oh she of little faith," Pete said, patting my head.

"Well, if you're done being overly presumptuous, I'm going to get the mail."

I was still laughing as I picked up the pile that lay inside the front door. Ryan's fan mail volume never ceased; it had actually increased since his fans had obtained a physical mailing address for the object of their affection.

Fortunately, the Seaport Post Office kept a running pile and delivered the trays of fan mail only twice a week. I laughed to myself when I weeded through the pile and still found a few that snuck through.

I used my finger to open up a plain white envelope addressed to Taryn Mitchell.

I gasped in horror as my eyes read the frightening message written on a simple, white piece of paper:

RYAN IS MINE
STAY AWAY FROM HIM OR DIE
BITCH

My throat tightened and I felt faint. Basic internal instincts made me want to run screaming. The nightmares were starting all over again.

"Why are you so jumpy?" Marie asked at the start of her shift. She was filling the cooler with bottled beer and every time she clanked the bottles together, I unconsciously flinched.

I took the letter out of my back pocket.

"Taryn, this is no joke! Did you call the cops?"

I folded it back up and shoved it deep in my pocket. "No, I didn't. What are the cops going to do? Besides, my fingerprints are all over it now."

She grabbed my forearm. "Does Ryan know?"

"No. I just got it in the mail today. I haven't talked to him today yet."

"He's going to flip. You are going to tell him, right?"

I looked away, feeling pressured. I hadn't intended to say anything to him. He already had enough to worry about.

"You can't keep something like this from him, Taryn."

Quite a few reasons not to tell him slipped into my mind. For one, Ryan was back in the gossip news. His rehearsals with Lauren happened to be photographed and candid shots were conveniently leaked to the masses.

Embarrassing stories were breaking over every media outlet that Ryan had rekindled his previous relationship with Lauren. New pictures of them hugging and being close were mingled in with old pictures from last year. The media was dusting off old photos and selling them as recent evidence.

To the untrained eye, one might not know the difference. To someone like me, who had spent countless hours researching the man I was sleeping with, I knew what was old and what was new.

Some of the magazines even reprinted comments he made years ago, putting them into new content to make it look like they had obtained the latest news directly from the source.

My mind was wandering when I turned the pub TV to watch *Celebrity Tonight*. Ryan's alleged affair in Florida was top-story news.

Marie marched over to me and snatched the remote out of my hand. "It's all crap and you know it," she said forcefully, changing the channel before I had a say in the matter.

Over the next few days, my mail was pleasantly devoid of horrid letters. I had hoped that the original letter was a one-time occurrence, but I worried nonetheless.

Unfortunately, Thursday afternoon, a new threat letter arrived in the mail. This one stated:

I'm going to cut you into pieces
Ryan is mine
End it now

The sound of car keys being dropped on the bar made me flinch again; my nerves were wound tight.

"Sorry, didn't mean to startle you," Kyle said. "Hi." He smiled innocently. "Is it all right if I have a beer? I promise I'll behave. See?" He opened up his coat to show me that he wasn't wearing a gun this evening.

I found myself getting lost in his mesmerizing smile and the comforting feeling of protection that swirled around him. For how spooked I was, I sort of wished he *were* packing a concealed weapon. I rolled my eyes at him and smiled slightly in return. Why did he have to be so damn gorgeous?

I twisted the cap off a bottle of beer and set it in front of him, slipping his money off the bar right after that. I wasn't about to give him free drinks, not after the scene he made here last time.

A few customers were playing pool and getting loud and rowdy. Someone dropped a pool stick on the floor; the sharp crack made me jump again.

"You seem on edge," Kyle muttered. "Is it because I'm here? If you don't want me here, I'll just have this one and then I'll leave."

"No, it's all right," I replied. "You can stay. Just as long as you don't start anything."

"Is he here? I guess I should apologize."

His comment caught me by surprise. *He wants to say he's sorry to Ryan?*

"No, he's not," I answered, disappointed that I had to say that out loud.

"Off filming again?" Kyle asked.

I glared at him, guessing that he already knew Ryan was in Florida. It was his job to know other people's whereabouts, and I knew Kyle was more resourceful than that.

Mike was guarding Ryan full time now, but he still worked for the same company as Kyle. I was pretty sure it was known who was guarding whom.

"Listen, I know I was an asshole the last time I was here and I just want to say I'm sorry," Kyle said sheepishly. "I really hope you can forgive me. It was wrong of me to act like that."

He was quite adorable when he groveled.

"It's okay. Just be cool about things, all right?" I tossed an empty beer bottle in the trash, wondering why I had a hard time holding a grudge.

"Okay. I promise," he swore, like a child being scolded.

We had another thick crowd for a weeknight and I was glad to be distracted from dwelling on the spooky threat letters. Even though I was trying not to keep tabs on him, I still glanced around the crowd to see where Kyle was.

"He's playing pool," Marie muttered on her way past me. "And he's watching you like a hawk."

I groaned, although in some bizarre way I actually felt relieved that he was on guard, ready to strike if I was in danger.

I was clearing off a table when Kyle approached to say good night.

"So is it okay if I stop in from time to time? I'm actually working not too far from here. If it's not cool, just say so. I don't want to cause any problems for you."

Kyle looked so humble, like he was really, truly remorseful. He finished his beer and put his black leather jacket on.

"As long as you don't specifically come here to cause problems for me," I warned, hoping he'd get the hint.

"You got it. Best behavior from now on," he vowed. "I swear."

He followed me back to the bar. "Before I go, I just want to make sure you're okay." He glanced around, determining how many people were within earshot before continuing. "You seemed really nervous before. Are you sure things are fine? Any of his fans giving you problems? I know you don't have a bodyguard assigned."

I thought about the new letter that was in my pocket and how terrified I was when I read it. I feigned a smile and lied.

"I'm okay, I swear," I answered immediately. I knew if I told Kyle about the letters, he'd insist on protecting me. That would never fly with Ryan.

"So his fans have been leaving you alone?" he questioned again.

"Yeah," I confirmed, hoping to cast off his concern.

"Hmm, that's good then." He nodded oddly, appearing distracted by a group of people carrying on by the poolroom. "Well, since everything is fine, I'm going to take off. Have a good night." He squeezed my shoulder lightly on his way to the door.

I MADE Marie go to the grocery store with me Friday afternoon; I was a little afraid to go out on my own. I was growing increasingly paranoid, and leaving the building was becoming more and more frightening.

"So, did you tell him?" Marie asked, buckling her seat belt.

"Tell him what?"

"About the letters? And about Kyle being in the pub last night," she reminded me.

I stared blankly out the windshield.

"Taryn!"

"Don't start. If I tell Ryan that Kyle was in the pub he's going to flip out, and I don't need him flipping out on me."

"You know he always finds out somehow. You'll just piss him off that much quicker if you don't tell him right away."

I huffed. I hated that she was right. Ryan was ridiculously jealous of Kyle.

"I'm trying to keep Ryan from getting hurt, Marie," I justified. "Kyle is a black belt. He's a walking lethal weapon. I'm surprised Ryan even attempted to fight him New Year's Eve."

"Men are so stupid." She laughed. "Testosterone and beer . . . makes them feel tough."

Horrible visions of Ryan fighting with Kyle just like he fought with that stunt actor on the set of *Seaside* flashed through my mind. I'd already seen Ryan made up to *look* like he was in a fistfight and I shuddered to think of the bloodied mess Kyle would turn him into if the two of them ever went at it for real. I had no doubt that Ryan could hold his own in a fight, but Kyle was trained in self-defense. Despite Ryan's best efforts, he didn't stand a chance to win that battle. I had to keep those two apart at all costs.

Unfortunately, Kyle was the least of my worries. Staring me in the face in the checkout aisle was a new glossy picture of my boyfriend gazing lovingly at his supposed rekindled love, Lauren Delaney.

The headline, in big, bold letters, announced to the world that the two were:

TOGETHER AGAIN!
Lauren admits, "I never stopped loving Ryan"

Those words embossed themselves onto my every thought. When Thomas cheated on me I'd at least had the luxury of being blissfully ignorant of it, but I felt even more demeaned to hear about it with Ryan *and* allow the lies to continue.

"HE'S BACK," Marie sang her words when Kyle walked through the front door of the pub Friday night. I was surprised that Pete let him in.

I watched as Kyle slipped through the crowd on his way to the bar.

"Hey, how are you?" He smiled and nodded at me, taking the last seat left at the crowded bar.

"I'm great," I lied. Deep down I was wondering if I'd made a mistake by telling him it was okay for him to come around. Kyle was safety and danger all coiled into one.

"Two days in a row," Marie muttered. She, too, was watching me out of the corner of her eye.

The cute brunette sitting next to Kyle tried to strike up a conversation but he effortlessly blew her off.

"Marie, you have to work his end of the bar. I can't be near him." I shook my head. "I don't even want to talk to him. Cory, go that way." We all shifted.

"Did you use your phone today?" Marie questioned, giving me a stern look.

I frowned and slid a Captain and Coke to the girl waiting at the bar. I still hadn't told Ryan about Kyle showing up.

"So what's it like?" the girl asked as she handed me a five-dollar bill to pay for her drink.

"What's what like?" I asked, having no idea what she was referring to.

"Being with him. Ryan Christensen?" She giggled. Her girlfriend looked just as eager to hear my answer.

I pressed my lips tightly together, holding back the desire to tell her off. Her intrusive question and the complete disregard for our privacy instantly irritated me.

"Hey . . ." Marie waved to the girl to come closer. "Did you ever dream about being with Ryan Christensen?"

"Hell yeah! All the time," the girl gushed.

"Just keep dreaming, then," Marie snapped back.

"Taryn, can I talk to you a sec?" Cory motioned. I followed him into the kitchen, grateful for the distraction.

"Hey, so what's up with that Kyle guy? Is he supposed to be here?" he asked.

"No, not really," I groaned, still completely irritated by the encounter with the female customer. "I don't know why he keeps coming around, either."

Even though I said it, I knew why Kyle was here. I pondered for a moment how different my life would be right now if I had met Kyle first. Would some random girl be asking me what it was like to be with my boyfriend if it was Kyle in Ryan's place?

That first day I met Ryan and he asked me if I was dating someone, what would have happened if I had said "yes, I am" like I always did when any other man asked me that same question? That probably would have been the last time I ever saw Ryan Christensen.

"Does Ryan know?"

"Know what?" I asked, distracted by my thoughts.

"About Kyle being here?" he reiterated.

"Oh, no. Not yet. But I'm going to tell him."

"Well, there are enough guys around here. We can toss him out if you want." Cory seemed to enjoy that idea a little too much. "I'd offer, but I don't think I could take him on my own."

I turned quickly when Pete came through the kitchen door.

"Taryn, I didn't know what to do about that asshole Kyle," he groaned. "I gave him shit about coming here but he said he'd be cool. Do you want him in here or not, because you know Ryan won't like this!"

Ryan certainly had enough watchdogs looking after me. I rested my hands on my hips, unsure of what to do about it. I didn't want any of my friends to get hurt or worse; I didn't do a weapons check tonight.

"I know Ryan will be angry; I haven't told him yet that Kyle has been here. I'd appreciate it if you didn't say anything to Ryan. Please let me tell him," I urged.

Pete shot me an angry look.

"Pete, I don't know what I can do about it. I own a public bar. I'm not going to call the police or anything like that. Besides, Kyle isn't causing any problems—probably because he knows Ryan isn't in town."

Pete became irritated. "I thought you made it perfectly clear to this joker the last time that he wasn't welcome around here, and yet he keeps showing up. Doesn't the guy know when to quit?"

"Apparently not," I muttered. "It's getting a little obsessive, actually. I mean, he knows I'm with Ryan. I don't know why he keeps coming around. Does he think I'm going to change my mind?"

I wondered for a minute why Kyle was still pursuing me. Why wasn't I a lost cause in his book?

"Maybe he's hoping," Cory replied.

"Well, you already have one PFA out on a wacko. You could always get one on him," Pete suggested.

I thought about how much of a hassle it was to get a protection order and the irony of having to get one against a bodyguard whose job it was to protect people.

"Just leave him go," I muttered. "I don't want a scene in my pub tonight. If he shows up again, I'll tell him to stop." Even though I'd said it out loud, I knew I would have a difficult time saying that to Kyle's face.

"Okay." Pete nodded. "Your bar, your decision. But say the word and we'll introduce him to the sidewalk."

IT WAS late Sunday afternoon when Ryan called. It was also time to tell him about Kyle, so I braced for an argument. Ryan was due to fly home in five days and I was hoping that the battle brewing between the two men could be avoided.

"Kyle has been showing up at the bar," I said. "I've been trying to ignore him, but . . ."

Ryan, of course, went ballistic. "Why the hell didn't you tell him to get lost, or do you like him coming around for you?" he yelled.

"No, I don't like him coming around. But I also own a pub; it's kind of hard to keep the public out," I snapped back. "Honey, I got a threatening letter in the mail slot the other day. I've been a little scared."

"I'm getting you a new bodyguard immediately."

"Ryan," I groaned.

"And I'm taking care of this Kyle bullshit once and for all," he said angrily.

Despite Ryan's attempts at warding off Kyle, two days later he showed up at the bar.

"My company wants to send me to Dallas," Kyle said somberly. "Some British diplomat needs coverage."

I tried to look surprised, even though I had expected something like this to happen soon. I studied the way his lips curled when he looked at me and I couldn't help but feel guilty for being the secret cause of his latest assignment.

"Great, at least you'll be a lot warmer there than here," I attempted to joke. "It was only thirty-six degrees out today."

He shrugged that off. "I'm turning it down."

"You can't do that. *Can* you do that?" Inside I started to panic, envisioning him staying in town and showing up to start something with Ryan again.

"I told you I wouldn't take any out-of-town assignments, Taryn," he reassured me. "I'm staying here to make sure you're safe and protected."

I gasped. His original charming personality was now turning scary. "There's no one after me. You need to take the assignment." I faked a smile and looked at him like he was being ridiculous.

"So you mean to tell me out of all those crazy fans of his there isn't one still scaring or threatening to hurt you? You don't need to lie to me, Taryn. I can tell by the way you've been so jumpy lately that something is going on."

My pulse quickened and I froze in place. I was starting to think that the only person I needed to be protected from was Kyle.

"Kyle, Ryan has hired another bodyguard for me. It's not your job to worry about me."

Kyle scowled at me. "I don't know why you felt the need to do that." I swallowed hard and chose my words, almost begging him to understand.

"Kyle, I'm not your concern. I'm not yours to protect. I know you know that." I hoped he could see the sincerity in my eyes.

Kyle's demeanor frightened me; it was obvious he was hurt and bordering on anger.

"I have a detective reviewing any letters I get that threaten me," I lied. "The detective thinks that the latest letters I've received are coming from someone who lives here, not someone who has traveled here."

Kyle shifted his weight on his bar stool.

"He also thinks that the sender is male," I continued, embellishing my lie and going with my hunch. "It's amazing how they can figure things out like that."

Kyle took a sip of his beer and set it on the bar. He looked away, then glowered at me. "Why didn't you tell me you were getting letters?"

"Kyle? Whatever it is that you're doing, please . . . please stop. It's not healthy for either one of us."

His lips twitched and he looked astonished. "Are you accusing me of something? You have something to say, just say it."

I tried to come up with an appropriate defense but I was powerless under his glare.

"Is this what you really think of me?" he asked warily. "Do you honestly think that I would do something like that? That I would be capable of hurting you?"

"Kyle, I don't know what you're capable of. You know I've committed my heart to another man, yet here you sit." If Kyle was going to be angry with anyone, I wanted it to be me.

"Taryn, I care about you. That's why I'm here. And it kills me to see someone as wonderful and beautiful as you are wasting your love on someone like Ryan." He gritted his teeth.

"You said to me once that I put myself between people who need protection and those who mean to do them harm." He looked me right in the eyes. "At least I don't make out with all sorts of women for a living. And one day when that man that you love so much has a slip of judgment and takes his acting too far with some other woman, who's the one who will live with regret? He'll only be sorry for a minute. You, on the other hand, will be shattered."

I looked away. His words stung like a thousand needles.

"I keep hoping, Taryn. Hoping that your eyes will open up and you'll see the heartache before it hits. Once he breaks you, it will take a strong man to put you back together. You deserve a better future than that."

My thoughts traveled a new course, back to the safe, familiar road that didn't lead to heartache. Maybe I'd be better off alone again?

"I'm here because actions speak louder than words," he said, suddenly looking hopeful.

His statements stoked up the fires under my deepest fears. As much as I wanted to cling to the thought of Ryan's undivided love, part of me still faltered.

"Can't you see he's trying to rip us apart?" Ryan's voice echoed through my heart, shouting at me not to listen to Kyle.

"I love you. Never doubt that," my love reminded me; the memory of his lips brushing mine when he spoke those words made my mouth tingle.

"Kyle . . ." I shook my head. "This . . . this has to stop. Please. I think it's time for you to leave."

He huffed, shocked by my reply. With one long gulp, he finished his beer and set the empty bottle down on the bar.

"Fine. I'll see you later," he muttered. Kyle gathered his keys and slipped his jacket on.

"No, you won't," I said as I stepped closer to him.

"Tell Ryan he will have to try harder if he wants me out of the picture," he muttered over his shoulder.

"Kyle, don't force my hand," I whispered. "Let go and walk away, with dignity."

"Is that what *you* really want?" he asked, his tone sharp but at the same time, pained.

"Yes," I stated without hesitation, although it pained me to say it. "Goodbye, Kyle."

I watched as Kyle stormed out of the pub. He never looked back.

"Everything all right?" Marie asked. She had been watching the entire conversation from the opposite end of the bar.

I nodded, hating myself for hurting him.

"Is he planning on coming back?"

"I don't know. I hope not. My nerves are so shot," I muttered. "I didn't even get my period this week from all of this stress."

I thought about Ryan's attempt to get Kyle assigned elsewhere and how that hadn't seemed to work. I reached in my pocket for my phone; Ryan needed to be informed before he flew home. I would never put him in harm's way.

CHAPTER 30

Rumors

RYAN STILL HAD his jacket on when he snuck into the pub through the kitchen door. He was supposed to call when he was on his way from the airport, but instead of a phone call, he'd decided to surprise me. He came right behind the bar and tossed me over his shoulder, carrying me off quickly into the kitchen.

He set me down to rest on one of the new stainless-steel counters and I wrapped my legs around his waist.

"Oh God, I missed you," he said while kissing me.

I giggled lightly. "I missed you, too."

He let me go long enough to hastily pull his jacket off.

"What do you think . . . of the kitchen?" I managed to mumble. His tongue was quite a distraction.

"Uh-huh," he muttered, kissing me harder. The kitchen was dark and his eyes were closed. "Looks . . . great." His mouth locked tightly on mine.

"It's good to be home," he finally sighed, giving us both a moment to breathe again.

It didn't take us long to grab his bags and make our way upstairs to the apartment.

"It's been a long day," Ryan said, yawning. "I haven't been sleeping well at all," he murmured on my neck. He pulled me tighter to his body and adjusted his head on his pillow. "I've discovered that I can't sleep without you in my arms. I've been forced to hug a pillow every night," he said sadly. "It's just not the same."

"I know what you mean," I whispered. "This bed is cold and empty without you in it."

He kissed me softly.

"Oh sweetheart, I know it's tough to be apart, but you know it's not permanent. I'm going to try and come home as much as I can . . . it's going to be hard, though, because we have a really tight shooting schedule. If you come down for a few days and I come home for a few days it won't be so bad. The next couple of weeks will fly by."

I sighed. Our relationship was like one giant hurdle after another, where crossing off each day on the calendar was the goal.

"What's wrong?" he asked, kissing my nose.

I shrugged, not sure of how to answer him.

"Tar, honey?" he whispered. "What's on your mind?"

"We're going to be like two ships passing in the night," I said, knowing we would be apart more than together.

"Hey . . ." Ryan propped his body up on his elbow. "Don't worry. I know this year will be rough, but everything is going to work out."

"I just don't want our *life* to fly by," I whispered.

"Some days it will, and some days it won't. We have to be thankful for what we have. Just think how all those families have to cope when one of their loved ones goes overseas for military duty. At least we get to see each other often and we can talk on the phone every day."

Ryan crawled onto me, playfully biting me on the neck.

"You worry too much. Besides, I have it all figured out," he murmured devilishly on my skin.

"Oh, you do, do you?" I snickered. I rubbed my hands over his shoulders and down his back to massage his muscles.

"Mmm-hmm," he murmured, kissing my cheek. "We're going to take it one day at a time—together."

I WAS still kissing him when I blinked. Our thirty-six hours together flew by and was quickly coming to an end. Ryan had a Sunday-night flight back to Miami.

"Hey, Mike." I hugged Ryan's faithful bodyguard when he came to pick Ryan up for their trip to the airport. "You taking good care of my man down there?" I asked.

"You know me, Taryn. I carry a big stick," Mike joked.

"Good. Keep all of those fans off of him." I laughed.

"Fourteen days," Ryan whispered in my ear. "Bring your swimsuit, 'cause I'm sneaking you off to the Keys for a day."

I grinned at him. "I can't wait. You have everything you need?"

"Yeah, I have enough clean clothes now to last me awhile. Kiss me, we've got to go." Ryan nuzzled me.

"Mike, don't forget Ryan's guitar." I picked up the case. "Do you want me to carry it out to the car?"

"No. Just stay inside, Taryn. The paparazzi are out there," Mike groaned.

"I love you, babe." Ryan kissed me. "I'll call you tonight when I get to the hotel."

The second the back door opened, cameras started to click. I saw Ryan quickly jump into the black sedan before our new steel door closed behind him.

THE BEGINNING of February brought bitter cold and a fine layer of snow and ice to Rhode Island. It also froze in place a few other annoyances—several paparazzi still lingered behind.

I was cleaning up the bar Tuesday night when Cory pounded on the front door. I had closed early on account of the bad weather. Alcohol and freezing rain never mixed well.

"Taryn, my car won't start." Cory breathed on his hands to warm them up. "Oh, and do you have any rock salt for the sidewalk? It's really icy out there."

I put my heavy coat and gloves on and grabbed the bag of rock salt from the office.

"Whoa!" I shouted as I slipped on the ice outside my door. Cory caught me before I hit the ground.

"Careful," he reminded me.

"Damn. It's like an ice rink out here." I stuck a plastic cup inside the bag and tossed salt all over my portion of the sidewalk.

"Told you," Cory teased. "You think you can give me a ride home?"

"Cory, I can't drive in this. It's too dangerous." I could barely stand without slipping. "Why don't you just crash here tonight," I suggested. "You can stay in the guest room."

"Hey, if you don't mind. Classes are going to be cancelled tomorrow anyway," he said, sprinkling more salt near the curb. "I wonder if Mario's Pizza is still open?"

I tried to walk back to the bag of salt to refill my cup but I couldn't get a footing on the patch of ice I was standing on.

"Help!" I whimpered. "I'm stuck here. I can't move."

Cory laughed at me. "What? Can't you ice skate?"

"Not in duck boots." I laughed.

"Here. Take my hand. I'll pull you to safety." He slid me across the ice. I laughed out loud because it was actually a lot of fun. "You need to buy boots with traction. Those things have no bite."

I started slipping again, so I grabbed his arm.

"Come on . . . I'll tow you over to the door before you fall and break an ass cheek out here."

"Very funny. Can you even break an ass cheek?" I asked.

"You want to find out?"

"No! Just help me to the door before I do, though."

Cory grabbed the shovel. "Even if you could drive me home, I'm picturing you stranded out here on the sidewalk all night. You'll be a frozen Popsicle by morning."

"Shut it or no slumber party tonight. I *was* going to make popcorn."

"This is going to be so much fun!" Cory used a feminine voice. "We can stay up all night and paint our nails and talk about boys."

The next morning the sun was bright and warm, melting some of the ice.

"Careful, Taryn," Cory warned. "It's still icy in some spots." He held out his hand to me.

We made it twenty feet down the sidewalk before three paparazzi descended on us.

"Who's the new guy, Taryn?" one pesky photographer asked. "Is this your new boyfriend?"

"No, absolutely not," I answered directly. My reply to that asinine question was now captured digitally.

"Why the hell do they keep taking our picture?" Cory muttered under his breath. We were tucked beneath the hood of my car trying to jump-start his truck with my Infiniti.

"They're taking *my* picture," I quietly informed him.

"Go sit inside your car," he groaned softly, trying to be stealthy with his comment. "This is ridiculous. Does Ryan go through this all the time?"

"Yeah." I nodded.

"Poor guy," Cory whispered. "This shit would drive me nuts."

"Okay, guys." I held up my hand to tell the photographers that I'd had enough. "Friend . . . ice storm . . . dead battery . . . you get the point, right?"

I saw the old Italian photographer shuffling along the sidewalk, trying to catch up to the other vultures.

"Jimmy Pop, be careful! It's really icy there. If you fall, you're really going to hurt yourself," I warned.

"You need help, Miss Taryn?" Jimmy asked me. His camera was slung over his shoulder instead of taking my photo. He was sincerely concerned.

"No thank you, Jimmy. Cory's battery is dead. I think we have it under control."

"Okay. How's Mister Ryan?" Jimmy's wrinkled face curled with his question.

"He's good, Jimmy." I smiled. "He is nice and warm in Florida. How are you?"

"Oh, my hands hurt," he moaned. "I guess you can't tell me when Mister Ryan is coming back? This cold . . ." Jimmy shivered and tossed his lit cigarette into the street.

"Jimmy," I whined lightly, "you know I can't say."

"I know." He came closer to me. His eyes scanned back and forth to see who could be listening.

"Be careful when you're outside," he whispered, cautioning me with his eyes. "You know what I tell you?"

"Yes, Jimmy." I nodded.

"Then go back inside, quickly, Miss Taryn."

"Okay, I will. If you ever want to warm up, you're always welcome inside my pub," I whispered back to him.

"Bless you, dear. Now go, quickly," Jimmy sighed.

Four days after Ryan flew back to Florida, it was reported in the tabloids that Ryan had ended our relationship and moved out. Pictures of Ryan looking annoyed and sad, getting into the black sedan while Mike packed the trunk with his belongings, were published.

The reason Ryan supposedly ended our relationship was captured in pictures as well: the unfaithful Taryn Mitchell—holding hands and frolicking in the snow with the cute bartender who works for her.

I was glad that I'd told Ryan about Cory staying over on the same night that it happened so he knew exactly why there were photographs of Cory and me together. It still didn't prevent the lies from being written:

Love on the Rocks

Ryan's rep may be denying the breakup, but there was no denying what we saw going on at the heartthrob's secret Seaport, Rhode Island hideaway over the weekend.

Ryan Christensen and his bodyguard were seen leaving at 7PM on Sunday, stepping out with several pieces of luggage and personal items. They then headed directly to the airport, where Ryan quickly departed back to Miami. "Ryan didn't stay long after personally collecting his things."

So does this confirm the breakup? Sure seems that way, since Ryan has been seen secretly hooking up with his newly single co-star, Lauren Delaney, in Miami. Looks like Ryan and Lauren's relationship is back on.

"Guess we won't see Ryan Christensen here in Seaport anymore. He broke up with her," the unfamiliar female customer sitting at the bar whispered to her friend, nodded in my direction.

I tapped a pitcher of beer for another customer, trying to ignore their conversation, but it was difficult.

"How could she be so stupid? I mean if she let that slip through her fingers, then she doesn't deserve him," the other girl whispered back.

I'd finally had enough. "Excuse me? We didn't break up. When are you people going to realize that those tabloids publish nothing but lies?"

"Tar, leave it go," Marie quickly interrupted my rant.

"No! I'm sick of this! I'm sick of people whispering about me in my own bar." I looked directly at the two girls who'd started my tirade.

"My boyfriend, who I am still with, is filming in Florida. He is working fourteen-hour days, seven days a week without a break, to make a movie for all of you ungrateful people to enjoy." I raised my voice. "And this is the thanks he gets?"

"Tar," Marie grabbed my arm, "you don't owe anyone an explanation about your personal life." Marie said that loud enough for most to hear.

"Where are *your* boyfriends, huh?" I asked the two girls. "Did you have sex with them last night? Do you have pictures? Come on—tell me . . . I have a right to know. It's only fair. You know my life; I want to know yours. If you're going to be out in public, then your life is no longer private either."

"Sorry, we didn't mean to upset you," one girl apologized.

"Ryan and I are people, just like you," I retorted. "Just because he makes a living as a working actor does not mean he gave up having a private life. You're entitled to privacy—so are we."

Between the false accusations, Kyle's irrational behavior, the lurking paparazzi, and being separated from Ryan, I was just about ready to go out of my mind. I couldn't wait to get on that plane and head to Florida for some fun in the sun with my love.

ONLY EIGHT more hours and two flights to endure before I finally got to see him. I pulled my white cotton shirt over my head and debated over what coat to wear. It was a balmy twenty-seven degrees outside my window, but it would be in the seventies when I landed in Miami. I put a thin top over my T-shirt, deciding it would be best to dress in layers.

I stopped to make sure the back door was locked before I rolled my suitcase down the alley. Of course when I stepped outside, Jimmy Pop and two other photographers were staked out, waiting to catch me doing something wrong. That was all I needed—one more photograph to set the gossip magazines ablaze with their lies.

If these magazines only knew how many lives they almost tear apart with their fabricated stories and false accusations. What a pathetic way to make a buck! I hated all of them and everyone who worked for them.

"You have a nice, safe trip, Miss Taryn," Jimmy Pop wished me well.

"Thank you, Jimmy," I said, giving him a brief smile for his kindness. He had his camera pointing down; he was the only photographer to leave me a moment of peace. Since I was leaving, the three photographers departed in the opposite direction. They had no reason to hang around my door any longer.

I rolled my suitcase down the slushy asphalt, pausing at the mouth of the alley where the snowplow had made mounds of dirty, watery snow. I wanted to keep my suitcase clean and dry, and this small trek down the alley was not helping. I took my time walking the last few feet that would put me in the street; the cold February air had caused some of the melting snow to refreeze, and I didn't want to have my picture taken slipping on the ice and falling down.

I lifted my suitcase over a small pile of snow and glanced up and down Mulberry Street for traffic.

Terror—absolute terror—blazed through me from the sight that my eyes took in. I froze in place, stifling the urge to scream.

Adrenaline coursed through my veins when I saw her, Angelica, sitting in her old, blue Plymouth Gran Fury not more than sixty feet from where I stood. The fear she incited slid through me like a hot knife in warm butter; she was out of prison and waiting for me.

Our eyes made contact; I could feel her hatred for me blast through the air and strike me where I stood, gluing my feet to the ground. This would be her moment, the time that she'd been waiting for, to finally take me out of the picture.

I saw her hand reach up and pull the gear shift down to put her car in drive. So much for slicing me into pieces. The thick steel bumper and crushing weight of her old car would flatten me like a steamroller. She pulled the old Plymouth away from the curb; her car slowly rolled to the stop sign.

My mind did the quick mental calculation to determine whether I could make it across the slushy, icy street dragging my suitcase before she could run me down. I was not safe on the sidewalk, either, and I was too far away from my back door to run; besides, I had a plane to catch. I had no choice; my car across the street in the lot would be my only sanctuary.

My eyes were locked on hers as I stepped out into the street; I wouldn't give her the satisfaction of looking away if she was going to run me down. I would not go out being a coward.

I was almost halfway across the street, but she hadn't moved an inch. *Why isn't she speeding at me?* I expected her to mash her foot down on the gas pedal and careen her car in my direction.

I allowed my eyes one brief glance at the opposing sidewalk when I noticed the silver streak in front of my eyes. If she didn't move, why did I hear tires screeching?

The searing pain in my stomach was what I felt first, pain like I had never felt before in my life. The battering ram that struck me instantly knocked the air out of my lungs. My fingers peeled away from the handle of my suitcase without any conscious effort on my part. I felt my chin smack down with force on a cold, flat surface. The contact made my cheek smear on the blur of shimmery silver.

Just like the time when I had watched Ryan film his fight sequence, I had the sensation of ropes pulling me sideways, followed by the feeling of flying. *Why am I rolling?*

The pain returned; a new pain this time cracked into my left hand and shot all the way up my arm, followed by a smack in the head. Instantly I was cold and wet, watching my life pass before my eyes.

The last thing I remember was hearing the jingling sound of my collection of keys when they landed on the ground.

Then . . . everything went black.

CHAPTER 31

Broadsided

I HEARD THE DARK shadow whisper "she's not breathing" before his lips pressed into mine. The shadow's warm breath was stale and lifeless, and tasted like a mixture of blood and cigarettes. I felt the shadow's strength when he touched my face, pinching my nose with force.

Ow, that hurts! Be gentle!

The wind that he blew into my chest burned my lungs like fire.

"Oh my God! Oh my God!" a female voice cried out. Her halo glowed like a sparkling rainbow around her head. "I tried to stop!" she sobbed.

Don't worry, heavenly angel. It's okay! I tried to say, but no words came from my mouth. I wanted to calm her, stop her from crying. *Why can't I speak to her?*

"Miss Taryn!" the male voice cried, blowing another gust of searing wind into my chest. His third gust filled my soul; I felt my breast rise to the sky toward the light. The wind scorched me from inside and I squeezed my eyes tight from the pain.

Everything was dark again; my body craved new air. My mouth and eyes flew open when my lungs pulled in a sharp breath on their own. I gasped repeatedly for more air; it couldn't come into my body quick enough.

Dazed and disoriented, my eyes tried to refocus on all the faces that looked down at me. Some faces were sideways, some were upside down. How peculiar! I tried to reason with these new visions but the burn in my chest and the taste of blood in my mouth overpowered those thoughts. *Who are these people? Why am I lying in the street?*

I turned my head to see who was talking to me. It was Jimmy Pop; he was kneeling next to me.

"Oh, Miss Taryn. Oi!" he cried.

"Oh, Miss Taryn! Stop taking pictures of her!" Jimmy yelled. He tried to shield my body with his own.

I wanted to get up; I didn't want to be lying in the cold snow and the street. When I tried to move, the pain blasted in my gut and radiated out toward my hips.

In the distance I could hear the screaming sound of sirens; the noise was coming toward me.

"Don't move, don't move! Stay still!" another voice shouted at me.

The shrill of sirens was more pronounced now. Their tones changed as they approached. I could see the red and blue flashing lights reflecting off the puddles on the wet street.

"Jimmy," I choked. "Jimmy." The blood in my mouth clogged my throat.

I looked at the old, Italian man kneeling next to me; his eyes were wrinkled and wet with tears.

"My purse . . ." I garbled. "Phone. Call Ryan."

"Move back, everyone move back!" I heard a man shouting. A new face appeared in my vision; this one, too, was upside down. I felt the leather of his gloves when he wrapped his fingers around the sides of my head. Even though his face was reversed, he still looked familiar.

"Don't try to move," he cautioned me. "Tell me your name."

"Taryn." I tried to swallow. The blood tasted horrible. "Taryn . . . Mitchell."

"Taryn, it's Officer Carlton. The ambulance is on its way. Are you allergic to any medicines?"

"No." I felt relief knowing I'd be rescued soon.

"Can you tell me what happened?" the officer questioned.

I could see from the corner of my eye that Jimmy Pop had my phone in his hand. He and another man were fumbling with it. If they would just hand me the phone I could call Ryan. "Give me . . ." I weakly asked, holding my arm out to them.

"Taryn! Do you remember what happened?" Officer Carlton asked again with more urgency.

"I was . . . crossing the street. She was . . . car . . . waiting." I tried to lift my left arm and point in the direction where Angelica's car was, but when I tried the pain shot down into my elbow. *My arm must be broken.*

"I didn't see." I tried to swallow. The blood was congealing in my mouth.

"Oh, Mister Ryan, Mister Ryan. It's Jimmy. Oh, come. You come quick! Miss Taryn, she's been hit by a car. Oh, oh, oh!" He started to cry.

New sirens joined in the mix of noise and confusion. They seemed to come from all directions toward me, and they had different tones.

"I'm alive," I mumbled, hoping Jimmy would tell Ryan the same. The police officer who was holding my head still kept asking me questions.

"Um, I'm on the pill . . . just birth control." I answered his question about what medicine I take. Someone covered me with a blanket.

"She's talking to the police," I heard Jimmy say in the phone. At least he knew I was alive. *Oh, Ryan,* I cried inside.

"Ambulance is here. You come now!" Jimmy ordered. "I don't know. I find out."

I was glad that the police made the crowd move away from me. There was too much going on; it was confusing.

"Tell me your name," a new voice asked. Latex-clad hands replaced the policeman's hands and I was looking at a new upside-down face. The paramedic was attending to me now.

"Taryn Mitchell." I tried to pick dried blood off my lip. It felt strange to talk; my lip seemed way too big. Swollen. My right arm moved with only the slightest bit of pain.

"I'm twenty-seven," I muttered, answering his age question.

He asked me the same questions about medicines and allergies. *Just get me off the damn cold street* is what I really wanted to say. My head was wrapped in some red rubber collar thing. It made me feel claustrophobic when they squeezed it to my cheeks. No longer could I glance at Jimmy Pop and the phone that connected me to Ryan.

I heard the ambulance driver tell Jimmy that I'd be transported to Saint Luke's Hospital, which was one town over. He conveyed the message to Ryan. I was so relieved that he knew where to find me. I'd never make it to Miami or his hotel . . . not today.

The ambulance crew rolled me to my side; I cried out in pain when they rolled me onto my arm. Slowly they rolled me onto my back and I was strapped down in place on a stiff board.

"I tried to cross the street. We have a stalker. She was waiting, in her car." I had to catch my breath. The pain in my stomach was excruciating. "I thought she was going to run me over. So I ran. I ran. I didn't see the other car. I wasn't looking." My words came easier now, even though my teeth were starting to chatter together and my lip felt twenty pounds over-inflated.

"Officer!" the paramedic shouted. I had to repeat my story.

"Angelica . . . Staunton. She's . . . stalking me and my boyfriend. She must have gotten out of jail. We have a restraining order; it's in my purse." I tried to point. It hurt to breathe. "She was waiting in her car, and she pulled away from the curb when she saw me. I thought she was going to hit me, so I ran. I didn't see." I swallowed hard. "I didn't see the other car. It was my fault."

I was glad to finally be up and off the street, even though I was lying on a stiff board. I know they tried to be careful, but I was still jostled a bit when they rolled me into the ambulance.

The cameras flashed repeatedly off the glass in the ambulance. *Great, more embarrassing publicity—just what Ryan needs!*

I felt a needle stick me in the arm, but the discomfort was minimal. Needles, tape, questions, shoes removed . . . my head swirled.

The sirens blazed to life and we were finally on our way to the hospital. *About time!*

I sighed, relieved we were moving. My eyes glanced over at the paramedic; he had menacing silver scissors in his hand. No sooner did the ambulance get going, he stuck the scissors into the pants leg of my jeans and started cutting.

"What are you doing?" I panicked as he cut my jeans, the same jeans I was wearing the first day I met Ryan.

"Stay calm, Miss Mitchell. I need to assess the level of your injuries."

I closed my eyes while he cut up the front of both legs of my jeans, all the way to my waist. Next he cut through the layers of my shirts, snipping my white lace bra open between my breasts. He cut my underwear and pushed the tattered, wet remains of my clothing out of his way, exposing my naked body. I felt like I was being raped and there was nothing I could do about it.

All my clothes were cut, one by one, piece by piece, from my body. Tears formed and dripped out of the corners of my eyes.

He started running his hands from the top of my head down every part of my body and I shivered with fear. He squeezed my arms, stopping at my left wrist when I cried out. *Damn, it's definitely rebroken.*

He was listening with his stethoscope and when he ran his hands over my ribs, the pain it generated made me moan in agony. He squeezed my legs; I was glad that it didn't cause any major pain. I could feel every touch of his warm hands. I was naked, fully exposed, and freezing.

He hooked me up to that annoying oxygen thing that fits in your nostrils. Although it was uncomfortable, it actually helped.

"I'm freezing." My teeth chattered. I was glad when he finally covered me with a nice, thick blanket.

"Unit 1784 inbound, ten to twelve minute ETA . . ."

"Is the driver okay?" I asked when he finished talking on the radio.

"Let's just worry about you right now," he flatly replied.

"What did I hit?" I murmured.

"It was an SUV, ma'am."

"I remember silver. Was it silver-colored?" My eyes squinted, trying to remember the details.

"Yes, it was." He nodded.

I sighed, relieved that I could remember.

The paramedic and his partner wheeled me through the glass doors of the emergency room, where I was immediately rolled into a curtained room. Nurses and doctors descended like flies and I was moved from the stretcher to the hospital gurney.

I spent the next five hours being poked, prodded, x-rayed, and MRI'd. I had a new IV stuck in the top of my right hand and a clip to measure something was snapped on my finger. Everything was taped securely in place. I had a rectal exam, a vaginal exam, was stuck repeatedly with needles, and they took my blood pressure with that stupid automatic machine a thousand times.

During the moments that I wasn't being poked or quizzed, I allowed myself to cry. I felt so alone; I just wanted to see Ryan. I needed him to hold me.

Eventually my left arm was wrapped in a cast, from my hand to my elbow. The doctor gave me a blue wrap because he said the color matched my eyes. I think he was just trying to calm me.

An older female orderly wheeled me back into the emergency room, returning me to the same little curtained area I was in before. A doctor and a nurse came in a few moments later; the nurse was pushing a large machine into the room with her.

"Ms. Mitchell, I'm Dr. Willsten. I'm the attending OB-GYN. We have the results of your urinalysis and you've tested positive for being pregnant. We're going to do an ultrasound of your uterus."

"What?" My thoughts spun wildly. I shook my head in disbelief. "Um, that's impossible. I can't be pregnant. I take birth control pills. You must be mistaken."

He smiled as he wrote something on a clipboard. "You know that birth control pills are not one hundred percent effective in preventing pregnancy. Have you recently taken any other types of medications? Any over-the-counter products?"

I remembered how sick I was after Thanksgiving, but that was weeks ago. "I had a bad sinus infection and bronchitis at the beginning of December. My doctor gave me antibiotics."

Dr. Willsten looked up from his paperwork and smiled at me again. "That will cancel out the effectiveness of the birth control medicine."

I heard a commotion coming from outside my room, distracting me momentarily.

"She's this way," I heard a female voice say. I pulled the cover up higher to my neck in case reporters or photographers were going to come ripping around the corner.

The weight of a thousand worries lifted off my chest when Ryan came running around the curtain. He rushed right to my side.

"Honey, are you all right?" He kissed my face, my forehead. I knew I had a busted lip. I could feel it was swollen. "Oh, honey," he cried out softly. His eyes looked me over to assess the damage.

Tears of relief streamed down my cheeks; all I could do was nod my head.

"I was just about to review the extent of her injuries with her," the man with the *Dr. Carlino* name tag announced. "Could we please get you to wait outside for a moment, sir?"

"No," I said fiercely, holding Ryan's hand with my good hand. "He stays. This is my boyfriend."

Dr. Carlino nodded. "We have reviewed all the test results and I'm happy to inform you that your injuries are minimal. Your left ulna is fractured above the wrist, but as you see, we've already addressed that with a cast. Your ribs are severely bruised, but luckily there are no fractures. You'll be quite sore for several weeks, though. The contusions on your skin will eventually fade. We will treat your injuries with pain management medications. Your lip and face are swollen from the impact, but fortunately it doesn't require stitches. And you've got a fair amount of bruising and what we call 'road rash,' but that will all heal with time. We expect you to make a full recovery." He smiled. "My colleague, Dr. Willsten, has been called in to assess the fetal risk."

I looked up at Ryan; he was trying to soak that one in.

I gasped in a few ragged breaths.

"Ryan, they just told me I'm pregnant." My voice was shaky with fear of telling him this news. "I'm sorry," I whispered. My eyes flickered back to his.

"Pregnant?" He shook his head slightly. "I thought . . ."

"The doctor said that the antibiotics I took a couple of weeks ago could have affected my birth control pill." I felt a tear leave my eye. "I'm so sorry. I didn't know."

"I'd like to do an ultrasound now," Dr. Willsten announced, rolling the cart closer to the bed.

My legs were draped in a sheet while the doctor inserted a long probe inside me. The anxiety of finding out that I was pregnant made my legs shake.

"Ow!" I winced from the pain.

"Sorry, I know it's uncomfortable." My pain didn't stop him.

The doctor was hitting a lot of buttons, taking some sort of readings. He marked an X at one end of a circle and another X on the opposite side. I was staring intently at the monitor, wondering how the hell he knew what he was looking it.

"You're about six and a half weeks along. Hmm." He looked at a little calendar and counted backward. "Christmas baby." He smiled at us. I felt Ryan squeeze my hand.

He clicked a few more buttons and we heard a strange noise over the machine's speaker. It was a fast whooshing noise.

"What is that?" Ryan asked hesitantly.

"That's the heartbeat," the doctor stated.

The machine printed out a picture, which the doctor handed to Ryan. "That's the embryo."

Ryan leaned on my pillow next to my head. A huge smile crossed his face.

"That's our baby? I'm going to be a father? Oh, Tar!" He kissed my forehead.

I was so scared to see how he would react. Nervous visions of him being angry and fleeing the emergency room were instantly replaced by calm and joy. I was so relieved that he seemed okay with the news. Our life had just made a monumental turn in a new direction.

Dr. Willsten spoke to another doctor on the other side of the curtain. I could only make out a few words, some of which were "continue to monitor" and "possible placental abruption." When he returned to speak to me, his face was stoic.

"Ms. Mitchell, we have a private room ready for you now. We're going to move you upstairs. We've noticed some abnormalities on the ultrasound. We're going to continue to monitor you overnight just to keep an eye on things. The impact from the accident was centered on your abdomen and we're concerned about your well-being. If all goes well, you should be able to go home in a day or so."

I was wheeled into a room with two beds, but they assured me that I would have the room to myself, considering our status. Random nurses kept passing by my door, all gawking in my room to get a look at Ryan.

Ryan pulled the guest chair over to the side of my bed and took my hand in his. "Honey, what happened?"

I swallowed hard, trying to remember the details of the last few hours. "I was leaving for the airport; I came down the alley. Just as I was ready to cross Mulberry, I saw Angelica sitting in her car."

"What? Are you telling me she's out of jail?" His voice bellowed his anger.

"Yeah. She was sitting in her Plymouth. I was terrified." My lips trembled. I felt like crying.

"She was on the other side of Mulberry where she always parks. Just when I got to the edge of the alley, she pulled up to the stop sign. I thought she was going to run me down." I scratched my fat lip. "I ran across the street. I was so stupid. I was watching her instead of looking where I was going."

Ryan softly kissed my cheek. "I love you so much."

"I must look horrible." I wanted him to stop staring at me for a minute. I attempted to place my new blue cast over my eyes. "Ow!" I cried out. Pain immediately shot into my shoulder when I moved my arm, forcing me to remember additional parts of the accident.

"You were hit by a car! I don't care how you look. I'm just glad you're alive."

I tried to smile. "Do I look like you did when you fought those bad guys?" I held the ice pack closer to my lip.

He smiled and nodded. "Yeah, just a little. But *your* makeup looks real." He trailed his finger over my cheek.

Of course we weren't alone for long. Two young nurses came into my room, smiling frantically at the sight of Ryan.

"Hi there! My name is Kerry," a slender brunette wearing bright purple scrubs announced. "This is Natalie. We'll be taking care of you tonight." Natalie was busy writing their names and the date on the dry-erase board on my wall.

While they tended to me, Ryan was off in the corner, making phone calls. He called his parents and spoke to his father. His parents were going to take the first available flight out.

I heard two men speaking briefly outside my door. Then a man in a suit knocked on my door and allowed himself entry.

"Ms. Mitchell, I'm Walter Krause, hospital administrator. How are you feeling?"

I was hit by a car. How do you think I'm feeling? This was just like the stupid questions that Ryan got asked every time he had to do an interview.

"I've been better," I muttered, looking at the IV that they'd inconveniently stuck in the top of my hand.

"Yes, well, I want to let you know that we will do our best to provide you with privacy while you are a patient here, but I hope you understand that we cannot guarantee policing all the corridors."

There was nothing in place to prevent any stranger from walking into the hospital and into my room.

My eyes flickered back to Ryan as he ended his call quickly.

"Mr. Krause, Ryan Christensen." Ryan held out his hand. "I have hired private security for Taryn. You'll inform *me* directly of any considerations or difficulties during her stay. I do not want you or any other member of your staff to concern her with those details. She needs to rest and heal."

"Of course, Mr. Christensen. That's why I'm here. Perhaps we can speak privately in my office."

"I trust your staff will comply with the medical privacy act?" Ryan stressed.

"Yes, of course. However, we are only governed to keeping her medical condition and records private. I will instruct the staff on proper conduct," Mr. Krause said.

"I'll be contacting my publicist to release a formal statement to the media. No other statements are to be made by any member of this hospital without consulting with me first. Is that clear?" Ryan's authoritative tone made me grin.

"Yes. I understand. Would you like to take a few moments to come to my office?"

"Thank you, but no, not at this time. Mike?" Ryan called out.

Mike, Ryan's bodyguard, came into my room.

"Mr. Krause, this is my security manager, Mike Murphy. He will be handling all security matters." The two men shook hands.

"I don't want any reporters or photographers on this floor. There will be a security team posted outside Ms. Mitchell's door at all times. We can have a discussion later or you can speak to Mr. Murphy directly for any security matters. Right now my priority is her." Ryan rubbed his hand across my head.

"Very well. We can talk later. If there's anything else you need, please don't hesitate to ask."

Mr. Krause seemed a bit perturbed with the way Ryan had just handled him. I didn't care. I loved Ryan's no-bullshit, take-charge attitude. It was one of the qualities that I loved the most about him.

Ryan barely nodded at Mr. Krause. He was stroking my hair, totally focused on me. The nurses were still waiting inside my room—for what, I didn't know.

"We're just going to check the fetal heartbeat again," one of the nurses said.

She rolled up my hospital gown and pressed the wand thing up into my bruised stomach. Soon we were able to hear the whoosh-whoosh noise of our baby's heartbeat again.

Ryan smiled gloriously and kissed my forehead.

"That's our baby in there!" he whispered his happiness privately in my ear. "I love you so much."

I was elated that he was fine with me being pregnant; he was actually beyond fine with it. I was able to relax and not worry; it made all the pain seem worthwhile. I smiled back at him with pure joy and love in my heart. He was going to be a father; I was going to be a mother. His blue-eyed baby was growing inside me.

I felt the nurse wiggle the microphone when the whooshing noise ceased; my attention immediately turned to her. The two nurses were looking at each other; neither of them looked happy. One of the nurses darted out of the room.

My smile faded and a sharp pain stabbed me in the belly button. I felt wetness gush between my legs. Pain rocketed into my chest from my bruised ribs when I tried to sit up. I panted in and out, hoping that shallow breaths would help me manage the pain.

"Something's wrong. I feel like something just popped," I breathed out at the nurse. I wanted to know what was wet between my legs. I tried to grab the top of the bedsheet so I could get my hand underneath it, but the stupid IV sticking out of my hand caught the bed rail. I felt the tube that was stuck in my vein poke me. "Ow!" I squeezed my eyes from the discomfort.

Just then another sharp pain stabbed me, this one so intense that it caused me to cry out in agony. The nurse pulled the sheet down past my feet, allowing me a split second to feel between my legs with my hand. Crimson blood was all over my fingertips.

The other nurse wheeled the large ultrasound machine back into my room.

Doctor Willsten came running. I was hooked up to a blood pressure machine in no time. As soon as the doctor saw the amount of blood, he quietly instructed the nurse to call for an O.R. suite. I was wise enough to know that meant surgery.

The doctor was performing the ultrasound of my stomach while one of the nurses monitored my blood pressure. Ryan stayed at the head of my bed; he was frozen in place. We were all listening intently to the whoosh-whoosh sound of the baby's heartbeat. Gradually it slowed in tempo until it abruptly stopped. There was nothing but silence. I felt faint.

In an instant, four people were in my room, lifting me up by the bedsheet to relocate me on a gurney. I was wheeled out of my room in a hurry.

"Where are you taking her?" Ryan cried out.

I reached my hand out to him, but a nurse was blocking Ryan from following me. The nurse stayed with him when they wheeled me out of the room.

Next thing I remember I was being rolled into a room with bright lights. People were hustling all around me. I was so confused and now sedated that I couldn't even speak if I wanted to. A nurse took each of my weak legs and propped them up in stirrups. A plastic mask was placed over my mouth and nose. In an instant, everything was black again.

MY EYES flickered when I started to wake up. It was hard to keep them open for any great length of time. Some sort of machine was beeping rhythmically in the background, lulling me back to sleep. I felt the cool rush of air streaming into my nose. *I must have that air hose prong thing stuck in my nose again.*

"Taryn. How you doing, hon?" some lady said loudly. "Can you wake up for me?"

I looked at her with one eye. *Who the hell are you and why are you shouting in my ear?*

"Hey, there. Time to wake up. We're going to take you back to your room now. You're going to be just fine." She smiled at me.

I was still groggy when they brought me back to my room. I saw Mike and another man perched on chairs outside my door. They stood up when the nurses stopped my gurney.

I could see Ryan sitting in a chair in my room; his face was in his hands until he heard the commotion in the hallway. When I saw him up close, I noticed his eyes were red and puffy. I could tell he'd been crying. Sitting across the room from him was the hospital chaplain.

The doctor explained that the impact caused my placenta to separate from my uterus and that the baby didn't make it. The doctor had to remove it all from my body, but he assured us that I'd still be able to have children.

The chaplain tried to give us words of comfort, using soft tones and encouraging us to believe in God's will. He said a prayer for the innocent life that left us today. Although I appreciated his efforts, I thanked him and asked him politely to give Ryan and me some privacy.

Ryan set his face on my chest and gently wrapped my bruised body in a hug; I draped my good arm up around him. I felt his tears as they soaked into my gown. We both sobbed uncontrollably, breaking down from the agony of our loss.

• • •

"THERE YOU go." Marie gently smiled at me as she finished wrapping a long scarf around my neck and face. "No one will see your puffy lip now."

"Are there a lot out there?" I motioned with my chin toward the window.

"A few," Ryan muttered, helping me with my coat. "Don't worry about them. They won't see you leave. Are you sure about this? I mean, I'll charter a private plane . . ."

"No, Ryan. Please? I want to go home. I just want to get out of this hospital and sleep in my own bed."

"But Marla said that . . ."

"I don't care what your publicist said," I raised my voice slightly. "I'm sorry, but I'm not going to hide somewhere. Maybe it would have been better if that damn car had killed me, or better yet, Angelica had run me over. That would be a better story for the media."

Ryan scowled at me. "Don't be so melodramatic."

"Marie, please tell the nurse I'm ready to leave and get me out of here . . . please?" I pleaded.

I was rolled via wheelchair to the loading docks where food and supplies get delivered to the hospital, all for the sake of avoiding the reporters and photographers who were hovering around the main entrance. I was so glad to slide onto the leather backseat of the sedan and finally be on my way home; it made enduring the pain of getting my bruised body in the car worth it.

A crowd of reporters, photographers, and onlookers blocked the alleyway behind my pub. Our driver had to honk his horn to get people to move out of the way. My blood was starting to boil with anger and frustration. All of this attention for what—to take more photographs of Ryan cheating on his rekindled love, Lauren, with "the nobody" from Rhode Island?

And to top off my glorious day, there was Kyle, standing dutifully by my door with other security men to hold back the throng of photographers. He took his sunglasses off and shoved them into his pocket when my car came to a stop.

Our stalker, Angelica, was still on the loose and yet there Kyle stood—willing to risk his own life to save mine.

His face was pained, and I could tell just by the way he looked at me and held his arms out to his sides that he was telling me "I told you so."

See this? All of this scrutiny . . . all of this incomprehensible, unwanted attention? More pictures to post with their web of lies? Haven't you had enough yet, Taryn?

Kyle's expression quickly changed when he glanced at Ryan. His contempt for Ryan was obvious, and the eye daggers that flew between the two men were mutual. I didn't know who hated whom more, but their hatred for each other was palpable.

"Come on, babe. I got you." Ryan held my hand and elbow, helping me out of the car. It was difficult to stand up. My knee was very bruised and stiff and the pain from my ribs shot down into my hips.

"Ow!" I winced.

"I won't let go," Ryan assured me. He helped me take a step. "Do you want me to carry you?" he whispered.

"No," I groaned and shuffled a few steps. I didn't want the photographers to capture him having to carry me and give them more reason to create new lies.

Kyle pushed past Mike and got right into Ryan's face. "Are you happy, Christensen? Now that one of your fans almost killed her?"

Mike quickly turned and intervened, blocking Kyle in the chest with his hands. "Hey, back off! Cool it, Kyle!"

"When is enough *enough*, Taryn?" Kyle cried out. Mike and another guard scuffled with him, pulling him back.

Ryan turned to deal with Kyle; the anger on Ryan's face was evident.

"Ryan?" I breathed out from the pain, diverting his attention back to me. "Just get me inside, please. Please?"

I wanted him to stay focused and ignore Kyle's accusations. Having Ryan miserable and brooding would be no help to anyone, especially me. I clutched his arm and leaned into his chest as he carefully led me to the door.

Ryan was only able to stay with me four more hours before he had to catch a flight and return to the set in Florida. He couldn't hold up production any longer; this film was a multimillion-dollar investment just to shoot. He had already been away for three days.

It felt as if another whole section of my heart were torn away when he left. It didn't matter that he called me every few hours.

Ryan's mom insisted on taking care of me for a few days, and Marie was in and out of the apartment twenty times a day as well. I was wondering when they both would get sick of watching me cry. My doctor finally prescribed antidepressants to help me cope.

Everyone in our inner circle knew that I had lost a baby. It took only three days after my discharge from the hospital for the rest of the world to be informed of the same. The media had a field day when the news broke. Speculation of my pregnancy stemmed from the fact that my room was in the neonatal wing of the hospital, but then was confirmed by some hospital informants who wished to remain anonymous. Those informants conveniently included the fact that I had lost the baby I was carrying . . . Ryan Christensen's illegitimate child.

Ryan's publicist released a statement that I was hit by a car while crossing the street and that no one was at fault for the accident. Every branch of the media also ended that same story with a blurb that Ryan's reps neither confirmed nor denied the pregnancy rumors.

Marla even made a special phone call to remind me to keep my mouth shut. Well, she didn't exactly say those words, but that was the message she delivered. I was tempted to tell her where she could shove her "public image management." My employees were also given gag orders and were reminded not to speak publicly to anyone about anything.

It was soon after that when Ryan and I had our first major fight over the phone, and his mom was sitting in the same room with me when it happened.

"What the hell did you say to Marla?" Ryan barked in my ear. "She informed me that she will no longer be speaking directly to you."

"Marla can go to Hell," I replied. "She's worthless in my book."

"Taryn, she's my publicist. I've had her for years now."

I huffed. "Ryan, she's so damn worried that I might speak to anyone about my accident yet she keeps allowing all those rumors about you having an affair with Lauren going? Oh, and what about the reports of you calling Suzanne to cry on her shoulder? I don't see her doing anything to squelch those lies either, so I let her know how I felt."

"What is she supposed to do?" he raised his voice to me again.

"She should do her damn job! She's supposed to protect your reputation, right? And now she also represents me?"

"You don't know what you're talking about. She can't stop what's printed," he snapped back.

"Like hell she can't. It took her no time at all to put out a public statement pretty much shading over the fact that I'm an imbecile who crossed a street without looking both ways, but she doesn't have anything to say about your supposed affairs? How about a big freaking public statement that says Ryan Christensen is not sleeping with Lauren Delaney *or* Suzanne Strass?"

"She won't do that," he said flatly. "And don't you dare ask her to do that, either."

"Why?" The tears from his betrayal came to my eyes.

"Because controversy is what's going to sell tickets."

I scoffed. "I can't believe this! My life, my reputation, they are all up for grabs, but Heaven forbid that we mess with ticket sales."

"Taryn, just stop."

"No! Screw that. I'm sitting here—banged up—broken—our first child is gone and I have to swallow it all because of ticket sales. You know what, Ryan? Fuck you!" I snapped my phone shut.

His mother's mouth dropped open but I didn't care anymore. He'd just informed me where I rated on his priority list.

Two minutes later he called back. I hung up on him and then turned my cell phone off. The tears were pouring out of my eyes. The pain from my ribs being bruised was no longer stifled by Percocet. I pulled a pillow over the top of my ice pack and wept uncontrollably.

"Taryn, honey." His mother tried to console me. "Don't get yourself so upset."

Her cell phone rang.

"I'm not talking to him right now," I sputtered through my tears.

"Ryan, you shouldn't get Taryn upset like this. She needs to heal." She moved her conversation to my kitchen, but I could still hear her.

"Son, she lost a baby. You need to be more understanding. She's in the living room crying her eyes out. She doesn't need this stress right now. I know, honey—you don't either."

Ellen came back into the living room and held out her phone. "He wants to talk to you."

"Tell him to ask Marla what I should say." I wiped my eyes with my shirtsleeve.

"*Taryn*." She used that stern mother tone with me. That was all I could take.

I grabbed the end of the couch with my unbroken arm and slid my body to the edge so I could stand up. "Ow!" I cried out, hunching from the pain that rocketed through my body.

"Just stay sitting," she reprimanded me.

"No, I need to stand up," I gritted through my teeth.

She tried to brace me, but there wasn't a spot on my body that wasn't bruised or busted. I managed to get my legs underneath me and I slowly straightened up. Ellen held out her phone with Ryan still holding. I took it from her hand.

"You know, when I was lying in the street, I was so relieved when the paramedics strapped me to that board and finally put me in the ambulance. It meant that I was no longer on display for the paparazzi to take my picture over and over again while I lay there bleeding. Then when the paramedic cut every piece of clothing off my body and I felt like I was being raped, I thought that *that* was the worst moment of my life.

"Then when the doctor told us that our child died inside me, I thought *that* was the worst moment of my life. But to hear that my life has to continue in a circle of lies and pain so that people go to see your movies, it just makes it all worthwhile. Thank you for that." I snapped Ellen's phone shut and handed it back to her. I locked my bedroom door behind me.

A few hours later, Ellen gently knocked on my door. "Taryn, honey? Are you hungry?"

"No, thank you." I had gone through an entire box of tissues from crying. I knew she had talked to Ryan about five times. Her phone rang every twenty minutes.

"Come on, sweetheart, you have to eat something. You haven't eaten all day."

I didn't care; I wasn't hungry, so I ignored her.

Ten minutes later there was another knock on my door. This knock was louder.

"Taryn, it's Marie. Open up."

I had to give Ryan's mom credit; she was resourceful.

"I'm okay, Marie. Just leave me alone." I didn't want to talk to anyone. I wanted to wallow in my own misery.

"Hey, Pete, it's Marie. I need you to come over to Taryn's and take her bedroom door down. She locked herself in. Just bring a drill and saw so we can cut the doorknob off. What? I should just kick it in with my foot?"

Marie smiled at me when I opened the door. She'd only pretended to call Pete. "That's what's going to happen if you ever lock yourself in here again," she threatened.

I heard Ellen talking on her phone, obviously to Ryan. She scurried for the living room when I came out of my room. She was giving Ryan a play-by-play account of my actions. He called his mom several times that night, but I refused to talk to him each time. I was so hurt that no apology could fix it.

The next afternoon, flowers showed up. Three dozen long-stemmed red roses accompanied by an "I love you—I'm so sorry" note. I left them in the box to rot. As if roses would make everything better somehow—perhaps give me a rosy outlook? Yeah, right! So much for a happy Valentine's Day. If his mother weren't here, they would have gone in the trash, but Ellen had found my crystal vase and spent a few minutes fussing with them.

"You know this is tough on him, too," she said, setting the rose arrangement on my dining table. "He is suffering along with you."

I knew she wanted me to see his side through my self-centered focus, but I was still so angry with him that I was only worried about protecting myself now. He obviously didn't care enough to protect my reputation, so I was on my own.

Ellen sprayed polish on a rag and started dusting my furniture. Something made her smile.

"Do you remember that time when Ryan called his father from here and told him that you took him fishing?" She turned to look at me.

"Yes," I said, recalling that evening quite clearly.

"He called me later that night when he got back to his hotel." She smiled. "He was so elated. He said, 'Mom, I found the woman I'm going to marry.' Of course I was thrilled for him, but as his mother I was also concerned. I mean he had only known you for a few weeks, but he was so sure right from the very start. Taryn, you know he loves you more than anything in this world, don't you?"

Her guilt trip was working. I tried to hold firm to my reasons for feeling betrayed so my position in this fight would be validated, but her one-sided conversation was pecking at my resolve. I started to feel like crap for being mad at him.

"He said last night that he feels completely responsible for the accident. After all, it was one of his demented fans that terrorized you, and you were on your way to see him when he couldn't be here."

"It's not his fault," I muttered. "He shouldn't think that."

"But he does," she assured me. "He cried so hard last night when I talked to him." Her voice trembled.

"He . . . he said he killed his baby." Her hand covered her quivering lips when she spoke the words, stifling her urge to cry. Ellen quickly dropped the dust rag and shielded her face in her hands when her tears broke.

Tears of my own cracked again and I watched her hurry away to the bathroom through my blurry eyes.

He didn't kill our baby—I did. I was the one to blame.

"Taryn, I'm so sorry," Ryan breathed in the phone when he answered my call.

I couldn't stop crying. I never knew I had so many tears to shed in one lifetime.

CHAPTER 32

Downward Spirals

I TURNED MY LAPTOP off when I'd had enough. New pictures were posted on the Internet of Ryan coming out of the back door of some exclusive club in Miami. His eyes were glazed over and he looked wasted, which angered me. Seeing gorgeous Lauren Delaney smiling in the same picture, just two steps behind Ryan, scorched my heart. Viewing the photos of Ryan guiding Lauren into the same car so they could head back to their hotel just about sent me over the edge.

He'd been partying a lot lately. Late-night cast dinners, rumors of the excessive drinking binges, private outings with Lauren, and his denials of it all over the telephone were piling up on me.

Photos from the set were leaked and posted all over the Internet as well. Clear shots of Ryan playing with Lauren's rings on her fingers, sitting so close that you couldn't slide a sheet of paper between them, made me burst into tears. It was hard to discern what interaction between them was for the film and what was . . . not.

And then there was the kissing . . .

The pictures of his lips on hers over and over again surrounded by words like "rekindled love" and "Ryan dumps Taryn Mitchell for old flame" made me deranged.

Ryan had informed me on several occasions that Lauren had a boyfriend, but every piece of photographic evidence pointed to that being complete bull. I wanted so badly to believe him. Some days I did; some days my faith wavered. It didn't help that all the tabloid websites stated that her relationship with Lucas Banks was over.

This absence from being in his presence drove the wedge deeper and deeper. Just knowing that he was spending so much intimate time with the last woman he had a relationship with before me was terrifying.

Every day he told me he loved me. Every day that we were apart seemed to last an eternity.

I had asked my doctor for a prescription refill, using the excuse that I was still in pain. Even though my body was healing, my mind was in pain. I was also starting to like the way the combination of antidepressants and narcotics made me feel numb.

Ryan seemed to be dealing with his own pain by drowning his misery in alcohol. I feared that he would slip and seek comfort in another woman's arms—someone who wasn't the source of his woes.

Ellen finally flew back to Pittsburgh. She had stayed with me for over two weeks, but she had to get back to running Bill's dental office. I was fending for myself fairly well, so there wasn't any need for her to stay. As much as I loved her, she was starting to get on my nerves.

As soon as she cleared out, Tammy moved into the guest room.

There were quite a few moments when I had the overwhelming urge to get on a plane and fly down to Florida to see just what the hell was going on down there, but I couldn't. My ribs were still bruised, my arm was in a cast, and I didn't have medical clearance to fly.

The large black-and-blue marks on my face were healing, diminished to a most unpleasant yellow tinge. My body and face had been covered quite extensively in road rash. Many spots were scraped and bruised . . . even my scalp. Those, too, were healing but the scabs that had formed itched.

And then there was the acute agoraphobia to deal with. Angelica was still on the loose, paparazzi still lurked around the corners, and I looked like shit from getting hit by a car. It certainly made hiding inside my apartment the most appealing of all options.

Through all of this, there was still one story that hurt more than any of them—and it was the biggest lie of them all. Articles were written and circulated all around the globe that said I had tried to trap Ryan Christensen by getting pregnant.

My supposed failed attempt at trapping him was reported as the reason why he went running back to Lauren's arms. It was so far from the actual truth, yet people were even talking about it on television. I was a gold-digging, small-town piece of trash who tried to use a superstar to get somewhere in life.

And here I thought I had it bad when Thomas dumped me. That was a bee sting in comparison to having the moon fall out of the sky and land conveniently on my head.

Marie and Cory were running the bar full time while I recuperated; I spent the majority of each day on the couch in a haze.

"Taryn?" Marie called out as she came through my door. She and Tammy both had their own keys to my apartment now. "Kyle is downstairs. He says he has something he wants to give you." Her expression was worried.

I thought I had seen the last of Kyle when I told him goodbye, but he still continued to drift in and out of my life. I was very apprehensive about seeing him again; part of me feared him.

Tammy led the way down the steps to make sure I wouldn't fall.

Kyle was sitting at a booth by himself; a brown bag was on the seat next to his hip. My two best friends stood behind the bar, watching his every move.

"Hi," he said curtly. "Look, I know you probably don't want to see me, but I got some things for you—it would make me feel a lot better if I knew you were safe."

I nervously sat down and rested my cast on the tabletop.

"I got you some stuff." He opened the bag. "Things you can keep in your purse or wherever, just in case."

The first thing Kyle took out of the bag was an ordinary can of wasp spray.

"This is better than mace and it sprays farther, too. Spray this in an attacker's face and they're instantly incapacitated. I only got you one can, but you should probably buy a few more."

I watched as he dug into the bag again. Kyle barely made eye contact with me.

"This is a strobe-light alarm with mace; it disorients and blinds an attacker," he muttered. "This is called a 'Screecher'—it's really loud. You can put it on your key chain or keep it in your car."

I was looking at one of the packages, wondering why I would ever need to use any of these things. I'd never needed them before; Ryan's fans had been keeping their distance.

"Just remember that you can't take any of this stuff on an airplane if you're going to fly anywhere. I was going to get you a Taser, too, but they're illegal in Rhode Island. Do you know any self-defense?" he rambled.

"Not really," I admitted.

Kyle didn't smile. "You should probably think about taking some classes when you're healed. I could show you some moves, but . . ."

He put all the items back in the bag and sighed heavily.

"Have you seen Angelica in the area?" he asked, quietly changing the subject.

"No." I shook my head. "I haven't been out of the house much. The two times I went out was to go to the doctor. Jamaal escorted me."

Kyle nodded. "Good. Mr. Jones is an excellent bodyguard and a good man."

Kyle looked nervous and depressed when he talked to me. "I've been trying to track Angelica down but she hasn't surfaced anywhere yet. I have a few people watching to see if she pops up on the map again. Just don't worry. I'll find her soon enough."

Kyle grabbed his keys from his pocket and started to slide out of the booth. "Okay, well . . . that's all. Take care of yourself."

He started to walk off but I stopped him.

"Kyle?" I called out, secretly wishing he'd stay just a bit longer.

He stopped abruptly in his tracks, but barely glanced back at me over his shoulder.

"Would you like to stay for a drink?" I asked apprehensively.

His eyes were so sad, and it pained me to know that I was the cause of his melancholy. As if I needed one more reason to be sad myself.

I grabbed the bottle of tequila.

"All you have to do is stamp on their foot real hard," Kyle chuckled, telling me about some self-defense maneuvers.

"So, in other words, hitting them over the head with this bottle wouldn't work?" I giggled. I was feeling quite tipsy from the beer, shots, and pain medicine.

"You could always use your big, blue club here," he teased, tapping his fingers on my arm cast. "Swing it hard enough and you could probably knock some teeth out with that thing."

I smirked at his joke.

"I'm not afraid. If someone wants to try and hurt me, I'm going to put up one hell of a fight. The majority of his fans are harmless, although I'm sure I'll have to deal with a lot more of them hating me over the next forty years. Oh well, whatever."

Kyle became awfully quiet.

"Hey, I remember what I wanted to ask you," I blurted out. "Where is the corner deli where you got that chicken soup?"

"Did you like it?" he asked, grinning at me.

"Oh yeah! It was delicious. You'll have to give me directions to that place."

He started to tell me what roads to take, but after the fifth turn I lost him. I was quite buzzed after that last shot.

"Can't you write it down for me? I'll never remember," I whined.

"You have a pen?" he asked.

I returned with paper and a pen and two more bottles of beer. Kyle started writing directions.

"You're a lefty, huh?" I teased, noticing he wrote with his left hand.

Kyle smiled at the paper.

"Did you know that I can write with *my* left hand?" I taunted. I pulled on the edge of the paper to mess with him while he was writing. "Yep, I'm ambidextrous. What do you think about that?" I tugged on the paper again.

He was grinning as he kept on writing. "I think we have yet another thing in common."

"No way! You are not." I took a sip of my beer, waiting for him to confirm this. He annoyingly kept silent.

As soon as Kyle finished writing, I slipped the paper out from under his hand. He tried to stop me from taking it but he wasn't quick enough.

In an instant, his whole demeanor changed. We were just having a fun time teasing each other, but now he seemed agitated.

Kyle looked at his watch and quickly downed the last of his beer. "I've got to go," he muttered and slid out of the booth.

I was completely confused by his abrupt departure.

"Well, thanks for the stuff." I patted the paper bag.

He was obviously distracted by other thoughts as he put his leather jacket on.

"I'll see you later. Get some rest," he ordered.

I watched as Kyle ran his hand through his hair on the way out the door. Marie and Tammy were staring at me, giving me the disapproving look that I'd spent too much time with Kyle.

Feeling guilty, I immediately went back upstairs and called Ryan.

"I still think you could make it," Ryan whined in my ear. "I'm sure there's an open seat on a flight."

I looked at the yellowish-brown marks that still covered my cheek through my slightly drunken eyes, thinking that no amount of makeup would ever conceal them. I was glad that we had finally moved on from the umpteenth Kyle argument.

"Ryan, I asked my doctor. He doesn't want me to fly for another two weeks. Besides, my face is still black and blue, or more like yellow and brown now. You can't be photographed with me looking like this."

"I don't care about that," he breathed. "But if the doctor is the one saying no, then I understand why you can't."

"Honey, I want to be there too, but a trip to L.A. isn't possible right now. I still have some pain in my ribs. I'm planning on watching the Oscars on television. I wouldn't miss your presentation for anything."

"I fly tomorrow, and then I have a rehearsal so I don't mess up my lines. I'm really nervous," he admitted.

"You'll do just fine. You're a pro at this." I tried to encourage him.

"This schedule is crazy. I leave out of LAX at nine the next morning. And then I'm scheduled to do some scenes later that night back in Miami," he groaned.

"No rest for the weary," I said.

"Tar, would you try to come down here in two weeks? Please? Since I can't see you this weekend, at least come down to Miami. I have something very special in mind for your birthday."

"Don't go overboard. It's just another day," I groaned. "Seeing you will be more than enough."

"Never mind what I plan," he whispered. "I'll get arrangements made for you to fly down here and I'm going to make sure you make it safely to the airport this time, so don't give me any shit about a bodyguard, okay?"

"All I need is for you to hold me," I said.

"Yeah, me too," Ryan whispered.

"Why are you talking so quietly? Is someone there with you?" I asked.

"No. Hang on," he said. "Hey, I'm gonna get going. I, um, ordered room service and they're here."

I thought I heard a woman's voice speaking in the background and what sounded like Ryan shushing her.

"Okay, well I guess I'll talk to you later then," I muttered. "I love you."

"Love you, too," he whispered quickly. The phone clicked abruptly. Ryan didn't even say goodbye.

The phone call I had with Ryan was still playing over and over again in my mind the next day. I knew he was flying to L.A. and he had a lot of things to do, but it still surprised me that he didn't try calling me. It was out of character for him.

I called him the following day, bothered that I hadn't heard from him. I tried to keep my annoyance out of my tone and kept my voice light and happy. Ryan was moody. He said it was because he was being rushed from place to place. He was also getting dressed for the Oscars.

Later that evening, I perched myself in front of the television to watch the Academy Awards. Ryan looked so handsome on the red carpet as he gave his interview. Of course, he was asked if he was there with anyone and his reply was, "No, I don't have a date!"

Date? How about your "one and only" girlfriend is still recuperating from her near-death experience? I grunted in anger. There was no private gesture to acknowledge he was thinking of me. I was still a secret he would never admit to out loud.

Several days later, we had another argument.

"Honey, why are there pictures of you hugging and holding Lauren's hand on the Internet?" I asked gently.

Ryan huffed in my ear.

"Taryn, you fucking promised me," he growled angrily.

"It's a simple question, Ryan. I don't hold Pete's hand or Gary's hand—ever. I just want to know why you felt the need to tow her along through some Oscar after-party."

"She was drunk. I didn't want her to make an ass out of herself while she was out in public," Ryan defensively answered.

Flashbacks of me asking Thomas similar questions coated my thoughts. Thomas always had a valid excuse too:

"Her car broke down and I couldn't just leave her stranded, so I gave her a ride home and then we just got to talking . . ."

"She was a girl I knew from school. She is going through some rough times right now."

"I had to do an estimate at someone's house. So what that I'm a couple hours late. Do I have to check in with you every ten minutes?"

I sighed loudly. "I thought Lauren has a boyfriend. Why wasn't he tending to her?" I asked.

"Because he's on location in New Zealand, Taryn," Ryan returned sharply. "Her *boyfriend*, Lucas Banks, is also filming." His tone made me feel like an idiot, as though I should've known that.

"I'm sorry," I apologized instinctively. My old habits of being insecure kept resurfacing. Thomas always had a knack of turning each argument around, blaming my lack of trust and neurosis for being the cause of our fights. "I just wanted to know what the circumstances were, that's all."

"You have no reason to be suspicious, Tar. It's just like the pictures of you holding onto Cory out on the icy sidewalk. I recall seeing *your* hand in *his* in those pictures. Just remember how quickly an innocent gesture gets taken out of context."

"You're right, but . . . I just don't want you to give Lauren the wrong impression either, Ryan."

"Are you going to be like this forever, Tar? Accusing me whenever I touch another human being?" Ryan snarled.

"No. But I will be like this when you're holding hands with someone you've already had sex with."

I tried to maintain my temper, and although I was unsure whether he'd had sex with Lauren when they supposedly dated, the fact that he didn't try to deny it was confirmation enough.

"And I know you well enough to know that if you saw pictures of *me* holding hands with some ex-boyfriend that I . . ." I took a breath, pausing to check the direction of my accusations. "With someone you didn't know or trust, smiling and canoodling at some over-the-top party with him, you'd flip out on me," I groaned.

"Yeah, you're right. I would," Ryan willingly admitted.

"And why would *you* have that reaction, Ryan? Would it be because *you* don't trust *me*, or because you don't want the entire world to have that impression of our relationship?"

"I trust you," he whispered.

"It's embarrassing and disheartening, seeing your boyfriend being affectionate with his ex-girlfriend off set," I said softly. "When you're filming, it's another thing . . ."

"If you would have just come out to L.A. like I asked you to we wouldn't be having this conversation. I was afraid of this . . . afraid of what the distance would truly do to us," Ryan uttered into the phone.

"Ryan, it's not the distance. I know you and Lauren hooked up last year and you dated her. She's familiar territory. I'm like this because I'm in love with you and I don't want to lose you to someone else." The thought of him slipping out of my hands and into Lauren's stabbed me in the heart.

"I figured you knew. No wonder . . ." he sighed. "I guess I messed up again. I should have told you."

"Well, put it this way: you just confirmed what I thought I knew," I whispered. "I wish you would've just been honest about what happened between you two. I'm just left here to speculate."

"What do you want to know?" he scoffed. "I'm sorry. We should've talked about this, but I didn't think it was a big deal, so either you trust me or you don't."

"Ryan, I trust you," I said, hoping he'd believe me. "But how could you think it wasn't a big deal for me when you know you're working on a romantic movie with some actress you screwed before? You never even told me about her," I reminded him.

He tried to interrupt but I spoke over him. I needed to get this all off my chest.

"You have to realize, all of these little, undisclosed secrets are what tears trust apart. Give me reasons to trust you, not reasons to distrust you, Ryan."

"Taryn, I said I'm sorry. I should've been honest about it, but I was afraid you would be angry and I didn't want to fight about it, so I didn't say anything. Now I've just made it worse."

I didn't want to push the issue any further. I hoped he got my point about honesty.

"Do you love me?" I asked.

Ryan sighed. "With all my heart."

"Then I trust you," I vowed.

"Do you really?" he questioned harshly. "Then can you explain to me why Kyle is in Miami?"

I was momentarily stunned from hearing Kyle's name come out of his mouth again.

"What do you mean Kyle is in Miami?" I retorted. "When did you see him?"

"He was on location with us this morning, Tar," Ryan growled. "Why is he here?"

"I have no idea why he's there," I insisted, trying to decipher Ryan's line of questioning.

"You'd better not be lying to me, Taryn," he stated forcefully.

"Ryan, I swear—I'm not lying. I have no idea why he's there."

"When was the last time you saw him?" he asked.

I thought about it for a moment. "When he came to give me that mace and stuff a week ago, and I told you about that. I've told you every time he's ever come around here. *I'm* not the one keeping secrets."

"Swear to me that you didn't know about him coming down here," Ryan breathed desperately.

"Ryan, I swear on my life that I have no idea why he is there."

"He irks the shit out of me. I don't know why he's here, but I'm going to find out."

There was a long pause until Ryan broke the silence.

"Taryn, I don't want to fight with you. I am just frustrated about . . ." It was silent again, and I didn't know if I should say anything or let him talk.

A million thoughts rushed through my mind. *He is frustrated with me and my insecurities. He is frustrated that I didn't come to the Oscars. He is frustrated that I lost his unborn baby.*

I mindlessly let the next thought slip out of my mouth to kill the silence.

"You're frustrated with me." It was a statement, not a question.

"I'm frustrated with *everything*, Taryn."

One single tear dripped down my cheek.

CHAPTER 33

Crushed

THE NEXT WEEK seemed to move along quicker. I was starting to feel better physically, and spending more time downstairs in the pub was better for me mentally. I didn't realize just how much interacting with people was good for my spirit.

My regular customers were glad to see me again and although many were concerned, some couldn't help but make a few jokes about the accident. I still wore my obnoxious blue cast as a constant reminder.

"Taryn, what are you doing?" Marie yelled at me.

"Just filling the coolers," I muttered.

"You're not supposed to be lifting and bending like that. Get away from there!" She tugged on my arm. "Go, sit. Take it easy. I don't want you getting hurt before your trip."

There was no arguing with Marie about the amount of physical labor that I tried to exert, but what she didn't realize was how good it felt for me to move and stretch again.

"Is it okay if I tap a beer?" I kidded with her.

"Fine, but no lifting heavy beer cases." She shook her finger at me.

I was feeling very apprehensive about my upcoming trip to Florida. Ryan was acting . . . weird, skittish. Since he was always working, our phone conversations had to be coordinated, but lately Ryan was over-the-top with arranging times when it was safe to talk.

Safe . . . he uttered that word during one of our conversations. Why all of a sudden is he worried about being *safe* when he talks to me? Was it because Lauren was constantly around him, even when he had spare moments of downtime when he wasn't filming?

Ryan kept me informed of Kyle's annoying presence, almost accusing me of being responsible for Kyle being there on occasion. Kyle had managed to spend a few days making his presence known on some of the filming locations . . . that was until Ryan put an end to it.

Ryan told me that he'd spoken to the head of Kyle's company directly and informed him that he wanted Kyle removed from the set immediately. He wouldn't tell me what happened, but something definitely went down between the two of them because Ryan was furious.

Kyle was to be ordered immediately to refrain from contacting me or attempting to see me in any way, shape, or form . . . permanently. I was sure that Ryan used his "no bullshit" tone with Kyle's boss.

I wished there were someone I could call to keep Lauren's lips off Ryan, someone to order her to stay away from him. I would have loved to use my authority to issue a "cease and desist" order on her.

I tried to constantly remind myself that Ryan was making a movie, that his kissing Lauren was no different from him kissing Suzanne. Sometimes I tried to swap out Lauren's head with Suzanne's just to keep my jealousy at bay, but since I had never met Lauren, it was difficult. I didn't know her, and therefore I didn't trust her.

Ryan constantly assured me that he loved me, but I couldn't help but think of my failed engagement and all the times Thomas "assured" me when he covered up his infidelities. Some experiences were difficult to shake.

It didn't help that Ryan's demeanor toward me had been different these last few days. He was nervous and weirdly excited that I was coming to Miami. Flight times, arrival times, departure times—all were carefully orchestrated.

My friends were behaving differently as well . . . smiling at me awkwardly all the time, as though they knew something I didn't. It sort of reminded me of the ambiguous looks they used to give me when they thought I was too stupid to realize Thomas was cheating on me.

The day finally arrived that I departed for Florida. This time I was going to make it there safely; Ryan was making sure of that. He hired a driver to get me to the airport and Jamaal, my new bodyguard—who was the size of an NFL linebacker—accompanied me the entire way. I felt better knowing that Ryan wanted me to arrive unscathed, especially since Angelica was still on the loose.

"I thought Florida is supposed to be sunny and warm?" I said to my driver, trying to break the silence. I glowered at the dismal gray skies that darkened the afternoon. The heavy rain was making trails down my window, obscuring my view of the landscape.

"It is, madam," my driver stated with a thick Jamaican accent. "But not today." He laughed.

"I feel like I should ask for a refund. All this false advertising." I laughed at my own joke, sensing that he either didn't hear me or didn't understand.

Downtown Miami was still teeming with life despite the inclement weather. I tried to pay attention to where we were driving while my fingers tapped along with the rhythmic sound of the windshield wipers.

I noticed the marquee on the Regency Hotel as we slowed. It was a relief to know that I'd finally made it and only a few more minutes separated me from being reunited with my love. I couldn't wait to wrap my arms around him and put an end to all my worries.

The steel garage door sealed tightly behind my car, shutting out the prying eyes and photographers that surrounded the hotel.

It was difficult not to feel like royalty when I had a hulking bodyguard holding out his hand for me to exit the limousine, my driver was handling my luggage, and hotel security was waiting for my arrival at the private entrance.

Butterflies coated my stomach while I slid the key card into the lock of Ryan's private suite.

"You can just leave my bags here," I pointed to the floor in the entryway.

"That's okay, ma'am, I'll take them to the bedroom for you," the bellboy nervously insisted.

"I can get them," I said. I wanted the bellboy out as soon as possible so that the second I saw Ryan it would be a private, intimate moment. I had been thinking about this reunion for days. I'd even strategically picked out my outfit—a simple cotton top and his favorite jeans. I was not about to waste a second of our time messing with layers of clothes as we got reacclimated. Besides, I didn't know if Ryan was lying and waiting naked in the bedroom. At least I hoped he was.

"No! Um, I have to take them!" The young man was adamant, almost shouting out at me. Before I had a chance to say no again, he quickly carried my bags off to the bedroom.

"Here you go," I said with a smile, tipping the bellboy ten dollars. He quickly snatched the money from my fingers and sprang for the door, not even making eye contact. I thought it was rude that he didn't even say thank you.

Ryan's suite was magnificent, of course. Private bedroom, enormous living room, and a large dining table with a lush fresh floral centerpiece made the room feel like an apartment.

"Ryan?" I called out, wondering why he didn't meet me at the door. I hurried to the master bedroom and opened the double doors. "Are you here?" I wandered around all the rooms, but he wasn't in the suite.

Where is he? We had agreed to meet here. I looked at my watch. I had expected him to be waiting for me, figuring he'd scoop me up in his arms and carry me off to the bedroom the moment we saw each other.

I tried his cell number, anxious to let him know I had arrived. My smile turned to a frown when his voice mail answered instead.

I took my thin jacket off, struggling a bit to get the cuff over my cast, and laid it over the back of the silk-clad chair.

Shimmery hues of black, blue, and cream-colored fabric caught my attention. Next to the polished mahogany dining table stood a long metal clothing rack on wheels.

I hesitantly approached, admiring the exquisite evening gowns that hung on padded hangers. I let my fingers feel the silkiness of the different fabrics. One striking dress stood out over the rest—the bustier top was made of buttery soft ivory leather, crisscrossing at the waist. Curiosity made me look. *Atelier Versace,* I read on the garment tag. I felt like I was committing a crime just by touching the dresses.

Stacked on the floor were dozens of shoe boxes—Jimmy Choo, Christian Louboutin, you name it. Every high-end shoe designer was represented.

Why does Ryan have women's clothing on display? Must be nice to be an actress—look at all the perks that come along with it. Wait, am I in Ryan's room or Lauren's room?

I turned around in confusion, then hurried off to the bedroom again, noticing Ryan's suitcases and his Gibson guitar. I double-checked the luggage tags and sighed with relief after reading "Shell-B Enterprises." *Okay, I'm in the right room.*

I reached for my suitcase and noticed there was an envelope lying next to it on the bed. *Hmm, that's weird. Did the bellboy leave a bill for something?* I opened the envelope and removed the folded paper. *Ah! Ryan did leave a note!* My eyes focused on the handwriting . . . but it wasn't Ryan's.

Morning Babe,

Sorry I wasn't here when you woke up. I snuck back to my room so we wouldn't raise suspicions. I know it's going to be difficult for you, but letting her know that it's over is for the best. I know you don't want to hurt Taryn's feelings, but you've let this go on long enough. She'll know why you ended it soon enough. I can't wait for dinner tonight when we can be alone again!

I love you too with all my heart!

Forever Yours

Lauren

Are you serious? No, this can't be happening! My brain tried to rationalize what I'd just read. *No, he wouldn't do this to me. Not today. Not on my birthday.*

I looked at the note again, trying to read it as it shook in my hand.

There was my name . . .

Taryn

I felt the weight of the entire world as it collapsed in on me, shattering every bone in my body. My heart was instantly torn to shreds and smashed into dust.

Lauren

. . . There was her signature, clearly encouraging *my* boyfriend to leave me. The rumors, the lies, the photographs—could they all be true?

it's over

. . . The words jumped off the page like a sharp dagger into my heart.

"No. Damn it. NO!" I cried out. "No! He loves me. Me, not her."

Did he really fly me down here to break up with me, or wasn't I supposed to see this little remnant of his infidelity?

How could he do this to me? Would he really be that coldhearted, leaving this behind for me to read?

Why not? After all, Thomas did it to me.

No, Ryan is not like that. He is a good person . . . who is cheating on me.

I started to hyperventilate. A million pictures flashed through my mind . . . Ryan kissing my hand, his smile that made my heart flutter, hearing his voice say he loves me a thousand times.

No, there has to be a rational explanation for this! There has to be! I staggered slightly, feeling dizzy all of a sudden.

My foot stepped onto something on the floor, right next to where my suitcase was placed. I bent to pick up the shimmery fabric. As I unraveled it, I discovered that in my hands was a pair of black silk women's panties. Like creeping death, more evidence of his infidelity unfolded to me. Visions of him with Lauren, making love to *her* in this bed right in front of me, snuffed out every one of my joyous memories.

My cell phone shrilled in my pocket, startling me. My pulse quickened and I recoiled, almost falling over my own feet.

"Hello?" I answered in between sobs.

"Is this Taryn Mitchell?" the male voice inquired abruptly.

"Yes. Who is this?" I muttered, wiping my cheek on my sleeve.

"It's not important. Write down this address," he ordered. His voice was gruff, muffled.

"What?" I asked, completely confused.

"He is with her right *now*," the stranger stressed. "We're taking pictures of them together. Get a pen."

While I listened to the clicking sounds of a camera, I scrambled to the desk and found a hotel tablet—the same stationery that Lauren used.

"Do you have a pen?" the man yelled.

"Yes, but I don't understand."

"You need to see the truth. Hurry. The hotel will get a taxi for you. Come to 2950 West Palermo Avenue—the restaurant on the corner. Shoot that . . . he's kissing her again! Ah! He is so busted! 2950 West Palermo."

"Who is this?" I asked. "Hello?"

I tore the paper off the pad and grabbed my purse.

"2950 West Palermo," I read the address to the taxi driver and then shoved the paper back in my pocket. The rain was coming down in buckets, causing the car headlights to glare off the windshield. The skies were pitch black from the storm blasting Miami. The dark and ominous clouds brought the wind, which caused the rain to blow sideways. Loud thunder started to rumble between the lightning flashes.

I sat on the edge of the backseat, staring wildly out the front window of the taxi. I saw the road sign indicating Palermo Avenue. My throat became tight with anticipation.

The taxi driver pulled over to the curb.

"2950 Palermo." The driver pointed at the tall office building. "That'll be fourteen-fifty."

I grabbed a twenty out of my wallet; my hand shook as I handed it to him.

"Do you want a receipt?" he asked in a rough voice.

"No," I said quickly, my hand already pulling the lever on the door.

I gave the cab door a shove and hurried through the rain toward the shelter of the entrance. Frightening thunder rumbled through the sky; the earsplitting crack made me instinctively duck while it echoed loudly off of the tall buildings. I flinched from the sound; knowing my luck, I'd probably get struck by lightning today, too.

I looked at the big numbers on the gray stone building . . . 2950. It was a bank with several floors of offices above it.

I was utterly confused. *What the . . . ?* Was someone playing a cruel joke on me—sending me on some wild goose chase? I pulled the paper back out of my pocket to double-check the address, but instead of the address, I was looking at Lauren's note again. The note I held in my hand was definitely not a joke.

Restaurant on corner, my memory informed quickly. I looked up and down the street, unsure of which way to go. I was in the center of the block.

Fueled by the evidence clutched in my hand, I started walking fast down the sidewalk. The rain soaked through my clothes; my wet feet slipped uncomfortably inside my leather boots. My hair that was once nicely done was completely drenched. I shivered from the wind and pulled my purse back up on my shoulder.

I wished I had an umbrella to shield me from the rain. I flipped up the little collar of my shirt just to keep the water from dripping down my back.

Two men were standing near the corner, huddled next to a building, wearing plastic rain jackets. Both of them held cameras with long, white lenses covered by a clear plastic sheath. Their lenses pointed toward the opposite street corner.

I looked across the street to the window. There was the restaurant and there was Ryan, visible from the street. My breath caught from seeing him. Rain dripped from my hair and down my face; my mascara bled and burned my eyes as I tried to focus through the downpour.

I saw Ryan lift Lauren's hand off the table. The two cameras clicked in a rhythmic hum.

He twisted the ring on her finger.

I felt the tears build in my eyes and unbearable pain cracked into my chest.

He picked her hand up and wrapped it in his, smiling at her before kissing her fingertips.

Horror and denial swirled through my soul like toxic fumes.

"No," I whispered in pain.

Then Ryan stood up from his chair, leaned across the table, and pressed his lips to hers. Right there in public . . . The cameras sounded like the knives that sliced my heart to shreds.

Anger, resentment, and pure hatred welled in me as the last fragment of my heart was torn from my chest. I made it halfway across the street before I was stopped by oncoming traffic.

A car came screeching to a halt, hydroplaning in the rain and missing me by inches. I was frozen in place; my eyes were locked on Ryan's face. No other vision mattered.

The driver honked his horn repeatedly, but I couldn't move. Part of me wished he would just hit me and end the pain once and for all.

Do it! Hit the gas and finish me!

Lightning flashed over my head but I didn't flinch this time. It would take a direct hit by a bolt of electricity to restart my heart.

The driver was impatient; his hand stayed on the horn longer the second time.

"Why?" I sobbed in the street. Losing our unborn child was nothing compared to the excruciating pain I felt now.

Right at that moment, it happened, before my very eyes: my greatest love turned into nothing more than another man I wasn't good enough for.

"Hey, lady! Get out of the street!" the driver yelled at me through his open car window, blaring his horn at me again. I glanced in his direction; his vicious tone distracted me.

"What the hell is wrong with you? Are you trying to get yourself killed?" the man continued shouting.

What the hell was wrong with me?

The lights of the oncoming traffic made starbursts in my blurry eyes. I was crying so hard that I forgot where I was for a second. My feet moved unconsciously; I followed the yellow lines, hoping they would lead me to a place where the pain would stop.

My fingers found a door handle in the dark. I dropped Lauren's poison-penned note, leaving it behind on the sidewalk. I didn't need it with me anymore. I had witnessed all the proof I needed with my own eyes.

"*Taryn!*" my memory called out in a muffled tone, strangely in the sound of Ryan's voice, but I couldn't respond to it. Darkness had already taken me under.

"Where to, miss?" some man asked me. "Miss?"

"Huh . . . home," I breathed.

"And where is home?" the man asked.

My lips quivered as I found the will to speak. "Airport."

Desolation and despair enveloped me again, choking my ability to breathe. All my hopes and dreams that involved Ryan were shattered.

My phone chimed that stupid ring tone, reminding me of his biggest lie that crushed my soul . . . he wasn't mine anymore.

I rolled the car window down and tossed out my cell phone, releasing his song to the wind.

"TARYN?" I heard a man's voice calling my name. *My mind must really be playing tricks on me. Now I'm hearing voices. So this is what a nervous breakdown feels like. At least I'm not crying anymore.*

"Taryn, wait up."

My legs trudged on their own, instinctively following the rest of the people hurrying around me. *If I follow them far enough, maybe the flashing lights will stop?*

"Hey. What are you doing in the airport?"

My eyes glanced over to my right; someone was talking to me. That was when I noticed Kyle's face.

"Stop taking her picture! Enough, guys!" he yelled.

I saw an arm press out in front of me, shielding me.

"Why are you soaking wet?" Kyle asked quietly. "Taryn, just keep walking." Something annoying was pushing into my back, forcing me to walk forward faster.

I felt cold and numb and utterly devastated. *Creeping death must be inside me now, devouring everything.*

Kyle glanced around my feet. "Where is your luggage?" he muttered.

I looked down at my hands—they were empty and trembling. The edge of my blue cast stuck out the end of my sleeve; water dripped from the gauze packing.

I couldn't remember if I was supposed to have anything in my hands or not. Instantly my chest tightened and it felt very hard to breathe.

"Hey, hey..." Kyle pulled me into his chest. "Calm down. Shh, it will be all right. I'm here."

I tried to block him with my hands. I wanted him to stop touching me. No man would ever touch me again.

He whispered in my ear, "Don't worry, babe. I'll take care of you. Let's get you home."

CHAPTER 34

Shattered

TARYN, SWEETIE. THANK God!" Marie rushed to my bedside. "It's gonna be okay. We're here." She wrenched her hands around my neck and shoulders to hug me.

Pete was frantically turning on all my bedroom lamps. It was dark outside, so I presumed it must be night again. My eyes were swollen; I had a hard time focusing them in the new light.

"Should I call nine-one-one?" Tammy asked in a panic.

Marie ran her hand across my face to wipe my hair from my eyes.

"Taryn, talk to me. Do you need to go to the hospital?" Marie's voice cracked when she asked.

Misery burst back into my chest and I started to weep again. I doubted any hospital in the world would be able to mend a shattered heart.

"I don't think she needs an ambulance, Tammy," Pete said from the other side of my bed. I felt him pet my hair.

"Oh, Taryn, it will be all right." Marie hugged me tightly. "Sweetie, what happened?"

"It's . . . over," I choked out. It was pure agony to say the words out loud.

Marie looked over at Pete and shook her head.

"Tell us what happened," Marie whispered.

"I saw him with her," I uttered between sobs. "I saw it with my own eyes. He touched her face, and kissed her hand, and I watched as he leaned over the table to kiss her. Right there in the restaurant for everyone to see." The magnitude of my admission crushed me again.

"Who, Taryn? Who was he with?" Pete asked gently.

"Lauren. He was with Lauren. All the rumors about them . . . they're true." I barely had the will to speak.

"Taryn, Ryan was filming," Marie spoke cautiously.

I stared at her face through my tears, wondering why she believed him.

"Sure he was. That's why the paparazzi were there," I muttered.

She grimaced at me. "What's all over your shirt?"

I looked at my chest, noticing yellow spots on the fabric.

"I think I threw up last night," I sputtered. Another crack of unbearable sadness struck my heart.

"Come on; let's get you in the shower." She tore the blankets off my body and wrapped her arm around my back to help me out of bed.

"Have you eaten anything?" Marie asked, walking me to the bathroom.

I felt confused and weak. I couldn't remember when I ate last. When I shook my head, the motion made me feel dizzy.

"Tammy, see if you can make something for Taryn to eat," Marie requested.

"I'm not hungry," I whispered. I deserved to feel the emptiness inside my chest. After all, it was the result of my own stupidity.

"Taryn, you have to eat!" Marie scolded, turning on the shower.

"What happened to your cast?" She peeled a big chunk of the casing off. The gauze padding was hanging out over my hand.

"I got it wet," I answered, pulling on a piece of cotton thread that hung out from the hole around my thumb.

"Pete, do you have any tape? Look at this. It's falling apart. I'll call her doctor tomorrow."

Pete came back with his toolbox. I wished he would have just cut it off instead of wrapping it in silver tape.

"Why didn't you call us, Taryn? We're your friends," Tammy said, pulling my sweatpants off my body. "You're not alone in this."

"Tammy, let's just get her washed." Marie pulled my T-shirt off over my head and tossed it across the bathroom. "We need to wrap her cast in plastic first."

"I'll go strip her bed, then," Tammy volunteered. "Are these her antidepressants? Here, Taryn, take this. Drink."

"Can you stand, or do you want me to run a bath?" Marie asked, pushing back the shower curtain.

I stepped into the shower, noticing that the bruises on my stomach were almost completely gone but I had a fresh black-and-blue mark on my thigh. I couldn't remember how I got that one.

The hot water actually felt good on my skin, although it stung a little on my face where I had been rubbing my eyes. I used my right hand to push the water through my hair, hoping that the stream would somehow reach my memories and cleanse them of the nightmares.

A few long strands of hair dislodged and tangled around my fingers like a spider web. Oh, how I wished they would have been strong enough to pull the misery from my mind before breaking away from my head.

Marie handed my toothbrush to me. "Brush your teeth while you're in there."

I let the water stream into my dry mouth, swallowing some to quench my thirst. I was feeling weak and tired and utterly miserable, so I leaned against the wall.

Will I ever find the strength to move on?

The shrill of a cell phone ringing startled me. I knew it wasn't mine. My cell phone was probably in pieces on a Florida highway by now.

"We found her," I heard Marie say. "She's in the apartment . . ." Her voice trailed off.

I knew it was Ryan she was talking to. I wondered why he even cared. Maybe he was feeling guilty for crushing me? I had no pity for him. He could wallow in his guilt for the rest of his life for all I cared.

The shower curtain pulled back slightly and Marie popped her head into the opening.

"You're not going to get clean that way." She frowned at me. "It helps if you actually let the water touch your body."

She pushed her sleeves up on her arms and turned the water diverter to shut the overhead shower off.

"Here, let me help. Sit down in the tub." Marie pushed the drain plug down and started to fill the tub with hot water. She swirled her hand around in the water by my feet.

"Sandy said that she's having a bunch of specials down at the salon this month. We should go get our nails done. She has this new foot soak stuff; she says it smells like peppermint . . ."

"Who were you just talking to on the phone?" I interrupted her.

She stopped washing my shoulders and put more soap on the sponge. Her lips pursed together and I knew she didn't want to say his name.

"I wasn't talking to anyone," she lied. "Here, wash your body." She squeezed some shampoo onto my hair.

"Sandy also told me about this new shampoo she got that has seaweed and plankton mixed in it, but I told her that it didn't sound very appealing. I mean, have you smelled the ocean lately? Who wants to wash their hair with crap floating in the o—"

"Marie, I heard you talking to someone," I interrupted again. "Please don't lie."

Her fingers froze for a moment in my hair.

"I love you, Taryn. We *all* love you. You are the closest thing I have to a sister in this world. And I know you are in pain right now, so I want to help you get past it so you can see things clearly." I felt her fingertips scrub my scalp.

"You know *exactly* who I was just talking to. I know you're upset, so I'm not going to say his name out loud, but he is the reason we knew to look for you," Marie admitted. "He called me. He called Pete. He begged us to get through to you when you wouldn't answer his calls. None of us even knew you came home."

"I don't want you talking to him anymore," I commanded hoarsely.

"Let's just finish getting you clean and then we're going to get some food into your body. You need to reexamine the situation with a fresh attitude, okay, sweetie?" Marie dismissed my order.

"Promise me you won't talk to him anymore. It's over," I whispered.

"I can't do that," she muttered.

"Promise me!" I begged, looking her in the eyes.

"No!" Marie said with conviction. "I will *not* promise that!"

"Then choose—right now—him or me!" I demanded with new tears in my eyes.

"Tammy? Can you get me a big plastic cup from the kitchen, please?" Marie yelled over her shoulder. "Wash your stinky pits. You smell like shit," she fired back, rummaging through the cabinet below the sink. "Here's a new razor."

I took it from her hand and threw it at the garbage can. "Those aren't mine. You can throw all of those blue ones in the garbage."

"Listen, I know you're hurting. And I also know you're miserable and confused. But don't piss me off on top of it."

Tammy handed her a cup. Marie repeatedly filled it with water and dumped it on my head to rinse my hair.

"I made spaghetti," Tammy informed while Marie was helping me get dressed. "That's about all the food she has in this apartment. I'll have to go grocery shopping."

"Thanks, Tammy," Marie said. "But I think it's time that Taryn resumes her life. Tonight we'll just relax and make sure she eats and takes her medicine. Tomorrow she is going to get out of this apartment and start pulling her life back together."

Marie tossed a T-shirt from the dresser to me. It was one of Ryan's.

"This isn't mine, it's his." I cast the shirt aside on the bed.

"So what? Put it on." Marie tossed it back to me. "Maybe you'll remember all the reasons why you love him and *used* to trust him?"

The sobbing started again. "I don't want to remember." I threw the liar's shirt at the wall. "The sooner I can forget, the better."

"Does it smell like him?" Marie asked, sniffing the cotton shirt she'd retrieved from the floor. "No? Well, I can fix that."

She took his bottle of cologne off the dresser and spritzed his shirt. Then she spritzed the air a few times, wafting the air with her arms.

"Stop! Don't do that!" I cried out. I didn't want to deal with anything that reminded me of him.

"Stop what? Stop remembering the man who loves you? Stop remembering that he exists?" Marie yelled.

"Marie!" Tammy barked. "Is that really necessary right now?"

"Yes! Yes it is! It's called 'tough love' and she needs to snap her ass back into reality as quickly as possible," Marie insisted, stabbing her finger at me. "Time is of the essence here."

She threw his T-shirt at me. "Put it on," she ordered—almost a dare.

"Go to hell," I spit my words at her.

Marie spritzed his cologne in the air again. The smell of his scent permeated the air, reminding me of happier times.

"So help me God, I will kick your ass if you do it again!" I screamed at her.

"Go ahead and try. You're so weak from starving yourself that a light breeze could blow you over," she sneered. "Put on Ryan's shirt."

"Why are you doing this to me?" I cried. "I flew all the way down there. I went to the restaurant that they told me to go to!" I started to hyperventilate.

"It's over! I saw it! I saw it with my own eyes. I saw him lean over the table to kiss her and watched as he shoved his tongue in her mouth. Right there in a public restaurant. Just like Thomas. Just like a fucking coward. He's a liar! All those rumors of him cheating on me with that whore were true. Why are you doing this to me?" I cried again.

"Because you're wrong and I can prove it," Marie sighed. "Come on . . . put a shirt on."

She led me by the hand to my computer, where my friends proceeded to circle around me so I couldn't escape.

"You need to see these." Marie opened an e-mail from Ryan. "Is this what you saw?" she questioned as she opened the files attached.

The first picture was the same view of what I saw in that restaurant window. There were Ryan and Lauren sitting at a table, visible from the street.

It was like living the nightmare all over again, seeing Ryan kissing Lauren. The searing pain made me look away.

"What time did you go to this restaurant, Taryn?" Marie asked.

"Why? What difference does it make? Didn't the cheating bastard *want* me to see this?"

Marie asked the same question again, emphasizing each of her words.

"I don't remember. Four, four thirty?" The tears were streaming down my cheeks. Tammy was rubbing my shoulders tenderly.

"Why did you even go here?" Marie pointed to the screen. "The plan was for you to go from his hotel to Key Biscayne."

A moment of total surprise slipped into my sadness.

"Key Biscayne?" I questioned her comment. "What are you talking about?"

"Never mind," Marie quickly dismissed.

"Wait, how do you know where I was going when I didn't even know?" I asked.

Marie ignored my question and tapped her fingernail back on the image of the restaurant window.

"How did you know Ryan was here?" she asked a second time.

"Someone called my cell and told me that I needed to come quickly and see what was going on with my own eyes."

"Who called you?" Marie's head whipped around to look at me.

"I don't know—some guy. He said I needed to know the truth."

Marie gave Pete a dreadful look. "Did he give you a name? What did he say exactly?" She pressed anxiously for answers.

"He didn't give a name. He said he was a reporter or something. He told me where Ryan was—even gave me the address. I had a cab drive me there."

"Shit, Pete. Ryan needs to know this." Marie flashed her eyes back to me. "Taryn, where did you think Ryan was?"

"I thought he was going to be at the hotel." I wiped my eyes. "He was only scheduled to film until two o'clock. I tried calling him but his voice mail picked up. I went into the bedroom to unpack and I found a love note from Lauren to Ryan."

Marie bowed her head in disgust.

"I know. Ryan found the letter on the sidewalk by the cab stand," she muttered.

"He was planning on leaving me," I sputtered. Tears streamed down my cheeks again from the pain of his betrayal.

"No, he wasn't," Marie insisted loudly. "I don't get it, Pete." She groaned, questioning him with her eyes. "Taryn, I asked Ryan point blank if he ever cheated on you and he said no, absolutely not," she stated firmly.

I scoffed. "And you believed him?"

"Well, there are other things. I can't say—I promised. Yes, I believe him."

"You're right. You don't get it. None of you get it!" I shouted, angry that my friends were siding with him.

"I saw them having dinner together. I read her little love letter encouraging him to break up with me. I found the whore's panties on his bedroom floor. I saw him touch her and kiss her with my own eyes! That's it, it's over! She can have him!" My throat strained from screaming. I had no fight left in me. "Turns out I wasn't enough after all."

Tammy wrapped me in her arms, gently trying to shush me while I became more and more hysterical. I was shaking all over.

"Taryn, come on. You have to admit this doesn't sound right. I mean, how would some *reporter* find out your cell phone number?" Pete asked.

"What does it matter?" I sobbed into Tammy's shoulder. "Feel free to go down there and break his face."

"No way! Not knowing what we know. I agree with Marie. Ryan wouldn't lie about this—not now. Somebody set you up . . . but who?" Pete pondered.

I glared at him. "Yeah, sure. There's some big conspiracy going on." I wiped my eyes. "What else could it possibly be?" I said sarcastically. I didn't understand why my friends were so gullible.

"Taryn, look at this picture. Is this what you saw?" Marie pointed to my computer screen.

"Are those the pictures he sent to cover his tracks? They could have been taken on any number of days."

"Turn around and answer my question! Is this what you saw?" Marie showed me another picture.

"Similar," I murmured. All the pictures she showed me were taken from inside the restaurant. *Why are there pictures of this quality from inside the restaurant?*

"No, this is exactly what you saw. Do you see that?" Marie pointed to a long, thin block at the bottom of each picture. "Ryan said all of these are date/time stamped as they film it."

The date and time matched when I was there. My birth date was on all of them. My pulse quickened from the shock.

"What's that?" Marie pointed to something gray at the top of the picture. It was hard to discern what it was.

"I don't know," I whispered.

"How about in this picture? Don't look at him kissing her." Marie covered them with her hand. "What is that?" She pointed again to something gray at the top of the picture. The elongated oval shape was more pronounced.

I gasped.

Marie turned to look up at me. "Do you see it now?" She smiled.

It was crystal clear what the gray thing was now . . . it was the microphone boom.

Ryan *was* on location filming, and the date and time stamps proved it.

"No, but why?" My vision became blurry and the room started to spin. "She left note . . . I read . . . wha? Not stupposed be filmin."

A high-pitched tone started ringing in both of my ears and I couldn't feel my legs. That was when the room tilted sideways . . . and disappeared.

"Taryn?" I heard the familiar voices urgently calling my name. Something cool and wet was touching my face. Something annoying was smacking my cheek.

"Hey, there. Welcome back." Pete smiled, dabbing my face with a cold washrag.

"What?" I tried to sit up. "What happened?" The room was still spinning slightly.

"You blacked out. You're okay. Here, can you drink this?" Pete held the cup to my mouth.

"Ugh! That tastes awful." I picked a small chunk of something grainy off of my tongue.

"Tammy crushed some vitamins into a cup of water. We need to get some nourishment into you," he said gently. "It's either this or we're going to take you to the emergency room."

I reached for the cup. "I don't want to go to the hospital," I muttered. "Reporters . . ."

The next hour was spent quietly getting me to eat and drink, and most importantly—to stay calm.

Parts of my trip to Florida flashed through my thoughts, but I couldn't remember all the details for some reason. Perhaps my last fragments of self-preservation and survival suppressed the memories deep in my subconscious to protect me from having a complete mental breakdown?

I remembered crying on an airplane. I remembered Kyle helping me into a car.

"I can't do this anymore," I whispered, staring blankly at my bowl of spaghetti. Tammy was sitting in front of me on the ottoman. She patted my leg.

"You need to eat some more, Taryn." Tammy nudged me. "Marie will get to the bottom of it."

I couldn't eat. Marie was filling Ryan in on my current state of mental collapse.

"Stop it, Ryan! She is not sneaking around with Kyle behind your back!" Marie said angrily. "Because you didn't see the state she was in when we found her, that's how I'm sure.

"Ryan, what part of *we had to kick your bedroom door in to get to her* is unclear to you? We almost called for an ambulance—she was that bad. Believe me, Taryn is far from happy and in love with some other guy right now. Yes, she knows I'm talking to you. I'm looking right at her."

I scoffed. Of course this would get turned around on me! My supposed infidelity with Kyle gave him an excuse.

"Ryan! Listen to me. Taryn said she found the note in your suite, and then right after that someone called her on her cell. This mystery caller is the one who told her where you were. He led her to believe you were cheating on her. I mean, how else would Taryn be able to find you when you were out on location?"

I watched Marie pace the floor while she talked to him.

"No, Taryn said he never gave a name. He told her that they were taking pictures of you, so I guess he was paparazzi?"

She moved the phone away from her ear. I could hear Ryan shouting.

"Ryan! Calm down, all right? Think. Who else has her number?" Marie asked.

She looked at me. "Taryn, do you remember if there was a name or number on your cell?"

"No, there wasn't," I whispered.

"Where is your phone? Get it for me."

I regretted my foolishness, but there was nothing I could do to change it. "It's on a highway in Florida," I admitted.

Tammy rolled her eyes at me.

"Ryan, I'm telling you, she didn't know you were still filming! . . . Well, did you *tell her* that your schedule changed?" Marie yelled back at him.

"He said the morning shoot got pushed back because Lauren was feeling sick but later she felt better, so they were behind schedule when they filmed the restaurant scene," she whispered to me. "He didn't get a chance to call because you were already on the plane and he was on location."

"I guess he was in such a hurry to see her that he forgot to throw her love note away?" I muttered, thoroughly disgusted with the lies. "Ask him how long he's been fucking her."

Marie gave me a dirty look and covered her phone with her hand so Ryan wouldn't hear me.

"Let him cover his tracks," I said scornfully. "Go ahead and believe him, because I sure don't."

Marie groaned. "Ryan, she hasn't been answering your calls because apparently she no longer has a cell phone. . . . Quit yelling in my ear!" she yelled back at him. "Stop it, Ryan! You love Taryn and Taryn loves you. She's a mess; you're a mess. You both need to chill out! Ryan, listen to the facts. Does *any* of this sound logical to either one of you?"

Marie spent another twenty minutes trying to calm him down. Eventually, she snapped her phone shut. "He's going to call back."

While she talked, my mind collapsed from the strain.

"When he calls back, tell him he can come and get his shit out of my apartment, because I'm done with all of this. I'm done with the lies, and the rumors, and the photographs, and having my boyfriend shove his tongue in some other girl's mouth when he thinks I'm not looking. It's over," my voice cracked. The familiar pain rippled through my chest again.

"Just calm down. Nothing is over. You're overreacting."

I felt patronized. "Get out," I seethed. "Just get out and take the rest of the Ryan Fan Club with you." I stormed past her, wishing my bedroom door weren't broken so I could slam it shut.

"Tar, don't be like this." Marie followed me.

"I don't get it, Marie. I thought you were *my* best friend? Aren't you supposed to be on *my* side? Or are you so blinded by worshipping mister actor man that you believe him?" I yelled at her. "Call him back. I'm sure he'll fuck you, too."

Marie gritted her teeth and before I could react, she slapped me across the face.

My hand covered the sting she left on my cheek. She smacked me hard enough that my eyes started to water. Tears formed right after that. Everyone I loved in this world had just betrayed me.

"Get a grip already, damn it!" Marie screamed at me. "I told you that if you ever screwed this relationship up I would kick your ass myself. And here you are, royally screwing up the best thing that has ever happened to you. Ryan loves you, you idiot! He's not screwing Lauren!"

Marie started to pace my bedroom floor. Tammy was trying to hold me as I sobbed on my bed.

"Pete! I'm gonna . . . !" Marie said emphatically, losing her patience.

"No, Marie, don't." Pete lunged forward. "Last resort . . ."

Marie held her breath for a moment before turning her glare back to me.

"If you want a future with that man then you need to stop thinking this way—immediately! Do you think that Ryan Christensen, the man who has been insanely in love with you since the first day he met you, would do that to you? Do you honestly think he would put you on a plane, fly you first class to stay in a luxury suite so he could *accidentally* let you see some bogus love note and break up with you?"

She gaped at me, waiting for my response. I had none.

"What was waiting for you in his hotel room?" Marie asked angrily.

"Marie," Tammy cautioned.

Marie waved her off. "Taryn?"

"Nothing." I sniffed. "Heartache and devastation . . . and some skanky ho's panties."

Marie groaned. "No, Taryn. I'm talking about the dresses."

"Oh, yeah . . . the rest of Lauren's clothing," I muttered. "A whole rack of her glamorous things. More evidence of her staying in his room."

"Taryn!" Tammy scolded. "All those gowns were for you."

I rolled my eyes. "I don't think so. Wait, how do you know about the dresses?"

"Versace, Vera Wang, Jimmy Choo . . . sound familiar?" Marie asked. "Please tell me you at least looked at the dresses."

"I did. I thought I was in the wrong room; I mean, why would Ryan have evening gowns on a rack?" I asked.

"They were for you," Marie insisted. "Ryan arranged to have a variety of dresses there—he wanted *you* to have your pick of what you would wear to dinner."

I looked at Marie, surprised that she knew all these details and shocked that the dresses *were* for me.

"And why do you suppose Ryan would want to dress you up in an expensive dress and Jimmy Choos? So he could leave you for Lauren?" Marie shook her head. "He made a ton of arrangements . . ."

"Marie!" Tammy and Pete both yelled at the same time.

Marie gave them both a reproachful look and continued. "To take you on a private, romantic dinner on Biscayne Bay for your birthday," she finished.

I felt my heart lodge into my throat.

Marie crouched down in front of me. "All of us want to see you happy, not miserable and broken like this. Ryan is so in love with you!" She smiled. "Don't give up on him."

"TAR, PULL your end over a bit more," Tammy said, fixing the clean sheet on my bed. "Marie, we need one more pillowcase."

Pete had gathered overnight bags together and everyone was staying with me. My friends weren't about to leave me alone.

"We could always play cards," Pete suggested. He looked hopeful.

Tammy fluffed the pillow. "That's up to Taryn."

I crawled onto my bed and pulled the quilt up over my shoulder. "Not tonight," I muttered.

Marie had her pajamas on already even though it was only nine thirty. She hopped onto Ryan's side of the bed and turned on his bed lamp.

"I'm sorry for slapping you." She snuggled behind me, patting my back.

"You really hit me hard," I whispered.

"I didn't mean to." Marie sounded remorseful. "You were getting irrational. I hope you forgive me. I promise I'll never do it again."

"That's what you said when we were fifteen and you told Adam Caldwell that I wanted to kiss him."

Marie chuckled lightly. "Well, you did."

"Yeah, but the entire baseball team didn't need to hear you," I groaned.

We both laughed.

"Ryan never called back," I said sadly.

"Give him time," she whispered. "He is just as upset as you are. He's trying to figure out who did all of this and film a movie at the same time. He's crushed right now, too." Marie sighed and fluffed the pillow up under her head. "Someone sure went out of their way to try and break you two up, that's for sure."

"I should have never opened that envelope on his bed," I sighed. "I thought it was a hotel bill or something at first. Maybe if I wouldn't have seen it . . ." I took a deep breath. "Ah, who am I trying to kid? Nothing changes the fact that Lauren wrote the note."

"Tar, Lauren didn't write that note. Ryan confronted her about it. He said Lauren's handwriting didn't even come close to what was on that paper. Even Mike was there to verify it."

I tried to remember what Lauren's handwriting looked like. I had seen it once on the card that I found in the front of Ryan's suitcase, on the day that Ryan told me he wanted to stay with me in the apartment.

"So the note *was* bogus and Ryan was really filming?" I asked. My chest was starting to feel tight again.

"Wait, back up," Marie said quickly. "Where was the note again?"

"When I went to the bedroom, the bellboy had parked my suitcase at the foot of the bed. The note was on top of his bed by my suitcase."

"It was on the bed?" Marie asked. Her eyes were all scrunched together as she questioned me.

"Yes. And the panties were on the floor, right next to my suitcase."

"If you were going to leave a note for someone who was supposedly still asleep, wouldn't you put it where they would see it, like on a table or the nightstand? How did it get on top of the bed?" she asked.

"I don't know. And it doesn't change the fact that there was some girl's black panties on his floor, Marie. Maybe he's not sleeping with Lauren, but he had some girl in his bedroom."

"Taryn, Ryan is not screwing around on you. Was his bed made or was it still slept in?" she asked.

"It was made," I said, wondering what her point was.

"Housekeeping," she said, drawing some conclusion.

At this point the damage was already done. The only thing left to question was whether the damage was irreparable or not.

"I've been feeling like all the odds have been stacked against us from the very beginning," I said. "As if that wasn't hard enough, fate keeps throwing Kyle at me on top of it. If it wasn't for him, I'd probably still be wandering around in a daze in the Miami airport."

"Taryn, what was Kyle doing in the airport?"

"You know, I asked him that on the plane. He said he was there on a job but his assignment was finished. Ryan said he saw Kyle on one of the sets last week. He called Kyle's company to have him removed, so Kyle wasn't supposed to be in Miami anymore. Ryan told me that Kyle was instructed by his company to stay away from me."

"I know," Marie admitted.

My wide eyes locked onto her face. I hadn't told her about Kyle being in Florida. That was a fight between Ryan and me that I kept to myself.

"You know the paparazzi took your picture with him in the airport. That's why Ryan is so pissed," Marie told me cautiously. "There are pictures of Kyle hugging you."

I threw the covers off and hurried to my computer. Pete and Tammy were in the living room watching Sunday-night television.

I searched one of the online sources for paparazzi photos that I knew of. It was hard to get past the vicious headlines.

"Oh, God," I groaned, viewing pictures of me looking like a drowned rat. "Does Ryan think I look happy to see Kyle in any of these shots?"

I studied the picture of Kyle hugging and consoling me. "Look, my arms are straight. I'm not even hugging him back. And here it looks like

I'm pushing him away from me. How could Ryan even think that I have feelings for this guy?"

"How could you ever doubt Ryan's love for you?" Tammy whispered.

"I never doubted Ryan before, but when I saw the love letter and the panties . . . and then got a phone call telling me that he was with the other woman at that moment—what was I supposed to think?" I retorted.

I looked back at the pictures on my computer. "When I was on the plane to come home, I guess I started to agree with Kyle. He said that all things happen for a reason and maybe it was better that all this happened now instead of having Ryan leave me after we're married and bring children into this world. That's usually when all the celebrity marriages end."

Marie groaned angrily. "That slick bastard."

I looked at a few more pictures, reliving the devastation I felt at the time they were taken all over again.

"The note said that he'd let this go on long enough. I didn't know what to believe." My fingers trailed down my computer screen.

Marie couldn't wait any longer; she punched a few keys on her cell phone. "Ryan, what did you find out?"

I knew Ryan had Marie's cell number; I never knew Marie had his.

"Housekeeping said there weren't any undergarments on the floor when they made his bed," Marie whispered to me. She told him she thought the bellboy must have put the note on the bed and expressed her suspicions about Kyle's involvement.

"He wants to talk to you." Marie smiled, holding out her cell.

"Hi," I whispered apprehensively. I didn't know how he would react to me.

"Hi," Ryan said softly. "Are you okay?"

"No," I admitted; the burn of remorse seeped into my chest. "I thought I'd lost you."

"Tar, honey . . ." He breathed heavily. "Why, I mean, how could you think that?" Ryan's voice cracked. "I yelled for you. I ran after you." His speech quivered. "I didn't know why you left me."

"The note . . . it said you were going to end it with me. I thought . . . you and Lauren." The tears streamed down my cheeks. "I was going to wait and show it to you and make you tell me to my face that she was what you wanted, but then some man called and I saw you in the restaurant . . . I didn't know you were filming . . . I swear I didn't know."

"So you were going to give up? Just like that?" Ryan asked.

"If Lauren is what you need to be happy, what's the point in fighting? Would it ever make a difference and change your mind if you wanted someone else? I've been there before, Ryan. Once one person in the relationship veers off course, there's nothing that can bring them back."

He was silent. I could hear him breathing. His lack of conversation frightened me even further, but I waited.

"How . . ." he choked on his words. "How can we ever . . . make it . . . if you don't believe in me?"

The hollow pain shot back into my chest. He was veering off course.

"I do believe in you!" I insisted. "I do." My words came in pleading whispers. "But how was I to take evidence that stated otherwise?"

Ryan's breathing became louder, labored.

"What happens the next time some fan sends some bullshit letter that you think is real? Are we going to be right back in this same spot again?" he snapped angrily.

"No, we won't, because reading some letter that arrives in the mail is a lot different than finding a love note from your co-star ex-girlfriend and silk panties that aren't mine on the floor next to your bed in your hotel room."

"I'm afraid now that you'll never be able to trust me," he muttered.

I could hear it in his voice and I knew him well enough to know he was trying to convince himself otherwise.

"That depends . . ." I uttered softly, wiping my tears.

"On what?"

"If you give me a chance to have a next time," I sighed, fearing his answer. If he wanted an out, here was his opportunity.

Ryan huffed in my ear. "I don't know," he murmured. "Tar, I'm an actor. This is what I do. If you can't trust me . . ."

I closed my eyes as new tears burned my face.

"What about you?" I asked, my tears clogged my throat. "Are you going to think I'm having affairs with other men when you're not around? You think I arranged to run into the arms of that asshole? I still don't remember how I ended up at the airport, Ryan."

I wiped the back of my hand across my eyes.

"I've seen the pictures of me in the terminal. Do I look happy in any of them? Because I thought they were an accurate representation of how completely devastated I was."

"I know," Ryan sighed. "I'm trying to get past the fact that it's Kyle in these pictures, but I can see how torn up you were."

For a moment, we were both silent. I was remembering the almost catatonic state I was in when those pictures were taken. Ryan was apparently logged on to his computer. Even still, one question remained unanswered.

"Just tell me, whose black panties were in your bedroom?" I asked, careful not to accuse him.

"Honey, I swear I don't know. I have no idea how they got there, but I can tell you that I'm going to find out. I swear to God there is no one else."

"You swear?" I asked for his vow.

"On my life," he confirmed. "Taryn, you know that I love you, but if you can't trust me, you have to let me know now."

"I want to trust you, I do. I love you so much!" I broke down again. "Please, please . . . just for one moment . . . put yourself in my shoes."

He breathed heavily. "Why do relationships have to be so damn complicated?"

I thought about every wonderful moment we'd spent together and the times when things became difficult.

"Our relationship only got complicated when we allowed other influences to affect it. Things were perfect when we stayed hidden away in our apartment."

Ryan laughed lightly. I hoped he was picturing holding me just as much as I was picturing being in his arms.

"So where do we go from here?" he asked.

I remembered saying the same line to him once earlier in our relationship when we were at a crossroads. There was only one reply that fit.

"We give it a chance," I whispered his line back to him.

CHAPTER 35

Answers

"MY ARM FEELS strange," I muttered, rubbing my hand over the skin on my left arm for the first time in six weeks. "It looks smaller, too." I pulled my shirt and coat sleeve back down to stifle the chill I got from the cold weather.

Marie took her eyes off the road for a second and smiled at me.

After the nightmarish last few days, I was finally able to start seeing things clearly.

"So tell me—how did you know where Ryan was planning on taking me for my birthday?" I asked, wondering how she was going to avoid answering. Marie had been very careful with her answers last night, skirting around subjects and giving me cryptic replies.

She was quiet for a moment. I could tell she was thinking about what to say before she said it.

"Ryan told me so we'd cover the bar while you were gone," she replied easily.

"Oh." I nodded.

Her reply seemed almost rehearsed. I sensed there was more to it than what she was willing to share, so, while we were on the subject, I tossed out my next question.

"And how did you and Tammy know about the evening gowns?" I stared at her while she drove.

She sighed heavily. "Ryan asked me to verify your shoe size because he wasn't sure if you wore a seven or a seven and a half. Considering how banged up you were, he wanted you to feel glamorous on your birthday."

Marie nudged me in the leg. "Do you have *any* idea how freaking lucky you are?"

I thought about her statement. Several reasons for me to feel lucky came to mind. First and foremost was the fact that the SUV didn't kill me.

She glanced over when I didn't answer.

"Do you know what Gary got me for my birthday?"

"I know he took you to dinner," I remembered. "Didn't he buy you a bracelet?"

"That was for our wedding anniversary. No, for my birthday we went to McD's and then he took me to CostMart so we could get a new air filter for my car. I got a cheeseburger and an air filter, Taryn."

"Did he at least change your oil, too?" I teased.

"No. And it took him almost two weeks to put the damn filter in my car."

I couldn't help but laugh at her.

"I tell ya, that Ryan Christensen is one hell of a romantic guy," Marie blurted, but then, very suddenly, she appeared to have said too much.

"What do you mean—romantic?" I asked, hoping she'd explain her interpretation of the word.

"Nothing," she muttered. "Just the dresses and stuff."

I felt terrible—Ryan never got to see his planning come to fruition. I stared at Marie; there was more to her thoughts, but she apparently had reasons not to share them.

"I really blew it, huh?"

Marie shrugged and shook her head. "If you would have only stayed in his suite for fifteen more minutes."

"Oh, now what?" I groaned, wondering what else I'd screwed up.

"You don't want to know," she dismissed.

She glanced over at me quickly, observing my "just tell me already before I kill you" facial expression.

"Masseuse, makeup artist, hair stylist . . . Ryan hired a team to pamper you."

"Oh . . . fuck . . ." The word slipped through my lips.

"Yep," Marie concurred. "Taryn, if you want a marriage to survive, you have to be willing to fight for it," she counseled.

"I think I've learned my lesson," I admitted. "Marie, you know I've been really worried. After the accident and with losing the baby, I knew he was blaming himself. Part of me still wonders how long we'll last before he moves on to a relationship that doesn't cause him pain."

Marie rolled her eyes and groaned.

"I wish I could be so sure about things as you all appear to be."

"If you only knew," she said under her breath.

"Okay! What the hell is *that* supposed to mean? I heard you mumble over there, so tell me already. What is it that I obviously don't know?"

"Come on, lady! Gas is on the right," Marie complained about the slow car in front of us.

"Marie!" I shouted.

"What?" she shouted back at me.

"Thirteen years we've been best friends. Thirteen!"

Marie's phone chimed, saving her from having to answer my question.

"Hey, what's up?" she said happily. "I'm telling you, Ryan, I'm willing to bet she told Kyle about your dinner plans. I'm sure that would have set him off. I'm waiting out in the car for Taryn; she ran into the store for bread." Marie covered her lips with her finger so I'd stay quiet.

"She just had her cast cut off at the doctor's and now I'm going to take her for a new cell phone."

Marie held the phone away from her ear again. Ryan was apparently upset about something.

"*Sorry!* I didn't know this required a security escort. Okay, okay . . ." she said sarcastically. "I'll make sure she calls that big refrigerator-sized Jamaal guy from now on. But it's too late now—we're already out. . . . You know she won't go for that. . . . Fine. Fine! I'll see what I can do. Okay! Jeez!"

Marie dropped her cell phone back in her purse. "He can be a real pain in the ass sometimes," she mumbled.

Things were not making sense to me. Why would Kyle get pissed if Ryan took me out to dinner? Even if Ryan took me to an expensive restaurant, which of course he would have, why would that set him off?

"Marie—what the hell is going on?" I said in a tone demanding an explanation.

She took a deep breath. She was silent for a long time before she answered. "Kyle was poking his nose around down in Florida."

"I know that," I admitted.

"Well, the part you probably don't know is that Kyle told a few people that *you* asked him to go down there. Word got back to Ryan that you sent Kyle to see if Ryan was cheating on you."

"You've got to be kidding me!" I groaned and rubbed my face. "You know I didn't do that, right? I swear I had nothing to do with him being there."

"I know. Ryan and I had a long talk about it. Mike checked with his boss at Protection Services. Kyle was reassigned immediately, but instead of going on the new assignment he took two weeks of personal time. That's when he stayed in Florida. Kyle knew you were coming."

"I can't believe Kyle would do all of this. What did he think? That I wouldn't find out?" I shouted. "How convenient that he was in the airport at the right time! He was probably following me."

"Ryan said he saw Kyle going in and out of Lauren's trailer a lot. I wonder if she was doing him?" Marie mused.

"No wonder Ryan was so mad the other day when I talked to him . . . Kyle was going after *all* of his women." Anxiety started to take me down again. "Marie, you know what . . . just take me home, please."

"No, I'm taking you for a new phone. You and Ryan need to keep in touch and work this out," she stated emphatically.

"Why? I haven't spoken to him since last night. You've talked to him more than I have. You keep saying stuff to me about marriage—heck, I'll be lucky if this relationship lasts another week."

"That's it! I've had enough of your negativity. God! Argh!" she groaned at me. "And you wonder why I slapped you last night. I want to slap you again right now. Taryn, just TRUST me!" she shouted as she turned the car ignition off.

"When we go in there, I think you should get a log of all the calls made to your number. We're going to find out just who the hell called you that day in Florida," Marie said as we walked toward the store. "Oh, and Ryan asked me to try and convince you to use his credit card to pay for the new cell. He wants to replace it for you."

I huffed as I opened the door. "I don't think so."

"Don't fight it. You need to get used to spending your husband's millions," Marie kidded me.

I scoffed at her comment. My mind was elsewhere.

"I wonder if *Lauren's* boyfriend knows that Kyle was inside her trailer?" I was thinking about Lauren's fidelity or lack thereof and if her boyfriend was pissed.

"What boyfriend?" Marie asked. She stopped walking.

"Isn't she involved with that actor, Lucas Banks? That's the guy she dumped Ryan for, right?" I figured Marie would be up on the latest celebrity gossip.

Marie drew in a big breath. "Tar, she hasn't been with Lucas for months. Lauren told Ryan that she and Lucas were still together and madly in love, but I just sent a link to Ryan's phone this morning of pictures of Luc and some model kissing in public to show him that Lauren has been lying."

"Why are you sending pictures?" I felt light-headed again. "Why does Ryan care about any of that?" My thoughts immediately returned to visions of Ryan and Lauren together.

"Ryan and I both think that Kyle didn't act alone in this. I think Lauren wants you out of the way so she could get back with Ryan," she said quietly.

The old, familiar burning feeling resumed into my chest.

The minute we returned to my apartment, Marie went right to work, analyzing my cell phone history and making calls.

"This is going to be harder than I thought," she groaned. "Customer Service is telling me that this number is a pay phone in Miami."

She drew another circle around the numbers on my cell phone call log and then dropped the pen onto my kitchen table.

"I guess I should call Gary. Are you feeling up to playing poker tonight? It's okay if you're not . . ."

"Yeah, I'm feeling up to it," I answered with a firm nod. "I need to get back into my familiar routine."

"Good. Okay then," Marie said as she stood up from the table. She looked at her watch and grabbed her coat. "Do you smell that? Whatever Tammy is baking down there smells fantastic."

"I know! Let's go beg for samples," I snickered.

I decided to stay in the kitchen with Tammy after Marie left.

Tammy pointed to a tray on the large cooling rack. "You can have one of those, too, if you'd like. I made extra."

I was eyeing the chocolate-dipped strawberries when my doorbell rang several times in a row. Marie had just left a few minutes ago; I wondered why she didn't let herself back in through the kitchen door.

"What did you forget?" I chuckled, opening up the new back door to my apartment.

My smile instantly faded to shock and panic when my eyes caught sight of Kyle. I leaned hard into the door, trying to close it as quickly as I had opened it, but Kyle shoved his heavy black boot in the doorway.

"Taryn, please! Just hear me out," Kyle pleaded. His fingers were wrapped around the edge, pushing the door open. I leaned all my weight into the door, but it was useless to fight him. He was so much stronger then I was. My planted feet slid on the smooth flooring.

"No!" I yelled. "Just go away and leave me alone!"

Kyle gave the door a good shove and it clocked me right in the forehead. I staggered back a step while still trying to maintain my hold on the door to block his entry.

"Taryn, come on. I just want to talk to you . . . give me a chance to explain."

Most of his body was already through the doorway. He shoved the door again, more forcefully this time, tossing me like a rag doll into the wall behind me. I quickly righted myself and lunged for the opposing door to the kitchen as my next means of escape.

I managed to grab the doorknob, but Kyle was quicker. His hand wrapped around mine tightly, preventing me from twisting the knob. He used his body to cram me into the door frame, trapping me in place. I kicked the bottom of the door with my foot.

"Please don't hurt me," I begged, pleading for my life. The grip he had on my hand was already sending messages of pain.

"I'm not going to hurt you," he whispered in my ear, chuckling slightly from my fear. "Just don't do anything stupid, okay . . . Taryn?"

I felt the doorknob jiggle slightly. I hoped Tammy would run for help instead of trying to rescue me. I didn't want Kyle to have two hostages.

I was absolutely petrified, fearing he was going to harm me, or worse—kill me. His aggressive stance and the way he breathed hard on my neck terrified me. I nodded quickly. It was the only response I could give.

"You don't mind if I check you for weapons, do you?" he said, slightly amused, taking the liberty to pat the front and back pockets of my jeans. "I'd hate like hell to get maced today."

My pockets were unfortunately empty. Kyle appeared to be pleased with that revelation, almost enjoying the fact that he'd caught me unarmed and completely helpless. I felt like the doomed rabbit, caught by my unlucky foot in the big bear trap.

My mind started to roll in fast forward, trying to remember the self-defense moves he'd told me about. His knee was pressed into my leg, holding me off balance. Could I stamp on his foot and then elbow him in the nose? *Just give me some space and I'm going to kick you right in the balls, you son-of-a-bitch!*

"You don't need to be afraid of me." He laughed, lessening the pressure of his fingers on mine, but still not letting me go. "Sweetheart, I'd never hurt you. I'm just worried that you might try to hurt *me*."

"Let go of me and we'll find out," I replied, a hard edge accompanied my tone.

"Feisty!" Kyle snickered in my ear. "How about you let go of the door so we can talk?"

"What do you want to talk about?" I breathed into the wood molding, still unable to move. My eyes caught the glowing green buttons on the security system keypad. I was pretty sure I could hit the police call button before he would be able to stop me. My fingers were only a few inches away from it.

"I came here to tell you that we caught Angelica. She was picked up in Florida and is being extradited back to Rhode Island on a bench warrant. Baby, she's in police custody now, so you don't have to worry anymore."

A tinge of revulsion ebbed up my spine when he called me "baby." Kyle eased up slightly on pressing me into the door. He effortlessly peeled my straining, clenched hand off of the doorknob.

"You can relax now," he said reassuringly, obviously pleased with himself. "I told you I would get her and I did. You're safe now."

"Am I?" I whispered; tears of fright were dripping down my face. I felt so fragile in his grip; it would only take one quick twist and he could easily rebreak my left wrist, which he now held in his powerful hand.

"Sweetheart, I would never hurt you. You have to believe me," he said softly, resting his forehead on my shoulder.

"Taryn, I had nothing to do with what happened to you in Florida," he said smoothly, convincingly. "I was there because Angelica followed you to Miami. Why do you think I was in the airport? My spotters lost track of her for a few hours, so I made sure you were protected at all times."

My breath hitched. Kyle was such a manipulator.

"She's really in jail?" I whispered, asking for confirmation that my *first* stalker was locked up thanks to my *second* stalker, who now held me captive.

"Yes," he said softly in my ear. "She can't hurt you anymore."

"What about you?" I asked, my breath stuttering from fear.

Kyle scoffed in my ear. "I'm not the one who broke your heart. He did that all on his own," he groaned and took a few steps back, finally releasing me.

I turned slightly to look at him. I was wondering if he'd be able to look me in the eyes while he spewed his lies. I found myself shifting from fear to anger.

"So which one of you came up with the panties idea? Was it you or Lauren who thought that one up?" I asked angrily as I rubbed my throbbing wrist. "It was a nice touch, actually. I didn't check the wastebaskets, but I'm pretty sure I would have found a used condom lying out in the open, too . . . am I right?"

"There you go, jumping to conclusions again," he said emphatically.

"How much did you pay the bellboy to deliver it? I hope you paid him well to be part of your devious plan, or am I to believe that Lauren masterminded the whole thing?"

Kyle stared at me incredulously, as if I were crazy.

"So you're telling me that pretty-boy was caught red-handed with some other chick's underwear lying about and yet he still managed to convince you that he *didn't* fuck around on you?" he asked, laughing while questioning my sanity. "Boy, are you gullible."

I looked down at the garnet ring that Ryan had placed on my finger, remembering the words he had engraved inside it—"My heart is yours." I became furious for allowing myself to fall victim to Kyle's underhanded plan.

"Ryan loves me," I said in defense while random memories and different voices flashed through my thoughts. *Taryn, you're the one he wants to . . . ; there are other things I can't say—yes, I believe him; better that all this happened now instead of having Ryan leave you after you're . . . ; if you only knew . . . ; get used to spending your husband's . . .*

"Ryan was going to propose to me," I whispered, finally realizing what everyone had been keeping secret. "You found out he was going to propose, didn't you?" My eyes locked on Kyle's, watching his reaction. Kyle's lips pursed together. I'd obviously hit a nerve.

"Ryan told Lauren, thinking it was safe to tell her about his plans since she was already in a committed relationship . . . and Lauren told you! That's why Ryan wants proof that Lauren lied about still being with Lucas."

It was all making sense now.

Kyle frowned. I could see the expression change on his face as he switched tactics.

"I don't give a shit about them. I only care about you. There is something here, Taryn." He gestured between us. "It's powerful, and I know that you feel it, too. Just give me a chance to take care of you . . . to love you like you deserve to be loved and have a normal life without all the public scrutiny, maybe even raise a family. You're kind and caring, smart and strong . . ."

"Oh, cut the bullshit, Kyle. You knew! Didn't you? Just fucking admit it!" I yelled at him.

"Admit that I knew what? That Christensen is all wrong for you? How being involved with someone in a different league unnecessarily risks your life every fucking day? Do you know how much it pains me to see the woman I love wasting her efforts on some sleazy, two-bit actor?"

My mouth dropped open from his admission.

"There, I said it. Now you know," he uttered in defeat. "I'm in love with you, Taryn."

Kyle took one step forward, but I held my hands up to stop him before he got any closer.

I was shocked. How could Kyle possibly be so in love me? We had *never* spent any quality time together, getting to know one another on any deeper levels. Our relationship was so superficial, we were barely even friends.

There was an attraction, but it was purely physical—at least it was for me, anyway—and we'd never acted on it. "*They scream that they love me . . . how could they even say that?*" I heard Ryan's voice say. Kyle was just as pathetic as some of Ryan's fans.

"You don't love me, Kyle," I said softly.

"Don't tell me how I feel!" he shouted angrily.

"You don't really want the shiny toy—you just don't want the other boy to have the shiny toy," I concluded. "You're jealous and angry that someone like Ryan would fish in the same pond as you."

"You don't belong in that world, Taryn! If you truly believed you did, you would have never left Florida. But you walked away, devastated, because deep down inside you know how easily you can be replaced," he said irately, pointing his index finger at me.

"I've had unemployed losers easily replace me, Kyle. Ryan's career choice has nothing to do with this. Besides, whether Ryan is still in the picture or not, it wouldn't matter."

Kyle's eyes narrowed, confused by my direction.

"I've submitted the driving directions you wrote for me and the letter I found in Ryan's hotel room to a handwriting expert," I lied. "That and the threat letters I got in the mail were all express-mailed this morning." I was getting better at this "acting" thing. I almost believed *myself*!

"You still think I wrote them? Doesn't matter; they won't match up," Kyle snidely remarked. His reply was too confident. It was as though he was prepared to have to answer this accusation eventually. "You can dust them for prints, too. You won't find mine."

"Why? Is it because you charmed some unwitting girls to do your dirty work?" I probed.

"I had nothing to do with that love note or any letters, for that matter," he barked.

I had never told Kyle about the letter I found in Ryan's hotel room until now. How did he know it was a love note?

I smiled. "You couldn't find any dirt on him, could you? That week you were there poking your nose around—you came up empty-handed. Ryan has been completely faithful to me, and when you couldn't find any evidence, you fabricated your own."

Kyle scoffed. "Maybe if you'd bother to open your eyes for two seconds and look at reality, you'd see that actors never stay in relationships for very long. They trade up every chance they get. The way I see it, things couldn't have happened at a better time. You needed a wake-up call to see how things really are."

"You're incorrigible!" I bellowed.

"You think that someone like Christensen is going to stay with you for the next forty years? I highly doubt it. There were so many hot women walking around down there on his movie set . . . he may be strong enough to resist now early on in this thing, but give it time and he'll cave. You should be happy that you didn't waste a lot of time on him—save yourself from further humiliation when he dumps you for one of his own kind."

I stared blankly at him for a few minutes while I concocted my next plan.

"You're right, Kyle. You're absolutely right," I sniffed, pretending to finally give up hope and faking sudden extreme sadness. I leaned against the wall. "I've been deluding myself to think that I could have a future with Ryan. How could I be so naïve? Lauren is gorgeous. I can't compete with her."

I wiped my eyes, hoping my acting was Oscar-worthy. "I'm going to end it," I murmured, nodding to confirm my decision. "Then I won't be in Lauren's way anymore and I won't get my heart broken again."

I took an embellished, stuttering breath. "I'm not even close to being in the same league. Lauren is so much more sophisticated and cultured than I am. She's a famous celebrity and I'm . . . nothing," I said sadly, playing up my self-deprecation. "A nobody from Seaport."

I inconspicuously placed myself next to the security keypad as I continued my dramatic performance.

"I can't blame *any* man for not being able to resist her. You're right . . . Ryan will be better off with her. I realize that now. Lauren knows what it takes to have a high-profile relationship. She's probably a much better lover than I am, too," I said, acting completely dejected.

Kyle scoffed. "I've had better," he muttered.

As soon as the words slipped from his mouth, he realized he had made a fatal mistake. "Babe, you are so much more desirable than she is! Don't ever put yourself down like that."

"Stop," I breathed out, ordering him to stay where he was. "I *know* I'm better than she is—after all, you just confirmed that she's nothing more than a manipulative whore. I'm surprised you two aren't madly in love with each other, considering that you are so much alike."

"Taryn," he crooned, taking another step.

My index finger hovered over the illuminated button on the security keypad. "Don't come any closer! All I have to do is tap it and the police will come immediately.

"Forced entry, the bruise on my forehead from when you hit me with the door, a few tears and you'll be handcuffed in no time. Can you still be a bodyguard with a police record?"

"Taryn, please. Don't. It was an accident. I'll lose my job," he pleaded.

"That didn't seem to concern you while you were fucking Lauren in her trailer or conveniently waiting to rescue me in Miami."

He raised his hands in the air. "Just hold on, all right?"

"I'm done holding on! Start talking or so help me I'm going to press it!"

I saw the desperate glint in his eyes. "She came on to me—not the other way around."

He was so full of it. "You're such a liar!"

"I'm telling you the truth! We had a few drinks. She threw herself at me."

I laughed. "And of course you took her up on her offer! Your final gesture to Ryan to make sure that if he *did* take her back, he got her back . . . used."

I heard my front door open; it was easy to distinguish subtle sounds in my home.

"And the letter?" I bellowed.

"The letter was her idea, not mine. She planned it. Just don't . . ."

"I'm sure you can run before the cops get here, but where would you run to? I'll petition the court to grant a PFA order on you. It probably won't take more than an hour or so—after all, this was assault," I mused, rubbing the tender spot on my forehead. "I wonder what a protection order would do to your career."

"Okay, okay! Just don't," Kyle begged. "I can't have a record. I'll lose everything. Baby, please . . ."

I wanted to slap him. "I'm *not* your baby. Kyle, how could you ever think we'd be able to have a healthy relationship with you hurting me like this?"

"I love you, Taryn. Everything I did, I did out of love. I just couldn't stand idly by and watch him *destroy* you. It was killing me."

"This isn't love, this is sickness. You destroyed me, Kyle. Not Ryan. You! You ripped my heart out!"

He shook his head. "I never meant to hurt you."

"Taryn, are you all right?" Pete yelled from the other side of the door.

"Yes," I quickly replied, watching the shock coat Kyle's face.

"The police are on their way. Is he armed?" Pete asked. I could hear the sirens.

Kyle's eyes widened with fear. "No," he uttered.

"He says he's not armed!" I yelled back to my friends.

Pete plowed the door open; he had my baseball bat in his hand, ready to swing. Marie was right behind him.

"You just keep away from her!" Pete threatened, waving the bat at Kyle.

Kyle backed up a step. "I'm not going to hurt her."

Marie tried to pull me out of the hallway and into the kitchen—to safety, I presumed.

"Taryn!" Kyle called out. "Please? I'm sorry! I can't go to jail."

Pete waved the bat at him. "Well, you should have thought about that a long time ago!"

I touched Pete's shoulder to calm him.

"Kyle, I'm sorry too, but I just don't trust you. If I let you go free, then what's to keep you from coming back and starting this crap all over again? You know I don't feel the same way about you, but yet here you are . . . *again*."

"I'll stay away. I promise. I'll leave you alone and never bother you again. I swear!" Kyle's pleading was urgent. He knew his time was running out. The police sirens were in the alley.

I had to make a decision, quickly.

"SO WHAT happened then?" Ryan asked.

"The police took our statements. They carted Kyle out to the patrol car real fast. Ryan, I told the police that I didn't want to press charges."

"You mean to tell me after all the bullshit that bastard put us through, you just let the son of a bitch walk?"

"Yes," I said somberly. I knew Ryan felt completely let down.

He huffed in my ear. "Be honest with me, please. Do you have feelings for him? Just tell me."

"*No*, Ryan. I don't. But I just couldn't send him to prison."

I could not condemn a man to that fate for simply wanting me.

"I didn't press charges because I was afraid," I continued slowly. "I was afraid that if I destroyed his life, he might come after us one day with a vengeance. He walked away a free man; he has no reason to ever retaliate. It's over," I sighed.

Ryan was silent. I could hear him breathing hard; he was stewing. I knew he wanted Kyle to pay dearly for every wrong he ever did to us, but in my mind, two wrongs never made a right.

"Ryan?" I called out to him, hoping to calm him so we could talk this out.

"What?" he asked in his irritated, short tone.

"After all of this, I can't have you mad at me, too," I told him; my words were more of a plea.

"I've . . ." he stammered. "I've got to go," he said grimly.

"Ryan?" I breathed out.

"I need some time to think."

A new, frosty tone etched his words. His gears that were once so easy for me to switch suddenly felt stiff, unmoving under my influence.

"Okay," I whispered as the burn of heartbreak slipped up my throat.

I slumped down into my chair at the big, round table. My friends all looked at me, confused as to why I was suddenly falling apart again after speaking to Ryan.

Marie's perplexed glare turned to anger. She pulled her phone out of her pocket and I knew just by her expression that she was planning on calling Ryan and reading him the riot act.

"Don't," I protested, wiping my eyes on a Mitchell's napkin.

MY HEART cracked wider when two whole days passed and I still had not talked to Ryan. I didn't call him either; part of me was deathly afraid to have my worst fear validated. Denial was a safer option, safer than the truth. Other than the two and a half days I spent in the pit of darkness after returning from Florida, this was the longest we had ever gone without speaking.

Ryan did manage to send me a text message, but it was short. I knew he was still in Miami filming the last scenes of *Thousand Miles* and that they were attempting to wrap filming this week. He was working fifteen-hour days. I could only imagine how uncomfortable things must be for him to film with Lauren . . . to pretend, to act in front of the cameras that he was in love with this woman who had so insidiously tried to destroy our relationship.

The devastation from my disastrous trip to Florida lingered in my heart, and every day it became more and more unbearable. I continued to beat myself up every spare moment I had for being foolish and gullible and for doubting Ryan's faithfulness. Had I scarred him so deeply that forgiveness was no longer an option?

Part of me couldn't blame Ryan for being angry with me; after all, how could our relationship survive if I didn't show him I could trust him?

But there were moments when he questioned my faithfulness, too, so why should I feel solely responsible for the current state of misery I was existing in?

And what about that leggy bitch down in Florida who still got to enjoy Ryan's lips on hers? Did Lauren have an ounce of remorse in her fake-breasted soul?

Tears slipped from my eyes as I tapped a pitcher of beer for a waiting customer. I thought about all the problems Ryan was dealing with—the troubles with Suzanne, and David, and the studio people, and Lauren, and Kyle, and losing an unborn baby . . . all these things that caused him pain had one common denominator—me.

"Taryn?" Marie reached for me, seeing my sadness.

I set the pitcher down on the bar and waved my hand to dismiss her attempt to console me.

I couldn't do this anymore to him . . . or to me.

Tammy stopped me as I hurried through the kitchen, grabbing me by the arm before I got through my door. My key was still stuck in the doorknob. She wrapped me in a tender hug as the magnitude of my grief reached its final peak and crashed down on me.

My knees buckled and I dropped to the floor, covering my face with my hands.

There was only one option left for me . . .

I had to let Ryan go.

CHAPTER 36

What Do You Say?

I WATCHED MARIE OUT of the corner of my eye as she answered her cell phone again while making a mixed drink for a waiting customer. Gary had been calling her at work these last few days, which was very out of character for him. Gary was never much of a talker, so I was surprised at how often he called.

I gathered through the bits and pieces of conversation that they were making plans for a family get-together; it sounded like several people were flying in from out of town. Marie seemed stressed, often getting angry with him when they spoke. She would become testy and then run off to the kitchen to yell at him in private.

I didn't ask what the problems were nor did I pay any particular attention to her personal business. The part of my soul that died last Thursday on a plane back from Florida just didn't care much about anything lately.

Ryan finally called me Friday morning, but our conversation was awkward, as though he'd called me just to be nice. I wasn't sure by the tone of his words if we were headed for the official breakup or if he called me just because he felt he had to. It didn't help my emotional stability that we only talked about how busy he was.

"No! It's just not a good time right now," he had stuttered strangely into the phone when I offered to get on a plane and fly to see him.

Ryan said he had just arrived in L.A. and was going through final fittings for his wardrobe for *Slipknot*. He had photo shoots and interviews, and the press tour for the premiere of *Reparation* was also just a few days away. Rehearsals and filming in Vancouver would start immediately after that. In addition, he was scheduled to start training for his role as a rock climber.

I would have flown around the world ten times if I knew I'd end up in his arms at the end, but he didn't want me to.

"My schedule is just crazy right now. I don't know when I'd be able to see you even if you did fly out," he had said, continuing his reasons why he didn't want me to get on a plane. "Don't get me wrong, I *want* to see you, it's just . . . bad timing."

Bad timing . . . this from the man who used to sneak off set to call and text me countless times a day now all of a sudden didn't have time for me. How quickly things change!

I almost called him back to ask if he still wanted me . . . if he could still love me the way he once did . . . but I couldn't do it. I was afraid if I pushed, his answer would be "no."

I remembered the solemn vow I made to him several months ago when we were on my rooftop: I would never break up with him—ever. I intended to keep that vow. If our relationship was over, he'd have to be the one to say the words out loud.

THE BAR was fairly crowded for a Saturday night. I went through the motions, mixing drinks and waiting on customers, but inside I was numb, lifeless.

I dried my wet hands on my bar towel, taking a moment to adjust the garnet ring I still wore on my right hand—as if it were a magic link to the only man I had ever truly loved. I had been through so much in the six months since Ryan and I started dating, it was a miracle that I survived. But it didn't matter. Right now I would have walked over hot coals and through blistering fire to be with him again.

"There's something to make *any* girl smile," Marie said loudly.

I felt my dead heart thump in my chest. I quickly looked in her direction, aching for the one face that would bring the sunshine back into my world.

To my dismay, Phil the Fireman was leaning on the bar. He was squeezed in between two customers who were trying to have a conversation around him. My silly hopes were for naught. I could feel that the final ending, that expiration date I had feared so tremendously, was a mere moment away.

"Hi, Taryn," Phil greeted me. His broad smile wavered when he noticed I didn't return his enthusiasm.

"Hi, Phil," I said glumly. I tried to make myself smile. I felt like such a hypocrite.

"Taryn, I need a new bottle of Jack," Cory said, snapping his fingers impatiently at me. "Fast."

I could have sworn that I'd put a new bottle out earlier, but then again I hadn't been paying much attention to details.

I was unlocking the back bar lower cabinet to get a new bottle for him when Marie backed up and stood at my side.

"Taryn, there's someone here to see you," she said awkwardly.

My pulse quickened and I felt flush. I jumped up from my crouched position, whipping my head around to see.

"Hi, Taryn!"

I instantly recognized the voice, but I was completely surprised to see the faces.

"Ellen? Bill? Oh my God! What are you guys doing here?" I leaned up over the bar. "Wait, let me come around."

I hugged and kissed them both.

"We were on our way to, um . . ." Ellen looked at Bill, apparently forgetting her words.

"Martha's Vineyard," Bill reminded her.

"Yes, Martha's Vineyard. We thought we'd stop by to see you first," Ellen said.

Marie rushed out from behind the bar. "Taryn, why don't you take them into the kitchen to talk? It's really loud out here. Cory and I can cover the bar for a while." Marie tugged my arm.

"Yes, yes, please let's." Bill placed a hand on my back and quickly guided me through the crowd toward the kitchen door. I could see him cringing from the volume of the music.

"I'm so glad you stopped here first. So you're going to Martha's Vineyard? Oh, you'll have such a nice time there," I gushed, thrilled to see them. It was the first time I'd smiled in days. "How long are you staying there?"

"Where?" Bill asked. He looked confused.

"On Martha's Vineyard?" I continued.

Bill and Ellen were looking at each other, unsure of who was going to answer.

Ellen smiled, but it didn't seem genuine. "Just a few days, honey. Just a few days."

Bill looked at his watch. He was acting a bit strange, like he was in a hurry to go somewhere.

"How long are you staying in Seaport? You know you are welcome to stay here. I hope you didn't get a hotel room." I didn't know why I was rambling. Bill's demeanor was making me edgy. It appeared that they weren't here for a social visit.

"We don't want to intrude," Ellen quickly replied. "We have a hotel room for tonight and then we, um, have much to do tomorrow."

"Oh, okay. Well, did you have dinner? We can go out to eat if you're hungry or I can make something for you to eat upstairs," I offered.

Why do they look nervous? They keep looking at each other. This is getting weird. I noticed the band had stopped playing, so it wasn't quite as loud anymore, but the volume of people talking out in the pub seemed to get louder.

"No, we ate before we came here," Bill somberly replied.

I felt my breath catch. My hand clenched my throat.

"What's wrong? I feel like you're going to tell me something bad." My eyes quickly toggled, assessing.

"He's met someone else, hasn't he?" I scanned their faces—waiting . . . trying to judge their reaction to my question. Ellen seemed startled.

"I knew it. He changed his mind. He doesn't think I can trust him anymore so he's moving on." Pain, agony, all too familiar, seeped back into my soul. It had taken him only one week to finally decide he'd had enough of me.

My eyes became moist and I felt the scorching burn roll up into my throat. Not only did I have to give up the only man I'd ever truly loved, I would also be losing two wonderful parents on top of it. I bit my teeth into my upper lip, trying to hold back a sob.

"Did he send you for his things?" I whispered, assuming his parents were here to pack up his stuff. Tears cracked and bled from my eyes from thinking about him moving out of the apartment. "He doesn't even want to talk to me anymore?"

"Oh, honey, no," Ellen quickly answered.

"Ellen, I'm so sorry. I'm sorry for disappointing you." I couldn't stop the tears.

"Oh, for God's sake," Bill huffed. He turned on his heels and hastily bolted for the door.

"Great. Now I've offended his father, too." I walked over to the large steel sink that Ryan paid for and ripped a few paper towels out of the holder to wipe my eyes. I had desperately hoped that Ryan and I would try to resolve things before finally calling it quits, but that didn't seem possible now.

"I think . . . I have a few boxes," I muttered, gasping for air between sobs, gripping the counter to hold myself up.

This is it—the moment of truth—it's officially over.

"Taryn, Ryan didn't send us. And I'm fairly certain that whatever he has to say to you he will tell you himself. You need to stop crying, because everything is going to be okay."

Bill popped his head around the cracked kitchen door. "Ellen, it's time. Let's go," he barked sharply.

I gasped from the shock. I must have really offended him. Bill didn't even stick around to say goodbye, go to hell, don't ever call my son again . . . nothing.

Ellen smiled at me and then rifled through her purse. "Let me freshen you up a bit first." She opened up her compact and started powdering my face. "Do you want some lipstick?"

I shrugged, completely confused by her actions. Maybe she felt my customers didn't need to know I was crying again? Maybe it was her final gesture of being nice to me since I'd never see her again?

Before I knew it, she was rubbing lipstick over my lips. *Great . . . she pities me. Her final final gesture is to get me pretty enough so I can go back out there and get hit on by some drunken asshole who is destined to be my loser husband, since I'm obviously single again.*

"There," she said, rubbing her thumb over my lip. Her hand combed through my hair, fluffing one side around my ear. "That's better. Are you ready to go?"

"Go where?" I followed her out of the kitchen.

My watery eyes had to adjust to the darkened pub atmosphere. Ellen immediately joined Bill, who was sitting down at a table for two near the poolroom with a drink in his hand. Apparently they weren't going anywhere. *What the hell is going on here?*

I stood there staring at them, completely dumbfounded by the last five minutes of my life, trying to make sense of it all. *I think I was just dumped by my boyfriend's parents who are here to move him out of the apartment, yet they are sitting here having a drink? What the . . .?*

An acoustic guitar strummed in the background as the band readied to play their next set. Bill glanced up to the stage. Maybe he wanted to stay and hear the band?

"I wrote this song for the woman I love," a very familiar voice announced over the sound system.

A shiver blasted down my spine and I gasped from the complete and utter shock of hearing *his voice. How could that be? He can't possibly be behind me . . . He's across the country in California!*

Quickly, I turned around, covering my mouth with my hands to keep from screaming out in surprise.

"I'm hoping she has the same reaction this time that she had the first time I played for her." He gently smiled.

There he was, sitting on a stool up on the stage, a very familiar Gibson guitar resting across his thigh. His smile widened when I smiled back.

"This song is called 'What Do You Say?'"

He started the soft melody. I stood there, shaking slightly, listening to his mesmerizing voice and his lyrics that touched my soul. My heart pounded in my chest.

If I could put back the pieces and make them right
I'd turn back the hands of time with all my might
You'd never think that things went wrong
If I took the pain away
And if I say that you complete me in every single way
If I shout it from the clouds above for everyone to hear
Could you ever believe me?
If I whisper to you sweetly

You say you need a reason
But I've never gone astray
Now if I can once again persuade you
To say yes to me today

There is just one more question left for me to ask
Before we throw it all away
What do you say?
Please say yes to me today

I gave you my heart, placed it in your hands
For our dreams of tomorrow, just like we planned
Together as one for the rest of our days
But if I'd only showed instead of told you
I would have taken this doubt away
If I scream it from the sky above
So everyone is sure to know
Could you ever believe me?
If I whisper to you sweetly
You cry out you need a reason
But we've never gone astray
Now if I can once again persuade you
To say yes to me today
There is just one more question left for me to ask
Before we let it slip away
What do you say?
Please say yes to me today

If you give me your hand, I'll wrap it in golden bands
For a long future together, I'd be a happy man
I'll hold you forever as our story unfolds
By my side
You've been my only lover, let the truth be told
If I scream it from the sky above
So everyone is sure to know
Could you ever believe me?
If I whisper to you sweetly

If I say I am your reason
And our love will light our way
Now if I can once again persuade you
To say yes to me today

There is just one more question left for me to ask
Before we throw it all away
What do you say?
Please say yes to me today

I stood there in complete awe, my feet frozen to the ground. Tears of joy, tears of pure love, dripped down my cheeks. I covered my mouth with my hands while the crowd exploded with applause.

Ryan set his guitar on the stand, let out a big lungful of air, and stood up. His eyes were fixed on mine.

Determination like I'd never seen before painted his face with purpose. His legs took long strides, rapidly closing the distance between us. He was headed straight for the big, round table in the middle of the bar.

I wondered for a split second if he actually saw where he was walking. Surely he had to see the enormous table in his way? His gaze was completely locked on my face.

His foot stepped onto the empty chair in front of him, lifting his body off the floor. His next step catapulted him on top of the big oak table, carefully stepping around people's drinks. He stopped when he reached the center.

All eyes were on him as he stood atop the table. It was so quiet in the crowded bar, you could have heard a pin drop. I could hear my heart hammering in my chest as I stared up at him.

"We've made a beautiful mess of things lately, haven't we?" He flashed that sexy crooked smile at me, which made my heart flutter.

I nodded, agreeing with him.

"But it's our crazy story," he stated. "It's been ours, only ours. There's been a lot of romance, sometimes way too much drama . . ." He raised his eyebrows and smirked. "Very memorable comedy, a few pulse-racing action scenes . . ."

He shrugged and sighed.

"We've also had our fair share of suspense and raw terror, and unfortunately gut-wrenching heartache, too.

"I think we've covered it all, everything except for being captured by aliens!"

I couldn't help but chuckle.

"But through it all you've loved me, unconditionally, and I know how fortunate I am to have your love.

"I don't want to live without you, not for one more minute, not for one more second. I want to spend the rest of my days living my story with you . . . only you."

He walked to the edge and jumped off the table, landing in front of me.

"It is here that I fell in love with you," Ryan whispered, taking my hands in his.

He dropped down on one knee.

"And as fate would have it, it is *here* that I humbly kneel before you and ask you to be my wife.

"Taryn Lynn Mitchell, will you marry me?" His glistening eyes, so blue, so full of emotion, gazed up at me . . . waiting patiently for my reply.

Only one word rang through my heart.

"Yes!" I nodded emphatically. My salted tears dripped across my lips. I said yes over and over again.

Ryan's smile was glorious. It took my breath away. He reached into the front pocket of his jeans and pulled out a ring. There was no box, no preshow.

He took my left hand into his and kissed my hand softly.

"Forever," he whispered, looking up at me, as he slid the ring onto my finger.

CHAPTER 37

Sparkle and Fade

"DO YOU REALLY like it?" Ryan asked when he caught me gazing at my engagement ring. I held my hand out to admire my exquisite diamond ring one more time. Even though my head swirled with thoughts, everything paled in comparison to the elation I felt about the amazing man who was holding me, his eyes begging for my response.

"If you don't, I could always get you something else. I mean, I won't be offended if you don't like it. You could pick one that you'd rather . . ."

I quickly lifted my head off of his bare chest and locked my lips on his, shutting him up before he could entertain more doubt.

"It's perfect," I reassured him. "Absolutely perfect."

He sighed. "Good. I'm glad." He smiled gently. "I wasn't sure. I looked at a lot of rings before I picked that one. I could have gone bigger with the center stone, but I presumed you'd feel anything *over* ten carats would be too much."

"You're right." I laughed lightly.

"There's an inscription in it, too."

"There is?" He had placed this ring on my finger so quickly that I didn't even have time to look at it.

He slipped his arm out from underneath our warm comforter and wiggled the ring off my finger. "See?"

I held it closer to my eyes, twisting the band so I could read it. Etched inside was one word.

"Forever," I whispered.

"That's right . . . forever," he said softly. "I'm only marrying one girl in my lifetime. Just like my father did . . . just like your father did. Our parents spent their lives together and worked through their problems. We will too."

I placed the ring back onto my finger.

"I am so relieved to hear you say that," I sighed out, drifting my fingers across his cheek. "But I'm even more relieved that you're just here with me. I thought I had lost you for good."

"Taryn, I know things have been totally fucked up between us lately." He paused and combed his hair back with his fingers. "But . . ."

"But we need to be more open and honest with each other," I quickly finished his sentence, whispering my words on his skin.

"Yes. Exactly," he agreed. "A lot more open."

I thought about the reasons my heart had ached just a few short hours ago. "You know a spectacular diamond ring on my finger doesn't resolve our trust issues, though."

"I know. And I am truly sorry. I should have told you about Lauren. We should have talked about it." He trailed his fingers down my back, straightening out a lock of my hair.

"Why don't you tell me now?" I softly murmured.

He fidgeted slightly underneath me. "There's not much to say, really. I met her when she screen tested for *Thousand Miles* with me. Production got pushed off a year and, well, we were both out in L.A., both single at the time.

"When I left to film *Reparation* she started seeing Lucas behind my back. A friend of mine called me in Chicago to tell me he saw them making out at the Chateau Marmont." Ryan frowned. Admitting that out loud seemed difficult for him.

"I thought we were exclusive. I guess I'm just old-fashioned that way—I only date one woman at a time. Needless to say, that was the end of that."

"Were you in love with her?" I asked, curious to know how deep his feelings were for her.

His eyes were thoughtful when he shrugged slightly.

"Honest and open," I reminded him.

He sighed. "Not really. I mean, I cared a lot about her. We were friends. It was new and fun for a while."

Ryan played with a long strand of my hair, twisting it around his finger. "The little bit of feelings I had for her are nothing in comparison to how I feel about you."

I was reveling in his words until he laughed lightly. "What's so funny?"

"You know we film out of sequence, right? Well, one of the final scenes we shot this week was of our big breakup," he snickered. "And man, was I ever in character for that."

I couldn't help but feel as though I was the one to blame for his breakup motivation. Guilt washed over me again.

"I'm so sorry for what I did to you . . . for doubting you," I said with much regret. "I hope you are able to forgive me."

His hand cupped my head to his chest. "No, Taryn. I did this. I put the doubt into your mind. Don't you dare feel bad."

"But I do. I ruined everything. All your plans . . ."

"Don't. I should have told you about her. I should have done more to put your mind at ease, but I didn't," he admitted. "Instead, I was angry with you for questioning my faithfulness. I realize that now. I'm just glad that I realized it before it was too late."

He squeezed me in his arms. "I need *you* to forgive *me*."

I wrapped my arms around him tighter, pulling him closer, while his warmth and presence stitched my soul back together.

"There's nothing to forgive," I whispered. "Only lessons learned."

Ryan softly kissed the top of my head.

My mind drifted as he held me. I thought about how I would handle the first moment I ever came face to face with Lauren Delaney. Our paths would cross eventually, now that Ryan and I were officially engaged. There would be a *Thousand Miles* movie premiere to attend in my future. My visions of that initial meeting were far from ladylike.

"Did Lauren ever confess?" I asked, recalling Kyle's eleventh-hour admission.

"She denied being involved . . . at first." Ryan scratched his brow. He seemed reluctant to continue.

"It's okay, just tell me."

"She cried—hard. She said she should have never let me go," he scoffed, "but my *intensity* when we were dating scared her, or some shit like that. Well, that was her excuse for cheating on me."

He pursed his lips with disgust. "After I told her that there was no way in hell I'd ever get back with her, she admitted that she was trying to keep me from making a huge mistake. She thought I was being impulsive and shortsighted with wanting to propose to you."

I adjusted my cheek on his arm, mulling over his last sentence. I also pictured Lauren pleading and begging with him to take her back.

"And then Taryn fell silent." Ryan rolled over onto his side and stared at my face.

I swallowed hard before speaking, burying my pained eyes in my pillow. "I can almost pinpoint the exact time in my memory when that conversation happened. It was when you told me you needed time to think."

Ryan pulled my chin up.

"I'm not going to deny that I didn't think about what she said. Not the part about her being a dirty, little tramp and wanting me back," he corrected. "The other part."

"And?" I asked hesitantly.

He was silent for a few seconds. "Look in my eyes," he instructed softly.

His request was confusing to me at first, because I was expecting him to say more after that. Instead, we lay still, gazing at each other for a very long minute. And then I saw it . . . it was all suddenly very clear to me. I saw our life together, our future, in brief snippets of time. I could not imagine being happy without him. I rested my hand on his cheek, guiding his lips to mine. When Ryan kissed me, life had meaning again.

"This last week, when everything turned to shit, that was a new low for me," he admitted. "The lowest I've ever been."

I laughed lightly. "I think *I* found a new level of low, ten floors down below the pit of despair."

Ryan chuckled in agreement. "So what do you think all that misery means?"

I thought about it for a moment. "Well, for me . . . I think it means that I can't imagine spending the rest of my life with anyone but you."

He softly kissed my lips. "So if we both feel the same way, and we're absolutely miserable without each other, then there can't be anything impulsive or shortsighted about it, can there?"

I smiled and shook my head. "No, I guess not."

The visions of a blissful future with this man I so desperately loved enveloped me in warmth. He was here in this room, in this bed, holding me once again!

How profoundly different this moment was from yesterday. The train that had been derailed, causing the unfortunate death of thousands of bits of my soul, was miraculously put back to right on the tracks again and all the dead were suddenly revived.

Ironically, it only took several seconds after that for the remnants of my memory, recalling when my heart was shattered underneath the train, to creep back into my throat. I stared at the ceiling to collect my thoughts.

"I know what our problem is. We've both been cheated on, dumped, and wronged so many times that our pasts are keeping us from moving forward."

Ryan slipped out a sliver of a laugh.

I gazed back into his eyes. "You thought that I was with Kyle—that there was something going on behind your back. And I thought you were going to leave me for someone like Lauren, who wasn't all banged up and wrecked. We lost faith in each other."

"I know. And I know these rings don't erase what happened between us." He adjusted the oval garnet on my right hand. "But they aren't just jewelry to me, either. Inside each of them is a message—a message of my commitment to you. I want you to be my wife, my partner, and my only lover, Taryn . . . forever. My eyes will never wander from you."

"Neither will mine."

"Then maybe we can help each other to trust more. Honey, neither one of us is a cheater. I've *never* done that to anyone I've ever dated—I'm guessing that you've never cheated on your past boyfriends either. We both know how much it hurts to be betrayed like that. So maybe we just have to always remember that it's not in either of our personalities to be unfaithful. And I can tell ya that once we both say 'I do,' divorce is *not* an option—ever. We work through the crap, okay?"

I thought about why I'd been living in the pit of despair and surviving through years of broken promises.

"I know, but infidelity is still a deal-breaker for me," I muttered. "You have to promise me that if I'm not . . . if you ever have that need, desire for something that our relationship is missing . . . if some actress . . ."

"You'll be the first to know—way before it ever comes to that. I promise." His fingers drifted down my cheek. "And the same goes for you too! We talk about it—we fix it, we don't let it break us apart," he emphasized. "Regardless of how many completely screwed-up, psychotic people try to meddle in our relationship."

"This time, I'm killing anyone who tries," I kidded. "Speaking of which . . ."

"What?" he softly urged.

"I want you to be completely honest with me and tell me if you are going to be working with girls you have intimate knowledge of. I know it's uncomfortable and you're going to be reluctant to hurt my feelings, but it will keep me from freaking out if I know all of the ugly details beforehand. I don't want to hear about it from other sources or see it on the magazine covers in the grocery store. Not knowing that kind of stuff and then seeing it on TV does not help me trust you." I figured that would help put my mind at ease.

"Deal. That list of actresses is very small, by the way," he added. "Okay, while we're being open . . . no more Kyle. I don't want him in the bar—or anywhere near you, calling you, bringing you gifts or soup—ever again. And the same goes for all the other guys who come sniffing around my future wife."

"Don't worry. I don't want to *ever* see Kyle again." I cringed, recalling the moment of terror in the pit of my stomach when he had me crammed in the door jamb. "I told him I'd get a restraining order if he ever came around again."

Ryan was dead serious when he put his foot down on the "Kyle and other guys" subject. There was no humor in his tone.

"You know, this double standard of yours isn't very healthy either," I said.

"What double standard? What are you talking about?"

"Oh, come on! You have to admit you are a lot more jealous than I am. I'm not allowed to accept soup from some guy but you get to kiss hot actresses? And then you got pissed at me when I questioned all the 'alone time' you were spending with your ex-girlfriend? You would have been completely unbearable if Kyle and I had a romantic past. Hell, you probably would have had a barbed wire fence and extra guard dogs installed around me if that was the case."

Ryan huffed loudly.

"Considering what comes along with the Ryan Christensen territory, I'd say I've been maintaining my understanding and jealousy fairly well."

"Yeah, you have," he agreed. "Sorry, I can't help it. It's just . . . I know how men think. Food, sex, sleep—not necessarily in that order either. I was on to Kyle the first minute I saw him. I knew the game he was playing."

"Ha! And you don't think women play the same games?" I changed my voice to imitate Lauren and batted my eyes at him. "'It's all right, Ryan. I'm happily involved with Lucas. You can talk to me. Here's a shoulder to lean your head on—right next to my boobs.' She probably checked out your crotch every time you had to kiss her just to see if she made your pants fit tighter."

Ryan laughed at me.

"You laugh! I'm serious!"

He rolled over, playfully grabbing my rear. "My crotch only bulges for you, dear."

"Yeah, right," I teased.

We spent a good portion of Sunday morning in bed, arms and legs entwined, enjoying the solitude and peace that came from being together.

Ryan looked at my alarm clock. "Come on . . . time to get out of bed. We have to get showered and dressed," he said, tossing his portion of the covers over my head.

"Why?" I asked, studying his face long enough to know he knew something I didn't.

He playfully grabbed my ankle, pulling me across the bed.

"We don't want to be late for *our party*," he chuckled, reaching for my hand. He helped me up onto my feet.

"What party? What are you talking about?"

"You really had no clue, did you?" he said, grinning in astonishment.

I narrowed my eyes, still not having a clue as to what he was talking about.

"That I was going to propose to you?" He tilted his head, smiling as he rubbed my cheek with his thumb.

I mashed my lips together and shook my head, slightly embarrassed. "I thought your parents came here to move you out of the apartment."

"I think I'm going to buy Marie and Tammy new cars." Ryan laughed lightly to himself.

An hour and a half later, we drove up to Marie and Gary's house to attend our private engagement party. Ryan's parents were already there, waiting for us.

I STILL could not believe that the last two days had really happened. Ryan and I were still madly in love, his symbol of his commitment clad in diamonds around my finger, my heartache was almost completely forgotten.

"I guess I should call Pete, find out what time they're coming for poker."

Ryan twisted the cap back onto the bottle of soda and put it in the refrigerator. "We're not playing poker tonight. It's just you and me tonight. We're going out."

"Out?" I was shocked. We had rarely ever gone "out" before.

"Yep. I'm taking you out on a date . . . a proper date," he corrected. "Go get dressed."

He pulled his jeans up onto his hips and grabbed a clean shirt off a hanger in the closet.

I liked him better naked. "So where are we going?"

"I have no idea. Out to dinner, bowling . . . it's your choice. We're going to try and have a normal date, even if I have to wear a disguise. I'm taking you out."

We drove to one of my favorite local restaurants. I looked at my watch, noting the time, so we wouldn't be late for our next stop.

Ryan tapped me in the foot under the table and snickered to himself when I flinched. We were sitting in a booth all the way in the back corner, well out of the way of most eyes.

"So, my beautiful fiancée," he teased, "where to next?"

I took a sip of soda to wash down my last bite of pizza, tapping my foot in rhythm against his.

"Movies," I answered casually. "George Clooney's latest flick is playing at the Galaxy Theatre."

Ryan tried to look unaffected, but I could tell he was freaking out thinking about being around crowds and the public. He even wrapped his scarf an extra loop around his neck to cover half of his face when we got up to leave.

He tugged my hand as we started to walk in opposite directions. "Um, honey . . . car is this way?"

I stopped and held my ground, pulling him toward me. "The theater is only three blocks down the street. See the marquee lights? It will be okay. Let's walk."

We held hands as we casually strolled down the empty sidewalk in the dark. No one noticed us; no one even knew we existed. It was wonderful.

I squeezed his hand tightly in mine, completely bewildered that he was finally here with me. My heart that was once so devastated with thoughts of losing him was now being stitched back together, like it was never shattered in the first place. His love for me was just the glue I needed, restoring me back to whole.

I knew I could never make the same mistakes again. My insecurities needed to be replaced with trust and assuredness. I would never doubt his love for me or his intentions to have a long life together. Still, I was afraid that if I blinked too many times, I would wake up from this wonderful dream of togetherness.

"That was good pizza," Ryan said, trying to stifle a burp but failing. His body was making all sorts of noises.

"If your fans only knew," I teased, giving him a nudge with my hip. "It would definitely *blow* your whole mysterious, sexy image thing! That was weak, by the way. I'm hardly impressed. I give that one a 2.7."

"See, this is why I love you. You don't judge my foulness, you grade it." He wrapped his arm over my shoulder, putting me in another teasing headlock. I reached up his jacket, retaliating by tickling him in the ribs.

Ryan nodded his chin toward the theater after he'd twined my fingers back into his. "I bet you a million bucks that George Clooney has his vile moments, too," he joked.

"There's no way I'm taking that bet. I'm smart enough to know that underneath the movie-star facades and special-effects makeup are nothing more than beer-drinking, burping, farty-pants men."

"Yep," he and his body agreed. "But put us in an Armani tux and we look good."

The Galaxy Theatre was one of our town's historic landmarks, having been in existence since the 1930s. It had the old-style ticket booth and fancy marquee lights illuminating the title of the feature movie. By the time we arrived, no one was in line.

We purchased a bucket of popcorn and a soda at the tiny concession stand and then made our way into the dimly lit theater.

"This place is cool," Ryan whispered, loosening his scarf just a bit. We had the back row all to ourselves. I noticed him glancing around at the interior—the art deco wallpaper, thick red velvet drapes bordering the stage, ornate chandeliers and sconces on the walls—all very reminiscent of an era when films shaped our society.

Ryan stuck his hand in the bucket of popcorn, laughing at the silliness of the old Tom and Jerry cartoon that played on the screen. He was able to enjoy an entire night out without any interference from the paparazzi or enamored fans.

"You know, when I take you to the *Reparation* premiere in a few days your theater experience is going to be much different from this," he whispered privately.

"I know," I said as visions of thousands of screaming fans passed through my thoughts. "And I'm ready for it."

"It will be your warm-up for the insanity yet to come in July," he continued, a hint of nervous apprehension and regret accompanying his words. I instantly knew he was referring to the *Seaside* premiere, which would be a three-week multi-country tour.

I rested my head on his shoulder to enjoy the movie, but even more so, this time we finally had together. Ryan softly kissed my forehead and whispered, "I love you." It was precious moments like these that made life worth living.

Unfortunately with all blissfully sweet moments, there must always be a few not-so-good ones mixed in between. I suppose it's what keeps the balance.

The very next day, I stood there in our bedroom, helplessly watching as he packed another suitcase. His bags held everything required to fulfill his basic needs . . . clean socks and underwear shoved around a stack of clean shirts and jeans, another script and some gum packed in his carry-on bag next to his laptop.

His other needs, those that could only be met by his lover, were hopefully fulfilled to the best of my abilities as well.

"You have my schedule in your calendar?" Ryan asked as he hauled his suitcase down the steps.

"Yes," I answered, confirming for the third time that my new phone was synched with his.

"I checked e-mail—all the flight itineraries are there. And there will be a car waiting for you when you land, Mrs. Bailey." Ryan smirked. "Marla's assistant is making the arrangements for your . . ."

"Honey, I know," I said softly, slipping my fingers into his front pockets to hold onto him for a minute longer. "Don't worry! I already talked to Marla's assistant, Trish. Everything will be fine. I promise to look smashing for each of the premieres." I beamed.

"Oh, and don't forget your passport."

"I won't."

"My parents and Nick and Janelle land at LAX an hour after you do, so you won't be alone for long. Oh, wait. What am I thinking? You won't be alone—the gang will be with you, which I'm glad of because I have almost three entire days of press junkets and appearances. Just remember to keep the hotel a secret, and . . ."

"Ryan..."

"What?"

"Honey, you're stressing out. You need to relax and stop worrying. I'll see you in L.A. tomorrow, I promise."

He let out a long sigh.

My eyes departed his face and glanced to the door when I heard a car horn honk.

"I love you," I murmured on his lips as he kissed me goodbye.

"I love you more," he said, pulling me in tighter.

"Go, be a movie star," I teased him. "I'll be on the next plane, right behind you."

Ryan held my hands; his thumbs rolled over both of my rings, twisting them on my fingers. It was his subtle way of reminding me of their engraved messages.

"I'll see you soon," he said sadly.

He kissed me one more time before slipping from my hands and out to the car that waited.

Acknowledgments

I'D LIKE TO thank the following people who've helped me turn this dream into a reality, listened to my lunacy, and guided me with a gentle hand:

First and foremost, a huge thank you to my husband, Cory, and son, Ryan, for giving me the time, space, and freedom to drift off into imaginary worlds every day. You've allowed me to realize that dreams really do come true if you point yourself in their direction. Having the complete support of your family makes all the difference in the world.

This novel would not be what it is without the tireless help from my dear friend, Janelle Storch. She read, critiqued, listened to me cry, told me not to give up a thousand times, brainstormed, tweaked, kicked me in the butt, and gave her time and support generously. Thank you for holding my hand during this amazing journey.

To my gals in the FP: Your friendships are invaluable and mean the world to me. Thank you for your support, your wisdom, and your unwavering love and acceptance. I am truly blessed to have each of you in my life. I cannot imagine having a better crew to make history with.

To my ninja editor, Amy Tannenbaum, thank you for believing in me. You had me at "hungrily devoured," but then again, I think you know that.

A huge thank you to the wonderful people at Atria Books. Judith Curr, you are an awesome woman and I thank you from the bottom of my heart for giving me a chance. And to your tireless team: Chris Lloreda, Kimberly Goldstein, Samantha Cohen, Alysha Bullock, Dana Sloan, Jeanne Lee, Paul Olsewski, Ariele Fredman, LeeAnna Woodcock, and Julia Scribner—thank you for making this novel all it can be.

A special thank you to my dynamo agent, Jane Dystel, and her equally fabulous cohort, Miriam Goderich, at Dystel and Goderich Literary Management. Thank you for giving me a shot and taking me under your beautiful wings.

To learn more about Tina Reber, visit her at:

Facebook
facebook.com/authortinareber

Twitter
@TinaReber

Atria Books/Simon & Schuster Author Page
http://authors.simonandschuster.com/Tina-Reber/409197896

Author Website
www.tinareber.com

Twitter Blurb Contest: Atria Books ran a Twitter contest asking readers to tweet a blurb for *Love Unscripted*. The winner's blurb is featured on the back cover of this book. For more twitter promotions, follow Atria Books at twitter.com/atriabooks.